AMBER CITADEL

Book One of The Jewelfire Trilogy

FREDA
WARRINGTON

WITHDRAWN
FOR SALE

EARTHLIGHT

LONDON · SYDNEY · NEW YORK · TOKYO · SINGAPORE · TORONTO

www.earthlight.co.uk

First published in Great Britain by Earthlight, 1999
An imprint of Simon & Schuster UK Ltd
A Viacom Company

Simon & Schuster UK Ltd
Africa House
64–78 Kingsway
London
WC2B 6AH

Simon & Schuster Australia
Sydney

A CIP catalogue record for this book
is available from the British Library

ISBN 0-671-02190-7

1 3 5 7 9 10 8 6 4 2

This book is a work of fiction. Names, characters, places
and incidents either are products of the author's imagination
or are used fictitiously. Any resemblance to actual people living or
dead, events or locales, is entirely coincidental

Typeset in 9½ on 11½ Meridien by
SX Composing DTP, Rayleigh, Essex
Printed and bound in Great Britain by Caledonian
International Book Manufacturing, Glasgow

Contents

Aventuria

Eisilion

Vexor

Thanmandrathor

os

Lapis Ocean

THE SERPENT
ISLES

Prelude I: The Hidden Beast

They wore the colours of twilight, the two who came to buy the Seer's knowledge. Long gossamer robes of violet, and over their faces grey veils, like mist. But he knew what they were: Aelyr. A male and a female, whom he'd never seen before and doubtless would never see again.

They would come to him now and then, the other-race, travelling from their own realm to seek his hut in the high, green mountains. They always sought the same thing. Knowledge of human affairs in Aventuria. And they paid well, so he gave them what they wanted.

Such commerce between human and Aelyr was strictly unlawful. But no one would ever know.

'Sit,' he told them. 'Some become dizzy and fall, you see. And the crystal is very thin, and the drop very deep.'

The hut was a basic, round construction of wattle and thatch with a floor of dark peat. Although the Seer had shooed out the goats and chickens that wandered through his ill-lit dwelling, the smell lingered. His guests were clearing their throats in quiet distaste. He smiled.

In the centre of the floor there was a well. It was deep and dark, bounded by a low wall, with a glint of water far below. The wall was capped by a disc of crystal, striped with clear and milky lines. The Seer took up his position in his tall chair while the Aelyr, slender and soft-moving as air, seated themselves on the low stools he indicated, facing him across the well. Although he could not see their faces he sensed their natures; the man taut and impervious, the woman pliable and persistent, like ivy.

The Seer had the appearance of a man in his thirties, with skin as brown as a nut, long hair that was fox-coloured but for a white streak at the front. He had a way of holding his head slightly to one side so that his hair fell forwards over his left shoulder. His skill was a demanding one, so exhausting that he had grown almost to hate it. He practised it only for others, never for himself.

'While I am in a trance you will see my visions, and I may answer your questions. But afterwards I will remember nothing. So note my answers well, for I cannot tell you a second time. And understand that I cannot see into the future. I can only see what *is*.'

He was aware of their hidden, alien eyes, fixed upon him through the veils. 'We hear rumours,' said the man, 'of disturbances in Aventuria. Some conflict, perhaps. What can you show us of it?'

'Conflict? When we have been at peace for nigh on two hundred years? Still. There will be a vision for each of you. Let us begin the chant I taught you . . .'

They helped to coax him into the trance. Their own input was vital, for the Seer could help no-one who had no energies of their own. But with Aelyr, it was always easy. His breathing became loud and shallow. His hands floated pale above the well, as if in water . . .

'The Bhahdradomen are rising.'

The words rattled from the Seer's tongue. His mouth was slack with trance, saliva pearling in its corners, his eyes opaque. Glamour lay silver upon his hair and skin, making him as radiant as the Aelyr who listened intently to him.

The man said, 'No.'

'Hush,' the woman said. 'Let him show us.'

The Seer's hands made shapes in the air. His breath stuttered in his throat. The cone-shaped darkness of his room was warm and close, vibrating with power, its thick animal scent transmuting to a sharper fragrance of storms and of wet electric earth.

'A rider. He rides to warn them,' came the hoarse words.

2

'But the hidden beast . . .'

His brown fingers pressed into the edge of the disc. The Aelyr watched. At first they saw only reflections of their own shapes in the crystal. Slowly the milkiness cleared until they seemed to be staring down into the black water of the well; and then the circle of darkness swelled, its circumference rushing outwards so that they gasped and swayed, losing balance. The well became a window onto night, swallowing the room, filling the world.

'This – this is for you.' The Seer pointed at the woman, but they both saw.

The scene swirled, paling from night to day. It appeared innocuous – a hill, covered with graceful houses and lush green trees – and yet the light was strangely flat, the shadows too still, the perspectives wrong. On the peak of the hill stood an edifice of snow-white marble, with tall columns and statues in niches along the roof. The structure was glorious, massive and yet joyously weightless, as if built of glittering frost.

'It's the theatre in Parione,' whispered the woman. 'The Old Royal Theatre. Humans can create such beauty when they wish.'

At first the scene was static. Then it began to move. Like a dream it was hard to make out clear details, but now they saw people around the walls of the theatre. A crowd standing ten deep, facing outwards, jostling and shouting soundlessly.

Further down the hillside a team of men and horses were climbing towards the great side wall of the theatre, hauling a huge engine; a battering ram. The people at the theatre surged forward, trying to obstruct it. Soldiers in green and officers in blue and gold rushed into the crowd with drawn swords. All without sound.

The Aelyr man gripped his companion's hand.

A path was forced through the crowd, the engine hauled into place. The ram swung back on its supports and crashed into the side of the building. Ugly cracks crazed

3

the marble. The rioting crowds flung themselves forward to stop it, only to be struck down, or run through with blades, or captured and chained.

Another blow. A statue fell from its niche high above and shattered on the marble flags. It was Nepheter, goddess of the poets, lying broken, betrayed.

The woman shuddered.

Helpless, the Aelyr watched the fight grow more desperate. The scene was disjointed, flashing forwards in time so that the struggle which must have gone on for hours was over in minutes. Those whom the soldiers did not capture or kill were driven off. At last there were none left. Bodies were dragged away, leaving streaks of blood on the snowy marble. And the destruction of the theatre went on. The whole edifice was crumbling to ruin.

'Enough,' said the woman. Tears soaked the gossamer of her veil.

'It's not real,' the man said sharply.

'Not real?' the Seer echoed. The hillside span away into the void. He pointed from the man to the well. 'Attend, my lord, for this is yours.'

The second vision was dark. Again the circle of the well rushed out to swallow them, but no light came, only wet, breathing darkness.

There was no revelation. No movement of armies, human or Bhahdradomen. No citadels fallings, no secrets spoken in subterranean lairs, no alliances being made. Only this.

Night. A forest. Rain rushing through the leaves and turning the grassy way treacherous. Above, the clouds parting to show the crescent of the celestial body that humans called Leaf Moon; no real light, only the faintest green glow to show the way for a lone, urgent horseman.

His horse was a swift roan with a dark mane and tail; the breed of horse that the nobles of Sepheret rode. The rider crouched over its neck, his cape and hair flying as he urged the horse on. Its hooves drummed the slippery ground,

4

and its snorting breath mingled with that of its rider; hot, desperate, near exhaustion.

'Where is he going?' whispered the woman.

'Riding to warn them,' came the Seer's voice, fractured as if he spoke the rider's own thoughts. 'The ones who don't yet know. Someone has to warn – darkness, misery coming and they don't know, won't believe. Must reach them. Get help. But I've ridden all night, my horse can't go on, and it's following me . . . They'll never let me deliver the warning. But I won't give up, nothing left to do, it's this or death . . .'

His horse was failing now. It kept slipping on the wet grass and mud as it galloped. The rider struggled to keep his seat. Branches waved like tangled arms against the sky. He was in a tunnel of trees which was closing before and behind him, and rushing after him, driving him on, slowly catching up, came the dark seed in the sky.

The Aelyr man jerked, swept along with him.

The horse stumbled, almost fell, and came to a trembling halt. Shaken, the rider looked around, gasping open-mouthed for breath. All was still, but for the soft rainfall. Perhaps they'd outrun it. Perhaps . . .

Both the Aelyr and the Seer felt his surge of terror. The sky boiled and exploded; some *thing* came crashing down through leaf canopy, a darkness that had glaring eyes and clawed wings. The horse screamed and bolted.

The rider remained in the saddle, a passenger, for two seconds. Then blade-like claws caught his shoulders, whipping him backwards off the horse. There was a moment of panic, of falling, with a flurry of leather wings and a hideous charnel stench all around him. He saw his horse's tail tasselling round and round as the animal surged away from him, lost. *At least it escaped*. That was his last thought. And then, cutting off the dry rasp of his final scream, a beak plunged into his neck and tore out his throat.

The dark bulk crouched over its prey on the forest path,

feeding, all enclosed now in a disk with frayed edges. The scene was held for a moment at the bottom of the well, and then it closed down to nothing behind a pane of thin grey crystal.

The Seer came back to himself, as usual, to find that he'd fallen sideways in his chair. His mouth was open, strings of saliva dripping on to his shoulder. His silver aura faded, leaving him feeling very old, collapsed in upon himself, suddenly wizened within his hot robes.

The silence that followed dragged on for a time. He couldn't see the Aelyrs' faces but he didn't need to; he sensed their shock, their questions. The man held himself like a wall against the vision's invasive quality, while the woman bent away from it like a willow in a gale. It was over. They began to collect themselves. Now they were going to be angry, because he hadn't shown them anything that made sense.

'Seer,' said the male. 'Tell us the meaning of what we saw. Was it real, an illusion, a warning?'

'I warned you,' the Seer replied with effort. 'I cannot interpret because I do not know what you saw.'

'You lie. What had the first scene to do with the second?'

'Don't,' said the woman, chiding. 'We shouldn't have come. There were never any guarantees. Look, he's ill.'

She came round to the well to help the Seer, holding a flask of sweet Aelyr wine to his lips. He was grateful to her ministration, but now it was over he wanted them gone.

'What have the Bhahdradomen to do with anything we saw?' the man persisted. 'The Bhahdradomen are exiled, destroyed. Whatever the connection between the two visions, this is a human disturbance.' His voice was soft, almost ethereal, but not gentle. It was cold; iced stone.

Recovering, the Seer sat up and said sternly, 'I had no control over what you saw. I don't *know* what you saw. I didn't ask you to come here, and I warned you of the

6

limitations before you paid me. Did I not?'

'Yes,' said the woman. He caught the faintest glimpse of her features through the veil. She radiated anxiety. 'But the theatre, Seer. We saw them destroying the Old Royal—'

'Don't speak of the visions! We agreed.'

The man said, 'But why would the humans destroy such a beautiful and ancient edifice, when they are so proud of it? It makes no sense.'

'Was it real?' the woman asked.

'Enough!' the Seer roared. 'You made your purchase. Now your visions are your responsibility, not mine. Take them away!'

The Aelyr started back, shocked, but quickly in possession of themselves again. 'And so we will,' the man said quietly. 'If we demanded more than you could give, we apologise. We thank you.'

Leaving them, the man turned and flung a few emerald coins among the exquisite liquors and silks they'd brought in payment. 'These are obviously problems between the humans,' he said. 'No concern of ours.'

'No?' said the woman, slipping her hand through his arm.

The Seer watched the door opening, watched the two twilight figures passing softly through into the night.

When they'd gone, he got up slowly and leaned down to pull aside a small curtain that covered the base of his chair. Beneath the chair was a golden cage and in the cage a silver-skinned figure of human shape, eighteen inches tall. This creature sat writing with a reed pen on a piece of parchment, in a script that no one but he and the Seer could read. The cage was for its protection, not its imprisonment. One or two of his clients had tried to harm it. Seeing him, it opened the door itself and stepped out.

'Have you recorded all my words of wisdom in the trance?' the Seer asked tiredly.

'I have,' said the silver companion, with a bow. 'Do you wish me to read it back?'

7

He sighed. 'Did I say anything of interest?' Always this little game.

His secretary shrugged, studying what he had written. The Seer had reams of these records, kept in a code of his own to guard them from unwelcome eyes. In days gone by he had pored over them for hours, trying to see a pattern in his ramblings. Now he never bothered. Not because he had found nothing, but because he'd begun to find too much. Yet he still kept the records. Mere habit.

Once he had planned to build a mansion with the money anxious travellers paid for his visions. Somehow he'd never got round to it. Now it seemed less trouble to remain in squalor and to take payment in liquor instead.

Stretching, he dragged his fingers through his streaked hair. He threw off the heavy robe, glad to be free of its heat, and stood there in breeches, bare-chested; a short, well-set man who appeared to be about thirty-five. He uncorked a flask of the Aelyr wine and took a swig.

He had lied to the Aelyr. Not in saying he couldn't interpret what they saw; he had no intention of trying. But in claiming he could not remember the images.

He put the wine aside, and poured himself a goblet of whisky instead. The wine was good, but too slow to intoxicate him. If he could get drunk quickly enough, some of the images and the sinister, penetrating atmosphere they carried with them would not lodge in his memory. So he hoped.

'I wish you wouldn't drink,' said the secretary.

Something flashed in the Seer's mind. 'I think I know who they were! Renegades – exiles – no friends among Aelyr or humans – no, it's gone.' He took a burning gulp of whisky. 'The image is gone. I don't know who they were.'

'Do you care?'

'Not really.'

'What would make you care?' The silvery man spoke rhetorically, his black eyes needle-sharp. 'Anyway, your

8

mutterings made even less sense than usual. "A rider. He rides to warn them." Gems like that.'

The Seer turned away.

'So I don't know where this came from, the statement you made at the start,' his secretary went on. 'Do you remember?'

'No.'

'Look.' The secretary pointed at a line of runes that looked oddly jagged, more sinister than the rest, seeming to vibrate on the page.

'I can't read your writing,' said the Seer, then wished he hadn't. As the secretary spoke, he felt the words filling his mouth again, irrational, sour, horrible.

'It says, "The Bhahdradomen are rising. *The Bhahdradomen are rising.*"'

Prelude II: The Dark Seed

'The King is displeased,' said the official. Grave, black-bearded and humourless, he had approached the playwright after the performance – as soon as the theatre had emptied – and cornered him behind the scenery.

'The King is at liberty to dislike my plays, Lord Poel,' Saphaeyender replied. 'It is not compulsory to be pleased by them.'

'He is more than displeased.'

'Might I enquire what, in particular, has incurred his disapproval?'

'Don't be disingenuous. You wrote and staged a play that made mock of King Garnelys.'

'If you choose to interpret it in that way. My play concerned a king who became increasingly profligate in his dotage, squandering resources on a mad project that no one needs, making slaves of his own citizens in order to do it. His name was not Garnelys.'

'But everyone knew what you were insinuating.'

'Yes. It's called satire.'

'You tried to make His Majesty look foolish.'

'Is he above criticism now? He had a fine sense of self-mockery in the past, I seem to recall. Have all his citizens not a right to call things as they see them? Or has our right of free speech been mysteriously spirited away without our knowledge?'

The official paused. His eyes were dark, carved hollows. 'Things are different now,' he said heavily.

Saphaeyender began to feel cold. 'Things are, indeed, different,' he murmured. 'The King has lost his sense of humour. Disaster.'

'For you.'

'I will not take the play off unless I am forced to do so.'

'Then you had better look for a new theatre,' said Lord Poel. 'Your royal licence is revoked. The King has chosen a new site for his monument.'

Saphaeyender laughed in disbelief. 'A new site?'

'A perfect site. It will stand on this very spot. The Old Royal is to be demolished to make way.'

'Demolished?' His heart raced, but he stood frozen, every fibre of him shrieking in denial. 'The most celebrated, revered, precious building in the city – destroyed—?'

'Preparations are being made,' the official said coolly, 'even as we speak.'

'The King wouldn't do that!'

'You brought this on yourself, Saphaeyender. If anyone is to take the blame for this, it should be you.'

'You wouldn't do this. The people of Parione won't allow it. *I* won't allow it. You will not do this!'

But now Saphaeyender knelt among the rubble of the theatre, weeping. He had crawled back here after the other protestors had dispersed or been arrested – those who had survived. His company was no more. Some of his actors had died trying to defend the edifice. The broken marble bruised his knees and the area was like a wound, a flat, festering ulcer.

Obscene destruction.

Rain poured down and soaked him, running down his face with his tears. He caressed the broken stones, struck them with his fists. He had lost more than the proud institution to which he'd dedicated his life. The theatre had been parent, child, and lover to him.

'Come on,' said a voice above him. 'Come away from here.'

He looked up. Leaning down to him was his closest friend, who at different times had been theatre manager, administrator, actor, creative muse. No longer.

11

'Eldareth. I can't—'

'They were looking for an excuse, that's all,' Eldareth said, taking his arm. 'This has been coming for months. The play was bound to be the flashpoint. You were never one for the quiet life, were you?'

'They are going to pay for this.'

'Yes.' Eldareth pulled gently at his arm. 'Come away with me, Saph, before they find you. Hurry. We are both wanted men.'

Chapter One. The Lost Mirror

Tanthe was daydreaming as usual.

She was working as hard as the villagers alongside her, hefting barley sheaves on to the wagon. Her sleeves were rolled up, chaff stuck to her hot skin, her back aching. The others were talking and laughing as they worked. The great black ox stood lazily between the shafts of the wagon, and four children played chase across the gilded stubble. Tanthe hardly noticed any of it. Her gaze was on the mountains above the meadow.

The sky throbbed with heat. Tanthe had to squint against the brightness. High in the peaks lived birds of prey, big silver wolves, flying things with leathery wings and lizard scales. Predators to challenge their living in the valley. Beyond the granite spine lay the ocean which she'd never seen; she could only imagine the grey waves crashing against the cliffs, far away. She wondered if the sky looked the same above Parione; the city of her dreams, further away by far than the ocean and hopelessly unobtainable.

Tanthe sighed. She was certain she'd been born in the wrong place. There had been a mistake . . .

Watching the sky, she saw a black dot against the azure. She caught her breath. The curving swoops of its flight were unmistakable.

'Dra'a'k!' she yelled.

Everyone stopped work and looked up. People came running from the far side of the wagon, her mother and father among them. As the creature swooped lower, she saw it clearly; its wide leathery wings, rudimentary feathers sprouting from its scaly skin, a huge vicious beak. Claws like black scythes, outstretched.

13

The four children screamed and scattered. One of them was her younger brother, Feryn. She held her breath in terror; they had no hope of evading the predator. It fixed its beady attention on the smallest girl and circled above her, keeping pace effortlessly. Tanthe ran towards her, shouting desperately, waving her arms to frighten it off.

The dragon-hawk ignored her. It folded its wings and dived.

There was the twang of a bow, the swish of an arrow through the air. The dra'a'k balked in mid-stoop, turning over and over, wings flapping uselessly. Then it fell to earth like a stone, landing a bare three feet from the terrified child.

Tanthe swept the girl up into her arms. The creature lay dead, staring at her with a round black eye. She'd never seen one so close before. Its colour surprised her; its scales were iridescent, turning from bronze to purplish-blue as the light caught it.

The ox was threatening to bolt with the precious load. Her uncle Ewain hurried to restrain it. Most of the others came running up the field towards Tanthe; the child's mother took her weeping daughter from Tanthe's arms, and the other children were quickly swept away by their parents. Feryn went running to his mother, seeming more excited than upset.

Then Tanthe saw that it was Rufryd who'd killed the raptor. Damn, she thought, it would have to be him acting the hero! He was standing near the wagon, setting another arrow to the string. But the sky was clear. Dra'a'ks were solitary hunters.

The villagers collected round the corpse.

'These things are getting too bold,' said Tanthe's father, Eodwyth, pushing at it with his boot. He trod its ribs down and wrenched out the arrow. 'They'd take a child as soon as a lamb. Come on, let's away home. Excitement's over.'

There was an air of shock over the villagers as they began to walk down the slope of the meadow, dishevelled

14

in their fawn breeches and sweat-damp, unlaced shirts. But soon they began to talk and joke again, clapping Rufryd and Tanthe on the shoulder and praising their quick actions. Rufryd strode off on his own, taking the praise with his usual mixture of arrogance and ill grace. Tanthe frowned after him.

The last few sheaves were thrown onto the wagon, the load secured. Feryn jumped up to ride alongside Ewain as the wagon began to sway along the grassy path to the village. Tanthe hung back to walk with her parents.

Eodwyth was tall, slim and strong, though he limped from an accident long ago, when a laden cart had rolled into him and crushed his leg. Tanthe didn't remember; it had happened twenty years ago, just before she was born. Tanthe had got her height and her midnight hair from him. Her younger sister Ysomir was more like their mother, Aynie; smaller, slim but rounded, their hair a warm deep amber touched with gold. Feryn, eight years old, was blond as the sun.

Eodwyth said, 'Well, love, we've earned a rest after that lot.'

'Was Feryn all right?'

'You saw him. Right as rain,' said Aynie. She came only just above her daughter's shoulder. Like Eodwyth's, her face bore lines from years of working outdoors, but they were lines of laughter, a sun-burned radiance. 'I don't think he realised the danger. What about you, love?'

'Oh, I'm fine, mum. No one was hurt. It's over.'

'Have you seen Ymmi?'

'Not for at least an hour.'

'I was a bit worried about her this morning. She was very quiet after breakfast.'

'I think she had one of her bad dreams last night,' said Tanthe. 'I'm sure she's all right.'

'Well, would you go and look for her? I can guess where she's vanished to but . . .' Aynie gave Tanthe a look, part disapproving and part amused. 'I would like

15

her home for supper. Don't be late. Be watchful.'

'Dra'a'ks don't attack adults, mother. I'll find her, don't worry.'

'You've worked well today,' said her father. Great praise from he who never flattered. 'Couldn't have managed without you. You'll do well.'

Some miles away, a being raised his head and felt distant ripples of human distress. The prickles of fear tingled on his skin like a fiery balm. Each day, as their fear spread and increased, he grew stronger. Refreshed, he pulled his cloak about him and continued along the verdant hillside.

His cloak had turned the same colour as the grass, camouflaging him. Within it, his own body was semi-translucent. His bones showed through the membrane of his skin and his face was a mere gel over the grey hollows of his skull, the frozen grin of his long shadowy teeth. The surface of his skin, though, had a sheen that echoed the green of the grass. He preferred to keep his form concealed, especially from humans. They reacted badly. They did not understand.

His name was Gulzhur, which in his own tongue meant Enabler.

At a distance, he kept pace with those he was charged with protecting. A troop of human soldiers on horseback. How strange it felt to be offering them protection, not death. Infinitely strange to be cooperating with humans, the age-old enemy, or at least offering the semblance of cooperation. Almost humiliating . . . still, only one small humiliation heaped on thousands since the War of the Silver Plains. And there was a curious pleasure in the game.

Gulzhur had worked for two hundred years to acquire his powers. Now he was one of the very few who could touch two realms at once, possessing the skill to call his little flock across an immense distance to do his bidding.

He'd had cause to summon them only rarely on this

journey, to his disappointment. There had been little resistance from the humans to their King's demands; they obeyed their monarch like sheep. So far, only two small communities had been uncooperative. Frustrating, playing this subtle waiting game. But when he had unleashed the *ghelim*! The dismay, horror and sheer disbelief radiated by the humans; and then their anguish, the wounds, the blood running from their torn flesh . . . Ah, such bliss. He supposed his satisfaction must be something like the release humans sought in their grotesque couplings, but infinitely deeper.

Enabler shifted a little between dimensions, emerging ahead of the mounted troop then stopping to wait for them on the hillside above the track. Only their leaders knew of his presence, and even what they thought they knew was not quite the truth. None of them understood how their hidden reinforcements were deployed, only that they came when needed. The soldiers had been told, and they believed, that their protectors were something else entirely. Gulzhur looked down on them with lukewarm contempt.

The journey had been fruitful, but it was nearly over. Only a few more tithes to be collected. Gulzhur sincerely hoped they would not be given up without a struggle. These humans were so meek and obedient, so trustingly eager to give all that was asked of them. Where was the challenge in that?

When her parents had gone, Tanthe turned and began to jog up the long golden slope of the field. Stubble cracked under her boots. The scent of warm earth filled her lungs. Bees droned and birds fluttered in the hedgerows. Behind her lay the patchwork sweep of meadows that lined the river valley, soft and fertile; but before her and on either side lay forest and wild mountains. No humans lived there; no one braved the savage coastline beyond but a handful of fisher-folk. Sepheret was the westernmost of

17

Aventuria's Nine Realms, Riverwynde the last village on the spur of land that Sepheret thrust into the Grey Ocean.

The afternoon simmered in warmth. But now and then Tanthe felt a cold blade of wind from the heights, and heard the eerie squawk of a dra'a'k. She had heard that Subterraneans mined those mountains, but she had never seen one.

Couldn't have managed without you. You'll do well. Her father could never know it, but his words made her heart sink. By them he meant, *you're fit to take over from me, and I know the farm is safe in your hands. I'm relying on you.*

But Tanthe didn't want to be a farmer.

She loved her family. She loved the village in which she'd been born and grown up, adored the wild land. She'd never been further afield than Havereyn, the nearest town, which was a day's walk away. And yet she'd always been restless. She dreamed of distant cities. One day she would have to leave; but how to tell her parents? They expected her to live her whole life here, as they had. To pair off with some youth and have children, who would also live out their lives in Riverwynde. How would they feel if she let them down?

She felt in her heart that her being born here was a mistake. She should have been living a graceful intellectual life in Parione, not breaking her back as a peasant on the tail end of the Nine Realms.

In the evenings, when the outdoor work was done, Tanthe would sieve the pulp of river reeds, and lay the rough sheets of paper to dry. She made ink, too, and encouraged the village children to read and write, so that one day they might write poetry and stories and philosophy, as the learned folk of the cities did. An unrealistic hope, but all she had. She read the poems and plays of great writers such as Saphaeyender until the books – such books as ever found their way to Havereyn – were falling apart. She even got Ymmi and others to dress up and act the plays with her for the entertainment

18

of the village . . . but people only laughed at her. It was kindly, tolerant laughter, but it made her feel hollow. Tanthe was sick of pretending. She wanted the real thing.

Shining Parione and the Amber Citadel. So far away, unimaginably far, like the realms of the Aelyr.

Near the top of the field, she heard voices. She'd guessed where they would be. Just under the woods' edge there was a sun-warmed hollow, and here she found Ysomir with Lynden.

They were kissing, and Lynden had one hand inside Ymmi's shirt, but Tanthe was quite relieved not to have found them stark naked. Ymmi's hair was a sun-streaked tangle, Lynden's glossy chestnut brown. Their sleeves were pushed up to reveal burnished arms, with chaff stuck to their sweat-moistened skin. They looked like another gift of the harvest.

'Stop that at once!' Tanthe barked sternly.

The lovers jumped violently and clutched each other, staring up like startled hares. Tanthe grinned. When Ysomir saw who it was, she glared. 'For the gods' sake, Tan! Did you have to frighten the life out of us like that?'

Lynden only turned red.

'Sorry. Couldn't resist. I was sent to fetch you home for supper.'

'Oh, we've got ages yet. Come and sit with us.'

'Are you sure? I'd hate to interrupt.'

'We weren't doing anything!' Lynden said quickly. He put his arm round Ysomir's shoulders and they nestled together. Tanthe found their affection vaguely touching and yet irksome, because she'd never experienced it, had no real interest in falling in love – not with anyone from Riverwynde, at least. Flopping down beside them, she stretched out on the ground and shielded her eyes with one arm.

'You sneaked off early, didn't you? You missed all the

19

excitement. A dra'a'k nearly made off with little Nerrie. Feryn had a lucky escape, too.'

Ysomir and Lynden were horrified. Tanthe quite enjoyed their reaction as she related the tale. 'Didn't you hear the commotion?'

'We heard the children squealing,' said Ysomir. 'I thought they were just playing. I can't believe it!'

'Oh, you were obviously far too busy to notice,' Tanthe said tauntingly. 'I hope you're taking Mum's advice.'

'What about?' said Ymmi.

'You know, *the* advice. So you don't have a baby before you want to.'

'Tan!' Ysomir cried. 'Stop it, will you! You're embarrassing Lynden.'

'No, you don't need to worry, Tan,' Lynden stammered. 'We're really careful.'

'Oh, you *are* at it then?' Tanthe said gleefully. 'Oh, don't look like that, Ymmi. I think it's sweet. I'm only teasing you.'

'Well, you've got a cheek. How would you like us to tease you about your love life – or the fact that you've never had one?'

'Because I choose not to. There are more interesting things to do in life than falling in love with your neighbours. If I lived in Parione, I could be an artist, an architect or a scholar. In the city they have things to talk about other than the price of grain or which meadow to put the sheep in. In Parione . . .'

Tanthe went on speaking her dreams, until she became aware of a shift in the atmosphere. There was someone else there. Tanthe took her arm away from her eyes and found Rufryd, Lynden's older brother, standing at her feet. He was a tall shadow, destroying the mood.

'Gods, is she on about how bloody wonderful the city is again?' Rufryd sneered. He sat down, resting his hands loosely on his knees. Like Lynden he was handsome, a couple of inches taller than his brother, with the same thick chestnut hair, but none of Lynden's kind nature. As children, Rufryd had bulled Tanthe; now she was old enough to stand up to him, she still found him intimidating, and hated him for it. There was a bitterness in him. His teasing, unlike Tanthe's, contained an edge of real spite. Even at Riverwynde's summer games, he had to be the one to run fastest, shoot furthest, jump highest, yet he seemed to find no joy in his own achievements. It infuriated Tanthe that although she, too, was fit and fast, she could rarely beat him at anything. 'I don't suppose she even mentioned the dra'a'k, let alone the fact that it was me who killed it.'

'I did, actually,' said Tanthe. 'Well done. As long as you haven't come to bore us to death boasting about it.'

'There's a thought,' said Rufryd. 'You should have told the dra'a'k about wonderful Parione. That would have killed it quicker than my arrow. You've never even been to a city, so how do you know it's so great?'

'Because I can read,' Tanthe answered imperiously. 'I learn things from books, unlike some.'

Rufryd, who could read perfectly well, only grinned at this. His and Lynden's father was Riverwynde's administrator; the family were well-educated, by village standards.

'You think you're so far above the rest of us, don't you?' he said. 'You belong in a city, because everything there is so superior to here. Not just any city. Only Parione itself is good enough for our Tanthe, because she's so clever. Why isn't the King clamouring for your talents at the Amber Citadel? He must need someone to tie up sheaves of wheat in court, and make paper for royal privy.'

Tanthe controlled her rising irritation. 'You're only jealous. I can quote all the major poets. You can't even pronounce their names.'

'These poets any use at dragging sheep out of a flooded river? Killing a dra'a'k before it takes the spring lambs?'

She retorted, 'Once a peasant, always a peasant, Rufe.

Don't worry your little head about anything beyond the bend of the river. It's too scary for you.'

Rufryd laughed, infuriatingly. Lynden said, 'Give it a rest, Rufe. Do you two always have to go on like this?'

'She starts it. Making a whole fantasy world out of rumours. Talking of rumours . . .'

He fell silent. The others looked at him expectantly. Lynden said, 'What? What have you heard?'

'Well, when I was in Havereyn last week . . .' Rufryd paused, sitting forward over his crossed ankles. 'Not sure I should say this in front of you, Ymmi. You get scared of your own shadow.'

'Don't bother, then,' said Tanthe, refusing to encourage him.

'But still, you're a big girl now. All right.'

As he began to speak, Tanthe tensed with the urge to stop him. Ymmi had always suffered nightmares. In childhood, Tanthe had often had to comfort her in the depths of the night. It took very little to frighten Ymmi; just the hint of something worth fearing could do it.

'It's very weird,' Rufryd said with relish, looking straight into Ymmi's eyes. 'Groups of riders, who look human but may not be, are going into the towns and villages and taking folk away. They come in the night and round people up, then pick out the ones they want to take. They tell you a fantastical story about where you're going, but it's lies. No one knows the truth, but no one dares to refuse. Because if you do, terrifying creatures appear out of nowhere, just like the Bhahdradomen used to when they ruled Aventuria. And the riders are coming this way.'

'That's enough!' Tanthe exclaimed. Ymmi's green-gold eyes were huge. 'Don't you dare mention that name! They're all dead.'

'Not too sophisticated to be superstitious, then?' said Rufryd. 'Saying the word might conjure them up. *Bhahdradomen.* There, nothing happened.'

Tanthe shivered. The sun was sinking, the light

deepening, blue shadows flowing into the gold. 'Where did this stupid rumour come from?' she went on furiously. 'I'll tell you. There's an event in a far-off town, something quite ordinary, but with each retelling it becomes more fantastic. It passes from village to village and by the time it reaches us, from some gap-toothed carter drunk on his own importance because he's made a couple of ralds at market, it's so distorted it's nothing more than an Aelyr-tale! Either that or you made it up.'

Rufryd shrugged. 'No. That's as I heard it.'

'Well, even you should know it's rubbish, then! Haven't you heard of the War of the Silver Plains? The enemy was destroyed two hundred and fifty years ago. If there are any left, they're too far away and too weak ever to trouble us.'

'No!' The word exploded from Ysomir's lips. Hanging tight on to Tanthe's hand, she began to speak urgently. 'That was my dream last night! The village was dark; there was just a streak of silvery blue light in the sky. We were all gathered on the green in the centre. We didn't know why we were there, but we knew something terrible was going to happen. Then there was a dreadful loud noise, a swooping, cracking sound like the wings of a dra'a'k, and something dark came down. It took Lynden.'

'Me?' gasped Lynden.

'You were dragged into the darkness, screaming. I woke up then, terrified. I've been having weird dreams like that since the spring, but that was the worst.' Her face was colourless and she looked through her sister as if in a trance.

'Why didn't you wake me up?' said Tanthe.

'I didn't want you to think I was being childish.'

'Don't be daft.' Tanthe turned on Rufryd. 'How could you do this to her?'

'Oh, come on!' said Rufryd. 'She overreacts to every-thing. It's time she grew up.'

'It's time *you* grew up. You were a pig to her when she was little and you're no less of a pig now! You knew what this story would do to her, so shut up before you do any more harm! Ymmi, who's going to bother coming to Riverwynde to steal us? We live on the edge of nowhere. No one cares about us. Come on, you know it was only a bad dream.'

Her words did not have the desired effect. Ysomir rose to her feet, shaking off both lover and sister. 'Don't sit there talking about me as if I were an imbecile,' she said. A tear ran silver down her face, but her fear did not seem childish. Rather it was as if she lacked a protective layer, and was raw to every possible horror that might befall. And Tanthe had never seen it so starkly before.

'Never mind,' said Ymmi. 'I know what's going on. Rufryd's trying to scare me, and the dream was just a coincidence. You've had your fun. Now leave me alone!'

She strode away along the hedge until she came to a gap, and there she slipped through and vanished into the trees. Tanthe and the two men watched her, stunned.

'I'll go after her,' said Lynden.

'No, don't. I'll go,' said Tanthe. 'You stay and talk some sense into your fool of a brother. If either of you possesses any.'

Tanthe followed her sister's path into the trees. She caught a brief glimpse of Ysomir's hair swinging in a bright tangle against her back. Then she passed out of sight.

Further down, a tongue of the woodland curved round the bottom edge of the field, and they often passed through it to take a short cut back to the village. So, Ymmi was on her way home, at least.

The trunks were almost black, dappled with bronze. The slanting sun intensified every colour, setting the under-growth ablaze with glowing greens, edging the beech leaves above her with flame. In a patch of clear sky she saw the rim of the Rose Moon, huge and pale red, while the smaller Leaf Moon was a waxing oval of mint green. The air cooled suddenly. Deep pools of shadow were creeping between the trees.

'Ymmi!' Tanthe called. No reply. She wasn't of a nervous disposition, yet all at once she felt shivery and worried. 'Wait for me!'

The abundance of sun and rain that had brought them a good harvest had also made the forest thick with new growth, so the familiar path was overgrown with shrubs and brambles. Tanthe repeatedly had to turn aside, to force her way through clawing bushes until she grew hot and dishevelled. She was angry now, with her sister as much as with Rufryd. This, on top of a day's backbreaking work.

Suddenly she had a clear feeling that she'd lost her way. The forest was close all around her, growing dimmer by the moment. Looking up, the sky was visible only as a few dull lozenges of light. She couldn't even find her way from the position of the moons, then. There was no glimpse of mountain or meadow to reorientate her, only tree trunks clustered thickly in every direction.

How did this happen? she thought. I know these woods so well – or thought I did.

She went on urgently, more frustrated than ever by the hampering undergrowth. A bush caught her hair like trophies on its forked twigs. Cursing with the pain, she ripped herself free and stumbled out of its grasp to find herself in a clearing.

The glade was full of blue twilight, silent, motionless. There was a pool at its centre, which seemed phosphorescent; white motes danced over it, and she saw that they were insects, shining like stars in the reflected light. Tanthe held her breath.

At the edge of the pool, side-on to her, crouched a naked figure. It was a young man, long-limbed, smooth and golden-pale. He seemed to be caught in a glow. Light flowed over the slender, perfect muscles of his arms and thighs. When he lowered a hand into the water, she saw bright ripples moving outwards from the tips of his fingers.

His hair was dark red, the colour of beech leaves. It was almost to his waist, and when he touched the water, skeins fell forward over his shoulders. Tanthe wanted to stroke the rich silk.

She stared, frozen. All her life, she had heard of such beings only in stories. Yet she knew at once what he was. Aelyr.

The man drank from his palm, meditatively, as if time were running slow around him. Drips fell like white fire back into the pool. Then he turned and looked at her.

His face was beautiful, shadowy, human-seeming. He looked startled, like a shy forest animal. Before she could think to say or do anything, he dived forward into the pool and vanished without a splash, without even a ripple.

Stunned, Tanthe leapt forward and stared down into the pool. Points of white fire glittered all over the surface. Instead of her own reflection, she saw the Aelyr's face staring up at her, his expression full of despair, one hand reaching up to her.

'If I could reach you,' said a voice, very faint. 'If you could help me . . . so hard . . .'

Entranced, she reached out her hand to his. In the same moment she had a flashback.

She'd been a child, perhaps Feryn's age. Her grandmother had given her a little mirror, a slice of clear rock crystal silvered on the back. And she'd loved the mirror until, one night in her candlelit room – after Ymmi had fallen asleep – Tanthe had looked into it and seen, instead of her own reflection, the face of a boy with bronze-red hair. Just staring at her. She'd been terrified, thrown the mirror down. But she'd never seen that strange face in it again. Forgotten about it . . . until now.

Tanthe's fingers touched the water. The surface broke up, and as it reformed the only face in the water was her own. She blinked. Suddenly the glade was normal again and, without the gleam of magic, very dark.

Something moved on the far side. Tanthe started, and in

shocked relief made out the figure of her sister between the trees.

'Ymmi!' Tanthe ran to her, across the grass on which the Aelyr had rested. They clutched each other. 'Did you see it?'

Ymmi nodded, looking pale. 'A man by the pool.'

'Aelyr.'

'We don't know that,' said Ysomir.

'He must have been! I saw him in the water. I thought he tried to speak to me . . . oh, I don't know. Never mind.'

Ymmi watched her for a moment, as if waiting for her to elaborate. When she didn't, Ymmi said, 'Did you come after me?'

'Of course. How can you make the best of a huff without an audience?'

Ysomir smiled. 'I wasn't in a huff. But I'm glad you came. I got lost, I don't know how.'

'So did I. Come on, let's try again together.'

'Do you know which way?'

'Downhill,' said Tanthe. 'I don't know what I was thinking of. All we have to do is head downhill.'

They walked arm-in-arm, shaken by what they'd seen. But now that the strange enchantment had vanished, the trees were suddenly accommodating, and soon they found the black, peaty thread of the path.

'Are you all right?' Tanthe asked as they went.

'Of course.' Ymmi sighed. 'You must think I'm such a fool. But my dream, and then what Rufryd said – I can't bear him seeing me frightened, it's so humiliating. I can't answer him back like you can.'

'I hate him,' Tanthe said fervently. 'I don't know why he's so vile. If it's any comfort, I think you scared Lynden more than Rufryd scared you!'

Ymmi flinched. 'Don't. The dream was so real. I can't bear to think of it. People don't understand why I'm timid when you're brave. It's easy for them to say, "Oh, she's afraid of her own shadow," but they haven't seen my shadows.'

27

They had reached the trees' edge. Lily Moon had risen, a small white coin, to join her two companions. Below them stretched a green meadow thick with blue wild-flowers that glowed in the dusk, and further down, the roofs of Riverwynde clustered beside the river. Tanthe felt a deep pang of hunger. Food, wine and company would be very welcome now.

'But you have nothing to be afraid of. I don't know how many times I've told you that.'

'I know, but I can't help my dreams. I just don't need Rufryd's stupid comments!'

Tanthe put an arm round her. 'I think all that's wrong with Rufryd is that he's jealous of Lynden.'

'Nonsense,' said Ymmi. But Tanthe was pleased to see her smile.

'So, how long have you and Lynden been fucking each other?'

'Tanthe!' Ysomir's indignation dissolved into laughter. 'Since Midsummer Day, if you must know. You don't know what you're missing.'

'But I don't care, because there's no one here I want. I suppose there'll be a handfasting soon?'

'Why soon? We're seventeen, we've got lots of time. But eventually, yes. We've known each other all our lives. Neither of us could ever want anyone else.'

'How nice to have what you want,' said Tanthe. 'I sort of envy you. You'll marry, and spend all your lives here. And what will you do?'

'What we've always done, of course,' Ymmi said, sur-prised. 'Lynden will tend the animals. He means to earn enough to buy a horse. There's nothing I like better than doing my stone-carving, but there's not much need for it round here. So I'll spin and weave and make clothes . . .'

'And you'll be happy?'

'Yes.'

'I wish I could be, so easily.'

'But you wouldn't leave, Tanthe, would you? Not really?'

28

Tanthe didn't answer. Something white was bobbing across the pasture in front of them; the tail of a hare in full flight. They stopped and watched as the animal raced past at urgent speed, her big hindlegs powering her flight, her ears flattened. The hare was sacred to their goddess; they didn't want to see her killed. But no predator came in pursuit.

'The goddess in flight,' Ysomir said softly. 'From what?'

At the door of their parents' cottage Tanthe said, 'Should we tell them what we saw?'

'The hare?'

'No, the other thing.'

'Admit we saw one of the Aelyr?' Ymmi laughed quietly. 'I don't think so, Tan. No one would believe us, anyway.'

'No,' Tanthe whispered, pushing the door open into light and the good smells of cooking. 'You're right.'

Their father's big grey hound, Gazer, came bounding up to greet them, thrusting his hairy head into their chest, trying to lick their faces. Tanthe put her arms round him. Gazer could be a grumpy old devil, especially with strangers, but they all loved him, none more than her father. As a child, Ysomir had ridden on the hound's back. Feryn still did, when he thought Aynie would not catch him at it. He was growing too tall, she said, and Gazer too old for such games.

'Anyone for Havereyn market next week?' asked Ewain over supper. He was her father's brother and he had always lived with them. Tanthe was extremely fond of him. He was as loud and cheerful as her father was quiet, and although he was older than Eodwyth he seemed content to remain unmarried.

'I'll go with you,' said Tanthe, ripping off another chunk of bread to mop up the last of her lamb stew. She was famished. Her feet rested on Gazer, who lay underneath the table looking up with pleading eyes. Now and then

29

Ysomir, whose appetite was modest, would slip him a scrap. 'Even though Havereyn is even more deadly dull than Riverwynde.'

'Without that deadly dull place we'd have nowhere to trade our produce,' said her mother. 'Ymmi, will you stop feeding that hound!'

Presently the men got up to clear the table, then Aynie brought a steaming dish of apples under a golden crust. 'We'll all go. Feryn's old enough now, aren't you?'

Feryn nodded emphatically.

'We can look at cloth for our winter clothes.'

Tanthe sighed, 'Mum, Ymmi's weaving is ten times better than theirs. There's nothing to do there but drink in the alehouse and talk about the price of cabbage. The streets are full of pig manure. They have no theatre. They wouldn't recognise a book if it fell on them. I don't think I ever found a book in Havereyn that wasn't being used as a door-stop. Cloth? You can't buy anything finer than sackcloth there and it's not surprising; it would be crusted with muck the moment you stepped into the street, so I suppose the only thing is to make cloth that looks as if it's crusted with muck to start with. They only have one colour of dye. Pig-shit brown.'

Her father was laughing. 'It's not that bad. Goddess's sake, love, they have to make a living. Same as us. What d'you expect?'

'I'd just like something a bit more cultured. Once in a while.'

'We must be the only village in all Sepheret that gets Saphaeyender's plays put on every solstice,' Eodwyth said. 'That's culture, isn't it?'

'I'm the only one who knows it,' Tanthe said darkly.

'That's unfair,' said her father. 'We appreciate your acting, you and Ymmi. So, what are we getting for Fallon?'

Fallon was the festival that marked the end of harvest and the beginning of autumn. Eodwyth's mother Helwyn, the village priestess, would lead a celebration to thank their goddess and god, Breyid and Anthar, for the harvest, and to reflect on the spiralling inwards of life towards winter and rebirth. Afterwards, Tanthe's other grandma, Freyna, would serve ale, cider and cakes and they would feast late into the night.

All across the continent of Aventuria, so Tanthe had learned, people revered the three-fold Earth Goddess and her consort, the laughing Lord of Corn, of Forests, of Animals, who gave his life to the land each winter and rose again in the spring. In every realm, although their names and forms might be different, they had basically the same deities. Folk in Riverwynde seemed to take Breyid at face value, as the sweet-natured, nurturing mother-goddess of the fields. Sometimes they invoked her spring-like Maiden form, Nephenie, to help in courtship or inspiration; at others they needed her Crone-form, Mahaa, the fierce wise woman who eased the land's passage through winter, and the human spirit through death. The villagers trusted absolutely in their goddess. So did Tanthe, yet she knew more; deeper secrets that she'd found in books and had confirmed by Helwyn. All goddesses were humanised faces of the Great Goddess Nuth, and the gods gentler forms of her consort, the primal Anuth.

Nuth was terrifying, because she was incomprehensible. She was Creator and Destroyer. She was the blackness at the beginning and at the end of time.

Few humans could face Nuth directly. Most needed their deities to have recognisable shapes. Helwyn's tradition held that at death, human and animal spirits entered Breyid's Summerland, there to await rebirth. But Nuth's followers (for she had her priestesses, Tanthe had read, in the city) believed that after death all spirits returned to the blackness of Nuth's womb. Whether they found rebirth or oblivion there was a mystery for the Great Goddess alone to know.

Tanthe, who could never control her enquiring mind, sometimes wondered what the Aelyr made of human beliefs. For she'd heard that they believed in no gods at all. And weren't they a race older and wiser than humans . . . more like gods themselves? There was so much to learn, Tanthe thought, so much she'd never find out stuck here. The least she could do at Fallon was to give people something to *think* about, not that they would.

'We haven't had time to rehearse,' Tanthe said tightly. 'Last year when we did *The Oak Tree of Pherenath*, people laughed at the sad bits. Idiots. I might read from *The Corn King* by Theotis instead. It's a poem.'

'It's a ruddy long, boring poem,' said Ewain. 'Revenge, is that?'

'It's a thousand times more intelligent than anything you'll hear in Havereyn, uncle.'

'At least you get to hear all the gossip from far and wide,' he retorted.

Eodwyth gave a short, disparaging laugh. 'For what it's worth.'

'Oh, the rumours fly round all right,' Ewain went on, cutting a piece of cheese and laying it carefully on top of his apple pie. 'The latest is the best I've heard in years.'

Tanthe felt a warning pang. She didn't want Ysomir upset again. 'Uncle, do you have to?'

He went on, ignoring her. 'What you make of the story depends on which version you hear. Something near unbelievable . . .' Tanthe held her breath. Ymmi went on eating small spoonfuls of apple. 'They're saying that the King's had some kind of quarrel with his son. But I don't suppose we'll hear the truth of it for another half-year at least.'

'Is that it?' said Tanthe in relief.

Ewain blinked at her. 'Isn't that enough? Who'd believe the King could fall out with his heir? There's more, though. Some kind of excitement in Parione.'

'What's that supposed to mean?' said Aynie.

'Well, one version is that the King's recruiting subjects to the army. He's taking folk from the countryside, handfuls or hordes according to who you hear it from. The other version is that, whoever is taking folk, they're not doing it legally and – listen to this – they may not even be *human*. Either way it's something to think on.'

'Ewain,' said Aynie, but he spoke over her.

'And it's coming this way. Must be, or the tales wouldn't have reached Havereyn.'

Feryn looked at his uncle with wide, excited eyes. Ymmi quietly put down her spoon. Tanthe was furious with Ewain. It was far worse hearing the story from him than from Rufryd, because her uncle was trustworthy. Eodwyth said sharply, 'Well, since it *is* unbelievable, I'd thank you not to repeat such nonsense in front of my children!'

Ewain looked hurt. 'Sorry I spoke. It's only what they're saying.'

Aynie sighed. 'When life's too quiet, people get bored and have to make up stories to entertain themselves. That's all.'

'Nobody would bother us out here,' said Eodwyth, 'but if there's anything wrong, the King will sort it out. He always does.'

'Here's to good old King Garnelys,' said Ewain, raising his glass. The others murmured with him.

Tanthe glanced at her sister, but Ymmi only gave a slight shrug, as if to say, stop fussing over me. I'm not a child and I'm not scared. But Tanthe didn't think Ysomir was childish; rather, she gave the impression of knowing something the others didn't.

Tanthe and Aynie were the last up, scouring and drying the big black pots. The kitchen was shadowy in the last flicker of the fire. 'Mother,' said Tanthe, 'Have you ever seen one of the Aelyr?'

Aynie stopped working. She gave a soft, startled laugh, then turned to her daughter. 'Well . . . yes, I have. Whatever made you ask that?'

33

'I just wondered.' Tanthe leaned on the window sill to look out at the night. Beyond their cosy house the world seemed so wild and empty, and this was just one tiny corner of great Sepheret, and Sepheret just one small realm of Aventuria.

'Years ago,' said Aynie, leaving beside her, 'before you or Ysomir were born, your father and I saw a procession of them in the woods. There were dozens of them.'

'Dozens!' Tanthe gasped.

'They were no taller than humans, very lithe and slim.' Her voice became dreamy. 'They were all in grey robes – except that these robes, when you looked at them, weren't grey at all, but of all colours. Beautiful subtle shades. The light around them was more of a pale glow, and it sparkled like a field of stars. They were performing some kind of ceremony. All these veiled figures moving slowly against this soft shining light . . .'

'What did you do?'

Aynie laughed. 'We backed away very quietly, and then we ran!'

'You ran away? I would have stayed and watched.'

'No, you wouldn't,' her mother said sternly. 'You don't understand. It was unnerving. The Hidden Folk aren't safe. They're not evil, they wish us no harm as long as we leave them be. But they're not safe. I've sometimes seen others, too; just glimpses. Why, Tanthe? Have you?'

Tanthe paused. 'I'm not sure.'

'It's not as strange to see them as some would have you think. They are real, after all. No-one will think you've gone mad. It's said that in the past, the folk of Sepheret were close to the Aelyr, and we used to mingle freely; the borders of our worlds were open to each other and we used to move in and out as we wished.'

Tanthe was astonished. 'How do you know?'

Her mother's eyes had become misty. 'Oh, it's just one of those legends.'

'But why aren't things like that now? What happened?'

34

Aynie shifted her shoulders, as if wishing she hadn't said anything. 'Good goddess, love, I don't know. If it's not in your history books, I don't know why you expect me to have the answer. Always full of questions, aren't you?'

She said it affectionately. Tanthe agreed with a rueful smile. 'Yes, well, I've got another. Mum, do you know what happened to that little mirror Grandma Helwyn gave me?'

Aynie frowned. 'Haven't seen it for years. I thought it was in your room. Why, have you lost it?'

'Oh . . . I expect it will turn up. Something reminded me of it today, that's all.'

Tanthe didn't know how to begin explaining what she'd seen. They were quiet for a moment. Aynie put her arm round Tanthe's waist and they looked out at the night. 'And what about the others?' Tanthe asked.

'Others?'

'Have you ever seen one of *them*? You know. Begins with B—'

'Don't say it, Tanthe,' Aynie broke in. 'No, they are never seen now. And you must never say that name! It used to be said they could read human minds. That if you called them, they would come.'

'I don't believe that.'

'True or not, they're best forgotten.'

'Sorry. Mum?'

'Yes, love?'

'Have you ever thought of leaving Riverwynde?'

Her mother blinked in surprise. 'No, I haven't. Why would I want to? I was born here. Your grandparents are here; three of them, anyway. I fell in love with your father here, our life is here. What is there for me outside?'

'Other landscapes. New people. Different ideas.'

'Oh,' said Aynie, as if the prospect held no interest for her whatsoever. Yet her eyes, searching Tanthe's face, seemed to tell a different story.

'Mother, would it be a disaster for you if I left, one day?'

A long silence. 'Well. I don't know. Would you come back? I know you think about it, Tan, but I've never really understood why. Everyone who loves you is here. We need you on the land. Of course, you're not a prisoner, no one can make you stay. But I can't for the life of me see why you would want to go.'

Chapter Two. Beyne

Helananthe left Parione in darkness, riding urgently through the slumbering streets.

She'd brought almost nothing with her, other than a good pouchful of ralds and precious stones. No royal trappings. Instead she wore plain riding clothes of brown, fawn and forest green. Her horse, too, was unremarkable. A skinny brown racer of the Torith breed, built for endurance rather than looks.

She was afraid. Not for herself but for her father, her lover, her brother. For Aventuria itself.

As she left the city behind, she thought of her love. So long since she'd seen him. After the destruction of the theatre, which he'd fought so hard to prevent, he no longer dared to show his face in Parione. And now she didn't know where he was.

The road into the countryside was dusted with the first grey light of dawn. Soon it would be busy. Helananthe turned her mount's head and galloped into the hills.

It was her father who'd told her to go. That was the first time she'd truly believed that their lives were in danger. Others had disappeared for arguing with the King, people had died or been forced to flee. But never, until her own dear father had begun to talk of exiling himself from the Amber Citadel, had she realised the enormity of the situation. Her father was still there, trying to reason with the King . . . for how much longer, she didn't know.

Now she was leaving Parione, not for her own protection, but to find an answer.

Helananthe had friends everywhere, made during her travels through the Nine Realms. But who among them could she trust not to side with the King, to betray her to him? In any case, she couldn't just hide. It wasn't in her nature. She needed to know the truth.

Riding up to a high promontory on Hethlas Rim, a few miles outside the city, she reined in and took a last look at her home. Many times she had paused on this vantage point, with the city lying in glory before her; never had it looked so breathtakingly beautiful as at this moment. As the sun rose, it flooded the grasslands and the river and the three hills of the city with melting golden light. The lower slopes lay in violet shadow, but the Amber Citadel sparkled. A lump rose in her throat. She could even imagine the theatre still there, the city basking in that perfect light . . . the King still at peace with himself . . .

Someone was watching her.

She started, a chill flashing over her shoulder blades. Glancing round, she thought she saw, on a wooded hill some distance behind her, a figure in a cloak and hood. Familiar black eyes pierced her. But no; it was an illusion, a tree stump.

Helananthe shivered. There *had* been something there. She took it as a warning.

At once, resolve set firm in her heart. Nudging her horse's sides with her heels, she turned him away and galloped towards the valley. She was heading south, through the realm of Paranios, to the ocean.

To the Serpent Isles.

Ysomir and Lynden were a mile down the river Aole, fishing. Rather, they were supposed to be fishing. They had even caught four sleek brown trout before their good intentions deserted them in favour of lovemaking.

Now they were lying naked and drowsy in the honeyed warmth of the afternoon. Long grass and reeds hid them from the world. A willow made a green bower over them.

'We always seem to lose our clothes when we're together,' said Ysomir.

'Are you complaining?'

She laughed. 'No. As long as Tanthe or Rufryd don't come looking for us.'

Lynden felt ashamed of the way his brother needled Ysomir. 'I don't know why Rufe's like he is. Even our father doesn't think much of him, sometimes.'

'It doesn't matter,' said Ysomir. 'He can't hurt me. You mustn't take any notice of my sister, either.'

'We should get handfasted. Then they'll stop teasing us.'

'Lyn, we're too young. We've got nowhere to live.'

'My father has all those rooms and no one in them. He'd love us to live with him. He might even smile occasionally. Come on, Ymmi. We know we'll always be together so why wait?'

'So why hurry?' she said, smiling, gently biting his shoulder.

'Not having doubts, are you? I love you more than life.'

'And I feel the same, you know that.' She rested her head on him, her amber hair spilling over his chest. He stroked the long, soft curls. It was five days since she'd admitted to her nightmare, just after harvest, and he was still worried about it.

'So what is it?' he asked quietly. 'More bad dreams?'

'Not really . . .'

'Tell me. We mustn't have any secrets.'

Ysomir breathed out, warm on his skin. 'I've had dreams that weren't about anything in particular. They were only scenes, like a forest, or a mountain-top, or a room in the cottage. But they had an atmosphere . . . something wrong. As if everything had turned cold and stopped, even time itself.'

Her words gave him a shiver. 'But why dream something so awful?'

'I don't know. All my life, whenever something's upset me, I've had nightmares. I've been chased by wolves and dra'a'ks, Aelyr and shape-changers. When my grandad Lan left the village, I had awful dreams about *him*, even

39

though he'd been kind to me and taught me to carve stone. I don't think anyone liked him but me. Yet still, nightmares.'

'Because you were upset at losing him.'

'Yes, but these dreams are different. I think I know what they're about but I can't explain.'

'Try, Ymmi. I may not be as bright as your sister but I'm not stupid.'

'I know you're not, you daft sod,' she smiled. 'All right. Do you know what the Xauroma is?'

'Sort of. According to Helwyn, it's the covenant between the monarch and the land. When the King or the Queen takes the throne, they promise to protect Aventuria. To make fair laws and to guard us against – well, against enemies. So the Xauroma is the promise, but at the same time it's more than that, it's something real. Like the wind is real. That's the part I don't really understand.'

'But I do,' Ysomir said. 'I can feel it. Can't you?'

'I don't think so.' As much as Lynden loved Ysomir, sometimes she foxed him completely.

'Yes, you can. It's there when we celebrate Midsummer Day, or Fallon, or Breyid's Day. Walking in the fields. When we make love. It's satisfaction and pleasure and beauty, everything in the right place.'

His lips curved. 'Yes . . .'

'Well, my dreams are of how I think it would feel if the Xauroma were broken. Cold. Dead. Meaningless . . .'

Lynden tensed, clasping her arms. 'Ymmi, that's horrible. Why are you thinking about things like this?'

'I wish I knew. I don't like it either. Are you sure you still want me?'

'Gods,' he said fervently, holding her slim warm body hard against him. 'More than anything. And I want to look after you, so you can forget all these fears and be happy. Look, everything's alive and warm!'

He kissed her, to prove it. A horse whinnied in a field near the village; his father's old cob, the only horse

Riverwynde possessed. But immediately, another horse answered, then another, startlingly loud and close at hand.

Lynden and Ysomir sat up in surprise. Peering through the veil of willow leaves they saw a line of eight horsemen riding along the track that came from Havereyn. The track curved out of the low hills then ran for a mile or so, roughly parallel to the left bank of the river on which they were sitting, until it reached Riverwynde; the end of the road.

The horses were like none ever seen in this district. They were dark brown, tall and well-bred with glossy coats and rippling manes. Six of the riders wore uniforms in deep shades of green; riding breeches, loose-sleeved jackets with leather breastplates over them, swords at their belts and high boots. They were three women and three men, each with their hair in a long, single plait. The two riders in front were clearly in charge. One man wore a green and violet uniform, with loose breeches, shining black boots, a jacket heavily frogged with gold and amber. Azure feathers swayed on his hat. The other man appeared to be a civilian, upright and austere in dark blue.

One of the green-clad riders bore a banner; a fiery jewel in a tree superimposed on an eight-spoked wheel, all worked in shiny deep gold on a field of indigo silk.

'That's the King's insignia,' gasped Lynden, parting the willow leaves. He was full of excitement, forgetting Ymmi's dreams.

Ysomir pulled him back. 'Don't, they might see us!'

'We'd better get dressed and go back to the village. Hurry up. I'll bring the fish and the rods. I've never seen the King's soldiers before. This is exciting.'

'But why would they be coming here?' she said.

Arthryn, father of Rufryd and Lynden, stood at the great central window of his chamber in the upper storey of the Village House. It was the only building in Riverwynde with two floors, so the view was excellent. Through the many small panes he could observe his whole domain; the green, the paths that wound away between the cottages, and the villagers – whose lives he was charged with ordering and protecting – going about their business. They appeared to move like lazy swimmers through the heat.

He nodded. They'd earned their rest. Being River-wynde's administrator was no easy task. Appointed to the task from Havereyn council twenty-five years ago, he had little power but much responsibility. Few were willing to assist his often dull work and since the boys' mother had died, twelve years ago, he'd worked almost single-handed. He could step down, if it became too much, but then what would he do? His position was his life. The endless work, which he undertook so that the villagers' lives might run smoothly, had become second nature. He couldn't see that responsibility had worn him out over the years, made of him a passionless clerk.

Sunshine and rain meant nothing to Arthryn beyond what they boded for the crops. The mountains harboured savage animals; he saw no beauty in them. The river was merely there.

All he cared for, really, was Lynden. Rufryd – Rufryd was the one who'd let him down when their mother died, showing no emotion but becoming savagely independent and hostile. Arthryn had never fully forgiven him for it. It was Lynden who'd come through. He'd only been five at the time but he was the one who'd shared Arthryn's grief, comforting his father as much as his father had comforted him. Rufryd was a disappointment. Lynden was precious, the youngest, the most promising.

This morning Arthryn felt restless. He despised rumours. Their existence implied that there were things he didn't know and couldn't explain; that he wasn't fully in control. Now, as he stood watching the valley, he saw a group of riders approaching along the track that led from Havereyn.

They entered the village, went out of sight between the

cottages for a few minutes, then reappeared at the far corner of the green. There were eight, riding in pairs on tall brown horses. Six in deep green, their officer in violet, green and gold, and a civilian in blue. All armed with swords and bows . . . The banner they carried was deep blue and bore a familiar symbol; the jewel, the tree, the eight-spoked wheel of the year.

They were King Garnelys's men.

Arthryn was pleased but puzzled. Since the defeat of the Bhahdradomen, Aventuria's once-massive army had dwindled almost to nothing. A minimal troop of a few thousand was kept, for ceremonial purposes in the cities, and to keep volunteers in training just in case the worst should happen. But in these peaceful days, the green-clad soldiers functioned mainly as a friendly, almost civilian police force. Even as such, they were rarely needed. Arthryn had never had to call them. Riverwynde sorted out its own problems. So why were they here?

Now as they approached his door they had acquired a train of followers. Villagers were running with them, mostly children, curious and excited. Arthryn prepared himself to meet them. He smoothed back his thick white hair, shook his grey robe and straightened the belt.

Footsteps on the stairs. Lynden came rushing in with Ysomir just behind him. 'Father!'

'I know, I've seen them. I'm on my way down. Call Megden and Colvin. Ask Freyna to bring ale, and find some volunteers to tend the horses.'

Arthryn stood at the Village House's impressive front door, waiting for the riders to dismount. The man who came striding towards him was big and heavy, his short black hair clasping a well-fed face with narrow eyes and large, shiny features. His clothes were a touch shabby from travelling. A gold star on his shoulder, set with a large sapphire, marked him as a civilian official of the highest responsibility, a Registat. One who carried out the King's commands.

And Arthryn knew him of old. They had once served together, as young men, on the council of Havereyn. His jaw tensed.

'Beyne!'

'Arthryn, old friend!'

The two men met before the arched doorway, grinning and slapping each other too heartily on the shoulders.

'Well, this is a rare honour,' said Arthryn. 'All who are loyal to the King shall come and go in peace. So, what brings you here?'

'Oh, an administrative matter. One of quite an unusual nature, however,' Beyne replied. 'It's good news, great news. I'm here on behalf of the King himself.'

'You've come from the Amber Citadel?' Arthryn was shocked. It was such a great journey that in all his life he'd met only one or two people who claimed to have been there.

Beyne cleared his throat. 'Not quite. Only from Skald. I am Registat, operating there both on behalf of the Duchy of Sepheret and, in this instance, the King himself.'

There were layers of falsity and threat in the statement. Everyone knew that the Duke and Duchess of Sepheret held no real authority. Lipservice was paid to them, important decisions referred to them, but the true seat of administration was not Luin Sepher – their ancestral home – but the mildly incompetent Council of Skald. The King, though; that was a far weightier matter.

Arthryn dipped his head, trying not to show irony or envy in the gesture. But as he led Beyne up the stairs to his office chamber, his stomach was in turmoil. *His talents were no greater than mine,* he thought, *so how did he rise so high when I have ended up in Riverwynde? By insinuating himself with the right people, which I could never bear to do.* 'I'm impressed.'

'Oh come,' Beyne said, as if he read Arthryn's mind. 'We are all in the service of King Garnelys, in no matter how humble a capacity.'

44

Arthryn made an heroic attempt to rise above his fury. 'Come, have a glass of wine. I've told my son to ensure that refreshment is provided for your men.'

He poured some wine, then the two men sat down on either side of his wide beech desk near the window. The chamber, his office, was plain and dowdy, its plaster yellowing between the sloping black beams. Shelves of dusty village records lined two walls. Arthryn sensed Beyne's smug disdain.

'Have you no assistants?'

'Only Megden, the old man who keeps house for me. And Colvin, who does the outside jobs and runs my errands . . .'

Beyne tutted. 'Only two assistants.'

'We need all hands on the land, not waiting on the likes of me.'

Beyne gave a rich laugh. 'Quite so. And the boy . . . that would be Lynden? I saw him by the river with a girl. They appeared to be wearing willow leaves, and not much else.'

'Oh well, these young folk,' Arthryn said offhandedly. 'She's his intended.'

'He seems a young man to be proud of,' said Beyne without inflexion.

'He is. Well, friend, what business brings you to the end of nowhere?'

'A formality,' said Beyne. 'Mere paperwork, in truth. Balancing the books.'

'I'll do whatever I can to sort it out. But I fail to see why it takes a man of your lofty rank to inspect Riverwynde's accounts.'

Beyne chuckled. 'You misunderstand. The *King*'s paperwork concerns the value of his subjects, not that of wheat or turnips. But come, we shan't talk business tonight.' Beyne raised his glass, his eyes shining with conspiracy. 'Tomorrow is time enough.'

Arthryn hid his dismay. 'You mean to stay overnight?'

'It has been a long ride from Havereyn. You would not

45

expect the horses to return without a rest.'

'Of course not.' Arthryn gave the semblance of a smile. 'It will be a pleasure to accommodate you, naturally.'

'And a pleasure to dine with you, and catch up on old times. My news will be cause to celebrate, believe me.'

When the soldiers came, Tanthe was helping Eodwyth and Ewain get ready for market. They were working in the barn, hot, busy, and annoyed by the sudden commotion that demanded their attention. Grumbling, they crossed the yard and went up the winding path to the green.

But as soon as Tanthe saw the green-clad men and women, her heart swelled. The horses were amazing. She'd never seen such beasts. Arthryn's cob and the stocky ponies she'd ridden in Havereyn could not compare. Village youngsters, proud and thrilled, were leading them towards the water troughs. And to see that symbol shining on every breastplate – the sign that represented Aventuria's radiant strength – Tanthe could hardly believe her dazzled eyes. These were people who'd come from *civilisation*. Forgetting her companions she walked slowly towards them, drawn as if by the Aelyr.

Ysomir appeared and slipped her hand through her sister's arm. 'Tan, what do they want?' she said worriedly.

'Let's go and ask them,' said Tanthe, never shy.

The riders were idling along the wall of the Village House. Megden, thin and stooped, was serving them food, while Tanthe's grandma, Freyna, followed on with a pitcher of ale. Tanthe went to the nearest, a rosy man with gingery hair. Ymmi hung back.

'Hello, where are you from?'

'Skald,' said the man through a mouthful of pie.

'You've come a long way. What are you doing here?'

He gave a sort of laugh, not very friendly. His accent was strange. 'Not for us to say. You'll just have to wait and find out.'

'But you've come on behalf of the King?'

'Who'd come to this goddess-forsaken hole if they weren't under orders?' He took a swig of ale and turned to make some incomprehensible remark to his companion. Both men burst into raucous laughter, apparently at her expense.

Tanthe was affronted. She moved away, taking Ymmi with her. 'I thought they'd be friendly,' she said. 'I thought they'd tell us about the city, and be full of heroic tales.'

'You want heroism?' said a tall female soldier. She was handsome, with cold dark eyes and a braid of thick brown hair. 'We're just doing a job. I didn't join the army for this!'

'For what?' said Tanthe.

The woman shrugged and turned away.

They went to the horses instead. The horses, at least, were companionable, blowing into their hair and resting soft muzzles on their shoulders. 'You've read too many books,' said Ysomir, smiling. 'I wish they'd leave.'

'Why? It's exciting.'

'Gods, you're as bad as Lynden,' said Ysomir. 'Grandma Helwyn doesn't think so.'

Tanthe looked round, and saw their grandmother standing in the centre of the green. Her russet robe hung gracefully on her tall frame, and her white hair was caught up in a moonstone clasp. She leaned on her staff, a long polished branch of white birch topped with a globe of moss-green agate. Their grandfather was beside her, stooped from endless gardening and still in his green-brown work clothes. He had the same air of calm watchfulness. They simply stood there, observing the soldiers. And because they were priest and priestess before they were grandparents, Tanthe and Ysomir felt too nervous to approach them.

Since the soldiers turned out to be unsociable, Tanthe wasn't too disappointed when none of them were billeted on her family. Instead, they had Lynden as a more than welcome guest for supper. No trout, though; Arthryn had

47

begged the catch in order to provide his old friend Beyne and the officer with a suitable feast.

Rufryd, Lynden told them, had tried to join the soldiers for a drink, but they hadn't wanted the company of villages. Rufryd was not pleased. Freyna ran an alehouse for the village which was nothing more than her big front parlour, open on request. The King's troop spent much of the evening there, behind closed doors.

But in the morning, Freyna came into Aynie's kitchen, looking serious. Like her daughter she was small and slim, her gold hair now mostly silver and tied back from her round, pert, wrinkled face. Tanthe was nervous of her grandmother. She was kind and humorous, but her temper could be alarming. Aynie's father, Lan, had felt the sharp end of it when Freyna had finally lost patience and thrown him out, ten years ago now.

Freyna waited until Ymmi was out of earshot, then she spoke quietly to Aynie and Tanthe. 'I didn't think much of that lot last night. Ordering me not to let the villagers in! I don't know what it is; they weren't rowdy. That would have been normal. Their manners are good enough but they're – sullen. In my day, the King's soldiers were good warriors and they were courteous. They enjoyed life, they didn't . . .'

'What, Gran?'

'They didn't *lurk*.'

Tanthe burst out laughing. Aynie tried not to. 'Sorry, Grandma. Sometimes the way you say things is so funny.'

'Oh, have your laugh. I'm serious. I'll be glad to see the back of 'em.' Freyna started to leave, then turned back. 'I know what's wrong,' she said quietly. 'They're not friendly because they *can't* be. They're waiting for their orders.'

'A formality.' Beyne looked at the desk's surface, tracing its grain with a finger nail. He wouldn't meet Arthryn's eye. 'Think of it as a small tithe, which you will be only too

48

glad to give. It's beyond my control. It is at the King's command.'

Arthryn's unease tightened to suspicion. He hadn't slept well. Beyne's bonhomie of the night before, his endless talent for talking – mostly about himself – without actually saying anything, had been tiresome enough. But this morning, as they got down to business, his serious yet slithery manner was worse. 'We've had a good harvest. I dare say it won't kill us to give a little extra. Garnelys is scrupulously fair.'

'Indeed. But the tithe he requires is not that of fruit or grain.' Beyne drew a scroll of thick paper from a pouch and pushed it towards Arthryn. 'It is human, I'm afraid. But think of it as a tremendous honour.'

Arthryn began to read the document. He checked the signature and the seal; it was a genuine command from the Amber Citadel. He couldn't understand it. He pored over each sentence of archaic legalese, piecing together its meaning until there was no doubt. Then he felt his blood draining away. His finger, resting on the offending paragraph, began to tremble.

'"One out of each seven heads of the unmarried population, or proportion thereof, aged between seventeen and twenty-five." This is a permission to take my young citizens away?'

'Permission and command.'

'For what purpose?'

'You don't actually need to know. It is joy enough to obey the King's will without asking questions.'

'Of course, but – come, you can tell me. Is this a conscription? Is there going to be a war? But against whom? We've been at peace two hundred and fifty years!'

'You are becoming agitated, my friend,' Beyne said coldly. 'There is no war. Between you and me, the King has instigated some great construction project in Parione and needs workers to accomplish it. Being scrupulously fair and beneficent, Garnelys is taking an even percentage

49

of the population from all across the Nine Realms. My jurisdiction includes Sepheret. I can hardly leave out Riverwynde, isolated as you are. It would not be fair on the other villages.'

'Of course. But—' Arthryn felt short of breath. He clutched the edges of the scroll. 'But we have very few people of those ages.'

'You have eighteen. I have a full list. And three of them must be spared. It's the King's—'

'Yes, yes. But we can spare no one.'

'I'm afraid you must.'

Arthryn stood up, wanting to defy this loathsome man but not quite knowing how. 'And if I refuse? What will the King do? It isn't his way to punish. He's a good man, not a tyrant.'

Beyne met his eyes. 'Please. Of course he is not a tyrant. He is there to serve Aventuria, not the other way round. Therefore, if he sees fit to gift Aventuria with a great new monument, what can those who are chosen to build it do, but go with a glad heart? To refuse him would be to betray the land.'

'I hope you are not accusing me of disloyalty.'

'I know you are loyal, Arthryn. I know you would be the first to do the King's will with great joy.'

'Then why have you brought soldiers?'

'They are here to take good care of the conscripts. Not to force obedience, because, clearly, obedience in this matter will be automatic.'

The words hung in the air. Arthryn stood there, dithering; he felt the world turning to mist around him, leaving him nowhere to go. 'Let me see the list.'

Beyne produced another scroll. Arthryn studied it. 'You've got some of their ages wrong,' he said, voice shaking. 'These haven't reached their seventeenth birthday. And these are older than twenty-five. I can show you the records to prove it!'

The official sighed heavily. 'Very well. I'll check them

later. Mark the ones who are eligible.'

'This girl is lame. These two were handfasted last month. There are only seven.' But Arthryn, putting black crosses by the names, irrationally felt he was sentencing those villagers to exile. His pen hovered by Lynden's name, and passed on. 'No, six.'

'So you're saying I am entitled to take only one?' Beyne said irritably, his pretence of friendliness evaporating. 'Damn it, this was almost a wasted journey. But I will have that one.'

'It's still one too many.'

Beyne looked at the list, then at Arthryn, his eyes narrow. 'You have begun to make a cross by Lynden's name, then changed your mind. Is he eligible, or not? It is an offence to deceive the King's representatives.' Defeated, Arthryn gave a minimal nod. 'He's a fine boy,' said Beyne. 'He'll do.'

Arthryn sat down heavily. 'No. Not him!'

Beyne's big-featured face creaked into a smile. Now the aura of his hard, cruel will came seeping like acid light through the cracks in the benign mask. Arthryn recalled how Beyne had always had gloating eyes for boys. He felt ill.

'Don't make the mistake of refusing. We will only use force if you make us. Don't blame me, old friend. I'm not a man of violence. I am merely a civil servant. Did you read the whole order? You will be recompensed.' Suddenly Beyne produced a purse and tipped a shower of coins onto the desk. They were discs of emerald, rimmed with gold, engraved with the King's crest. 'Fifteen ralds, for his family.'

'You can't buy my son,' Arthryn said at length. 'He is not for sale, not even to the King. Look, it's a lot of money. You take it instead! I'll sign that I've received it. But don't take Lynden, I implore you! Take Rufryd!'

In the laden silence, Beyne smiled. 'Your older son? That's acceptable to you? Interesting.'

Arthryn sat paralysed, aghast at himself. What was he doing? But he couldn't take the words back. All he could think of was Lynden. Horrified, he watched himself losing control as if it were happening to someone else.

'Just take anyone but Lynden.'

Beyne began to shake his head. Arthryn's fury broke loose. 'When we worked together on Havereyn council, you were never above taking a bribe! Isn't that how you've climbed so high? Wouldn't the King be interested to learn of your past corruption?'

Beyne's face became still and poisonous. At last he spoke, his tone grating. 'Very well, I will forget I heard you make that worthless threat. But if it means so much, I'll choose someone else. Have the young people gather on the village green in one hour's time. If they have any special skills, tell them to bring examples of their work. Lynden had better be among them, so that no one suspects; but to reward your generosity, I promise not to take him.'

Beyne scooped the coins into his own pouch, and made him sign the receipt.

'How many others have you . . .'

'From my allotted area, I've gathered approximately one hundred and eighty young people. On my return I will be taking them to a holding camp at Afthan Horn, near Skald. From there, others will take them on to Parione. It's doubtful they'll ever come home again. They are highly privileged to be chosen for the King's great project, my friend.' He got up, bowed, and gave his old colleague an icy, knowing smile.

It was only when he'd gone, and Arthryn had stopped shaking, that he understood what he'd done. Saved his own child from an unknown fate at the expense of someone else's. And he knew, horribly, that Beyne had done this everywhere, that Riverwynde was simply the last stop on a long, corrupt trail.

*

The horses were ready. They'd been fed and watered, groomed by the village children until they shone. Now they were in full tack, each with its rider holding its bridle. Tanthe stood with her family, part of the crowd on the green waiting to see them off. Feryn sat on Eodwyth's shoulders, thrilled, and Gazer was sitting at his feet. Tanthe felt strange; disappointed but still yearning for unknown glories.

Suddenly the Registat Beyne strode out and stood on the steps of the Village House with Arthryn and the officer at his side.

'On behalf of his majesty King Garnelys,' Beyne began cheerfully, 'I wish to thank Riverwynde for your hospitality. You have all been waiting, I know, to learn the reason for our visit. Well, prepare to celebrate. The King is doing you a great honour. One of you – just one at this time – is to be selected to join a new force who will serve the King as artisans.'

There was a spattering of applause and cheering. Beyne held up his hand. 'No volunteers. The selection will be made by us. The following people will present themselves . . .'

The officer, his feathered hat in one hand and a list in the other, read out seven names. 'Lynden and Rufryd Arthryn-sons.' Three of their neighbours, two youths and a girl. Then, 'Ysomir and Tanthe Aynie-daughters. At the King's command you will gather in the centre of the green and submit yourselves to inspection.'

They hesitated, giving each other curious looks. Beyne beckoned and Aynie whispered, 'Well, you'd better go.'

Ysomir hung hard on to Lynden's arm, pale and shaking, as Beyne looked them over. She stood out like the sun among the others, she was so lovely. Tanthe held her free hand. Lynden simply looked puzzled. 'This is stupid,' he whispered. 'Why can't the King get his artisans somewhere else?'

Rufryd stood apart from his brother, looking bored.

'They've heard about you, Lyn. Better just give yourself up.'

'Shut up!' Tanthe hissed.

The black-haired official moved back and forth, eyes narrow. He seemed to be enjoying himself. 'Any special skills?' The other three shrugged and mumbled, offering nothing.

'I've studied the classic writers, and I teach the children,' Tanthe said proudly. Beyne looked at her as if she had two heads. Close up, his eyes were cold and sneering. She recoiled, suddenly unnerved.

'You'd better stay here then, hadn't you? Next.'

'I'm good at archery and running,' Rufryd said, looking straight into Beyne's eyes.

'I'll bet you are,' said Beyne. 'With those long legs.' Then his gaze moved to Lynden and slid very slowly, almost lasciviously over him. Ysomir looked at Tanthe in bewilderment. 'Well?'

'Er, nothing really,' said Lynden. 'I'm good with animals. They seem to like me.'

'I can imagine.' After a long pause, he moved to Ysomir.

'I weave quite well,' she said. 'And stone-carving.'

'Stone-carving?'

'I made this.' Ysomir produced a figure of the god Anthar that she'd chiselled from a lump of jasper, a few inches high but capturing all the god's exuberance, his horns and his cloak of leaves wonderfully detailed. Beyne took it from her, and showed it to the officer.

Tanthe tried to lip-read their conversation. It seemed that Beyne kept looking at Rufryd – *oh yes, please take him!* – as if considering strength over dexterity, but the officer seemed more impressed by the stone figure. Finally they seemed to reach a decision. Her heart jumped. Both men nodded, and Beyne came towards the group.

Ysomir caught her breath. She was holding so desperately on to her lover, Tanthe knew, because of the dream. Ymmi was convinced they were going to take

Lynden away from her.

'You,' said Beyne.

His large hand fell on Ysomir's shoulder.

'Don't touch her!' Tanthe cried. 'What are you doing?'

Beyne gave her a cold, contemptuous look. She felt the weight of his power, and was afraid. 'A feel for stone is the one skill the King needs above all others. You are . . .'

'Ysomir,' Ymmi stammered. 'Daughter of Aynie and Eodwyth.'

'Good. Well, Ysomir, let me explain. You're a very lucky young woman. You're going on a journey. You've been chosen to work in Parione.'

'Parione?' Tanthe gasped.

'You can't do that!' Lynden exclaimed, clutching Ymmi. 'She's going to be my wife!'

To Tanthe's horror, two of the soldiers came forward and roughly pulled Lynden away. Another pushed her backwards, isolating her sister. Tanthe started to tremble with fury. Ymmi looked stunned as the Registat went on, almost as if bored. 'Two of my women will accompany you to your parents' house. You will be allowed to take a small quantity of personal belongings, and to say your goodbyes. But you must be quick. No use prolonging the agony, eh, my dear?'

'But I don't want to go!' said Ysomir, terrified, breathless.

'Take me instead,' Tanthe demanded. 'I want to go to Parione. I volunteer.' They ignored her and she lost her temper, trying to push through to Beyne. 'Are you deaf? I said, take me!'

The soldier who had pushed her now turned and struck her, and she fell to the ground, her face stinging from his heavy gauntlet. The world spun, then people were leaning over her in concern, and the soldiers were taking Ysomir away.

Ewain helped Tanthe up and they ran home, half a minute along the path. Lynden followed her, but at the door a soldier stopped him going in. Tanthe slipped into the kitchen and there found her mother in tears, her father and brother distraught. Arthryn was with them. Aynie kept saying, 'I don't understand. They can't just take my daughter like this!'

'They can, I'm afraid,' said Arthryn. 'I'm so sorry, Aynie. It's the King's command. It's a great project at the Amber Citadel. She won't be alone. It's an immense honour.'

Aynie said, 'Yes, I can see that, but why her?'

'Sod the honour!' said Eodwyth.

'Sod my father, teaching her to carve!' cried Aynie.

'I'm sorry,' Arthryn said again, looking at no one. 'I did everything in my power to dissuade them. It could be worse; he wanted to take three! There's nothing we can do.'

'Isn't there?' Tanthe said under her breath.

They heard Lynden's voice outside the cottage, shouting to Ysomir. Arthryn went out to him, and Lynden fell silent.

The soldiers barely let Ysomir speak to her family. They stood close by as she collected a few garments, hairbrush, facecloth, towel, and put them in a small bag. They let her hug her mother but no one else. Then they whisked her away, seating her on a horse before one of the female soldiers, the one Tanthe had tried to speak to. Tanthe caught only a few glimpses of Ymmi's pale, shocked face as all this happened. Tanthe was beside herself, feeling that it should be her in her sister's place – but only for Ymmi's sake, because this was not the way she'd wanted to go to the city. This was wrong.

As the mounted party began to leave, Arthryn did something strange. He rushed to Beyne's horse, forcing the official to rein in. Tanthe, standing close, heard Arthryn's low, passionate words but didn't understand them. 'It's happening, isn't it?' He gripped Beyne's saddle. 'The Xauroma is breaking down. The corruption touches everyone. It's touched you, it's touched me. We're tainted. Tell me how it happened!'

'Nothing has happened,' Beyne hissed, leaning down. 'Don't question the King's wisdom, you provincial penpusher. Don't spew your guilt on to me! Swallow it and do your job.'

Something unspoken passed between the men's eyes. Arthryn's hand fell.

Beyne kicked his horse hard, forcing Arthryn to jump out of its way. Silently he went into the Village House, turning his back. Then the troop were moving off, Ysomir with them.

It had happened so quickly. No one could grasp it.

'I was always so proud of her,' Aynie said at Tanthe's shoulder. 'Now I wish to the gods and goddesses that she'd been born slow or lame, anything to prevent this!'

'Where's Ymmi gone?' Feryn kept asking, growing frustrated when no one would answer him. At last Aynie seized his hand almost angrily and bundled him home.

A few minutes after Beyne's party had left, Arthryn reappeared. Lynden came running out of the Village House behind him and came to Tanthe, shaking with misery and rage. He'd been locked in, he said. It was Arthryn himself who had kept his son from saying goodbye to Ysomir. Kept him from making a scene.

'I don't understand,' Lynden raged. 'They can't do this!'

But Arthryn said nothing. Only stared into the distance with narrow, dry eyes.

Then the villagers' anger began to rise. Suddenly they were all turning on their leader, the man they trusted, blaming him. Eodwyth and Ewain started it, but soon all the rest were shouting too. Tanthe was too shocked to join in. She was glad her mother had gone back to the cottage with Feryn.

'It's the King's will,' Arthryn kept saying, his hands raised to keep the peace. 'Come, we're talking of our beloved King Garnelys. When has he ever ill-used any of

57

his citizens? He loves us. This is an honour, Eodwyth. His orders . . .'

'I don't care what the King's blasted orders are,' said Eodwyth. 'I'm not letting them take my daughter. I'm going after them.'

'No,' said Arthryn. 'Don't act rashly.'

The villagers began to come forward, a hesitant trickle at first. Opposing the King's representatives was unthinkable. Tanthe shouted, 'There are a hundred of us and eight of them! What are you afraid of?' and then the rest came surging after Eodwyth, forming a loose, enraged crowd. Some ran into their houses as they went, emerging again with staves, axes or bows, even fire pokers or kitchen knives. Only the old and the very young stayed behind. Tanthe and Lynden ran side by side, unarmed.

'This is madness!' shouted Arthryn, following the crowd. 'I forbid it!' But the group set off along the path that the King's men had taken, and he was left behind on the edge of the village, forlorn, powerless.

The trail left by the horses was easy to follow, the line of churned ground marked by heaps of fresh manure. Rain clouds had crept across the sky, darkening the morning. The mounted group had not had time to travel more than a mile. Within minutes they came in sight again, just at the curve of the track where it bent away from the river and passed towards the low hills. They were moving at a jog trot through the gloom. Running, the villagers began to gain on them.

Excitement rose in Tanthe's chest. What would the soldiers do, stop and surrender? Break into a gallop? Or would they turn and fight? Someone was going to be hurt. But the men must give Ymmi back. They couldn't win against this mob.

'Hold!' her uncle cried. 'Give us our young woman back! Hold or we'll attack!'

The riders turned in their saddles to look back. Tanthe could see Ysomir, a blurred shape in her cloak, but couldn't make out her face.

Beyne snarled. 'Go home. Don't make idiots of yourselves.'

Someone fired an arrow at the King's men. It curved towards them and swished close to Beyne's head. The atmosphere blackened. Tanthe heard the *weep* of swords being drawn. Then five of the main riders peeled off the main group and came galloping into the heart of the mob.

Everyone scattered. She saw her uncle swinging a stave, heard the painful thud as it connected with a rider's backplate. The man kept his seat, but his plunging horse knocked two women to the ground. There were several seconds of chaos. The villagers, untrained, came back in swinging their weapons wildly but not without effect.

Tanthe, unarmed, hovered at the edge of the fight. She noticed that Rufryd was keeping well out of the action, just standing there with folded arms and a strange grim look on his face, as if he thought this was all incredibly stupid. Tanthe's rage flared. She started towards Beyne's group – towards Ysomir – knowing it was foolish, not knowing what she'd do when she got there. To her shock, she found Lynden and a straggling group of villagers running with her. They were fired up now, shouting.

Beyne snapped an order. He and the remaining riders moved off at a canter, outpacing the villagers. Tanthe shouted, 'Ymmi!'

A dark shadow sailed above her. She looked up at the sky and saw a small low cloud. Or – not a cloud, but a strange thickening of the air, like dark oily bubbles forming in a mist.

Her father caught her arm. He'd seen it too. Around them the shouts and the chaotic fight went on. Suddenly the five attacking riders broke away from the skirmish and went galloping fast after their companions – as if they knew something was about to happen, and were fleeing before it did.

The bubbles of darkness exploded.

59

Out of them came a swarm of monsters. Thin bodies, spoked wings, lashing tails tipped with barbs. In colour they were scar-red, patched with green corrosion. Their heads were ugly, with tiny eyes and gaping beaks, and their claws were vicious, catching in clothes and hair, tearing flesh.

Tanthe fell headlong and hit the ground, pulled down by her father. She saw Lynden fall a few yards away. Heard a man give a horrible scream.

All turned dark as night. Rain began to fall. It was only later that she found it wasn't rain at all, but specks of blood and of the creatures' saliva, which left tiny burns on her cheek and her hands and all over her clothing.

For a minute or more, endless, the world was filled with the dark bustling of a nightmare. Tails like razors lashed at her head. The monsters dodged and whirled out of reach of the swaying staves and axes. Nothing touched them. The last of the villagers dropped to the ground and covered his head, defeated.

Tanthe forced herself to glance up. She thought she saw a figure, half-seen as if part of the battlefield itself had risen up to form a ghostly human shape. It moved slowly, turned, and looked at her with the veiled face of a skull. She buried her head.

Slowly the sounds began to diminish. Silence fell. Clean air swept in. Tanthe looked up and the sky was clear; overcast still, but clean. The monsters and the horsemen had all vanished.

She and Eodwyth staggered up, helping each other. Eodwyth was limping; he'd run too hard on his bad leg. 'You all right, Tan?' he said.

She nodded. 'I think so, Dad.' She made to rub her face but he caught her hand.

'Don't touch your eyes. Their spit stings. You'll blind yourself.'

Around them the other villagers, dazed, were also rising to their feet. Lynden sat up, dejected. His hands hung between his knees and his head was bowed; Tanthe saw blood in his hair, blood running in rivulets off his chin. She started towards him.

One of those who had fallen did not rise again. Her father stumbled to him, turned the body over, and let out a long howl of despair.

It was his brother. Tanthe saw the face of her beloved uncle Ewain, white and open-eyed, a terrible wound in his scalp, another in his shoulder. As if a great claw had rent and pierced him. His whole torso was wet and purple with blood.

The pall of twilight was colourless, static with a deadly atmosphere. Tears ran down Tanthe's face. She gripped her father's shoulders but neither of them said anything.

A man, their neighbour, who a few days ago had helped them bring the harvest home, said gently, 'Some of us will bring a stretcher from the village, and take him back. Go home, Eodwyth.'

'No,' said Eodwyth. 'I'll wait with him. Go back with Lynden, Tanthe. I'll see you later.' She didn't want to leave him, but she could see he meant it. He needed to be alone with his brother.

She went to Lynden and helped him to his feet. 'It's my uncle,' she said quietly, as he saw her father kneeling by the body. 'How am I going to tell Mum?'

'Gods. I'm sorry.'

'Come to our house,' Tanthe said. 'I'll bathe and dress that wound for you.'

Lynden nodded. 'They ate our fish,' he said.

'What?'

'That bastard Beyne and the troop officer – they ate the trout Ymmi and I caught, and then they took her!'

Tanthe put her arm round him. She couldn't answer.

As they walked back towards the village, Rufryd suddenly appeared beside them. Tanthe didn't want him there. She was too angry to say anything to him.

'How is he?' Rufryd asked, meaning Lynden. 'Badly hurt? Answer me!'

'Why should I?' Tanthe exploded. 'You didn't do a thing to help!'

'Because it was bloody stupid of you lot to try! Look what happened!'

'Dragon-hawks. We *would* have got her back if it hadn't been for them.'

'They weren't dra'a'ks, Tan,' said Rufryd.

'Of course they were. What else?'

'Dra'a'ks don't attack in flocks, and hardly ever come this far down off the mountain; they certainly don't appear and vanish in midair. You know their prey is usually animals or small children; they don't attack adults then leave them to die, or make wounds like that. They were too big. Didn't you see the colour of them?'

'They must have been a different type, like there are different types of bird.'

'Dra'a'ks can't be trained to protect human troops!'

And Tanthe knew all this, but couldn't bring herself to admit it. It would raise too many impossible questions. 'Trained? Don't be ridiculous.'

'They looked like dra'a'ks, but they weren't,' said Rufryd. 'They were . . . I don't know. Something worse.'

Gulzhur stood looking down at the battlefield for a long time after the humans had staggered away. He always liked to linger a while, relishing the devastation. He felt satiated and glowing, yet the scent of blood was still delicious, and pulses of warmth still rained on his flesh, emanating from one remaining man who was kneeling over the corpse. Only one death, but so much pain.

At length Enabler reluctantly turned and went on his way, his hood concealing his translucent face and the grinning skull beneath. These humans, at last, had shown spirit and given him a fight to savour. Perhaps, in time, they would give more.

Chapter Three. A Game of Amber

From a chamber tiled with amber, white marble and black onyx, high in his fortressed palace, King Garnelys surveyed his kingdom. He was alone. Waiting for news, he stood at an arched window with his forehead pressed to a small, cold pane. The city of Parione spread gloriously below him, all the way to the violet-hazed horizon.

Parione was the greatest city of Aventuria, spilling over the long wide skirts of three hills. It was beautiful in a profligate yet stately way, like a meadow that had exploded into a mass of creamy flowers. Its streets were wide and airy with buildings of pale and honey-coloured stone, handsome without severity. Trees, gardens and fountains, art galleries and workshops filled the curving streets. Around the city the landscape was velvety green, the sky above soft and evocative. Always beautiful, Parione's sky, whether rosy with sunlight or swollen with rain. Down there lived his thousands of beloved subjects, who adored their King.

Dominating the city on the highest, steepest hill stood the Amber Citadel. Within its great outer wall were two more walls rising in concentric oval rings, each housing different levels of royal guards or staff, until at the centre rose the palace of King Garnelys and Queen Mabriahna. The Citadel had been built one thousand seven hundred years ago of the loveliest honey-coloured marble that the quarries of Napheneth could yield. Stone full of crystal, that in all lights shone the colour of deep golden amber.

Once the Citadel had needed to be fortressed against enemies. Now and for the past two hundred and fifty years, the monarchs of Aventuria ruled over a peaceful, united realm. Yet the great continent, Aventuria, had not always been united, and certainly not peaceful. The earliest days were lost in mist and myth; the earth running with jewel-fire – the untamed semi-sentient energy of rocks, stones, rivers of lava – until the Aelyr mage Nilothphon (according to legend) tamed the energies and so made the land habitable for humans. But of the people who first blinked in the light after the Goddess birthed them, little was known. They were hunters, followers of the stag god. In those days the realms had no names and no boundaries; it was said that the Aelyr first taught humans the basics of civilisation, but Garnelys rejected the idea. Ridiculous to think that humans had evolved nothing for themselves. It was the warlike people of Torith Mir, with their endless raids on their neighbours, who forced the other tribes to cooperate and to grow in knowledge. The men and women of the lands that were to become Noreya, Eisilion and Paranios fought fiercely to drive the northerners back. But one tribe, under their leader Maroc, fled into the south, there to establish the first city by the warm Lapis Ocean and the first realm, Azura Maroc.

Garnelys had visited that land. He'd travelled widely in his young days (as his granddaughter Helananthe now travelled – or rather, *had* travelled) to learn about the realms of which he would be King. He'd found Azura Maroc a hot, florid country of jewel-colours, still full, as in the ancient days, of astronomers and scientist-philosophers who lazed in the shade in their gorgeous robes, holding forth endlessly and cleverly but never doing anything practical. A spent force. Once, Azura Maroc could have called the rest of Aventuria its empire. Over aeons its people had forged the trade routes, mingled with the Aelyr, helped the other realms to establish themselves under their own Kings and Queens. But glorious Azura Maroc had fallen, some two thousand years ago, overcome by plague.

The plague had coincided with the first appearance of

the Bhahdradomen. Some said that the hollow-eyed invaders came from a blackened land far across the ocean; others that they'd crawled up from holes in the earth. That they'd been waiting for the plague, or even caused it. For it was left to Thanmandrathor and Paranios to repel the invaders at terrible cost, while Azura Maroc languished in devastation. The Golden Age was over.

Then the centre of civilisation moved to vibrant Parione. Each realm was proudly independent; they had their quarrels – with each other and with the Aelyr – and Torith Mir remained a menace in the north. Yet it was a fruitful time, an age, if not of gold, at least of silver. Until the Bhahdradomen came again. And again.

Each time they were defeated they returned in greater force, persistent as cockroaches, devastating as locusts. Over two hundred years they spread their blackness over the continent and for two hundred more they remained. Every realm in turn fell to the horror. Garnelys could not even imagine the nightmare of those times; no one could. At last there was only Parione left. All the other realms turned to the Amber Citadel as their last hope; and it was only when the others gave up their kingships to Parione, and united under a single monarch, that they were able to turn the tide and drive the Bhahdradomen out in a long, terrible, thunderous war, culminating on the Silver Plains of Thanmandrathor.

Two hundred and fifty years of peace and healing had passed since then. Garnelys liked to think of it as the Heliodor Age; the land glowing like a jewel in the sun. Because the monarchs of Parione had ruled wisely and well, the other realms had remained happily subject to them, mindful of the need to stay united. It was a proud achievement, the union of the Nine Realms.

Except that Garnelys himself had done nothing to achieve it. His inheritance had rolled into his lap, ripe and complete, a golden apple. So he must do something to leave his mark.

From his vantage point the King cast his brooding gaze over the city's other two hills. They were of equal height and formed a rough triangle with the Amber Citadel, affording him a good view of each. The hill to the right was crested by the rounded, pearly temple of the Goddess Nepheter. On the other had once stood the city's main theatre, the Old Royal, one of Parione's oldest and loveliest buildings.

Now, alas, it was gone.

Garnelys looked narrow-eyed at the scene. The hill-top was denuded of trees, scarred and flattened. Ugly. His citizens had fought and lost life and freedom to save the theatre; people still stood and wept to see the naked earth where it had been, but he was dry-eyed. It was their own fault. If only they had kept faith with him when he first announced the great project. If only that snide playwright Saphaeyender had not mocked his plans in his so-called satire, and the audience had not laughed in such delighted recognition.

His relationship with his subjects had changed the day he ordered the demolition of the theatre. That act had tainted their trust with disbelief and fear, killed their mockery dead. And he felt no regret. Only a minority opposed his plans, but he'd had to act decisively to show that dissent would not be tolerated. One day, when they understood, they would forgive him and sing his praises. He knew they still loved him.

The conscriptions were going well, after all. The people of Paranios and watery Mithrain had submitted willingly enough. So had the fair-headed folk of Noreya, land of forests and of impenetrable forest-lore, and even the slithery people of Eisilion, with their fox-god and snake-goddess. And how easily the clever, lazy dreamers of Azura Maroc had given up their young people, even trying to send more than he had asked for!

From what he'd heard, the hunters of Deirland and the farmers of Sepheret were also cooperating. He'd anticipated trouble from Torith Mir and so Garnelys, ever subtle, had recruited from there many of the new officers he needed; men and women who weren't afraid to be fierce, strict, even harsh. The lure of power seduced them most effectively. The last realm from which he'd anticipated resistance was Thanmandrathor; and yet those people, usually so brave and loyal, had had the effrontery to organise petitions and protests against their King! Hard to enforce conscriptions in such a vast realm. But, damn them, they would submit. He'd always admired their honourable nature, never expected to have it turned against him. Traitors.

Garnelys stared hard at the hill, imagining the scene as it would look when the project was finished. His mind was empty of all else. He did not even think about the imminent, dreadful arrival for which he waited. It was hard, these days, to keep his mind on anything but the project.

His long, gnarled arm reached out and plucked the bell-pull, summoning the attendant who was on duty outside the door. 'Have Laphaeome sent to me,' said the king. 'Have him bring the drawings.'

Laphaeome came swiftly. The door of golden oak opened to admit his white-robed and hooded figure, coming in with quick gliding steps, carrying rolls of paper under his arm.

'Your Majesty,' said the architect, bowing. 'You wish to see the latest refinements to the plans?'

'If you please. You will pardon me if I have interrupted your work.'

'Not at all, sire. My purpose is to anticipate and serve your wishes.'

'As you always do.' Garnelys's sombre mouth creaked at one corner into a smile; the same expression was reflected on the architect's pinkish-pale face. It was a bland face, Garnelys thought, too regular and soft-featured to have any real character, but the eyes were black and sharp with intelligence. These days, Garnelys felt more in accord with

67

Laphaeome than with any member of his own family. 'Spread the plans on the table.'

Laphaeome did as he asked, covering the round, marble-inlaid surface with drawings and weighting their corners with books. He always wore thin black gloves; explaining that the ink irritated his skin; in fact his hands looked slightly deformed, but the King was too well-mannered to comment. The ink diagrams showed cross sections of stone blocks, of trenches and foundations and lifting machinery. But the one that held the King's attention was that of the tower itself.

'The height,' he said, tracing the grey lines of the sketch. 'How are you progressing with the problem of achieving such a great height?'

'It has proved a challenge, sire . . .'

Garnelys glared hard into the architect's eyes. 'A challenge that must be met.'

Laphaeome broke the eye contact, dipping his head. He spoke softly and reassuringly. 'I was going to say, sire, that although it has proved a challenge, we have overcome all technical obstacles to construction. The mining of the stone is going well; opposition from the Subterraneans so weak as to be nonexistent.'

Garnelys tutted. The Subterraneans were a small, obstreperous race who thought that they alone had a divine right to mine and quarry the earth. Once Garnelys had eagerly absorbed knowledge of the non-human races; now the mere idea of their existence irritated him. They made his world too complicated. 'Then do not mention them to me!' he hissed.

'Your pardon, sire. We are almost ready to begin laying the foundations.'

'When?'

'In four days' time, sire, to be precise.'

'Good,' said the King, letting go of his breath. 'Good.'

'The refinements we have added here, you see . . .'

As the architect spoke, Garnelys raised his eyes from the

68

drawing to the hill beyond the window, visualising so strongly that he could actually see a tower soaring up and up against the sky until it pierced the very dome of the heavens. A tower of blond marble – the colour of yellow beryl, the colour of the sun – embellished with moonstone and sunstone and amethyst. Garnelys caught his breath with the glory of it. His Heliodor Tower.

It would be a monument to the Goddess, like the phallus of Her consort piercing Her veil, symbolising the divine origin of life; but it would also be Garnelys's legacy to Parione, his offering to the gods, his own memorial. Thus, in the only way possible, he could be sure that the people of Aventuria would never forget him.

That was his great terror. That in his long reign he had done nothing bold, nothing decisive, nothing memorable, and that his name would die with him. He was seventy-seven, he might have left three years or thirty, but it would never be enough.

'Excellent. Now, from the beginning; take me through each step of construction . . .'

Laphaeome's voice, as he explained each detail, was very quiet. Over it, almost drowning him out, the King heard noises from beyond his chamber. Footsteps in the corridor, hushed troubled voices. His right hand tightened into a fist. This was the moment he'd dreaded. He didn't want to face them but they were coming closer and their burden would not be denied.

He closed his eyes, concentrating on the architect's voice. A curtain fell across his mind so that he could perceive nothing clearly through its grey weave. He was sinking through it. He recalled suddenly a day – last year in the summer – when he'd announced his project to an over-joyed populace; their cheers, their laughter, the love and trust that radiated from them. 'This great tower will be the wonder of the world. This is our gift to you, the people of Aventuria. Those of you who are chosen to build it shall be immortalised.' Then the cheers, the shouts, the celebration!

Garnelys clung to the memory.

Three sharp raps at the door brought him back to himself. The attendant admitted Lord Poel, who came in white-faced but stiff and sombre. Garnelys could see the attendant and the door-wardens staring, aghast, upset but trying to control themselves. Even the voice of the emotionless Poel cracked like parched earth as he spoke. 'Your Majesty. Captains Valnys and Kerowen of the Royal Guard.'

Garnelys looked up. He saw in the doorway the two captains, in their violet and green dress uniforms, holding their feathered caps in their hands. Their faces were grim. Behind them – only half seen in the dark corridor – were four royal guards, bearing a laden stretcher.

'Your Majesty,' began the taller man, Valnys. 'We came here with all haste—'

'Wait,' Garnelys broke in sharply.

'Sire?'

'Can you not see that I am otherwise occupied? You will wait until my business with my architect is finished. Laphaeome, go on.'

Kerowen's face did not change, but Valnys's plainly betrayed his shock. He hesitated before bowing his head in stunned acquiescence. 'Sire.' The architect, who had paused, continued explaining how the tower was to be built. Seeming unflustered by the interruption, he neither hurried nor skipped any detail.

Laphaeome went on for fifteen minutes. The Captains waited; still at first, then beginning to twist their caps in their hands and to glance at each other. The bearers grew tired and restless. Lord Poel glared and they all stood to attention, holding their breath, stiff with apprehension. Only when Laphaeome had finished did Garnelys dismiss him. With his gloved hands the architect rolled the plans, tucked them under his arm, and left as if nothing were amiss.

'Well?' said Garnelys.

Lord Poel nodded at the captains. Valnys glanced

uncomfortably at Kerowen. The two came forward with grave faces and folded hands. 'Sire,' said Valnys, his voice shaking. 'We found his hiding place in the crypts of the temple in the lower city. We did our utmost to bring him alive, but he fought long and valiantly. It was I who ran him through. For that I beg your forgiveness. If we have served you ill, we shall accept our punishment.'

The King exhaled. 'No, Captain Valnys. My command was to bring him here in any condition. His crime was of the gravest nature: betrayal of Aventuria. You will receive the rewards due to you.' But Garnelys had noted the suspicious, fearful looks that Valnys and Kerowen had exchanged. Why, why did they doubt him?

'Come,' said the King, beckoning the stretcher-bearers into the room. 'Lay him on the marble dais at the rear of the chamber. I had it placed there in readiness. The events surrounding his death will be kept secret, on pain of death, do you comprehend? I wish no shame to attach to his name. It shall be announced only that he died of a tragic illness.'

In silence, the soldiers carried their grim burden past him. On the stretcher, covered in a cloth of purple and gold, lay the body of Prince Galemanth, handsome even now, with his long dark hair brushed back from his strong, pallid face. He had been forty-nine. As Garnelys studied that familiar face a dart of blackness went through him, yet it seemed very far away. He knew, and yet could not *feel*, that this was his heir upon the bier. His only son. Dead.

Later, as darkness fell outside, King Garnelys brooded over the pieces on a metrarch board. Of course, his move was obvious. He advanced his golden tower to the far side of the spider-web squares, and claimed victory.

'Sire, I hardly think I can compete with your strategy.' His opponent, a young male conscript, spoke in a nervous whisper. 'Do you desire another game?'

'Yes, let us play again. You provide an exacting challenge, Tryonis.' Garnelys was absorbed by the game, not ready to relinquish that feeling. With trembling fingers, the fair-haired lad gathered up the pieces and began to replace them in two opposing curves, one of amber, the other of blue lapis. Tower, sun, star, the three moons, hierophant, priestess, serpent, the warriors on their tiny horses . . . The only sounds in the chamber were the clicking of the pieces on the polished board and Garnelys's own breathing.

Sudden, muffled voices outside the door shattered his peace.

The attendant came in and announced, 'Your Majesty, Her Majesty Queen Mabriahna.'

He heard his wife come in, yet he kept his eyes fixed on the metrarch board. He wished to think about nothing but the relationship of the pieces on the intersecting nodes of the web. Tryonis looked up anxiously, then leapt to his feet and bowed. Garnelys snapped at him, 'Sit. Make your move.'

'Sire.' The young man obeyed, flushing with confusion.

'My dear,' said Mabriahna.

Garnelys did not respond.

She came closer, her skirts of yellow silk swishing on the tiles. 'My dear,' she said softly, 'I have come to see the body of our son. Will you not send this young man away?'

He looked up slowly. Her overskirt was striped with black, her stomacher and full sleeves trimmed with black and silver, her grey hair immaculately swept back and held with a cluster of opals. Her face, though reddened and scored with grief, was composed. She possessed a natural dignity that nothing could take from her, and she had done her crying in private.

'I'm in the middle of a game. No one is preventing you from viewing the body.'

She stared at him. She took in a small breath, and the wounded shock in her eyes was so discreet he barely saw

72

it. 'I wish to talk to you alone.'

'There is nothing to be said that cannot be said in front of this servant or any other.'

He saw her long graceful throat as she swallowed. 'Well, then so be it. I will not argue with you in front of our subjects, nor in front of our son.'

At the rear of the chamber, twelve thick white candles had been set on tall sconces forming an oval around the bier where Galemanth lay. Their light spun a dim cocoon on the darkness. Mabriahna passed into this solemn space, shadows spreading from her fingers as she reached out to touch her son's face.

The conscript's hand was shaking as he moved one of his moons. The King knew he was confused and afraid, yet he felt no sympathy. The blue and gold pieces blurred in his vision. Mabriahna was silent for a time, then she spoke, her voice close to breaking.

'When did you hear that he was dead? Did you know before they brought his body?'

The King sighed. 'Yes. I received the message a few hours before they brought him to me.'

'You did not tell me,' she whispered.

He did not reply. She said more forcefully, 'How could you not tell me?'

'How could I?' he exclaimed. He slid his priestess forward to sweep Tryonis's moon off the board.

A long pause. Then she spoke as if talking to herself, 'At least he is here. At least we know for sure. Not like Helananthe. I only see her rolling on the bottom of the ocean, with her hair floating around her like seaweed. Fishes gnawing at her and sea-snakes twining round her. I can't bear to think of how she died, but I can't stop dreaming of it, imagining it.'

'Mabriahna.' He wanted to silence her.

'Galemanth hadn't got over it. I doubt that he ever could. But at least he is here. I can see him and touch him and know for certain this is real. How did he die?'

'A fight. A sword-wound. It was quick, they told me.'

Another pause. Then, '*Why* did he die?'

He rose abruptly. Tryonis and Mabriahna both started, waiting to see what he would do as if they were afraid of him. Why this fear, he wondered in irritation. He walked heavily to the bier and went in a slow circuit around it, looking at the body from every angle. His handsome son, his only child. 'If you must speak, do so softly,' he whispered.

'I asked you to send the boy away,' the Queen answered stiffly. Then she took his hand. Hers felt like fire, while his was cold and rigid as wood. 'Look, beloved. This is our son.'

'I know.'

'Yet you seem as if you don't! Why are you not shocked? Have you wept at all? We don't weep in public but with each other . . . yet you never came to me. You have not been to my chamber for two years and more. It must have been quite gradual, the change, for I cannot remember a point at which I realised something was wrong. What has happened to you? Why have you changed?'

'I haven't,' replied Garnelys. Her questions were like the constant stinging of a summer fly, insignificant yet maddening. He felt a great black weight of rage gathering inside him. 'All that I do is to safeguard Aventuria.'

'And what about all that *I* do? We are meant to rule jointly. Have you cut me from your counsel and all your decisions, to safeguard Aventuria?' Her question did not merit an answer; she did not seem to expect one. Mabriahna moved to the far side of the bier and stood looking at her son's waxen face. 'Is it true that you made the pallbearers wait while you finished talking to an architect? And now you sit playing metrarch rather than face what has happened!'

The steel anger in her voice increased the heavy black cloud within him. He closed his eyes and pinched the skin between his eyebrows, feeling that the blackness must

74

explode or kill him. 'All that has been done is for Aventuria's sake.'

When he looked at her again, Mabriahna was looking at him differently. Her lips soured, and there was horror gathering in her eyes. 'Tell me you didn't have him killed.'

Garnelys sighed. The pressure in his soul grew, blotting out all else. His hands began to shake. 'I could no longer trust him,' he said woodenly. 'The Nine Realms would not have been safe in his hands. He betrayed us, Mabriahna. That is why I have no tears for him.'

She recoiled, her face a map of revulsion. Staggering, she steadied herself on the edge of the bier and her voice rasped out like torn metal, 'You killed him!'

Queen Mabriahna pressed a hand to her tormented face, and fled the chamber.

A long silence followed her departure. The King stood motionless, not feeling, not thinking, not even seeing clearly. The room with its reddish glow and flickering flames looked unreal.

'Sire?' came the nervous voice of Tryonis. 'Do you wish to continue our game?'

The King turned and walked to him, the candles casting a monstrous, leaping shadow from his feet. He towered over the boy, and his eyes were blood-black marbles in his gaunt, aquiline face. The playing pieces went skittering onto the floor as he seized the conscript's shirt. The boy cried out in terror. 'No. No more games. I have other needs now.'

A hidden panel in the wall swung open into a short corridor. At its end, a twisting staircase led down into a cell, one of countless similar in the rambling structure of the Amber Citadel. Tryonis struggled, but despite his age the King's height and strength were far superior. Garnelys barely noticed his pleas for mercy through the rushing in his ears. This must be done. The truth must be known.

The cell was ten feet square, cold and rough-hewn with walls of dark, sweating rock. Chill air flowed through a low, black archway on the far side. The only furniture was a wooden post bolted to the centre of the floor, with cross members and dangling metal straps. Garnelys knew his way in the pitch darkness; with sure hands he strapped the boy to the post. All the time he cried out with fear of the darkness, but the king ignored the noise. Once the boy was secure, he lit a lamp mounted on one wall. The rock shone darkly. Hanging in the straps, the youth was white and writhing with terror. As Garnelys turned to the iron rack and selected his favourite knife, he caught the pungent scent of urine.

'Sire, I beg you – whatever I've done, don't punish me.' Then, pathetically, 'Will someone tell my mother?'

Garnelys had grown used to blocking out their cries. He raised the knife and began to chant, channelling the intense energy that the Aelyr called *gauroth*. A large quartz crystal, dark as smoke, was fixed to the top of the post, protruding above the victim's head. As Garnelys chanted, it began to glow.

The straps were so designed that the more the victim struggled, the tighter they became. Realising, the boy writhed harder in panic. Tight bands clasped his shins and thighs, upper arms and wrists, ribs. He sweated. Panic radiated from him in hard waves with his heartbeat; and with each pulse, the crystal glowed brighter. Dark *gauroth* energy filled the cell, spinning a cone of power.

Chanting faster and faster, the King stepped forward and lowered the knife to the boy's throat. In the same intent, quiet manner as that in which he'd played the board game, Garnelys pressed the point into the tender flesh, and made a shallow cut like a smile over the windpipe.

The man screamed.

The cone contracted, whirling faster and faster. The smoky quartz pulsated. Voices seemed to echo from it, sighs and moans, and they were answered by a much greater crystal, far below in the roots of the Citadel. All the sounds blended into one eerie dissonance; the chanting,

76

the boy's screams, the bodiless groans of pleasure.

'Speak,' said Garnelys. He watched the blood trickling down over the conscript's collarbones. Red. Wet. He heard the crack of bone. Tryonis gasped and pleaded, caught in agony and the unravelling horror of wondering how long this would last before he died.

The energies throbbed, feeding on the pain and the blood.

'Speak!' the King cried, directing all his will into the tormented body. 'Speak to me, Galemanth!'

The boy swooned, but the long red slit in his throat twitched and opened like a mouth. From it issued the voice of the King's son.

'Kerowen, Valnys. You are good men, you have been good friends to me. There is no need for this. My quarrel with my father is no concern of yours. It will all be resolved in time.' There was a pause. Then, *'No, I will not go with you. I am not a child to be coerced, nor a hound to be brought to heel. I will speak to my father when he is ready, not – very well, if it is a fight you want—'*

The *gauroth* showed Garnelys the past in vivid, harrowing detail. His son, a brave swordsman, fighting in the dark chamber of the temple of Nuth. The fatal blow dealt by Valnys, who then jumped back in distressed horror at what he'd done. Galemanth falling, dying, reaching out – *'Tell my father . . .'*

'What?' Garnelys shouted. 'What?'

'This is the wrong path,' whispered the red slit. *'Father, you have made a mistake and now I will not be here to guide you out of it. I will always love you. But forgive you – never.'*

'Then reveal the future to me!'

'All was revealed at my death. The secrets that monarchs of Aventuria learn only when they ascend the throne. I know your shame and I want no part of it!'

The boy raised his head and stared at the King with his son's dead eyes; coldly yellow-green as two peridots, full of deathly accusation.

Uttering a howl, the King lurched forward and plunged

the knife into the boy's guts, just as Valnys had slain his son. Blood pumped out from some deep, essential artery. Garnelys dropped his knife and thrust his hand into the wound, feeling the hot blood spurting over his hands, feeling the dying agonies of his victim, breathing deep of all the smells, even the stench of ruptured intestines. He gasped in relief. The *gauroth* was sated, and now he felt his own tension draining away. The energies he'd summoned had fed both his strength and that of the land; the explosion was over, and with it the black storm in his soul was gone.

Garnelys stepped back, swaying. Blood dripped from his hands. Tryonis was dead. How pitiful he looked, his young life destroyed, wasted . . . the King trembled, horrified at what he had done and yet numbed against it. He didn't always kill them, but sometimes it couldn't be helped. He felt drained. Sad, hopeless, and yet purged . . . perhaps able to sleep tonight, after all.

There was a soft sound behind him and the figure of Laphaeome drifted to his side. Strange, how the architect always knew where and when to find him, and how he seemed to understand him completely.

'These sacrifices are sad, but essential, your Majesty, just as in the ancient days,' the architect said gently. 'I will see that all this is cleaned away. You go and rest.'

The King nodded. At last, to his own surprise, he felt tears coming. A single drop ran down and dripped from his chin to form, in the lake of blood at his feet, a tiny clear pool.

Dawn in Riverwynde saw the still grey aftermath of the battle. Dew lay silver on the wide flat stretch of grass where Ewain had died, and blood lay there too, staining the ground and jewelling the spiders' webs with dark garnets. The villagers stood silently at the place. Nothing like this had happened in living memory.

The sun rose over the river and began to burn off the

dew. The hills and the sky were softly golden. It was going to be another fine, hot day.

When the villagers had paid their respects in the place where Ewain had been killed, Helwyn the priestess led them in procession back to the village. There they interred him in the wooded hillside burial ground where their ancestors lay. As always, the priestess and priest led the rite – even though it was their own son they were burying. Tanthe's grandfather, Osforn, reminded her of an oak, gnarled but enduring, while her grandmother was a birch, white and graceful as she moved round the circle, calling the blessing and protection of the elements. Her voice wavered but did not break. *'May the winds blow kindly on him, the gentle rain nurture his roots, the sun give of her warmth and the rich earth be as the womb of Nuth . . .'*

Priestess and priest were acting as channels of the nature deities Breyid and Anthar, welcoming their child back into the earth. But never had anyone dreamed they would have to perform such a rite for their own son.

A soft breeze blew through the trees as the villagers circled the grave, throwing in small gifts and flowers, each paying a tribute. *'Ewain was a kind man.'* *'He was always ready to help.'* *'If I was sad he would make me laugh.'* It broke Tanthe's heart to see how bitterly her parents wept. Two of her family were gone at a stroke. That should have been me, not Ymmi, she thought. I could have coped, it would have been an adventure for me, but she's not strong enough.

How can I think of leaving my parents now, when they've lost so much?

When the time came to fill in the grave, Eodwyth planted a birch sapling there to mark the place. His brother would live on in the tree and never be forgotten. Life springing from death.

After the burial, as she strode the thin grassy paths between the cottages, Tanthe realised that everything felt different. Her grandparents walked with dignity, but their

79

eyes were distant and they spoke to no one. Her other grandma Freyna walked with Aynie and Eodwyth, Gazer trotting along beside Feryn, but Tanthe hung back. The village was somehow out of shape, hostile, no longer like home. Nothing would ever be the same again. Where there had been laughter and camaraderie, there was silence. Evil had touched them, they'd been bitterly betrayed, but they were all too terrified to acknowledge it. Too afraid even to ask why it had happened.

Entering the cottage, the first thing that met Tanthe's eyes was the circle of plaques hanging on the kitchen wall. Ysomir had carved them from moss-green stone to represent the eight spokes of the year. Hazelnuts and pumpkins for Darkeve, which was the new year and the gateway to winter; holly and mistletoe for Hollynight, the winter solstice; snowdrops for Breyid's Day, daffodils for Estrae, may blossom for Firethorn, roses for Midsummer, wheatears for Lunagh, the beginning of harvest, and apples for Fallon, the autumn equinox. The plaques mocked her with their naive beauty. Tanthe remembered a young Ymmi sitting at the kitchen table with their granddad Lan, her honey-brown head bent over a lump of rock as he showed her how to hold the chisel . . .

Tanthe closed her eyes, turned away. She went straight out again and sat instead on the green until it was time for them to assemble in the Village House. The villagers crowded into the bare hall on the lower floor, as Arthryn's assistant Megden passed among them with cakes and glasses of mead.

Presently Arthryn called them to attention. 'A tragedy has befallen us,' he began. 'We have lost two of our dearest citizens. All inhabitants of Riverwynde are equally valuable to us, there are none we can afford to lose; yet none of us will ever forget the goodness of Ewain or the beauty of Ysomir, our fairest maiden—'

'She's not dead,' Tanthe said, loud enough to be heard.

Arthryn glanced uncomfortably at her and continued,

'However, we must not get these events, tragic as they are, out of proportion. Ysomir, as her sister rightly points out, is alive and furthermore has been chosen to help in a glorious project at the King's command. Whilst I fully appreciate your feelings, your attempt to bring her back was ill-considered.'

'Well?' called Eodwyth. 'Did you see the things that attacked us? Where did they come from?'

Arthryn cleared his throat. He hesitated, as if uncertain whether to tell the truth or not. 'Beyne explained it to me. We all know of the Mediators, sorcerers who helped to bring peace after the War of the Silver Plains. Well, the Mediators are helping the King in his project. As the army is not yet large enough to send great forces of armed men to the outer Realms, the Mediators send those creatures with them as a – a reinforcement in case of trouble.'

Tanthe glanced at Rufryd and Lynden, standing at the side of the room, but they were silent.

'You're lying!' shouted someone.

Arthryn seemed flustered. 'That's what Beyne told me. I have no other explanation.'

'Why didn't you warn us?'

'I tried! I did everything to persuade you not to go! And even I didn't know what these creatures would be like! I'm sorry. But who are we to question the King's wisdom, or think that we know better than him what is good for Aventuria?'

'But why would the King use such monsters against his own people?' Aynie said. 'Can we be sure it's really the King behind this?'

'I'm as sure as I can be,' said Arthryn.

'Resign!' called someone else. 'Let Helwyn take your place!'

The priestess rose in her white funeral robe, leaning on her staff of pale wood. 'I would not take Arthryn's place, even if I could,' she said wearily. 'It's not his fault. What has happened today is that we've been shown a truth we would rather not acknowledge. For as long as we are left to ourselves, our lives are peaceful, the Xauroma intact, our rulers benevolent. We are free. But when someone interferes, suddenly we find there is nothing we can do about it. To whom can we appeal? To Arthryn? You've seen that he has no power to help us. To the council of Havereyn, then? Or the Duchess of Sepheret? No, for they have no true power either. The council of Skald, from which Beyne was sent, rules us – but again, they are only taking orders from the King.

'And the King is not a fool; he knows that not all will be happy to be torn from their homes, yet he's so determined to have his way that he sends soldiers and dra'a'ks to enforce it. How can we appeal against that? This is the truth. We are not free. We are like children, entrusting ourselves to a single all-powerful parent, and completely at the mercy of that parent's good will.'

A stunned silence met her words. Eodwyth said, 'What can we do?'

'I don't believe we can do anything,' said Helwyn. 'We have trusted the King all our lives. If we stop trusting him, what do we have to take the place of that trust? Nothing. I want my granddaughter back, as you all do – but we would only tear ourselves apart, trying to find her. There's no sense in more of us dying. My advice is that we go calmly about our business. Let the strand of life be unbroken.'

She sat down again, to a murmur of voices.

Arthryn said, 'I can add nothing to that. If you won't listen to me, at least listen to the wise words of our priestess. It would be wrong to oppose the King. Let's try to feel honoured that Ysomir was chosen.'

Aynie was weeping. Eodwyth put his arm round her. There was a general, subdued muttering, but no one spoke up. Tanthe couldn't contain herself.

'So you're going to do nothing?' she exclaimed. 'You're going to let them take my sister, and resign yourselves to never seeing her again? *I* can't!'

'I know it's hard, but Helwyn has spoken the truth,' said Arthryn. 'Life must go on.'

'Until the next time.'

Tanthe looked at her father and mother, but they only gazed back at her with hopeless eyes, shaking their heads to quiet her.

'Helwyn's right,' said Aynie, wiping her nose. 'All I want to do is run after Ymmi. But I can't. I have Feryn to look after and we can't leave the farm. Your father can't travel far with his bad leg, anyway. There's a dozen reasons we can't go. Sometimes you have to do the hardest thing of all, which is to accept.'

'We've got to do something! We must get her back!'

'Tanthe,' Eodwyth said roughly. 'Isn't it enough that your uncle died?'

'He's right,' said Freyna. The sharp humour that usually gleamed in her eyes was dead. 'Keep our heads down and get on with things.' She tried to take her granddaughter's arm, but Tanthe shook free.

'You cowards!' Tanthe yelled – at everyone, not just her family. 'You can't just give up!'

The others only turned away from her, her parents included, their heads lowered. They were silent with the stoic resignation that sustained them through the worst of winters and dra'a'ks attacks. Typical Riverwynders! She'd never felt more of an outsider. The only person to look Tanthe in the eye was Helwyn, a fierce look that was both chiding and meaningful.

'Tanthe,' she said softly. 'Don't insult them.'

'I didn't mean it, but—'

'They are dealing with this as they feel they must. And you must do the same.' She touched her granddaughter's shoulder, and moved on.

In the late afternoon, Tanthe went alone to a favourite wild corner of the woods and made a little shrine to Breyid. She built a cairn of stones, and inside it laid wheat ears and wild flowers. Tanthe cried as she worked. It was the first time she'd allowed herself to shed tears.

She loved this little grove, surrounded by oaks and by feathery arkh-woods, the sacred tree that was so beneficial to women. Its bark prevented pregnancy, its leaves eased all pains of the womb. Tanthe had never had a lover, but here she had often pleasured herself with her own hands, dreaming of lovers in far-off Parione, or even of the forest-god Anthar in his cloak of leaves.

The last thing on her mind now, though, was pleasure. She sat with her head drooping in front of the small shrine, asking Breyid to protect Ysomir.

'Help us,' she said. Her hands still itched from the tiny venom burns. 'I know what I must do. But I want to know it's the right thing. For mother and father, not for me. Guide me.'

A few days ago, everything had seemed perfect, and yet it had all been about to go wrong. It was as if Rufryd and Ysomir had known, in their different ways.

The light in the grove was rich and deep, all emeralds and molten reds and dark blues. Slowly she became aware of a strange paleness creeping in, a crystal glow from an unseen source.

Tanthe heard a noise, like someone taking a breath very near.

Her heart leaped. She looked around wildly. There seemed to be voices murmuring all around her and she turned dizzy. 'Who is it?' she cried. 'Show yourself!'

She heard the breath again, this time running out in a sigh. It seemed to be only a foot or two from her ear. '*Ohhh.*'

The world began to spin around her. She felt that her face was touching the sky, that she was close enough to kiss the spinning moons. And at the same time she was falling, the trees tossing like waves, the grass turning to gossamer beneath her. Her scream came out as a dry rasp. A male face smiled at her, framed by darkest auburn hair, a beautiful smile that seemed to mock her with its softness.

Then there was a brilliant flash, white fire piercing her eyes. It was the flash of a weapon. She was sure she was about to die. The Aelyr were going to kill her. Somehow, without meaning to, she'd offended them, or trespassed on their territory.

No. Breyid and Anthar, help me!

The world gave a shuddering jolt beneath her. All was still again, and she was lying on the grass, dazed. She sat up, putting her head in her hands. After a moment she pushed her hands back over her hair, breathing deeply, checking that body and limbs were intact. She was unhurt, only shaken.

A brightness on the altar caught her eye.

Tanthe leaned towards it and saw, lying on top of her offering of wheat and flowers, a slim white object. It was a knife, about six inches long, with a blade of white crystal and a silvery handle that was inscribed with symbols of a blazing sun and a triple moon. It was exquisitely beautiful, unearthly, so delicate it looked as if it might melt in her palm. It lay half out of a scabbard of silvery leather, sewn with tiny clear jewels in a diamond pattern.

She'd never seen an Aelyr knife before. But she recognised it for what it was.

'Am I meant to take this?' she asked aloud. 'Is it for me, or is it an Aelyr offering to Breyid?' Nothing answered her. 'I could be committing some dreadful blasphemy. If so . . . I'm sorry. But I need all the help I can get.'

Biting her lip, she reached out to the knife, only for it to dissolve and vanish under her hand. Tanthe snatched her hand back and scrubbed her fingers on her thigh as if she'd touched poison.

She was trembling. Nothing there. Yet it had seemed so real. Are the Aelyr playing tricks on me, she thought, or am I going mad? That was stupid of me. Taking anything of theirs is playing with fire, the stories say.

Again she wondered what had happened to the small crystal mirror Helwyn had given her, years ago.

The weird light had vanished. All was quiet again. Tanthe was left with a pounding heart, and a dull ache gathering behind her eyes.

She stood up unsteadily, thanked the goddess for her attention, and walked slowly back to the village. How different it seemed; closed, unfeeling, unreal. It was nearly dark, and no-one was abroad; they'd all retired early, out of respect for Ewain. But near the Village House she saw a shadow, someone moving softly along the wall of the barn and the kitchens at the rear of the House. Seeing her, he hurried away as if to hide.

'Lynden!' Tanthe called softly.

He stopped and waited for her, resigned. She pulled him into the recess of the kitchen courtyard, and in the dim twilight saw that his face was white, his eyes sore and encircled by shadows.

'You didn't say a word at the meeting,' she began. 'I thought you might have supported me! Don't you want to get Ymmi back?'

His head drooped. He leaned against the wall in a posture of total despair. 'Gods, Tanthe. You wouldn't ask that if you knew how much I wanted it! But what was the point of saying anything?'

'If you had the guts to stand up to your father—'

'For what? All I would have done was embarrass him! It's pointless.'

'I know.' Tanthe put her hand on his shoulder, trying to comfort him. 'They're scared.'

'It's more than that. It's like the priestess said, it would be mad to defy the King. We've tried it once and look what happened.'

'Yes, and I understand that my parents can't up and leave the village, however much they want to. But there's nothing keeping me here. My grandmother told me to do what I believed was right, just as if she knew what was in my mind. So. I'm going to go and rescue my sister. That's all I know.'

Lynden took a long, deep breath. His expression became resolute. 'In that case, I'm coming with you.'

Tanthe was half-worried and half-pleased. 'Are you sure?'

'Yes. I'm scared, too, but I don't care. I want Ymmi back. I'll die if I stay here without her, so it's the only thing to do.' He looked across to the kitchen window, which was dark. 'Come inside. There's no one up.'

In the kitchen, while Lynden fumbled to light a candle, Tanthe sat at the long scarred table. In the pool of candle-light, he poured two mugs of ale and sat opposite.

'It won't be easy,' said Tanthe. 'It could take weeks, even if we can borrow or steal a couple of horses along the way. I'm not even sure of the best way to begin. But we should go tonight. The sooner the better.'

'Not easy?'

It wasn't Lynden who'd spoken. An inside door creaked faintly and out of the darkness stepped Rufryd. He came into the candlelight and leaned on the table, glaring con-temptuously at Tanthe. 'Not easy? Have you any idea how hard a journey like that will be?'

'This is a private conversation,' she said angrily. 'Just like you to lurk around, eavesdropping.'

'I didn't need to,' said Rufryd. 'You were right under my window, talking at the top of your voice, as usual. If you think you're taking my little brother on this mad journey, you've got another think coming.'

'Rufe, mind your own business!' said Lynden.

'You're crazy. It's tough enough walking to Havereyn. How d'you think you'll carry enough food to walk for days at a time? How will you survive in the wilderness between realms? What will you do if your boots wear out, or you fall ill, or wild animals attack you? Do you know how far Parione is, or even where it is?'

'Of course I do,' said Tanthe.

'Draw a map, then.' Rufryd pushed a stick of charcoal at her, and a scrap of paper on which Megden had scrawled a list of tasks. 'Go on.'

Tanthe, furious, turned the scrap over and began to draw. Riverwynde. Hills. Havereyn. Afthan Horn. Mountains, the river Skaldwater, the town Skald beside it . . . then what? She paused, then completed what she thought was a good likeness of Aventuria.

'That's rubbish,' said Rufryd, grimly pleased. 'You've missed out a whole realm and a mountain range. You love Parione so much, but you don't even know how to get there.'

She threw down the charcoal. 'Well, you do better!'

'I don't need to. Father has maps in his office chamber. I'll fetch one.'

Rufryd lit a second candle from the first, and took it with him. While he was absent, Tanthe said, 'What on earth is he playing at?'

'He's just being Rufryd,' Lynden sighed.

'Listen to him if you want. I don't care. I'll go alone!'

'No, Tan. He's not going to talk me out of it.'

A few minutes later, Rufryd came back and dropped a large scroll in front of Tanthe. She began to unfold it; it was a superb map, beautifully drawn in black ink on fine white linen. But Rufryd was holding some smaller scrolls, and he looked pale in the candlelight, as if he'd had a shock.

'I found these on Father's desk,' he said.

'What?' said Lynden.

Rufryd sat on the bench seat beside his brother. 'According to this, Tanthe's family should have been paid fifteen ralds for Ysomir.'

'How much?' she gasped.

'Fifteen—'

'Well, we weren't. Paid, that's obscene!' she exclaimed. 'Let me see.'

'This seems to be a copy of the receipt, with my father's signature on it,' said Rufryd.

'Arthryn sold my sister?' She was ready to leap up and do murder.

88

'But he's not like that,' said Lynden.

'It's true, he isn't,' Rufryd said, shaking his head. 'Whatever else our father is, he's not dishonest. More likely he gave the money back to that slithery official.'

'Why?'

'Look at this,' Rufryd said flatly, smoothing out a list of names. 'The ones with crosses are us lot who were called on to the green. He marked my name, but changed his mind about Lynden. Lyn was there, but father must have known damned well he was safe. Of course, he wouldn't give a bean to keep me.'

They all stared at each other. 'No,' said Lynden. His eyes shone with bitter rage. 'No. If I thought it was true, I'd kill him.'

Tanthe caught hold of his wrists. 'And if they'd taken you – then I'd've had Ysomir sitting here agonising, instead of you! What does it matter now? Arthryn's too set in his ways to act. They all are. But I'm not.'

'You're insane,' said Rufryd.

'Well, *I* don't give a sod for your opinion. You're a coward like all the rest.'

'Really?'

'Really.'

'You're wrong, your royal high-and-mightiness. You needn't think you're taking my little brother on some mad journey into the wilderness on his own. If he's going, I'm coming with you. To protect him.'

'Oh, gods!' Tanthe put her hands to her head in despair. 'That's all I need. Now it *will* be a nightmare.'

'That's what you get for calling me a coward. You can't stop me.'

'Well, then, you'd better start getting ready,' she said viciously. 'We're leaving before dawn. I must leave a letter for my parents, but Breyid alone knows what I'm going to say to them. I hope my grandmother can explain; I think she'll understand, at least.'

With his hand resting on the King's order, Lynden said

quietly, 'If we'd been married already, they couldn't have taken her.'

'We weren't to know.'

Rufryd pulled the papers from his brother's grasp. 'Well, I know what I'm leaving for father.' His eyes shone viciously. 'I'm going to pin this lot on the front door. People will start seeing it at first light. Then everyone will know exactly what my father has done.'

Chapter Four. Flame and Flight

Dawn found Tanthe, Lynden and Rufryd tired and footsore on the gentle hills above Havereyn. As the first golden light warmed the shadows, they sat down on a rock to rest and examine their blisters. They'd kept off the road to avoid other travellers, which had made the walk harder, and seemed to have been a waste of time. They hadn't seen or heard another soul on the road all night.

It had been a strange journey. Leaf Moon and Lily Moon had guided them, casting double shadows and the faintest glow. Tanthe had often been out at night, but not like this. Rarely without Ysomir, and never with the knowledge that she wasn't going home. Every sound in the night made her jump. With each step she had the feeling that something was watching them, and the feeling persisted until sheer physical tiredness took its place.

Tanthe prided herself on being fit, but she was already wondering if she could really hope to walk two thousand miles – never mind find her sister and bring her all the way home again. She sighed, massaged her feet, then un-stoppered a flask of apple juice and drank deeply. The flasks they'd brought of fruit juice, water and cider were nearly empty already. In their rucksacks they each carried enough food to last four or five days, a change of clothing, salt to clean their teeth, soap, towels, bandages. They had hunting knives on their belts, bows and arrows on their shoulders. Rufryd's bow was a particularly fine one he'd made himself, of wood and bone. They wore their weatherproof winter cloaks, which would be good to travel and sleep in when the weather grew colder. For the time being, though, the cloaks were too heavy and hot.

Despite the discomfort, Tanthe was excited. Infinitely better to be active than to stay at home, hoping for the best but not knowing what would happen to her sister.

'How much money have you got, Tan?' asked Rufryd.

'About thirty cateyes.' She took the coins out of her pocket and counted them; small, iridescent brown-gold stones that were rimmed in bronze. A hundred of them made one spinel, a blue stone clasped in silver, of which ten made a rald. She'd seen spinels rarely, and ralds only twice. Beautiful, sparkling grass-green discs, circled with gold . . . Money meant little in Riverwynde, where they bartered more goods than they sold.

Rufryd made a sound of disgust. 'Lynden and me have got fifty between us. It's not going to get us far, is it? Probably wouldn't even buy a loaf of bread in Parione. Meanwhile that pig Beyne has our fifteen ralds in his pocket.'

'It wasn't ours. I wouldn't even want to touch his filthy money.'

'No, but we could have used it to buy horses. At this rate we'll end up barefoot and starving in the middle of nowhere before we get within two thousand miles of Parione.'

Every time Rufryd opened his mouth, Tanthe wanted to hit him. She was the one who had to restore Lynden's hopes each time Rufryd trod them into the ground. But he was right. She got angry with him because he spoke the blunt truth. 'No, we won't,' she said. 'We're young and fit, we know how to hunt and forage. You're going on like an old woman. No, sorry, that's a huge insult to old women.'

That, mercifully, silenced him. He tried to give a sarcastic smile, but his face darkened with annoyance.

'Come on,' Lynden said impatiently. 'Are we going through the town, or round it?'

'We may as well go through,' said Tanthe. 'We need to refill the flasks and buy some bread. We've done nothing wrong, no one has any reason to stop us.'

'Yet,' said Rufryd.

By mid-morning they were walking along the main street of Havereyn, feeling conspicuous although no one took any notice of them. Tanthe disdained the town for its air of drabness, yet she felt a secret frisson of excitement at being anywhere larger than Riverwynde. The houses, built of beams and reddish-brown bricks, stared down at them from the windows of their protruding upper storeys. The thick, untidy thatch of their roofs was dark brown with age and rain, except for the odd splash of gold where it had been replaced.

The farmers' market was in full swing when they arrived in the big, central square. The lanes were churned to mud, as usual. The complaints of cattle, sheep and pigs mingled deafeningly with human shouts. Then Tanthe remembered, with a pang, that she and Ymmi should have come to market today with Ewain.

Life must go on, but she doubted that anyone from Riverwynde would come to market until tomorrow at the earliest. Trying to relax, she stopped by a street vendor's stall to have the flasks refilled with cider and spring water. That took ten of their precious cateyes. Lynden was looking at a pen containing three chestnut horses; she saw him exchange a few words with the man at the gate.

'He wants five ralds each,' Lynden sighed as he came back.

'Ridiculous.' Rufryd clapped his brother on the shoulder. 'Well, even if he'd take five for the lot, we couldn't afford it.'

'Forget it,' said Tanthe. 'We've got to walk, that's all there is to it.'

Turning, they began to walk through the crowd. Suddenly Tanthe felt a set of thick fingers jabbing repeatedly into her shoulder. Annoyed, she swung round and found herself face to face with a tall but stooped man of around seventy. His hair was a long tangle of silver, his grey eyes glittered, and his wide grin revealed a selection of lopsided teeth.

'Tannie?' he said. His breath smelled of stale wine. 'My little Tannie?'

For a moment she couldn't think who it was. Then, with a creeping sense of amazement, she realised. 'Oh, gods. Granddad?'

It was her mother's father, Lan, whom she hadn't seen for – she couldn't remember. Eight years, at least. The family no longer had anything to do with him.

'What's this old boy want?' said Rufryd. 'Come on, Tanthe. Tell him to get lost.'

'I can't,' she stammered. 'It's my granddad.'

'What?'

'Here for the market, are ye?' said the old man.

'Er, not really.'

'How's Aynie? I never see you any more. That's not fair, is it? I did wrong by Freyna, I know that, but I never did wrong by you. Come home, come and talk to me. Landlady has a nice pot of stew on the go all day, plenty for all.'

Tanthe's stomach growled. She realised that her grandfather might help them; indeed, he was the only one who could. She looked at the other two and said, 'All right, then. We'd love to.'

Rufryd and Lynden looked at her in horror. 'What are you doing?' Rufryd cried. 'We can't, we've got to go!'

Her estranged grandfather took her hand and was happily tugging at her to follow him. 'We can't turn down the offer of a free meal and a rest,' she whispered. 'He might help us!'

As she spoke, she noticed Rufryd's gaze moving over the crowd behind her. Suddenly his face changed, becoming anxious. 'Okay,' he said. 'You're right. Let's go with him, quickly.' He began to shepherd Lynden and Tanthe with Lan, so hurriedly that he was almost treading on her heels.

'Careful!' she exclaimed. 'What's got into you?'

'I've just seen Colvin in the crowd. The bloke who does

94

all my father's donkey work. If he sent anyone after us, it would be him!'

Tanthe's pulse quickened. She glanced back, saw the unmistakable figure of Colvin, who stood a head taller than most of those around him. His broad body was turned side on to them, his thick brown hair and beard obscuring most of his face. Colvin wasn't the brightest of people, but he was fearsome.

'Did he see us?'

'I'm not sure. I don't think so. Maybe we should lie low at your grandfather's for an hour or so. Trouble is, the longer we stay here, the more likely it is that people will turn up from Riverwynde wanting to stop us.'

'But we can't just keep going without rest!' said Tanthe. 'Look how tired Lynden is.'

Lynden frowned, and said nothing.

Lan, oblivious to their conversation, took them to a tall, narrow house in a back lane, which smelled ripely of cooking and other, less savoury odours. His room was in the top storey, gained by several flights of alarmingly steep stairs. 'Sorry about that,' he wheezed. 'I call it the north face of our stairs. Now, you wait there while I get us summat to eat – and drink, eh boy?' He gave Lynden a huge wink.

'Smells like you've already started,' muttered Rufryd.

'I know you,' said Lan, wagging a thick finger at him. 'Arthryn's boys. You pampered little buggers!'

With that, he left the room and they heard his staggering footfalls on the stairs. Tanthe held her breathe, certain he would fall. When he didn't, she relaxed and looked around. The room was quite big but bare and ill-lit, with a plain bench and table, one hard chair, and a bed. A discoloured piece of muslin hung half-way across the window. The table and the windowsill were covered with small stone figures of Breyid and Anthar.

The last she'd heard, Lan had set up home with a well-to-do cloth trader and seamstress called – what was it? Lisset, or something.

'That's really your grandfather?' said Lynden. He sat on the bed, sleepy-eyed.

'Yes. My mum's father. Don't you remember him? He left the village about eight years ago. He and Freyna decided to go their separate ways for some reason. It was all quite friendly.'

Rufryd laughed. 'I've heard about your grandfather. He was drinking the profits, so Freyna threw him out. Very friendly. He won't be any use to us.'

Tanthe glared at him. 'Why not? He's not a bad man, just—'

'Drunk.'

'Shut up. He *will* help us!' she said between her teeth.

'How?'

'He might be able to tell us something.'

'I don't know about you but I could just fall asleep,' said Lynden, yawning deeply.

Lan returned with a tray bearing four bowls of stew, a huge loaf of bread, and pitchers of beer. He must have negotiated the stairs with the skill of long experience. Tanthe and the others fell on the meal like wolves; she sensed her grandfather watching them with curiosity, but she was too hungry and too tired to explain herself.

'That's it, eat up,' he encouraged with uncomprehending good humour.

'That was wonderful,' Tanthe said at last, mopping her bowl with the last scrap of bread. 'Are you living here alone, Granddad? What happened to Lisset?'

He laughed. 'Oh, she threw me out four year ago.'

'I wonder why,' Rufryd murmured.

'Took up with some merchant, twenty years younger than her. Quite a girl, Lisset. Breyid bless 'er.' He shrugged, and took a long drink of beer.

'But this place, it's . . . it's awful,' said Tanthe.

Lan looked wounded. 'It suits me. What's wrong with it? I see m'friends.' He waved at the stone figures. 'I make a few cateyes with me stone carving. I like a drink, what of

96

it? Don't go on at me like your Gran!'

'I'm not.' There was a soft snore. Lynden had fallen asleep on the bed. Tanthe found herself struggling to stay awake. She and her grandfather sat on the bench, while Rufryd tried to get comfortable on the upright chair. 'Granddad, we need help. A few days ago, a man called Beyne must have come through here with some soldiers and conscripted some of the younger people. He probably passed through again yesterday.'

Lan frowned. 'Whatsisname?'

'Beyne. Never mind, you must have seen or heard about what happened. What reason did they give for taking people? Did they say where they were being taken?'

'Where who was being taken?'

Rufryd said lazily, 'Give it up, Tan. He was probably too pissed to notice anything.'

She ignored him. 'Please, Granddad, it's really important.'

'I don't know nothing about no soldiers.'

'Well, they came to Riverwynde and took Ymmi.'

'Who?'

'Ysomir. My sister.'

He smiled broadly. 'Little Ymmi. How is she? How's her schoolwork?'

'She's left school. She's grown up, Granddad. She's very good at stone carving too. That's why they took her, they said.'

'I taught her that.'

'Yes, I know. That's why the soldiers took her. To help with a building project in Parione.'

'I knew a man went to Parione once. Mind you, he reckoned he'd been to the Serpent Isles, too. Ruddy liar.' He blinked weary eyes and peered at her. 'Are you Ysomir or Tanthe?'

Tanthe let out a sigh of exasperation and sorrow. Plainly her grandfather was too addled to have noticed anything outside his own small world. 'Tanthe. Look, do you mind if we sleep for an hour? We're all very tired. Can you wake us up at midday?'

'Course, my chick.' He patted her leg. 'You get some rest now.'

Tanthe lay down beside Lynden and fell immediately into a deep sleep.

She woke violently, what seemed to be one second later, to find dusk filling the grimy window. Her grandfather was sitting by the hearth, drinking from a jug of wine with his left hand and worrying the fire into life with a poker in his right. She leapt off the bed with a cry, at which Rufryd and Lynden also woke and looked round stupefied.

'Granddad! I asked you to wake us at midday! What time is it?'

She heard the boys swearing. 'Shit,' muttered Rufryd. 'Might have known this would happen. I should have stayed awake!'

'I don't know. Is the sun going down, or coming up? Going down, I think. You were sleeping like babies, I didn't like to wake you. You're not going, are you?'

'We must,' she said, shrugging on her cloak and ruck-sack, as the others were doing. 'We've got a long journey.'

'Oh, that's nice,' he said, smiling and nodding.

'Come on,' said Rufryd.

But Tanthe hesitated. She felt tears pricking her eyes. She couldn't bear to see her grandfather living in poverty, hardly aware of what time of day it was. 'Granddad, you're not well. Why don't you go back to Riverwynde? They'd look after you there. You need help, and mother would be glad to see you again, I know she would.'

He stood up, his eyes suddenly blazing. 'Help? What d'you mean, girl?'

'You don't have to live like this—'

'I don't need any help!' he growled. 'No bugger's going to look after me! I had all this nonsense with Freyna.'

'Well, I'm not surprised!' Tanthe exclaimed. 'You drink too much.'

'I'll drink what I ruddy well like and I'll live where I ruddy well like!' he roared. To her shock, he took aim with the wine jug and flung it at her. But his aim was bad and it flew instead towards Rufryd. Rufryd ducked, and the jug smashed on the wall behind the table, showering the stone figurines with wine and broken clay.

'That's it,' Rufryd said grimly. 'Let's get out of here.'

He hustled his brother and Tanthe to the stairs. Upset, Tanthe shook off his hand and stumbled as quickly as she could down the uneven stairs. Blinded by tears and the gloom she nearly lost her footing several times, but somehow she made it to the bottom and out into the alley. She was sobbing, trying not to let the other two see. Lynden put his arm round her.

'Don't, Tan,' he said helplessly. 'It's all right.'

'It isn't, though, is it!'

The alley was deserted. Outside, it was still quite light. Rufryd looked up and down, then took the map out of his rucksack. 'Don't shed any tears for him, Tanthe,' he said callously. 'Just because he's related to you doesn't mean he's not an evil old git.'

As she stood there, trying to compose herself before she lashed out at Rufryd again, she heard her grandfather's voice, faint but coming closer. 'Tanthe! Don't go, love.' He came rushing out of the doorway after them. 'I'm sorry.'

She couldn't speak. She pitied and disliked him, when all she had wanted to feel for him was love. To her discomfort, he gave her an awkward, drunken hug, enveloping her in a cloud of acrid breath. 'It was a good day when you arrived,' he said into her ear. 'You're a good girl. It's all true, what you said, but I'm too old to change. I'm sorry, love. Take this.'

He pressed a small leather bag into her palm, turned away, and staggered back inside the house, waving vaguely as if to send them on their way. Tanthe looked inside the bag and gasped. 'He's given us seven ralds!'

She started after her grandfather to thank him, but

Rufryd held her back. 'Don't. He'll probably have forgotten who you are by the time you catch him up.'

'Okay,' she said, wiping her eyes and cheeks. 'Well. Now we can buy a horse, at least. But where did he get so much money from?'

Rufryd laughed. 'Selling his statues? Nah, he must have conned it from Mistress Lisset before she threw him out. He probably has a pot-full under the bed. One of those who likes to live in squalor and hoard his wealth.'

Tanthe said nothing. Sometimes she hated Rufryd so bitterly that she wanted to kill him.

The market was long over when they reached the square. Street-cleaners were busy, not so much sweeping away the mud as smoothing it into a more attractive pattern, while music and light spilled from taverns around the market square. The three travellers stopped at a street vendor to buy slabs of meat and gravy on trenchers of bread. They were all starving again.

The vendor, in response to their enquiry, told them where to find the man who had been selling the horses. It was a small farm on the eastern edge of the town, which was the direction they needed to travel in. 'Maybe he'll sell us all three for seven ralds,' said Rufryd. 'He was asking too much for them.'

'And maybe he's sold them already,' Lynden said gloomily.

'One will be better than nothing,' said Tanthe. 'At least it can carry our rucksacks and cloaks.'

As they walked through the quiet streets, Tanthe looked up at the sky and saw three dra'a'ks fly over, silent and stretched out, like reptilian swans. She shivered.

When they found the farmhouse – a typical Havereyn dwelling of brown brick and thatch – they immediately saw a paddock to one side, containing a single thickset chestnut horse. There were other horses in a higher field, but this was the one that had been at market. For a moment she was tempted to steal the horse and just make off with it; then there would be fewer witnesses if anyone came asking questions from Riverwynde. But a shadow moved in the field, and she realised that the farmer was there, filling a water trough from a bucket.

'Evening,' said Rufryd as they approached. The farmer, a short wide man with reddish hair and a grumpy demeanour, looked up suspiciously. 'How much did you get for the other two?'

'Why d'you want to know?'

'Because we're interested in buying this one, if it's sound and hardy.'

The horse was nuzzling at the farmer's shoulder. He caressed its head protectively. 'What work would you be putting him to?'

'We're travelling to Skald to sell some shrine figurines,' Rufryd said easily. He leaned on the fence, putting one foot on a haybale that was lying half under the lowest strut. 'Need a horse to carry the baggage. Light work. My brother here would half-kill anyone who tried to mistreat him, I promise you.'

That was true, Tanthe knew. Lynden loved animals.

'Aye. Well, come in the paddock and have a look at him. He's called Flame,' said the farmer. He opened the gate for them. Lynden and Tanthe went inside, but Rufryd stayed where he was, watching. Beyond the farmland, a line of wild hills lay along the horizon, glowing in the last rays of the sun. They must follow Ysomir into that unknown country.

The horse stood about fourteen hands – a large pony, really – and was good-natured with friendly dark eyes. The farmer shooed him round the field to show his paces; a steady, clean trot and canter. Flame quickly circled to them and chewed at Tanthe's cloak, making a slobbery green mark and blowing grassy breath all over her. 'He's five ralds. That's what I got for the others.'

'For both of them, maybe,' Rufryd said, looking candidly at the farmer. 'We'll pay two.'

'Four. That's my last offer.'

'Three. That's ours.'

The farmer stood tapping his foot, narrow-eyed. Tanthe wished that Rufryd wouldn't always be so offensively sure of himself.

'All right. Three.'

'If you throw in the tack.'

'With his headcollar, bridle and saddle and grooming brushes, that will be one rald extra.'

'Yes, yes, we'll pay it,' Tanthe said quickly, thrusting four of her grandfather's coins at him. 'Thank you so much, you've saved our lives.'

The farmer actually grinned at her. As he went to fetch the tack, Rufryd exclaimed, 'I could have talked him down if you hadn't stuck your nose in!'

'Why don't you stay in Havereyn and get a job on the market!' she snapped. 'You obviously have the soul of a trader.'

'I'm just trying to preserve our money! Anthar's Horns, this is all the thanks I get.'

'Well, we don't have all night to stand here bargaining.'

Lynden hissed, 'Gods, will you two stop it!'

As the farmer buckled on the bridle and showed them how to secure their rucksacks over the back of the saddle, Tanthe was growing increasingly anxious to leave. They'd spent hours in Havereyn and she felt that the place was dragging stickily at them, as if they were flies in treacle. Too late, they became aware of a big, bearded figure approaching them through the twilight. Even Rufryd had grown complacent and forgotten to keep a look-out.

'Hold there,' came Colvin's deep, booming voice. 'Your little adventure's over. Arthryn's sent me to bring you home.'

'Shit!' cried Rufryd. 'Go home, Colvin. Tell my father to go to hell!'

Colvin shook his big head and kept coming. Lynden clutched Tanthe's arm; he'd gone white, and she felt a spear of panic and dismay go through her. Colvin's fists were like great fleshy rocks. 'I can't do that. I've got my orders.'

As Colvin reached the gate, Rufryd snatched up the hay bale and threw it into the big man's stomach. Colvin staggered back. At the same moment, Tanthe vaulted into Flame's saddle and sent the startled horse charging towards the gateway. She was unused to riding and almost lost her seat at once, but by gripping the mane she clung on. To her horror, Colvin jumped into her path, grabbing for the bridle. Flame shied; he missed. They were through the gate, but she looked round to see Colvin making a grab for Lynden. She turned the horse and rode at him again, her teeth set in rage.

She caught a glimpse of the farmer, still in the field, hurriedly closing the gate as if to protect himself.

This time the big man jumped out of her way, caught his booted foot awkwardly and fell onto the rutted ground in front of the gate. She saw Rufryd dragging Lynden out of his way and giving him a shove. 'Run!' Rufryd yelled. 'Go, Tanthe! Both of you, go!'

Catching her breath, she turned Flame and sent him at a gallop in the direction of the open countryside. With the rucksacks weighing him down, he wasn't the swiftest of mounts, but it seemed a breakneck speed to Tanthe. Lynden followed her, running flat out. As she pulled Flame to a halt and helped Lynden up behind her, Tanthe looked back, her heart in her mouth. She saw Colvin climbing to his feet, Rufryd looking small and defenceless in comparison. But he was quick and his opponent was slow. Swift as light, Rufryd unlatched the gate, jumped onto it and swung it hard into Colvin's guts.

Taken by surprise, Colvin went down, winded. Tanthe heard the clang as the gate juddered on its hinges. Then Rufryd was running, running like a hare to catch them up. And he could run; he'd always won the summer races at home by yards.

Tanthe urged the horse on. Two of them in the saddle was an uncomfortable arrangement and they were both hanging on grimly, but Flame was strong and steady. She glanced back once more to see that Colvin was still down. The farmer was bending anxiously over him. It was the last she saw of them. Looking ahead, she went galloping on towards the deceptively gilded hills and the wild unknown.

Alone in her chamber, Queen Mabriahna lit candles and incense on her small shrine to Nepheter. The gesture felt hollow. In the last two years she seemed to have lost all sense of the goddess's presence. Even lost all sense of herself as a channel of Nepheter's wisdom. She felt lonely and afraid.

Mabriahna sat woodenly on the edge of a couch. Her hands felt like ice and she was so cold she could barely move, yet she did nothing to warm herself. For the time being she was drained of tears, but for all her grief nothing had changed. Her son was dead. And – the knowledge sat in her mind like a canker, but she couldn't bear to actually frame the words – her husband had killed him. Garnelys the Good, who from the moment they'd met at the age of sixteen had been her dearest friend and true love.

Sometimes she began to wonder if she had imagined all those years. His sweetness and kindness, his laughter, his gentle wisdom in ruling Aventuria, his delight in his son and his grandchildren. Never had he expressed a word of disappointment that no more children had followed Galemanth. No, they had simply been glad of the Goddess's single gift.

The change had begun about three years ago, she recalled, falling on them as a fine web that grew darker and thicker as the days went by. Garnelys had always had his introspective moods, so at first she didn't notice. But imperceptibly those moods had darkened. His visits to her chamber – which had once been frequent and joyous for them both – grew infrequent until they ceased altogether. Her desire still burned bright but for him it was cold ashes, and he would not tell her why. When she tried to ask, he would turn aside her questions with wounding anger.

Soon she discovered that he was making decisions without her. King and Queen were meant to rule jointly, representatives of Dionys and Nepheter on earth; but because he was the heir to the Sapphire Throne and she was his consort, there was nothing she could do. If *she* had been monarch in her own right, she could have taken control, kept him from harm's way until she found out what was wrong.

Mabriahna had no experience of hardship on which to draw. She had gone from a loving family – her parents were the Duke and Duchess of Mithrain – to a loving husband. Her life until now had been smooth. What could she say to a husband who'd changed from companion to icy stranger, when his intransigence repelled her at every turn?

If the change had started when the news came about Helananthe, that would make sense. Helananthe had been the older child of Galemanth, a bright and adventurous young woman who one day would take the throne. But Helananthe – furious about the demolition of the theatre – had quarrelled with Garnelys, and fled, and was reported lost at sea.

Queen Mabriahna still did not understand why she had been on that ship, or what she meant to do in the Serpent Isles, if that was indeed where the voyage was taking her. Last winter, less than a year ago, the news had come. The ship had sunk with all hands.

The royal family had been devastated by her loss. Helananthe's mother had gone back to her family's castle in Eisilion, taking her small son with her. She still refused to see anyone. Galemanth, deserted and grief-stricken, had gone from rational debate to acrimonious conflict with his father the King. But that was not the beginning of the King's black moods. No, they had begun months before the shipwreck.

Somewhere in that time, the architect Laphaeome had appeared. The Queen was still not clear when he'd arrived, or where he'd come from. Only that he'd replaced her as the King's closest confidant. What do they talk about? she wondered. She hardly knew Lord Laphaeome, yet she was bitterly jealous of him.

It was soon after the architect appeared that Garnelys had conceived a wild project, which would use up vast wealth and human effort. Many of his long-trusted advisors had tried to talk him out of it. 'It's far too costly and wasteful,' they told him. 'It is not needed. The peace of your reign is legacy enough.'

Blind, he called them. Disloyal. And now they were all gone, replaced by hollow, self-seeking people that Mabriahna would not have allowed to set foot in the palace. His long-serving chancellor had been replaced by the austere, granite-faced Lord Poel. The vibrant, wilful commander of his army had been removed from her post in favour of General Grannen, a man from Torith Mir who was utterly unfitted for the task. He despised the army's role as guardians of peace; he craved war, against the Bhahdradomen, against anyone. And Garnelys couldn't see it.

Mabriahna groaned. Destroyed the theatre, now destroyed even his own son.

She raised her head and looked out of the window, only to see the terrible wounds in the hill where the foundations of the Tower were being built. She shut her eyes again quickly. This was madness. Her whole world had turned to chaos.

Now the only family they had left was their grandson, Helananthe's little brother Venirryen. He was Garnelys's sole heir; all their hopes for Aventuria rested in him. But he was only eight, and far away with his mother. At least he was safe . . . safe, from his own grandfather?

A light tapping at her door roused her from her thoughts. She quickly smoothed her skirts and sat upright, calling, 'Enter!'

She expected a servant. Instead it was Garnelys who came in, hesitantly at first, then with a rush that brought him to his knees at her feet.

'My dear,' he said throatily. 'Oh, my dear. Forgive me.'

He took her hands, and rested his head on them in her lap. He seemed his old self again, as beautiful as he had been in his youth, his long sculptured face full of light and framed by the pale flowing wings of his hair. He kissed her fingers with dry lips. She saw that he had been crying, after all.

A huge wave of emotion passed through Mabriahna. Was he better? She hardly dared to hope. She craved reassurance that their son's death had been an accident after all.

'It's all right,' she said gently. 'You feel that if you even begin to express your pain, it will break you into pieces. I feel the same.'

'Yes. You always understand me.'

'Don't you remember, love,' she began softly, 'how dear he was as a little boy? How he learned to read upon your knee? How we would walk with him in the garden, and I would be angry that you let him march along the top of the walls like a soldier? But he never fell. He was so fair, so sweet in nature.'

'Yes.' Garnelys was shaking. 'Oh gods, our son . . .'

'He was a good son and would have been a good king after you.'

At that, his trembling stopped. His hands stiffened in hers.

'I know that you did not will his death,' she went on. 'I was wrong to accuse you. I did so, and you did not deny it, because we were both distraught.'

Garnelys sighed, rose slowly, and walked around the large room, with its yellow, white and gold draperies.

When he looked at her his face was gentle, but deeply troubled. 'You must understand, my dear. His death has almost destroyed me. Yet it could not have been otherwise. He crossed me, he disagreed with my policies, he supported the protests against my plans, he ran away and began to plot against me.'

She watched him gliding towards her. 'He was grief-stricken over his daughter,' she said thickly. 'All children quarrel with their parents.'

'But I am not *any* parent. My only true child is the land. You knew that when you married me! All that I have done is for the good of Aventuria. The covenant between the land and the king is the Xauroma. I *am* the Xauroma. I must safeguard that at *any* cost. Even that of my own son.'

'So you did—'

'Yes, but you see why. For Aventuria.'

She was trying and trying to understand, to communicate with him. 'But in the past, you and I used to discuss these problems and listen to each other. Did you never wonder if – for a moment – if your son might be right?'

'Of course. But he wasn't. He plotted with Helananthe and that accursed Saphaeyender to discredit me. He would have destroyed all that I had created.'

'I don't believe that.'

'But you must. It's the truth.' He sat beside her and took her hands, pressing them to his heart. 'My dear, this is so hard for you and I beg you to forgive me. But I need your support. You must believe me.'

And she desperately wanted to. To know that he was still the gentle, wise man she had married, that even this horror was for the best. To trust him again.

'Oh, my dear,' she said softly. 'I want that more than anything. But you must know that you are sometimes like a stranger to me. You frighten me.'

He pulled back, frowning. 'I – frighten you?'

'I think the burden of the crown is too much for you

108

alone. Let me help you again. Galemanth would have helped you, but as he is gone, you must think of the future. Think of little Venirryen, who is your heir now.'

She saw the shadows coming into face, as if he were ageing before her eyes, but she plunged on, determined to speak while he was still listening to her. 'I have too much to think of with the Tower to consider Venirryen. He's a child. I am not planning to die in the near future.'

'My dear, forget this Tower. It will take too much energy from the land, too many people to build it. Parione is beautiful enough without it. Rebuild the theatre instead, and all this trouble will end.'

Suddenly he gripped her arms, startling her. 'But without the Tower, what will there be left to mark my reign? Who will ever know that I existed? Don't question me, Mabriahna. This is treachery!'

'No!' she gasped.

As he gripped her, the split sleeve of his robe gaped, and on the white shirt beneath she saw a bloodstain. 'What's this? You're hurt? How?'

He glanced down at the stain, rearranged the sleeve to cover it. As he did so, she saw dried blood under his fingernails. Then she knew, horribly, that it was not his own blood. 'We will never speak of this again.' His whisper was a deadly threat.

He rose, and now the darkness had taken him over completely. He was a looming shadow, his long face carved with a cold, black ambition and an anguish that was centred so completely upon himself that it left nothing for her. He was gone from her again, and she was more terrified than ever.

'No, Mabriahna,' he whispered in a voice as chill, lightless and empty as a cave. '*You* are the stranger.'

Gulzhur, sitting on a moonlit hillside, held a piece of haematite and polished the oily surface. He disliked working with stones, they were too much part of the earth. Their fiery energy, the provenance of humans and Aelyr and Subterraneans, disconcerted him. But there were some stones, at least, with which he felt affinity. Blendes full of metal ore, massive dark rocks without crystal structure, pyrites, sulphur, the iron-grey cogwheels of bournonite. All that was oily and fugitive.

Dark rainbow ripples shifted on the flat surface of the stone. Enabler gazed into the depths, losing focus, his mind beginning to fall . . . and then he was in the void. He was walking along an infinite black path under a luminous black sky.

'Facilitator?'

Another figure was coming towards him, as pale as he was grey and camouflaged.

'Enabler,' said the pale figure. They pressed palms, forming a brief X-shape at chest-level. 'Where are you?'

'Somewhere near a town called Skald,' said Gulzhur. 'I am bored. I need a greater challenge.'

'All too easy, isn't it? I walk freely in the Amber Citadel and no one ever questions me. They all believe that I am who I say I am. Again and again I ask myself, how did humans ever defeat us? You may be bored but I am enjoying myself beyond description.' Facilitator smiled in glee.

'You are taking imitation of humans too far,' Gulzhur said sourly. 'Let us not forget that they *did* defeat us. That we move in secret because we are still so weak.'

'Ever the realist, Gulzhur.'

'Of course. Someone must be. How goes it with the King? You have him under control, Zhoaah?'

'No, no,' Facilitator said excitedly. 'If you think that, you misunderstand completely. All that he does, he does of his own volition. All I have ever done is to ease his path; by being there, by listening, by understanding, when his human counsellors would not. I give him tiny nudges in the right direction. When he needs a particular piece of advice, I'm there ready to lay it in front of him. I anticipate his moods. That's the beauty of it, you see? I don't control the King, I simply give him what he needs.'

Gulzhur nodded tolerantly. He was much older than Zhoaah. 'I know. My words were ill-chosen. You are finding some reward for your labours, I trust.'

Facilitator's eyes burned. 'Human pain,' he said. 'Amazing, how easy it was to relieve the King of his inhibitions. Hatchling's play.'

'It's a beginning,' Gulzhur said drily. 'We have a long way to go. Humans do not have enough pain in them, to pay for what they have done to us.'

Chapter Five. The Aelyr's Gift

Rufryd was cursing his decision to act as nursemaid to his little brother. Two nights spent trying to sleep under hedges was only surpassed, on the third morning, by a downpour of rain. Lynden was grown up, and surely Tanthe was tough enough to keep him out of trouble? But for all his misgivings, he knew in his heart that he couldn't have let Lynden go alone. So he cursed Beyne instead, and, more than anyone, his father.

After their flight from Havereyn, they avoided the villages and farms that clustered in the fertile valley of the Aole, travelling on the uplands rather than the main tracks. The landscape of cultivated fields gave way to wiry grassland, scattered with boulders.

'What lengths do you think Arthryn would go to, to bring us home?' Tanthe asked, once they'd calmed down and got their breath back after the exhilarating escape from Colvin.

'I don't know,' Rufryd answered honestly. 'The old bastard is weak, but he's also stubborn. I would say he's probably given up by now, but you never know.'

'Don't talk about Father like that!' Lynden retorted. 'He doesn't want us to put ourselves in danger. He was being protective, that's all!'

'Of you, maybe. No, don't kid yourself, Lyn. All he's thinking about is the embarrassment of his villagers being seen to disobey the monarch. Of *him* being seen as not in control of his own sons.'

'That's not true.'

'Wake up, will you?'

Tanthe broke in, 'You must remember, he'll be under

pressure from the rest of the village to bring us back. At least Colvin can go back and say he tried. My grandmother understood why we had to do this. Maybe she'll furnish Arthryn with a good reason to leave us alone, so he'll save face.'

'Why are you standing up for him?' Rufryd said savagely.

'I'm not. Quite honestly, I think we'll have far worse things than Arthryn to worry about.'

They hadn't spoken much since then. The further they went, the more it became apparent that they would never get on, and the more isolated and far from home they felt.

Now they were making their way through a shallow, flat ravine between upswept scarps, with clouds looming in grey peaks above them. The ground was covered in loose stones, which slowed them down as Flame had to pick his way carefully over them. Even though the horse was sure-footed, he sometimes skidded and Rufryd had horrible visions of him falling, laming himself and crushing their provisions into the grass and mud. Tanthe was leading Flame, Lynden walking ahead and Rufryd behind, hoods up and heads down against the rain.

In theory they had agreed to take turns riding Flame, but in practice, they rarely rode. It had become, Rufryd observed, a rather stupid competition between them. To sit on Flame's back was to admit exhaustion, and none of them wanted to seem less hardy than the others.

It still wasn't cold enough for their cloaks, but given a choice between being too hot and getting soaked, being hot won. But now Rufryd felt damp with sweat instead. When one of his boots began to leak, he cursed the day that his brother had ever fallen in love with Tanthe's sister.

He couldn't say quite what it was that he so disliked about Tanthe – apart from everything she did and every-thing she said. The arrogant way she carried herself, her back straight and her head high, as if she were looking down on everyone; her stubbornness, her temper, the way

113

she tried to humiliate him at every opportunity. Her pretensions to be something she wasn't, her ridiculous worship of a way of life and a city she'd never even seen . . . on second thoughts he could say *exactly* what he didn't like about her. And yet there was a curious pleasure in baiting her, trying to knock her back to earth. Always had been, even as children.

Emerging from the end of the ravine, a long gradual climb brought them to the summit of a hill, capped with long, flat rocks. To Rufryd's frustration, there was a sheer drop below, so they would have to work their way forward in a series of long zig-zags rather than a straight line. The map didn't show obstacles like this.

'That map of my father's is useless,' he said.

'Oh?' Tanthe lifted an eyebrow. 'Before we left you were boasting about how wonderful it was. Maybe your map *reading* is useless.'

'You reckon you can do better? You didn't even know which way was north until I showed you with the compass!'

'Look, you can't expect a map of the whole Nine Realms to show every little hill!'

Lynden said quietly, 'Can you two manage to have a single conversation without arguing? Let me see the map.'

'It's stopped raining,' said Tanthe. 'Let's have a rest. You look like you need one, Lyn.'

They sat down on the damp rock, while Flame found a patch of grass to graze on. They were high up, and the world looked very lonely; a great sweep of wild grassland vanishing into a grey haze. There was utter silence. A single hawk hovered, small against the sky. The air was clear and sharp with the scent of rain.

Rufryd experienced a few moments of perfect calm. All at once it felt wonderful to be miles from Riverwynde, away from the drudgery of his directionless life and the continual, oppressive presence of his father. This was the first time he'd been beyond Havereyn. The world seemed

huge and full of possibilities he'd never even guessed at . . .
and so precious and beautiful, so hard won from their
enemies by Garnelys's ancestors.

That made it doubly hard to believe that the King could
ever do his people harm.

'So where are we?' said Lynden, struggling to flatten the
scroll.

'On the Torland Moors. About . . . here.' Rufryd pointed
to an area, empty but for a few sketched-in hills, that lay
about halfway between Havereyn and Skald.

'Oh, gods,' Lynden sighed.

'What's wrong? I haven't got us lost yet. You could see
Skald from here, if it wasn't so hazy. We're going to loop
down to the base of this hill, then across the valley there.
The map shows woodland, and a tributary of the Aole with
a little bridge across it, which we'd better not miss unless
you want to swim.'

'That's not what I was bothered about. Parione is two
feet away. We've travelled about half an inch.'

There was a brief silence. Rufryd leaned back on his
elbows. 'We told you it was a long way. We can travel at
about three miles an hour, for perhaps ten hours a day,
assuming we don't fall ill or have any other hold-ups. So
we can cover, say, thirty miles a day, but the actual
distance will be less because of the uneven terrain, or
having to retrace our steps because there's an obstruction
the map didn't show. So we're unlikely to reach Parione
in less than seventy days. Then there's winter. We aren't
likely to be there before Breyid's Day, even if our journey
goes perfectly.'

Lynden hung his head. 'I know that. I know!'

'You still want to carry on?'

Tanthe was glaring at Rufryd, but he ignored her.
Lynden was quiet, looking at the rain-lashed landscape.
Eventually he said, 'Ysomir hasn't been given any choice,
has she?'

Two nights later, they had made it across the Torland

115

Moors without mishap and were walking along gentler trails through a dense but friendly-feeling oak forest. They were growing exhausted, though. It was the monotony of walking, as much as anything. They needed a day of rest in a good inn, plenty of food, hot baths . . . Rufryd didn't mention his desires to the others. Tanthe would seize any scrap of evidence to prove he was soft. And Lynden, feverish with determination, would have walked in his sleep if Rufryd had let him. They would have to rest eventually, if only to stop Lynden killing himself.

The evening was warm, tinted with the soft reds and golds of early autumn, when they came upon a clearing with a perfect crystal pool, fed by a spring. At one side, between two thick, knotted trees, they found a little shrine; a pile of stones that had been built by a traveller years ago. Now it was falling apart, covered in old leaves and lichen.

'Let's stop here,' said Tanthe, letting out a long breath of relief. 'My feet are killing me.'

They made camp, removed Flame's burdens, groomed and watered him and tethered him to graze at the edge of the woods. Then they took it in turns to bathe in the pool, Rufryd and Lynden politely averting their eyes as Tanthe went in first. Rufryd heard her gasp with mixed pleasure and pain as she first plunged into the crystal-cold water; and somehow he caught a glimpse of her bared shoulders and small, rounded breasts as she tipped water over herself, the pool a blaze of gold behind her, and her face and dark, thick hair silhouetted against a flaring corona of light. Hurriedly he turned and sat with his back to her; but whichever way he looked, her image stayed imprinted on his eyes.

Deep in the night, Tanthe opened her eyes. She felt alert and yet somehow she knew she was dreaming, or at least in a strange state between sleeping and waking. Nothing felt quite real. She stood up, looking around her. The whole wood was bathed in a strange glow, each tree glimmering as if sprinkled with jewel-dust. The colours were rich and yet misty; leaf-green, emerald, holly. Tanthe began to move forward as if sleepwalking. She saw the little shrine that they'd found the night before, but now it was different. It looked newly-built and covered in fresh flowers, white daisies and purple iris and yellow buttercups. Amid the petals she saw something gleaming.

It was the Aelyr knife again. The blade shone silver-white, the scabbard glittered with crystals. On its pommel was a big rounded stone, silvery and translucent, with layers of iridescence in its depths. Tanthe caught her breath. She had never seen anything so beautiful. She longed to touch it, but recalling what had happened last time, she dared not. She had felt the anger of the Aelyr, and thought she was about to die.

She stretched her hand towards the knife, her fingertips hovering a few inches above it. She touched it; it remained. The pommel felt cold against her fingertips. Cautiously she picked it up – and as she did so, a shape moved above her.

She froze in shock. A few feet away, facing her across the shrine, was the Aelyr male. He seemed half in bronze shadow so she couldn't make out his face in detail; just the gleam of an eye, the dark fiery hair curling over his shoulders. He wore a tunic of silky stuff so delicate that it hardly covered him. Tanthe stared in a mixture of wonder and fear at his tawny gold, near-naked body. There was a glow around him; he looked unreal, beautiful, frightening. He met her eyes, then walked away through the trees.

Clutching the knife, Tanthe ran after him. She seemed to move through honey; he kept looking back, to make sure she was following. She saw him on the edge of the pool, firefly lights glittering around him; then he leapt forward and was gone, his image held for a moment on the air before fading to nothing.

'No,' Tanthe breathed. She rushed forward, fell to her

knees beside the water. Looking down, she saw not her own face in the surface, but his. A strong, beautiful face with glowing eyes, and expression of despair.

'*Keep the knife. It will help protect you.*' The words were in her head, but his lips moved with her.

'Who are you?' Tanthe cried.

'*Trapped here. Trying so hard to reach you.*' He reached out, closing his eyes in effort.

'Why? Please speak to me!'

'*Taken years – you don't see—*' He was struggling to speak, his image breaking up, reforming. The glow that contained him swelled like a pressure wave, probing, malevolent. Tanthe felt that if only she could touch him she could save him; bring him safely through to this world. She reached out her hand—

Something seized her. Dragged her forward. Her whole arm was underwater, she couldn't keep her balance . . .

She screamed, wrenched backwards, and woke violently.

Rufryd was standing over her. 'Tanthe?' he gasped. 'What's wrong? You were shouting, you scared the wits out of us.'

All was still. She found herself lying yards from where she'd fallen asleep, close to the edge of the pool. The shrine which was just as it had been before; covered in leaves and lichens. The shimmer of magic had given way to a dull cold dawn.

Sitting up, she winced as a pulsing pain hit the back of her eyes. Her fists were cramped around something that was hurting her palms. The knife! She uncurled her hands to find a small, dull knife in a very old and worn scabbard that was covered in lines of broken stitching. The tiny holes where the stitching had been were filled with grime. The stone in the handle was a dull pebble. Shock and disappointment filled her.

'Oh, gods,' she groaned. 'What a dream.'

'What's that you've got?'

She flexed her hands. 'This? Er . . . some old knife I picked up. I think it was on the shrine.'

'Let me see,' said Rufryd. He reached out for it but she snatched it away.

'It needs cleaning up.'

Lynden was sitting up, rubbing his face. 'I had a nightmare, too,' he said.

'What was it?' Tanthe was alarmed. Her most distinct impression of the Aelyr was his distress, the sense that he'd made a desperate struggle just to communicate with her.

'I don't know. These horrible white figures were trying to grab hold of me. I don't want to think about it.'

'Anthar's balls,' said Rufryd. 'Who'd have an imagination? Come on, let's have breakfast and get moving.'

For once Tanthe was grateful for his blunt practicality. Shaken, she needed banal reality to steady her, and was desperate for a long draught of cold, sweet-sour berry juice to ease her dry mouth. While Lynden sorted out their rations, she went behind a tree to relieve herself – and to examine the knife. It was a dreadful old thing, the blade blunt and pitted. She felt like throwing it away. Instead, she wrapped it carefully in a piece of rag and put it in the inside breast pocket of her jacket.

Her right sleeve clung to her skin, soaking wet.

That evening, they came upon a large, busy village called Forthryn Seal, at the intersection of three roads. It was a friendly place; people greeted them as they passed, seemingly accustomed enough to travellers to pay them no particular attention. At the centre they came to a large inn, the Golden Hawk. They stopped on the wide street and looked up at its walls of sand-coloured brick, its large windows and overhanging, tousled thatch.

'We should stay here tonight,' Tanthe suggested.

'Getting too much for you, the hard life?' Rufryd said with a mocking grin.

'No,' she said icily, 'but it seems stupid to go and sleep in a wood when we're here, with enough money to stay. But the important thing is that we could talk to people. See what we can find out about Beyne's activities. Lynden?'

He looked tired out and eaten up with worry, his eyes too large, shining through his unkempt fringe. 'I don't know. I'd rather press on.'

Rufryd put a hand on Lynden's shoulder. His only redeeming feature, Tanthe thought, was his concern for his brother. 'So would I, but she's got a point. You're obviously done in, Lyn.' Lynden gave him a sour look. 'We all are. We'll travel faster tomorrow for a good meal and a rest.'

A cheerful stable girl took Flame from them and led him into the courtyard, leaving Tanthe and her companions to enter the inn. The taproom was clean and cosy in the light of spherical lamps hanging from the ceiling beams. It seemed a popular place, already noisy with customers. The air was laced with the smell of beer, of roasting lamb and potatoes and buttered vegetables. Tanthe's mouth watered. She would never admit it to the others, but she felt as if she could sleep for a week.

Having ordered food and drink from a welcoming landlady, they sat down at a big, oblong table, hoping that some of the villagers would join them. As she relaxed, Tanthe began to have flashes of last night's dream, remembering the Aelyr's face, the sheer strangeness and terror of the encounter. She couldn't shake it off. So she was glad of the distraction when – as they finished wolfing down a much-needed meal – two men of middle years, tankards of beer in hand, asked if they minded company.

The newcomers were both thick-set and rosy faced with curly brown hair, like most of the people of Forthryn Seal; one, introducing himself as Athed, was talkative and indulged in much tutting and head-shaking, as if he didn't know what the world was coming to. His companion, Dwyorn – who was older and going grey – let him do most of the talking, nodding philosophically at intervals.

After some pleasantries about the weather, the harvest and the finer points of the Golden Hawk, Athed asked, 'Where are you travelling from?'

'Near Havereyn,' said Rufryd through a mouthful of potato.

'You've come a way. Got business around here? Oh, don't answer if I'm being nosy. Nosiest folk in Sepheret, we are.'

'We're going to Skald,' said Tanthe, repeating Rufryd's lie. 'To, er, to sell my grandfather's stone carvings.'

'I'd like to see them carvings,' said Athed. 'How much do you want for them?'

That threw her. They had nothing to show, of course. But Rufryd said smoothly, 'They're all spoken for, I'm afraid. Special commissions. We're not even allowed to unpack them until we get there.'

Tanthe breathed a secret sigh of relief. Only now was she beginning to wonder how much trouble they would get into if they were found out. She was sure the King himself would understand, if he knew the circumstances, but one word to the wrong person, perhaps a friendly drinker in an alehouse who turned out to be an official like Beyne . . .

'Oh, well. Skald, is it?' Athed stroked his beard with his index finger, smoothing away a blob of beer foam. 'You should be careful there.'

'Why?' said Tanthe.

More head-shaking. 'There's a lot of army activity there. They've been taking a lot of conscripts. They say it's for some great monument the King's building in Parione but I don't know . . .'

Lynden, who had looked in danger of falling asleep, was suddenly alert. 'What do you mean?'

Athed shrugged. 'Well, it could be a cover. Maybe there's a war started that we don't even know about. They say there's a bad atmosphere in Skald, a lot of new officers sent from Parione who aren't the sort the King would usually have. They're nasty, they throw their weight around. That's not our local guard, is it? They're meant to be our friends and protectors. My brother used to work in the garrison at Skald and he said a better bunch of lads and lasses you'd never meet. Not now, though.'

'Maybe the King thought they were getting soft,' said Dwyorn. 'Hard to keep 'em in full training, just to sort out petty disputes between farmers.'

'So, did you get the conscriptions as far out as Havereyn?' asked Athed.

Tanthe nodded, swallowing hard. 'That's the King being fair,' she said, trying to sound neutral. 'Not taking too many from one place. My sister got the short straw. What about you?'

'They took my older son and my niece, and ten others,' said Athed gloomily, staring into his beer mug.

Tanthe was shocked. 'I'm sorry.'

'Now that's an odd thing to say, considering it's meant to be an honour,' said Athed, in a tone that told her he felt exactly as she did. 'We should be celebrating. Gave the families five ralds for each. Compensation, they said.' He blew through his teeth in disgust. 'Could hardly get a decent horse for that. Money's all very well, but it's got no hands and it can't work.'

'Did you know you were meant to be paid fifteen?' Rufryd said softly.

His head jerked up. 'What?'

'I saw a piece of paper I wasn't meant to see. Whatever Garnelys needs them for, he's trying to give the families a fair reward. But it's not reaching them. You can wager your life, the rest of your money was pocketed by some official. You know, bribes over who was taken and who wasn't. Someone is making himself rich by carrying out the King's will.'

The man shook his head. He sniffed. 'Well, Garnelys wouldn't like it. I'm sure he never intended that. No doubt he's got the best of intentions but . . . I would surely like my son back.'

As they spoke, a group men and women were gathering round to listen, some of them taking the empty seats. Tanthe was powerfully aware of their worry and confusion. It was the same as at home. *Garnelys would never harm us . . . We want to help him, of course . . . but what is happening?'*

Dwyorn leaned forward and tapped the table. 'They say this project is so great, it will take half the able-bodied folk in the land to build it, and that the second wave of conscription is already coming. Next time it won't be one in seven, it'll be one in three, then one in two, then everyone who can walk.'

'Don't exaggerate,' said Athed. 'It would ruin us.'

'I'm not,' he said. Tanthe saw a glint of intelligence in Dwyorn's eyes that made her shudder. He wasn't spinning tales; he was making a coldly realistic prediction. 'And yes, it would ruin us.'

'But Garnelys wouldn't do anything to harm Aventuria,' Tanthe said cautiously, testing their reaction. 'The monarch makes a covenant with the land that he can't break. It's been so since the days of Queen Hetys. Like you said, it's supposed to be a great honour to be chosen for the project.'

The shrewd man gave a cynical snort. 'They would say that, wouldn't they? They're not going to say, "Come and have a miserable time lifting rocks". They want the chosen ones to go happily, not dragged kicking and screaming.'

This brought a stark, painful vision of Ysomir into Tanthe's mind. Dwyorn continued, 'Not that I'd say anything against good old King Garnelys. He probably is doing it for the best. But these folks in their amber palaces, they don't realise how we live. They'll take everyone off the land, and won't even know what they've done until they start wondering why there's no food on their tables nor clothes on their backs!'

123

That caused a burst of laughter, dispelling the tension. In the surge of voices, Athed leaned forward and pressed his hand on Rufryd's forearm, looking keenly from him to Tanthe. 'My friends, as you're on your way to Skald, would you do me a great favour? I don't mean any disloyalty to Garnelys, but when it's your own kin who get called up it's a different matter. If you can go up to Afthan Horn, will you try and take a message to the camp? Ask for my son Beorwyn and tell him . . . tell him we're thinking of him and if there's any way he can come home—'

'What?' Lynden broke in, frowning. 'What camp at Afthan Horn?'

'Well, they told us the conscripts were being taken to a holding camp there, to wait until they'd gathered everyone from Sepheret. Then they'd all be taken on to Parione together—'

'When? When?'

'I don't know, lad.' Athed looked put out by his vehemence. 'They took our people up there about fifteen days ago.'

'And you think they're still there?'

'I'm hoping so.'

Lynden was already on his feet, glaring at Tanthe and Rufryd. 'If we can get there before they leave, we might—'

'Yes,' said Tanthe. She was up, pushing her way out from behind the table and taking Lynden by the arm. Her heart was pounding as she pulled him aside. 'Shush. Sit down. Don't tell everyone.'

'Sorry. But we've got to go!'

'Sit down,' she repeated firmly. 'I'll go and pay for the meal. Then we'll leave – quietly. We don't want people to know what we're doing . . . just in case.'

Tanthe went to the bar, paid and got the flasks refilled, explaining that they would not be staying the night after all. Her hopes of a long sleep in a comfortable bed, followed by a hot breakfast, were evaporating, but Lynden was right. 'Rufe!' she hissed.

'Oh bugger it.' Rufryd rose with clear reluctance. 'Okay, I'm coming.'

'Don't look so fed up. A few hours might make all the difference to catching up with her. How much further is it?'

'We'll have to check the map. About a hundred miles, I think.'

'That'll take three days!' said Lynden, bright-eyed.

'Two, if we push it.'

They still had all their belongings with them as they'd decided to eat before going to their rooms. As they left the inn's warmth, Athed shouted after them, 'Hey! His name's Beorwyn. Don't forget!'

'We'll do our best,' Rufryd answered.

They hurried to the courtyard where Flame was stabled, tacked him up and secured their rucksacks on his back. It was dark and raining as they led him out into the road. A strong wind blustered through the village, scattering leaves all around them and taking their breath away. Their plans for the night ruined, now they would have to keep going on sheer determination.

Rufryd stood trying to read the map under the Golden Hawk's outside lamps, swearing as he wrestled the wind for control of the crackling linen. 'All right,' he said. 'It's easy. As long as we stay on this road we can't go wrong. Tan, get the storm lantern out of my pack. We'll light it before we go.'

They set off, heads down and cloaks fastened against the wind. Soon they were beyond the last of the cottages and following the thin rutted track between the trees. The small circle of light from the lantern danced on their surrounding as they went. After several hours, nearly asleep on her feet, Tanthe felt that the small sphere of earth, grass and trees in which they moved had become the whole of reality. She was miserable, tired, aching all over.

It would be worth it if they got Ymmi back at the end . . . but how? After the cold, intransigent way in which Beyne had taken her – almost gloating – they wouldn't give her back just for the asking.

'What did he mean, a second wave?' said Lynden. 'They wouldn't take anyone else from Riverwynde, would they?'

'That's not the issue,' said Tanthe. 'It's not just Riverwynde's problem, is it?'

'I can't understand what Garnelys is doing,' Rufryd put in. 'Everyone always says he's kind and wise and never makes mistakes. And nothing's ever happened to disprove that. Our lives are easy, we're left alone to live as we want, everyone's happy.'

'Thanks to our father sorting out all the problems,' Lynden put in.

'And my grandmother,' said Tanthe.

'But what problems?' Rufryd exclaimed. 'I tell you, the odd village squabble or dra'a'k attack is nothing. If you compare that with how things were before the War of the Silver Plains, you'd realise we lived in Paradise. Gods, the stories about how life was under the Bhahdradomen—'

'Don't!' Tanthe cried.

'What?'

'Don't say that name. Especially not in the dark.'

'Superstitious, Tan,' he said thinly. 'You can't be an intellectual city dweller while you're a superstitious peasant.'

'I don't care. Just don't!'

They walked on in silence for a few minutes. Then Lynden said, 'I can't start worrying about the whole of Aventuria. All I want is to get Ymmi back and take her home.'

Again and again as they walked, Lynden felt that they were being followed. The skin of his back crawled. Grey wraiths dashed across the corners of his vision, and he thought he heard whispers and soft footfalls just behind them. But if ever he stopped to listen there was silence and nothing to be seen in the quiet shadows of the forest.

They walked steadily for a night, a day, and another night, taking frequent brief rests for food and a few winks of sleep. Flame plodded on patiently, occasionally stumbling from tiredness. He'd already dropped some weight. Lynden was concerned for him. He would often caress the horse's ears as he led him, whispering, 'Sorry, lad. I know you need to rest. Just keep going, it won't be much further.'

By the second dawn they were numb with tiredness. They kept walking automatically, afraid to stop in case their aching bodies refused to move again. Tanthe and Rufryd were even too tired to bicker, for which Lynden was grateful. He loved them both, but too often he felt like banging their heads together.

There was a golden light ahead. As the trees ended, the path swung to bring them in sight of a magnificent hill. It filled the landscape, so breathtaking that they stopped in their tracks to stare up at it. Gilded by the autumn sunrise to melting shades of green and golden-red, the hill thrust up before them like a plateau that had tilted and sunk into the earth; a gentle slope running up from their left to form a peak that jutted proudly above the steep, carved drop of its right-hand, eastern face. Woodland clustered around its skirts on the shallow side.

'That's it,' Rufryd said in tired relief. 'That's Afthan Horn!'

Lynden's gaze followed the undulating green slope up to the peak, but could see no sign of anything that resembled an encampment. The sheer face, which was of bare, pleated rock, fell to the path on which they were travelling, then fell again down into a steep valley. Below, he saw the loop of a river and the glitter of roofs. The buildings were blue-grey, dour and magnificent, tiled with slates the colour of dark sapphires. On both sides of the river bank the houses were tiered along the hilly banks, half hidden by great trees and wrapped in a bluish haze.

'That must be Skald,' said Tanthe excitedly. 'It's the first city I've ever seen. It's beautiful. I wish we had time to go and explore.'

'Well, we don't,' Lynden said anxiously. 'Can you see any sign of the camp?'

'It's a big area,' said Rufryd, looking up at the Horn. 'It could be anywhere.'

'We'll ask someone, then.'

They went on, breakfasting on stale bread, oat cakes and goat's cheese as they went. Soon they came to a fork in the path; the right-hand looped round the steep face, the left-hand track led up onto the shallower slope. It looked new but well-used, the flints churned up by hooves and wheel-ruts. At present, both roads were deserted.

'Up on to the hill?' said Rufryd.

Lynden nodded. Instinct told him that was the right way to go. He could imagine Beyne's mounted party jog-trotting along the rutted path, Ysomir slumping tired and miserable in front of one of the riders. Anger and fire ran through him.

The hill, once they began to climb, was steeper than it looked. Toiling up the slope, they passed through green meadows where sheep and goats grazed, and narrow strips of woodland. The grass glittered with dew. Lynden realised that his boots and breeches were soaked, but he was past feeling any discomfort, or caring about the landscape's beauty.

As they climbed Afthan Horn's long flank, the westerly landscape came into view. They could no longer see Skald from here, only the hill flowing down from its crest into miles of green meadowland. Two or three miles away to the west was the edge of a thick dark forest which ran, as fast as Lynden could see, north and west all the way to the horizon.

An hour's climb brought them up onto the highest point of the saddle, where the ground flattened out at last. To their left, a wide section of pines had been cut down; the starkness of the raw stumps shocked him. Then Lynden saw the fence. It was built of rough logs, at least ten feet high and solid, with an odd glitter along the top.

Lynden's heart began to race. 'There it is,' he said through dry lips.

'Wait,' said Rufryd, gripping his arm. 'That's a hell of a fence. Doesn't look like they want anyone going in or out.'

Lynden suddenly saw what was glittering on top of the fence. Shards of broken glass. 'Anthar's balls,' he whispered.

'An army camp means warriors. Warriors have swords, bows and spears,' Rufryd went on. 'Beyne and his crew weren't messing about when they took the conscripts. We could all get killed.'

'Do you have to talk to me as if I'm an idiot?' Lynden said hotly.

'We're not,' said Tanthe. 'We just need to be careful.'

'Well, it would be daft to try and take her by force, wouldn't it?' said Lynden. 'We'll have to negotiate. Tell them she must come home because her mother's ill, or something. We could offer them something in exchange.'

Rufryd sighed. His eyes were shadowed and he looked dishevelled, unshaven and exasperated. 'Like what? One rather small, slow horse?'

'I'd rather they took me than her. I'll offer myself!'

'Over my dead body,' Rufryd said grimly. 'Soon we're going to find out just how stupid this journey was.'

'Are we just going to stand here, or are we going to take a closer look?' said Tanthe.

Alert with anxiety, all tiredness forgotten, they approached the fence. They went right up to it and peered through any narrow gaps they could find. On the other side, angular shadowy shapes were visible against the grass. Tents.

Nothing stirred. There was no sound other than the chirping of birds and the distant bleat of sheep. There were only a few tents left, their oiled sides flapping sluggishly, but many brownish circles in the grass where others had been taken down. Shock and disappointment flooded Lynden, and he sank to his knees.

'No,' he gasped. 'There's no one there. They've gone. They've taken her!'

Tanthe was beside him, pulling him to his feet. 'Come on, Lyn. Don't give up. We knew this was a long shot. If we find out when they left, we might still catch them up!'

His head aching and his eyes stinging, Lynden rose wearily and pulled Flame's reluctant head up from the grass. They followed the fence for fifty yards, came to a corner, turned and followed the second side. Halfway along they found a great gate standing open.

Now they could clearly see the churned ground where the camp had been. They stood in the gateway, stunned. Lynden saw Tanthe turn away, and knew she was crying, and didn't want the others to see. He felt the same.

'Hoy!'

The shout took them by surprise. A man emerged from a small hut, just inside the camp's entrance. He was of middle height, stocky and strong-looking, wearing what Lynden took to be a basic version of the King's uniform; dark green breeches, creamy-brown linen shirt and a green tunic with the tree and eight-spoked wheel imprinted in gold on the shoulder. 'Morning,' said the soldier, strolling towards them. He was unarmed, and didn't seem unfriendly. 'Looking for something?'

'We were on our way to Skald,' Tanthe began at once, 'and we met a man on our travels who said his son was here at the camp. He asked us to deliver a message.'

'Well, yer too late. They've gone.'

'We can see that. When—' her voice wavered, and she cleared her throat. 'When did they leave?'

'Five days ago.'

'Five days!' Lynden cried, before he could stop himself.

'And – and they've gone to Parione, have they?'

The soldier sniffed. 'If they're lucky. Parione or the mines.'

130

The word was a physical blow to his stomach. 'What mines?'

'Look,' said the soldier, coming closer, 'You're not the first relatives we've had up here, trying to talk their way in to see their family members or take them home. I'm very sorry for you. But it's the King's will, it's the law, and there's nothing anyone can do about it. Some friendly advice; one, the Registat doesn't like this sort of thing, and I'm expecting him up here any minute to make his inspection. Two, we're expecting a new conscription order any day, so if you three don't want to be part of it, I'd scarper if I was you.'

Lynden stood facing the man, wild-eyed. Tanthe was pulling at his arm. 'Come on. Let's do as he says. We'll go and have a rest, and decide what to do next.'

He went with her, flattened by misery. The three of them walked on along the fence. 'Five days?' he said. 'I don't understand. How could they have got so far ahead of us?'

'Easily,' Rufryd answered. 'They were mounted. We were crawling along at a snail's pace on foot, probably covering twice as much ground as we needed to because we didn't know the way. If every time Beyne conscripted in a particular place, he sent the conscripts straight to Afthan Horn to wait, they must have been ready to leave as soon as Ysomir arrived. Riverwynde was last on his list. She was probably here less than a day.'

Lynden said nothing. He had no strength left to express his fears.

Just as they reached the far corner of the camp, a party of horsemen appeared suddenly over the rim of a dip in the land. Four fine brown horses, three riders in cavalry uniform and the leader in plain but well-cut dark blue. Lynden recognised him. Beyne.

The official reined in, his bloated face creasing into a hard, calculating stare.

'What's this? I know you. I remember you very well.'

131

Tanthe whispered, 'Oh, shit.'

Beyne rode close to Lynden and leaned down. 'You're not as pretty as I remember. You'd clean up, though. Were you hoping to join your little girlfriend? If only the King had relaxed the quota sooner, I could have accepted volunteers. The good news is that I'm authorised to conscript you all, if you wish. The bad news is that as you'll go where you're sent, you're most unlikely ever to see her again.'

Beyne laughed, silently, gloatingly. Lynden was paralysed. Then the official straightened up and signed to his men. 'Take them!'

Lynden lost control. All his exhaustion, misery and disappointment coalesced into rage and there was a black veil falling over his eyes.

'You bastard! You goddess-forsaken *bastard*.'

In dread, Tanthe heard the words burst from Lynden's mouth. Said in anger it was a terrible insult; it meant one who had turned away from the Goddess and so made himself motherless. Beyne's face darkened with rage, but before he could move, Lynden seized his leg and toppled him out of the saddle.

Tanthe gasped. Rufryd said, 'Let's run for it,' and she was already leaping onto Flame's back. Beyne just clung on by seizing his horse's mane. He teetered in midair with one foot in the stirrup, ungainly and struggling, until one of his men helped him back into the saddle. It gained the others a few seconds; Tanthe was urging Flame into life and pulling Lynden up behind her.

Thankfully, he didn't resist. He seemed almost out of his mind with shock but he clung to her as they fled at a gallop, along the fence, then leaving the camp behind and crossing an open meadow. Rufryd was running alongside them, swearing in between laboured breaths.

'Thanks, Lynden. You bloody idiot.'

'It's not his fault!' Tanthe cried.

The mounted men were in pursuit. It was obvious they could catch up in seconds, but instead they were following at a controlled hand-gallop. Just enough to keep their prey running.

'This is a game to them,' she said. 'They're trying to wear us out.'

'They'll kill poor Flame,' Lynden said in anguish. 'It's hopeless.'

'No!' Rufryd shouted. 'This way.' He altered course slightly, so they were heading for the forest.

Flame ran gamely, but he was exhausted and couldn't compete with the speed of the other horses. Fear dried Tanthe's mouth and cramped her stomach. Lynden was hanging grimly round her waist. They heard the drumming of hooves as the horses gained on them.

'It's no good,' Rufryd gasped. 'You go on.' Yards from the edge of the trees, Rufryd stopped dead. Tanthe turned in the saddle to see him facing back towards their pursuers, setting an arrow to his bow. He let fly; the arrow arced cleanly through the air and sank with a thud into Beyne's chest.

Beyne let out a strangled grunt, doubled over, pitched out of the saddle.

'Gods, he's killed him!' Tanthe breathed.

'Keep going!' Rufryd yelled. He was running frantically after Flame now, but the mounted party had come to a halt. Tanthe's brief hope of stealing Beyne's horse was dashed as one of the men grabbed its reins, while another jumped down beside the fallen leader. The remaining two men were aiming crossbows.

A couple of shafts sang past Tanthe's ears. Then Flame was plunging in among the trees, down a steep bank, leaping across a ditch at the bottom and nearly losing his footing in the thick undergrowth. Hauling himself up on the other side, he slowed to a walk and dropped his head. His sides were heaving like bellows. Tanthe found her hands greasy with his sweat.

'Get down,' Lynden said. 'He's had it. Poor sod.'

They dismounted, and Lynden took the horse's reins. Rufryd came scrambling after them. Around them the trees grew thickly, with twisted trunks and a low, dense canopy.

'They're not following us,' said Rufryd, trying to catch his breath.

'Are you sure?' Craning her neck, she could just see the party where they had halted, a few yards from the forest's edge. They were staring grimly at the trees, shaking their heads. Then – with Beyne lying over the saddle of his mount – they began to move off the way they had come.

Tanthe found herself shaking violently. She bit her hand to stop herself bursting into tears with sheer terror. The moment passed and she caught her breath.

'Lyn?' she said, her voice trembling. 'Are you all right?'

'No, I'm not bloody all right,' he said, staring fiercely at the ground. 'I wish that arrow had been mine!'

'Come on,' said Rufryd. 'Let's get as deep into here as we can, so we'll be sure they never find us.'

'Why did they stop? I thought two of them would follow us, at least.'

They were making slow progress between the close-set trees, over ground that was thick with the fallen leaves of many seasons. Rufryd glanced sideways at her, grim-faced. 'Don't you know where we are?'

'Some blasted forest.'

'The Forest of Ardharkria. That's why they didn't follow us.'

Tanthe went cold. Even reading the name on the map had always given her a shudder of dread. No one came here; Ardharkria was deeply feared, and it harboured nameless entities that were barely touched on even in the darkest of Aelyr-tales, for fear of invoking them. That was what she'd always heard.

'Very funny.'

'I'm not joking. Now don't go superstitious on me, Tan.

The tales about this place will protect us. We're going to need that.'

'Now we've killed someone, you mean?'

'We?' he said strangely. 'I did it, not you.'

'But we're all going to get equal blame for it, if we're caught!'

'Then let's not get caught,' Rufryd said harshly. 'Let's hope they believe this place is full of ghouls and monsters.'

'And what if it is?' she exclaimed.

'We're perfectly safe here. They're just stories.'

'You don't understand,' Tanthe said through her teeth. 'There *aren't* any stories.'

Despite her fears, there seemed to be nothing untoward in the forest. The sun shone warmly through the leaves, which were just beginning to turn russet and yellow. Tanthe began to forget her instinctive dread. Maybe Rufryd was right, it was only the weaving together of rumours over the centuries that had created monsters where none existed. It was foolish to be superstitious, and she'd always been the strong one, comforting Ymmi's fears. The forest seemed warm and friendly. Only the thickness of the fallen leaves and the closeness of the gnarled, flaky trunks made it seem, if anything, too warm, soft and enveloping.

'Something's following us,' said Lynden, rousing her from a reverie that was perilously close to sleep. They had been walking for two hours or more.

'What?' she exclaimed.

They stopped, peering all around them through the trees, listening hard. There was no sound but that of falling leaves pattering around them. Not even birdsong.

'There's nothing there,' Rufryd said at last. His voice sounded unnaturally loud.

'That's it,' said Tanthe. 'We have got to stop and rest. Lyn, I think you're hallucinating because you're so tired.'

'I don't want to stop,' Lynden said blankly. He looked drunk on despair.

'You've got no choice, little brother,' said Rufryd. 'If they'd followed us, they'd have caught us by now. So we're safe, for the time being. First decent place we find, we're going to sleep before we drop dead.'

Soon they found a small hollow sheltered by an oval of trees, and decided to camp there. Tanthe was past caring whether she slept in a haunted forest or on Beyne's doorstep, she was so tired. There was only a thin layer of leaves and the earth beneath was dark, soft and peaty. They found Flame a patch of grass and made him comfortable, shared a drink of cider and some bread, then rolled themselves in their cloaks to sleep on the warm clean earth.

She lay awake for a few minutes, the whole of the journey whirling uncomfortably in her head. Again and again she saw Beyne falling, and she thought, *we killed him, we are murderers now, they'll come after us* . . . then her mind sank into merciful unconsciousness.

Deep in sleep, she became vaguely aware that she was struggling. A nightmare in which she couldn't breathe. She began to panic, fighting to surface into consciousness, but the more she fought the worse it became. Tiny vicious pains stung her scalp, and she could feel the earth caving in beneath her head and shoulders. Her head was being pulled, dragged into the earth, crumbs of soil falling in on to her cheeks—

In horror she tried to sit up, but something was gripping her hair, gripping it so hard that it nearly ripped from her scalp. All was dark and she felt tiny claws or jaws scraping her skin. The earth all around her and below her was full of a ghastly, busy scuffling.

A scream ripped up from her lungs, but as her mouth opened it filled with earth. The ground was closing over her face and she was sinking deeper. Suffocating. Drowning in the earth.

Chapter Six. Sunstone and Shadow

Ysomir stood on the long wooden platform, clutching her cloak around her and shivering more with trepidation than cold. Although she was in the midst of a crowd, she had never felt more alone. A lamp hanging from a post swung in the slight breeze, shining brightly on their hair while leaving all else in shadow.

Behind her was the bare hut, where they'd been given food and hot, honeyed tea as they waited. In front was a long, high-sided wooden carriage, with two powerful draught-horses harnessed in tandem between its shafts. Its eight wheels ran on rails, and the rails were two thin silver ribbons vanishing into darkness.

She'd never seen such a vehicle before today. It was about thirty feet long, with a row of small windows cut into its planked sides. The windows had shutters; no glass. The horses that drew it were tall, velvety brown beasts, with black legs and muzzles, large mobile ears, thick necks and muscular hindquarters. They stamped at the hard-packed earth that lay between the rails, impatient to be off. The driver sat high up in a cab built into the front, hunched up in thick furs and holding the reins loosely as he waited for orders.

Some yards behind this conveyance stood a second, also ready to leave. Ysomir had already watched three similar ones move off into the night, rolling easily on the rails. Now her turn had come.

'Clever, that,' said a voice beside her. She looked round and found a great, sleepy-eyed bear of a man beside her. He was twice her size, with thickly curly black hair and a glint in his eyes that alarmed her. She wanted to escape him but she didn't know how.

'What?'

'Running the carriage on the rails. Easier for the horses to pull, you see.'

'Oh.' I don't care, she thought, edging away. I want to go home.

'Next lot!' the guard shouted. 'Don't rush. There's a seat for everyone. Privy at the rear. Breakfast when we reach Mananneth.'

Ysomir waited her turn with the other conscripts, as they had their names ticked off on a list then climbed up the steep step into the wagon. Inside, they had to sit in two long rows facing each other, their knees almost touching. To her dismay, she found the bear-like man opposite her. Most of the others, like her, looked very young and as worried as she felt. Four guards – a female and three males – climbed in after them and seated themselves by a small stove near the back. The stove was unlit, but she wondered how warm it would keep them when the weather turned cold.

The chief guard – a man of around fifty who seemed neither threatening nor concerned about his charges – slid the door shut with a heavy thud, and shouted to the driver that they were ready. As the carriage lurched forward the lamps suspended from the ceiling swung wildly. The shadows rotated around the walls. Ysomir clutched the edge of her seat, dizzy with fear. With a great creaking and shuddering, the vehicle began to roll into the night.

Soon the shadows settled to a steady vibration. Travelling at the pace of a steady trot, the vehicle's motion was level and far smoother than the ordinary horse-drawn wagons that had brought them here. But still it was punctuated by shudders and jolts that soon made her bones ache.

It was hard to avoid the eyes of the man opposite her. She tried looking at the walls, the ceiling, the floor; but every time she glanced at him, his gaze was still fixed on her. She winced, desperately uncomfortable. She closed her eyes but sleep would not come; it only made the rattling noise of the journey seem more intense, hallucinatory.

'This is something, isn't it?' said a fair young man next to the bear. 'Never sat in anything like this before.'

'The King must be very clever, thinking of a carriage like this,' said the dark-haired girl beside Ysomir. 'I'd still rather be home with my lover, though.' She fingered a locket at her throat as she spoke. It was a beautiful thing of silvery moonstone.

'Not me. I want to see Parione. My name's Lath.'

'I'm Serenis.'

The young men and women around Ysomir began to talk, exchanging names and telling of the villages and towns from which they'd come. They tried to involve her in the conversation, but she could not bring herself to join in. She was too homesick, too anxious. All the same, she found the murmur of voices comforting. Presently they began to sing old folk songs, some of which she knew and others that were unfamiliar. That lulled her and she half-dozed, with memories running through her head like dreams.

It was a blur, the way she'd been taken from Riverwynde. It had happened so fast, events running out of her control as if she'd become a piece of gossamer with no weight, no voice. Being hoisted onto the saddle of one of the cavalry-women, clutching a little bag containing her belongings, not even allowed to say goodbye to Lynden . . . not even realising how final the parting was. She'd been numb. Simply not believing that this was possible. Her nightmare had been of Lynden being taken from *her*, not the other way round.

As they'd left the village, something weird had happened. The villagers had come running after them; some of the horsemen had turned back to confront them. There had been shouts, the chilling sounds of a fight . . .

then the sky had gone dark and she had sensed a vile presence, but the horse-woman had followed Beyne's orders, and carried her swiftly away from the scene.

Since then she'd been haunted by nightmares of what might have occurred. No one would answer her questions. More than the pain of being taken from her family, she had the anguish of not knowing if any of them were hurt . . . or worse.

By the time they'd reached Havereyn, the shock of her abduction was beginning to sink in. She was worn out and saddle-sore, but the King's party – hardened travellers – had stopped only for brief rests. They weren't unkind to her, only indifferent, but their rough manners and the simple fact that they were strangers was enough to fill her with fear.

Ysomir had been confused, thinking that there must be something unusual, even special, about her to have been chosen by the King. But when they reached the town, there were more mounted soldiers and a group of young people from Havereyn and the surrounding villages who, like herself, had been chosen. Then she realised she was not unique at all. She was only one of a herd. The knowledge was at once comforting and alarming.

All her life she had been cared for by her family. No one – apart from Rufryd – had ever said a cruel word to her. She'd always felt different to them, thin-skinned and too exposed to the dark face of life, but they understood and had always protected her.

Now there was no one who cared or even knew her.

At Havereyn, the recruits had been piled into horse-drawn carts and transported at a jog trot along the road to Skald. The road, a mere track paved with flint, was so rough that she thought the motion of the cart would shake her to pieces. Some of the others were excited, some were upset and crying. But Ysomir was silent, closed in on herself, neither speaking nor weeping. She thought the journey would never end.

They had stopped for a few hours each night and slept in makeshift tents beside the road, but it was never for long enough to recover from the day's exertion. She felt worn thin by fatigue. The food was edible, but never enough, even for her small appetite. On the first night, the commander issued a stern warning that anyone trying to escape would be severely punished.

'Why are we prisoners?' one young man had called out. 'We've done nothing wrong.'

'You're not prisoners,' the commander had barked. 'You're at the King's command and that means obeying the rules, you lazy country oafs. Your lives are going to be different from now on, so get used to it.'

Ysomir had lain awake on the chill ground, looking through the open end of the tent to the wild hills beyond and thinking, all I have to do is get up and walk, and in a few days I will be home . . . Later that night, a young man – the one who had spoken out – had tried it. The guards caught him and beat him; she heard his cries. In the morning he appeared, bruised and bleeding, with chains on his wrists and ankles. A warning to the others. But they were a peaceful people who trusted their King; it wasn't in their nature to rebel or ask too many questions. Suddenly it struck her that these soldiers from the city knew that, and despised them for it.

It took them six days to reach Afthan Horn. She was shocked by the size of the camp; it was a town of tents on the hillside, swarming with hundreds of young men and women. The crowd alarmed her. She still couldn't get used to it, but there was no escape. The camp was surrounded by unscalable fences.

Here they were officially signed into the King's service. Their clothes were taken away and they were issued with uniforms; brown leather boots, loose breeches of a hard cloth, shirts of the same dull greeny-brown, a leather tunic and a dark green cloak. They were each given a small rucksack for their rations and personal belongings. Ysomir and the others from Havereyn were at the camp for only one night; at dawn, they were on the move again, in the charge of different officers. She was relieved to see that the narrow-eyed, sinister Beyne was staying behind. Yet he seemed her last link to Riverwynde. Now they were being taken further into the unknown, and with every step her hopes of going home receded.

By evening, the conscripts had been brought to the base of the hills on which Skald and Afthan Horn stood. That was where the strange silver rails began, and the guards began to load them forty at a time into the great carriages.

'Don't be sad,' said a voice. Her eyes flew open. The huge man opposite her was leaning forward; afraid he was going to touch her, she pressed back against the carriage-wall. 'I'm sorry,' he said. 'But you look so alone. I just wanted—'

'Leave me alone,' she said, huddling deeper into her cloak.

'But don't be afraid. I'm Beorwyn Athed-son. What's your name?'

She didn't answer. She invoked Breyid and Anthar to make him vanish, but he remained there, his eyes fixed on her. 'What's your name?' he said again.

'Ysomir Aynie-daughter. Please, I'm trying to sleep.'

He didn't seem to hear her. 'I'm from Forthryn Seal. Where are you from?'

'Riverwynde.'

'Where's that?'

She turned sideways, trying to find a comfortable place to lean her head. There was none. The back of the bench was hard, and the girl next to her kept lolling on to her shoulder.

'Where's that?'

At last she sensed he'd given up. There were no more questions, to her relief. But throughout the endless night, her neck and head throbbing with pain, she remained miserably awake.

Every few hours, the carriage stopped for the recruits to stretch their legs, rest and eat. Once or twice a day they would stop at a way station where the horses and drivers would be changed, the privy cleaned, fresh food and water taken on board. It was always a relief when they were allowed to stretch out on the grass, wrap themselves in their cloaks and sleep for a couple of hours. Their carriage and the one behind travelled in convoy, but occasionally they saw the one ahead of them in the distance. It became a game between the conscripts, making light-hearted bets on when they would next spot it again. Their spirits were high, and there was a camaraderie developing. Ysomir wished she could join in, but all she could think about was Lynden. And perhaps even more than him, she wanted Tanthe.

About five days into the journey, they halted beside a narrow river on a broad, lushly beautiful green bank, with hills all around and a line of mountains in the distance. She hadn't looked at a map of Aventuria since her schooling ended and had only the vaguest idea of where Parione was or what lay in between.

As she sat on the river bank, nibbling at her food, she began to think about the city. Perhaps it would be beautiful. Perhaps she would like it, and when her conscription was over, she could send for Tanthe to join her there . . .

'Do you want my cheese?'

Her unwanted companion was standing over her, holding a greasy white lump in his paw.

'What?'

'I watched you. You don't eat enough. You can have mine.'

'No – no, thank you, I've had enough.' She got up hurriedly and made her way back to the carriage, where the others were assembling.

'Won't you talk to me?' said Beorwyn, following her.

'Leave me alone!' she cried, and he did, looking at her baffled.

It was the nearest she came to tears, but she swallowed the feeling and sat as near as she could to the four soldiers who guarded them. As the carriage moved off again, some of the folk near her began to talk about Parione. How beautiful it was, how glorious the Amber Citadel, how their journey would be worthwhile in the end. They repeated far-fetched stories with Ysomir knew weren't true; they speculated on the nature of the monument they would be helping to build.

As they spoke, she noticed that the guards were laughing, not pleasantly. 'Parione?' said one. 'They'll be lucky!'

His tone shocked her out of her numbness. Her head came up. 'What do you mean?' she said.

They all stopped laughing and stared at her. 'Who told you you were going to Parione?' said the guard who had spoken. He was tanned and quite handsome, with chestnut hair like Lynden's and very blue eyes.

'The – the man who conscripted us. Registat Beyne.'

'Oh, well. He never told a lie in his life, did he?'

She felt her cheeks turning hot. She felt she would rather be dead than trapped in this hot, crowded wagon, breathing the ripeness of human bodies. 'Where are we going, then?'

'That's not for us to say, now is it? But you'll be surrounded by the riches of the earth. You'll be covered in jewels, all right!'

The four laughed uproariously. Ysomir pulled her hood as far over her face as she could, and tried to sleep with her hand hiding her face.

In the evening, when they stopped at a way-station to rest, she turned away from the crowd, intending to get as far away as she dared. On the hillside, a few yards above the cluster of huts and stables and the long wooden platform, Ysomir saw a little group of trees. As soon as she'd drunk the soup they doled out, she climbed slowly towards them. All she wanted was to be alone for a time.

144

The night was blessedly cool and odourless. Leaf Moon was just peeping over the horizon, nearly full. It looked, tantalisingly, just as it did at home.

For a few moments she had her wish. Then she sensed someone following, and the blue-eyed guard appeared beside her.

'Not thinking of making a run for it, are you?'

'No. Of course not.'

'Only you wouldn't get far before wolves or dra'a'ks ate you.'

'I need some air, that's all. That big man with the beard won't leave me alone.'

'That Beorwyn? He's a bit simple, if you ask me.' She went on walking and he kept pace with her. 'Look,' he said, 'I'm sorry if I upset you before. We were just larking around. We get bored stiff making these runs.'

'I'm quite bored, too,' said Ysomir. She swallowed hard. 'I'd rather be at home.'

'I know. So would I, to be honest. If only I had the money, I could buy a commission and be near my wife. My name's Jenorn. You're Ysomir, aren't you?'

'You should know that, after ticking me off on all those lists. Jenorn . . . where are they taking us, really?'

'I'm not sure. But it's probably to Napheneth.'

'What's that?'

'It's where they quarry the stone. Not as glamorous as Parione, that's all.'

'Oh.' At this moment, she was too tired to care where she went. But now they were at the trees and she'd been deprived of her wish to be alone. Jenorn's presence made her feel awkward.

'Did you say Napheneth?' The new voice made her jump. Someone was already there, leaning back against one of the tree trunks, half-hidden by the twilight. It was the dark-haired girl, Serenis. 'I don't want to go to a quarry!'

Jenorn stopped and shrugged. 'I don't know for certain.'

'You must know,' said the girl indignantly.

'Look, it's not up to me. I don't make the decisions.' He went closer to her, holding his palms open in a gesture of conciliation. Ysomir saw her chance to leave. 'I've just been telling Ysomir, I want to be with my wife but I've got no choice, either.'

'My lover and me were going to be handfasted soon,' said Serenis.

Jenorn put his foot on a thick tree root and leaned on his knee. 'I'm sorry. I know how you feel.'

'So do I,' Ysomir said, so softly they didn't hear her.

'Now all I've got is a picture of him,' Serenis went on, clasping her locket. 'When can we go home?'

'I don't know. Let me see that.'

She lifted the locket to show him. Ysomir saw the flash of pale crystals, glowing intensely in the moon light. Jenorn lowered his head close to her throat, balancing the jewel on his fingers, opening it to look inside then snapping it shut. He caught his breath. Ysomir was suddenly embarrassed, sensing a flirtation between them that she didn't want to witness.

'This is beautiful. It's very valuable, isn't it?'

'Yes. Very.'

Ysomir turned to walk away, still hearing their voices.

'Give it to me,' said Jenorn.

'What?'

'In return, I can make your journey a lot more comfortable. I can make sure you don't get sent to Napheneth.' His voice was thick with greed. Ysomir stopped in her tracks.

'I don't care. I'd rather die than part with it.'

'If you refuse, I can make your life so miserable you'll wish you *were* dead.'

Serenis gasped in disbelief. 'Don't be stupid. It's all I've got of him.'

'I'm taking it, whether you like it or not,' Jenorn said viciously. 'It's my way out of here!'

'No!' she cried, her voice rising in alarm. 'Get off me, get *off*!'

Ysomir saw Jenorn pulling hard at the chain that held the locket, holding Serenis's shoulder with the other hand. When she tried to fight back, he thrust her hard into the tree trunk and she yelped in pain.

Ysomir ran back to them, shouting, 'Stop it! Leave her alone!'

When Jenorn took no notice, she seized his arm and tried to pull him off. The guard's face swivelled towards her, blue eyes ablaze. His fist swung like a sledgehammer into her chest and she fell back, hitting the ground so hard that for a few seconds she was dazed and winded.

Through the cloud of hissing stars in her head, she heard Serenis scream.

A shadow reared over them. There was a roar. Suddenly she saw Jenorn rising into the air, and dangling above her, held by two great fists. Beorwyn's face was distorted with rage, his whole form shaking; then he flung the attacker across the glade. The guard crashed into the trunk of another tree then smacked painfully onto its roots, leaves raining around him.

Ysomir staggered to her feet and found Serenis in her arms, shaking. There was a red line round her neck, but the locket was still in place. 'Are you all right?' Ysomir said.

Serenis clung to her. 'Are *you*?'

Jenorn tried to get up, but as soon as he did so, Beorwyn seized him and smashed him back against the trunk again, one hand squeezing his throat. The guard began to go purple. He was trying to splutter words of rage, but his anger collapsed into fear. His nose was pouring blood.

'Never touch her again,' Beorwyn said calmly. 'If anyone hurts her, I'll kill them. Motherless worm!'

When he finally let Jenorn go, the guard fell to his knees, coughing and gagging. Ysomir simply stared at him, feeling ice-cold inside. Beorwyn turned to her, his big hands hanging by his side. 'Forgive me, Mistress Ysomir,' he said. 'I know you don't want me by you. But I won't let anyone harm you.'

147

Ysomir had no idea what to say or do. Jenorn hurried past them, giving the two women a grim, bitter look as he passed, almost running to get away from Beorwyn.

'Thank you,' she said faintly. 'But it was Serenis who needed help, not me. I hope you don't get into trouble for hitting a guard.'

'I don't care.'

'He deserved it,' said Serenis. 'Bastard.'

'They want us to get back in the carriage now,' said Beorwyn.

'All right.' They began to walk back, the two women supporting each other. Serenis was slightly shorter and more slender than Ysomir, yet she reminded her of Tanthe. How odd it felt, to have defended someone else, when others had always defended her . . . and were still doing so, it seemed. Beorwyn was a couple of feet away, protective but unobtrusive.

'You think I'm stupid, don't you?' he said sadly, addressing Ysomir.

'No, Beorwyn. I think you're anything but stupid.'

'I'm not like Jenorn.'

'I know.'

'You don't need to be afraid of anything while I'm here.'

Near tears, she put her hand on his arm, to show she understood. He smiled, like a child. 'But not just me,' she said firmly. 'You can't look out just for me, and no one else.'

He nodded. 'If that's what you want, Mistress Ysomir.'

'Looks like you've made a friend for life,' Serenis whispered ironically. 'Now, you come and sit with Lath and me and our friends. Don't be on your own. And Ysomir—'

'Yes?'

'Thank you. I don't know what would have happened if you hadn't been there. I would have died if I'd lost this locket.'

Nothing more was said about the incident. Jenorn

evidently refused to make any complaint against Beorwyn, knowing that a worse complaint would be made against him. And to protect Beorwyn, Ysomir and Serenis also said nothing. But when the carriage set off once more, Jenorn was no longer on board. His place had been taken by a sour-faced female officer, who had apparently swapped with him from the other carriage. Ysomir was relieved, but her main feeling was a kind of quiescent despair. What was happening, that a soldier of the King would try to rob and abuse someone in his charge?

And Ysomir had thought herself a sound judge of character, but found out in one fell swoop that she had misjudged both Beorwyn and Jenorn.

Some good had come out of it. She'd emerged from her broken shell, and found friends. They all needed each other in this strange adventure. With Beorwyn there, a gentle bear-like presence, she felt safe.

The days passed.

The carriages slowed, the horses labouring up an incline. Even with the stove alight, it was growing very cold. The conscripts stuck their heads out of the windows to see a steep wall of mountains ahead. Ysomir tasted snow; the flakes melted on her lips and settled in big white clots on her hood.

'Close the window shutters,' said the chief guard irritably. 'It's bloody freezing. Don't worry, we'll be over the Whiteveil Mountains well before winter sets in.'

The Sun Chamber was a long, vaulted hall, with slim columns that branched and interlaced like trees to support the arched ceiling. All was panelled in flakes of amber, so the whole chamber glistened rich, translucent gold. A great window behind the throne showed, in blue and gold and green, Queen Hetys offering up a symbolic jewel to the Tree of Life.

The Sapphire Throne was a tall double chair clustered with lapis, blue spinel and sapphires. King Garnelys sat easily there, one elbow resting on the arm and his chin on his hand. In a flowing robe of midnight blue, with a stiffly quilted and embroidered yoke and sleeves slashed to reveal silver, he was wise, regal, unassailable. His hair, flowing white around the powerful hollows of his face, was held with a platinum circlet on which there sparkled a large blood-red almandine. His eyes were dark and appraising.

His council were seated in tiers along either side of the Sun Chamber, one hundred and forty men and women in all, elected by the citizens of Parione. They filled the chamber with jewel-colours in their court clothes; amber, lapis, beryl-green, amethyst and jet. Royal guards in indigo and gold were positioned at the double doors and all around the hall. General Grannen stood to the King's right, Lord Poel to his left with his aide Derione beside him. Lord Laphaeome was just behind them. But the Queen's seat was empty.

The doors were open; on the threshold stood a small crowd of citizens, anxious for an audience with their monarch.

'Sire,' said the steward who stood before him, 'may I present the list of petitions. The Actors' Guild, that you pardon Saphaeyender and Eldareth and allow them to return to Parione without fear of punishment. The Stone Masons' Guild, that your conscription of unskilled labour compromises their ancient rights and privileges. Priestesses from the Temple of Nuth, that armed men entered their inviolable sanctum at your command. A member of the Stone Masons' Guild speaking on behalf of the Subterraneans, who protest that ancient treaties between humans and Subterraneans have been grossly violated.'

'Let them come forward,' said the King.

He listened as, one by one, the factions expressed their grievances. He nodded with grave understanding, just as he had always done. He sensed their nervousness as they stood before him, not to praise him but to complain. Yet they weren't afraid; their faith in his mercy was absolute.

'I have heard you all,' he said at length. His tone was mild. 'Now I give my judgement. Let me ask you this; do you love your monarch?'

'Aye, sire!' said every voice in the chamber.

'Do you believe that your King has a bond forged with Aventuria, that gives him an insight and wisdom no other human possesses? That that is why I am charged with serving Aventuria?'

'Aye!'

'Then live by your belief.' Black diamond harshness came crackling into his voice. 'Trust me when I say that all I do is for your benefit. All your petitions are dismissed.'

Murmurs of dismay broke out. 'Sire—'

'Those who question me, question the covenant of King and land. They attack the Xauroma. They are traitors! Surely none would dare stand in the Sun Chamber who is disloyal to the Amber Citadel?'

There was a shocked silence. The petitioners were looking at each other with wide, fearful eyes. Garnelys heard the crisp slap of his guards' hands flying to sword-hilts. Grannen stood like a granite wall, feet planted wide; Lord Poel was marble, ice-cold.

One black-robed priestess looked at Laphaeome and said quietly, 'Sire, will your Mediator not mediate for us?'

She met the King's eyes. He saw that she knew the truth; that he'd run his son to ground in her temple and had him murdered there. He lifted a finger. Two guards seized her and dragged her away.

'This audience is at an end,' said Garnelys. 'All rights of petition are suspended!'

The factions moved out of the chamber in hushed alarm; the council members were silent, watching the King expectantly. Suddenly their presence irritated him beyond reason. They were there to discuss and advise; traditionally the monarch acted on their advice, but he was not obliged to. He'd ignored them when they advised against the Tower. He needed them not at all.

'The council also, is suspended,' he said. 'You will not sit again until the Tower is finished!'

One hundred and forty faces turned to him in disbelief. He rose to leave before anyone should have the audacity to object; but none dared. They rose and bowed as Garnelys swept out of the Sun Chamber. He had never felt more isolated, as if he were not in the palace but alone on a mountain-top; yet never before had he felt such a craving for this solitude.

'Sire?'

He'd left the others behind and was striding down the long, blue-shadowed corridor towards his private metrarch chamber. Then Laphaeome was beside him, soft-moving, white as milk. 'Is all well?'

'Never better,' said Garnelys. 'I should have done this before. Poel and Grannen are advisors enough. I don't even need them. Only you and the Tower. Happy the day you came to me.'

'I knew you needed me, sire.'

'Do you think, Laphaeome, that they can still love me now that they fear me?'

Reaching the chamber, Garnelys crossed it and went straight through the hidden door, down the steps into the cell. There he fingered the straps that dangled on the empty frame, stroked the dull brown crystal. The cell smelled coppery-sweet with blood, and of something burnt.

'Naturally, sire. They love you as they would a stern parent – and respect you all the more.'

'I don't want them to know.'

'About what?'

He stroked the post in a turmoil of lust and loathing. 'About the people I bring here. Was this your idea, or mine? I can't remember.'

Garnelys's memories of the last three years were oddly imprecise. He hated to dwell on the start of it, the black depression and fear that had begun to overwhelm him.

But one day, like a guardian spirit, Laphaeome had come to the palace.

He had presented himself as a mage from the Serpent Isles, a quiet community who had earned themselves the title of Mediators for their role in settling the War of the Silver Plains. He was travelling through Aventuria, Laphaeome had explained; he had come to pay his respects to the King; he could sense the King was troubled.

'Sire, I can guide you out of this storm,' Laphaeome had told him, so gentle, so resolute, 'if you will only trust me.'

'Trust between my people and yours is unquestioned,' Garnelys had replied. More than that, his faith in Laphaeome had been instant and absolute. They'd talked for hours.

'I sense that you have lost your way. You need strength. I can show you ways to gain that strength, to find the answers you need.'

'Sorcery?'

'There's no great mystery to it, sire. All things vibrate with their own unique energies, so the Aelyr have taught us. Trees, plants, our minds, the crystals and stones in the earth. It's a matter of attuning yourself with a particular energy and making it work for you.'

'This sounds a matter for the priestesses of Nuth, not for me.'

'No, this is a realm you should explore. Some energy forms, the Aelyr say, are damaging to the human mind and should never be invoked; but I will tell you now, sire, that they are wrong. There are certain energies called *gauroth* that indeed are dark, strong and difficult to control. But not damaging. The Aelyr fear them only because they are so powerful. Learn to focus them through a particular crystal and you will gain everything you need. You will require a boy . . .'

'A boy?'

'Or a girl. *Gauroth* feeds on emotion, you see . . .'

Now Garnelys remembered the conversation with a

chill. Invoking the energy had come easily, to his delight; controlling it was a different matter. He'd sought a cure for his ennui; answers to the mysteries of life; guidance; and at last, the secret of eternal life. But the answers that spilled from the cut throats of his victims had been chaotic, nightmarish, mocking, like the shouting of a madman through a roaring storm. *Gauroth* only came in response to pain. It was a thing of horror, unless you could master it.

Often it had ended in frustration, with only a hurt or terrified or dead victim. But now and then, clear, liberating words of prophecy came tumbling out, like jewels.

Slowly, erratically, the jigsaw had assembled itself in the King's mind. Build a tower to the gods and you will never be forgotten. Build it forever and you will live forever. And Laphaeome, with his great store of mage wisdom, knew how to build it.

Garnelys's father Aralyth had told his son that he would never make a great ruler. Now Garnelys was going to prove him wrong.

The energy the King raised, he always earthed into the Xauroma. That seemed important. What better way to strengthen the covenant that had begun to feel so fragile?

Above all, though, summoning the *gauroth* was addictive. His blackness built up and up until he could bear it no more; all that brought him relief was the explosion of his victim's pain, sometimes of their blood or their very life.

'You are thoughtful, sire.' Laphaeome's voice brought him back to the present.

'It's all right,' said Garnelys, thinking aloud. 'In the ancient days, blood sacrifice was made each year to ensure the fertility of the land. It was a powerful ritual. This is only the same as that; I am returning to the ancient ways, to ensure our survival.'

'Yes, you are exactly right, as I have always told you.'

'But the council wouldn't understand,' said the King,

fingering the straps. 'That's why I had to get rid of them. I feel as if a great weight has fallen from me; now I don't answer to anyone but the gods.'

Chapter Seven. Ardharkria

'Tanthe!'

The shout seemed to come from very far away, muffled by the earth. Her struggles were becoming feeble, her panic dissolving into a dream-state where she seemed to be in another place, another time, being dragged backwards into terrifying darkness.

Her right arm, waving in the air, was seized by a strong hand. The hand was trying to pull her upwards but failing; her hair was caught, enmeshed deep in the ground. The pain in her scalp so excruciating that it shocked her back to consciousness. Now someone was digging frantically in the ground around her head, brushing soil from her face. She felt a strange sawing motion behind her skull. Her hair was dragged so painfully that tears flooded her eyes and she tried to cry out, could only gag and retch.

Then, as if she'd been loosed from a sprung trap, her head came free. It was Rufryd who'd freed her and was now lifting her up. She sprawled forward, coughing violently, spitting the earth from her clogged mouth. Her cloak, which had been wrapped around her when she fell asleep, was in a twisted heap beside her.

'Gods, Tanthe,' he gasped. He passed her a flask of water, which she took gratefully to rinse her mouth. She spat out the first two mouthfuls, then took a long, desperately needed drink. Her lungs were sore, her scalp on fire. As she caught her breath, she saw his face in the moons' light; he was deadly white, and still gripping his large, sharp belt knife in his right hand. 'I'm sorry,' he said. 'I had to cut your hair. I heard you cry out and—'

156

She rose to her knees in sudden horror. 'Lynden,' she said hoarsely.

Rufryd's eyes widened. He turned and scrambled to his brother's side in half a second. Lynden was lying hardly six feet away from them, apparently asleep. But as they reached him, Tanthe saw that the ground was boiling and shifting around him, as if thousands of tiny creatures were burrowing underneath it. His whole body was slowly becoming immersed in the soil. At least his face was clear, so he could still breathe. Tanthe grabbed his hands and began trying to haul him upright; at that he woke, and stared at her in baffled fear.

'What—'

'Shush, don't panic. We'll get you free.'

Meanwhile Rufryd was burrowing under Lynden's head, sawing through his hair, which had grown long on the journey. Lynden yelped with pain. Tanthe grabbed the Aelyr knife from her pocket and began to work at the other side of his head. To her immediate dismay, she found that the blade was useless, weak and blunt. Why had she expected magic from it? In annoyance, she stuck it back in her pocket and used her belt knife instead.

As the last strands of his hair parted, Lynden broke free of the imprisoning ground and sat forward like a rag doll, gasping with pain. He drew breath, then sprang to his feet in shock.

'What was it?' he said, leaning on Tanthe. 'What happened?'

They stared at the ground in revulsion. Where he had been, there was a deep impression of his body. And in that impression, dozens of segmented maggot-like insects were at work, questing, burrowing, digging. Rufryd picked one up and held it gingerly on his palm. The creature was two inches long and as thick as his thumb, luminescent greenish-white in colour with segmented eyes and vicious hinged mandibles. As it curled into a defensive ball, they saw that it had hundreds of tiny, writhing legs.

'What the hell are these things?' Rufryd said softly.

'I don't know.' Lynden's voice was sour with disgust. 'I thought I knew every animal and insect there was at home. I've never seen anything like that before.'

His older brother raised his eyebrows and gave a tight little smile. 'At a guess, I'd say we were about to be a breeding ground for their little ones.'

'Drop it. For the gods' sake, let's get out of here!' Lynden said, running to Flame. The horse was untouched and grazing peacefully.

'Are you all right, Lyn?' Tanthe asked, following him.

He gaped at her. 'Gods, they got you too. I didn't realise. What happened?'

'They nearly killed me,' she said, trying to wipe the dirt from her face. Her hands were shaking. 'I woke up suffocating.'

'You must both be restless sleepers.' Rufryd went to help Lynden with Flame as he spoke. 'You'd half-thrown your cloaks off in the night. I was still wrapped up in mine so it made it harder for the little bastards to get hold of me. I felt a stinging pain like something tugging my hair. I think that's what woke me. Then I heard Tan making this awful noise, like she was being strangled. I found her being sucked into the earth. The only way I could get her free was to cut her hair.'

Tanthe put her hands to the back of her head, found a hacked-off tangle. She didn't know whether to scream or cry. 'What have you done to me?'

'I said I'm sorry!' Rufryd rounded on her angrily. 'I saved your bloody life! If you can't say thank you, just don't say anything.'

She swallowed. Now she was indebted to him, and she hated it, and she couldn't bring herself to frame words of gratitude. Or rather, she wanted to say *something*, but the words clogged in her throat.

'I knew we shouldn't have come into Ardharkria,' she said stiffly. 'Goodness knows what else is in here, waiting

158

for us.'

'It was this or get arrested.'

'Please don't start arguing again.' Lynden was hurriedly tightening the straps of Flame's saddle. 'It'll be dawn soon. Let's move on.'

They did so, treading the forest floor in shaken silence. Presently Rufryd said, 'Tan, I don't know what you're worried about. Your hair didn't look that great to start with.'

'Piss off.'

'I reckon I've improved it. And mud's good for the skin, you know.'

'I know why those maggoty things didn't bother with you,' she retorted. 'They didn't like the taste of smug bastard. Gods, I'd kill for a hot bath.'

Every now and then, when she was thinking of nothing in particular, the horror of it would rush up and envelop her. It was a formless impression of being dragged backwards into darkness, not understanding; feeling only fear and helplessness. It lasted just a moment or two, but for that brief time it would overwhelm her utterly before subsiding out of her grasp.

Tanthe dredged her memory for some key to the horror. She wished she could ask her mother, 'Did something frightening happen to me as a child? Did I bury myself in a silo of grain, or get locked in the shed, or nearly drown?' and Aynie might throw light on the darkness. 'Ah yes, when you were three . . .' But Aynie wasn't there to ask.

They wound on through the forest for three uneventful days. According to the map, they had passed out of Ardharkria and into the Forest of Sepher. Although this detour would take them some miles out of their way, they were still heading in the general direction of Parione. Sepher had no evil reputation that they'd heard of, but they took to sleeping propped upright against tree trunks, taking turns to keep watch. Sometimes they saw luminous eyes in the darkness, but nothing came near them. Lynden was nervous and haunted, constantly insisting that they were being followed; Rufryd was becoming irritated with him. Tanthe could have done without the tension growing between the brothers.

They supplemented their rations by hunting, building camp fires to roast the rabbits or big woodland birds that Rufryd killed. Tanthe hated to admit it, but of the three of them he was by far the best archer. She watched him one morning, silhouetted against the glow of a sunrise which turned the whole glade to molten gold; noticing how long and well-shaped his legs were, what a pleasing curve his calves and ankles made as he braced his feet apart to take aim. His slender waist lengthened and the muscles in his forearms stood out as he lifted the bow. His hair, blowing back from his face, shone like a burnished chestnut. He was completely intent upon his quarry, a large brown rabbit which was grazing obliviously forty feet away.

Lynden let out a cry before Tanthe realised anything was wrong. Out of the trees to their right a big grey shape came bounding, twice the size of a wolf. Flame neighed in shrill alarm, rearing against his tethering rope. The creature was growling fiercely. Tanthe caught a glimpse of open jaws, thick fangs, a red, dripping tongue. Before she could even take a breath, let alone move, it raced past her and launched itself at Rufryd.

Taken by surprise, he fell backwards with a shout. His bow and arrow bounced on to the grass. The beast pushed him down with huge forepaws, and with a hideous growl fastened its jaws on his throat.

Incredulous, Tanthe realised what the creature was.

'Rufe!' Lynden cried. He was setting an arrow to his own bow, but Tanthe stayed his hand.

'Don't!' she said. Lynden protested, but she was running forward, calling, 'Gazer! Leave him. Come on, lad, *leave*.'

She reached Rufryd and put both hands on the great hound's collar. Rufryd's eyes were screwed up, his face

160

white with fear. She couldn't see any blood. At her command, the hound reluctantly opened his jaws and let his victim go. Then Tanthe hauled him off and shoved him away, telling him sternly to lie down.

Gazer snuffed at her and began to whine with joy, his tail swaying. His head was level with her chest.

'Lie down!' she repeated, and he obeyed, looking up at her with innocent brown eyes as his tail thumped the ground.

Pushing her ragged hair off her face, she turned to Rufryd to see him sitting up and rubbing his throat. There were red teeth-marks, but the skin was intact. Lynden was kneeling anxiously beside him. 'Gods,' Rufryd said hoarsely. 'What was that?'

'It's my father's wolfhound.' She brushed tears out of her eyes. 'Don't you recognise him?'

'I didn't have a chance, did I? I always tried to keep out of the bloody thing's way.'

'I don't know why he attacked you. Perhaps he thought you were threatening me.'

'Well, get the damned thing away from me! He was always growling at anyone who wasn't part of your family.'

Lynden said quietly, 'This is what was following us. I'm sure of it. For days. Maybe your father's come to take you home . . .'

'I don't think so.' Tanthe rested her hand on Gazer's head. His long tongue came lashing wetly at her wrist. She listened intently for the sound of humans crashing through the undergrowth after the hound, but she heard nothing. It seemed Gazer had travelled alone. 'Are you all right, Rufe?'

'Yes,' he answered grudgingly.

'Gazer doesn't mess about, you know. I've just saved your life. So now we're even. But, "If you can't say thank you, don't say anything."'

'Yes. Right.' He jumped to his feet, retrieving his bow.

161

'Assuming you didn't train him to attack me in the first place.'

'If only I'd thought of it. I'd have got rid of you years ago.'

'Ha ha. What the hell's he doing here? How did he find us? Don't answer that – he must have smelled you a hundred miles off.'

Tanthe pulled a face at him. 'Maybe he escaped and followed our scent.' She bent down to Gazer, rubbing and scratching his hairy neck. 'Good boy. What do you want, eh? What's this?' Her fingers, moving round his collar, found a small leather tube. Inside was a scroll of paper. She drew it out, unrolled it, and found a message in her father's handwriting. She read aloud.

'"Dearest Tanthe, I hope this finds you safely. We understand why you're doing this and we wish we could be with you. Aynie and me are worried about you. When we lost one daughter we didn't expect to lose both – but still, this isn't a plea for you to come home, at least not until you've done what you must. We know why you had to go and we thank Breyid for your bravery. This is to tell you that no one else from the village will try to stop you. Instead, we want you to take Gazer with you. He will help protect you against the dangers you may face. Your grandmother fears that something worse has begun than we could have guessed at. We need to talk to you. Come home safely, with Ysomir if you can. Until we meet again, Breyid and Anthar walk with you both. Your loving parents – Eodwyth and Aynie."'

Tanthe was crying by the time she finished reading the note. Gazer sat panting beside her, grey as a ghost yet solid, warm and patient. He tried to lick the salt from her face. She pushed his great head away. 'Oh, gods. Dad sent him after us. He loves this hound so much, it would nearly kill him to part with it.'

'Well, it's reassuring to know he loves you more,' said Rufryd.

162

'Come and make friends with him. He's not dangerous once he knows and trusts someone.'

Lynden befriended Gazer immediately. But when Rufryd approached, the hound's lips rose over his teeth and a howl bubbled from deep in his throat. Rufryd started back, cursing.

'Give him your hand to sniff,' said Lynden. 'Give him a bit of food.'

'Speak gently to him,' Tanthe added.

'Are you sure this is a dog, and not Arthryn?' Rufryd sounded sardonic and bitter. 'Licking up to Lynden but trying to take my throat out? Can't see much difference, myself.'

Lynden's expression darkened, but he said nothing.

Eventually, reluctant as he was to grovel to his attacker, Rufryd won Gazer over. The hound accepted a scrap of meat, let himself be petted, and even gave Rufryd's hand a lick.

When they resumed hunting, Rufryd discovered Gazer's worth. The hound flushed out the prey for him, then retrieved the corpse when his arrow had flown to its target.

'All right,' Rufryd admitted, some hours later as they were walking along a forest path with their supper tied over Flame's saddle. 'I was a bit harsh on the old boy.'

'You're talking about the hound, I assume,' Lynden said thinly. He'd been brooding for hours.

'Of course. I wouldn't be talking about Arthryn, would I?'

'You know, you've got no right to be so bloody rude about our father.' Lynden's tone startled Tanthe; she hadn't realised how angry he was. 'I've had enough of it. You'd better stop, or—'

'Or what?' If anything, Rufryd sounded even angrier. 'What can you do to stop me saying what I think? Father is a mean-minded, cold-hearted, petty coward. I know why you don't want to hear it, Lyn. The truth hurts.'

'He's a good man. He loves us. He doesn't deserve this.'

'Doesn't he?' Rufryd's expression was a sour, savage contortion of a smile. 'He loves you, his little golden boy. I don't suppose you remember much about how he treated me after mother died. Like I was worthless, less than a rat in the grain store. You can never do anything wrong for him; I can never do anything right. He hates me. Now what kind of father is he, what kind of man, that can be so partial over his own sons?'

'Gods, Rufe. You sound as if you're jealous of me! You can't be. That's ridiculous.'

'I'm not. I'm just trying to open your eyes. He's weak. He's emotionless. He's not fit to have responsibility for Riverwynde; he's proved that once too often with Ymmi.'

'Don't drag her into this,' Lynden said furiously. 'Don't you understand how grief-stricken he was, losing mother?'

'So he took it out on me?'

'No. I won't listen to this. He's a good man and you're wrong!'

'Oh, he's good to you, Lyn. He gave Ysomir away, to keep *you*.'

A long, bitter silence.

They came to a lake; a broad, golden lake that mirrored the hues of the evening sky. The air was clear and mild but fragrant with autumn. The oaks at the wood's edge glowed in gorgeous shades of red, and between them and the margin of the water lay a broad, flat bank of springy grass. It spoke to Tanthe of relaxation, peace, and sleep.

'This looks a good place to make camp,' Tanthe said brightly. 'I'm starving.'

'Sounds good to me,' said Rufryd. 'Lyn?'

'Fine,' he snapped, stalking off to tether Flame. 'Do whatever you want.'

Rufryd scowled after him. 'I don't know what he's in such a huff about.'

'Losing Ymmi, being in the middle of nowhere, and his

164

brother having a go at him. Isn't that enough? You two had better make it up. I can't stand this atmosphere.'

'Oh, can't you? Well, you know what you can do. Sod off home.'

A flame of rage went through her. 'I would if I could. Quite honestly, I'm not surprised your father can't stand you. I should have let Gazer rip your throat out.'

As she turned to walk away, meaning to gather firewood until she calmed down, he said, 'Tanthe, I'm sorry.'

She turned back. 'What?'

'I said I'm sorry. I didn't mean it. But it's not Lynden who's got to live with knowing he killed a man. It's not you, either.'

Her mouth fell open. She didn't even want to think about how it felt. 'You might have just wounded him,' she said lamely.

'And that's meant to cheer me up? Never mind. Let's get this fire made.'

After they'd built a good fire, they took it in turns to bathe in the icy shallows of the lake, then huddled in front of the flames to warm up. Tanthe had scrubbed one set of breeches, shirt and undergarments in the lake, and put on the clean ones – as clean as they could be from being rinsed in streams, at any rate. The clean clothes felt cold and stiff, but they soon softened from the warmth of the fire and her body. While she began to roast their supper, the boys did their own laundry, kneeling yards apart beside the water and ignoring each other.

They dined well on rabbit and pheasant, Gazer included, with a good pile of woodland berries for the humans. A spring, rushing down a narrow gully into the lake, provided them with sweet, clean water. Afterwards, Gazer flopped down to sleep beside the fire. Flame had made peace with the great dog and grazed placidly.

Rufryd and Tanthe sat facing the fire, the lake on their

right and the woods on their left. Lynden was on the opposite side of the blaze, still not talking to them; Tanthe couldn't even see him through the fire-glow. Craning her neck, she saw that he'd wrapped himself in his cloak and lain down to sleep with his back to them. She was sorry he was still upset, but she didn't see what she could do to mend anything. If it hadn't been for the brothers' argument, she would have felt perfectly contented, for a few hours, at least. The spines of her own hostility seemed blunted.

Then she had another flashback. Falling backwards, darkness—

She shook it off, but Rufryd had noticed. 'What are you staring at?'

'Nothing.' Then she thought, he's older than me, he might know . . . 'Rufe, do you remember, when I was a child, did I ever have an accident?'

He blinked in surprise. 'All the time.'

'I mean something out of the ordinary. Like nearly drowning?'

'Not that I know of. You were always falling over or into something, then bouncing up again. Nothing stopped you, even though you were the clumsiest kid in the village. What's this about?'

'Oh . . . It doesn't matter. Clumsy, that's a new one.'

'Comment withdrawn. I've had enough arguments for one day.' He tilted his head towards Lynden.

'Was it all true, that your father hates you? Why?'

'Dunno. Don't suppose he's obliged to like me. Lynden's the baby and he's more like our mother; he's special, I'm a disappointment.'

'How? You beat us all at archery and nearly every other sport. You never let us forget how good you are.'

He laughed. 'Yeah, and you know why? I was trying to wring a single word of praise out of my dad. But I never have.'

'I don't understand.'

166

He exhaled. Finally he said, 'Truth? I was just as devastated at Lynden when our mother died. But I couldn't show it like he could. I went off on my own instead, and I thought my father would understand, but he didn't. He thought I didn't care.'

'But you were only a child.'

Rufryd shrugged. 'He still expected us to think and behave the same way he did. He thinks I let him down.'

'Couldn't you talk to him?'

'You must be joking.'

'So that's why you've always been so vile!' she said. 'Because your father treated you badly, and you're angry about it.'

'Right,' he said acidly. 'What's your excuse?'

'I'm deliberately vile to you because you bullied me – and when you couldn't get away with it any more, you bullied Ymmi. I thought you didn't get on with your father because you were just horrible to everyone. If I'd understood, things might have been different.'

'Really? Look, Tan, I'm not proud of it. I wish it hadn't happened and I'm sorry. But I'm grown up now. I don't blame Arthryn for anything. I have no feelings for him at all.'

'He hurt you.'

'Not physically.'

'But still, he hurt you.'

'I'd rather not talk about this, if you don't mind.' He clasped his hands round his knees, not looking at her.

'You are the most annoying person I've ever met.'

'What a coincidence.'

She took out the blunt little knife and began trying to scrape the grime off the scabbard with its dull tip. Presently Rufryd spoke again. 'I often felt I'd like to kill him. If he'd been bigger than me and he'd beaten me, that would have made it easy. But now I have killed someone – I know I couldn't do it. It didn't make me feel good, killing Beyne. Only for a few seconds, anyway. Then I just felt . . . unclean.'

167

Tanthe laid her hand on his shoulder. He didn't respond, but he didn't shake her off either. 'I'd feel awful, too,' she said. 'But they'll treat us as if we're all responsible, if they catch us.'

'This is bad,' he said. 'Humans haven't killed each other since before the War of the Silver Plains. Then your uncle – what's happening to us?'

'I don't know.' She had no idea of how to console him. 'People do have fights and kill each other sometimes.'

'In the city, I take it. How do they deal with killers there?'

'Sometimes they're executed. Sometimes they spend a long time in prison. Sometimes they're let off. It depends why the killing happened. You were defending us so we can save Ymmi; isn't that a good reason? Sorry, Rufe, I know I'm not helping.'

'No,' he said quietly. 'You are. Show me that knife you're messing with.'

Exhaling, she handed it to him. Fire flashed dully on the blade as he examined it. 'Odd-looking thing.'

'It's useless, not even decorative.'

'Why did you pick it up, then?' He gave it back to her and she sheathed it and put it away.

'Because I think one of the Aelyr gave it to me.'

Rufryd looked at her, his eyes narrowed sceptically. 'You are joking.'

'No. I might have been dreaming. But I really have seen one of the Aelyr, and the first time at least, I was wide awake.'

'Where?'

'In the woods by Mountain Meadow. You know, where we take the short cut? It was the end of the harvest, that day you upset Ymmi. I ran after her and we both saw the Aelyr by a pool.'

'You never said anything.' He sounded almost indignant. 'What did it look like?'

'Why would I have told you?' Tanthe laughed. '*He* was

very beautiful. He was naked and crouching down by the pool's edge, with long hair streaming over his shoulders and down his back.' She smiled, remembering, and her voice became softer. 'The colour of his hair was incredible, a dark, dark red with strands of fire in it. There was a glow round him, and when he bent down to drink, even the water seemed to turn to light in his fingers. It was . . . I don't know how to put it. It was as if time was passing at a fraction of its normal speed, as if he'd come from another realm and was carrying the aura of it with him. Then he dived into the pool and . . .' she decided not to tell him the rest. 'He vanished. Just vanished without a sound.' She noticed Rufryd's expression. 'You don't believe me, do you?'

He raised his eyebrows. 'No, if you say you saw it, I'm sure you did.'

'Don't be so condescending. My mother believed me. She's seen them herself, she said it wasn't that unusual. I know what I saw! He wasn't particularly pale or ethereal. No, he was very physical. He'd be about the same height as Lynden, lean but very strong-looking. His limbs were beautiful and the light moved over them as if he were wet . . .'

'You fancied him, then,' Rufryd broke in.

Tanthe re-focussed her eyes. She'd been in a dream. 'Does that bother you?'

Rufryd coloured and stared at the ground. 'Of course not.' She'd never seen him so embarrassed before. She was startled, and thrilled to find a new way to tease him.

'Well, the Aelyr was the loveliest male I've ever seen. I can't help that. When I saw him again – and it might have been a dream, but I don't think it was – he was wearing this silk garment so thin he might just as well have been naked, and his chest—'

He glared at her, eyes glittering. Tanthe was mildly alarmed by his reaction. 'Spare me the details. You're drooling.'

169

'He was a living work of art, Rufe,' she said, deliberately provoking him now. 'Any woman would have wanted him.' Talking about the Aelyr, remembering him, was bringing a strange heat to her stomach. But to see that Rufryd felt threatened by her passion took her aback.

'I s'pose human men aren't good enough for you, then. Like Riverwynde isn't good enough for you.'

They both seemed to be holding their breath. Tanthe said very softly, 'I thought I heard you apologise for being nasty to me. Do you really find me so hateful, for having ambitions?'

He sighed. 'For the gods' sake. You don't get it.'

'What? You saved my life. I can't be that bad.'

Rufryd leaned forward to put more wood on the fire. A plume of red sparks shot up. When he sat back again, he was so close that his hip and his elbow were touching hers. 'And you saved mine.'

'Thank you.' For some reason, she began to tremble.

'Thank *you*,' he echoed. And he rested his hand on her leg, just above her knee.

Tanthe had trouble drawing breath. 'By the way, I've got nothing against human men, or against Riverwynde. The idea seems quite tempting at the moment.'

'The idea of what? Home, or a human man?' His breath was warm on her cheek. From the corner of her eye, she could see his hair and his eyes glinting in the fire-glow.

'Er,' said Tanthe. She felt hot. She thought she had meant home, but talking about the Aelyr had had a strange effect on them both.

'Tanthe,' he said throatily. As he spoke, his hand slipped onto the inside of her thigh. The warm pressure of his palm sent a delicious ache all through her body. 'I admit it. I'm jealous of your Aelyr lover.'

'He's not my lover. I didn't think you even liked me.' She found herself pressing closer to him, one hand creeping to his shoulder, the other to his chest so she was half-embracing him. He felt so warm. The natural scent of

170

his body was earthy and wholesome, arousing her simply because it was so familiar.

'I don't,' he whispered into her neck, smiling. 'I can't stand you. It's just that I really, desperately want to fuck you. Ever since the first time I saw you bathing, so beautiful, but long before that—'

'You watched me?' Tanthe's intellect told her to hit him, but her body was not listening. Instead, the mixture of humour and lust in his voice drew her deeper. She could hardly catch her breath for desire.

'Didn't mean to. I couldn't help it. But don't tell me you've never watched me, because I've seen you.' And he was right, she had watched him too. With his eyes gleaming darkly under his thick silky fringe, he looked as desirable to her as the Aelyr.

'We can't do this,' she gasped. 'Lynden—'

'He won't hear a thing.'

Rufryd lifted his other hand to her cheek and kissed her. His lips, his tongue; every touch sent flames of sensation through her. She opened her mouth to him, felt him stiffen and utter a faint gasp at her response. Heat ran through her, gathering between her thighs, demanding relief. All her ideas and plans were about to collapse. This was meant to happen with some great poet in distant Parione, not in a forest with Rufryd of all people, but she didn't care. Now his hand was pulling at her laces, delving onto her bare flesh. To her amazement he was gentle, his palms flowing over her stomach and breasts. She would never have thought he was capable of such tenderness. Pushing herself deeper into his grasp, she felt her thighs interlocking with his, and the long, hard swelling at his groin pressing into her. She pushed off her boots with her feet, as he hurriedly unlaced her breeches then began on his own. Trying to shed her shirt, she felt something in one of her pockets.

A practical gift from mother to daughter, which she'd practised using but never needed for real until now. The flexible little dome of rubbery arkh-wood, to prevent conception. With his help, she shed her clothes. Then, while he broke away from her to throw off his own, she seized the moment to slip the dome into place.

'What are you doing?' he whispered.

'What do you think?' she hissed.

'Oh.' He smiled at her, and they fell naked on to her spread cloak. How strange this was. Rufryd seemed completely different, animated with a mixture of wonder and arousal. His body felt wonderful under her palms, strong and hard, his thighs like rough silk with their light covering of hairs and the phallus standing proud and thick from the dark bush at their juncture; like the forest god, Anthar. He slipped his fingers between her hidden lips and stroked her there, making her ache and burn to have him inside her.

'You're beautiful,' said Rufryd.

'So are you. When did you change your mind about me?'

'Who says I have?' He eased himself above her, the rounded shaft pushing insistently and deliciously between her thighs. His excitement increased hers. Urgently she guided him inside her. As he slid deeply in they both gasped, pausing a moment as if neither of them could believe it; and then the sacred rhythm began. They were half-animal and half-god, struggling, sweating, murmuring. And when their bliss peaked at last in scarlet flames, Rufryd cried out, surrendering his whole self into her body; and Tanthe rose and fell with a spasm of joy as profound as pain, seeing nothing but red light behind her eyelids, like a fire-tipped arrow loosed across the heavens, touching the ecstasy that had created the universe.

Lynden had tried to sleep as Tanthe and his brother bickered. He wrapped his hood tightly round his ears but couldn't keep their voices out; dozed for a moment then came wide awake, aware that something had changed. He

172

listened. He opened his eyes, half-sat up, then froze in complete, overwhelming disbelief. He could see, in wavering silhouette through the heat-haze, that they were kissing. Worse – *oh no, please no* – they were starting to make love.

Dismayed and embarrassed beyond words, Lynden curled up and pretended to sleep. They seemed to make hardly a token effort to be quiet; every gasp, moan and laugh rang clear in the quiet air, assaulting his ears. When he heard their cries of joy as they climaxed, he turned and stared up at the stars, his hands pressed to his forehead. Pain filled him; his own arousal shamed him.

How was this fair? They had hated each other all their lives; now suddenly they could conveniently ignore the past just to sate some passing twinge of lust. Yet he and Ysomir, who'd loved each other more than life, were forced to be apart.

Lynden's eyes stung and watered. He longed to see Ymmi, to hold her, stroke her hair . . . to make love to her. In theory, because she was under the King's care, she was in no danger, but his heart told him that was all a lie. Fear for her tore at his chest. They should be travelling on through the night to find her, not wasting time so those two could lie there indulging selfishly in sex.

What if I never see her again? he thought. What if we never have the chance to make love again, or to be handfasted? How am I supposed to bear it?

There was silence for a time, pierced only by the fluting of an owl and Gazer's soft snoring. Then voices, sighs. Gods, they were starting again!

Lynden's misery turned to blinding anger. He couldn't take this. Furious, he sat up, grabbed his few belongings together and bundled them into his rucksack. The fire hid his actions, but they were paying him no attention anyway. Although he hated to leave Flame behind, it couldn't be helped.

'Curse you, sod you both,' he said through his teeth. 'I

don't need you, I'll find Ymmi on my own!' Flinging the rucksack onto his shoulder so violently that it bruised him, he forged off into the darkness alone.

Chapter Eight. The Blue Stallion

'I didn't finish telling you my story about the Aelyr,' Tanthe said sleepily. 'In my visions, the knife was different, exquisitely worked and covered in jewels. The Aelyr only seemed able to speak to me if I saw him in a reflection, like the surface of a pool, and even then I could hardly hear what he was saying.' She frowned. 'He told me the knife was for my protection. There was something about him being trapped and trying to reach me . . . He seemed really distressed, but there was nothing I could do about it. I wish I could find out who he is.'

'It was just a dream, Tan,' Rufryd murmured. He didn't want to talk about mysteries. 'Maybe you saw him for real the first time, but after that it was only a dream.'

'I wish I could explain it so easily. Never mind.' She ran her hand affectionately over his thigh.

They had slept in each other's arms, with Tanthe's cloak beneath her and Rufryd's as their cover. Her body felt so warm and smooth against his and he wanted her again, but dawn was casting a silver net over the lake, and if he was honest with himself, he felt too tired to make love in the chill of the morning. Three times they had entwined last night . . . Rufryd smiled in delicious contentment at the memory.

'Well, I don't know how we're going to explain this to Lynden,' he said.

'If we get up before he wakes, we won't have to. But does it matter?'

'He'll be embarrassed, and he'll think we've gone mad, that's all.'

'Have you?' She put her chin on his chest to look at him.

Her hair, falling in dark, ragged layers around her face, made her look unutterably seductive; her green-blue eyes shone vividly. 'Gone mad, I mean? Are you going to get up and act as if this didn't happen?'

'Only if you do.'

Gazer barked, but they ignored him.

'Don't turn it back on me. Can you get into the habit of speaking to me in a civilised fashion? It's going to be tough for you.' She grinned sardonically, but she was serious.

'Tough for *me*?'

'You'll only get what's coming,' she said.

'I hope so.' He pulled her towards him and kissed her. 'Last night was wonderful.'

'It was my first time,' she said.

'I know. You were going to save your sexual energy for some perfumed intellectual in the city, and not end up rolling around on the ground under a peasant. Oh dear. All that frustration for nothing.'

She bit his chest, just hard enough to hurt. 'Far from it. I'm happily acquainted with my hands, thank you. What about you? Tell me. I won't be jealous.'

He had nothing much to boast about, so he told the truth. 'There was the weaver's daughter, Ellin. Then a girl I saw a few times in Havereyn, until she got handfasted to some merchant.'

He hoped Tanthe would be jealous, but she only laughed. 'Ellin? Was there anyone she *didn't* sleep with?'

'Only Lynden, I think.' Rufryd pulled a face. 'All right. I haven't had much in the way of experience, either. To be honest, I was more concerned with my archery and hunting, because there was no one I was interested in . . . except you.'

She gave a gasp of amazement. 'Is this a test to see how gullible I am?'

He wrapped her in his arms, so he didn't have to meet her eyes as he spoke. 'Tan, you don't understand. I've loved you for years.'

She held her breath. Then she murmured, 'Bloody funny way of showing it.'

'Couldn't admit it, could I? It was easier to pretend I loathed you, than make a fool of myself. Maybe it's time we grew up a bit.'

She was very still against him. He felt moisture on his chest; her tears. 'Oh, Breyid. I don't know what to say, Rufe. Maybe we should grow up. Whatever I used to think about you, I trust you with my life, and out here – all we've got is each other. We ought to get up and relight the fire.'

'In a minute.' Gazer began to bark again. The sound grew louder.

'It's cold, and our clothes are going to be damp—'

Rufryd's face was suddenly enveloped by Gazer's large wet tongue. Spluttering, he rolled away, choking on the stench of the hound's breath. Tanthe, laughing at him, sat up and tried to wrestle Gazer off.

She stopped laughing suddenly, and froze.

'Rufe,' she said. 'Lynden's not there.'

'Probably gone for a pee in the woods.'

'No. His cloak and rucksack have gone.'

Rufryd leapt to his feet and stared at the spot, on the far side of the dead fire, where Lynden had been sleeping – or so he thought. 'Lynden!' he yelled.

There was no answer. Only a flight of rooks, clattering up through the branches in fright at his shout. Flame was there, but Lynden and his belongings were gone.

Pressing a hand to his head in despair, Rufryd swung round to face Tanthe. 'Oh, gods, Tan. What's happened to him?'

Towards afternoon, Lynden found a lane winding through the forest. It was too narrow to be called a road, too thick with grass for many travellers to have used it. Yet it was a path of a sort. Reassured to find some sign of civilisation, Lynden set forth upon it. Tiredness was overcoming him and he knew he must rest soon, but not yet, when every step took him nearer to Ysomir.

Autumn was coming early here; he could see the darkening sky through the branches. Rain-clouds cast grey gloom over the day and a blustery wind was tugging at the red foliage. He felt leaves brushing past his hair and his face as they fell. Again and again they startled him. He was tense, on the verge of fear. When he looked, there were no leaves where they should have fallen, and yet the sensation of things whispering past his face went on . . . Was he walking through cobwebs? Lynden ran a brisk hand over his face, but the feeling came again, and with it a faint murmur of voices.

The shadows between the trees seemed to move. He had to hold himself back from running, bitterly regretting his impulsiveness in leaving his brother and Tanthe behind. There were dangers in the wild places, not always visible. They'd already had a taste of that.

Then his feet struck something bulky in the grass. Lynden went sprawling over it and fell headlong on to the ground. He lay shocked and winded, but after a pause he rolled away from the object that had fouled him and got to his feet. He was shaking badly now, possessed by a visceral knowledge that he was about to uncover something appalling. He looked down. The light was poor, but still enough to reveal what the object was.

A corpse. He'd fallen over a corpse.

Gasping, wide-eyed and trying not to retch, Lynden forced himself to look. It was a youngish man, dressed in good clothes, obviously from a wealthy household. But his face was grey, his throat so badly torn that his head was half-severed, his jacket pricked with blood as if some clawed beast had killed him.

Lynden had rarely seen death so he couldn't judge how long the man had lain there. There was a musty-sweet smell rising from him and the blood was dried and old, the edges of the neck wound shrinking. A few big, jewel-green

178

flies wandered over the sunken skin of his face.

Clamping his hand over his nose and mouth, Lynden drew away and leaned on an oak. He was alone with no map, alone with whatever the forest held . . .

He felt his self-control fraying. He held on desperately, invoking the protection of Anthar; visualising with all his strength the forest god striding through the trees, a green light shining around his antlers and his cloak of leaves. The forest shuddered. Lynden sensed a wild energy gathering around him. His head span; again he heard voices murmuring, louder now. Something gold and grey and glittering whirled in the clearing. Now outside him. Now inside.

The world tilted. Lynden stumbled, losing consciousness. When he came back to himself, he was kneeling on the roots of the oak with pain blossoming in his head.

Gasping, he dragged himself to his feet. Everything looked the same, but he felt different. It was as if an extra sense, slumbering in his mind, had suddenly woken. He felt raw and over-sensitive, as if the real world might at any moment peel away to reveal something he didn't want to see.

'Anthar, help me,' he whispered. 'What's happened to me?'

Gradually the feeling receded, and his pulse began to steady. Then a hot, snorting breath struck his neck.

Lynden yelled in terror, leaping forwards and twisting round to see his attacker. He fumbled for his belt knife. He was certain that he was about to die but determined to go down fighting.

The creature behind him – shying backwards and equally alarmed – was a horse. It had on a saddle and bridle of polished leather, chased with gold and lapis, but the reins were broken and the saddle twisted round onto its belly. The animal wheeled and trotted a few paces into the trees, turning again with head high and nostrils flaring. Lynden swore. Willing his heart to stay inside his

179

chest, he followed the horse. A short way into the trees, it stopped and waited for him, allowing him to approach slowly and with soft words.

'All right, gently now. Where are you from? Is that your poor master out there?'

The horse was a beauty. He'd never seen one like it before, except in the pages of Tanthe's books. It was tall and refined, its neck and tail highly arched, its head amazingly fine-boned with huge, soft dark eyes. The head and legs were dark, but the coat was roaned with white which gave a bluish effect. On the hindquarters, beneath the black fountain of the tail, there was an exquisitely marked wedge of white stripes. Lynden glanced under the lean belly to check its sex. A stallion.

Lynden carefully stroked the velvety muzzle, working back to stroke the neck and shoulders as he won its trust. He cautiously gathered up its reins. 'That's it. Poor lad. Have you been here all this time, watching over your rider? I wish you could speak to me.'

The horse calmed him. It was such a relief to have the company of another living creature. He checked the buckles of the bridle, removed the saddle and examined the creature's back. No sign of sores. He patted and groomed the stallion with his hands, encouraging its blood to flow.

With a horse – especially one like this, bred for speed – he could travel swiftly. He might overtake Ysomir's captors long before they reached Parione. Hope and excitement swelled inside him. 'Well, will you take me?' he whispered, stroking the creature's big, responsive ears. 'I'm sorry about your master but there's nothing we can do for him. I wish I knew your name. I'll call you Blue for now.'

Blue rested his head on Lynden's shoulder and blew hot grassy breath into his ear. Scratching the horse's cheek, Lynden looked back at the body of the rider. He felt guilty, finding it then just leaving it, but the important thing was to find Ymmi. As his gaze drifted over the dead man, he saw a white folded paper protruding from the top of one of his riding boots.

Holding Blue's reins, Lynden bent down and drew out the paper. A message, scratched in a hurried hand on creamy parchment.

'*To the Elders of Forthryn Seal or Havereyn – to any who find it –*

'This is a warning to all people dwelling west of Skald in the realm of Sepheret. An order has come from the King authorising his Registats Beyne, Feroyn and Mathane to conscript young people into the King's service for the construction of a great memorial. In the name of the Xauroma, we warn and adjure you: *Defy the order*. Do not let your people be taken away! Resist, call an end to this madness before it is too late. *Those that are taken are going into slavery and death*.

'Our King is no longer the man he once was. Yes, he still walks in Garnelys's image, in Garnelys's brain and body, but he has changed. Much as it grieves us to make this statement, we must; our beloved King no longer acts in the best interests of Aventuria. He has ruptured the Xauroma.

'Few will believe us, we know. But for all our sakes, you *must* believe before it is too late. His granddaughter is dead, he wars with his only son. It is rumoured that even his small grandson is in hiding, in fear of his life. The King's project is madness, it will kill thousands of his own people. Let the people of Sepheret not be among them! But only if we stand firm will our children, our brothers and our sisters, survive.

'The authors of this warning must remain unknown for fear of reprisal. But in the many names of Goddess and God, we swear that it comes from a true source.'

Lynden stood clutching the message, frozen with denial. A man had died trying to deliver this warning . . . An odd, crisp feeling filled his skull, like a sifting of ice particles. He clutched his head in discomfort . . . and then it was as if he saw a faint vision, as if he actually *remembered* what had happened.

He saw Blue galloping along the forest path, the rider urging him on, desperate to deliver the message but already knowing he was doomed. A flying thing was following, gliding between the trees, a dark shadow bristling with fangs and claws . . . now dragging the rider backwards out of the saddle, dropping to the ground. Feeding. Then wheeling coldly away, task finished. And something else overlaid on that, shadows whispering in another dimension. A figure with fox-red hair and two figures veiled in twilight on either side of a well; a tiny being with silver skin . . . Vague, but full of meaning that was gone as soon as he thought he'd grasped it.

Lynden went dizzy. The vision ended.

Slavery. Death. Ysomir.

His worst fears were written there in black and white. He almost collapsed under the weight of it, leaning back against Blue's warm flank while his head swam and his lungs heaved. Now he knew that his forebodings had been more than anxiety. It was as if everyone in Riverwynde had known but couldn't admit it. If the Xauroma were damaged, how could they *not* feel it – but how could they even begin to acknowledge it?

He let out a few sobs of shock, then mastered himself. If the message were true, then the situation was far worse than they'd dreamed. It affected the whole of Aventuria, not just two families in one tiny village.

Lynden put the saddle on to Blue's back, tightened the girth and mounted. Rufryd and Tanthe should know. It wasn't fair not to tell them . . . but he would lose precious days if he went back for them. Then he remembered Rufryd's harsh words, the way he'd fallen carefree into

182

Tanthe's arms as if the quarrels hadn't happened. No, sod them. The most important thing was Ysomir.

Lynden turned Blue's head to the north-east. At first the horse fought him, not wanting to leave his master even now; then suddenly he took off at speed, nearly losing Lynden under a low branch. He wasn't going in the direction Lynden intended.

With some difficulty, Lynden slowed him, stroked his neck and spoke calmly. To his relief, Blue began to settle down. Lynden turned him in the right direction and they set off again, this time at a steady canter. Blue was keen and responsive; once they got clear of the forest, they would fly.

Towards evening, the character of the woodlands began to change.

Without the map, Lynden had no way of knowing that his path had taken him out of benign Sepher and back into the Forest of Ardharkria. Slowly the oaks began to give way to beeches, tall and widely spaced. The ground between the trees grew uneven, scattered with fallen branches and leaves. Beneath lay the sort of dark soft earth in which he and Tanthe had nearly been buried by the voracious insects.

The beeches gave way to trees he did not recognise. They grew ever taller and darker, with their branches thrown in a wild, bare tangle against the sky. There was no sound but Blue's hoofbeats, no colour. No grass, no fallen leaves. The forest became dark, damp and cavernous, eerily devoid of life. Again he felt the strange energy buzzing in his head, and this time it was like a voice warning him to turn back, an overwhelming sense of danger.

He was riding down a gully with trees standing on high banks around him, making him feel dwarfed, lost. Their roots stood out of the earth like claws, clasping rocks that were white as bone. Lynden felt as if he were winding his way into underground caverns. He could still see the sky above, yet he was overwhelmed by the feeling that he was being drawn deep into the earth. The air was dark and stiff with menace. There was no vegetation, not even the tiniest woodland plant or toadstool.

He halted Blue, and looked back the way he'd come. But the path, instead of leading uphill, seemed to tilt even more steeply downhill than the way he was going. His mouth went dry with panic. In the shadows under the tree roots, he saw luminous eyes staring at him.

Swallowing thickly, he sent Blue onwards. Never before had he experienced such an acute awareness of danger. It was like another sense. Like the time he'd known that Gazer was following them, inexplicable but real – and this time, far worse.

There was a pale shape standing on the side of the path ahead of them. Some kind of animal. Lynden rode on, trying to conquer his irrational fear. But Blue stopped dead, tossing his head and showing the whites of his eyes. It was all Lynden could do to keep him from turning and bolting.

The animal was the size of an ox, and superficially resembled one; four limbs, solid barrel of a body, a lumpen head. But there was something wrong about it. Its coat glowed an unpleasantly luminous white, and the flesh that slithered over its great muscles seemed oddly bloated. Lynden watched its lips drawing back over its peg-like square teeth and heard its loud, ponderous chomping as it gnawed at the tree trunk. With strips of bark hanging from its jaws, it swung its great head to look at him. Its eyes were whitish-blue, ringed with pink, containing the dull curiosity of a cow – but overlaid on that, something so inimical and alien that his stomach twisted in revulsion. And further along the gully, there were two more of these beasts.

Blue stalled, digging his toes into the earth. Lynden hardly had the strength to keep him from whirling round and fleeing. As he tried to decide what to do, a pale figure appeared next to the beast. Lynden didn't see where it came from. It simply materialised from the air, like an apparition.

The figure was human shaped, but like no human he'd ever seen. Its cloak was the same colour as the ground – dark, mottled with grey and brown – and its face was the same, yet with a raw sheen like an underground fungus, and weirdly rudimentary, as if it had been pulled from clay. Lynden stared, feeling that he'd lost all grip on reality. The skin was yet semi-translucent, so that the shadow of the skull was hinted at. The effect was of a double image, with no clear features.

The overall impression was so disorienting that Lynden gaped in fascinated horror, unable to look away. He was certain he had wandered into a waking nightmare.

The figure spoke. Its voice was quiet, expressionless but with a quality of thickness as if it were not speaking its own tongue. 'What is the meaning of your presence?'

'I – I'm lost,' Lynden blurted.

It wasn't only the figure's appearance that horrified him. Its very presence seemed to be draining away his energy, leaving in its place a helpless, soul-sapping misery.

'You are breaking the agreement. No humans here.'

'I don't know of any agreement. I don't mean any harm. Tell me the way out and I'll go.'

'There is no way out.'

The figure raised a slow, pale arm. The sleeve slipped back, revealing a long, spindly white hand with seven fingers. Lynden stared. Seven—

Screaming, Blue spun round and fled at a gallop. Something happened in Lynden's mind; it was as if another, clear power took over. He sensed a bustling in the air behind him, a cold, malicious power swooping in to destroy him. Holding the reins under his knees, he set arrow to bow, his hands moving deftly. He turned in the saddle and loosed the arrow into the air – just as, behind and above him, a monster came bursting out of a knot of cloud. It was like a dra'a'k yet unlike, just as the ox was unlike any ox he'd seen. It was bigger, covered in loose skin of reddish hue, its long beak open and lined with tiny sharp teeth. Its wings flapped like sluggish sails.

Lynden's arrow crunched into its breastbone. The monster stalled in midair, turned over and crashed to the ground – just like the dra'a'k Rufryd had killed at harvest – inches behind Blue's rump. The cry it gave was almost, but not quite, human.

The stallion was running flat out now. Lynden could only hang on to the pommel, one arm looped through his bow so he didn't lose it. The forest flowed past in a blur. His hands and feet were tingling, his head throbbing, his blood draining sickly away. The brief fire that had saved him faded, leaving only strengthless revulsion, as if he'd touched a mystery so alien his body and mind had no defence.

He must get back to Rufryd and Tanthe. His anger at them no longer mattered. They must be warned before they blundered into this.

Tanthe and Rufryd sent Gazer after Lynden. Afterwards, they realised that without the hound they would never have found him.

They dressed quickly, made Flame ready, scattered the remains of the fire. Then Tanthe took the hound to snuff the place where Lynden had been lying, the last time they saw him. 'Find, Gazer,' she commanded, rubbing his hairy head. 'Find!'

Gazer loped off at such a speed that she had to call him back, and tether the rope from Flame's halter to his collar, so she could hold him. Gazer set off again, straining, arching against the rope, almost dragging Tanthe into a run.

Lynden's route took them almost directly east, back into Ardharkria. The soft light of morning grew leaden and heavy, and the trees stood blackly against the stormy

186

luminosity of the sky. All day they followed the trail, eating and drinking on the move.

When they came across the body of a man lying on a narrow, overgrown path, Rufryd turned white with dread. But it was not Lynden. Their discovery of the corpse shook them, made the whole forest shimmer with hostility.

Gazer seemed to lose the scent and ran in circles. Tanthe held her breath, certain something dreadful had happened to Lyn here. But soon the hound caught the trail again and led them onwards.

As evening gathered, despite turns taken at riding Flame, Rufryd and Tanthe were both footsore and ready to drop. But Gazer pushed on single-mindedly, stopping only to lap from streams.

'We've had no chance to hunt, so we can't even feed the hound after all this exertion – never mind feed ourselves,' Rufryd said grimly. 'I'll kill Lyn when we find him. I'll bloody well kill him.'

They came to the top of a steep bank, beyond which the forest fell into a dark, damp, overgrown valley. Tanthe wrestled with Gazer, trying to persuade him to an easier route down the drop before she broke her neck. The valley was silent, oddly lifeless . . . although she felt no real sense of danger, the atmosphere was unpleasant.

A sudden sound made her jump. Something was crashing through the undergrowth below, coming towards them. Gazer went wild, barking, hanging on the taut end of the rope with his forepaws clawing at the air. Tanthe couldn't hold him. She let the rope go before she fell.

A horse came bursting out of the trees, galloping towards them with its ears back, eyes white-ringed, foam flying from its mouth. As it came flying up the bank, forcing her to leap aside, Tanthe caught a brief glimpse of the rider who was slumped on its neck. Lynden.

'Rufe!' she yelled. But he was already running in the same direction as the stampeding horse, looking back over his shoulder. As the beast drew level with him, he seized its reins, and was nearly dragged off his feet. He ran with the horse, struggling; and as he dragged it at last to a reluctant halt, Lynden tumbled forward and landed on the ground at his feet.

The horse – a rarefied, athletic blue roan with dark points – stood with its head down and its sides heaving. Gazer, meanwhile, was staring down into the valley, barking and snarling at something unseen.

Tanthe angrily called him to heel. As she ran to Lynden, she felt an uncomfortable warmth against her left breast.

Rufryd was kneeling beside his brother. 'Lyn? Lyn, it's us!'

'He's breathing,' said Tanthe, dropping down on the other side and loosening Lynden's shirt. 'Give me his water flask. Is he injured?'

'I don't think so . . . can't see any wounds or bruises.' As she unstoppered the flask and moistened his face, Lynden groaned and half-opened his eyes. He began trying to sit up, so Rufryd lifted him and supported him on his knees. 'Feel how hot he is, Tan! I think he's ill.'

'Damn. And I'm so clever. I didn't even think to bring a simple medicine like willow bark.'

Lynden stirred, murmuring. He coughed, looked dully up at Rufryd, and began to shiver violently. 'Rufe,' he said.

'Yes, it's all right, we're here. What possessed you to go off on your own?'

'Ardharkria. The Forest—' Lynden struggled and panted, thrashing at the air with his right hand, trying to point into the depths of the valley from which he'd come.

'Calm down. Yes, you stupid sod, we're back in Ardharkria.'

'Perfectly harmless, you told us it was,' Tanthe said briskly. 'Rufe, we have to find a village. He's feverish, he needs proper care! Oh, I hoped this wouldn't happen, one of us getting ill.'

'Can't you feel it?' said Lynden through chattering teeth.

188

'Feel what?' asked Rufryd, looking worriedly at Tanthe.

Lynden frowned. His head thrashed from side to side. 'I can't explain. Feelings – visions – like fire and ice on my skin – like sand sifting through my brain. Why can't you feel it?'

Again Tanthe became aware of the heat against her breast. It was almost painful.

'I don't know, Lyn,' said Rufryd. 'Just keep calm and we'll take you somewhere more comfortable.'

'We must leave here. Listen to me.' He clutched Rufryd's arm, trying to pull himself up. 'It's why Ardharkria is forbidden. I saw them. I saw them.'

Tanthe reached into her pocket, and exclaimed in pain as the object there stung her fingers. It was the Aelyr knife, and it was so hot she could barely hold it. Carefully she drew it out and took it from its scabbard.

Behind her, Gazer was still snarling viciously at some unseen enemy in the valley.

'What, Lyn?'

His chest heaved. Sweat ran down his fine-boned face. 'Bhahdradomen.'

'Gods,' whispered Tanthe. 'Rufe, look.'

She held out the Aelyr knife, balancing it on top of the scabbard to protect her palm from the heat. The blade was no longer dull but shining silver-white; and the stone on the pommel was no pebble but a bright moonstone, glittering with fugitive rainbows, throbbing with a pale, brilliant, warning light.

Gulzhur stood for a time, looking at the body of the winged beast. He poked it with his foot. The *ghelim* was dead; so he thought. Then it stirred, croaking its pain in an almost human voice. The muscular fibres of its chest cavity were already beginning to force the arrow out of the wound. Gulzhur seized the shaft, broke off the head that protruded from its shoulder, and wrenched it out. It came free with a soft sucking noise.

The beast screamed, flapping. Its words were unintelligible.

A brown-cloaked figure had joined Gulzhur and stood quietly beside him. At length he spoke uneasily. 'Enabler, this is unfortunate.'

'Indeed, Rhu. I have lost one of my troop. Will you keep the *ghelim* here while it recovers from its wound?'

Rhu blinked. Years of living in Ardharkria had given his face a grey-brown sheen, like bark. 'Of course, Enabler, but that's not what I meant. Humans never come here. Never.'

'Ah, he was just a boy. Doubtless he has died of fear by now. If not, his stupidity will catch up with him before long.'

'His shot was not stupid,' Rhu said mildly.

'Pure chance,' spat Gulzhur. Inwardly he was furious, but he never let fury master him. 'That was luck, not skill.'

'Still, it's strange,' said Rhu.

'These are strange times.' Gulzhur looked up through the bare twisted branches to the flat grey sky. He smelled bare earth, sap, and the sweet metal of ox-flesh. It was time to tell them. 'Everything is changing, Rhu.'

Rhu's fellows were gathering around them, moving silently from the shadows, almost human-looking in their browns and greys. They watched Gulzhur with pond-green eyes, half-suspicious, half-hopeful. The handful of visits he'd paid to them in recent weeks had made them uneasy and resentful; why, after centuries of isolation in hostile territory, were they now graced with a visitor from the homeland? Still, even after all this time, they recognised and respected his status.

'You are a long way from home, Enabler,' said one.

'Home?' said Gulzhur. 'Yes, a long way, and I have much to tell you. We have suffered in exile long enough. The old regime is gone. Aazhoth's time is over. Those such as Aazhoth, who have bent to human demands, colluded with humans to keep us in exile – we will follow them no more. We have a new leader now. A true hatchling of the Ancestor. Under him, we will never again refer to a scrubby island on the far eastern corner of this continent as "home"! Aventuria is our home!'

Rhu and the others stirred. They'd been quiescent for too long to show much fire. But their time would come. These pockets of his people had not been left across Aventuria for nothing. 'A change must come,' Rhu said. 'We can't stay within these boundaries much longer. Once the trees are gone, our flesh-oxen will need new pastures. It's hard to control them.'

'You shouldn't have to control them,' said Gulzhur. 'They should roam free, as in the days of old.'

'What would you have us do?'

'Nothing as yet,' said Gulzhur. 'Be quiet here, don't arouse human suspicion. I will be in this area a few days and I will visit you again before I depart. I come to bring you hope and to tell you – be ready!'

And he felt the red energy begin to grow among them. Waves of pain from the groaning *ghelim* fed their excitement. Not as powerful as human pain, but still arousing.

'And this new leader,' Rhu said, 'you come at his command? How did he take power? Did he seize it, or take it by consensus? Who is he?'

Gulzhur smiled, turning away. 'All I can tell you is his name. Remember it,' he said. 'His name is Vaurgroth.'

Chapter Nine. Luin Sepher

Tanthe ran to fetch Gazer, and with some difficulty persuaded him to leave off barking at his invisible quarry. She hardly had the strength after walking all day, but she had physically to haul him with her. Her heart thumped with the effort.

'Sod you, Gazer, come *on!*'

She wouldn't admit to being afraid, but Gazer's belligerence, Lynden's terror and the bright glow of the knife – tucked now through her belt – made her feel disturbed and vulnerable. It was beginning to rain and the forest was drenched in an eerie slate-blue gloom.

'Where did you find the horse, Lyn?' Rufryd was asking as she reached them, with the reluctant Gazer at her heels.

'Back there – I found a body,' Lynden said, gesticulating weakly. 'The horse was near the body. Must've been his master. Found this.' He pushed a piece of parchment into Rufryd's hand, and tried wildly to get to his feet. 'Ymmi's in danger. We have to find her!'

'Yes,' Rufryd said, trying to subdue him. 'Calm down. That's what we're doing.'

He read the note, then passed it to Tanthe. The words were a long slow sword cutting through her spirit; a warning of slavery, betrayal, death.

'Can you get Lyn onto Flame's back?' she said, lowering the paper. 'We need to leave.'

'Right. Though I don't know where the hell we're going.' Rufryd helped Lynden up, but his brother turned pale and fainted as soon as he was upright. Rufryd hoisted his inert form across Flame's saddle, while Tanthe caught the blue stallion.

'This is a noble's horse,' she said.

'You may as well ride him.'

'No. He's too tired.'

'Or you're too scared.'

'No. But I don't fancy him running away with me, like he did with Lynden,' Tanthe said acidly. But she put her foot in the stallion's stirrup, and nervously mounted him. He danced under her until she gathered the reins. Then she tied Gazer's rope to a ring on the saddle so he couldn't go loping off. They set off, heading eastwards, hoping to escape Ardharkria; Rufryd leading Flame, Tanthe's mount pulling skittishly ahead. Darkness was falling and she felt too weary to fight any danger that might pursue them. Behind them was silence, but the forest and the sky seemed to be watching, poised.

Once she felt more confident on the horse, she took the knife out of her belt again. It was cooling. Before her eyes, it turned from milk-white to pebble grey. Shaking her head, she tucked it back into her pocket.

'It's not our horse, anyway,' said Rufryd. 'We can't keep it.'

'I don't see why not. Whoever owned it is dead.'

'And he had a family, and they should be told what happened to him.'

'Yes, but not at the expense of us getting even further behind Ymmi! You read the message.'

'Yes. And whoever sent it needs to know that it never reached its destination.'

Tanthe was startled by Rufryd's attack of conscience.

'You're saying that taking the horse would be stealing?'

'Exactly. Stealing and worse.'

'I never realised you were so honest.'

'Well, there's a lot you don't know about me, isn't there?' he said shortly. 'You must have found that out last night. We've got to get help for Lyn. We have to take the horse back to its rightful owners. Though how the hell we're going to find it . . .'

Tanthe knew from his tone there was no arguing with him. She was frightened for Lynden. She'd never dared to think that one of them might actually die on this journey.

'We could try this,' she said. And she dropped the stallion's reins, and let him find his own route.

Immediately he speeded up, neck arched, ears pricked, and took a different angle through the trees. Tanthe clutched his mane, then caught the reins again to slow him down. But he was a smooth ride and she felt safe on his back. Apart from the odd restraining tug, so that the others could keep up, she let him have his head. He was going home.

'Hoy! Hold!'

The shout jolted her violently to alertness – that, and Gazer's deafening outburst of barking, which made her mount shy. She'd been dozing, she realised. Shaking herself, she sat up in the saddle and made out – in shadow on shadow in the wet night – a path winding steeply uphill through the trees, and the peak of a hill standing ahead against the sky. Two white lights, one on either side of the path, dazzled her.

'Halt! Our bows are trained on you. What is your business?'

'Don't shoot!' Rufryd's voice. 'We have a sick man here!'

Tanthe was shocked by their aggression. In the small part of Sepheret she knew, people were usually friendly to strangers. For a second she was tempted to unleash Gazer in self-defence. Instinct, though, told her not to, that they would only shoot him first.

She managed to pull the stallion to a halt; despite his own tiredness he danced on the spot with impatience. The two lamps came swaying towards them. To her dark-attuned eyes the light was blinding. Squinting against it, she made out two tall, youngish men striding towards them, each holding a loaded crossbow on one arm and a

194

lantern on the other. They were all in black; full breeches and jackets that were elaborately padded and gleaming with dark brocade.

'Dismount!' one yelled. 'And shut that dog up!'

Tanthe obeyed hurriedly. As soon as her feet touched the ground, her legs nearly gave way; Rufryd caught her. She held Gazer's collar to quiet him. She could hardly see the men's faces through the lantern light, but one of them came suddenly into view, exclaiming in amazement at the sight of the horse. 'Halcyon! What the—'

The man turned to stare at Tanthe and Rufryd. His square, strong face, lit eerily by the lantern, fixed dangerously upon her. His voice was smooth yet hard, like glass. 'This is our brother Arhan's horse. How do you come to be in possession of it?'

'We found him running loose in the forest,' Rufryd answered. 'Or rather, my brother did. We were bringing him back.'

The two men looked at each other. The other was young but thin and gaunt, with over-bright, haunted eyes. 'Found him? Then where is our brother?'

'We also found a body. Whether it was him or not, I couldn't say, but he was wearing clothes much like yours. If so, I'm sorry. But now my own brother is very ill and needs care.'

'Please help us,' Tanthe added. 'We think something attacked him in Ardharkria. We've travelled all day to find help.'

'Great Anthar's horns,' said the man. His narrow eyes gleamed with moisture, but he still looked at them as if they might be thieves or murderers. 'Who are you?'

'Just travellers,' said Rufryd. 'It's a long story.'

'We don't mean any harm,' Tanthe added.

'Don't you know where you are?' said the man.

'Not really, no,' she said, becoming angry. 'But I'm sure it's not a place that no longer pays reverence to Breyid the Healer!'

'All right.' Finally he disarmed the crossbow and lowered it. His mouth thinned. It couldn't be called a smile. 'Very well. As you took the trouble to bring our horse back and give us this sorry news – come up to the house and be welcome. I am Calamys and my brother here is Pheilan. I know that our parents will be more than happy to accommodate you.'

The house came into view as they laboured up the steep path. It was on the very peak of the hill, hemmed by great, jutting boulders. Tanthe saw the silhouette of towers and turrets against the rain-washed sky, roof tiles gleaming darkly, tall dusky windows punctuated by beams and gables and large windows with tiny leaded panes. She'd never been so close to a building of such size. It looked intimidating yet beautiful, in an eerie way.

'Welcome to Luin Sepher,' said Calamys.

Tanthe swallowed. She'd often heard the name Luin Sepher whispered as if it were impossibly remote and mysterious; she'd never dreamed she would come here.

An archway, hidden in the juncture of two high walls, led them into a courtyard with stables along three sides. The doors were shut, but when the stallion lifted his head and let out a high whicker, he was answered by a dozen other equine voices. Tanthe touched Rufryd's arm. 'All these horses!' she whispered.

Rufryd lifted Lynden from Flame's back and supported him. Lynden blinked in the lantern light, coughed, then went into a convulsion of shivering. 'It's all right,' said Rufryd, wrapping his cloak more closely around him. 'We're safe, you'll soon be better.'

'It was in the sky,' Lynden said hoarsely. 'Killed him. Bhahdra—'

'Shush. It's all right.'

While Pheilan led Flame and Halcyon into the stables, Calamys took the others through an arched door into a hallway and thence into a large kitchen. When the heat

196

from the wide fireplace hit her, Tanthe also began to shiver. She hadn't realised how chilled she was until then. Calamys pulled on a woven strip that hung down the wall, a distant bell rang, and after a minute a slender middle-aged woman came rushing into the kitchen, tying on an apron as she came.

'Meris, we have visitors. One of them is ill. See to him first, then make up beds in the guest wing for the others. They would appreciate hot drinks and food before they retire, I should imagine. And wake Lady Amitriya to attend . . .'

'Lynden,' said Rufryd.

'To attend Lynden.'

'Yes, sir,' said Meris.

Calamys turned to Rufryd and Tanthe. He was no longer hostile, but had a slightly disdainful air of authority. 'If you can overlook her eccentricities, my aunt has her skills, not least healing. Go with Meris. Ah, but if you would be so kind as to leave the dog outside . . .'

Tanthe laid a protective hand on Gazer's head, torn between gratitude and suspicion. 'He needs to eat and rest, too.'

'Of course. I'll get the stable boys to feed him and make him up a bed in the hallway. A fine hound,' Calamys added. 'Deserving of respect.'

Half an hour later, Lynden was tucked up in a big four-poster bed, looking lost in the thick covers, his face as pale as the pillow. Rufryd and Tanthe waited anxiously beside him, while Meris held his head up and the Lady Amitriya fed him sips of a hot tincture that smelled bitter with herbs and sweet with honey.

She was elderly, thin and stooped, with a hank of unkempt white hair and an astonishing aura of energy. She barely spoke to the newcomers and Tanthe, nervous of her, didn't know what to say. Her body was sheathed in a loose dark blue robe, embroidered with moon symbols. She seemed, as Calamys had hinted, rather odd.

'That will bring his fever down,' said the Lady, when Lynden had swallowed the last spoonful of mixture. 'He will sleep now.'

'Have you any idea what's wrong with him?' Rufryd said.

She shrugged, her bird-like face devoid of expression. 'People get fevers. I expect he has caught a chill.'

'We think something might have attacked him.'

'There is no wound upon him. An animal?'

'Well, he said . . . he saw something in Ardharkria that was . . . how can I put it . . . not human.'

Her black eyes gleamed keenly. 'Fever plays many tricks on the mind, my dear. We who live on the edge of Ardharkria dismiss such foolish rumours.'

With that, Lady Amitriya gathered her bottles of tincture on to a tray, and left the room. Meris said, 'I will take you to your rooms now, as Lord Calamys requested.'

Lord, thought Tanthe. She'd known Halcyon belonged to a nobleman, but hearing that word sent a flame of anxious excitement through her. How were they expected to behave, as guests of nobles? Meris, meanwhile, was helpful but indifferent, making plain that although she was a servant, she was still more of a lady than these peasants.

Her attitude was guaranteed to rouse Tanthe's pride. But for now, all that mattered was sleep.

'One room will do,' said Rufryd.

Tanthe looked at him.

'I'm staying with Lynden,' he explained. 'I'll sleep beside him. The bed's big enough.'

'Of course,' she said, smiling weakly. 'Get some sleep, then. Don't try to stay awake all night.'

Rufryd embraced her and held her close for a few moments. 'You were brilliant bringing us here,' he said into her ear. 'Good night. Make the best of a real bed.'

She whispered, so the servant wouldn't hear. 'Rufe . . . the note Lyn found. Shouldn't we tell them?'

'Tomorrow. Go! Sleep well, Tan.'

Lynden was floundering under a soft white weight. The great pallid ox was crushing him, its bulk enveloping his body, forcing him into the ground where thousands of insects gnawed at his flesh. The earth was so cold, making him shiver. And it was so hot, making him thrash and sweat and gasp for breath. The Bhahdradomen face stared down at him, and between its seven-fingered hands it held Ysomir.

'I'm taking her away now,' it said in a thick voice that seemed to creep right inside his membranes. 'She will be my bride instead.'

Lynden yelled hoarsely, 'No! Ymmi!'

Someone was holding him. He became aware that Rufryd was beside him, his face sheened with candle-light, and that they were in some weirdly cavernous place that made no sense. Lynden tried to climb out of bed, realising there was no time to waste.

'Lynden!' said Rufryd. 'What are you doing?'

'We've got to go and find Ymmi.'

'Yes, but not now. You're ill, you stupid sod! This is the third time – try to relax. I'm here.'

'Yes,' said Lynden, understanding, falling back into the soft, enveloping bed. It was all right. Rufryd was there. He tried to fight sleep but inevitably he slipped down again . . . and there the hallucinations and the nightmares were still waiting.

Tanthe was woken by someone sitting heavily on the edge of her bed. She opened her eyes and found Rufryd looking down at her. He was in a blue robe, and his hair was damp and his chin freshly shaved, but there were shadows under his eyes.

'Are you ever going to wake up?' he said.

She pushed herself up on her elbows. 'What time is it?'

'Mid-afternoon. You've been asleep for at least fifteen hours.'

'Oh.' She dropped her head back. 'Gods, I needed it. Last night I was unconscious before my head hit the pillow.'

She sat up, noticing for the first time the room in which she'd spent the night – and half the day. She'd never seen such a place, with a high ceiling, a fireplace, rugs covering the floor. The walls were ivory, but the fabrics – bed cover, canopy and curtains – were all in blue and black, with a feathery pattern like a peacock's tail. She'd seen pictures of peacocks in her books about Parione.

'How's Lynden?' she asked.

Rufryd exhaled. 'He had a rough night. He woke me four or five times, trying to get out of bed to find Ysomir.'

'Oh, no.' She closed her eyes. 'Is he any better now?'

'His fever's still up and down. He's had some lucid moments; he was able to get to the privy by himself and to have a hot bath, so he was more comfortable at least. Lady what's-her-name gave him some more medicine. Now he's sleeping quietly . . . but I don't think he's going to get over this quickly, Tan.'

She shook her head, and put her hand on his knee. He placed his hand over hers. Selfishly, she was almost relieved. The prospect of a few days' rest was unutterably tempting.

'Have you spoken to our hosts yet?'

'Only the ones we saw last night. But I gather we're invited to dinner.'

'Gods, I hope we can have something to eat before then! I'm famished.'

'We only have to call and Meris will bring a tray for you. I had two sorts of cheese, beer bread, warm cakes full of fruit and the best mead I've ever tasted.'

'Oh, stop! Call her! No, wait a minute.'

'What?'

'Rufe, I suppose you realise who these people are, don't you?'

'Does it matter? They're wealthy and they're helping us. We'll find out tonight.'

'Oh, work it out! The name of the house, Luin Sepher. Three sons, the Lords Calamys, Pheilan and the one who died – as far as we know – Arhan. Their parents are the Duke and Duchess of Sepheret.'

He looked startled. 'And?'

'They rule Sepheret! We're their . . . subjects, I suppose.'

'So they are very good to their subjects.' Rufryd smiled, as if to shrug it off. 'Come on, Tan. Not worried by it, are you? You know you're a noblewoman at heart. You were just born in Riverwynde by mistake.'

'Of course we're as good as they are! That's not what I'm saying. If you can stop mocking me long enough to listen – we'll have to be very careful about what we say to them.'

'About why we're so far from home?'

'Yes. Because they must have condoned the King's conscription. It couldn't have happened otherwise. So if they know about Ymmi and why we're going after her, they'll know we're breaking the law. And if they know about Beyne . . .'

Rufryd lowered his head, looking at their entwined fingers. 'But perhaps they didn't condone it. What if the King gave them no choice? The message, Tan. Why was one of their sons carrying a warning message?'

'I don't know. But I think we have to get out of here just as soon as Lyn is strong enough.'

'I'll go along with that. But until then, let's make the best of it, eh?' He slid his hand under the bedcover and over her bare thighs.

'Rufe, don't.'

He withdrew his hand. 'Not having second thoughts, are you?'

'Don't be daft!' Smiling, she stroked his cheek. 'It's only that I haven't bathed yet. I must stink of sweat and horses.'

'So bathe afterwards.' He buried his face in her neck, tickling her there with his tongue and making her laugh. His body was warm and hard; she couldn't resist. 'It's not so bad. I'll hold my breath,' he said, sliding into bed beside her, smiling as she hit his chest in mock indignation. 'Stop complaining. You smell wonderful to me.'

Tanthe was trembling as Calamys led them into the great dining hall. The walls were panelled in black wood, with a narrow, leaded window set into each panel along the right-hand side. The ceiling was high and arched, supported by curving, ornately carved beams of the same dark wood. Although at least a hundred candles blazed along the walls and on the long table, the blackness absorbed most of the light. The atmosphere was one of brooding solemnity and grandeur; she felt out of her depth, but determined to show she was equal to it. This felt like the first test of her ambitions. She must pass at all costs.

At the far end was a great, blazing fireplace. The family were waiting there to greet their guests. They looked so stiff and formal, she flushed with mortification to think that a few hours ago, she and Rufryd had been romping lustfully in one of their aristocratic beds.

Meris had brought fresh clothes for them. Rufryd was wearing simple dark breeches and a white shirt, and she had on a long, midnight blue dress. Even though it was too big for her, it was the most luxurious garment she'd ever seen, let alone worn. Alone in her room, she'd looked at herself in the mirror in despair; her hair – thanks to Rufryd – looked like a crow's nest. But she'd done the best she could with the comb, pomade and clips provided by Meris. With her hand through Rufryd's arm, she carried herself with all the dignity she could muster, feeling as if their exertions were written all over them.

She thought Calamys handsome but too fleshy, with a square face and narrow black eyes. He always seemed to be listening, appraising, not speaking his true thoughts.

'Tanthe,' Calamys began, 'My mother the Lady Alorna, Duchess of Sepheret, wishes to meet you. Mother, may I present our guests Tanthe and Rufryd from, er, a village near Havereyn.'

Tanthe wasn't sure if she was expected to curtsey. Instead she gave an awkward dip of her head, and clasped the proffered hand, which was long, bony, and smooth as silk.

The Duchess was a tall, angular woman, with white hair swept into an immaculate shape and adorned with a net of blue stones. Sapphires, Tanthe guessed. But, she observed, the Duchess was no taller or more impressive than her grandmother Helwyn, apart from her clothes. It was all Tanthe could do not to stare blatantly at the Duchess's dress, with its boned bodice, puffed sleeves and full skirt. The ground was black silk, embroidered with shimmering shades of blue in thread and tiny lapis beads. The effect was of combined richness and restraint. It made her borrowed dress, which she'd thought so luxurious when she put it on, look like a cast-off.

'My father, Lord Dannion, Duke of Sepheret.'

The Duke was also tall but stoop-shouldered; she couldn't decide whether he was arrogant, or simply shy. His face – gaunt like his youngest son – had a quality of remoteness, and his eyes were grey and watery. He nodded but did not shake their hands. He and Pheilan were also in blue and black; there were no other colours to be seen. They wore full knee-breeches, silk stockings, jewelled slippers and lavishly-worked tunics with slashed sleeves.

'My mother's sister, Lady Amitriya, and my younger brother Pheilan you have already met . . .' Like his father, Pheilan had an air of remoteness, a slight nerviness which he hid by being aloof. The Lady Amitriya, with her unkempt hair and shapeless robe, looked nothing like her sister, or indeed like the rest of the family. She was as quick and restless as a bird, and her expression was sourly ironic. 'And this is my wife, Lady Esamir.'

The wife of Calamys wore a looser style of dress in shades of dark blue, with a leaf pattern sewn in silver beads. Her frame was large but seemed wasted, as if her big bones needed more flesh. She had an oval face with slanted blue eyes, a full sulky mouth, honey-brown hair flowing to her hips.

Tanthe misheard her name.

'Oh, my sister is called Ysomir!' she said. Rufryd pressed his foot warningly on her little toe.

'How amusing,' said Lady Esamir with a slight smile, 'the village folks giving their children such poetic names. There's nothing at all wrong with country names like Nerrie and Freynie, is there?' They all laughed politely, except Amitriya, whose face would have curdled milk.

Tanthe wondered why 'village folk' shouldn't have whatever names they wanted, but as she couldn't say that, she said nothing. The Duke spoke before the silence became awkward.

'I understand that you brought news of our son Arhan's death.'

'We – we don't know for sure if it was him,' Rufryd said quickly.

'We had some men ride out this afternoon to find him and bring back the body.' He gave a long, audible sigh. 'Alas, it was our son.'

'I'm sorry,' Tanthe and Rufryd said together. Tanthe added, 'I hope we did the right thing, bringing his horse back.'

'Of course you did,' said Lady Alorna. 'And naturally you may stay until your companion is fully recovered from his fever. It's the least we can do to show our gratitude.'

'We had suspected for some time that he was dead,' Lord Dannion said heavily. 'This is the confirmation we had dreaded, but still a great shock to us.'

Tanthe said cautiously, 'Have you any idea, er, how he died?'

'We rarely go into the wilder parts of the forest. An animal. There are wild cats . . . who can say?'

She thought his answer strangely glib and lacking in curiosity. Wild cats would not kill a human, certainly not

204

one on a horse, and dra'a'ks did not come this far from the mountains . . . Rufryd stepped forward and gave the Duke the note that Lynden had found on the young man's body.

'I'm afraid this message never reached its destination, sir,' he said. 'It's a shame it didn't, before—' Now it was her turn to give his arm a warning squeeze. 'Well, before.'

The Duke read the note, passed it to his wife; then Calamys, Pheilan and Esamir read it in turn. None of them said anything; their faces were impassive. Tanthe had read that the high-born thought it bad form to show their emotions; she was impressed. Were they grief-stricken by Arhan's death and failure? Who could tell?

'But where were you going, that you found him?' the Duchess asked.

Rufryd cleared his throat. 'We had been to Skald to sell some stone carvings. I thought we could take a short cut through the forest but I, er, misread the map. I quarrelled with my brother and he went off on his own. When we caught him up, he'd found your horse but he was ill. The horse brought us here.'

Tanthe held her breath, waiting for more questions. But Lady Alorna only said, 'I see.' She took the message from her sister Amitriya and dropped it on the fire.

'Now,' she said, with a smile of polished warmth and grace, 'I believe that dinner is served. Meris will show you to your places. Do feel, for as long as you stay with us, perfectly at home.'

'Thank you,' said Tanthe. It would be impossible to feel any such thing, of course, but the sentiment touched her. She caught Rufryd pulling a face behind their hosts' back, and she glared at him, to say, *behave*.

The atmosphere over the dinner table was polite but distinctly strained; Tanthe felt it in every break in the conversation. At first she thought it was their presence, but after a while she was less sure.

She and Rufryd were famished, and the food was delicious. The courses were so small and delicate she thought they would never eat their fill, but one came after another, and by the fifth she was more than satiated.

As each dish was brought in – by Meris and two young boys – Lady Alorna explained slowly and in great detail what it was called and what ingredients had gone to make it. 'First we have soup of carrots and nutmeg; this green herb is parsley . . . Ah now, these are tartlets of minced meat with a layer of apricots encased in pastry. The way cook makes them is a most ingenious adaptation of the traditional recipe . . .'

At first, Tanthe thought the family were being condescending, talking to their country guests as if they'd been raised on a diet of root vegetables. Most of these dishes were new to her, it was true. Presently, though, she realised that they only spoke to their guests, not each other, and that they were doing so to fill the silence. She reminded herself that they had lost their son, they couldn't be expected to laugh and joke.

'Ah,' said the Duchess. 'Now this is my husband's favourite. Jugged hare.'

Rufryd and Tanthe exchanged a quick look. Tanthe swallowed. 'I'm sorry, but we can't eat hare.'

'Oh, why not?'

'The hare is sacred to Breyid. We don't kill or eat it.'

'Of course. I forgot, we don't have quite the same practices as those who work on the land. Meris, remove the hare and bring the pheasant, please dear.'

The Duke said nothing, but his lips thinned as his favourite dish was removed. Tanthe was embarrassed. 'Please, don't let us stop you eating it, it's just—'

'No, no. We will not cause offence to our guests. Our goddess, the family goddess of the duchy of Sepheret, as it were, is Nephenie. She has no sacred animals.'

Tanthe saw her chance to prove that she was not an ignorant peasant, that she was as knowledgeable as her hosts. 'Yes, Nephenie is another name for Nepheter, the goddess of Parione. But she is also the maiden aspect of

206

our mother Breyid, as Mahaa is the crone. Nephenie of the poets. She's very important to me, too.'

'Our father is the one for poets,' said Pheilan, swirling dark red wine round his glass. 'He has a great library, from which he emerges only to eat.'

A brief silence, brittle as glass. 'Yes, Nephenie, Nepheter,' said the Duke. 'You are quite right, my dear. As Saphaeyender said of her,

> *Silver muse, your shafts beguile*
> *Alike the lord in lofty tower*
> *And shepherd on the wooded rise.'*

Tanthe continued,

> *'Fair, the rosy-fingered moons*
> *Who spin their webs of radiance*
> *On all the world, and none despise.'*

'Wherever did you learn that?' Calamys said disdainfully.

'We can read, even in Riverwynde. Saphaeyender is my favourite poet. I know all his work.'

'And his plays?' The Duke seemed pleased. It was the first sign of animation he'd shown. 'Which of his plays is your favourite?'

She paused. She only knew two, which she and Ysomir had acted endlessly in their childhood, until the books fell to pieces. '*The Oak Tree of Pherenath*,' she said quickly.

'Pah!' said the Duke. 'It's not his best. An early, fumbled attempt. The structure of *Eskadale* shows real maturity, the master at the height of his skills, don't you find?'

'Erhm . . .' Tanthe had never heard of it. 'Yes, but . . . I like *Oak Tree*'s naivete.'

'Good point,' said Lord Dannion.

Calamys leaned forward, eyes fixed knowingly on Tanthe. 'In what way do you feel *Eskadale*'s maturity manifests itself in contrast? Which characters in the later play best demonstrate the point?'

'Erhm . . . Iagis and Thion . . .'

'That's *Arkenfell*, not *Eskadale*.'

She was suddenly out of her depth. Not even knowing the characters' names, she couldn't bluff her way through it. 'I'm afraid I haven't read it,' she said finally. 'I couldn't always get the books I wanted.

'Well, we should do something about that,' said the Duke. 'Send more books to the villages.'

'They'll use 'em for goat feed,' Calamys said under his breath. Tanthe glared at him but he leaned towards her again and said, 'So which of the three writers is the greatest; Saphaeyender, Theotis or Amahlliah?'

Tanthe felt she was poised over a great void; her own lack of knowledge. Once she thought she knew everything; this was an appalling way to find out she was wrong. She'd read some work by the second, but hardly anything by the third. 'I don't think it's fair to judge,' she said coolly.

'The revered Lady Amahlliah is considered to be the greatest, of course,' said the Duke, 'But I hardly think the plays Saphaeyender has written recently can be surpassed.'

Tanthe's mouth fell open. Before she could stop herself she exclaimed, 'Saphaeyender is still alive?'

'But of course. I thought you would have known.'

'I thought – I just assumed – he died years ago.'

'He is your favourite writer, and you didn't know?' said Calamys. 'Tanthe, you're blushing.'

'And you're trying to make a fool of her,' Rufryd said belligerently. 'Leave her be. Half the children in our village wouldn't be able to read if it wasn't for her; who have you helped with your education? You idle—'

'Rufe, don't!' Tanthe whispered. She pinched his leg under the table.

'Ah, here is dessert,' the Duchess said loudly. 'A cheese-cake, flavoured with rosewater and decorated with crystallised rose petals . . .'

She trailed off, staring at the doorway. The others looked up. Meris came in carrying a large dish, but another figure was following her into the room. Lynden.

Silence fell; Meris quickly put down the dish and hurried out. Lynden was dressed in breeches and a shirt, but he was barefoot and had put on the shirt inside out. He walked slowly, not quite steady on his feet. There were deep circles under his eyes, and his expression was tired, grim, but perfectly rational.

The family stared at him as he walked up to the table. Tanthe didn't know what to do; neither, apparently, did Rufryd.

'Please forgive me for intruding,' Lynden said. He stood next to his brother, supporting himself with one hand on the table. 'I had to come and warn you, and it won't wait.'

'Lyn, you should be in bed,' said Rufryd.

'No, I'm feeling much better. I'm not out of my mind.' He looked at the Duke and Duchess. 'I'm sorry, but someone must tell you before it's too late. There are Bhahdradomen in your forest.'

There was a protracted, stony silence. To Tanthe's shock and mortification, both the Duke and the Duchess rose from their seats without expression and strode swiftly out of the room. Esamir and Pheilan stared fixedly at their plates; Lady Amitriya watched Calamys.

'No,' Calamys said thinly, when his mother and father had gone. 'Of course there are no Bhahdradomen. You probably saw the Leyholmen; they are woodcutters, dependants of my parents who are allowed to make a living in the forest.'

'I know what I saw!' said Lynden.

'You had a fever. You were hallucinating.'

'No. It was the Bhahdradomen I met who *made* me ill. It seemed to suck all the strength out of me.'

'There are no Bhahdradomen in Ardharkria.' Calamys's tone was dangerous. 'Peasant superstition.'

'And the note we found on Lord Arhan?' Rufryd put in.

'What note?' Calamys said, meeting his gaze. 'There was no note.'

'All right. Then what the blazes is this?'

From a pocket, Rufryd took a rounded pale object, an inch or so across. Tanthe's mouth went dry; it was one of the insects that had nearly buried her in the forest. Rufryd placed it on the table in front of Calamys. It was dead, but Esamir stared at it, her shoulders rising with revulsion. Throwing her napkin down, she fled the room.

'Put that abominable thing on the fire. How dare you?' Calamys was trembling, rage cracking his cold exterior. 'This conversation has not taken place.'

He rose and strode out after his wife, leaving the three alone with Pheilan and Lady Amitriya.

'I'm sorry, I don't know what to say.' Tanthe put a hand to her hot face. Rufryd shrugged and threw the offending insect into the flames.

'Don't be,' Amitriya replied. 'It's not you. Dinner ends like this as often as not in this house, doesn't it, Pheilan?' She gave a sinister laugh as if at a private, black joke. 'Sit down, Lynden, and help us with this cheesecake. Shame to waste it.' Hesitantly, Lynden obeyed.

'I don't understand,' he said. 'I know what I saw. Why won't they listen to me?'

'Don't talk. Eat,' she said, pointing the serving knife at him. 'Blabbering about things he didn't understand is what caused Lord Arhan's death.'

Half an hour later, Tanthe and Rufryd took Lynden back to his room, talking in hushed voices as they went down the long, creaking corridors.

'This was a mistake,' Lynden said. 'We shouldn't have come here. That horse could have helped me catch up with Ymmi. Now we're back where we started.'

'You're forgetting that we had no choice,' Tanthe retorted. 'You were ill.'

'I'm fine now.'

'You're not. You still need rest. We're not leaving until I'm certain you're not going to drop dead on us!'

'Don't be daft. I know what was wrong with me. It wasn't a proper illness, it was . . .'

Rufryd said, 'How do you know it was a Bhahdradomen you saw? You've never seen one before, have you? So how can you be sure?'

Lynden sighed. 'I can't explain. Something happened to me when I found Arhan's body, I felt I could see things I shouldn't . . . oh, never mind. I just *knew*. Are you telling me I imagined it?'

'Maybe.'

'Like I imagined you and Tanthe were arguing one moment and having it off the next?'

'Ah. I didn't think you knew.'

'I should think the whole bloody forest knew!'

'Keep your voice down. That isn't why you ran off, is it?' Lynden said nothing. 'You stupid idiot!'

'Oh, Lyn,' said Tanthe.

'Yes, all right, it was stupid of me,' Lynden conceded. 'But if you expected me to lie there all night listening to that while Ymmi's—'

'Lyn, I'm sorry.' Tanthe put her hand through his arm. 'We never meant to upset you. It just—'

'Happened, yeah, I know.'

They had reached the open door of his room. 'We'd better talk about what we're going to do in the morning,' she said.

'Come in, then.' Rufryd looked up and down the corridor to make sure no one was about; they filed in, and Lynden turned up the oil-lamp beside his bed. 'The sooner we go, the better. I don't like these people, they give me the creeps.'

As he spoke, the door creaked on its hinges and slammed shut. They all started and turned. Calamys and Pheilan stood barring the door, and the lamplight glinted on the blades of their short swords.

Calamys turned the key in the lock and smiled, like a dra'a'k.

'I'll do worse than give you the creeps,' he said in his icy, polished drawl. 'Now, it's time to tell us who you really are and what you are doing here.'

Chapter Ten. The Jewels of the Earth

A damp, chill winter was already underway when Ysomir and her companions were brought to the quarry.

Clots of snow whirled through the air, plastering the sides of the carriage, melting almost as soon as they landed. Through this veil she saw great cliffs rising up on either side, bleak and ghostly. The ground between them was all grey mud cut into tiers, square grey lakes criss-crossed by ridges. Snow lay lightly on the ravaged earth, dissolving into the edges of the water.

'I think this is where they were bringing us,' said Ysomir, hugging Serenis as they squeezed their faces into the carriage window. Her spirit quailed. But the journey had been so long and tedious, she'd long ago lost hope of escape. 'This must be Napheneth.'

Serenis's face fell in dismay. 'Great Anthar's prick! It's bloody horrible!'

Whatever the situation, her tone of indignation always made Ysomir smile. There was something so loveable about Serenis; she had an ability to make people laugh, without ever trying to.

Since the incident with the soldier who'd tried to steal Serenis's locket, Beorwyn had protected them in a world that seemed ever more hostile. She and Ysomir were inseparable, while Lath and the others who'd shared the carriage throughout the journey had become like family. They looked out for each other. They needed to, to protect themselves from the guards' bullying. The further they went, the worse each new assignment of guards seemed to be. What had happened to the proud, cheerful soldiers that her grandma Freyna had described so fondly? These men and women were indifferent, opportunistic, sometimes cruel. It was only Beorwyn's presence that kept them at a distance and made the journey bearable.

The carriage creaked to a halt beside a complex of low wooden buildings. The door was opened. Ysomir and Serenis watched great blocks of stone being hauled on flat wagons from the cliffs, appearing through the curtain of snow and vanishing into it again. Under the icing of snow, the stone had a creamy colour. The sight of it made Ysomir's heart lift; she had always loved stone, loved its coolness under her fingers as she made her carvings.

Two women, bundled up in shawls and rosy-faced from the cold, climbed on board and distributed steaming mugs of soup. The conscripts took them gladly, and a murmur of conversation began. However desolate the outside world, this rectangular wooden space had come to be a warm refuge, a place of comradeship and safety, the nearest thing they had to a home.

As Ysomir sat with their hands clasped round their mugs, Beorwyn began to sing.

The dark days of winter be endless a-turning
The bright days of Firethorn be so far away
It's a snowdrop on Breyid's Day as cracks the earth open
Then soon will our feet dance
Upon the new grass, and our hearts
All with passion be burning . . .

His rich, deep voice filled the carriage; other voices joined in harmony. Even the guards joined in. The sound was exquisite; Ysomir closed her eyes and smiled, feeling that perhaps, after all, she could bear what had once seemed unbearable.

When the song finished, Beorwyn leaned over and touched her hand. 'The King would never do wrong by us,' he said. 'Whatever he wants with us here, it must be for the best.'

214

'Yes,' she said, wanting to believe it.

'Right,' said a voice. There was a heavy thump of boots as an officer jumped up into the carriage, shattering the mood. The conscripts sat up, alert and anxious. The newcomer was red-haired, as big as Beorwyn and clad in scuffed leather, with a short sword at his side.

'You – and you—' he began pointing to all the largest and strongest-looking members of the party, most of whom were male. Beorwyn was the first one he indicated. 'Follow me. You're for the quarry. The rest of you – all the nimble ones who won't mind squeezing through a few tunnels' – he grinned with ghastly amusement – 'stay on board. You're for the mines.'

Ysomir and Serenis stared at each other.

'No,' said Beorwyn. 'I'm not going. My friends need me.'

'You've got no choice, mate,' said the officer. Beorwyn shook his head stubbornly. 'I'm not standing here arguing. Off.'

'No!' Beorwyn roared. And he rushed at the red-haired man, flinging him off the carriage and leaping after him. Everyone rushed into the doorway to watch; the guards forced their way through, cursing and shoving people out of the way. For a few moments Ysomir could not see what was happening. She was held where she was by the crush. At last she forced her way to one of the windows and, kneeling on the bench seat, stuck her head out.

The two big men were confronting each other in the snow-slicked mud beside the track. Beorwyn swung his great fist at the officer's chin and felled him; but when the man came up again, his sword was in his hand. The carriage guards set on Beorwyn and he flung them off like children; but more guards were pouring out of the huts to assist, and even Beorwyn could not fight them all.

Ysomir watched in misery as they overpowered him and clamped chains to his feet and ankles.

'He only wanted to stay and look after his friends!' she cried, as the red-haired man jumped on board once more.

215

He was panting, his livid face clashing with the colour of his hair. 'He's just bloody lucky we didn't kill him. Right. Let's try again. The ones I picked for the quarry – off *now*!'

As the carriage – now half-empty – lurched into movement again, her last sight of Beorwyn was of him standing like a chained bear in the midst of six guards, his hair matted and tears running down his cheeks. His gaze met and held Ysomir's; she couldn't call out to him, couldn't even wave; then he was gone.

The mines lay another ten miles further on, as far as she could estimate the distance. The landscape in between was all ravaged, carved out of mud, coated in snow.

At last the conscripts were brought to another huddle of low buildings on the side of a bleak hill. Dismounting from the carriage with her small rucksack in her hand, Ysomir found herself looking down a long, scarred valley. Only the hill peaks on either side were touched with green beneath the veil of whiteness. Their skirts were pitted with dark holes. Nearby lay a vast heap of small, grey rocks.

One of the guards saw her looking. He plucked one of the stones off the heap and threw it to her. 'Here. That's what you'll be mining. Jewels fit for the King!'

For the first time, males and females were separated and shown to their quarters. A fierce-looking female officer with grey hair and arms like tree trunks led Ysomir and the others into a long, plain barrack room with rows of narrow beds. Half the beds were already occupied; the young women leapt up and stood to attention as the officer entered.

'I can't live here,' Serenis whispered. 'It's not fit for a pig!'

Ysomir couldn't see much wrong with it. It was clean, no plainer than the room she'd shared with Tanthe at home, and after weeks in the carriage she was simply glad to see a bed. But the officer heard. She swung round and clipped Serenis across the head, her eyes blazing. 'You'll live here and like it, unless you want your head shaved and your rations withheld!'

Serenis stepped back, shocked. Ysomir grasped her arm.

'You're in the King's service now,' the officer addressed the whole group, her voice cutting roughly through the air. 'My name is Teseyna. All I require of you is obedience and hard work. For as long as you are here, I am your mother, your goddess, and your monarch!'

When she had gone, Serenis said in a low but defiant voice, 'Funny. I don't remember my mother being the Death Crone.'

A ripple of soft laughter went around the dormitory.

'Welcome to Harphaneth,' said someone. 'Realm of mud, jewels and maggots.'

It took Ysomir hours to fall asleep that night. In the light of Lily Moon, which shone in a long crystalline shaft through the window beside her bed, she looked at the piece of rock the guard had thrown to her. She wiped off its coating of dirt, then took the chisel from the bottom of her rucksack and began to scratch at its dull coating. In the scratches, lines of brightness shone. She went on working until she'd cleared a space an inch square. Under the grime was a window of amethyst-coloured crystal, swirling shades and tiny rainbow sparkles frozen into the rock. It was like looking into another world; one into which she wished she could escape. The rock was like an unformed goddess-figure in her hand. She went on working at it until the chisel fell from her hand and she slept at last.

In the days that followed, her little secret carving was all she had to take her mind off the drudgery of the mines.

They were made to walk down long, deep shafts into the earth, through tunnels where they must bend almost double to pass. Deep down, the tunnels levelled out and there they must stay for ten or twelve hours at a stretch, chipping at walls of rock to shell out the nodes of crystal. Ysomir, already used to being permanently cold, damp and worn out, bore it. But those who panicked or refused to go were punished.

The first time it happened – when a small, blonde girl, who looked hardly old enough to be there, recoiled in terror at the closed-in blackness of the mine – Ysomir and Serenis tried to protect her from Teseyna's wrath. They, too, were seized by her fellow officers and beaten close to unconsciousness. Ysomir would never forget the expression on Teseyna's face as she brought her thick arm down, again and again; sheer, sadistic glee.

It was this that broke her spirit. Not only the pain itself. But that another human being, in this peaceful beneficent realm, Garnelys's kingdom, should take such pleasure in causing it.

This would never have happened if Beorwyn had stayed with us, Ysomir thought in misery afterwards. But she knew that the idea was false; even Beorwyn would not have been allowed to protect them. He would have been overpowered and punished even more brutally.

The overall commander of the mine was a harsh, merciless man, and all his officers, male and female alike, seemed to have been selected for their viciousness and tireless energy in enforcing discipline. Many of them, it was said, came from the land of Torith Mir, where such savagery was inbred. But there were others from Eisilion, Noreya, even Paranios itself, who were just as bad. The cheerful, trusting nature of the conscripts – which made rebellion unthinkable in the first place – could hardly have been more thoroughly betrayed.

Now the miners were quiescent. They worked, they accepted their rations, they fell with relief into their beds at night. When the others slept, Ysomir would take out her half-formed stone figure and work on it until sleep overcame her. Its shape offered itself to a lush figure with down-tilted head and flowing hair. It was her goddess, Breyid, in violet crystal; the protector and healer.

'D'you think this will ever end?' Serenis asked, on the

seventh day. They were sitting together, resting their backs against the tunnel wall as they took their brief lunch break. The tunnel was head high and supported by wooden struts. Their lanterns, hanging on poles that they'd stuck into the earth, cast overlapping circles of light on the rugged walls. They'd been working ten yards further along than the others, so they were alone. 'I've been thinking about what Beorwyn said. You know, that the King is doing this for the best and we should be happy to serve him, blah blah blah.'

'Well?' said Ysomir. Serenis's face and hands were smudged with dirt. Ysomir had ceased to be fastidious about eating with soiled fingers.

'I don't believe it. The King doesn't know, or he doesn't care. Either way, we've been lied to.'

'But when did the lies start?' Ysomir said softly.

Serenis sighed. She sat forward, rubbing her back, then jumped to her feet. 'All I know is that I've got to go for a piss. This cold does dreadful things to me.'

'Don't bother going all the way back to the privy,' said Ysomir. 'Just go further down the tunnel.'

Serenis hesitated, looking into the pitch-black mouth that lay beyond the bend on which they were working. 'Nah. I'd rather have a nice long walk.'

She grabbed her lantern and set off towards the privy, which was near the mine's entrance. Ysomir heard Lath and others greeting her as she passed them.

Alone, Ysomir leaned her head back and tried to rest for the few minutes she had left.

'Human,' a voice whispered, right by her ear. 'Don't be afraid. I'm a friend.'

She nearly hit the tunnel roof in shock. Her heart bounced, her head snapped round to see a little greyish figure standing beside her. He was human in form but less than two feet high, muscular and naked, with a head of thick black hair.

'Don't cry out,' he whispered in a strange-sounding,

reedy voice. His face was round and flat-featured, with enormous dark eyes. But they shone with intelligence, and his expression was wholly human; anxious, vulnerable. As her lantern-light moved over his skin, she saw that he was not grey but silvery. 'Please. I need your help.'

'Who are you?'

'I am of the Zampharei, whom humans call Subterraneans or – when they are feeling less respectful – maggots. Whatever you have heard of us, it's not true.'

'I've heard nothing,' Ysomir said, her mouth suddenly dry. 'I've heard people use the word "maggots" – I'm sorry if it offends you – but no one said what it meant.'

The Subterranean slipped his tiny hand into hers. His fingers felt amazingly strong, but he was too small and slender to offer any danger. He stirred her compassion as would a child. 'Please help me,' he said.

'What's wrong?'

'My friend has had an accident. He is down there—' the tiny man pointed into the darkness of the tunnel, where Serenis had refused to go. 'I can't lift him.'

'Wait, I'll get someone else to come with us—'

'No. I don't trust the other humans. But I trust you. You look kind.'

Nervously, Ysomir got to her feet and picked up her lantern. But she hesitated.

'If you help me now,' the Subterranean said, 'I will help you later. You don't want to be in this place, do you? I will help you escape.'

Hope thrilled through her. 'But not just me. My friends—'

'Never mind them now. Come, quickly! I will show you a wonder.'

The silver figure took her hand and led her swiftly along the tunnel. A few yards on it came to a dead end, but he led her instead into a rounded side-passage that was too small to have been carved out by humans. He trotted along upright, but Ysomir was forced to bend double. The passage angled downhill, snaking this way and that. Despite the cold, she grew hot with anxiety.

'What happened to your friend?' she asked.

A long pause. 'Ah. A fall. You will see.'

For five minutes – which seemed much longer – they wound through the passage. Ysomir felt a growing urge to turn back; if she was late starting work, she would be punished. Then the passage opened unexpectedly on to a round chamber. As Ysomir straightened up in relief, her lantern-light danced on the walls and she gasped in amazement.

Every surface was covered in huge, sparkling amethysts. It was as if they'd stepped into the heart of a geode. Their jutting points dug into her feet; they flowed over the walls and clustered on the roof, reflecting a thousand shining hues of purple and lavender with every shift of the light.

'It's beautiful!'

'There is no beauty greater,' said the Subterranean. As he stepped away with his back to her, she saw that his thick black hair grew over his shoulders and down his spine.

She looked around for his injured companion, saw nothing. 'But where's your friend?'

'Oh, that was just a story I told to bring you down here.' He turned nimbly to face her, his eyes gleaming like jet.

'Why?'

'I said I would show you a wonder.'

She watched him, feeing ever more uneasy yet unable to tear herself away. She didn't want to seem rude, or cowardly. 'Thank you, it *is* wonderful, but I should go.'

'Of course, but as you've so kindly come this far with me, do me the courtesy of listening for a moment.' There was an edge to his voice that alarmed her, rooting her there. He touched the wall, caressing a thick, pointed shaft of crystal. 'These are our kindred spirits, all the crystals and stones, base and precious. They are the eggs of the earth;

221

they give birth to beauty, magic and spirit-connection. But they are more, far more than humans can ever know. Every stone has its own energy, its spirit, its *roth*. It has lain buried in the earth for such aeons as you cannot comprehend. If you rip it from the earth it suffers! Did you know that?'

'No,' said Ysomir. 'Suffers . . .?'

The child-like friendliness of his voice transformed into a malevolent rasp. 'Do you care? Do you hear its screams of agony as you tear it from the body of its mother the earth – from its companions who have resonated with it for millions of years? Do you feel its anguish? My people do. Every stone you murder, we share its pain.'

Ysomir looked frantically at the mouth of the passageway, feeling trapped and desperate.

'Only my people are meant to mine the stone,' he went on. 'It has always been so. Only we, the Zampherai, have the knowledge and the permission of the stones themselves. We know how to take them gently, without damaging their matrix or the spirit within; we know how to heal the earth afterwards. And if the stone gives not permission, then we leave it in peace. Would you know to do as much?'

She shook her head. 'I'm sorry. But I don't want to be here, I didn't know—'

His mouth opened in a grimace. His teeth glittered; she saw that they had tiny points, and his eyes blazed with malice. 'Trespassers, all of you! My people have always been the miners of the Nine Realms – until you humans grew too greedy and impatient to deal with us. Humans came to us from your King. They said they wanted gem stones and honey marble for a monument – but they wanted too much at once. The earth could not have withstood such an onslaught. Always in the past humans have acted on our advice, but not this time. They would not listen. They had not the patience to wait; they had no intention of recompensing us. Instead they decided to rob the earth and us, to breach the treaty by which we have operated for hundreds of years. When we refused to deal with them, they came with their army of slaves and took what they wanted anyway. They are raping us. Raping the earth. They are stabbing the body of the Mother through the very heart!'

He turned to Ysomir, pointing a silver sharp finger at her. '*You* are raping us. For that crime . . . this.'

He looked up at the sparkling roof as if listening; there was a pause. She half-turned to flee, but he said, 'Don't run, unless you want to die.'

As he spoke she heard the explosion.

A heavy thud like a thunderclap, muffled yet painful to her ears. The whole cavern shuddered, throwing her on to the floor. The sharp facets of the crystals bruised her in a dozen places. Her lantern went out. Then came a sinister rumble that swelled, died away, swelled again; and into the cavern came a rush of air and dust, mingled with the stench of smoke, raw earth, and unknown miasmas. She lay coughing, unable to move.

'There are dangers in these mines,' said the voice of the silver man above her. 'There are pockets of bad air that burst into fire. None should come down here who know not the dangers; for the Zampherai will turn the dangers against trespassers until you are all gone. Go back and warn them!'

The voice grew faint and ceased. When Ysomir looked up, she was in pitch blackness.

'Hello? Are you there?'

No answer. Shaken and in panic, she climbed swaying to her feet and began to pick her way to the entrance. The air choked her; she felt that she would be lost underground, die for lack of air. That was surely what the Subterranean had intended.

There was no Beorwyn to protect her now.

She staggered along worm-hole passage, feeling her way along the walls, testing the ground cautiously before each step. 'Is anyone there? Help me!'

She thought she heard voices whispering, swirling along past her at waist height; she pressed herself back against the wall. Then all was quiet, but for a sound like dry rain. After a while she realised what the sound was. Particles were falling from the roof, pattering onto her head and hands.

The thought of being buried alive petrified her. She broke into a run, heedless of what lay ahead, coughing on the stench. At least she could breathe. A cold, clean draught was blowing from somewhere, and she saw a faint glow.

The light grew stronger as she came to the end of the passage and turned into the main tunnel. She'd found her way back! Her heart leapt with relief. And then she came round the bend – where she and Serenis had been sitting less than fifteen minutes earlier – and saw the source of the light.

Where she and her companions had been working, there was a heap of rubble and a ragged hole, above and to her left, through which winter daylight fell. The explosion had torn out the side of the hill. Directly in front of her, where the tunnel should have been, there was only a great heap of churned clay and rock.

Her hand flew to her mouth. Sick disbelief held her there, frozen.

Finding her voice, Ysomir shouted and shouted for her friends. She stuck her hands in the clay and tried to dig, tearing her fingernails, finding nothing but clods of earth and stone. Finally an answer came from somewhere above.

'Stop yelling, you idiot! Get out before the rest caves in!'

She looked up and saw a thin figure climbing up towards the light, pausing to call out to her. It was Lath. She felt the ground shaking, the patter of earth becoming a deluge, and she ran to the collapsed side wall and began to climb over the rubble towards the hole.

Rocks and earth slid beneath her. Her arms and legs

ached viciously. But above her was the bleached, icy light and she climbed towards it until, mud-soaked and gasping for breath, she emerged from the ruined mine.

There was a big group of people standing around the hole on the hillside. Lath gave her his hand and they helped each other over the churned, trembling ground. As they staggered clear, she looked back to see the edges of the hole falling in, the whole rubble pile sliding backwards to fill the shaft, like a mouth swallowing itself.

'No,' she said, choked by sobs. She looked around wildly, but could see no familiar faces. 'Didn't the others get out?'

'Just you and me,' said Lath. Loosing her hand, he reeled away from her and sat down in the mud with his head in his hands. But Ysomir was too shocked to comfort him.

'But Serenis might not have been buried,' she said. She spoke to no one in particular and no one answered her. 'She went up to the entrance, she might have escaped . . .' Ysomir began to walk through the crowd, in one direction and then another, hoping that by a miracle she would find her friend. She passed close to a knot of officers, including Teseyna and the commander, but they took no notice of her.

'Third time this had happened,' the commander was saying furiously. 'The maggots cause these explosions, the little bastards. If you slugs were more vigilant—'

Teseyna pointed. 'There!' she said.

Ysomir turned, glimpsed a small silver-grey figure with a mop of black hair, peering at the officers from behind a rock. Gloating? It didn't look quite the same as the one that had lured her into the cavern, but she couldn't be sure. It was hardly visible against the mud, but two men were already running towards it, swords drawn. The Subterranean ducked down, but too late. One of the soldiers grabbed the creature by its shoulders, lifted it bodily into the air and flung it on to the ground near the officers, so that it was in full view of everyone. As it tried to get up, the commander swung his sword at the creature's neck.

Ysomir could not look away in time. She saw the sword connect, heard the sickening crunch of blade through bone, saw the matted black head go flying and the body crumple with blood fountaining from the neck stump. She staggered away, doubled up with disgust. How did this brutality wipe out the Zampherai's crime?

'Every damn one of them,' the commander shouted savagely. 'Every one of those bastard maggots you come across, kill it!' He stood, face distorted, chest heaving. 'Now. Details for digging that lot out.' He poked his thumb towards the mine. 'I want this section operational again within two days. Those maggots are not getting the better of us.'

Hours later, when the last of the bodies was being dug out, Ysomir was still haunting the hillside. Almost everyone had helped in the excavation, but most had now gone to their quarters. Lath had been taken to the sick bay. A freezing rain was falling, but she no longer felt cold. She walked back and forth over the clods of mud and there – as the rain washed the caked soil from the line of corpses – she found Serenis at last.

Ysomir fell to her knees, stroking her friend's cold flesh, weeping uncontrollably.

'Why couldn't I save you? What am I going to do without you? Serenis, Serenis, don't leave me.'

Her fingers found the precious locket, and she took it from around her friend's neck. The crystals from which it was made, she assumed, had been lifted gently from the earth by a Zampherai's sympathetic fingers. She would never look at any jewel in the same way after this. She opened it and looked at the face of Serenis's sweetheart, who would now never see his love again. He looked a little like Lynden. Only a little.

'I'll keep this for you, Serenis,' she said, slipping it into

226

her pocket. 'I'll keep it safe. It's all I've got of you now. I'll go and tell Lath I found you. I suppose he already knows, but I'll tell him anyway. Goodbye, love, Mahaa take you gently into the arms of Nuth. Breyid and Anthar bless—'

Cruel fingers dug into her arms, dragged her upright and shook her. It was Teseyna. The officer's face was caked with clay, her hair damp and straggling, her expression ferocious.

'Where the hell have you been, you little shit?'

'Here, all the time—'

Another shake, a shove. Drained of strength, Ysomir fell to her hand and knees and received a kick in the leg. 'Get up, slug. Commander wants to see you.'

Ysomir stood before the commander in his small, bare office. She was so exhausted she could hardly stand up, so flattened by grief that she felt like a figure made of paper, unreal. Teseyna had left them alone.

'Aynie-daughter,' he said. Sitting behind a makeshift desk, in the light of a single candle, he too looked tired and aged by the day's events, though no less intimidating. 'You escaped the explosion.'

'I – I survived it, sir.'

'How?'

Her voice nearly failing with tiredness and fear, she told him about the Subterranean, repeating everything she could remember the silver man saying. The commander listened with steepled hands and unfeeling, narrow eyes. 'He – he asked me to warn you that – that they will go on sabotaging the mining until it stops.'

'So, you come to me as the maggots' mouthpiece. I might almost think you were siding with them.'

'No! They killed my friend. But—'

He leaned forward. 'But?'

He knew he was frightening her, and seemed to be enjoying it. *It's probably the only fun he's had all day.* Ysomir heard the words as if Serenis had spoken them.

227

And suddenly she was no longer frightened, but angry. 'How many more people must die before you stop? You say we're serving the King but does he know about this, or the conditions you make us work in? You can't go on plundering stone out of the ground like this. It's breaking the Xauroma. I can't, I won't do it any more. I don't care what you do to me.'

She braced herself for a violent response, but his mouth crimped in amusement and he shook his head. 'Oh, we're an expert on the Xauroma, are we? That's a big word for a peasant from the arse-end of Sepheret. Aynie-daughter, you've told me nothing new. I hear it every damn time something like this happens. Threats, terrorism – we'd be fools to give in to it. That maggot lied to you. The real truth is this. The maggots have had a monopoly on mining in Aventuria for centuries. They have earned fortunes and held the human race to ransom over it. It was time for it to end. Spirits in the stones? Bullshit. All they're sore at is having a little fair and healthy competition.'

'I don't believe that.'

'So. Sympathising with terrorists. Refusing to work. And then there's this.'

He took something from a drawer and placed it on the desk in front of her. In dismay, Ysomir saw that it was her carving of Breyid.

'Did you carve this?'

She nodded, wondering what she was being accused of.

'It's very good.'

'Give it to me!' she hissed in sudden distress. Seeing his thick fingers curved possessively around her goddess, she felt violated. She made a grab for the figure but he snatched it out of her reach.

'Ah-ah. Temper. We have all had a difficult day.'

'What gives you the right to go searching through my private belongings?'

'This is failure to disclose information. Why didn't you tell anyone you could do this?'

'I did!' she said. 'I told them in Riverwynde and I wish I hadn't. That's why they took me!'

'Well, no one told me. Typical. You were supposed to restate your skills to each change of guard detail.'

'No one told us. I thought the officers knew everything.'

'If only.' His eyes were taunting. 'Lumps of raw stone like the one you used for this are worth money. You must have stolen it.'

'A guard gave it to me, I didn't know.'

'Ignorance is no defence. Stealing is a very serious crime.'

'And you are not stealing these rocks from the earth in the first place?'

He stood up, his chair scraping on the bare boards. He towered over her and despite her defiant words, she felt sick with fear. 'The maggots can't presume to know better than the King what's best for Aventuria, now, can they? And neither can we.'

She stared at the edge of his desk. When his hand fell onto her arm, she came near to collapsing with dread. But he only lifted her hand and pressed the carving into it. 'Keep it. A going-away gift. For all the punishments you've earned, you're a privileged woman, Aynie-daughter.'

She glared at him, her eyes questioning. 'How so?'

'I've no further use for you, but I've been instructed that they need more stone carvers in the city.' His gaze, meeting hers, was sardonic, displeased, yet bitterly amused. 'Get out of my sight. Sleep. Tomorrow you're being sent to Parione.'

229

Chapter Eleven. Lady Amitriya

The lamp-light flashed on the metal of Calamys's sword, glinted in his hard, demanding eyes. Rufryd glanced around for a weapon, but his own knife was on the far side of the room, stuck in his belt which was hanging over the back of a chair. It would have been little use against a sword, in any case. Pheilan looked less sure of himself, but that might make him more impulsive than Calamys. It would be foolish to try anything; Rufryd knew he'd only end up dead or wounded. Furious, all he could do was to put himself in front of Tanthe and Lynden.

'Speak,' said Calamys. 'Peasants from Havereyn do not wander about in Ardharkria. Who are you?'

'Might as well tell him,' said Lynden.

'Why should we?' Tanthe exclaimed. 'This is a free country, you can't threaten us like this!'

Calamys sneered. 'I can do whatever I please in my own house.'

'We've got nothing to hide,' Lynden said flatly. 'My betrothed, Tanthe's sister, was conscripted. We're trying to find her and take her home. That's all. Everything else we told you was true, except about going to Skald.'

'So, you are acting contrary to a Royal decree.'

'Yes,' said Lynden. 'Wouldn't you?'

Tanthe put in, 'Your own brother was carrying a warning against complying with the conscriptions! Where did that come from, if not this household?'

'Arhan's actions were nothing to do with the rest of us. But you three . . .' his gaze raked over them. 'We hear rumours that our local Registat, Beyne, was shot by three renegades answering your description. What do you think? Shall I hand you over to the authorities in Skald? Or shall I save you all that misery and kill you now?'

The sword twitched in Calamys's hand. Rufryd tensed. If he could seize the bed-cover, fling it over Calamys and Pheilan, disarm them in the confusion – then, he thought, we'll have to flee, with no time to take Flame and Gazer, nor even our cloaks and bows. But that was preferable to letting this sneering aristocrat butcher them all.

Pheilan stood squarely in front of the door, expressionless but wide-eyed. Calamys came closer. His sword tip danced near Rufryd's throat; Rufryd swallowed his anger and didn't flinch. His lordship was a bully, and the dreadful thing was that Rufryd recognised himself. The tip touched Tanthe's throat, then Lynden's. They all held their ground and stared defiantly at him.

'You saw,' said Calamys, meeting Lynden's gaze, 'nothing in the forest.'

'I know what I—'

'No.' The sword-tip drew a pin-prick of blood from Lynden's throat. You saw *nothing*. Understand?'

'What are you afraid of?' Lynden said through his teeth.

The blade pressed harder, denting his skin; he turned pale.

Rufryd couldn't take any more. He had to act. Tanthe squeezed his arm, as if she knew and was trying to hold him back – then someone pounded on the door. Pheilan started forward, almost jumping into the air. Calamys turned, cursing, lowering his blade.

'Who's that?' he whispered. 'Quiet, don't let them in!'

'Calamys!' came a female voice. The latch rattled. 'I know you're there. Open this door!'

Pheilan quickly sheathed his sword and turned the key. Calamys hissed, 'I told you not to—' but it was too late, Lady Amitriya came bursting into the room like a small blue and silver whirlwind. Her hair was wild, her face hawkish with rage.

231

'What in Nephenie's name do you think you are doing, you idiotic pair of rogues?'

'Teaching them. Warning them. Aunt, this is nothing to do with you!'

'Is it not? Leave our guests alone!'

To Rufryd's pleasure, she ignored Calamys's blade and clipped her nephew across the side of the head. He ducked away, reddening.

'Get out!' she growled. 'Put that blade away. Never unsheath it inside the house; how many times were you taught that? I will deal with this.'

Glowering, Calamys thrust his sword into its sheath and stomped out, followed by his brother. Tanthe immediately began fussing over the blood on Lynden's neck but he pushed her away, saying, 'It's nothing. It itches, that's all.'

Lady Amitriya stood glaring at them. Light from the corridor made her hair a feathery halo, and there was a touch of insanity in her eyes. Calamys held no fear for Rufryd; this tiny woman was more unnerving by far.

'All we asked of your household was care for my brother,' Rufryd said. 'We've done you no harm. What in the gods' names have we done to deserve this?'

'You've broken the taboo,' said Lady Amitriya. 'You *never* speak of what's in Ardharkria. Understand?'

'No,' said Rufryd.

'Go to sleep.' Her sheath-like robe billowed as she turned. 'Calamys won't trouble you again tonight, I promise.'

At breakfast, it was as if nothing had happened.

They were invited to eat with the family as they had the night before, as if they were still welcome guests, and the Duke and Duchess treated them as politely as they would a visiting party of nobles. The Duchess even patted Lynden on the arm, asked him, 'How are you feeling today, dear?' and constantly made sure that he was eating enough.

Only Lord Calamys's veneer of civility had any touch of falseness about it to Tanthe's sharp senses. He stabbed fruit with his knife then offered it to them with a suggestive gleam in his eyes, as if presenting them with their own, dripping hearts.

The previous night, they had all three slept in Lynden's voluminous bed, Rufryd in the centre, he and Tanthe taking it in turns to keep watch. But no one disturbed them. Once, when Rufryd had briefly kissed her on the lips, Lynden – whom they'd thought was asleep – had said, 'Don't even think about it,' making them laugh.

Now Tanthe decided to play the family's game and made polite conversation. Rufryd did so too, but his tone was laced with sarcasm and he seemed determined to act more of a yokel than he really was. Lynden remained silent throughout the meal.

Afterwards, Lynden rested, Rufryd went to the stables, and Lord Dannion invited Tanthe to see his library. It was like entering a breathtaking hall of wonders, containing treasures she'd only dreamed of seeing. Lord Dannion, seeming pleased to find an enthusiastic student, showed her pristine copies of Saphaeyender that she'd never seen, with exquisite illuminations; plays and poems she'd longed to read, writers she'd never even heard of. Entranced, she forgot the incidents of the previous night; even, very nearly, forgot the purpose of their journey.

She liked Lord Dannion, but his inner self was unapproachable. She dared not talk to him of anything but literature.

In the afternoon, Rufryd came to find her, bringing with him the ripe scent of the stables and cold air on his clothes. 'Lynden's much better today,' he said. He spoke quietly, trying not to attract the attention of Lord Dannion, who was reading at a table by the window. 'He's been looking at the horses with me. We should think about leaving first thing tomorrow.'

Tanthe, who had been immersed in *Eskadale*, tore herself back to reality. 'Yes. Flame and Gazer should be well rested by now, too.'

Lord Dannion interrupted, clearing his throat. 'I am not certain that you can leave.'

'What?' said Rufryd.

'You will have to consult Lord Calamys on that matter.'

Amazed, Tanthe began, 'But, your lordship, you don't have any reason to keep us here, surely—'

'Speak to my son. I have nothing else to say on the matter. Sorry—' the last word dissolved into another croaky *harrumph* as Lord Dannion buried himself once more in his book.

'We're going to have problems,' Rufryd said. He, Tanthe and Lynden stood looking over the door into Flame's stall, while Gazer sat on the cobblestones beside them. Dusk was gathering into a clear, chill evening. 'They don't want us to leave.'

'Because I mentioned the Bhahdradomen?' said Lynden. 'Gods, I wish this had never happened. If you two hadn't started screwing each other—'

'Hey, don't blame us!' Tanthe cried. 'You and Rufe arguing about your father had quite a lot to do with it, I seem to remember!'

'Whatever,' Rufryd said blackly. 'We're stuck here now. Calamys is just waiting for us to try, so he's got an excuse to slaughter us.'

'We could go now,' said Lynden. 'While they're not expecting it.'

'Not that easy,' said Rufryd. 'The gate to the courtyard is locked. Calamys has riders constantly patrolling the hillside, when he isn't out there himself. Our bows have been put in the weapon store and we have to ask before we can get them back. Besides, even if we escape from him, he'll get the authorities in Skald to send someone after us instead.'

'Then we'll have to use cunning instead of brute force,' said Tanthe, patting his shoulder.

Rufryd grimaced at her. 'Enough of the snide remarks, if you want any sex tonight.'

'Ooh, threats, is it?' Tanthe grinned.

Lynden rolled his eyes and said impatiently. 'Well, have either of you got any bright ideas?'

'At least we know where we stand with Calamys,' said Tanthe. 'It's the others who worry me. The way they are so nice, but won't talk about anything that really matters. I think we should lull them a bit to start with. You could have a bit of a relapse, Lyn, so they think we wouldn't even dream of leaving for a few days. Meanwhile, we look for gaps we can slip through.'

'This is hopeless,' said Rufryd.

Tanthe felt a spurt of her old anger at him. 'Until you think of a better suggestion, just keep quiet!' She turned away from them, crossed the courtyard, and strode back into the house on her own. She was frustrated, anxious, and annoyed that neither she nor Rufryd could come up with some bold means of escape.

The house was dark and quiet; she was growing to dislike its eeriness. The family lived in little pockets of light, and half the time there was no one to be found at all. Her footsteps rang as she walked down a long, dusty corridor. She thought she would go back to the library . . .

A hand closed on her arm, causing her heart to bound violently with shock. Dizzy, she span round to find Lady Amitriya in a small doorway, clutching at her. The old woman's face was intent, and despite her bird-like frame there seemed a terrible and frightening power about her.

'Come with me.'

'I was, er, going to the library.'

'Never mind that. I need you. Come!'

It was the last thing Tanthe wanted to do, but she dared not refuse. The Lady Amitriya sent her ahead through the doorway, up a claustrophobic stone stairway that she thought would never end. The only light came from the afternoon dusk filtering through small embrasures. At last they came out onto a round wooden landing, and Tanthe realised they were part-way up one of the towers.

Above their heads, the top section rose dizzily for another fifty feet. The walls were painted white, but discoloured and flaking with age. Another spiral staircase led upwards, set to one side of the tower and made of black wrought iron, rusted and fragile in appearance.

'I'll go first,' the Lady said. 'Don't look so worried, dear, it's perfectly safe.'

She led the way up the iron stairs, which creaked and swayed alarmingly as they climbed. Tanthe clung to the cold rail, trying not to notice how the restraining bolts moved freely in and out of the crumbling plaster. The tower was tall and cold. As they neared the top, she saw a hatch above her head, and through it a patch of blue-grey sky. What if she was to be imprisoned up there? What if the stair structure collapsed, stranding them both in the turret?

Lady Amitriya reached the top and stepped on to a wooden floor, turning to give Tanthe a hand up. As she followed, Tanthe saw that the turret was roofed by a dome of glass, and three-quarters filled by an imposing structure of brass. There was a thick cylinder, resting on a base, with thin struts curving around it on different planes.

Tanthe had no idea what it was. She'd thought her books had taught her all she needed to know, but after her recent humiliation she was no longer sure of anything.

'What – what is it?'

'I'll show you, dear. First, look at the view.'

Tanthe drew a breath of amazement. The roof of the house was below them. The dome offered an astonishing panorama of the landscape beyond.

It was magical. She had never seen such a view before. It seemed the whole realm was laid out before her, in fold upon fold of hills and forests, shimmering in misty tints of greyish-violet and bloomed with silver by the subtle lights of the sky. One side of the sky was still flushed with red, and all three moons had risen. Leaf Moon was full; Rose and Lily in their waxing crescents, casting the faintest multiple shadows so that every feature seemed to have infinite depth and complexity.

Tears stung her eyes. She pressed her face to the glass, her breath misting its cold surface. 'Aventuria,' she said.

'Yes,' said Lady Amitriya. 'But now, look through here.'

She beckoned Tanthe to one end of the brass cylinder, and made her put her eye to a small cup shaped eyepiece. Tanthe squinted, trying to focus. Then she gasped aloud.

A new revelation. One small section of the forest rushed towards her, in incredible closeness and detail. She could see individual branches, even the last leaves clinging in clusters to denuded twigs.

'A telescope,' said Amitriya. 'Mine. I wanted you to understand.'

'What?'

'How perfect is this land. How precious. How unthinkable it would be to lose it, either through greed or fear. Here . . .' She guided Tanthe's right hand to a protrusion on the side. 'Turn this knob to adjust the focus. Now look.'

She tilted the cylinder, and now Tanthe found Rose Moon filling the whole of her field of vision. No longer a flat disc, it was a sphere floating in the sky, with the most incredible patterns etching its surface. Not merely patterns but mountains and craters and a webbing of veins that must surely be rivers . . .

Amitriya helped her swing across to study Leaf Moon. It was a smooth sphere with colours like bruises under ice, subtle tints of green that were hardly there at all when she saw it so close. And Lily Moon, purest brilliant white, with even brighter starbursts that exploded outwards in criss-crossed lines. It was like marble, like opal, too perfect to be real.

She stepped away from the telescope, tears blurring her eyes. 'This is the most amazing instrument.'

'Lenses of purest, clear rock crystal,' said Amitriya. 'I polished them myself. Years of work, it took me to build

237

this. "Miraculous are the fruits of the earth, all the fiery jewels and formless stones therein."'

'Saphaeyender,' said Tanthe, smiling.

'There's more to see,' said the Lady, pulling her down towards the eyepiece again. 'Look to the eastern horizon.'

'It's dark.' An ink-line of hills, a silver-dusted sky.

'But far beyond it lie the Whiteveil mountains. You have heard of them, I take it?'

'Of course.' Tanthe knew they would have to brave those mountains to reach Parione.

'Beautiful but wild, savage, unforgiving. You should go soon, if you want to cross them before winter. Now—' Before Tanthe could challenge her remarks, Amitriya swung the telescope downwards.

'Ardharkria,' she said. 'Tell me what you see.'

'Forest,' said Tanthe, slowly moving the cylinder, studying the endless undulating spread of trees. Their branches were stark but eerily lovely in the moons' light. And then there was a patch of darkness.

She was past it before she realised she'd seen it. She eased the telescope back, adjusting the focus. There was an irregular shadow within the forest, roughly oval but with many protruding arms, where the trees were dead and there was no undergrowth. That was why it appeared so dark; the bare soil showed through the naked trees. The area was a stain spreading on the forest.

Something about it struck revulsion through her heart. She had a flashback of being dragged back into the earth, buried. 'What is it?' she exclaimed, jerking away from the telescope.

Amitriya peered through, then straightened up again.

'That is the thing we don't talk about.'

'Where the—' she could hardly bring herself to say the word, 'where the Bhahdradomen are.'

A low, disturbing chuckle came from Amitriya's throat. 'That's it, my dear. Where the Bhahdradomen *aren't*.'

'So Lynden wasn't imagining things.'

'I wish he were. I wish he were.'

Tanthe stood leaning on the telescope, trying to get her breath. She felt overwhelmed by strange emotions, mostly fear.

'I don't understand. I thought they were exiled from Aventuria. What are they doing there?'

'You must never tell any of the family that we have had this conversation. But I am going to tell you the truth now.'

Tanthe went to the window and looked at the stain – which she would never have noticed without the telescope, but which she now couldn't miss – as Amitriya spoke.

'They have been there for as long as I remember. Yes, they masquerade as the Leyholmen, a harmless wood-cutting people, to any who should accidentally stumble upon them. But some, like your Lynden, see them for what they are. It's a miracle he escaped with his life.'

'My hound knew as well,' Tanthe said softly.

'If the truth be told, we all know. That's why Ardharkria is so dreaded. But many of us are not allowed to admit it. Dare not admit it.'

'Why are they there?'

'I cannot say for sure. But it is my belief that when the War of the Silver Plains ended, the peace treaty had secret clauses. The Bhahdradomen were allowed more than their barren land across the Straits of Vexat. They were allowed to keep certain small pockets of land within Aventuria itself. As long as they abided by the treaty and did not stray beyond the agreed boundaries, they were allowed to stay.'

'I can't believe it,' said Tanthe.

'What do you know about them?'

'Not much,' she admitted. 'Just that they were a dreadful and terrifying enemy. Look what they did to Lynden!'

'Do you know the Creation story?'

'Yes,' said Tanthe. 'My grandmother Helwyn taught it to me. She's our priestess.'

'It's so old that no one knows who wrote it. But it has some lines near the end that I'll wager you've never heard.' Then Amitriya began to recite the story, and the rhythm of her voice, while the night darkened behind her small, wild silhouette, filled Tanthe with an awe she would never forget.

> Before the beginning of all things
> There was only Nuth
> And Nuth was the blackness of the universe
> And Nuth was the silence of the universe
> But in the immeasurable void
> Before time began
> Nuth was lonely.
> She looked into the void
> Which was as a mirror to Her soul
> And She fell in love with Her own reflection.
> She separated Her reflection from Herself
> And saw that He was the other half of Herself
> And She named Him Anuth
> And their love created time.
> From their passion blazed forth
> The fiery sun
> And the stars of the firmament
> Then from Her body Nuth brought forth the moons
> Great and cold
> And She brought forth the earth
> Blue with oceans, green with forests.
> And She brought forth the crystals of the earth
> Of all Her children the most perfect
> Full of fiery energy, yet everlasting.
> Then She gave birth to the Aelyr
> Who were proud and loved Her not.
> And at last She brought forth humans
> Quick and frail, to teem the earth
> Alone of all Her children returning
> The love of their Great Mother

Then Nuth rested.
All that is, comes from Nuth and Anuth
Even the Eaters, the mimics
Not from Her womb; not with love did She create them
But from matter She threw aside.
A nub of clay, left over from earth
She rolled between Her fingers and discarded
But it became an egg
And from it crawled the Eaters
And away into the swamp they crawled
For all She touches is filled with life.

Amitriya stopped. Tanthe filled in the remaining lines, and Amitriya joined in again, so they spoke them together.

All came from Nuth
And at the end of time
All shall go back to Her
And Her great black wings
Encircle Her children returning
To the great black circle
Of Her womb.

They were quiet for a moment. Then Tanthe said, 'I take it the "Eaters" are the Bhahdradomen. No, I've never heard those lines before.'

'Whether or not you believe they are literally true, they are a way of explaining how a race so inimical to our own came into being. Nuth made them. Mistake or not, they are part of the earth.'

'But she didn't give birth to them. They came from a bit of dirt she flicked away.'

'Indeed. But my dear, that is the attempt of a primitive poet to make sense of the inexplicable. We don't really know where the Bhahdradomen came from. They claim to have been in Aventuria first. If that is so, then where were they when humans first formed tribes, and began to

241

settle the land? They are liars, of course.'

'"The earth was wild in those days",' said Tanthe. 'I keep finding that line in history books. I always wondered what it meant.'

Amitriya's answer sent strange flickers through Tanthe; parts of the story she knew, others she'd never heard before yet she seemed to recall them like a long-forgotten dream. 'In the ancient days the earth ran with fire; mountains erupted, rock flowed like molten gold. It was the sentient energies of the earth raging jealously against the rise of the new, quick life-sparks that were animals and humans. The earth raged for thousands of years, so the legends tell us. Meanwhile, the Aelyr – who are like us in shape yet different, so far ahead of us in knowledge and wisdom – take credit for taming the earth. They learned the secrets of the earth's myriad *roths*, its energy-forms, and calmed them, and made bargains that would enable both mankind and Aelyr to live here in peace. Now, did they do it out of the goodness of their hearts, or to exert their magical prowess? I incline to the latter view. For it is said that in the early days, the people of Eisilion worshipped the Aelyr as gods, but the Aelyr came from their own realm, which some call Verdanholm, and they descended on Eisilion in fury and destroyed their temples and smashed the sacred statues. So ever after, the people of Eisilion have viewed the Aelyr as demons.'

'I never knew that,' said Tanthe. 'Why did the Aelyr do it?'

'I don't know,' Amitriya said tersely. 'They never were in the habit of explaining themselves.'

'My mother said that the people of Sepheret were once close to the Aelyr. Friends. I can't believe it; they seem so elusive – "not safe", my mum said – but is it true?'

Amitriya's thin mouth twisted. 'So I've heard. I know they are real; I have seen them myself, and I have met those who have spoken with them. But condescending and distrustful of humans – oh, greatly so. You must have

242

read of the days before the Realms, when humans lived as tribes and wandered freely across the land?'

'Of course,' said Tanthe. 'And how they began to form settlements, and give names to their lands, but so long ago that no one can be sure when it actually happened. But they only knew peace, until the warlike tribes came down from Torith Mir and tried to conquer them. Mounicaa and Arbal were two of the first names recorded in history, the first leaders to unite the tribes and drive the invaders back to Torith Mir. The first Queen and King, I suppose.'

'The first heroes, at least.' Amitriya nodded. 'Then there was Maroc, as infamous as they were famous, for he was said to have fled the fighting and taken his people to the south, where they founded Azura Maroc. And their first city, Lapiszul, was the birthplace of ancient wisdom.' Amitriya's eyes shone and she caressed the telescope. 'The first astronomers were there, who looked at the sky not only in wonder but in the determination to understand the rhythms of the sun and moons and stars. It's said that the Aelyr aided them. The citizens of Parione are secretly still a little jealous of the Azura Marocians. They wish to believe that civilisation was born in Parione, but it is not so; Parione is great, but Lapiszul was first.

'The other realms came slowly into being, spreading out from the south and the centre. After Paranios, Mithrain with its lakes and watery elementals, then Eisilion and Noreya, and later Deirland and great Thanmandrathor. Noreya, the realm of trees, was constantly raided by Torith Mir, land of dead forests; and although Maroc had been branded a coward, it was in the end the Azura Marocians who brought Torith Mir to heel. Not through war, but through trade. Torith Mir, for all its savage landscape, was rich in amber and jet and precious stones. Parione itself was first established on the trade route from Azura Maroc to the north, which ran through the fertile golden bowl of Paranios. And Silana was Parione's first Queen, and she it was who turned it from a settlement to a great city.

243

'But while all this went on, Sepheret was still a wild land of tribal hunters, followers of the ancient stag god. This realm was remote, and had no name, no ruler. Now, there was a man who had worked hard for Queen Silana and performed many heroic acts on her behalf, so she decided to reward him with a kingdom of his own. His name was Sepher. She gave him this land, and he named it after himself, and he and his family and many, many folk from Paranios and Mithrain came here and began to build towns and farm the land. And that is how my family came to be here; we are King Sepher's descendants, now reduced to the rank of Dukes. And the tribes who were already here dwindled and interbred until they were wholly absorbed by the newcomers.'

Tanthe felt a shiver. 'So, was that why the Aelyr of Sepheret withdrew?'

'Not all Aelyr are the same. Perhaps those in particular felt close to the hunters who were one with nature, and resented the invasion of agriculture and villages.'

'But that means I might have Paranian blood!' Tanthe exclaimed. 'Ancestors from Parione!'

Amitriya snorted. 'You almost certainly have, as if there's anything special about it. I suppose the first awareness that not all Aelyr are the same came when the Marocians began to mine in Torith Mir. For the stones were protected by the race called Subterraneans, who in turn were protected by Aelyr. It caused a conflict between the Aelyr of the south and the north. Those of the south, who helped the people of Azura Maroc, supported humankind's right to share in the jewel-fire of the earth, while those in the north, who helped the Subterraneans, opposed it. But the Aelyr of Torith Mir were defeated, and withdrew to Verdanholm, and then the first agreement between Subterraneans and humans was forged, allowing us to take stones from the earth providing the Subterraneans did all the mining. Then for centuries Aventuria flourished, while the friendly rivalry grew between Azura

Maroc and Paranios. The Nine Realms were beautiful, fertile in every way, and peaceful . . . Then came the first invasion of the Bhahdradomen.'

'After the plague,' Tanthe murmured.

'Yes. Azura Maroc's days of glory were ended by the Grey Death. That was when the Bhahdradomen first appeared, although there are stories of them in Aventuria long before then, living disguised among humans until disaster weakened us. It's said, also, that it was the Aelyr who found a cure for the plague. But all the Aelyr received in return from humans was ingratitude.'

'Ingratitude? Why?'

'Obvious, is it not?' said Amitriya. 'Sometimes people do not want to be helped. They want to have saved themselves. I imagine that they had had enough of their faces being rubbed in the superiority of the Aelyr, the constant insinuation that humans could achieve nothing alone. The more the other-race did for us, the angrier we grew with them. As you can see, there has been no single factor in the withdrawal of the Aelyr from this world, but many.

'And again, it's said that the Bhahdradomen, having ruled and defiled Aventuria for three and four hundred years, would never have been defeated without the Aelyr on our side. Yet afterwards, the resentment between our two races grew ever more vitriolic. It was said openly that the Aelyr only fought with us to save their own skins, for they have no love for humans.'

Tanthe was shaken. 'I had no idea there was so much ill-feeling against the Aelyr.'

'It would be terrible, would it not, if the Bhahdradomen came again and the Aelyr, this time, *didn't* help us? They're not obliged to. Treaties were drawn up, forbidding the two races from interfering in each other's affairs.'

'But you don't think the Bhahdradomen will come again . . . do you?'

'Let's look at the facts.' Amitriya seemed almost to be

relishing the conversation. 'The Bhahdradomen, unlike the Aelyr, are inimical to us in every way. They cannot live without destroying all that sustains us. They have no conscience; what they need, they take, and when they decided to gorge themselves upon Aventuria they felt no touch of pity for the humans or animals who lived here. They hate us and they are jealous of us. They brought us to ruin and it was only when the Nine Realms united under Queen Hetys that we found our strength! Yes, the Bhahdradomen were soundly defeated and the survivors driven into Vexor. And yet . . .' She pointed a thin finger at the stain on the forest. 'There they are.'

Tanthe tried to swallow against the dry thickness of her throat. 'I don't know what to say. I never realised how little I knew, until I came here.'

Amitriya squeezed her arm. 'Don't worry. All our knowledge is a spider's web, really. Mostly gaps.'

'That's why I want to go to Parione! To find out what's true and what isn't. I couldn't make people at home understand that.'

Amitriya's eyes glittered, but she seemed to think better of saying anything.

'This is awful.' Tanthe waved a hand at Ardharkria. 'The Bhahdradomen, I mean. I can't believe the King would put us in such danger!'

'Believe that the King is not as perfect as we would all like to think. Ever since the War of the Silver Plains, the monarchs of Aventuria have paid the Dukes and Duchesses of Sepheret to keep quiet about the enemy in their midst. We do not speak of it, not merely because to do so would result in the people being angry and rising against the Duchy and the Bhahdradomen, but because it would also result in us losing a large proportion of our revenue. The whole of Sepheret would be the poorer. And again, we do not speak of it because we are ashamed. And then again, because we are afraid.

'The stain has begun to spread. Oh, the Leyholmen are

quiet and they know their place; they know that if they tried anything, humans would turn on them and destroy them. But even in defeat they are still . . . what they are. The human soul sickens and fails, just to look upon them. They are outgrowing their territory. Their flesh-animals eat everything in their path, leaving nothing but sour, infested soil behind them. They are creeping into fresh areas of the forest, and how can we stop them, so few of us? We have asked the King for help, but our pleas are ignored. This problem, officially, does not exist.'

'Gods,' Tanthe said. 'I don't, I really don't know what to say.'

'We are frightened. Dannion and Alorna and Esamir are terrified. Calamys acts as he does because he, too, is terrified.'

'They've got no reason to keep us here, then.'

'Only that you may spread the knowledge of our shame.'

'What if we promise not to say anything? Why should we? All we want is to find my sister!'

'And meanwhile, to see that—' Amitriya pointed a claw-like finger toward the shadow '– eat the whole of Aventuria? The King will not help us, because the King has lost his mind. It was I, and Arhan, and Pheilan, and a man named Eldareth, who tried to send that warning to the rest of Sepheret. But somehow, the Bhahdradomen knew and they killed Arhan before the message could be delivered. And Dannion and the others, of course, would never have allowed it to be sent in the first place.'

'Gods, I hope we didn't get you into trouble with them!'

'They don't know it was me. They wouldn't do anything if they did. Nothing is discussed, nothing is admitted, do you see?'

'But they—' Tanthe stopped, thinking of the creatures that had appeared from nowhere and killed her uncle. 'You can't be telling me that the King is hand-in-glove with the Bhahdradomen! I don't believe it.'

247

'No, I don't think that he is. Not consciously, at least. But I think something is happening that is out of his control.'

Night had fallen, but the moons' light turned the landscape to one of crisp, shimmering wonder. Tanthe was quiet for a while, looking at the beauty, imagining the stain spreading and turning it all to death. She was conscious of Amitriya's gaze burning into her. 'I feel awful,' she said at length. 'I feel sick. I can't take in what it means. I'm scared.'

'This is just the beginning.'

'What do you want us to do?'

'I'm old, travelling would kill me. You are young and strong. I can get you out of here, if you will promise to do something.'

'What?'

'Help Aventuria. Help stop this.' Tanthe nodded, biting her thumbnail to stop herself weeping, as much that Amitriya had confided in her as anything. She felt a gentle hand on her arm. 'Come, you need a drink. I'll make you something hot and strong.'

'I need it,' Tanthe said as she stepped on to the precarious iron stairs. 'My lady, won't we be in the same danger as Arhan was?'

Amitriya paused and looked beadily at her. 'We're all in danger, my dear.'

When Tanthe had gone, Rufryd told Lynden to go after her. Then he set off alone to explore the house for a way out. All the main doors were solidly locked and bolted, the windows at ground level too small to be climbed through. But at the end of a long, low corridor, he saw Calamys emerging from the weapon store and slipping out of a small side door onto the hillside. Rufryd flattened himself against the wall until Calamys had gone; then he entered the weapon store.

A wizened old man, sitting on a stool inside the entrance, leapt up and began telling Rufryd he must not take anything. Rufryd simply strode past him and took his bow and arrows, ignoring his impotent protests. His bow was all he wanted. He would not take anything that did not belong to him.

With no clear plan, Rufryd stepped on to the dusky hillside and looked around him. There was no one in sight. A mass of boulders lay to the right of the door. It was tempting just to run for it, but without the others it would be pointless. He'd walked a short way downhill and stopped to look around when he heard a voice behind him.

'Shot, trying to escape.'

It was Calamys. He'd stepped from behind the boulders and was pointing a loaded crossbow at his heart. Cold sweat sprang to Rufryd's neck; he saw Calamys's finger beginning to squeeze the trigger mechanism.

As the bolt flew, Rufryd ducked and flung himself forward. He clasped his attacker's thick legs, tackling him to the ground. The crossbow went flying; they wrestled, but Rufryd swiftly found that his opponent was a poor fighter. In seconds, he had Calamys pinned face down on the grass, arms twisted up behind his back. Calamys gasped in helpless rage and pain.

'You're the one with the fancy weapons, but you don't know how to fight,' Rufryd said into his ear. 'Try to harm any of us again and I'll get you first. Try to keep us here and I *will* kill you. I've killed before. It won't be so hard the second time.'

'Let me up,' Calamys grated. 'I've work to do. If you kill me my family will take worse revenge than you can imagine!'

Rufryd sucked in a breath. 'Ooh, I'm scared now.'

'You stupid bastard! Yes, you could do it – and leave my family one less person to guard the forest!'

'From what? The woodcutters?'

Rufryd shifted his grip, meaning to force the truth out of him. But as he eased off briefly, Calamys gave an unexpected twist and threw him off. He seized his crossbow. Rufryd made a grab for his ankle but couldn't hold him. Calamys went stumbling off down the hillside, stopping to reload at frantic speed. Rufryd jumped up and followed. The clear ground ran like a tongue down into the line of trees, which curved up on either side of them. As the sky darkened, the moons grew brighter.

'Tell me the truth, Calamys!' he called harshly. 'What are you all so afraid of?'

There was a crashing noise, and Rufryd saw a big, pale animal emerging from the trees on their left, below him but above Calamys. It was like an ox, bulky and grotesque, with four sharply curved horns. It was too heavy for speed, but sheer momentum was carrying it down the hill as it charged towards Calamys, head down.

'Look out!' Rufryd shouted.

Calamys looked round too late. He tried to dodge away, but one long horn caught him in the side, tearing the thick material of his doublet. He cried out and bent over, staggering to keep his feet, blood spilling over his hands. The bull lumbered on a few paces, braked with its hooves digging into the turf, and turned to charge again.

It saw Rufryd, swung its ugly head, but made for Calamys a second time. Awkwardly he lifted his crossbow and fired, but the bolt stuck in the creature's thickly-fleshed shoulder, only enraging it. Calamys seemed rooted to the spot. Rufryd set arrow to bow and took aim. What would it take to penetrate its hide?

His arrow flew in a swift clean arc and pierced the animal's eye with an audible crunch. Its legs gave, and its bulk shook the ground as it fell.

By the time Rufryd reached it, it was dead. His arrow had sunk deep into its brain. There was something repulsive about its pale, unnatural flesh; he'd never seen such a creature before. He gripped the shaft and heaved at it until it slid free, coated in tissue and gore.

'Steak for dinner?' he said drily.

Calamys turned away, retching. 'We never eat them. Never,' he panted, wiping his mouth. 'Help me.'

Looking this way and that to make sure nothing else was about to attack them, Rufryd put his arm under Calamys's shoulders and, taking most of his weight, helped him up the hillside.

'What the blazes was that?'

'We must keep them under control,' Calamys gasped as they went. 'The oxen. They consume everything. They must be culled.'

'Are they yours? Or are they wild? Or . . .'

'They belong to the . . . the Leyholmen. There's an agreement that they don't let them wander out of the allotted area, but there are too many, they take liberties. We *must* keep control.' Calamys's voice was tight with rage. His fist was pressed into his side, but the blood flowed redly over his fingers.

'Calm down. You're making the bleeding worse. Not your day, is it, Lord Calamys? First I beat you squarely in a fight, then I save your life.'

They had reached the side door. Calamys gave Rufryd a bitter glare containing no forgiveness, but before his lips could frame any angry words his face bleached to white and he passed out, a dead weight in Rufryd's arms.

The family gathered round Calamys's four-poster bed, while Tanthe, Rufryd and Lynden clustered in the doorway. Lady Amitriya had dressed his wounds, and Calamys was lying propped up on the pillows, pale but alert and grim-faced. His mother and wife were on either side of him; Lord Dannion and Pheilan hovering anxiously at the foot of the bed.

Tanthe stood with her arm through Rufryd's. He'd whispered to her what had happened; although he'd made little of it, she felt very proud of him.

'He has lost some blood, but the wound is superficial,' Amitriya said briskly. 'He will heal swiftly, as long as he rests. Have you told your parents, nephew, how it was that you escaped with your life?'

Calamys said grudgingly, 'Rufryd shot the beast.'

'We thank you,' said Lady Alorna, looking up at him. Tanthe noticed how pale and strained her face was, how human she was under the polished shell. 'We can't thank you enough.'

Rufryd shrugged.

'All the thanks we want is for you to let us leave,' Tanthe said. 'We want to go with your blessing, not sneaking out in the night with people following, trying to stop us or kill us. We're not your enemies.'

'I saw nothing in the forest,' Lynden added. 'I've nothing to tell anyone.'

Calamys glowered. Lord Dannion and Lady Alorna looked at each other.

Dannion said heavily, 'This must be Calamys's decision. He knows best.'

'Oh, and what state is he in to make such a decision?' Amitriya cried in exasperation. 'You sit among your books all day, taking responsibility for nothing! Will you not for once look above the parapet and admit what is going on outside? At least Lord Arhan was brave enough to take action, even though he perished for it! You may be too inert and too craven to change anything, but at least do not prevent these young people from trying!'

The pause that followed was painful, sharp with tension. Suddenly Pheilan said acidly, 'If you can turn a blind eye to the – the Leyholmen, it can't be so hard for you to turn a blind eye to these travellers, too!'

At last Lady Alorna said softly, 'Very well, let them go.'

Dannion exhaled. 'Yes, yes, if Calamys has no objection. I shall miss Tanthe, we had such a splendid day.'

'You're fools, all of you,' Calamys said. 'They would have been of more use helping us here than riding to their deaths in Ardharkria. Have you any idea how hard those damned oxen are to kill? And Rufryd does it with a single

252

arrow. Still, if you would have it so, do what you will. It will bring disaster.'

'As if the disaster is not already here?' snapped Esamir.

'We'll do more than merely allow them to leave, won't we?' said Amitriya firmly. 'We will give them all the help we can.'

Chapter Twelve. Serpent and Seer

Helananthe was dreaming about her lover when the ship began to sink.

She woke suddenly in her bunk and felt the ship listing, straining against some violent force. Over the noise of the wind and the tortured creaking of the vessel, someone was hammering at her door.

'Wake up, my lady! All on deck immediately!' It was the first mate's voice.

'All right!'

Rolling out of bed, she dragged on her shirt and breeches, pulled on her boots and ran out on to the deck, still buckling her belt. The prow of the small ship reared to meet her then lurched away to one side, almost flinging her over the rail. She saved herself. The first mate was clinging on beside her, his face set in a helpless grimace. The ocean was grey as granite and heaving weirdly, like a vast slow serpent flowing alongside them, all in one direction. The sails were straining, the crew struggling desperately to turn the ship. She saw figures high in the rigging and eerily silhouetted against the glowing sky.

'What's happened?' shouted Helananthe.

He shook his head. His eyes were wild. 'We're lost.'

The ship tilted ominously. A wave burst over them, drenching them with chill water. 'Should we not launch the lifeboat?' she said.

'It would do us no good, my lady.'

Losing patience with him, Helananthe struggled forward to find the captain. Huge charcoal columns of cloud towered in the sky, like the fingers of a gigantic hand. The whole vessel was surging forwards faster and faster, while the sea swelled high on one side and fell away on the other. Holding firmly to the rail, she glanced up and saw the captain at the wheel. His grey hair glittered with water and his eyes were glassy.

Nearing the prow, Helananthe saw the sight that transfixed him. Suddenly she was able to make ghastly sense of their predicament. A great whirlpool seethed in the waves and the ship was caught in it, being dragged in a helpless downward spiral towards the core of the vortex.

She clung to the rail in panic, but the ship itself was beginning to break up. It was a small trade vessel, not built for this onslaught. Its timbers shrieked as the force ripped them apart.

The ship was spinning faster as she was sucked down. The crew were screaming, falling from the rigging, tumbling overboard. Sea water exploded over them and swamped what was left of the ship, sweeping Helananthe overboard.

All turned black. Helananthe felt herself sinking rapidly, deafened by the clamour of water in her ears. Great bubbles of air surged up past her, the last breaths of the dying ship. She thrashed in panic, but there was no time to feel fear; it had happened too swiftly. Only a spurt of sorrow, that the crew had all met their deaths because of her. The chill shock of the water had stopped her breath. Her lungs and head were bursting . . .

Raging, she gave herself up to death.

Father, I'm sorry. I failed.

Suddenly in the void she saw her father's face, pale as death, his eyes closed. *Oh gods, not you too. He has killed us both, his own son, his own granddaughter . . .*

An aeon seemed to pass.

Helananthe saw a shining green disk floating towards her. She was still in agony, her head and lungs on fire, yet the pain seemed distant. She was tied to the bulk of her body by the merest thread, which was about to break.

She stared at the green light. It came closer and closer.

She could make no sense of it . . . until it resolved itself into a jewel; a multi-faceted jewel, flashing beams of light through the black water. And she saw, as if in a nightmare, that the gemstone was lodged in the forehead of a huge, scaled snake.

The great head passed right underneath her, then rose, colliding with her. It was nudging her upwards!

The sucking force of the water was still trying to pull her down to the ocean bed, but the sea-snake thrust its nose under her helpless body and eased her out of the flow.

Light glimmered all around her. The darkness was full of jewels, weaving around her. She felt herself moving. The water flushed to a deep emerald, and in the shimmering light she saw the snakes clearly; a dozen long triangular heads and sinuous necks, their scales shining. And each one was a different hue; ice green, sea-blue, turquoise, aquamarine, all intertwining in a watery dance.

Helananthe awoke on a beach. The sand was white, and the rising sun already warm. She felt like a grounded whale. Her clothes lay sodden on her and she was draped in seaweed.

As soon as she stirred, explosive coughs shook her body. She tried to sit up, wincing as the light wrapped a band of pain across her eyes. Her skin burned with salt and she was crusted with sand . . . but she was alive.

Nepheter's tits, she thought, I survived. Gods . . .

She looked around quickly for other members of the crew, but the beach was deserted.

She closed her eyes. They'd become her friends, the crew, though she'd never been able to tell them who she really was or why she needed to sail to the Serpent Isles. She'd commissioned them and they had trusted her . . . and for their pains they were dead.

A fine princess I am, she thought, lying here like a dead fish.

A weird memory flashed through her mind.

The sea-snakes . . . did I dream them?

'Who are you?' said a voice above her. 'How did you get here?'

Her eyes flew open and she saw a man standing over her. He was slim, pale skinned, dressed in a white cloak with a pattern of moons sewn round the edges in silver. He looked familiar.

'Shipwreck,' she croaked. 'Where is this?'

'Kethna,' he said. 'Largest of the Serpent Isles.'

And at once she knew who he was. 'Rathroem,' she said. 'Don't you remember me?'

'Gods,' he whispered, starting.

'I'm Helananthe.'

His hands flew to his mouth, then fell slowly. 'Princess Helananthe!'

'The one and only.' She almost wept with relief. Controlling herself, she climbed stiffly to her feet and regarded Lord Rathroem. He was one of the Mediators; he'd befriended her when he had once stayed at the Amber Citadel, ten years ago. She was considerably taller and broader than him. Even as a young girl, her awe of him had been tempered by the fact that she could have lifted him up and spun him round as easily as she did her small brother. Not that she'd ever dared . . . She smiled ruefully. 'Yes, it's me. Have I changed so much in ten years?'

'You're even taller. Covered in seaweed and sand, no, I did not recognise you. My dear – your highness – how did you come to be here?'

'No titles. Just "dear" will do. This is where my ship was bound. I was coming to ask your help. By some miracle I am here, but the others – they can't have survived.'

'I'm sorry,' said Rathroem. 'Did you lose anyone—'

'Close to me? No,' she said quietly. 'I was travelling alone. The others were the crew I had chartered to bring me here. I barely knew them, but they were good people. A whirlpool swallowed us.'

257

'These waters were ever unpredictable. Three moons will raise mad tides and currents . . .'

'I'm sure they do, but I don't wish to stand here discussing the science of it, Lord Mediator! I see you haven't changed.'

'Forgive me.' He dipped his head in contrition. 'You must be exhausted. Come, I'll take you to the College. Are you able to walk?'

'I'll manage.' She hurt all over, but the last thing she wanted was to be carried on a stretcher. 'I'm more resilient than the ship, it seems.'

Rathroem led her across the beach and a stretch of white sand dunes, then through a forest of ferny trees where strange birds piped in the lush canopy. Presently they reached a cluster of white villas in a clearing. A stream rushed between banks of glittering moss, curving round the side of the buildings then surging away into the forest towards the ocean. The air felt humid and deliciously warm. As they crossed the stream on a delicate wooden bridge, Helananthe looked down and saw, sitting on a rock, a blue frog like a tiny sapphire. Never before had she felt so vividly glad to be alive.

At the beginning of the voyage, she'd been sad that her lover could not go with her. Now she was glad she had travelled alone; she could not have borne to lose him, however hopeless their future. She said, 'It's lucky you were on the beach just then. Was that coincidence?'

Rathroem shrugged. 'I often walk there. I was watching for the serpents which have been sighted along the coast of late. They are such a lovely sight, but they always seem to presage some crisis or other.'

She stopped in her tracks. 'Sea-serpents. Gods, I thought I dreamed it! They rescued me. They brought me here!'

Rathroem gazed at her. His eyebrows rose in dry surprise. 'It is well-said that they know more than humans ever could.' Then he bowed. 'Welcome to the Serpent Isles, your highness, and to the College of the Mediators.'

'Have I changed?' she asked again as Rathroem led her through the long, cool cloisters to the guests' sleeping quarters. 'Be honest.'

He laughed. 'I remember a large, awkward girl of seventeen who was abrasive, even aggressive at times, but warm-natured at heart. On occasion she bemoaned her size and her face, confiding her fears that she would never find a man tall enough, nor one who would find her attractive. Well, now I see a woman who would seem to be strong and graceful where once she was awkward, confident rather than abrasive. There never was anything wrong with your face; in all – under a light coating of sand and seaweed – you would seem to have become a very handsome woman.'

'Flatterer.'

'Never. By the way, did you find a man tall enough?'

Helananthe lowered her eyes. 'Yes. But since he is a commoner, I shall not get to keep him.'

'Ah. Your father remains intransigent?'

'To the end,' she said under her breath.

'We have no staff, no assistants,' said Rathroem, leading her into an airy room with white walls and a terracotta floor. 'We do all the work ourselves. I apologise if you find our standards inferior to those of the Amber Citadel, but we live very simply here.'

'Don't apologise,' Helananthe replied. 'You know I don't stand on ceremony. Show me a bed and a flagon of whisky and I'll be perfectly content.'

His mouth twisted in amusement. 'You will need to rest after your ordeal.'

'Not yet. I came here to ask a question and I must know the answer. Just lend me a dry robe, if you have one big enough. Then I'll be ready.'

Rathroem brought her a robe, a towel and a large jug of hot fruit tea, laced with honey and liquor. He returned after fifteen minutes, by which time Helananthe had rinsed the sand from her face, and replaced her sodden clothes with the robe, which came to mid-calf. Reasonable, she thought, looking down at herself; the Mediators had no mirrors. She'd scraped back her honey-coloured hair and tied it in a braid which hung damply down her back.

'I see the tea was to your liking,' he said, noting the empty jug.

'Healing nectar. Come to Parione and sell it under royal licence! You would make a fortune – if you cared about wealth.'

'Which we don't. Are you sure you want to talk to us immediately?'

She drew a breath. Her brush with drowning had left her exhausted, but that was the least of her concerns. 'Yes. I can't rest until I have an answer. Do I look presentable?'

'Perfectly. Our magic nectar's brought a healthier colour to your face, at least. I have told my colleagues you are here. They're waiting for you.'

He took her to a meeting room, a round chamber with pale walls. In the centre was a floor mosaic, showing the three moons, interwoven with a border pattern of leaves and gemstones. The mosaic was surrounded by a circular bench, on which six senior Mediators had already seated themselves, two men and four women.

Rathroem took his place as the seventh, and they rose and bowed to their princess, respectful rather than deferential. Garnelys was not their King. They were a self-governing community and had been so for hundreds of years.

Compared to the Mediators, who were all slender, soft-moving and quiet, Helananthe felt herself to be a large, loud presence. She studied them shrewdly, until Rathroem caught her eye.

'I think my question has already been answered,' she said, her voice echoing though she tried to keep it quiet. 'But still, let's begin.'

'We are honoured to receive her royal highness the

Princess Helananthe,' Rathroem began, 'who has come as an emissary from her grandfather King Garnelys. Shall we sit down?'

Helananthe sat alone at one side of the circle, facing the seven. 'Before you make any more assumptions,' she said coolly, 'Let me correct you. The King did not send me. In fact I came on behalf of my father, the King's son, Prince Galemanth. Alas, I now believe my father's life to be in danger; worse, I fear that he is dead.' There were gasps of dismay, but she went on firmly, 'You earned the title Mediators and the trust of Aventuria in the War of the Silver Plains. I hope that trust holds true.'

'Always,' said Rathroem, echoed by the others.

'I came to ask a question. The future of Aventuria may depend on it.'

'We will answer it as best we can.'

'A man named Laphaeome has entered my grandfather's court. The King has taken him on as – well, as a confidant, a companion, a counsellor. I couldn't say exactly what he is to my grandfather, but his official post is now that of Royal Architect. This man has advised the building of a huge monument, which he designed himself. The result has been disastrous, though Garnelys cannot seem to see or accept the fact, even from his own family.

'The point is that this Laphaeome, who led my grandfather into this ruinous venture, claims to be a Mediator. He has the appearance and the manner of a Mediator; Garnelys trusts him, and Garnelys is not stupid. He won't hear a word against Laphaeome. But I – I don't know what to think.

'Tell me, do you know of such a Mediator? Did my grandfather send for him, or did you send him to us, for some reason?'

The Mediators looked gravely at each other, shaking their heads. Helananthe felt a shadow fall on the room.

'No,' Rathroem said at last. 'The name is unknown to us. Of the few Mediators travelling the Nine Realms, none bears that name, and I can't see that any would have reason to use a false name. And none of us has left here for five years or more. Certainly no one has been sent to the Amber Citadel.'

'That is all I needed to know.' Helananthe's exhaustion swamped her, and her head swam. She almost collapsed; Rathroem hurried to support her. 'I knew it,' she gasped. 'As soon as I walked in and saw you, I knew that Laphaeome was false. He looks like you and yet . . . something is wrong. What I don't understand is why my grandfather can't see it!'

'Don't distress yourself. You need to rest.'

'No – no, I'm all right. I just need some fresh air.'

The others rose and bowed their heads respectfully as Rathroem helped her out of the meeting room. 'Are you sure you don't want to go back to your room?'

'Not yet. I need to talk to you alone. Can we go into the garden?'

'Of course.'

He led her to the mossy lawns behind the College, and they strolled side by side along the stream, with plumed birds calling in the branches above their heads. The air was humid and fragrant with the scents of vegetation. Helananthe breathed in deeply, and felt calmer.

'I find the gardens so tranquil,' said Rathroem.

'It is beautiful here,' she agreed. 'Healing. You were born here, weren't you?'

'Born to the Serpent Isles and to the vocation of Mediator.'

'Is it lonely?'

'Not at all. No lonelier than being monarch of Aventuria, at least.'

They followed the stream through the forest until they came to a waterfall. There they stood without speaking for a while, watching the water surging down the cliff-face into a silver pool that was edged with shining rocks. Then Helananthe spoke.

'The strange thing is that I was always closer to my grandfather than to my father. Father had a streak of granite in him that scared me. As I grew older he was always fretting about who was going to marry a big plain girl like me, who would make a suitable alliance and one day my consort on the throne . . .'

'And did he find anyone?'

'Oh, yes. Just the right young duke, whose marriage to me would strengthen the alliance of the Nine Realms and who'd make an inoffensive king. There was only one problem. We hated each other. I refused to marry him. So I was not my father's favourite person for many years. I spent most of my time with the army to keep out of his way.'

'And your mysterious lover?'

'I don't know what's become of him. A long story. I'm trying to accustom myself to the possibility that we may never meet again.'

'So you are alone?'

She laughed. 'Rathroem, I hope this is not an offer. I'd flatten you!'

He looked away, trying to keep a straight face. 'It is not, I assure you.'

'Anyway, Galemanth has been angry with me more often than not. Garnelys, though, was so warm and kind. I would always go and talk to him when I couldn't talk to my father. That's why the change is so hard to understand.'

Rathroem frowned. 'In what way has he changed?'

'Garnelys is a good king. Too good, if anything. He has always worried too deeply about his responsibilities; he cares too much, so my grandmother says. I think that's where the problem began. I first noticed it three years ago, when I came back to the Citadel after several months away. He'd become withdrawn and short-tempered. Intellectually he was as sharp as ever, and physicians found nothing wrong with him, so we were sure there was no illness.'

263

'A malaise of the soul, then.'

Her face hardened. 'If that's so, I can find no pity for him now. He began to treat my grandmother abominably, ignoring her, insulting her. And my father said that such a streak of blackness in his spirit could not have appeared from nowhere; it must always have been there. He told me that Garnelys's warmth and fairness were not the whole truth about him, that he'd always had dark moods and moments of cruel behaviour, as far back as Father could remember.'

'But when did this streak come to the surface? Before Laphaeome arrived, or after?'

Helananthe paused to think, shredding a waxy white flower she had plucked. 'Before. Months before. But somehow, Laphaeome turned up at just the right moment to feed on my grandfather's mood. And then they conceived of building a huge monument to the Goddess and God. It would be his memorial, his gift to the people of Aventuria.'

'Is that wrong?'

Helananthe laughed bitterly. 'Oh, the news was welcomed with great excitement when it was first announced. Even I thought it was a good idea. But my father immediately saw it for what it was. A great waste of the earth's substance and of human life. He begged Garnelys to cancel the project, but the King was obsessed. Anyone who opposed it became an enemy. And that included my father.

'Garnelys has got rid of all the good staff who have served him well for years, and replaced them with brutal, ambitious arse-lickers – oh, excuse my language, but there's no other way to describe them! People who did the slightest thing to displease him vanished.'

'Vanished?'

'I'm as sure as I can be that he had them killed.'

Rathroem sat down on a rock as if he could not believe what he was hearing. 'The King is doing this to his own people? The Xauroma—'

'Is gone. A broken promise.'

'The sea-snakes. That's why they're restless! Helananthe, don't weep.'

'It's spray from the waterfall!' She sat down beside him, but turned her face away as she went on. 'The last straw was the theatre. Saphaeyender put on a play criticizing the King's behaviour, so Garnelys tore the theatre down and began to build his monument in its place.'

'The Old Royal? But I loved that theatre. Garnelys loved it. He took us there to see *Arkenfell*, do you remember? He wouldn't—'

'That's what everyone said. But he did it. Forty people died trying to defend it. People loved Garnelys so much they couldn't believe any bad of him – until that moment. The King is making himself more and more isolated, and where there was trust and happiness, we have only fear and brutality.'

'Gods,' Rathroem whispered.

'My father sent me away for my own safety; he was thinking of leaving, too, but trying to resist the idea. And the strange thing is that it was only this conflict with Garnelys that made my father and I stop quarrelling. It brought us close, for the first time in our lives. He was a good man, Galemanth. Why do I keep saying *was*?'

Rathroem waited for her to go on.

'My life was in danger too, but I couldn't waste time hiding. So I came here. But I almost feel that when the ship sank, it was no accident. Somehow Garnelys knew where I was going, and he tried to kill me.'

'By causing a whirlpool? My dear, there are no mages capable of doing something so drastic, not even the Mediators. And your King is no *roth* mage.'

'I know it's not rational. But it's what I felt. So if I go back and find that my father is dead, I will be desolate, but I won't be surprised. *Garnelys is killing his own heirs*. What does that mean?'

'I can't say.'

'I thought . . .' She was struggling. Rathroem laid his hand on hers. 'I thought that if Laphaeome was truly a Mediator, there might be an underlying, rational explanation for all this madness. I hoped you would shed light on our darkness.'

'I cannot. Not yet. We are not gods, we don't pretend to be seers. We were chosen to Mediate purely because we were neutral in the War of—'

'Rathroem, shut up. I don't want to hear your excuses.'

'Fair enough. But there's no point in you expecting to think of an answer before you've had a good long sleep.'

She smiled tiredly at him. 'You don't live completely in the ether, then. At the risk of being misconstrued again – take me to bed, Rathroem, before I pass out and you have to carry me.'

Helananthe slept solidly through the rest of that day and the next night. Towards morning, her sleep was disturbed by nightmares of thrashing against the whirlpool, while her father's face came drifting endlessly towards her.

She surfaced hard, fighting her way from under the bed cover as if from under the sea. For a few moments she couldn't remember where she was. Then the weight of her responsibilities descended on her, and she fell back on to the pillow.

Someone knocked at her door. 'Come in!' she called, propping herself on one elbow and trying to smooth her hair. As the door opened, a burst of fresh sweet air blew in. She remembered the jewelled serpents, and felt calmer.

'Good morning, Princess,' said Rathroem. He brought a tray, and she looked lustfully at the plates of golden biscuits, porridge, fruits and cheeses.

'I must warn you, I eat a lot.'

He grimaced. 'I remember. You were always stealing my food.'

'Because you would have left it otherwise!'

He placed the tray on her lap. 'Do you want me to explain what everything is?'

'No. I don't care what weird fruits you grow here. I eat anything.'

As she ate, Rathroem sat expectantly in a chair beside her bed, his hands folded in his lap. Helananthe began to grow impatient with him.

'Have you spoken to the others?' she asked.

'You spoke to me in confidence, so no, I haven't. But they want to know if you are asking us to mediate.'

A mouthful of biscuit almost went the wrong way. She swallowed hard. 'Between whom?'

'Yourself and the King.'

'I think that would be a bit pointless, don't you? It's gone far beyond mediation. He is still the King, remember. I have no power.'

He was silent, watching her with dark brown eyes. It was impossible to tell his age; he had a sort of translucency about him. So like Laphaeome . . . but where Rathroem was guileless and clear as diamond, Laphaeome in her memory seemed muddy and deceptive.

'Well?' she said. 'Don't sit there staring at me.'

He shifted. She could be imperious when provoked.

'Helananthe,' he said, 'Have you ever seen a Bhahdradomen?'

She looked at him in surprise. 'No. How could I have seen one? They are not allowed to set foot over the Vexat Straits.'

'Well, I have seen them, and I still could not necessarily recognise one.'

'What do you mean?'

'Their natural form is roughly human in shape. I mean that they have a skull, four limbs and a spine. But their form is . . . how can I put it . . . malleable.'

She put the tray aside, her appetite vanishing. 'Go on.'

'Consider a chick that has just hatched from the egg. If the first thing it sees is not its mother hen but your hand,

267

it will take your hand to be its mother. It will imprint upon you. Well, the Bhahdradomen are like that. But in their case, the imprinting is more extreme. They can actually grow to look like the creature with which they have been placed. They call the mutated ones *ghelim*.'

'I've heard something like this before,' she said softly. 'I thought it was a children's tale.'

'No. It's true. The real adepts can change their appearance at will. Not drastically, but enough to fool human eyes. And where their art is imperfect, they will still be taken for what they purport to be, because of their ability to penetrate the human mind and influence it. There will always be some humans they cannot fool, of course, those who can see the truth through the veil of deception. But there are many more of us whom they *can* fool.'

Helananthe got out of bed, paced across the room and back. 'Gods. You think Laphaeome is . . . it's impossible. Grandfather would not be so easily tricked!'

'Who knows? You say he has grown obsessive, and obsession clouds the mind.'

'But how has this creature impersonated one of you?'

'I don't know,' said Rathroem. 'I'm only guessing.'

'I knew there was something about Laphaeome. Something wrong.'

'How old would you say he was?'

Helananthe shrugged. 'It's hard to say. Hard to look at him properly. I can't tell how old you are, either. However, for his knowledge of architecture and the way he speaks, I would say he is at least forty years old.'

Rathroem cleared his throat. 'Forty-three years ago, a Mediator vanished in Aventuria. Suppose the Bhahdradomen took him and used him to imprint one of their own upon him?'

'But that's madness. What did they think they could achieve? They know they have no hope against us. If they breach the treaty, they will be crushed.'

'Perhaps they don't care. They have lived in exile for two hundred and fifty years and now they are restless. If the Bhahdradomen are rising – and I'm not saying they are, but if – you would be well-advised not to ignore the possibility.'

'But it's not possible. Garnelys isn't a weak character. This has all come from him, and even if Laphaeome is what you say, then I think Garnelys is using *him*, and not the other way round!'

Rathroem's eyebrows rose eloquently. 'That's quite a thought.'

'I must talk to my grandfather.'

'Will he listen to reason?'

'That's the trouble. Everyone who has tried to reason with him for the past three years has died for their pains. My grandfather cares about nothing other than his project. How are we to make him listen, or act?' Helananthe sat down on the edge of the bed. 'I must go home,' she said. 'I don't know how, since our ship was destroyed.'

'We have our own vessels,' Rathroem said. 'We can put one at your disposal.'

She sighed. 'I'm almost sorry you said that. How tempting to stay here; if I'm thought to be dead, I have no responsibilities! No, I must go back. But if I can't reason with the King – then what?'

'I can't tell you what to do. I can only offer advice.'

'Considering you're so useless, I can't believe I'm going to ask this,' she said acidly, 'but when I go, will you come with me? Perhaps you could reason with him, after all. Will you try?'

'Yes, Helananthe, because you are my friend,' he said. 'But only as observer and negotiator.'

'Be careful, Rathroem,' she said, half-serious. 'Your neutrality could become severely irritating.'

The Seer's home was a mere hovel, a ramshackle round cottage set near-invisibly into the side of a hill. Goats

269

grazed on its turf roof. Sheep and chickens wandered in and out of its musty interior.

Helananthe was close to exhaustion as she climbed the last stretch of grass towards the cottage. The journey had taken weeks. A voyage from the Serpent Isles on a small, swift Mediator vessel; then a long trek from the south coast to the Serpentine Mountains north of Parione. It would have been faster on horseback, but Mediators did not ride. And now Helananthe, too, was disguised in the white, hooded cloak of a Mediator.

The door stood open, so she knocked instead on the wall. The wattle frame shook alarmingly.

'Yes?' said an irritable voice. 'Who is it now?'

The Seer appeared, wiping his hands on a piece of grubby sacking. His rust-red hair, streaked with white, hung forward over his shoulder. His eyes were narrow with tiredness and a miasma of stale alcohol rose from him.

'We require your services,' said Helananthe.

His eyes opened wide. 'Mediators? But you despise Seers! Charlatans, the lot of us.'

'Not you,' said Helananthe. She put back her hood. 'Anyway, I'm not a Mediator. Good day to you, Fox.'

She didn't know his real name. She had nicknamed him that on a previous visit, and he had never objected. He did not know her true identity, either – or pretended he didn't, for she suspected he knew more than he would ever admit. It was three years since she and her lover had last come to the Seer; that time, to see if there was any chance they might marry. The visions had indicated against it.

'Ah. It's you,' he said brusquely. 'Come in, my lady, but don't wipe your feet; my clients generally prefer to do that on the way out.'

Helananthe followed him into the dark, dung-scented interior. She saw something small and silver dart through the gloom, and conceal itself under the Seer's chair. His secretary. Rathroem, hovering into the doorway, said, 'I'll wait outside.'

As he walked away to sit on the green hillside, Helananthe turned to the Seer and said, 'You're probably wondering why I'm here.'

'No,' said Fox. 'And I would consider it a courtesy if you'd refrain from telling me.'

'You're hungover, aren't you?' Helananthe said grimly.

The Seer shrugged. 'Have you anything in the way of a cure?'

'I'd suggest water and willow, or feverfew.'

'That's not what I meant. I prefer payment in kind; I don't suppose—'

Helananthe reached into her purse and brought out six ralds. 'I've only brought money, I'm afraid.'

He sniffed, examining the gold-rimmed discs of emerald. 'It'll do.'

'Oh . . . and this.' From under her cloak she brought out a flask and offered it to him.

His eyes lit up. 'Serpent Isles whisky! That's more like it.'

'To remain sealed until after our session.'

'Of course!' Businesslike, he led her to the well in the centre of the hut. 'Sit down. To achieve the full effect of the trance, you must chant with me, like this—'

'I remember,' she said, seating herself on a low stool. 'By the way, tell your secretary to come out; I know he's there, and I don't want him making notes.'

The Seer's eyes gleamed in annoyance, but the pewter-skinned little man emerged from beneath his chair, gave a sardonic bow, and jumped up to sit cross-legged on the arm of the Seer's chair.

'Now, Fox, don't be so brusque with me,' said Helananthe. 'You've been busy, haven't you?'

He paused. 'Very busy.'

'What sort of people have been coming to you?'

'All sorts. More Aelyr than human.'

She tutted. 'Now, you know you are not meant to See

271

for Aelyr; any more than they are allowed to probe into human affairs.'

He gave a tight smile. 'They bring exceptional liquor. Who's going to tell on me?'

'I've already forgotten you said it. So, all these people; what have they been seeing?'

He sat down in his tall chair on the other side of the well, glaring narrowly at her. 'You know I can't tell you that.'

'Of course. Client confidentiality.'

'No. I don't *know* what they've been seeing.'

'Really? Not even a little glimpse?'

The secretary said, 'What d'you think is making him drink so heavily?'

'Shut up!' The Seer looked angry. 'You're right. No matter how hard I try not to, I always see something. It's enough to drive anyone mad.'

Helananthe sat forward. 'You've been seeing terrible things, then?'

'I can't tell you. All visions take their toll on me. They steal a little bit of *ethroth* out of my soul to create themselves.

Seeing the genuine pain behind his eyes, she softened her tone. 'Then why don't you stop?'

'Because people keep coming. Because I can't stop. Because I have to do it. Now, if you want a reading before you make me so angry I throw you out – stop asking questions!'

She leaned towards him, elbows resting on her knees. 'I don't mean to offend you. But perhaps your skill would cause you less pain if you faced it instead of turning away from it!'

'Well, how glib,' Fox hissed. 'You expect me to take on all of Aventuria's pain?'

Helananthe caught her breath. Tension snapped between them. 'Pain?' she repeated softly. 'I don't want to take it on, either. But I *must*.'

'Don't lean too far forward,' the Seer said crustily,

pointing at the disc of striated crystal that capped the well. 'If you break my *zaharoth* crystal, and I have to fish you out of the depths, it will cost you more than six ralds. Now, watch your reflection. Breathe deeply. When you feel ready, join in my chant. And don't expect to see anything that you expected to see . . .'

His words were canny. As they sank into trance, the crystal surface peeled back to reveal no vision of Garnelys, nor of her father; nothing of Laphaeome, nor her lover. Instead she found herself flying vertiginously over a broad, round hill. Its crown was bare but thickly surrounded by gnarled, dark oaks, its flanks bounded by ancient walls now held together only by wreaths of ivy, silvery streams snaking through gullies under the shadow of massed bramble and dark holly . . .

Helananthe felt herself falling. She caught herself with one hand on the edge of the well, and the vision ended.

The Seer had slumped in his chair. For a moment she thought he'd fainted, and she jumped to her feet in concern.

'It's all right,' said the secretary. 'He always does this.'

After a moment, the Seer hauled himself upright and pressed a hand to his head. 'Now the questions start afresh,' he said wearily. '"Oh, Seer, what did this mean? What did that mean?"'

'No,' said Helananthe. Her heart swelled with an odd sense of relief and purpose. She found more ralds and dropped four into his hand, gave four more to the secretary, who looked at her in surprise. 'No more questions. Thank you, Fox. Now I know exactly where I must go, and what I must do.'

Chapter Thirteen. Moonstone Fire

A damp, misty morning was breaking as Rufryd, Tanthe and Lynden entered the courtyard. Gazer sprang up and bounded over, his great tail waving as he ran in circles of delight around them. In the centre of the courtyard, a stable boy stood holding the bridles of three magnificent horses.

One was Halcyon, whom Lynden had called Blue. The other two were of similar build, with long arched necks, fine heads with great dark eyes, large mobile ears. Their bodies were slender, their legs hard and powerful. One was a burnished red that glowed vividly in the dawn, the other a dark brown, but their heads, manes and legs were velvety-black, their tails raven banners.

'This one's Redbird,' said the boy, handing the reins to Tanthe. 'And this is Sunhawk.' Rufryd took the brown gelding from him and began to make friends.

They were leaving Flame behind. Lynden had already said a quiet goodbye, emerging from the stable sombre and red-eyed.

They'd been given generous provisions, fresh clothes – padded black garments embroidered with blue, over which they wore their own, heavy cloaks – and extra weapons; a sword each and a fresh supply of arrows. Only Amitriya and Pheilan had come to see them off. Pheilan looked very pale and nervous, his larynx bobbing in his long throat.

'I wish I could go with you,' he said. 'I wish I'd gone with Arhan, then he might not have died.'

'Does Calamys know you tried? I mean, to help warn us against the conscriptions?' Tanthe asked.

'I'm sure he does. It's never mentioned. He knows I'm too afraid of him to do anything else.'

Amitriya tutted. 'This is what I'm up against. People who would rather live in luxurious terror than take a risk and fight!'

'But how did you know the, er, the things that the message said about King Garnelys?'

'From a dear friend of ours called Eldareth, who was lately in Parione. He came and told us. He said that in all the Nine Realms, no one dares speak out against the King. My dears, this began months, even years before it touched you. Don't imagine that Aventuria is still the benign Kingdom you have always believed it to be. It might have only taken the Duchy of Sepheret to defy the orders . . . but Alorna and Dannion refused to act.'

'But it wasn't their fault,' said Pheilan. 'They were under terrible pressure from the army and the Registats in Skald. My parents are powerless, in truth. So is Calamys. That's why he's so angry.'

'Where's this Eldareth now?'

'We don't know. He was already fleeing for his life. Perhaps he is dead. Go.' Tanthe put her foot in the stirrup and gingerly mounted her red mare, marvelling at her beauty, and the richness of her trappings. The saddle had a deep seat with a high pommel, shaped for comfort. Redbird arched her neck, responding to the bit as Tanthe collected the reins.

'I don't know how to thank you for giving us so much,' she said.

'I've given you nothing,' Amitriya said shortly. 'A passage to your deaths, maybe. Some advice; you will of course avoid the part of the forest I showed you. But the Bhahdradomen there are not especially dangerous; it's the others, the ones that appear from nowhere, the ones you don't see until it's too late.' Lynden went paler as she spoke; Tanthe thought of her uncle, the monstrous beings that had swooped from nowhere when they tried to attack the soldiers . . . a flicker of dread went through her. 'I'll make an offering to Nephenie for your protection. But if all goes well, head east, cross the Whiteveil Mountains as soon as you can.'

There seemed to be nothing else to say. Rufryd and Lynden were both in the saddle and ready to leave. Pheilan unlocked the gate to the courtyard, and they rode out in single file, Lynden leading and Rufryd at the rear. 'Good luck. Blessings,' he said. 'Come again and be welcome.'

The gate closed behind them with a final-sounding clang. The house of Luin Sepher stood tall and impenetrable behind them; Tanthe thought longingly of the books she'd never read, the deep soft beds and delicious food they'd left behind. They began to ride down the hillside, fog folding thick and cold around them. The grass was grey and wet, the sky veiled, the trees like ghosts.

Soon they were in the woods again. Rufryd, navigating, took them some way north before turning east, avoiding the shadow of dead forest where the colony of Bhahdradomen were. As they went, Tanthe explained everything that Amitriya had told her.

'I still can't believe it,' she said. 'Our monarchs have let them live there since the War of the Silver Plains? Who could tolerate that, if they knew about it?'

'I'm starting to think I'd believe anything,' said Lynden.

He looked older, Tanthe thought. His glow of youth was still there, but tarnished by reality.

'Pheilan told me about the insects,' he went on. 'They're found in the soil where the Bhahdradomen are, or where they have been. The adults burrow into the soil, and they bury dead or sleeping animals in which to lay their eggs. The maggots feed on the corpses, and when they reach a certain stage of development, they emerge from the ground and crawl up grass stems. There they go into a dormant stage, a hard chrysalis. The oxen that the

Bhahdradomen keep come along and eat the vegetation and swallow the maggots in their casing. They pass through the animal's gut until they are dropped in a different place. It's how they spread, you see? The casing breaks open and an adult comes out. The adults burrow into the soil . . .'

She shivered, fighting off another flashback. 'How did Pheilan know all that?'

'He and Amitriya found it out for themselves,' he said. If I could forget how I felt when I saw that Bhahdradomen, it's quite interesting. Makes me wonder how much else there is that we've never been told.'

'I dread to think.'

Tanthe almost understood the Duke and Duchess, burying themselves in the comfort of books or food. Now, she felt, they weren't going only to find Ysomir. They were going to find the truth, and it was knowledge she didn't want.

'We can't avoid going back through Ardharkria,' Rufryd said. 'Not unless we go a couple of hundred miles out of our way.'

'We should be all right, as long as we don't go through Leyholmen territory,' said Tanthe. 'And don't go to sleep lying down on the ground. But I think Lyn should decide. He was the one who had it worst.'

'I'll be all right,' Lynden said brusquely. 'You don't need to cosset me! If they come near us . . . I'll know.'

Fog persisted all day. Tree trunks loomed solid through the greyness, glistening with moisture. Soon they noticed how utterly silent it was; apart from the soft rhythm of the horses' hooves and the occasional fall of a leaf, there was no sound at all. They only saw one sign of life all day; a yellow-eyed lynx, watching them from the branch of a tree. Gazer snarled, and the cat hissed and fled vertically up the trunk.

The soft going and the undergrowth meant they could

progress no faster than a jog-trot. It was easier than being on foot, but by nightfall they still had not cleared the forest. Saddle-sore and worn out, they found a sheltered hollow where they untacked the horses and let them graze. They fed Gazer on a joint of lamb their hosts had given them, and dined on the food that wouldn't keep for long; bread, butter, cheese, herbed meat rolled in pastry. For later in the journey they had salted meats, dried fruit and biscuits.

They settled down to sleep, propped against the trunk of a big, smooth beech tree. Gazer pressed himself alongside Tanthe's thigh, his big head between his paws. Lynden took the first watch. Tanthe's turn was next, then Rufryd's.

'Wake me after a couple of hours,' Tanthe told Lynden firmly. 'You need the sleep more than I do.'

Lynden settled down in his cloak, tired of being nursemaided and determined to watch for as long as the other two. For an hour or so, he was calmly alert. But gradually, tiredness and boredom got the better of him. He dozed, convinced he was fully awake; a dog barked, there were strange sounds and movements around him, but it was too far away to disturb him. But then, a strange vision; figures moving through a watery blue light, and a warning screaming in his mind, *they're coming, they're—*

He only realised he was asleep when he came violently awake. Someone was shining a blinding light in his face. Confused, he squinted against the light and saw a face grinning down at him, hideously underlit by the lantern. The fleshy, mean-eyed face of Beyne.

'Rufe!' Lynden croaked.

'No one's going to help you,' said Beyne. 'Don't move.'

'What?' Tanthe cried suddenly, waking up. 'Gazer? What's happening? Lynden!'

In the glow of Beyne's storm-lantern and several others, Lynden saw a troop of mounted soldiers surrounding the trees, some aiming crossbows, others with swords drawn.

Beyne said coolly, 'What's happening is that you are under arrest.'

Rufryd was awake by then. As he and Tanthe shook themselves out of sleep, they took in the situation. Tanthe dropped her head on her knees and groaned. Rufryd swore.

'Don't use that language to me,' Beyne said, moving to glare down at Rufryd.

'I thought I'd killed you.'

Beyne kicked him in the thigh. Rufryd curled up in pain. 'You nearly did, you motherless piece of filth. We have good healers in Skald. Still, the charges against you are just as grave. Attempted murder, defiance of royal decree, evading arrest. I'm sure I can add a few more to that list. Horse-stealing, from the look of things. Get up, keeping your hands well away from your weapons.'

When they were slow to respond, he yelled, 'Get up!'

They rose slowly, hopelessly. 'Gazer?' called Tanthe, looking around. 'Where is he? Why didn't he warn us?'

One of the soldiers turned and raised his lamp. The light fell on to the forest floor a few yards away, illuminating a grey, motionless hump. A crossbow bolt stuck out of the hairy flank.

Tanthe almost screamed. 'Oh gods, what have you done to my hound?'

'We shot the vicious mutt. He attacked us.'

Tanthe put her hand to her mouth. Tears flowed from her eyes. Lynden had never seen her cry like that before, not even when Ysomir was taken. His throat tightened and he closed his eyes. This is all my fault, he thought. If I hadn't fallen asleep . . .

'Now,' said Beyne, cruel and silky, 'you are coming back to Skald to answer for your crimes. It's over.'

They walked in misery through the forest; three of the soldiers leading their horses, while Tanthe, Rufryd and Lynden were made to go on foot. Their wrists were bound in front of them and tied to the saddles of three of Beyne's riders. All their weapons had been confiscated and loaded onto the back of Halcyon's saddle. Beyne had made them saddle up the Sepher horses before they moved off; it was plain he meant to confiscate both the fine horses and their valuable trappings when they reached Skald.

'This is my fault,' Lynden said after a time. 'I fell asleep.'

'It could have happened to any of us,' said Tanthe, from the other side of a mounted soldier. She was in between Lynden and Rufryd as they were pulled along, three abreast. 'We shouldn't have made you keep watch so soon after you were ill. I just don't know how I'm going to tell my dad about Gazer.'

'Shut up!' snapped Beyne.

Rufryd swore under his breath. 'It was bad enough thinking I'd killed the bastard,' he murmured. 'It's worse finding out I didn't.' Beyne didn't hear him, but the men leading him and Tanthe both snorted with laughter.

'Is something amusing you?' Beyne said savagely.

'No, sir.'

'Frog in my throat, sir.'

When dawn came, the fog lingered, wreathing the dripping branches and drooping leaves. The leader of the soldiers said something; Beyne rode impatiently beside him and said, 'What d'you mean, Kraes? Can you read a map or can't you?'

'Pardon me, sir,' said the leader. 'I only meant that it's further to the edge of the forest this way. We'd be out quicker if we headed due east, then turned south back to Skald.'

'Are we going the right way?'

'Yes, sir. South-east, directly towards the town.'

'Then continue.'

'It's just that the men don't like Ardharkria.'

'I noticed,' Beyne said sourly. 'The Ducal family of Sepheret are a bunch of mad eccentrics whose only remaining power is to spread rumours about their domain so ludicrous that only peasants believe them. There's nothing in Ardharkria to fear.' He cast a sneering glance over his shoulder at the prisoners. 'Peasant rumours.'

Tanthe loathed him bitterly. She felt that when they shot Gazer, they might as well have shot her.

The forest was motionless, muffled. The trees seemed to lean over them, parched, thirsting for relief or revenge. Tanthe felt oppressed, as if she were trapped in Ardharkria and would wander in circles until she suffocated. The soldiers, she noticed, were growing tense and jumpy, glancing around as if seeing things from the corners of their eyes. She kept surreptitiously working at the ropes around her wrists, trying to get a hand loose.

There was bare peat underfoot. No leaves on the trees. Skeletal branches scraped at the mist. The trees were dead, even their bark stripped from them.

She felt the Aelyr knife – which they had not discovered – growing warm against her breast. Lynden drew a sharp breath.

Amid the trees, off to their left, there stood a group of figures, colourless in the fog. Their garments were ragged, grey with age. Tanthe glimpsed strange greyish faces, eyes green as mould. They looked human and yet something was not right . . . Gathered in a group, they stared at the mounted party as they rode by.

'Ignore them!' Beyne ordered. 'Anyone would think you'd never seen woodcutters before!'

'No,' said Lynden. He pulled against the rope, and was nearly dragged off his feet by his captor's horse. 'Can't you see what they are?'

'Lyn, calm down,' Rufryd said. 'It's all right. They're not going to take on this many of us, are they?'

'But look at them.' His voice rose. 'Anyone can see they're not human.'

The heat of the Aelyr knife stung Tanthe's skin. The soldiers were glancing warily at Lynden. The suppressed hysteria of his voice was infectious.

Tanthe couldn't feel the waves of horror that Lynden had described, nor see anything obviously dangerous about the passive woodland folk. Yet the heat of the Aelyr knife stung her breast, and she felt her blood hammering.

A movement caught her eye. She looked up and saw, in a tree just ahead, a big creature like a dra'a'k clinging there between branch and trunk. Only it was not a dra'a'k. It was too big. Its scales and its drooping, leathery wings were tinged with rust-red. It watched them with the same impassive intelligence as the woodcutters, its long, toothed jaws set in a smile.

'Anthar's prick, what's *that*?' said the leader, whom Beyne had called Kraes. His horse shied and stopped, so the whole party came to a shambling halt behind him. All the animals were nervous. Tanthe saw Redbird and Halcyon trying to rear, soldiers struggling to control them. The horse to which she was tied swung its haunches round and nearly knocked her over.

'For the gods' sake, Kraes, don't you *know*?' snapped Beyne. He lowered his voice, but the forest was so quiet Tanthe heard him clearly. 'It's one of the creatures sent by the Mediators to protect our backs. You've seen them before.'

'Never so close,' Kraes stammered.

'It's friendly. To us, at any rate. Now, get control of your horse and lead on!'

Tanthe was puzzled. She'd read of the Mediators in her history books; they'd negotiated the peace treaty between human and Bhahdradomen after the War of the Silver Plains. They were benign and neutral.

The horses went a few paces, snorting, sweating, colliding with each other as they tried to bunch together. In between trying to keep her feet and avoiding being crushed, Tanthe was working urgently to free one of her hands.

Then one of the Leyholmen left the group and came towards them. He looked different to the others; more a traveller, in a voluminous cloak the same elusive grey as the fog. He leaned on a staff and his face was hidden by a deep hood. The knife burned. A sense of wrongness went through her from head to foot. She glanced at Lynden, saw that he was deathly white and sweating. Rufryd, also looking at his brother in concern, caught her eye.

'Look, it is the Mediator,' Beyne said in a tone of relief, too loud. He booted his horse's flanks and rode forward to meet the cloaked figure. He dismounted, and the two dipped their heads to each other in greeting. Lynden was shaking his head, eyes wild.

'Lord Mediator,' said Beyne.

'Lord Registat,' responded the cloaked one.

'What brings you here? I thought you were guarding the troops across the Plains of Menroth.'

'Until the new conscriptions, I have little to do.'

'Of course. Then, how can I help you?'

The Mediator angled his staff and pointed it at Lynden. 'I want him,' he said.

Tanthe caught her breath.

'What?' said Beyne.

The Mediator pointed to the dra'a'k-like creature clinging to the tree. 'He wounded one of my creatures most grievously.'

'Well, I am sorry to hear that, but I can't give him up. He's my prisoner.'

The cloaked man's tone sounded reasonable, but it had a curious edge to it, Tanthe noticed, that seemed to creep right inside her skull. 'Come now, Lord Registat. One token of appreciation for all the help I've given you. That's all I ask.'

'Lord Mediator, be reasonable. I'm sure the King is rewarding you more than generously for your help.'

'I want him,' came the voice from within the hood.

'The boy is mine.' Beyne's tone hardened. He moistened his lips. 'He must be dealt with by the due process of the law—'

'No!' The cry burst from Lynden's throat. His brown eyes blazed, his drained skin seemed to shine. Tanthe wrestled frantically to free herself, desperate to reach him. 'Can't you see what they are?' he cried. 'Look at them, look at them! How can you not see?'

He wasn't protesting at his own fate. Tanthe wasn't sure he'd even heard Beyne arguing over him. He went on shouting, beyond controlling himself. The soldiers all stared at him. Beyne swung round, furious.

'Shut him up!' he roared.

The soldier in charge of Lynden jumped down from the saddle and tried to restrain him. Lynden elbowed him in the stomach, sending the man reeling on to the ground, and went on shouting, 'Look at them! Count their fingers! Are you blind? Don't use your eyes, then, but *feel* their energies. For Breyid's sake, use your instincts!'

His words had a terrible effect. His fear infected Tanthe, stripping illusion away; suddenly she could see clearly that these woodcutters were not human, couldn't understand how she had not seen it. All around her the soldiers were blank-faced with terror.

It was as if Lynden's voice, far from being hysterical with fear, had taken on a dreadful power to reveal the truth. The humans stared at the Leyholmen and at the Mediator and they *saw*.

Age-old, malevolent intelligence, hunched like shadows with vulture wings. Horror sucked at Tanthe's heart. It was irrational, like a phobic loathing of spiders, yet she couldn't suppress it. She wanted to scream and run. Her left hand came painfully free of the rope and she groped for the Aelyr knife in her pocket.

The stone on the pommel was so hot it nearly burned her, but she managed to grasp the cooler, padded hilt. The blade shone like diamond as she took it out.

Her captor was too busy trying to load his crossbow to notice what she was doing. She sawed through the rope, then dodged round the back of his horse to free Rufryd.

284

They ran to free Lynden – who seemed not even to notice they were there – before the soldiers realised they were loose.

The Leyholmen were moving forward. Horses were milling wildly, Beyne yelling for control. The fog pressed in like darkness; the figures were unarmed but they moved soft as mist, radiating a chill that sapped the spirit, turned hands and legs numb so that crossbows and swords fell to the ground.

'Let's get our horses!' said Rufryd, shaking Lynden. 'Quick, before they bolt!'

The soldiers leading Halcyon, Redbird and Sunhawk had let them go, more concerned with saving their own skins. The troop was disintegrating. Two of the horses broke away and fled, their riders urging them on into the forest. The leader's horse reared and Kraes lost his seat. As he hit the ground, a figure leaned slowly over him, pointing a hand with too many fingers like a pale blade towards his heart.

Beyne's nerve broke. His yells turned to screams. He began to back away from the Mediator. The cloaked figure simply watched, leaning on his staff – but Beyne's face was wrought with ghastly recognition, as if his very soul were being torn out and shredded. Tanthe stared, horrified. Then the Mediator came forward, as if it had changed position without moving; Beyne fell, and she saw its fingers, its seven fingers, plunging into the Registat's heart like a knife into rotten fruit.

Wraiths were all around her. She didn't even see where her attacker came from. He was suddenly there, rising over her, a smothering spectre. Her legs gave way and she fell; and although the Bhahdradomen seemed weightless she was being suffocated. Drowning, losing all feeling, threshing . . .

The knife throbbed in her hand. She brought it upwards in a wild thrust. It met no resistance; she'd only stabbed thin air.

But the creature let out a hideous shriek. It lurched away from her and she glimpsed it, clutching its chest with both hands, its face a mummified mask of horror. Yellow plasma spattered on to her hands, stinging. Gods, she *had* stabbed it!

Its shrieks were hideous. The noise cut through her skull until she was forced to put her hands over her ears. It was screaming high-pitched words she didn't understand. *'Aer-roth. Mnelim, mnelim!'*

The Aelyr knife shone brilliant in the gloom. The bright orb pulsed and sparkled. Her attacker fell and was silent, but its wails were taken up by a dozen other voices cutting the air into ribbons of pain. Tanthe saw the Mediator near Lynden, as if he'd started towards him then stopped, frozen, to glare at her. Gasping for breath, she sat up and showed him the knife in a defiant gesture.

The Mediator raised his head. For a moment she saw a blurred skull of a face, white eyes piercing her with hate, fear and calculation. Then, as if the fog had swallowed him, he vanished.

All around her, horses were churning the ground as the last of them bolted; their whinnies meshing with the shrill cries of the Bhahdradomen. Tanthe curled up in a tight ball on the ground, rigid.

'Tanthe!'

Rufryd was shaking her. 'They've gone!' he said. 'What did you do?'

She sat up, jumping violently when she found the Bhahdradomen corpse lying right next to her. It seemed small, desiccated. Its mouth was still frozen open with its last scream. She saw others, which might have been mere eddies of mist, vanishing into the fog-cloaked dead forest. Their shrieks faded.

'It was this,' she said, holding out the knife. Its brightness was beginning to dim. 'Went straight into its stomach, like piercing a bubble.'

Tanthe saw that their three horses were trying to race

after the others, and that Lynden was fighting to control them on his own. She and Rufryd ran to help.

Two of Beyne's men lay dead; Kraes and another. The earth around them was already beginning to boil with insects. Tanthe looked away, repelled.

A few yards away lay Beyne himself. His bulky body was on its back, his eyes staring glassily upwards and a scarlet hole gaping in his chest. His plump face was set in a horrible grimace, a last outpouring of frustrated malice.

'Now he's dead, for certain,' Rufryd breathed. He took Sunhawk's reins from Lynden. 'Are you both all right?'

'Yes, I'm fine,' said Lynden, who looked anything but. 'As soon as the Bhahdradomen left, I was all right.'

'I'll let you know when I've stopped shaking,' said Tanthe. Her mouth was so dry she could hardly swallow.

Rufryd gathered up the reins and swung into the saddle. 'So let's get the fuck out of here,' he said.

By nightfall they were out of Ardharkria and crossing a rolling stretch of meadowland. They'd ridden hard all day. It was only when they left the trees behind that the sense of nightmare receded, and they managed to collect themselves.

In the morning, after a good night's sleep and refreshment, they felt renewed. The air was sweet, the sky clear, the grass springy underfoot. Riding on again in daylight, they began to talk about what had happened.

'I wish I could have gone back and looked for Gazer,' said Tanthe. 'I want to know he didn't suffer.'

'Well, we're not going back there just for a dog!' said Rufryd.

'He's not just a dog!' she flared. 'He was one of our family and my dad's best friend! He entrusted him to me and I did a great job of looking after him, didn't I?'

'I'm sorry, Tan. I didn't mean to sound heartless. But we can't go back.'

'I know that!' she said. 'It doesn't stop me feeling awful.'

'Gazer was doing what I should have done,' Lynden said wretchedly. 'Trying to defend us.'

'Don't keep punishing yourself about it,' said Tanthe. 'Even if you'd stayed awake, there wasn't much you could have done about Beyne turning up. I know you were scared yesterday, but your being scared saved us.'

'He wasn't the only one,' Rufryd put in. 'What is it with you, Lyn? You were like someone else. You start shouting that those people aren't human, and suddenly I see what you mean – and I'd rather not have known, thanks. It was horrible.'

'It was no bloody fun for me, either,' Lynden retorted. 'I couldn't help it.'

Tanthe said, 'Well, if you hadn't, we'd have been locked up in Skald by now.'

'And if it hadn't been for your knife . . .'

'Funny,' she said. 'This rotten little knife that won't cut butter as a rule, suddenly slashing through ropes and sending the – the Leyholmen screaming for the hills. Are you still convinced I found it by accident, Rufe?'

He shrugged. 'But what makes you so special, to be given a gift like that?'

'So, you don't think I'm special.'

Rufryd groaned. 'I didn't mean it like that! I'm just asking – oh, never mind.'

'Now we know,' said Lynden. 'Those creatures that attacked us at Riverwynde and killed Ewain were Bhahdradomen. The King . . . is using the Bhahdradomen against his own people.'

'No,' said Rufryd. 'I can't believe things are that bad.'

'Even if it's so – Beyne didn't know,' said Tanthe. 'It was obvious he didn't know! When he realised, he practically dropped dead with horror. He kept calling that thing "Lord Mediator". But the Mediators were human, and they didn't take sides, but they were good and fair judges. They were *human*. It doesn't make sense.'

'I'm damned if I know what's going on,' said Rufryd.

'What if the King doesn't know what he's dealing with? He should be warned!'

Rufryd sighed deeply. 'Oh, Tanthe. Who do you think we are, to tell the King anything? If he *has* got anything to do with Bhahdradomen, he knows all about it, believe me. And us trying to work out what he's doing is just hopeless.'

'Well, I can't give up.' After a few moments she added. 'By the way, let's not keep calling those things by name. Just in case they answer.'

For once, Rufryd did not mock her. She actually saw him shiver.

Gulzhur stared into the oily surface of the haematite, but the trance came hard. He was alone in the dark wood, hunched over a mixture of anger and triumph. Trying to take stock.

He had been forced to kill Beyne. The soldiers who'd escaped didn't matter; no one would listen to their crazed tales. But Beyne had *known*.

Curse the boy, the one who'd ripped apart the veils of deceit. There was always some damned human who knew. And Ancestor curse the girl who wielded an ancient weapon he'd hoped never to see again. She had killed one of Rhu's people with it. But worse by far had been the fear unleashed by the pulsing *Aer-roth*, igniting an ingrained race-memory of terror. Because even Gulzhur feared the weapon, he dared not follow to take revenge. Not yet. But one day, when her guard was down . . .

'Enabler?'

The plain took wavering shape around him. Zhoaah was there. 'Facilitator.'

'I can barely see you. Are you well?'

'Tired, my friend. I have just learned a sobering and much-needed lesson.'

'About what?'

'Overconfidence,' said Gulzhur. 'Forgetting the lessons

289

of the past. The weapons that defeated us are not all lost, nor are all humans blind.'

'What has happened?' Zhoaah asked, worried.

'I'll tell you in due course. I have too much to consider. But don't concern yourself; it is a minuscule setback in the scheme of things. All is finished here; I am on my way to your side.'

They were out of Sepheret now, and entering the realm of Deirland. The first stretch, the Vale of Elphet, was easy, with wide flat swathes of grass over which the horses could canter easily for hours at a stretch. There were sweet streams, hedgerows, fruits, plenty of birds and rabbits to hunt. The horses were an endless source of wonder; fleet, willing, sure-footed and hardy. Their dream of reaching Parione began to seem realistic after all.

As they travelled, the country grew more rugged; no farmland, only bowls of wiry grass rimmed with jagged rock, stands of wild grey forest. Tanthe was astonished to find how sparsely habited Deirland was, wilder by far than Sepheret and so lonely. In the twilight she often sensed shapes moving around her, heard voices whispering; but when she turned, nothing was there.

She thought a lot about the conversation she'd had with Lady Amitriya. Couldn't forget the image of the old woman speaking the Creation poem with the blue night behind her . . . and everything they'd discussed, gods and legends and realms, now took on individual colours and atmospheres in Tanthe's memory. When she thought of Sepheret she associated it with the blue and black of Luin Sepher, and the white of its ivory walls. And if that were so, then Deirland's colours were the grey of mist, the greyish-green of dew-soaked grass and the brown of dying bracken.

'I don't feel that Breyid and Anthar belong here,' she said one late afternoon as they rode through the falling dusk. 'Not in the forms we know them, anyway. Do you?'

'You do think about some weird things,' said Rufryd. But he spoke quietly, as if trying not to disturb the hush of the forest. The trees were wide-spaced so they could see a long way between the tall ashen trunks; and in the distance, a hunting party was passing soundlessly through the trees, a line of bluish silhouettes in the mist. Some were on foot bearing spears, some mounted on wiry horses; men and women in deerskins, their arms bare and their hair wild. Tanthe and her companions stopped dead to stare at them. The Deirlanders looked like ghosts, hunters from the ancient past before the realms had names. As if moving through water they passed with dreamy slowness, the mist around them streaming like a faint blue aura.

Something came crashing through bushes and fallen leaves, jolting Tanthe from her trance. The hunt's quarry erupted right in front of her as if it had surged out of the ground; a massive stag, with branched antlers flung up to the sky. The horses shied in alarm; the stag skidded to a halt and stood there a moment, dark flanks heaving. His bold eye stared straight into Tanthe's, dark and fearful yet knowing; and for a chaotic moment she felt, *knew*, that this was not simply an animal but the Stag God of Deirland, the most primal manifestation of Anthar – of Anuth himself – hunter and hunted in one magnificent form.

And beside him, a white doe with eyes black as Nuth.

Then stag and doe were gone, racing away to their left. The Deirlanders turned in pursuit. Although they passed within fifty yards of the spot where Tanthe, Rufryd and Lynden stood, they took no notice of them; only flowed by in near-silence, their deerskin cloaks flying.

'They won't catch them,' said Lynden, very soft.

'No,' Tanthe breathed.

'Not this time,' said Rufryd. His eyes shone with excitement and awe, and his hands tightened on Sunhawk's reins as if he wished himself with the hunters. They watched until the ghostly figures were swallowed by the dusk. Then the three of them rode on their way, not speaking of what they'd seen. No words to explain how a simple hunt had been transformed by twilight and mist into ineffable, eternal ritual.

A few days later, as they came up onto the vast Plains of Menroth, a cold, blustering wall of weather came from the north, lashing them with rain and hail. The horses went with their heads down, ears flattened, manes hanging like dripping string; at night there was no better shelter than the odd gorse bush. Their fires would not light. They slept as best they could, wrapped in their weatherproof cloaks, but the damp seemed to seep into everything. Tanthe became used to being cold and uncomfortable, to the constant smell of damp clothes and wet horses. It would have been a long detour south to the nearest town, so, not wanting to risk being captured again, they struggled on.

If she and Rufryd had not quite returned to their former state of hostility, in these conditions it was hard to be in the best of tempers. Beset by the weather, and mindful of Lynden's feelings, they had not made love since leaving the house. That alone made them both tense, although by nightfall they were too tired to do more than sleep.

Chilly winds blew and black clouds rolled across the sky. The nearer they came to the Whiteveil Mountains, the more bitter the climate became, as if winter were not a season but a physical domain into which they were running headlong.

Beyond the plains came low hills, covered in scrubby grass and boulders. Here at least was some shelter. For six more days they travelled and each day the mountains drew closer; a white line at first, then a jagged wall, gradually resolving into an overwhelming barrier. The snowy peaks were luminous against the louring black clouds.

Now the mountains towered over them. The greatest peak, to their left, was wreathed in cloud, its western face sheathed in bright ice, its southern flank in cold shadow. Mount Ishte. Around it the mountains stood in silent, monumental grandeur.

'Once we're among them, there's no turning back,' said Rufryd.

They were climbing a grassy, rock-strewn hill. Above them, the slope turned to bare shale. The afternoon was dry but the air smelled of snow.

'They look so much higher than the mountains at home,' said Tanthe.

'Yes, and who was ever stupid enough to go up into the mountains in winter? Sensible people were huddled by the fire, drinking ale and moaning about the weather.'

Riverwynde seems so far away, Tanthe thought, remembering last Hollynight when all had been normal. It seemed a lifetime ago. How desolate, not to be with their family for Hollynight . . . how would her parents feel as they lit the red and gold candles to celebrate the rebirth of the sun?

'We made it in time,' she said. 'It's not winter yet.'

'Not in the lowlands, no.' Rufryd reined in and turned to face the others, one arm resting across the pommel. 'Look, we did our best. But there was no way we were ever going to beat the bad weather. To be honest, I think we'd do better to ride south, find a friendly village, and stay there until spring arrives.'

'No!' Lynden cried fervently. 'And lose the whole season? That would be insane!'

'And trying to cross these mountains in winter isn't? Tan, what do you think?'

'I expect you're right, but I still think we should go. The weather may hold for days. And if we don't risk it we'll waste so much time. Come on, Rufe, you know we have to keep going.'

'How did I know you were both going to say that?' Rufryd said in resignation. 'All right. Well, we don't have to do any mountaineering, anyway. According to the map, there's a pass along the base of Mount Ishte. Menroth Pass. Should take about four or five days to get through.'

'Better make a start, then,' said Lynden. Halcyon tossed his head, snorting at something unseen in the air.

Tanthe saw the first snowflake come whirling out of the sky and land on Redbird's mane. It stayed there for a second before melting; the size of her little fingernail, a perfect, six-sided crystal.

By the time the snow began in earnest, they were too deep into the mountains to turn back. They'd seen the clouds thickening, dark and heavy with their load, but they'd urged the horses on, hoping to find shelter before it set in. They were climbing the saddle that lay between the first two peaks, but the angle was far steeper than it had appeared from below. The path wound upwards between fallen boulders and standing stones that looked as if they had been placed there deliberately by some long-vanished race.

The horses went on at a steady walk, but they were edgy and unhappy, snorting at the snowflakes, tossing their heads.

'This is just a flurry,' said Lynden.

'I hope so,' Rufryd answered, half-joking. 'I can't feel my feet.'

Tanthe's face began to ache with the cold. Her fingers were stiff, even in the thick gloves Amitriya had given her. The snow fell steadily, silently, dusting the bare rocks at first; then building up in ever thickening layers until every stone wore a thick white cap. The path was fetlock deep, then hock-deep.

A wind sprang up, blowing the gossamer layers into drifts. The horses hated it. They pranced and skidded, turning their heads this way and that to evade its cruel coldness.

'We have to stop,' Rufryd said finally.

They took shelter under an overhanging face, with a

stack of boulders on one side to protect them and the animals from the worst of it. There they ate some of their carefully preserved rations, and fed the horses with handfuls of oats that they'd brought from Luin Sepher for times when grass was scarce. It wasn't enough.

'I've lost track of time,' said Tanthe, 'but I think tonight is Darkeve, isn't it? My grandparents will be leading the ceremony at home. We should light a candle for the Crone, and ask to be blessed with her wisdom.'

'You can,' Rufryd said. 'I'm too cold to move. I'm sure she'll understand.'

'You're so irreverent,' Tanthe said.

'Maybe, but I'd rather not sit contemplating our dead ancestors while we're up here. Happy New Year,' he added sardonically, kissing her frozen cheek.

All night they sat huddled together for warmth, listening to the wind moaning through the peaks.

When morning came, the sun broke through and they saw just how high they had climbed. Mountains rolled away from them in every direction, but Mount Ishte seemed further away than ever. Tanthe simply hadn't appreciated the scale. All was blindingly bright. The snow flashed gold and tiny diamonds from the sun, but the shadows were blue. The boulders behind which the horses had sheltered were garlanded with icicles.

'It's beautiful,' she whispered.

'I wonder if Ysomir saw this?' said Lynden.

'I doubt it,' said Rufryd. 'There are several passes. Unfortunately the map doesn't say which is the easiest. I just brought us to the nearest.'

'We'll blame you, then,' said Tanthe. He grimaced, and kissed her.

They had barely readied themselves and set off before the clouds rolled in again. Billows of snow blew across their path, growing so deep now that they were struggling along at a snail's pace. They had to dismount and lead the horses; Tanthe took both Redbird and Sunhawk so Rufryd could walk ahead to trample a path for the others. Tanthe had never been so exhausted nor so achingly cold in her life; she could see Lynden was suffering too, though he never uttered a word of complaint.

The gigantic landscape seemed so hostile, so unutterably wild. It was the domain of the crone-goddess, Mahaa. She asked silently for mercy, wishing they'd thought to make an offering before they set out.

At about midday, she thought her pleas had been heard. The storm died down and they found themselves looking across a flat valley towards another, gentler peak. In between lay a field of glittering snow that looked almost too perfect. But Mount Ishte had shifted several miles to their left and seemed further ahead of them than ever.

'How did that happen?' Tanthe said.

'It's a lot bigger and further away from us than it looks,' said Rufryd. 'Anyway, we're still heading in the right direction. Let's press on. This looks like a frozen lake.'

Lynden said, 'Be careful,' as Rufryd set foot on it.

There was a sinister creaking noise. Rufryd stepped back hurriedly, just as the whole field cracked and fell away in a flurry of sparkling mist. He slipped; Tanthe and Lynden both caught hold of him by reflex and saved him from falling over the edge. Shocked, they found themselves on the edge of a chasm, watching the snow-crust fall away with a soft rumbling noise into the void.

The chasm was not wide, but it was very deep.

Tanthe turned hot, and sweat trickled down her spine. To have come so close to losing Rufryd . . . His hand came fumbling on to her shoulder, trembling.

'There's no way across,' he said. 'We must have gone wrong somewhere. I had no idea this would be so hard.'

'It's all right,' she said, trying to sound reassuring. 'We'll retrace our steps and try another way round.'

As they went, a fresh blizzard blew up. The gale flung veil after veil of snow into their faces; they couldn't see, couldn't find their way, could barely even breathe. They found themselves floundering their way through thick drifts. The horses' coats were clotted, their manes and tails roped with snow. Tanthe felt ice forming on her eyelashes, her very eye-sockets aching with cold.

The endless, featureless whiteness played tricks on her eyes. There seemed to be pale shadows moving in the curtains of snow. When she stared straight at them, they vanished; but when she looked away they were there again. Dread clenched in the pit of her stomach. She felt a familiar pressure against her breast. The Aelyr knife was pulsing. She couldn't reach it; her gloves were too thick and her hands too numb. Lynden gasped. His eyes widened, he put a gloved hand to his forehead.

'I've got that feeling I had in the forest,' he said. 'As if there are Bha—'

'Don't say it!' Tanthe exclaimed.

'I keep thinking I see them. Following us.'

'Where?' said Rufryd. 'I can't see anything!'

They paused. There was no sound but the snow hitting their cloaks.

'Let's just try to go on,' said Tanthe.

They struggled on for an hour or more, with the pale shadows appearing and fading, a constant dread worming through their physical struggle. The horses were restless, as if they sensed it too. Their eyes were rimmed with white and they kept tossing their heads, slipping on the treacherous surface.

The animals had had enough. The horses grew slower and slower until they stubbornly turned their backs on the storm and refused to go on. Meanwhile, the wind was sculpting a wall of snow directly across their path.

'Oh, shit,' Rufryd breathed, his teeth chattering. 'Now we can't go backwards or forwards. I'm so sorry.'

'No,' said Lynden. 'It's my fault. I should have listened to you.'

'Never mind whose fault it is,' said Tanthe. Her face was so stiff she could hardly speak. 'Let's think about how we're going to survive until the storm dies down.'

'We're going to be buried if we stay here,' said Rufryd.

All was white, a blank nothingness swirling with grey-white flakes in every direction. She noticed, suddenly, that her sense of dread and of being followed had vanished. It seemed an almost tempting idea, Tanthe thought, simply to lie down and sleep in the soft downy blanket . . . A thrill of despair went through her. For the first time, she felt that they might actually die.

The pale shadows were coming towards them through the snow, closing in.

Lynden moved between Tanthe and Rufryd, pressing his gloved hands on their arms. 'Gods,' he whispered. 'I thought they'd gone, I never felt them coming!'

The horses stood like statues. Tanthe felt the Aelyr knife pulsing – not hot this time, but stone-cold.

The shapes drifted towards them in silence. They were hard to make out. Pale grey shadows hardly seen against whiteness.

They seemed to move through the air and through the walls of snow, as if they were reflections, or moving in a different dimension. They came floating quite slowly towards Tanthe and her companions. She watched them through the falling veils as if in a dream. Disoriented, mesmerised, she stood paralysed on a blade-edge of fear, seeing too late the weapons in their hands.

Now the pale ones were all around them. Tanthe could not count them; they seemed to slip in and out of reality. They were covered head to foot in veils that shimmered grey, white, violet, back to grey. Some had delicate, silvery bows, others spears or swords that were like clear glittering ice.

'What kind of fools would brave the Whiteveils in winter?' The voice was quiet, crystalline, icy, and it seemed to come from everywhere at once. 'Only human fools.'

One of the veiled ones stepped forward and touched

Tanthe's shoulder with a spear tip. It was the lightest of touches, and yet she felt a fearful chill dropping through her, worse than the cold of the mountains.

'Come,' said the voice. 'Your journey is over.'

Chapter Fourteen. The Heliodor Tower

Before dawn, when all was drear and bitterly cold, Ysomir was pushed onto a horse-drawn carriage to begin another long journey along the snaking silver rails. She was wrapped in her cape, her rucksack clasped against her. Three guards huddled around the stove in the back corner, cutting out the heat to the rest of the travellers. The carriage was nearly empty. Seven other faces looked blearily up at her, but there was only one she knew. Lath.

She sat next to him, relieved to see a familiar face.

'I didn't know you were a stone-carver,' she said, her breath clouding the air.

'I'm not. They need carpenters, commander said. I don't care. I'm just glad to be out of this place.'

He stared across the carriage with lifeless eyes. He's still in shock, Ysomir thought, he shouldn't be travelling; but no one seemed to care about that. All yesterday's churned mud was frozen and coated with glittering ice. As the driver urged the two big horses into life, the conscripts watched wordlessly as the bleak slopes of the quarry, looming coldly against the sky, dwindled and vanished.

Ysomir thought of Beorwyn. Would anyone tell him about Serenis or the explosion? Would they think to tell him where she, Ysomir, had gone? Of course not.

The landscape was unfamiliar, but at least there were trees again.

Lath was naturally thin, but now he was almost skeletal. His pale, mousy hair hung lankly around his long face, and the skin around his dark brown eyes was pinched with exhaustion. His spirit had been crushed by yesterday's disaster. But after a few minutes, he took Ysomir's hand.

'Thanks,' he said.

'For what?'

'Coming to tell me about Serenis last night. For sitting with me. I think I would have given up and died if you hadn't been there.'

'Don't give up. Serenis wouldn't want that.'

'I miss her,' said Lath. 'I still can't believe it.'

'Nor can I,' Ysomir said quietly. 'She made me laugh, like my sister used to. I almost feel she's talking to me sometimes, telling me not to be so bloody stupid.'

Lath smiled. 'Yes, that's Serenis.'

He began to weep suddenly. Ysomir held him, her chin resting on his bowed head. Some of the others looked at her, but she stared defiantly straight through them. These people all looked starved and worn down by work, with no excitement or hope in their eyes. She felt almost nostalgic for the earlier journey, when Beorwyn and Serenis had been there and they'd even found things to laugh and sing about.

Winter was sweeping over the landscape; the little they saw of it, for the window shutters were kept closed against the cold. The trees were bare, their damp black branches frozen in crone-like stances against a white, icy fog.

It was the time of the Crone goddess, when the earth fell into death-like sleep. Ysomir imagined Breyid in her crone-form, Mahaa, the wise one, ancient, terrible and powerful.

'Lath, we should ask Mahaa for strength,' she said.

He sat up, rubbing his eyes. 'Yes. If she won't help us, no one will.'

'Hold my hands,' said Ysomir. 'We'll close our eyes and call her, feel her power. Don't shut the winter out but open yourself to its strength.' She began to chant,

> 'Great Mahaa
> Behind your ebony gates
> Ruler of Death and of Winter

301

> *Midwife of our birth and re-birth*
> *Beginning and end*
> *Darkness of midnight, darkness of space . . .'*

With Lath's chilly hands in hers, she stopped fighting against the cold but gave herself to it, feeling the chill air on her face, extending her awareness to the snow-filled clouds and the deep, dormant tree roots.

> *'We your children call to you*
> *Open your raven wings*
> *Enfold us*
> *Let your strength and wisdom fill—'*

A hand fell on her shoulder and shook her. Her eyes flew open and she found one of the guards glowering down at her.

'Stop that! Invocation is forbidden.'

Ysomir was speechless, but Lath – previously so passive – reacted with a burst of rage that astonished her.

'Since when has invoking our goddess been wrong?' He stood up, taller than the guard but much slighter, his fists clenched. Ysomir pulled at his arm, terrified that he would be hit or punished.

The guard only grimaced. 'I don't make the rules,' he said sourly, stomping back to his seat.

Lath sat down again, shaking with anger. 'Have these people even given up their goddess, now?'

She whispered, 'I'm sure they haven't. But calling the energies of the goddess or god to help us is a form of magic. It changes things.'

'All it would have done for us is made us stronger,' he replied under his breath. 'Is feeling anything but helpless and miserable forbidden now?'

'I *do* feel stronger, don't you? But some people can call the energies so strongly that it makes changes in the physical world, too.'

Lath's eyes widened with curiosity. 'Can you?'

'No, of course not. My grandmother can. She's our village priestess. She's a wonderful healer. And my grandfather Osforn has such a magical way with plants, though he never says much. He's the priest, of course . . .'

'Are they Seers?'

The question took Ysomir aback. 'I don't think so. Do you know, I never asked either of them what they could and couldn't do? But they worked with plants and herbs mostly. Helwyn had a beautiful orb on her staff but I don't know that she ever used it for magical things. I don't think she felt for stones; I heard her telling my mother once, their energy was too much an Aelyr one, too cold. I wish I'd asked what that meant.'

'Carpenters, my folk,' said Lath. 'What they do with wood, that is magical. I can make a door or a cupboard, but I can't make wood shine and sing like my father can. Don't think I'm much good at anything, really.'

'That's not true, Lath,' Ysomir said, but she was still thinking of her grandparents. She would have done anything to see Helwyn; she tried to capture her white hair, the way she stood as she invoked the goddess and god; so proud and tall. Her breath lodged in her throat. Memories of Darkeve, of Hollynight, of Breyid's Day when the first snowdrops poked through the glistening snow . . .

'Ysomir? You all right?'

'I was thinking, you can know someone all your life and yet know so little about them. There's so much I should have asked, but I never thought of it. I never dreamed that one day it would be too late.'

Twelve days later, they arrived in Parione by night.

Ysomir did not even realise where they were at first. She had been dozing, but something woke her; a soft commotion outside, made up of horses' hooves, wheels rattling, sounds changing as if they were echoing off buildings. She heard marching feet, voices, snatches of music.

303

Waking fully, she turned and opened the nearest window shutter, only for half-a-dozen voices to be raised in protest. 'Shut that ruddy window! Raised in a barn, were you?'

Before she obeyed, she caught a glimpse of a sloping street, shadowy hills rising on the side she could see, great buildings of marble standing between tall, leafless trees. Lights shone along the street and in the high, remote windows. Snow glistened on the roofs, but in the gutter it had turned to brown slush.

'What does it look like?' whispered Lath.

'Very big. Very cold.' Ysomir pulled her cape around her as a spear of intense loneliness passed through her from head to foot. She couldn't say any more. Never had she felt such a powerful desire to go home, nor such an intense conviction that she'd never see Riverwynde again.

At last they came to a halt, and the door was pushed open with the heavy grinding thud that she'd grown to hate. Ysomir and Lath joined the line of conscripts as they jumped one by one out of the carriage.

Ysomir was last. As she stepped down onto the flag-stones, the sight that met her gaze overwhelmed her.

A magnificent hill soared upwards before her, crowned with a great, curved wall that seemed to dwarf even the hill on which it stood. Glimmering lights threw a ghostly glow up the edifice, white at the base, melting into pale yellow and then a dark gold that was almost lost on the darkness. She saw that the wall stood about a hundred feet high but was unfinished, with irregular blocks of stone protruding from the top. The whole was covered in a black fretwork of scaffolding. She could see human figures moving on the scaffolding, tiny as spiders.

Ice crystals were sifting down against the glow, but she was so used to the cold she did not even feel it. There were torches everywhere, their long white flames moving in glittering lines up the hill, flaring on the wall like arrows pointing to the heavens. There were conscripts everywhere, voices shouting, the noise of hammering and of creaking ropes. As her eyes grew keener in the dark she saw a team of figures hauling a great block of stone up the hill, another block being lifted up the scaffolding on a massive pulley.

It was a tower they were building. A huge tower the colour of the sun.

Ysomir's heart convulsed with different emotions. Fear, amazement, breathless awe.

She turned and saw, less than half a mile away, another hill crowned with a great, fortressed palace. It was almost in darkness, but for the faintest glimmer of gold outlining a complexity of walls and spires.

The Amber Citadel!

She turned to share the sight with Lath, only to find herself alone but for a guard, the one who'd reprimanded them on the carriage. He shoved her in the shoulder.

'Get moving, girl! Don't bother gawping. You'll see so much of this place you'll be sick of it after a few days.'

He hurried her after the rest of the party, along a paved path that wound halfway up the hill. She was out of breath by the time they reached a wall of sandy rock set into the hillside. There the guards ushered them through an arched gateway. Heavy, barred gates clanged shut behind them; ahead was a tunnel, as dark as the mines.

This tunnel led deep into the hillside, branching off into a maze of smaller corridors. The one down which Ysomir and her party were taken had many small caves off either side, with doors of iron bars. Glancing through, she saw cells with three or four thin mattresses lying on the floor. Some were occupied. She heard water dripping, voices, the sound of raucous laughter echoing in the distance.

She reached out and gripped Lath's hand.

'This is a dungeon,' she said softly. 'Like in the books Tanthe and I used to read together.'

'This is worse than the mines,' Lynden said shakily. 'I don't want to be here.'

'It's not a dungeon, you idiots,' the guard said harshly behind them. 'These are your quarters. Only the best for Garnelys's subjects. Welcome home.'

Ysomir was separated from Lath, and put in a cell with three other women.

'Who's this, then?' they said, turning to stare at her with hungry, hostile eyes.

'I'm Ysomir.' She tried to smile, to show she was friendly.

The women surrounded her. 'That's a fancy name for a piece of shit,' one said.

They prodded her, mocked her, seized her rucksack and scattered the contents all over the floor. When she tried to protest, they drove her into a corner with threats, coiled violence simmering in their eyes. They frightened Ysomir more even than Teseyna had done. She retreated deep inside herself, stopped reacting.

'She's a bit simple, if you ask me,' said the shortest of them, breathing foul breath in her face. 'Nothing to say? What d'you say to this?'

She punched Ysomir in the stomach. Ysomir collapsed in agony. Sneering, her cellmates turned away and left her to help herself.

If anything could have tipped her over the edge of misery into anguish, it was this. Yet in a strange way, she was almost relieved. She could not bear to make another friend like Serenis, then lose her.

Ysomir was too different; she still had some innocence and freshness about her, in spite of the long journey and the mines, and she wasn't a native of Parione but a peasant; almost a foreigner. However individual her cellmates had once been, they had developed a look; lank hair, drawn, belligerent faces, haunted eyes. Their bodies were wasted, but their arms were strong and rope-like. They were veterans. From the few unguarded remarks they made, she found out that they'd been put to work on the Tower last summer. In that time they'd had to dispense with all niceties of good behaviour and kindness, just to survive. They had grown tough shells, so to them Ysomir seemed a soft, defenceless thing.

They each had a thin mattress on the stone floor, on which Ysomir tried and failed to sleep through the long, chilly night. Sanitation was a bucket in the corner without even a screen for privacy. By morning, both Serenis's locket and her carved goddess had vanished, but she was too afraid to say anything.

When they found out she could carve, that only deepened their hatred and envy. It meant she would be on lighter duties. For that, she must be made to suffer during their rest hours.

Ysomir knew she must become like them, or die.

Tanthe could have dealt with them, she thought, staring into the bowl of watery porridge that passed for breakfast. I don't think I can.

The communal area, where they took meals, was a big dark cave lit by torches and lamps and lined with trestle tables. It was so crowded with young men and women that there was barely any elbow room. But at least here she could escape from her cellmates.

And in a few months' time, would she look as they did – wiry, desperate, brutal? Would she, in turn, be tormenting frightened newcomers? Never, she thought. For a moment she wished she had died in the mine with Serenis. And she thought of Lynden, how they should have been handfasted by now. She wondered if he was thinking about her still, or if he had found someone else . . . No. Unworthy thought. There would never be anyone else for either of them, she knew that.

A salt tear fell on to the grey mass in her bowl.

'Don't cry into your porridge,' said Lath, sitting down next to her on the bench.

'Why not?' said Ysomir. 'It's the only thing that gives it any flavour.'

'Eat it, then. It's freezing outside, and we'll be spending twelve hours out there. That's what my cellmates said.'

'What are they like?'

He shrugged. 'Bad-tempered, unfriendly, and dying on their feet, by the look of them. Yours?'

'Same. They don't sing many songs about the joys of working in the service of good King Garnelys, do they?'

Lath's mouth curved up at one corner. 'You sound like Serenis,' he said.

A bright day was dawning, snow falling in powdery flecks from a passing swathe of cloud, as the working party were brought out on to the hillside. The cold began to bite into Ysomir's cheeks immediately, then to penetrate her uniform. It would only get worse. They were driven by guards up a steep path towards the summit, the unfinished Tower looming ever closer. In daylight its curved wall glowed the most exquisite pale gold, frosted with tiny glints of light. Below its massive base, though, the hillside was churned up, raw and ugly. Scaffolding teetered skywards all around it; she wondered how high they planned to build it.

She and a handful of others were led away from the main group. Lath gave her an anxious wave as she went. On the far side of the tower, there was a flat area with smaller blocks of stone stacked on it, and here a short, strongly-built stone mason began to allocate tools, designs and blocks for the carvers to work on. They stood shivering as he instructed them. He was brisk and businesslike, but not unpleasant.

From here, almost at the summit of the hill, Ysomir had her first clear view of the Amber Citadel. She even forgot the cold for a few minutes. It was truly amber in colour, a warm melting gold, but it was not pretty and symmetrical as she'd imagined. Rather, it had a raw magnificence, with its thick crenellated walls rising one inside the next, and at the centre a tangle of roofs and turrets. You could see how it had grown age by age, one style layered on another, the elegant palace at the very summit fused with older, castle walls. And the King and Queen lived there . . . She couldn't believe she was so close to them. It seemed unreal.

'. . . staring at, girl?' said a loud voice. 'Did you hear a word I just said?'

She started. The stone mason was in front of her, scowling, waving a rolled-up piece of paper in her face.

'Sorry. I was just . . .'

'Never mind. Here's your design. Get on with it.'

She unrolled the plan, trying to hold it flat against the raw wind. Her teeth chattered. The design was lettering, but only half a word; it seemed to be part of an inscription. She knelt down by the block she had been shown, and started work.

It was hard. She'd never worked on such a large scale before, never in such bitter conditions. She began to work wearing gloves, but couldn't control the tools accurately enough; so she discarded them, and endured frozen, bright red hands instead.

She worked painstakingly, terrified of making a mistake. After a couple of hours she was already exhausted and chilled to the bone, her hands numb with exertion. And there were still ten hours to go.

Above her, all day, she heard the creaking of ropes, the pounding of footsteps on the scaffolding and ladders, voices shouting, rock grating against rock as the massive blocks were hauled into place. The wall grew slowly. A few times she heard cries of pain, yells of rage. There was one break for hot soup, another for a lunch of bread, stew and stale cake. The food was poor, but by then she was so hungry she would have eaten anything.

By the time dusk fell and the shift ended, Ysomir felt as if two days had gone by. She ached all over, and her arms were so tired she could barely lift them. And her cellmates called this 'light work?' How much worse must the others be feeling?

309

Thinking of her cell mates, she quailed. A cold, red, winter sun was setting behind the Amber Citadel. She wished she could just walk towards it and keep going . . .

But she was being herded towards the gate in the hillside, and the night shift was streaming out wearily to begin work.

Lath was silent at the evening meal, his face etched with strain. 'Are you all right?' Ysomir asked.

'Everything hurts. I can hardly move. Look.' He opened his palms and they were red-raw.

'How did you—?'

'Rope-burn. A block slipped. Fell on to the man next to me and broke his leg. I heard it break.' Lath shook his head, swallowing hard. 'They dragged him away. You probably heard him screaming.'

'I thought you were meant to be on woodwork.'

'There was nothing for me today, so I have to do whatever else they tell me. I've never been so cold in my life. You sweat at first, then you feel like you're covered in ice.' His voice fell. 'I have to get out of here.'

She held his hand. 'Try to bear it, Lath. If you try to escape, you'll only make things worse.'

'How much worse could it get?'

As he spoke, Ysomir noticed a strange figure walking along between the tables on the far side of the room. The figure was wearing a long charcoal-grey cloak, the hood so deep that his face could not be seen. He was tall and apparently male, and from the knotted look of his long hands he was clearly of a fair age.

'What?' said Lath. She tilted her head, and he looked round to stare at the newcomer. She was not sure when he had entered, but a hush had fallen, as if everyone was aware of him. The figure spoke to no one, only moved softly between the tables like a spectre. Ysomir was filled with a sudden dread that stopped her eating; whether it was the figure itself or the others' palpable fear that infected her, she couldn't tell.

310

She dared not even ask her neighbours who it was. She suspected they wouldn't answer. Presently, the cloaked one stopped behind a handsome young man, tapped him on the shoulder, and beckoned to him. The young man paused, open-mouthed; then he got up and followed the figure out of the cave.

Even when they had gone, the hush persisted. The level of conversation rose, but the voices were subdued and laced with anxiety.

Later, the dreaded moment came when everyone was shut into their cells. Ysomir curled up on her mattress, hoping the others would ignore her. They seemed less interested in tormenting her tonight; too tired, perhaps. She was on the point of sleep, when she felt a booted foot pressing into her shoulder. She jerked awake, heart pounding.

'Did you see him?' It was the shortest, most aggressive of the women, Ede.

'Who?' said Ysomir.

'Old grey-bones, the torturer, we call him.'

'Who is he? Where was he taking that boy?'

'He comes and chooses people and takes them to the Amber Citadel,' said Ede, a menacing edge to her voice. 'The King wants them.'

'What for?' Ysomir felt she was being baited, but she was compelled to ask.

'Nice get-out, being chosen to serve the King, isn't it?'

'Is it?'

'Except that the King tortures them to death.'

'What? I don't believe that!'

'It's true. Enough stories come back out of the Citadel. They say the King's gone raving mad.' Ede paused for a chest-racking cough, spraying Ysomir with spit. One of the other women threw a boot at Ede and snapped, 'Stop that racket!'

'In fact,' Ede went on, catching her breath, 'They say that old grey-bones *is* the King. He comes down here

311

himself, because he likes to see his subjects suffering.'

Ysomir didn't know what to say. She was too tired to think; all she wanted was for Ede to leave her alone. 'Do you believe it?' she asked.

Ede gave a short laugh that turned into a painful cough. 'It's the truth. I'm just warning you, farm-girl. I'm pretty sure he'll come for you.'

'Why?'

'Because he always chooses the prettiest ones, male and female. Takes 'em quick, before their looks go. The torturer's coming for you, *Ysss-omir*.'

'You're just trying to frighten me!'

'Torturer's coming for you,' Ede repeated lightly, moving away and lying down on her own mattress. And every hour, Ysomir was woken, if not by Ede's cough, then by one or other of the women whispering, *'Old greybones is coming, Ysss-omir.'*

In the morning, Ede was shivering with fever, too sick to work. Ysomir, never one to be vindictive, wanted to stay and nurse her, but such an indulgence was not allowed. She was ushered out with the others, to brush two inches of snow off her work before she could begin again.

As she went to take her first desperately-needed break, a man – who had just come off one of the pulley gangs – collapsed right across her path. She jerked back in shock. His skin was white, his lips blue, his hands red with dead white fingertips. A guard marched over, yelled at the man to get up, kicked him in the ribs. The kick rolled the man on to his back, but he only stared up at the sky with sightless eyes.

Two people fell from the scaffolding on the same day; she saw them both fall. Another died of frostbite, and she feared that she and Lath would go the same way. By her fifth day at the Tower, coughs and fevers were running wild through the conscripts, claiming one or two lives every night. But a trickle of new workers kept arriving, healthy and innocent, to replace those who died.

Ede got better, but her deep cough persisted, and she was made to go back out on the scaffolding long before she was well enough to work.

'I'm quite looking forward to dying,' she told Ysomir one night, as they sat side by side on their mattresses. 'It's the quickest way out of here.'

'Don't say that. I can't believe I'll never go home.'

'Wait until you've been here as long as we have.'

The cold, it seemed, had numbed both Ede's desire to bully and Ysomir's fear of her. They were not friends, but they communicated.

'I can't believe the King would allow this, if he knew how bad it is!'

'Which King are we talking about? Beloved Garnelys, who treated his kingdom like a precious, exotic flower? Or this Garnelys, the madman? You peasants come here so wide-eyed, saying "I can't believe it, the King is so perfect!" He can't *not* know. We're on his doorstep.'

'I thought – we were always told he was good – we never had any reason to believe otherwise, until Beyne came.'

'Let me tell you something, farm-girl. Parione was like Nepheter's summer-land on earth until two years ago. I was an actress, or rather I was going to be one. I was studying with a theatre company; I hoped I'd work at the Old Royal one day.' She gave a savage laugh. 'Should have been careful what I wished for; I'm working where it *used* to be. Anyway, everything started changing. Not suddenly. It was quite slow at first. The King had a project, he wanted volunteers. When it was first announced, it sounded so wonderful, but we had no idea what the price was going to be. People volunteered, but not enough it seems, so then it became compulsory, if you were chosen you had to go to the quarry whether you wanted to or not. The atmosphere changed. Suddenly the army was growing, and it was everywhere, and it was as if they'd been

313

recruiting bastards for officers on purpose. People start protesting. Saphaeyender puts a play on, that says everything we wanted to say, but so elegantly. Oh, that showed the King all right. Next thing we know, he knocks the theatre down.'

'My sister wanted to see it, so badly,' said Ysomir.

'The King stops being seen in public any more. There were even rumours his own family quarrelled with him. His granddaughter dies in a shipwreck, and what a coincidence, Prince Galemanth dies too, a few months later. An illness, they say, but then came all these rumours the King himself had his own son assassinated, right in the Temple of Nuth. You know, I'm past caring now. Saphaeyender put his finger on it. Yes, he did. And look what happened.'

She turned away, curling up under the thin cover. Ysomir suspected she was weeping. She whispered, 'Ede?' but got no reply.

On the sixth day, as she laboured on her third block of stone, a supervisor whom she'd never seen before came to inspect the masons' progress. He was wearing a light grey cloak with the hood up, and black gloves. He stopped beside Ysomir and she saw that his face was nearly as pale as the snow, with undistinguished features and very dark eyes.

'Don't let me stop you working,' he said.

Her wrists ached and her hands were numb. It was all she could do to hold the chisel and hammer. 'Thank you, Lord—'

'Laphaeome,' he said in a soft, smooth voice. 'The architect.'

Ysomir stood up, astonished. 'You designed this – this tower?'

'And how pleasing it is to see our citizens working together to make the King's dream a reality.'

In her head, Serenis's dry voice said, *'That's one way of*

314

putting it.' To her remorse, Ysomir realised she'd spoken the words aloud.

'You are not happy to be sacrificing your time and skills for the King?'

His black eyes bored into hers. A wash of fear went through her. 'How – how high is the Tower to be?' she stammered.

His eyes seemed to leak into her, like ink. 'It will pierce the heavens. It has been a most interesting exercise, the logistics of designing both such a remarkable monument and the method of construction . . .'

Ysomir wasn't sure whether the voice belonged to Serenis or herself. 'And did your calculations including working out how many people will die before it's finished?'

Laphaeome's dark wet gaze made her skin crawl. 'As many as it takes.' He moved round and inspected her work; three large letters gouged into the frosty face of the rock. 'Surely the stone mason has not passed this? It's not up to standard.'

'It's the cold,' said Ysomir. 'Look at my hands. I can't hold the tools properly. It's the same for all of us. You make us work for too long!'

'If your skills do not meet the standard, you will be put on to less exacting duties,' Laphaeome said impassively. Then he was gone, gliding away like a ghost.

When Ysomir returned that night, almost asleep on her feet, her cellmates came to tell her that Ede had collapsed on the scaffolding that afternoon, and died a couple of hours later. Both were hoarse, red-eyed and beginning to cough.

Ysomir went to look at Ede's body. She recovered Serenis's locket from one of the pockets, and felt like a grave-robber. 'Whichever one of you has my goddess,' she told the other two, 'you can keep it. I hope it brings you blessings.'

Later, as she sat with Lath in the communal area, she had no appetite. She drank glassfuls of water and hot herb tea, but could not swallow a morsel of food. She pushed her dishes towards him and argued with him until, reluctantly, he ate her meal as well as his own. Her chest ached, and the noise of the area seemed deafening.

'Ysomir, you're not going down with this 'flu, are you?' he said worriedly.

'I don't know.'

'Are you cold?'

'Yes, but I'm always cold.' She was holding herself rigid against the shivers that threatened to rack her.

'Gods,' he said. 'It took one of my cellmates yesterday. The guards don't give a damn. Please don't leave me.'

'I met the architect today. The one who designed the Tower.'

Lath stared at her in disbelief. 'Are you sure you're not ill?'

'Really. He said it's going to pierce the heavens, whatever that means. Only someone as strong as Beorwyn could survive the labour they expect of us. "The Tower is an age-old pinnacle in the ocean, against which we are thrown like sea creatures, wave upon wave until our shells are smashed and our bodies washed away on the tide. But for all that are lost, more come, wave upon wave, to be smashed in their turn against the merciless Tower."'

'Who wrote that?'

'I just made it up. It's been in my head all day. Lath . . . if you ever meet my Lynden, tell him . . .'

The whole room was wavering. She seemed to be looking down a tunnel of dark, shimmering colours. The charcoal-cloaked figure came into view, drifting across her field of vision, then stopping and turning to look at her. He seemed to be in the centre of a heat-haze, looming above her, surrounded by colourless flames.

She couldn't see his face. Only the shadow of the hood. He stretched out a long, gnarled hand to her, and there was nothing she could do to resist his command.

'You,' he said in a deep, aged voice. 'Come.'

She heard Lath gasp, 'No!' but he sounded as if he were miles away. She was rising dizzily, resting her hand on old grey-bones' arm; and he was leading her into darkness, along a deep dark tunnel that wound down and onwards forever . . . until the ground itself turned liquid beneath her feet and Ysomir, consumed by fever and by swirling nightmares, fell headlong towards the core of the earth.

Chapter Fifteen. Silverholm

Frozen to the bone, Tanthe stumbled through curtains of whiteness, Rufryd and Lynden beside her. Their captors moved like ghosts against the snow, but the occasional prod of a spear-tip was real enough. They had climbed a long way, and then begun to descend a wide flank. The slope was steep; her feet were constantly skidding down through the snow, and her legs trembled with the exertion of staying upright. All she could hear was her own gasping breath.

She couldn't see the horses. Where were they? Every time she tried to look back, one of their shadowy captors would push her onwards. But at last, the snow veil parted briefly, and she glimpsed the horses ahead of her, their coats so clotted with snow she could barely see them. They were being led down the slope by three near-invisible figures.

Were these people Bhahdradomen or not? They roused no mind-spinning revulsion, and Lynden didn't seem distressed. Yet they radiated a quiet, glassy chill that was disturbingly unhuman.

Their captors were leading them down into a ravine, where the slopes formed a deep V between two intersecting mountain walls. Above them soared the peaks, wreathed in cloud, making Tanthe feel as small as a gnat. As the incline grew steeper, she found herself leaning into the wall, supporting herself with her hands. Only the build-up of snow under their boots kept them all from falling. Below them, the horses were struggling in white flurries.

Once we're in the valley, she thought, how will we ever climb out again?

When they came to the bottom unscathed, their captors led them along a path that was treacherous but mercifully flat. Tanthe had her hood up, her head bowed, all her attention fixed on keeping her feet.

She realised, suddenly, that there was no snow on the path. The blizzard had died down; she could still hear the wind but it sounded muffled and far away. Her face began to tingle and burn.

Putting her hood back, she looked around.

The slopes still rose around them but they were bare rock; above, she could see the yellowish glow of daylight through a thickness of snow, which appeared to be resting on a ceiling of ice. Ahead of her, the horses went skittishly, snorting clouds of breath on to the air. She looked back, saw what seemed to be the tunnel entrance where the ceiling began. Two of the white-cloaked figures were turning handles to haul a huge, translucent wedge of rock across to block the aperture. Above it was a broad ledge, gained by a curving stair set into the left-hand wall. And from the ledge, two cloud-pale faces were staring down at them.

'Rufe,' Tanthe said through stiff lips.

Rufryd and Lynden looked back, took in what she had seen, said nothing.

A hundred yards further on, the tunnel curved and opened out into a breath-taking cavern. They emerged onto a wide ledge about halfway up, overlooking the soaring space.

Her first impression was that the whole place was carved of ice; shining, crystalline, touched with rainbows. Below and above, Tanthe saw a complexity of different levels – some appearing to float in space – connected by twisting walkways and steps. The ceiling arched high above, translucent, gleaming. A wondrous, echoing cavern of white ice. And yet the air felt *warm*. The warmth made her shiver.

The light was soft and clear, enhanced by white lamps

that glowed everywhere. Tanthe saw people moving on the other levels, too far away to make out clearly. Her heart jumped with a mixture of excitement and fear.

Without speaking, their captors brought them along the ledge and down a gentle slope to a wide, semi-circular platform. It was protected from the drop only by a low rim of stone. Here they halted, and for the first time Tanthe was able to count them. Seven. Not ghosts but solid, real figures. Yet even in clear light they seemed spectral.

'Welcome to Silverholm,' said one. His voice was low-pitched and full of quiet power. 'We shall put up our spears now. You are too tired, I think, to engage us in a fight.'

Then he and the others began to put back their veils. Tanthe, Rufryd and Lynden exchanged looks of amazement. The faces revealed were long, pale and oval, with strong noses, small mouths, dazzling violet-blue eyes. Not beautiful, exactly, but so striking she couldn't tear her eyes away. It was hard at first to tell male from female, though Tanthe swiftly picked up a more masculine cast to some of the faces. Their skin was pearly, their hair long and straight and ranging in colour from white to palest gold. The man who had first spoken, who seemed to be their leader, had hair so white-blond it had almost a blue sheen.

The three who had led the horses took them away through an arch in the wall. The leader saw Tanthe's look of concern.

'Your horses will be well-cared for,' he said. 'But the mountains in winter are no place for them. Surely you must have known that.'

'We didn't ask for your opinion,' Rufryd said heatedly, 'and since you've captured us, we don't owe you any explanation, either.'

The man raised his thin, arched eyebrows. 'Captured? Rescued, I would say.'

Several more of the pearl-skinned folk had come to

relieve the party of their cloaks, and Tanthe gave hers up without taking her gaze from the man's face. 'Who are you?'

The man smiled haughtily. 'We are the Shaelahyr. The Aelyr of the Whiteveil mountains. My name is Elrill.'

'Aelyr?' Tanthe's heart accelerated. Her companions breathed out in quiet shock.

'Whatever you have heard of us, we are not cruel or inhospitable folk. We wish you no harm. If we had not brought you here, you would certainly have perished in the storm. I'm afraid you will be compelled to stay here awhile. Not by us but by the weather.'

Lynden's head came up. 'For how long?'

'For as long as winter lasts,' said Elrill. 'The thaw begins usually between Estrae and Firethorn.'

'Firethorn! That's nearly summer!' Tanthe swallowed a pang of despair, but Lynden's eyes burned.

'You can't stop us leaving!' he said.

The Aelyr answered firmly, 'You are going nowhere until the winter is over.'

'No!' Lynden cried. There was a swish of metal and, to Tanthe's dismay, he stood brandishing his short sword at Elrill's chest. The Aelyr's face turned hard as ice. Lynden pivoted, snaking his blade at the other six Aelyr who were gathered loosely on the ledge. His face was flustered. 'You can't keep us here. We'll fight our way out!'

He lunged, but a slim blade came ringing out of every Aelyr scabbard. Metal clashed. The three humans were ringed round by cold Aelyr faces, by glass-sharp swords. Rufryd drew his own sword and rushed to his brother's defence, but they were outnumbered. Elrill simply glared at them in blazing cold fury.

Without thinking, without drawing her own weapon, Tanthe tried to put herself bodily between the Aelyr and her companions. It was that or watch Rufryd and Lynden be killed.

'Stop!' she cried, raising her arms. A sword whispered

321

past the back of her hand. She did not even feel the cut until it began to itch, and the blood ran down her wrist.

Elrill seized her elbow and dragged her aside. A flick of an Aelyr sword and Lynden's blade clattered from his hand; then Rufryd, with four sword-points at his throat, was forced to throw down his own weapon. Two Aelyr males held their wrists firmly behind them; Lynden's face was feverish and desperate, Rufryd's grim with rage. Tanthe held her cut hand, her blood dripping on to the pristine white rock.

'So, this is your response to our hospitality,' Elrill said savagely, picking up the discarded weapons and handing them to a white-haired young male. 'More than rude and foolish. You fight badly, also.'

'Just a moment,' Tanthe said, furious. 'You know nothing about us! I know Lyn shouldn't have attacked you, but he's desperate. We all are, and – *ah*—'

A grunt of pain broke from her as she was seized by a man and a woman, her arms pulled behind her and tied with cords. Outraged, but weakened by the long ordeal in the blizzard, she couldn't defend herself. The Aelyr were deceptively powerful.

'Take them out of my sight,' said Elrill, turning away.

Six Aelyr took them through winding tunnels to a cave on a lower level. The cave was oval and about thirty feet across, with lamp-light flaring on walls of shiny white crystal. The horses were there, tethered to slim columns of rock at the rear of the cave. Lynden let out a sigh of relief. Someone had untacked them, and an Aelyr woman was there, doing her best to dry them off with a cloth. Their coats steamed.

Tanthe wriggled against her captors. 'Let me help with the horses! I'm not going to do anything!'

The Aelyr ignored her. Impassive and eldritch, they dragged the three to another column which stood to the right of the entrance, and lashed them to it with their hands behind their backs. Their cloaks and rucksacks had already been taken; now they were stripped of their remaining weapons, even – to Tanthe's distress – her Aelyr knife.

The female flung blankets on to the horses and left hurriedly without speaking. Two Shaelahyr men remained to guard the prisoners, standing at the open entrance with spears. Tanthe, Rufryd and Lynden were left there with their backs pressed to the column, bound so tightly that they could not move to sit down or even to see each other without painful contortions. The air was lukewarm, and they were all shivering as they began to adjust to the higher temperature.

'Thanks, Lyn,' Rufryd said tightly.

Lynden bowed his head. 'They can't keep us here.'

'You know, I do believe they might have been trying to save us from ourselves. We're worn out and so frozen we were about two hours off dying. So you choose that moment to demonstrate to the nimblest fighters in all the realms just what rubbish we are at sword-fighting!'

'Oh, shut up!' said Tanthe. 'Leave him alone. Gods.'

A pause. 'You all right, Tan?' Rufryd asked. 'How's your hand?'

She'd been trying to ignore the throbbing pain and the blood. 'Funny. You two start the fight and I'm the one who gets injured! No, I'm not all right. I'm starving, my feet are on fire, and I'm desperate for a pee.'

'Same here. I'd take that as some sort of proof we're still alive.'

'At least they untacked the horses and put blankets on them,' said Lynden.

'Probably stolen the saddles and bridles,' said Rufryd.

'I'm sure the Aelyr don't do undignified things like stealing.' Tanthe tried to ease the ache of her arms. She was growing more uncomfortable by the moment. 'But what are the horses going to be fed on?'

'What are *we* going to eat?' said Rufryd. 'Not very nice, these Shaelahyr, are they?'

Tanthe didn't answer. Her instinct was to defend the Aelyr, to keep their magical image intact in her own mind, but she couldn't. She leaned back against the column and closed her eyes, trying to rest.

'Scared?' he said.

'No.' She exhaled. 'Well, just a bit.'

'They think they're so far above humans,' Rufryd said in a low voice. 'So bloody superior.'

A new voice, clear and echoing, said, 'That's what we think, is it?'

Tanthe's eyes came open. It was Elrill, walking towards them in pale breeches and a long tunic, with his snowy hair floating about his shoulders. He emanated a cool radiance that made him seem even less human than he had at first impression. His face was smooth but his eyes glittered with blue fire.

'I trust your tempers have cooled?' he said.

'Yes,' said Tanthe, before one of the boys could say something they'd all regret. 'Could you untie us, please? We're unarmed, we're exhausted, and we don't mean you any harm, I swear.'

Elrill gazed thoughtfully into her eyes. The look darted right through her. Then he held out his hand, and on his palm lay her knife; grey and dull, adorned with a pebble.

'What's this?'

'A knife,' she said. 'I would like it back. Sentimental value. It's too blunt to do any harm.'

'Where did you get it?'

Half-annoyed and half-frightened, she tried to keep her emotions out of her voice. 'Why do you ask?'

'I want to know if you realise what it is.'

Her mouth tightened. 'All right, it's an Aelyr knife. I dreamed that an Aelyr gave it to me; Rufryd thinks I just found it. When there are, er . . . certain dangers it . . . it warns me.'

The blade caught the light, and the pebble turned briefly to moonstone; she was not sure if she had imagined it.

Elrill said, 'It's a defensive weapon called a *mnelir*, set with a *liroth* stone. The Aelyr of Verdanholm make these; I would say it's about a thousand years old. No one finds these lying around.'

'I don't know what to tell you,' said Tanthe. 'I have no idea who the man was in my vision, or why he gave it to me. But I'm telling you the truth! I didn't steal it, if that's what you think.'

Elrill gave her a long, appraising look; she wondered what he was seeing. Then he pressed his forefinger to the blunt tip. 'Do you trust me?'

'Do we have any reason to?'

He produced the scabbard and sheathed the knife. Then, leaning towards her, he slipped it into the side pocket of her black, Sepher jacket.

'A token,' he said. 'Have it; it's harmless against Aelyr, and I trust you to take care of it. Can we trust *you*?'

'Yes. Lynden only acted on impulse because he was upset.'

Rufryd nudged her foot with his. 'Tan, don't start apologising on other people's behalf!'

'No, she's right,' said Lynden. 'It was stupid of me. I'm sorry, Lord Elrill. I swear it won't happen again; only let us go.'

'I'll do so, if you promise to tell me who you are and what your business is, travelling in possession of an Aelyr knife, Sepher horses and all the trappings of the Duchy of Sepheret. Did Eldareth send you?'

'No,' said Tanthe. 'We don't know this Eldareth. But we'll tell you everything, if you'll only untie us and let us rest first.'

'Tan, we're not obliged to tell these people anything!' said Rufryd.

This time, she dug her foot into his. 'Ignore him, Lord Elrill. Rufryd is determined to stay tied up so he's got something to be angry about. But we have nothing to hide.'

Elrill sighed. His gaze moved over Lynden and Rufryd, and he flicked his hand at the two Shaelahyr who were guarding the entrance. 'Let them loose.'

The knots were untied, and the three stepped away from the post in relief. As blood rushed into Tanthe's frost-bitten hands, her sword-cut began to pulse viciously. The pain was so intense she couldn't speak. Her companions stood rubbing their wrists. From their expressions, they were suffering almost as badly.

Elrill turned his beautiful blue-violet eyes on to Tanthe. 'I believe you. Truth is written all over you; you couldn't dissemble if your lives depended on it. So, rest and eat and warm yourselves. Then you can explain to me why you are braving such dire weather to wander in the realms of the Shaelahyr.'

The 'rooms' to which they were taken were small caves, scooped out of the rock, with just enough space for a mattress on a low pallet, a chest that doubled as a table, and a folding screen to place across the entrance. Outside ran a ledge that overlooked the main body of the cavern, protected from the drop by a waist-high wall.

The caves were of the same milky rock crystal. Although Tanthe had first taken it for ice, it was dry, smooth and cool to the touch. The table and pallet were of silvery oak; the bed cover and the screen made of a warm white silk, woven with subtle frost-flower patterns and tiny jewels.

The Aelyr gave them a room each, returned their cloaks and rucksacks – although not their weapons – and brought them fresh garments to change into later. Before they rested, though, Lynden insisted on seeing that the animals were fed and watered.

Tanthe and Rufryd went with him, and found the Aelyr female who had been with the horses before now throwing down a bed of fine straw for them. She looked at the humans, cool and wary; they looked back at her, fascinated by the unhuman sinuosity of her movements, the long pure white fall of her hair. Eventually Lynden blurted, 'Where do you get straw from?'

She looked at him with slanting sapphire eyes and no hint of warmth. 'This is what we use for our mattresses. We have stores of grain and vegetables, brought up from the lowlands before winter sets in. Did you think we lived on air?'

'No. I don't know what I thought.'

'Your horses will be well-fed and cared for,' she said, stroking Halcyon's neck. 'So, Elrill considers it safe for you to wander free in Silverholm?'

'Of course,' said Tanthe, suddenly realising that the Aelyr was nervous of them. 'We're perfectly civilised, don't worry.' She told her their names.

'I am Cyl,' said the Shaelahyr.

Half an hour spent attending to the horses put them all in better spirits. Tanthe caressed Redbird's soft muzzle and scratched her neck, silently apologising for bringing her into this. Thank Mahaa the horses were uninjured. And if anything could calm Lynden, it was Halcyon.

By the time they went back to their quarters, exhaustion was catching them up in earnest. Back in Tanthe's room, Cyl dressed her wound with healing moss and a bandage, then brought her a rock-crystal tumbler full of honeyed, hot tea. As Tanthe thawed out, the tingling of her feet and hands eased at last.

She had never been so close to an Aelyr before. Even her mysterious auburn-haired male had never seemed this close or real. They *were* different. Cyl was a creature of snow, remote and humourless, with a presence that was delicate and tangibly alien. Tanthe couldn't pin it down, but it was there; thrilling, perilous, other.

'They said the snow had trapped you, and they found you just in time,' said Cyl. 'Are you warm enough? We keep Silverholm cool, so that the bitter cold outside is less painful to us.'

Tanthe sat on the edge of the low bed, thinking

longingly of lying down on it. 'But how do you heat such a place at all? I've seen no fires.'

'There are streams deep beneath the earth of boiling water and liquid rock. We draw our heat from them.'

'You do feel the cold, then?'

'Why, do we seem unfeeling?' Cyl's extraordinary eyes shone like blue fire into Tanthe's.

'Well, I wasn't sure,' Tanthe said sharply, almost wanting to dislike Cyl for her coolness. 'Forgive me if my questions offend you, but you are the first Aelyr I've spoken to properly. I expect I seem crassly nosey to you, but I am genuinely interested.'

Cyl blinked, surprised. 'In fairness, I am not used to humans, either. Yes, we do feel the cold. We are better than humans at controlling our reaction to it, that's all.'

'Then why do you choose to live here?'

Cyl's gaze drifted away from Tanthe's, haunted. 'That is something you should ask Elrill. But to put it simply, we love the solitude and the purity. None trouble us here.'

'You bear arms, though. Against whom?'

The blue stare came back to her, now imperious and chill as the mountains. 'Who are you asking these questions for, Tanthe?'

Tanthe gasped. 'No one.'

'Are you sure?' Cyl frowned a little, blinked, stared again.

'Of course I'm sure! Why are you looking at me like that?'

The Shaelahyr broke the contact. 'As you said yourself, there is a difference between genuine interest and crass intrusion. Rest now; I will wake you in time to bathe before our evening meal.'

She stalked out, leaving Tanthe ruffled and indignant. She glared after the Aelyr woman for a moment, then went next door to find Rufryd and Lynden together; Rufryd stretched out on the bed, Lynden sitting on its edge, hands cradling his hot tea, head bowed. They'd obviously been arguing.

A white cat with slanting blue eyes sat on the chest; as Tanthe entered, it mewed and stood up to be stroked.

'That's an impressive bandage, Tan,' Rufryd said, propping himself up on one elbow.

Tanthe went to fuss the cat. It butted its head blissfully against her palm. 'I've just had the most bizarre conversation with Cyl,' she said.

'Well?'

'Oh, I don't know. I probably said all the wrong things. But I refuse to tread on eggshells, if they won't make any attempt to be friendly back!'

'Careful what you say,' he said gravely.

'Why?'

He tilted his head at the cat. 'I reckon Cyl's changed shape so she can spy on us.' He made a mock hissing noise; the cat stared at him, gave a squawk of alarm, and fled the room. But her claws found no purchase on the ice-smooth rock and she skittered out of the entrance, sliding sideways as she tried frantically to turn the corner. Rufryd fell back on the bed, almost crying with laughter. Lynden shook his head in exasperation.

'For the gods' sake, Rufe!' Tanthe snapped, trying to keep a straight face. 'There was no need to terrify the life out of that poor cat.'

'I didn't know she was going to react like that,' said Rufryd. 'Touchy lot, aren't they? Oh, calm down, Tan. It's bad enough these Aelyr having no sense of humour. The horses are in a nice warm cave, eating their heads off, and we've been promised a long sleep and a hot bath. Things could be worse.'

'You're feeling better, then.'

Lynden said, '*And* he seems to have forgotten what Elrill told us.'

'I know how you feel, Lyn.' Tanthe sat down beside him. 'But we can't travel through this, whatever happens. The gods know, we've tried!'

His brow furrowed. 'I can't just give up.'

'No one's talking about giving up.'

'Ysomir needs us. Next spring might be too late!'

'I'm as frustrated as you are, but we'll get nowhere by starting fights with people who are trying to help us.'

'Imprison us, you mean,' Lynden said darkly.

Tanthe was exasperated. 'Are you sure you're seventeen, Lyn?'

'What?'

'Because you're acting as if you're seven! Grow up!'

'Tan,' said Rufryd, 'I've just had this argument with him. I'd rather not hear a word-for-word repeat of it. For Breyid's sake, let's get some rest.' He turned on his side, with his back to them. 'Stick the screen across on your way out.'

Tanthe was woken, hours later, by music.

The room was filled with a strangely glowing twilight. Someone – Cyl, she assumed – had placed a white lamp on the chest beside the bed, but veins of light shone within the walls themselves. It was like being in an underwater cave, full of dim, icy light.

And the music . . . soft fluty sounds that might have been instruments or voices braided with sharper, metallic notes, ethereal but underpinned by a rolling bass that seemed to come from the roots of the mountain itself . . . The sound drew Tanthe out of bed. She put on one of the garments Cyl had left, a simple robe, and went out onto the ledge.

The cavern was dark, but glittering with thousands of firefly lights. Below she saw many Shaelahyr, sitting on round ledges on a dozen different levels, and all playing instruments; pipe, harps, lutes, finger-cymbals, long curved horns, others she'd never seen before. Their hair and skin shone like pearl against the darkness. Where light caught highlights on the ledges, the rims shone like crescents floating in space.

A Shaelahyr woman came up to her, but it wasn't Cyl.

This woman was smaller, with silvery hair that caught violet lights, and eyes the colour of amethyst. The edges of her hair glowed as if feathered with starlight. 'Did you sleep well?' she asked. 'I'm Metiya.' And she actually smiled, a joyful impish smile.

'Wonderfully, thank you. Hello, Metiya.'

'Come, I'll show you where to bathe. We will soon gather for *sertance*, our evening meal. Elrill asks that you join us.'

'Will Cyl be there, or has she had enough of us?'

Metiya burst out laughing and slipped her hand through Tanthe's arm. 'Don't judge us all by her. She is determined to win a wager we once made, that one of us could make her smile.'

She led Tanthe along the ledge and over a vertiginous walkway to an open arch. Tanthe smelled steam laced with delicious fragrances. A labyrinth of corridors gave onto an airy, glassy cave, in the centre of which was a bath almost large enough to swim in.

At the far end, a statue of an Aelyr maiden stood clasping a giant shell, from which water gushed, steaming, into the pool. The bubbling pool lay on a level with the marble floor, washing away into a concealed channel as it was constantly replenished.

To Tanthe's amusement, the bath was communal. Lynden and Rufryd were already immersed; seeing her, Lynden turned faintly pink but Rufryd grinned. Tanthe shrugged, gave Metiya her robe, and slid naked into the pool to sit on the submerged shelf beside them.

The heat made her gasp. Enveloped by foaming water and by green, spicy fragrances, she tipped her head back in pleasure. The hot water soaked the ends of her hair, caressing her neck and scalp. Her bandaged hand got wet, but she didn't care. She pulled the bandage off and found the cut already closed.

'Towels,' said Metiya, indicating a soft white pile on a marble bench behind the statue. 'When you are dressed,

331

we'll take you to Elrill.' She gave a friendly grin and left them.

'Gods,' Tanthe sighed. 'This is wonderful. This is the most delicious thing I've ever felt.'

'For once, I can't argue with you,' said Rufryd.

Lynden carefully avoided looking at her, but Rufryd watched her openly, a slight smile on his lips. Tanthe watched him, too; the water glistening on his strong shoulders and streaming over his chest.

'I never dreamed such a place as this existed,' she murmured. 'These people are *Aelyr*. I mean, I always knew they were real but I couldn't quite fully believe it until now. Guests of the Shaelahyr . . .'

'Don't get too comfortable here, will you?' Lynden said sourly.

'We won't,' Tanthe said, annoyed with him.

'Show you two a bed and everything else seems to go out of your minds.' Lynden rose out of the water, turning his back to them as he climbed out and wrapped himself in a towel.

'If by "everything" you mean my sister, of course I haven't forgotten her.' Tanthe spoke evenly, not wanting to start an argument. Lynden didn't reply.

When they had dragged themselves reluctantly from the bath and dried off, they returned to their rooms and put on the Aelyr garments; soft trousers, long loose shirts and tabards, all made of figured, jewel-scattered white silk. The material was thin yet deliciously warm. Tanthe felt wonderful. All she needed now was food. The nightmare of the mountains seemed to have taken place a year ago.

Seeing Rufryd, she laughed.

'What?' he said.

'You look so strange. Those ethereal garments, with your weather-tanned face and hands sticking out of them. It sort of spoils the effect.'

'Thanks. I was going to tell you that you look wonderful, but now I won't bother.'

'Are you ready?' said Cyl, waiting on the walkway outside their caves. She and Metiya were there together. 'Elrill and Liyet are waiting for you.'

A thrill went through Tanthe. Music echoed from the blue-black vault of the cavern, its harmonies flowing along unexpected paths into exquisite dissonance. It drew her into a trance. She walked with her hand through Rufryd's arm, but she was hardly aware of him or of Lynden walking in front of them.

The two women led them to a walkway that twisted upon itself, spiralling down to a wide disk of rock that seemed to hang suspended over the void. Elrill was there with fifteen or so Shaelahyr around him, all sitting cross-legged on cushions. Their hair gleamed like ice and starlight. In darkness the cave behind them seemed vast, and it was impossible to believe that harsh winter was outside. Lamps gleamed everywhere like moons. Skeins of light glittered within the rock itself. This place was another realm; unearthly, cool and slow-moving. She could see the musicians on other levels, playing with a languorous self-absorption as if to please not Elrill's party, but themselves.

Elrill and the other Aelyr looked utterly relaxed. They were lounging, talking to each other, drinking wine. Metiya and Cyl sat on the fringes, giving the humans up to their leader. There was no air of formality, but still Tanthe felt nervous.

'Greetings to you,' he said, looking up. Again his strangeness and the colour of his eyes struck her afresh; she couldn't hold such intensity in her memory. There was a white cat draped over his shoulder; she, too, stared at the newcomers with eyes of the same blazing violet. Another cat dozed by his thigh, and a third came wandering up to mew at them.

Next to Elrill sat a tall and striking woman with serene blue eyes and an alert baby in her arms. 'This is my companion, Liyet,' he said, 'and our son Theliell.'

Liyet smiled. The Shaelahyr were not all made of ice,

333

after all. 'Sit with us, and be very welcome,' she said. 'You are hungry, I hope.'

Cautious, they sat down on three vacant cushions he indicated; Tanthe on Elrill's right, Rufryd and Lynden to the left of Liyet. None of them could take their eyes off the child. Theliell had the same long, serene face as his parents and startling azure eyes. He did not cry or gurgle; he simply *watched*, uncannily like a small adult. Liyet saw Tanthe staring; embarrassed, Tanthe said the first thing that came into her head.

'Are there many children here?'

'Not many, no,' said Liyet. 'We live long and breed slowly. We are finite, as I expect you know.'

'Er – no, I'm sorry, I don't. What does that mean?' Immediately Tanthe felt she was straight out into deep water again. Why can't I keep my mouth shut? she thought. But Liyet answered calmly. 'A human comes into existence only when he or she is conceived. But Aelyr souls pre-exist. Therefore our number is limited; we can't simply decide to have a child, there must be a soul, a spark ready to come to the physical plane. But then, if the spark choose us, we cannot deny it, either. He or she *must* come into being.'

Tanthe was stunned. 'So – you – er, didn't actually choose to have Theliell?'

Liyet laughed, glancing at Elrill. 'No, but we knew he was coming. And we would never have chosen *not* to have him, because for him to come to us is the most wondrous privilege.'

'Yes, I can see that, but . . .'

'No one knows how many Aelyr souls there are still to be born. But our number has, in the end, a limit.'

Tanthe looked at Liyet, open-mouthed. Before she could think what else to ask, Elrill said, 'This is hardly a subject to discuss with humans.'

'Didn't that cause the schism between us at the start,' Liyet countered, 'the jealous guarding of secrets?'

334

'Ah, here is the wine,' said Elrill, cutting off the argument.

Then Tanthe almost leapt out of her skin. A silver-skinned man no more than eighteen inches high, dressed in a green tunic, was offering her a glass of wine.

'I don't bite,' he said indignantly.

Elrill and the other Aelyr laughed at her shock. More of the tiny figures were pouring onto the rock, bearing dishes of food which were far bigger than they were. Tanthe, Lynden and Rufryd watched in astonishment as the little men and women walked here and there among the guests, setting down the dishes. The silver folk were slender, with thick black hair, dark eyes and perfectly proportioned bodies.

'They are Zampherai,' said Elrill, as if that explained everything.

'Who?' said Rufryd.

'Surely you know of them. Subterraneans.'

'I've heard the name,' Tanthe said. 'Never seen them before. I didn't realise they were so—'

'Good-looking?' said one of the silver-skinned men at her elbow.

She'd taken a quick sip of wine, which tasted sublime. When he spoke, she nearly swallowed it the wrong way. 'Exactly,' she gulped.

He gave a sarcastic smile, and trotted away.

'They are our helpers,' said Elrill. 'We could not live here without them. Do you think we created this place with Aelyr sorcery?'

'I don't know,' said Tanthe.

'The Zampherai built it. They are the miners, the magicians with crystal. Come, help yourself to food. You're hesitating.'

Tanthe said, 'We have a folk story about a boy and a girl who went into the Aelyr realm and never came home again, because they ate the food. Saphaeyender wrote a beautiful version of it.'

'You are still on earth,' Elrill said, chuckling. 'This is earthly food. What a lovely conceit, that Aelyr want humans so much they would drug them with enchanted food to keep them!'

Tanthe took a morsel off the dish in front of her. It appeared to be a plum, stuffed with something like goat's cheese. But the flavours – dark and savoury, laced with hot spices and unfamiliar herbs – took her by surprise.

It was very good. She took another; Rufryd and Lynden dubiously followed suit. Soon the dish was empty, and the Zampherai were refilling their wine-glasses, and bringing a plate of tender rolled leaves, stuffed with a delectable nut mixture. The Aelyr ate sparingly; Tanthe was embarrassed that Rufryd and Lynden were giving their best impersonation of famished hounds.

'You are feeling better after your ordeal,' said Elrill.

'Very much,' said Tanthe, her mouth full. 'Thank you.'

'So. You promised to tell us who you are.'

'But how do we know we can trust you?'

'Perhaps you can't. I've no way of proving it. There has been friendship between human and Aelyr, but there's been enmity as well, and much misunderstanding. We feel no great affection for you, but we feel no hostility either. We don't particularly want you here. You have nothing we covet, if that's what worries you; not even your fine horses. We helped you because you were in a dreadful mess, and despite your ingratitude.'

'We've said sorry. We are grateful.'

'You and your people didn't have to be so heavy-handed about it,' said Rufryd.

'We captured you because we didn't know who or what you were, and the open mountainside was hardly the place to stand discussing it.'

Tanthe said, 'Whatever impression Lynden gave, we're harmless. We have no hostility towards the Aelyr. Quite the opposite.'

'Well, your outburst is forgiven,' said Elrill. 'It was quite the worst display of sword-fighting I've ever seen.'

'We're farmers,' Tanthe said tightly, wanting to explain that she was not really a farmer, but . . .

'For farmers, then, you weren't so bad, but you have so much to learn.' Elrill paused. Music rose in the gap, voices fluting in a strange language, making the hairs stand up on her neck. 'First, tell us your story.'

Tanthe looked at Rufryd and Lynden. They shrugged. Then, between them, they told Elrill everything. All the way through, he and Liyet exchanged looks; when it came to the story of the Bhahdradomen in Ardharkria, their expressions were of shocked dismay.

When they had finished, Elrill shook his long head. 'Ah, it is worse than we had feared.'

'You've heard about this?' said Rufryd. 'When?'

'We have heard rumours in the lowlands for over a year that your King has been issuing strange commands . . .'

'Did you do anything about it?' Rufryd asked. Tanthe sensed an accusation.

'The Aelyr do not interfere in human affairs,' said Elrill. 'I hardly think you would want us to. In fact, we are forbidden to do so, by mutual agreement. Would humans dare to interfere in ours?'

Rufryd looked stormily into his wine. 'It seems to me that something appalling is happening, and there's no one to help us.'

Elrill said, 'And yet, if it was really so appalling, I would have expected our friend Eldareth to have come here and warned us. Yet he hasn't.'

'Who is this Eldareth?' said Rufryd. 'They mentioned him at Luin Sepher.'

'Many things. He has been an actor, a writer, a traveller. Eldareth is one of the few who would dare, not merely to speak out against wrongdoing, but to take action.'

'He was trying to warn us in Sepheret, apparently,' said Tanthe.

'Yes, that's Eldareth. And yet he has not been to us. I

fear he may have put his life in danger once too often.'

Elrill sounded genuinely sad. Tanthe warmed to him. His words excited and terrified her. 'All we set out to do was find my sister,' she said. 'This all sounds so complicated.'

Elrill laughed. 'But surely you see that, even if you find her, you will not be allowed simply to take her? You'd need an army! You're brave, my friends, but too naive for words.'

Tanthe, Lynden and Rufryd were silent. How painful, knowing he was right.

'More wine,' Liyet said gently. 'My heart aches for you.'

'What is it, then?' Tanthe asked. 'The Bhahdradomen?'

It felt strange using the word. But surely they were safe here.

'The Bhahdradomen may be restless, but they are too weak to dare an open attack on humans, let alone the Aelyr,' said Elrill.

'They had a go at us,' said Rufryd.

'Only when you recognised them for what they were.'

'When Lynden recognised them,' Tanthe said quietly. 'Yes, that's true to some extent. But I think they first attacked us when we tried to take my sister back – I mean, I couldn't say exactly what attacked us – but the thing is, Beyne unleashed them on us and *he* didn't know what they were. He genuinely didn't know. He thought he was dealing with the Mediators.'

There was a long silence. Liyet said gently, 'Tanthe, I sense that you want answers from us. I'm not sure we can give any.'

'The Eaters ever were mimics,' said Elrill. 'We must be on our guard – but still, I'm convinced they have no true strength. They may slip about like snakes, biting here and there, but unless their fortunes change drastically they are not our first concern. No, the problem seems to be with your human hierarchy. Is your King's ambition sane, or has he lost his grip on reality?'

Tanthe was uneasy. She recalled the note, warning the people of Sepheret that Garnelys had gone mad, but to hear it from the lips of another, not wholly friendly race – it was as if an outsider had insulted a member of her family. 'Are the Aelyr qualified to judge human sanity?' she said softly.

'This is not an Aelyr insult.' He gave her an arch, chilling look. 'I am speculating, according to what you have told us. My friends . . .' Elrill leaned forward. 'The Aelyr are supposed to keep their distance from human affairs. But the Shaelahyr . . . well, we are more involved than common sense would allow.'

'Why?' asked Tanthe.

'We have our own realm, Verdanholm, but Earth is dear to us. Different factions of the Aelyr have argued over the centuries; many believe we should withdraw from the world completely because humans cannot tolerate us. But we say that we have more than a right, we have a duty to stay here. Some Aelyr dwell in both Earth and Verdanholm, passing freely between them. But the Shaelahyr . . . well, we were banished from Verdanholm for . . .' He paused; the other Shaelahyr were looking at him with raised eyebrows. 'Well, let us say for loving this world too much.' His lips thinned; he obviously wasn't going to tell them every secret. 'Do you not know your history?'

Tanthe bristled, but she was more glad than ever of her talk with Lady Amitriya. 'I like to think I know something.'

'Well?'

'Well . . . In the ancient days the earth was wild; all the energies of the stones and crystals were in a state of chaos. Rock ran in molten rivers, mountains thrust up from the earth, chasms opened and spewed fire—'

'Ah, do you know why?'

'I was told,' she said, annoyed at being tested and determined not to fail, 'that the *roths* of the earth are

339

sentient in their way. They wanted neither humans nor Aelyr walking upon them, who had endured for countless aeons before the beasts appeared.'

Elrill smiled. 'Yes, that is the story, though how far changed by myth even the Aelyr cannot say. But a great Aelyr, a wise *roth* mage named Nilothphon, is credited with healing the Earth. He first discovered the secrets of jewelfire, and learned to speak to the stones and calm them, and thus made the land habitable. In return for letting humans live in peace on the surface, the earth *roths* asked for guardians who would stand between them and the living races.'

'The Zampherai!' Rufryd exclaimed. To Tanthe's surprise, he was listening raptly.

'Though the Zampherai would deny that the Aelyr actually created them, of course,' Elrill continued. 'But I'd say that the Aelyr showed great care for the world, wouldn't you? We were peacekeepers and teachers, as the early tribes spread across Aventuria and began to form the realms. Many Aelyr lived on Earth in those days, in Sepheret and Torith Mir, in Azura Maroc and in Paranios, which was as beautiful as Verdanholm. It's said that by our very nature we were far ahead of humans in wisdom, and that we taught them many of the skills they needed, and that, in jealousy, they turned those skills against us and tried to drive us out.'

'It's also said,' Tanthe flashed back, 'that the Aelyr have a high opinion of themselves and are not above rewriting history to prove it. But I wouldn't know about that.'

'Tanthe!' Rufryd said under his breath.

Elrill looked shocked. For a terrible moment she thought he was going to throw them out onto the mountainside. Then he broke into laughter, while Liyet and the Shaelahyr around him pulled ironic faces.

'A fair point,' he said. 'The truth is slanted on both sides, it seems.'

'I'm not taking sides,' said Tanthe. 'My mother brought

me up to think of the Aelyr as wonderful and mysterious. And I've heard that the Aelyr didn't withdraw for a single reason but many, one of which was human ingratitude. Perhaps we were fed up with the Aelyr taking credit for everything.'

'Understandable, indeed,' Elrill said, smiling straight into her eyes. 'And I'm enjoying your candour. But some of us stayed. Now, I couldn't say whether we originated in this world and later moved to Verdanholm – which humans could not enter – or the other way round. However, it's clear that humans and Aelyr could not agree on history, philosophy or belief, nor even on how we should live in the world.'

Tanthe thought of Amitriya. 'Someone told me that the people of Eisilion used to worship the Aelyr. But you destroyed their temples, everything!'

'And now the Eisilionians hate us, and we are the villains. Why?' Elrill gave her a dark look. 'Because they, like you, don't understand why we did it. We're not gods. We don't want to be worshipped. It was perfect idiocy on their part to worship us! They would not listen to reason, so they had to be stopped. Regrettable.'

'So it is true you have no gods?' said Tanthe.

'It's true, indeed. We acknowledge all the myriad *roths* of the universe. It's just that, unlike humans, we do not put names or forms to them, nor make festivals around them.' Tanthe wanted to challenge this veiled criticism, but Elrill went on. 'Still, the human traditions at least pay reverence to the cycles of nature. The Bhahdradomen pay reverence to nothing at all but their single god, the Ancestor, the primal Egg from which they believe their race first hatched.'

'But where did they come from?' asked Rufryd. 'I heard that it was from a land far across the Lapis Ocean to the south, a land they had to leave because they'd destroyed it. They came to feed on Aventuria instead.'

Elrill nodded. 'A land named *Hellaxis*, a blackened, dead

place where humans sometimes wish each other, meta-phorically. It may be real, it may be only a story to explain the Bhahdradomen, it may lie deep underground or in another realm altogether. Since the Bhahdradomen keep their secrets, we don't know. Still, the Eaters came from somewhere. A few at first, then in wave on wave, until the tide overwhelmed us, and they ruled Aventuria for three hundred years and more.'

There was silence on the ledge; the music turned eerie and mournful. 'Those were dark days, terrible days,' Elrill went on. 'But I was telling you before of Nilothphon, the mage who calmed the earth. The agreement he made was the earliest form of Xauroma; all the leaders that followed, even the ancient ones such as Mounicaa and Arbal, created Xauromas of a kind, their promise to cherish the land which nourished them in return. Queen Silana, when she founded Parione, renewed that covenant most powerfully with the help of the Zampherai. But the greatest Xauroma of all was forged by Queen Hetys when she united the Nine Realms against the Bhahdradomen. and that Xauroma, which still protects Aventuria today, was renewed by King Maharoth, successor to Queen Hetys, when he finally triumphed over the enemy on the Silver Plains.'

Tanthe said, 'Whatever the quarrels between humans and Aelyr, we stood together against the Bhahdradomen, didn't we?'

'Without each other's help, none of us would have survived,' Elrill said. 'The Shaelahyr acknowledge that, even if some Aelyr do not. Still, we won, and the Eaters have spent the last two hundred and fifty years in exile on Vexor, beyond the Vexat Straits. Allowed to remain there on condition that they never attempt to enter Aventuria again.'

'I'm not sure King Maharoth didn't show them too much mercy,' said Rufryd, 'after what we've seen. Secret deals, to let colonies of them stay on the mainland!'

Elrill and Liyet exchanged looks, seemingly more concerned than they had been at the start. 'It is disturbing,' said Elrill. 'The truth about the Xauroma is that although it is powerful, it's also fragile. It's not merely a covenant between the monarch and the land, but a complex web between humans and Zampherai and Aelyr. If it begins to break down, then the Bhahdradomen might crawl through the gaps.'

Lynden gasped. Tanthe saw that he'd gone white; she, too, turned cold.

'I don't mean to alarm you,' Elrill sighed. 'Aventuria has been a green and golden cradle of peace for two hundred and fifty years. That's all you've ever known. I'm sorry you've had such a savage awakening from your innocence. Still, I am certain that the Bhahdradomen, however resentful they undoubtedly are, remain crushed. Their leader Aazhoth believes very firmly in toeing the human line for the sake of a quiet life. He would never try anything.'

Tanthe didn't feel wholly reassured; neither did Rufryd, from his expression. Lynden pressed his fingers to his temples. 'They *are* trying to come back. I can feel it.'

Liyet touched his arm, concerned. 'How clearly do you see this?'

'Not clearly at all. It's just a bad feeling that comes and goes. I wish it wouldn't.'

Elrill spoke gravely. 'Well, if you wondered why we still arm ourselves when we have no enemies – it's always wise to be prepared for the worst. I hope you will accept my assurance that you are safe here for as long as you stay. Can we put our rather unfortunate beginning behind us, and be friends?'

'Yes,' said Tanthe, her throat tight.

'So we're not prisoners?' said Lynden. 'We are free to leave?'

Elrill looked up into the vault of the cavern, and exhaled. 'The weather will only grow worse. With or without your horses, you will die if you leave. I can assure you, you are going nowhere until the spring.'

Lynden lowered his head. He squeezed his eyes shut; Tanthe shared his spasm of pain. But this time, he made no objection. Rufryd put a hand on his shoulder.

'When spring comes,' Lynden said hoarsely, 'will you help us then?'

'As far as we can,' said Elrill. 'We live pleasantly here. Since we all do our share of the work, you will be expected to do yours, of course. But one thing we can do for you in return, since you are trapped here, is to do something about your appalling lack of skill with the sword. Let us teach you the Aelyr style which is, I'm bound to tell you, infinitely superior to the human.'

Tanthe was alone, undressing for bed. She felt tired, frustrated that their search for Ysomir was delayed, but resigned to it. Never in her most outlandish dreams had she thought the Aelyr would capture her, shelter her, even teach her . . .

Her screen moved, and Rufryd's face appeared round it. 'Are you planning to sleep on your own?' he asked softly.

She smiled. 'I'd rather not. Come here.'

'Well, I don't know.' He folded his arms. 'I'm not sure I've got the energy to make love to you.'

'Don't torture me.'

She held her arms out and he went into them with a sigh of pleasure, kissing her face, biting her neck, trying to pull off his clothes without letting go of her. When at last he was naked and he slid into the bed beside, he was already erect. Her forest god, warm and hard and eager.

'I don't think I can hold back for long,' he breathed. 'It's been such a long time.'

She cupped his buttocks, pulling her against him. 'Nor can I. I've really missed you.'

She was already open to him, aching, as he slid inside her. Delicate fires ignited, so exquisite they were almost

344

painful. They joined fiercely, hurriedly, with more heat than affection; when Rufryd began to come she was with him, welded to him, all the guilt, fear, and frustration of the journey dissolving in their climax.

The second time was slower, more tender. Finally they lay watching the strange crystal lights rippling in the ceiling, letting the sweat cool on their limp bodies.

'You're an animal, Tanthe.' Rufryd gave her a sleepy kiss. 'I like that in a woman.'

She smiled. 'I hope Lynden didn't hear us. He seems so alone. I hope he'll be all right.'

'Well, he's learned his lesson about running off on his own. He knows we're stuck here, he's just got to accept it.'

'I can't believe we're here. It's like a dream.'

'So they really exist, the folk of the other-world. Can't say I like 'em much.'

'They're different, that's all.' She was quiet for a moment, thinking of their talk with Elrill. 'I'm less frightened of them than I was.'

'Who, the Aelyr?'

'No. I mean the Bhahdradomen. I can say the word now. You heard what Elrill told us. They creep around because they have no power.'

'No power at all,' Rufryd murmured, falling asleep.

The next morning, Lynden was on his own with the horses, trying to forget the muffled cries of bliss that seemed to emanate from Tanthe's room in the night. As long as he was taking care of the animals, at least he felt useful.

'Lynden?' said a soft voice.

He looked up from examining Halcyon's feet and there, resting her hand on Sunhawk's withers, was Elrill's companion Liyet. She was tall and radiant, as he'd expect a goddess to look. The uncanny child was not with her.

'Good morning, Lady Liyet,' he said, nervous.

'Just Liyet,' she said, moving around the horses towards

him. 'You're troubled, Lynden. Is there anything I can do?'

Her beautiful eyes pinned him; he had no idea what to say to her. 'Thank you, my lady, but I don't think so.'

'You can talk to me.' She came closer. 'You spoke last night of seeing the Bhahdradomen for what they are?'

Lynden swallowed hard. Then he found himself telling her everything; his strange experiences in Ardharkria, his unbidden visions. 'I don't know what's wrong with me,' he said hopelessly.

Liyet touched his shoulder; her hand was warm and soothing. 'Lynden, I know what it is. You've picked up some form of *ethroth*.'

'What?'

'Last night Elrill spoke of the energies of the earth. It isn't just the stones that possess those energies, but everything. We Aelyr have no gods; rather, all those entities you regard as gods, we regard as vibrations. All things have their own powers, their special characteristics, their thought-forms or spirits, which we call *roth*. Some of them float free – especially where there has been a traumatic event – waiting to attach themselves. Those we call *ethroth*.'

Lynden was stunned. 'How can I get rid of it?'

She stroked his shoulder. 'My dear, it won't harm you. It's already helped you, from what you said.'

'That's one way of looking at it,' he said grimly. 'I'd still rather be rid of it.'

'But you can't, because it has opened up a channel in you that was there all the time. You could be a Seer, if you trained yourself.'

'Gods, no!'

'What are you afraid of?'

'I don't know,' he said, shuddering. 'I don't know.'

Liyet laid her hands on his arms. It was the first time any woman had touched him – apart from Tanthe with her sisterly hugs – since he'd lost Ysomir. He confessed, 'I keep seeing Ysomir . . . in love with someone else. But that figure is like Death. I don't know what it means. All it does is torment me!'

Liyet leaned towards him, kissed his forehead, and held him steady with the placid aquamarine of her eyes.

'Learn to use the *ethroth*, Lynden. Don't let it use you.'

Rufryd could never admit it to his brother, but their stay in Silverholm was the happiest time he'd ever known.

The sword-master, Alraen, was small, willowy and pale as frost; he looked as if a gust of warm air would dissolve him. But when he fought, he was a lightning-whip.

Rufryd entered training with a flippant, overconfident attitude; his sword skills were only a bit rusty, he thought, and this was just a way of passing the time. Disgusted to find they would be using wooden practice swords and not real weapons, he said so aloud. Within five minutes, Alraen had knocked the arrogance out of him.

'This is why we use the wooden swords on which you pour scorn,' Alraen said, standing over his bruised, winded pupil in the training cavern. 'So that I do not kill you!'

It took Rufryd and Tanthe many days to adjust to the relentlessness of the training. There were no fights at first, only endless repetitive exercises. Boring, exhausting, frustrating. All that kept them going was the competition between them; they urged each other on with mockery, because neither was going to be the first to give up. And slowly, Alraen's discipline began to take effect. The exercises became no longer dull, but a dance of meditation.

It was Lynden, though, who made the swiftest progress. He never complained. Instead he threw himself into the training and stuck with it almost obsessively. When the other two were resting – lounging in the hot bath, exercising the horses through the ice-crystal corridors of Silverholm, eating with the Aelyr or enjoying their unearthly music – Lynden would go for extra practice sessions. He was growing single-minded and serious, rarely smiling. Rufryd was concerned for him, but nothing he said made any difference.

'If we must stay here,' Lynden said, 'the least I can do is get myself ready to rescue Ymmi.'

So Rufryd left him to it. Winter passed slowly, strangely, yet pleasantly enough. The Shaelahyr remained a mystery to him, but he didn't think too deeply about them. He left philosophy to Tanthe, happy to let her murmur her thoughts as they lay in each other's arms after making love each night.

Soon, to his humiliation, Rufryd found himself losing sword bouts to his baby brother. That spurred him on to greater efforts; but Tanthe seemed to reach a certain level and stick there, unable to get the hang of certain manoeuvres. Rufryd watched her becoming more annoyed with herself by the day.

'Too much sex,' she announced, when they had been at Silverholm for thirty days. 'It's dulling our edge. It's impossible to fight well when you've got a stupid smile on your face.'

'You speak for yourself,' said Rufryd. 'I'm doing fine.'

'No, you're not. You're too complacent.'

'I always beat you.'

'So? Ymmi could beat me, for all the progress I'm making. I think we should abstain for ten days.'

'What from, training?'

'No, from sex, you idiot!'

Rufryd was dismayed. 'Tan, it took years for Alraen to become an expert. You can't expect to reach his level in a single season!'

'I don't. But I've got to try something.' She grimaced at him over her shoulder as she walked away. 'Gods, what a miserable face, Rufe. It's only ten days!'

He sensed a trace of her old haughtiness, but he gave in gracefully. Perhaps, when she came sliding into his bed after ten days, he would tell *her* that abstaining was such a good idea, he wanted to carry on.

Seven days passed; still Tanthe made no improvement. Rufryd only smiled and said nothing, then, for some reason, she stopped speaking to him.

By the eighth morning, Rufryd was beginning to think the horses were better company than Tanthe or Lynden. Quietly annoyed with her, and bored with his lonely nights in bed, he grumbled to Sunhawk as he walked the gelding along the corridors. Bringing him back into the stable-cavern, he was startled to find one of the Shaelahyr there, stroking Redbird. It was Metiya.

'Your horses are so beautiful, Rufryd,' she said, turning to him with a smile. 'You don't mind me talking to them, do you?'

'Of course not, Metiya. Go ahead.'

Rufryd felt awkward; Metiya was so delicate, like a white willow, her silver hair flowing over her shoulders, her long pale face that could have been sculpted from snow. Her sweet-natured, bubbly charm did nothing to make her seem more human. Next to her he felt too tall, too rough and earthy. 'Er – I wish we could get out of here to exercise them properly,' he said. 'I go up to the entrance sometimes to see how the weather is, but the snow just gets thicker and I nearly freeze to death.'

'But you can see the weather without going outside,' she said. 'Come, I'll show you.'

Metiya took his hand, led him out of the cave and to a narrow archway near the bath-house. Stairs spiralled up through a chimney of rock, emerging into a small cave with one wall of clear crystal. The air was warm. She led him to a marble bench and said, 'Look. I sit here sometimes and watch the mountains.'

The view, Rufryd saw, was stunning. The cave was high in the mountainside, the clear wall undercut so no snow had landed on it. Warm air from a vent wafted over the window to keep it clear of frost. Outside the mountains rolled away in bleak splendour; huge, thunderous, shrouded in snow.

'That's amazing,' he said. 'Beautiful.'

She laughed in delight at his reaction, and sat very close to him, her thigh pressing against his. 'You're beautiful, too,' she said. 'Your hair's so dark, and your skin is like amber.'

'Oh,' said Rufryd. 'Is it?' He was acutely aware of the Aelyr woman beside him; her breasts filling her silk robe delightfully and pressing into his arm . . . She raised a hand and stroked his cheek with a milk-white finger. He began to think he should make his excuses and leave.

'Do you like us?' she said. 'The Shaelahyr, I mean.'

'Er . . . well, I like *you*.'

'Good.' She pressed closer; he didn't seem able to detach himself. But he was completely taken aback when she straddled him, put her arms round his neck and kissed him deeply on the mouth. When her tongue touched his, he clasped her head and responded fiercely.

'Have you ever made love to an Aelyr woman?' she whispered as the kiss ended.

'Er, no, I . . .' Her body felt light on his, her skin cool to the touch, but her thighs were warm on his through the layers of silk. His heart was beating rapidly.

'I've never had a human man,' she whispered, pulling at the laces of his trousers. 'I want to know what it's like.'

'I think you're going to, any second now.' Rufryd groaned, beyond resisting her. She was naked under her robe, her secret hair like spun silver and her delicate flesh moist as she sheathed him inside her. 'Oh, gods, Metiya . . .'

It was delicious; swift and overwhelmingly erotic. Afterwards, he and Metiya went down to the bath, stripped off their dishevelled clothes and luxuriated in the hot water. Rufryd stretched his arms along the sides and tipped his head back. Now he felt appallingly guilty.

'You are thinking of your human lover,' said Metiya. 'Will she be jealous?'

'Not if she doesn't find out.'

'The Aelyr think of jealousy as a human emotion, but we lie to ourselves. We are not so different. Just different

350

enough to find each other enigmatic and very beautiful . . .'
She slid towards him in the hot water as she spoke,
grinning mischievously. 'Thank you, Rufryd, for satisfying
my curiosity.' She embraced him, her breasts pressed to
his bare chest and the hot wet ropes of her hair clinging to
his skin as she kissed him.

'Only jealous if I find out?' cried a loud voice above
them. Rufryd opened his eyes and saw Tanthe standing on
the side of the bath in her training gear, a towel in her
hand. 'Actually, I couldn't care less. Have him, Metiya.'
Her eyes blazed and she flung the towel hard at his head.
'Two days, Rufe!' she shouted as she marched out. 'You
couldn't even wait two days! *Bastard*!'

Storming out of the bath-house and along the ledge
outside, Tanthe had no idea why she felt so angry. She and
Rufryd were not handfasted, they had made no vows, they
were free to take any lovers they wanted. So why this
blinding pain in her eyes and her heart?

She remembered what Alraen had taught her. Never act
in rage. She cleared her mind, drove the anger out of
herself like arrow of poison. Then she went to the training
cave and said, 'Alraen, will you fight with me?'

'You have only just finished your practice,' said the
master, studying her.

'No. I haven't finished.'

'Very well.' He handed her the long wooden blade and
they saluted, and began to circle, to parry. Then all
Tanthe's emotion sprang into her arms and she matched
him stroke for stroke. And suddenly she did it. Grasped the
move; swung and twisted her sword, ended with the point
lightly touching his throat.

She stood back, flushed and gasping. He bowed respectfully and gave her a wry smile.

'At last,' he said. 'It is not good to fight when you are
angry, but sometimes it helps.'

Later, when she was back in her room, stroking a white

351

cat and trying to collect her thoughts, Rufryd came to find her. He looked sheepishly round the screen and said, 'Tanthe?'

'I did it,' she said, fiercely triumphant. She straightened up and faced him. 'I killed Alraen.'

'What?'

'Not literally. I mean I got the hang of that stupid move at last!'

He looked at the floor. 'You should have taken it out on me instead.'

'No,' she said. 'I might *really* have killed you.'

'Tanthe, I'm so sorry.'

'Two days until we stop abstaining,' she said, her voice turning hoarse. 'You couldn't wait two miserable days. Or is it just that you're bored with me?'

'It wasn't that at all! It only happened that once. I didn't go looking for her; she sort of jumped on me and I got carried away. You know how it is.'

'I see.'

'Tan, don't cry.'

'I'm not! It doesn't matter!'

'But it does. I wouldn't have hurt you like this for anything.'

Tanthe was calm, but her eyes burned. 'What was she like?'

'What do you mean?'

'Was it different, with one of the Aelyr?'

'Well, all the bits were in the same place. I don't know.'

'You're hopeless.'

He shook his head contritely. 'If it taught me anything, it's that I want you, not anyone else. It's you I love, Tan. Please forgive me.'

He seemed devastated to have hurt her. Because of that, and because she had forged her pain into a sort of victory in the training cave, she softened towards him.

'Rufe . . .' She touched his arm.

'Did abstaining actually help?' he asked.

'I don't think so. It clearly didn't do *you* any good. Being furious with you helped a lot more.'

'You should thank me, then. Joke!' he added.

A smile pulled at the corner of her mouth. He said softly, 'Do you still love me?'

'I don't know.'

'Are we going to be all right?'

'I don't know,' Tanthe said. 'I just don't know.'

'Tan, please . . .' he reached for her but she pulled back.

'Not yet,' she said softly. 'I need to go and have a think.'

Tanthe wandered for a long time through Silverholm, finding her way through deeper passages she'd never explored before. The Zampherai were still working here; she saw a few of the silver-grey figures in the shadows, but they ignored her. And then she was alone. There was something unutterably soothing about the dimly glowing, ice-blue silence.

She was no longer angry, but she wasn't sure what she felt. How much did she actually love Rufryd? As a soul mate for her entire life? Or just as a dear friend to sleep with for a while? She didn't know. All she knew was that part of her soul had turned cool, protecting herself, not fully trusting him any more.

She wondered what was happening in Riverwynde, what her parents were doing. And what was going to happen when winter ended. For now she could see no end. It was as if Elrill had fed them enchanted food and would keep them for ever.

Some way ahead, the passage swelled into a rounded area, with a raised curve of quartz that served as a seat. Tanthe started; someone was sitting there, staring at her.

She could only just make him out in the shadows, but it seemed to be an Aelyr male in a short, grey tunic. Not one of the Shaelahyr. His hair flowed dark red against his pale gold skin, and she knew him.

He seemed to be looking at her, but as she came closer

he rose and turned away. She broke into a run, calling, 'Don't go!'

But when she reached the place, he was gone. Tanthe swore; tears of frustration sprang to her eyes. She turned round and there, under the translucent sheer surface of the wall, she saw him.

Catching her breath, she went up to the wall and stretched out a hand. He mirrored her action, his fingertips meeting hers in the crystal plane. His face, heart-achingly beautiful, almost touched hers, forehead to forehead.

'Who are you?' she cried.

His lips moved, but she couldn't catch what he said. 'I can't hear you,' she said. 'I'm Tanthe.'

'Tanthe,' he echoed.

She fumbled in her pocket and produced the knife. The moonstone on the pommel glowed brightly. 'You gave me this,' she said. 'I know what it's called. *Mnelir*. It saved my life.'

He nodded. A tear ran down his cheek. 'I want to touch you,' he said, his voice very faint and far away. 'So hard to reach you. I keep trying.' Suppressed pain racked his face. 'I will keep trying.'

'Yes,' she said urgently. 'What can I do to help you?'

He said something, but his voice was only a faint buzz of sound.

'I can't hear you!'

He glanced behind him. 'They're coming,' he said. The wall seemed to rush upwards in a pale flame; then it turned opaque, and he was gone. Tanthe stepped back, dizzy. She struck the rock with her fists.

'Don't do this to me,' she cried. 'Don't keep vanishing!'

Frantic, she explored the nearby corridors for fifteen minutes, searching on ledges, in caves, on walkways. But there was no sign of him. She pressed her hands to her head, close to tears.

'Tanthe?' she turned and found Elrill behind her. He said, 'You look lost.'

'You made me jump!'

'Forgive me. Tell me what's wrong.'

'I met an Aelyr – I don't know his name – I was talking to him and now I can't find him.'

He looked kindly at her, humouring her. 'Was it so important? I'll help you find him if I can. Don't tell me, fair hair, violet eyes . . . it may not be easy to narrow it down.'

'No, no,' she said. 'He wasn't Shaelahyr. He's very distinctive. You couldn't miss him. Long dark red hair, much darker skin than yours – a pale gold colour – and brown eyes. He's the one I told you about, the one who gave me the knife!'

'Ah.' Elrill frowned.

'Is there some way he could really be here, or that we could find out who he is?'

Elrill's expression had changed. He was looking at Tanthe with a deep, shrewd gaze of suspicion, and all his tolerant warmth towards her seemed to have vanished. 'Tanthe,' he said firmly. 'Indeed, I could not miss him. And I can promise you that there is no such Aelyr here, nor has there ever been.'

She drew a breath, and stepped away from him. 'He's from Verdanholm, isn't he?' she said. 'They're your enemies.'

'Not enemies, exactly,' Elrill said coolly. 'However, you are quite right in assuming that I would not want to summon such an Aelyr here, even if it were possible, which it isn't.'

'But he's harmless. He's in trouble of some kind.'

'That's a shame.'

'But you're not going to help me?'

'Tanthe . . .' Elrill looked at her strangely for several seconds; his lips parted, he shook his head minimally so the light caught blue on his hair. Then his face hardened, and she felt that their friendship had ended, and she didn't know why. 'No, Tanthe. I wouldn't know how to begin. This is not the time.'

Chapter Sixteen. The Shadow of the King

Ysomir woke in a bed. Not a hard pad with a thin cover, but a deep soft mattress with thick pillows, blankets and quilts. Her head ached, her throat was sore and her nose so thick she could hardly breathe. She drifted, thinking that she was at home, and that her bedroom had been miraculously transformed by enchantment into a bower of gold leaf and marble.

'Tanthe, did the Aelyr do this?' she said. Her voice was a croaky whisper.

'What, dear?' said a grey-haired figure, bending over the bed.

'Grandma?'

'No, dear,' the woman said sadly. 'I'm Namane. Physician to His Majesty's staff. I'll be looking after you until you're better. You're in the Amber Citadel.'

'How . . .?' She tried to sit up, only to be shaken by coughs. Bands of pain squeezed her head and chest.

'You were brought here last night.' The physician was a big woman of perhaps sixty, with a round, attractive face. She turned away and poured steaming liquid from a jug onto a greenish powder in a glass. She stirred the mixture, held it to Ysomir's lips. It tasted bitter and grainy, but Ysomir swallowed it, having no choice but to trust her. 'This will give you some relief. You're lucky; you'll live. This 'flu is nothing to those who have a warm bed and plenty of rest, but it's killing those poor beggars on the Tower like rats. Not that they'll improve conditions. Just bring more poor sods to replace the dead. I don't know what we've come to.'

Ysomir finished the medicine. It eased her throat, at

least. Looking round, she found herself in a chamber, about fifteen feet square, with walls of soft gold and a floor of black and white marble, strewn with silky rugs in shades of blue, lavender and burnt gold. She had never seen such luxury. She stared at everything in amazement, thinking she was still dreaming. Even the quilt on her bed was made of padded blue satin, worked with a pattern of moons and lilies in white, gold and green.

'Who brought me here?' she asked.

Namane didn't answer. Turning to replace the phial of green powder in a bag in the floor, she blew softly through her teeth. '"Lucky",' she murmured. 'Unfortunate choice of word. The longer you're ill, the better.'

'Why?' Ysomir's memory was returning; the cold, dank tunnels, the cloaked and hooded figure who had come to claim her. It all seemed a wild nightmare.

The physician shook her head. 'Things have changed here . . . but it's dangerous to ask questions. I don't know anything for certain. My duty is to care for the health of the royal staff and guests, nothing more. No questions.' She busied herself tidying and closing the bag. 'Some have disappeared for less.'

Ysomir lay back on the pillow, drowsy again. 'A man in a cloak brought me here. I saw him take others before me. They never came back. People said it was the King. Was it, really?'

Namane lowered her head; it might have been a nod. 'I can't say. You passed out on the way. He brought you to me in his arms. Touching.'

'The folk in the Tower had a nickname for him,' Ysomir whispered. 'Old grey-bones. The torturer. That's not King Garnelys, is it?'

Namane closed her eyes, her face stiff with pain. Then it passed and she said decisively, 'No. No. You rest now, dear. A maid will bring you a light breakfast in a few minutes. Try to eat it. I will be back in a few hours' time with more of that disgusting medicine. You are in the lower guest quarters, by the way; not that that will mean anything to you. Enjoy your 'flu while it lasts.'

Her time spent working in the mines and the Tower had taken their toll. Drained by cold and fever, Ysomir could make no sense of her situation. She floated, feeling safe, soporific, cocooned.

That night, as she lay fevered and hallucinating, sounds wove themselves into her dreams; cries and moans, echoing from somewhere outside her room.

Ysomir got out of bed and went to the door. It was locked; that was no surprise. She called out, but no-one answered; finally she went back to bed and covered her ears with the pillow, but she could not blot out the sounds. A woman wept intermittently, through grief or fear, Ysomir could not tell which; a man cried with physical pain, on and on the whole night, until his voice faded to nothing. She never heard him again.

The servants who brought her meals next day were taciturn, radiating suppressed fear. There was no ease or joy in the Amber Citadel, it seemed. Even the air seemed taut with anticipation.

The following night, still fevered, she dreamed that a dark grey figure was leaning over her bed. Then, in a wedge of light through the open door, she saw two silhouettes and heard Namane arguing with someone. 'She's still weak, she's not ready yet.'

It happened again the next night, and the next; but Ysomir could never rouse herself enough to make out whether it was real or nightmare, Namane's potions made her sleep so deeply.

Gradually she began to feel better. She was able to get out of bed and sit in a chair, wondering at the luxury of her prison. But after a time, even that began to pall. She asked Namane for paper, pen and ink to stave off her loneliness, and Namane obliged. It had been one of Tanthe's favourite childhood games for them to write letters to each other as (Tanthe said) the citizens of Parione did; to pretend they were great ladies who had servants to deliver their messages across the city. Now Ysomir began to write to Tanthe in earnest, describing her experiences in heartfelt letters that she had no means of sending. *'I miss you so much. Here I am in the city you always dreamed of seeing, and I wonder if it is at all as you imagined . . .'*

On the evening of the tenth day, when Ysomir was feeling almost normal again, Namane came in and leaned on the dressing table, her head bowed and her strong arms shaking with tension. 'I can't do this job any more.'

'Namane?' Ysomir rose, hurriedly folding the letter she was writing and tucking it into her sleeve. She wanted no one, not even the physician, to read her scribblings. 'What's wrong?'

The physician turned. She was almost grey with despair; Ysomir was confused.

'I'm sorry,' Namane sighed. 'I can't put this off any longer. I've pushed your illness to the limit with the King, but he's grown too impatient. He insists on you being taken to him, well or otherwise.'

Ysomir bit her lip. 'I am well,' she said. 'But I still don't understand. What on earth would the King want with someone like me? There must be a mistake.'

Namane shook her head, red-eyed. She caressed Ysomir's chin and said only, 'Goddess go with you, my dear.'

A maid came and dressed Ysomir, after she'd bathed, in a dress of ivory silk, with an over-skirt and stomacher of pale gold satin. Ysomir marvelled at the clothes. They were like the pictures in Tanthe's books! She almost laughed, then, at the madness of her situation. Even Tanthe had never fantasised about being presented to the King and Queen.

'What am I doing here?' Ysomir said aloud, suddenly dizzy with the enormity of what was about to happen.

The maid stared at her with a long, expressionless face, and didn't answer. She was plainly unhappy at being made to dress up a peasant as a courtier.

'I've done the best I can,' the maid said at last, when she'd finished arranging Ysomir's hair. 'Do you want to see yourself?'

She turned Ysomir to face a full-length mirror. A stranger stared back at her. A pale, haunted nymph, looking out-of-place and fragile in the unaccustomed clothes. Her hair was gathered up with a cluster of opals from which it rippled, gleaming, over her shoulders.

'You look beautiful,' said the maid, in a tone more of despair than pleasure.

An equerry and a guard, both in the indigo and gold livery of the palace, came to escort Ysomir to the royal chambers. They passed along echoing corridors hung with portraits, up several grandiose flights of stairs. Neither of the men spoke to her. She was caught between taking in everything, remembering it for Tanthe, and anxiety at what awaited her. Lamplight shone on warm stone walls, on panels of amber and gold, on the gilded frames of paintings.

At last the two men stopped in an ante-room at a high, ornate door. The equerry went in; the guard waited with her. As she stood there she realised that the huge portraits that lined the walls were of Aventuria's monarchs. She knew these faces; she'd seen engravings of them in books. Queen Silana, who had founded Parione. Queen Hetys, who had united the Nine Realms as one. King Maharoth who'd won the War of the Silver Plains. His descendant Queen Devinda, her son King Aralyth. And then Devinda's grandson, Garnelys himself.

Ysomir stared at the portrait. It showed a beautiful young man of great kindness and dignity, clothed in blue velvet, holding the staff of office which was topped with a crystal sphere. A crown of nine jewels was on his head, to symbolise the unity of the realms. His hair flowed over his shoulders in two raven wings and his features were strong, with high cheekbones, a firm mouth, a curved blade of a nose. He radiated warmth, gentle strength, surety of purpose.

Her heart leaped into her throat. He was everything she and Tanthe had dreamed of . . . how could such a man, whose soul shone openly in his eyes, possibly mean harm to anyone?

The door opened. No lamps were lit within. The guard led her through into a corridor and left her there, with no instructions, no word at all. The darkness was sudden and complete. As her eyes began to adjust, she looked round to see what she should do next, but the men had melted away and closed the door behind them.

Ysomir saw a windowed niche at the far end of the corridor, an arch of blue night against which stood a tall silhouette. The figure was gaunt and imposing, the folds of his dark robe hanging stiffly like those of a statue. Her throat tightened. She began to walk towards the silhouette, drawn as if she'd surrendered her own will. As she approached, trembling, he turned slowly to look at her.

She glimpsed the outline of his carved, hollowed features, the feathering of white eyebrows, the dark orbs of his eyes. Her breath rushed to the top of her lungs and hovered there. *His eyes*. They were pits as dark as blood, and they seemed to emanate a black energy that stole her strength.

His gaze hung on hers and reeled her in.

Ysomir recognised the face in the portrait. This was her King, older and thinner, but unmistakably the same man. Beloved Garnelys, whom she and Tanthe had been taught to love . . . yet something was different. Not his age, but his soul. His inner self was there in his eyes as if he couldn't hide it, innocent light warped to cruel darkness. It was as if he regarded her and saw, not a frightened human being but a fragile morsel, a gold-winged moth to be drawn into his web and sucked dry.

'Ah, child,' he said. His voice was soft but deep and powerful, rough-edged. 'At last.'

'Your majesty,' Ysomir said faintly. She bowed her head, made a semblance of a curtsey. She didn't know what else to do. She was caught between terror and awe because, whatever his nature, he was still her sovereign.

'I have waited many days for this moment. You fell ill when you were brought here. You are recovered now.'

It was more a statement than a question. 'Yes, thank you, your majesty.'

'Good. Your name?'

'Ysomir Aynie-daughter, your majesty.'

There was a long silence. His gaze moved over her. The look was not sexual – it did not even occur to her that it might be – but slow and strange.

Eventually he said, 'The correct address, after the initial greeting, is "Sire".'

'I'm sorry, sire.'

'Not that it matters.' He reached out a hand – a long, bony hand that she recognised – and pinched her chin between his thumb and forefinger. She winced inwardly, not daring to evade his grasp. 'Where are you from, Ysomir?'

'Riverwynde, sire.'

He frowned. 'Where is that? I've never heard of it.'

'In the – the west of Sepheret. It's only a very small village, sire. My family are, er, farmers . . .'

He didn't seem to be listening. 'You are a handsome race in Sepheret. I noticed you immediately, but even so, you are more striking than I remember.'

Now she knew for certain that it was the King himself who had haunted the conscripts' quarters under the hill. Looking for . . . what?

She stammered, 'Sire, I – I am overjoyed to be chosen to work in the palace. I will serve you as best I can.'

There was a twitch to his thin lips, almost a smile. 'I don't require you to work. Ysomir, you are . . . exceptional.' His hand fell away and he gave a deep sigh.

The chain of fear pulled harder. 'Sire?'

'Can you play metrarch?' he asked, surprising her. 'Of course not. Farmers have no inclination for such pointless, cerebral pastimes.'

The remark made Ysomir indignant, which helped her to rally her strength. 'Actually, I can play, sire. My sister and I learned from a book. She made the board and I carved the pieces. I may not be very skilled, but I know the rules.'

'Well.' Again he nearly smiled, but the expression did nothing to lighten the demanding weight of his gaze. 'Come, then. Entertain me a while.'

The chamber to which the King took her was lushly adorned in golden stone and veined marbles. In shape it was two joined ovals, the main one some thirty feet across and the lesser one half that size. The main area was well-lit and had tables, chairs, and a couch, but the smaller chamber was bare, like a temple, and dark. A stone block in its centre looked less like a table than a bier. It was empty, yet an atmosphere of death hung on the room. Ysomir stared at the candles that stood around the bier on tall black holders. They were unlit, their mournful half-melted shapes garlanded with stiff ropes of wax.

'My son Galemanth lay there,' said the King. 'We buried him last autumn.'

Ysomir let go of her breath and caught another. So it was true, the Prince was dead. 'I'm very sorry, sire.'

'The Death Goddess will come for us all, will she not? To some sooner than others. Come, pay no attention. Sit here with me.'

He led her to a small table that stood in the square bay of a window. The edges of the recess were draped with embroidered fabrics, but the curtains were open. Dozens of small diamond-shaped panes threw back reflections of the room, of the King's gaunt figure and Ysomir's anxious face, but beyond the glass was blue night.

The King made her sit facing the window. Her eyes refocused and she saw, like a great shadow in the night outside, the jagged outline of the Tower.

A wave of dread rushed through her, and she quickly looked down at the metrarch board.

'Help me set out the pieces,' said Garnelys. 'I always have the amber, you have the lapis. My prerogative to move first.'

All the time they played, he seemed to be watching her. His eyes did not just follow her, but leaned on her with a physical weight. He was like a great, taloned dragon-hawk, whose mind moved on some alien level beyond the reach of reason. Ysomir tried to think of nothing but the game, admiring the pieces, wondering if she could ever carve something so perfect.

'You lied to me,' said the King.

Fear swamped her. 'Sire?'

'You told me you did not play well. Where did you learn such a strategy?'

'I – I never found it that hard a game.'

'Metrarch? Not hard?'

She blushed, feeling she'd said the wrong thing. She couldn't tell whether he was amused or angry.

It could only get worse. A few minutes later, the King raised his hands in the air and said, 'Ah! The moon-tower trap!'

She stared at the alignment on the web, and swallowed drily.

'You've beaten me,' he said.

'Sire, I'm terribly sorry, I didn't mean – I shouldn't have made that move—'

'No,' he said. 'It is the first time in months I have found someone who played better than me, and did not let me win. Never let me win, do you hear?'

She nodded, her pulse racing.

He smiled at her. There were points of warmth in his eyes and she began to think that she could like him after all. Was this all he wanted, a companion to stave off his boredom in the evenings? She began to relax a little.

'Let's play again,' he said.

As she began to set the pieces in their opening positions, there was a rap at the door and the equerry came in, followed by three tall men.

'Your majesty, forgive the interruption, but your presence is requested urgently. Lord Serpeth, the Duke of Eisilion, General Grannen and Lord Poel are here to see you.'

The men brought draughts of cold air in with them, making the lamp-flames flicker. The King rose to his feet, turning from Ysomir as if she'd ceased to exist. The men gave her only the briefest of sideways glances; she felt, mercifully, invisible.

She knew their names. Names read in books or heard on her travels, like untouchable figures from myths. Yet here they were in the same room as her, real people.

The first one, Lord Serpeth, was in his forties, tanned and golden haired, wiry and muscle-roped as if he spent all his days on horseback. He had a face like a lynx, and the coldest green eyes she had ever seen. His realm, Eisilion, was in the north-west, wild and sparsely populated.

Lord Poel . . . she racked her brains. He was a big man, almost square in shape, his black and white robes adding to the picture of stiffness and gravity. His face was long and stern, his black hair and beard crisply curled. She disliked him on sight; he looked pompous, cruel. He was an official, the highest in the city, the one who put the King's orders into effect.

The last man, General Grannen . . . now that name she had heard on the journey. He was the high commander of the King's army, but had only been in the post for two years. He was robust, grey-haired, his eyebrows two sweeping inverted Vs above granite-coloured eyes. He was full of energy yet very still, coiled. No pomposity about him, only a stone-cold ruthlessness. Her companions had described him as *that Torith Mir bastard*.

Grannen, she realised, had masterminded the conscriptions. Because of him she'd been torn from her family, and Serenis had perished in the mines, and others were dying every day to build the Tower . . .

'Sire, the situation is close to crisis,' Lord Poel was saying softly. Ysomir looked blankly at the metrarch board as if she couldn't hear. 'Only half the conscripts are likely to survive the winter. Because of continuing disobedience in Thanmandrathor, we have many fewer recruits than we should have had from that Realm. It's thrown our calculations into disarray. We cannot conscript more until the spring. Is there any possibility that work on the Tower could be halted until such time . . .?'

'No,' the King said crisply. 'Work must continue. *It cannot stop.* If you are incapable of carrying out my will, you will be replaced by others who can!'

'Sire, Lord Poel is being overcautious.' Grannen spoke soothingly, but a cold look flashed between him and Poel. 'Work will continue. As long as the wagon-tracks out to the west and south are kept clear, fresh conscripts can be brought through in all but the worst of weather. We've lost many, it's true, but these people are soft and unused to discipline. Those who survive will form a force worthy of you. Our chief cause for concern is not loss of conscripts but the persistent unrest in parts of Thanmandrathor and other isolated pockets. However, the problem is in hand. Once their obstinacy is crushed, the flow of recruits will be restored.'

The callousness of his words turned Ysomir to ice.

Lord Serpeth bowed. 'Your majesty, I come to pledge my loyalty and that of all the people of Eisilion. If ever you should have need of us, we will come in force.'

Garnelys clasped Serpeth's arms warmly. 'Cousin, I thank you. It's all I ask, for my subjects to do my will and trust me! Come, we'll go down to the meeting chamber to discuss these matters in detail.'

The men swept out of the room, but their collective aura

of power and implacable will remained. Ysomir shuddered under its weight. She didn't fully understand the conversation, but . . .

You understand, said the dry voice of Serenis. *What it means is that the slaves are restless, but if they dare to rebel, Lord Serpeth will be there to help Grannen crush them. For which news the King is joyously grateful!*

Ysomir was alone. No one had told her what to do; as far as she knew the guards were still outside the door, and she dared not try to leave. But the King's meeting might take hours . . . Her head ached with tension, and she longed for the warm oblivion of bed. A cold draught from somewhere was making her shiver. She became aware of a faint, disturbing sound, like someone moaning, sobbing.

Looking quickly around the room, she saw on the wall to her left a long tapestry stirring as if the air was blowing from behind it. She went to it, lifted the edge, and found that it concealed a door which was not properly shut. Chilly air came from behind it, carrying the weird, agonised moans.

Ysomir peeped through. On the other side it was dark, and there was a tang of metal in the air. She gagged. The smell was that of blood, mixed with the aftermath of storms, and a static that felt like fur on her skin. She didn't want to go in . . . but if someone was in distress, she couldn't leave them.

Taking a lamp from a side-table, Ysomir went into the darkness.

She found a narrow stair that spiralled downwards. Holding her breath, she descended the uneven steps. This seemed a much older part of the Citadel, heavy and thick with age. She came out in a chamber that must lie below and to one side of the one she had left; but this was dark, damp, grave-cold. Nothing in it but a plain bench, a central post that was hung with chains and straps, and a rack of instruments. Knives, pincers . . . what on earth were they for? A spurt of denial went through her. The disk of

367

lamplight caught stains on the floor and glints from the big, brown crystal that squatted on top of the post. The room was thick with the taint of blood and tortuous energies.

Ysomir stood there open-mouthed, horror winding round her heart. Every instinct told her to flee, but she could still hear the phantom voice, and now it sounded like dissonant humming, punctuated by unearthly screams. It drew her out of the chamber to a narrower, older stairwell on the far side, downwards again through the dank gloom. As she descended, the noise grew louder. The darkness smothered her yet she couldn't stop.

She emerged at last into what seemed to be the very heart of the Citadel. Was she inside the hill itself? She was in a domed chamber, and something huge was moving in the darkness. Holding up the lamp, she jerked backwards in astonishment.

The chamber was almost filled by a massive, rotating sphere. And from this sphere emanated the eerie, almost-human voices.

Ysomir dropped the lamp. She pressed her hands over her ears, but she couldn't block out the sound. Sobs shook her whole body. The voices were not loud, only piercing and anguished, clawing her soul down to share their misery. Pain, pain, and terrible energies lashing out. The force of it flattened her to the chamber wall.

The sphere was a huge polished mass of crystal, very dark, with glints of red in its depths. It rotated on a base of polished stone as if floating on a film of water, and it pulsed with energy like a dark moon. She was transfixed, held there by the slow spinning of the globe, the scarlet fires diving through its depths, the glints of luminosity that swam to the surface and vanished again. Waves of discord and torment lashed her, until she fell to her knees and cried out.

'What are you? What can I do to help you?'

Someone grabbed her upraised hands.

Ysomir nearly passed out with terror. Looking up wildly, she found a pale, hooded figure standing over her. Her lamp burned low but it had not gone out; in its light she could just make out his face; yellowish-pale as bone, with soft features and dark, shrewd eyes. He must have been in the chamber on the far side of the sphere all the time.

She tried to scream and couldn't. She struggled but he held her fast, drawing her up to her feet.

'Don't!' she gasped. 'Let me go!'

'Hush. Be calm. I'm not going to hurt you.' His voice, too, was soft but penetrating. She felt immediately calmer. 'You are not supposed to be here, are you?'

'But what is it? Why is it so full of pain?'

'I don't know,' he said. 'I am not supposed to be here either.' His pale mouth curved in a slight smile.

Despite her shock, his presence made her feel safer. 'I've seen you before,' she said.

'I am Laphaeome.'

'The architect of the Tower?'

'I have that honour. And you, if I remember, are Ysomir. But what are you doing here?'

Haltingly, she told him. 'I meant no harm. I thought I heard someone—'

Laphaeome took her arm. 'Come back upstairs. The first thing you must learn is never to question the King.' He pushed her before him up the long spiral stair and she went numbly, carrying the lamp. The moaning of the sphere diminished until she could barely hear it; but it was still there. 'He has his reasons for all he does, but the best way to keep him sweet is simply to humour him at all times.'

The architect ushered her back into the main chamber, and closed the hidden door behind her.

'I don't understand what he wants me for,' she said.

'He is growing old. He is lonely.'

'But all the others—'

'Others?'

'The ones he took from the Tower before me. Where are they?'

'Ysomir,' Laphaeome said gently, 'You and I are only here to serve. We cannot begin to understand the intentions of one who is so far above us. But what have you always believed about the King?'

'That he's good. That he loves us.'

'Then you must go on believing it.' White-robed and soft-moving, Laphaeome put his hand under her elbow and led her to the door. His hand in its black glove was oddly shaped. 'Go back to your room. If you cannot find the way, ask someone.' He spoke kindly, and she was simply grateful to be given permission to leave. 'Go on. If the King comes back and asks why you left, I'll take responsibility, so don't worry.'

As the days passed, they began to fall into a pattern. Ysomir was usually left alone in the day, seeing no one but the taciturn maid or Namane. She spent the time writing, or looking out of her window onto a stretch of snowy courtyard, beyond which there lay a high wall of honey-coloured stone. No chance of escape – but where would she go, even if she could?

In the evening, the equerry would come and take her to the King's private chamber, where he would demand nothing of her other than several games of metrarch. Sometimes their meetings would be interrupted by Poel or other court officials; at others, the King would simply grow tired and distant, and tell her at last – often not until the early hours of the morning – to leave him.

Each time she saw him, he seemed different. Sometimes brooding, almost as if a massive dark beast crouched on his shoulders. Sometimes sharp and cutting as glass shards. At others he would be benevolent but vague, as if he were not really aware of her.

She never dared to mention what she had seen behind the hidden door. But she often thought of the great, groaning sphere, turning endlessly below their feet.

For ten days or so, her life followed this pattern. She was never able to drop her guard; just when she felt slightly more at ease with Garnelys, his mood would change again, unnerving her. He seemed to be watching her more intently every night, wanting something of her that he couldn't put into words.

This evening, as they sat playing, the King looked paler than usual. He won the first game, but instead of expressing satisfaction as he had before, he stared at Ysomir as if she had offended him.

'You let me win,' he said.

'No, sire, I did not. I promised I never would.'

His eyes, black caves lit by tiny red fires, devoured her. 'Very well. Set the board again.'

She did so, her fingers trembling, afraid of the consequences if she did not make an effort to win. But what consequences? So hard to think clearly with his great, gaunt form looming before her.

As they went on playing, she sensed the King growing more and more restless. Beads of sweat formed on his high forehead.

Eventually she plucked up courage to speak. 'Sire, you don't look well. Should I send for someone?'

The effect of her words was incendiary. He glared up at her, his eyes aflame. 'No!' he roared. He leapt to his feet, towering over her. 'Don't speak!'

He seized her wrist. His hands were like knotted steel, crushing her bones. Blinded by shock and terror, she hung like a puppet as he shook her, yelling, 'Be silent! Don't make a sound!' His voice fell. 'Not a sound.'

He was breathing hard as he pulled her towards the side wall, lifted the tapestry, opened the concealed door. Icy darkness clustered around them. She smelled the chill tang of copper, static, and blood.

Garnelys dragged her over the threshold. Ysomir was paralysed. The echoing moans of the sphere suddenly filled her head, and she felt she would rather die than step into the stairwell. Stars danced before her eyes.

Then he stopped.

He pulled her back into the main chamber, slammed the door, and leaned on the tapestry with his hand pressed to his forehead. Ysomir stumbled away, clutching her bruised wrist. Garnelys ignored her. He went to the rear of the chamber and began to pace round and round the bier, his whole body shaking. 'No,' he said. 'Not her. Not yet.'

She looked wildly at the doors to the chamber. Two guards stood outside . . . would they stop her if she ran? Was there any use in trying?

Garnelys came towards her and she backed away.

'Why do they always cower?' he said. 'Why are my subjects afraid of me? Am I monstrous? Is that how I'll be remembered?'

Ysomir only stared at him. 'Answer me!'

'You told me not to speak, sire.'

His voice fell and he pointed at her chair. 'Sit down, child. Wait there. Don't leave.'

Ysomir obeyed. She sat down at the metrarch board, cradling her wrist, watching the King as he opened the chamber door and said a few quiet words to the guards. A few agonising minutes passed by, then one of the guards brought a young man to the room, and left him there.

Ysomir didn't know him, but she recognised him from the Tower. He was skinny and freckled, with reddish hair hanging lankly over his forehead. Once he'd been handsome, but now he was hollowed out by the cold, the backbreaking work. The fine court clothes in which he'd been dressed could not hide the fact. A deep cough shook him, rattling in his chest as he tried to suppress it.

'Your majesty?' he said, wide-eyed as Ysomir had been. His gaze flicked at her, then fixed on his King again.

'Come with me, boy. I need you.'

Garnelys led the young man to the door in the wall. It closed and the tapestry fell into place behind them; Ysomir heard footsteps on stone, fading to silence.

She sat staring at the metrarch board, fiddling with the pieces, her hands trembling.

Whatever he's doing with that boy, said Serenis's acid voice in her head, *I don't think he's making love to him.*

After a time, she heard a faint cry. Then another. Her head jerked up.

'I've got to help him,' she said aloud.

'Don't,' said a voice at the door of the chamber.

Laphaeome was in the room, seeming to glide rather than walk towards her. He wore a long white robe with a hood, beneath which his face was oddly luminous. His appearance made Ysomir almost jump out of her skin.

'Did the King tell you to stay here?' he asked in a low, crisp voice.

'Yes.'

'Then stay. You must never disturb the King's private business. But you know that.' He sat down opposite her. Strangely, she felt she could confide in him.

'Please help me. I don't know what to do. I'm so afraid.'

'Of what?'

'The King.'

In the pause after she spoke, there was a distinct scream from beyond the concealed door. Tears sprang to her eyes. Laphaeome showed no reaction.

'What is he doing?' she said. 'He behaves as if he's—' she daren't say the word, *mad.*

'It's not what it seems,' said Laphaeome. 'How do you think he rules a vast land like Aventuria, or maintains the delicate bond of the Xauroma, without magic? The King is a great and accomplished *gauroth* mage. It is not for us to question his actions. His methods are arcane beyond our comprehension.'

The screams went on, high, distinct, desperate. She hugged herself, tears streaming down her cheeks. 'I don't care. I can't listen to it!'

She was on her feet and just as quickly, Laphaeome was

in front of her, holding her arms. 'Let me go!' she cried. 'I've got to help that boy, I don't care what happens to me! Goddess, what is wrong with you?'

'No,' he said softly, smiling. 'Sit down.'

He had a strange smell, faint and musty, like long-dead leaves. All her strength seemed to go out of her and she obeyed, shaking with outrage, yet helpless as if a spell had been cast on her. And she heard Serenis's voice say in her head, *Don't eat the poisoned honey*.

The architect sat facing her. And the more the boy screamed, the more benign he looked.

'I never heard that the King was a sorcerer,' she said. 'No one ever told us that.'

'There is a great deal you don't know. And even more that you will never know.'

As Ysomir watched him, she had the impression that long white worms of energy were crawling from his eyes and into her brain. She dropped her head, closing her eyes against it. But the whole chamber seemed to be filling with a darker force, a static that hurt her teeth and covered her with spider-silk. And she could hear Serenis telling her. *Get out. Anthar's balls, woman, if you want to save yourself, get out now!*

'Why is he doing this to us?' she gasped.

'Serving your King is not painful, surely.' The architect sounded amused. Ysomir's consciousness expanded with a ghastly vision; the whole of the Amber Citadel was awash with evil. Laphaeome, Lord Poel, Grannen, Serpeth, even Namane, all of them clustering around the King, bolstering his delusions, helping him to spin his sticky dark web . . .

'Who are you?' whispered Ysomir.

The architect became very still. His black eyes seemed to change size, swelling, contracting. It was as if he knew she'd seen the poison inside him, but in trying to terrify her, he only revealed the full truth of himself—

A sound disturbed them. The moment flared and was

lost. Breaking contact, Ysomir jerked her head up and saw the concealed door opening.

The King stood in the doorway, his chest heaving, his mouth open and down-turned, his eyes tipping up under the lids. There was blood on his hands, a red stain on the front of his robe, gore trailing from the hem of his robe.

Ysomir stumbled to her feet, gagging on a scream that wouldn't come. Her skirt caught the metrarch board and the pieces went skittering over the floor.

Garnelys pointed at her. 'Get out,' he said. He began to come towards her, and she saw the blood on his trembling hand, lying thick and red in the creases. 'Go!'

She fled.

The corridors veered around her, cavernous and endless, glimmering with dim lights. She was lost; her chest heaved as she struggled for breath, her limbs ached, but she ran and ran. In her mind it was not the King following her but Laphaeome, pale and smiling.

The corridor ended in a pair of tall, golden doors. She clasped the handle and flung herself through. Slammed it behind her. On the other side was a huge drawing room with a shining floor, another doorway on the left revealing a bed-chamber, a great canopied bed – and a woman, dressed in fine striped silks, standing in the doorway between the two rooms and staring at her in shock.

Ysomir pressed back against the door. Her chest ached with exertion. She couldn't speak.

The woman, now walking slowly towards her, was silver-haired, imposing and dignified. Her face was powerful like the King's. Her dress was so stiffly sculpted it seemed to sail with her, like a ship. Yellow and silver and black blurred across Ysomir's vision.

She fell forward, and the noblewoman caught her. The next thing she knew, she was lying on the cover of the huge bed, panting for breath as the room faded then reformed around her.

'That's it, deep breaths,' the woman said. 'Don't try to sit up. Poor dear.'

A cloth, damp and wonderfully cool, was pressed to her forehead. Slowly Ysomir's strength began to return, and her head stopped swimming. She looked up at the woman and saw that her face was beautiful, strong, but carved hollow like the King's with strain. She looked familiar.

'What is your name?' the woman asked, her voice rich.

'Ysomir.'

'I am Mabriahna.'

'Oh, goddess!' Ysomir gasped, trying to sit up. She made it on to one elbow. 'You're the Queen! Your majesty—'

'Yes, but never mind.' A hint of sternness. 'Tell me who you are, and what you were running from.'

'I – I can't. I'm sorry, your majesty, I had no idea whose chamber this was.'

'Obviously. But don't call me that. No titles, dear. Tell me.'

Ysomir couldn't begin to explain. Not to anyone, especially not to the Queen. Horror welled through her and the only words she could utter were, 'The King.'

'Gods.' To Ysomir's surprise, Mabriahna sat down heavily on the bed beside her. 'You don't need to say any more. Poor child. Did he bring you from the Tower? You are so pretty, but you don't look right in these clothes. They never do.'

Ysomir began to sob. She felt she was losing her mind. 'There was blood on him.'

'I know. I've seen it.'

'He was going to take me, but he took a boy instead. I heard him—'

Mabriahna cradled her, rocked her as she wept. When her tears subsided, the Queen brought her a glass of wine and held it to her lips, then smoothed back strands of her hair, for all the world like her mother.

'I don't know what to say to you, Ysomir,' the Queen said at last. 'I can't stop him. The gods know, I've tried. I can't protect you from him. I have lived alone for years now. I used to pray that he would come to me; now I pray that he will not.'

Ysomir was silent. After a moment the Queen went on. 'I can understand why he spared you. Even with your face swollen with tears, I can see how lovely you are. There is something special about you.'

'No. My sister is special. Not me.'

'Is she at the Tower?'

Ysomir shook her head. 'No. She's still at home. I miss her, but I'm so glad she's safe.'

Mabriahna did not ask where 'home' was. 'I can't promise that the King will spare you for ever. If he would not even spare his own son, nor his granddaughter . . . none of us have any hope.' She raised her strong, sharp chin and stared across the chamber with bleak eyes. 'None of us.'

'But what is he doing?'

'I think,' Mabriahna said slowly, 'that he believes he is feeding the Xauroma. He knows it is dying, so he is trying to feed it energy.'

'With people's lives?' She thought of the screaming sphere.

'All is energy. Magic is no more than subtle vibrations in realms we cannot see. So the Aelyr say. But it's too late, and no one can make him understand . . . all those who tried to argue with him are gone now. He replaced them with men who are as cruel and as reckless as he has become. I used to trust in the Goddess. Now I cannot find her any more . . .'

Ysomir sat up, and twisted round so she was sitting next to the Queen on the edge of the bed. 'Ma'am?' she said warily. 'That man, Laphaeome, the architect . . . do you know him?'

'I have seen him. I don't wish to know him.'

'Where is he from?'

'He is one of the Mediators. Have you heard of them?'

377

'I can't remember.'

'They are mages from the Serpent Isles. They visit us occasionally.'

'Are they human?'

'The Mediators? Yes, of course they are human.'

'But . . . Laphaeome isn't.'

Mabriahna said nothing for a moment. Then, 'Hush. You aren't well. One imagines all manner of things when one is not well. It is not good to think on these matters. There is nothing I can do now. Nothing.'

Silence fell between them; a vast, unbearable silence. More than ever, Ysomir felt alone, adrift. *She's given up*, said Serenis. *No good talking to her.*

Ysomir was wondering what to say when someone pounded on the door. She and the Queen clutched each other involuntarily.

'You have no guards on your door!' Ysomir said.

'I sent them away. They irritate me.'

Mabriahna pulled away from her, collected herself and stood up. The door opened and King Garnelys stood there, dark against a nimbus of light from the corridor.

'So here you are,' he said, looking past his wife to Ysomir.

'And here she stays,' Mabriahna said calmly.

'I want her to come with me. I want to talk to her.'

Ysomir stared at them; her King and Queen, facing each other with stiff determination, in conflict over her. This, she thought, Tanthe and Lynden will never believe in a thousand years!

Garnelys looked different. He had changed into a clean robe, but it was more than that. He was like the man in the portrait; the light had come back to his eyes, and there was a strength and radiance about him that made her want to throw everything else aside and love him. His hair flowed silver over his shoulders and he looked like her true King. But still that edge of uneasy hunger lingered in his face.

'The girl has suffered enough for one day,' said the

Queen. 'If you want her, you will have to knock me down to take her. Not that you would surprise me.'

Mabriahna stood, arms folded, gazing squarely into her husband's face. Ysomir held her breath.

'How could you think I would ever hurt her?' he breathed. 'Very well. Keep her. But I will come back for her soon.'

Chapter Seventeen. Eldareth the Wanderer

Tanthe sparred with Lynden under the training area's icy crystal dome, enjoying the contest. The pale, hard wood of their blades flashed as they circled, dodged and struck. Sweat gathered under her shirt. She felt breathless, nimble and strong; exhilarated. Her hard work throughout the winter was bringing its reward at last.

Tanthe smiled as they fought. Lynden seemed to be enjoying himself too, returning the look. She swept her blade under his guard and touched his arm, scoring a point.

At that, his expression changed. His lips pulled back, his eyes glittered, and he went mad.

His attack took Tanthe by surprise. He surged forward, swinging his sword with skill and incredible speed. Off-guard only for an instant, she gathered her wits and defended herself, just too late. He feinted, drove in under her guard, and dealt a bruising blow to her breastbone.

'Disqualified!' called Cyl – one of Alraen's senior students – who was refereeing their bout.

The blow was hard enough to wind her. Tanthe stepped backwards, coughing for breath.

'Anthar's balls, Lynden!' she cried. 'You're supposed to pull back!' She rubbed at the tender spot, wincing. 'We're meant to be practising, not trying to kill each other!'

Lynden looked horrified as he came to her. 'Gods, Tan, I'm really sorry. I don't know what came over me. It was as if you were someone else, and I was so angry I couldn't see.'

Cyl said, 'I think that's enough for today. Alraen will want to talk to you, Lynden.'

As the Shaelahyr woman took their weapons from them and walked away, Tanthe took his arm and pulled him to the side of the arena. 'If you're going to start blanking out like that, you shouldn't be fighting,' she said tersely. 'What have I done to make you so angry?'

Lynden bit his lip. 'It's not you. It's Rufe.'

'What's he done now?' They went into the changing area, a smaller cave that linked the arena to the communal bathing room.

'He suggested that one of the Aelyr girls is interested in me, and since Ymmi isn't here, what am I saving myself for?' Lynden flung his shirt on to a marble bench. 'Why can't he understand? I don't want anyone but her!'

A flame of rage leapt through her. Tanthe waited for it to subside, then she gave a resigned laugh. 'He's probably just trying to cheer you up, Lyn.'

'Why are you defending him?'

'Just giving him the benefit of the doubt. I've had a lot of practice at that.'

'I know,' Lynden said grimly. 'He told me what happened. You caught him with Metiya. I could have killed him.'

'Oh, it's all right, Lyn. It was weeks ago and I'm sure it hasn't happened again. He was so sorry afterwards, I had to forgive him.'

Lynden was gazing darkly at her. 'But are things the same between you?'

Tanthe was silent. At last she said under her breath, 'Not quite the same. No. I love him, but I can't quite forget about it.'

'That's it, isn't it? How would Ymmi feel, if she knew I was enjoying myself with someone else? I can't. I wonder what she's doing. Every day that goes by, I feel more afraid that she might be dead by now.'

'Stop that.' Tanthe put her arm round his shoulders and shook him. 'Ouch, you really bruised me, you know.'

'Sorry,' he said.

'Had any more of your, er, vision things?'

'No, but . . . It's like an open door in my head. I'm afraid of what might walk into it.'

'Don't be afraid, Lyn.' His words disturbed her.

'That's what Liyet told me.' Lynden combed his hair with his fingers and looked straight at her, his brown eyes very bright. 'Do you feel that you don't know the Shaelahyr any better now than when we first arrived? They look at you as if they know something, but won't say it.'

Tanthe exhaled. 'You're right. Funny thing is, I get on quite well with Cyl now, but I still don't feel I really know her. And Elrill doesn't seem to like me any more, but he won't say what I've done wrong.'

'How long have we been here?'

'Let me think. We arrived just after Darkeve. Now we're about halfway between Breyid's Day and Estrae . . . so, about sixteen weeks.'

'Gods. Is this thaw ever going to start?'

Lynden had been asking that question every day, it seemed, when he was not morosely silent. 'Come on,' said Tanthe. 'Let's put our cloaks and boots on over our training gear. We'll go up to the entrance and take a look.'

That cheered him a little. Tanthe and Rufryd both found it hard work, trying to keep Lynden's hopes up, and Rufryd was the quickest to lose patience with him. She and Lynden walked through the halls and corridors of shining quartz, watched by a scattering of Shaelahyr and their attenuated white cats.

As they walked up the gentle slope of the outermost tunnel, wintry air flowed down to them, chilling their hot skin and making them pull their cloaks tight around them. At the entrance, Tanthe ran up the stairs to the ledge above the door and looked through a panel of transparent rock. All was white.

'Doesn't look any better,' Tanthe said, coming down again.

'Let's open the door and look outside.' Lynden began to work at the handle of the pulley.

'Must we? We'll freeze!'

'No. It feels warmer.'

Groaning, Tanthe took the other handle, winding in the ropes until the tall vertical slab of rock that formed the door began to slide open. A wedge of chill air muscled in, and a clot of snow fell from above and landed on her head.

'Shit!' she said. 'Half of that went down my neck!'

Outside was the snow-wrapped white V of the mountains, looking just as it had for the whole winter. Mount Ishte rose in splendour against a pearl-bright, overcast sky. 'Oh, don't go out there, Lyn. Let's get this thing closed, before Elrill comes and complains.'

'No, Tan.' Lynden took a few steps along the path. 'It *is* warmer. Can't you feel it? Look, the snow's falling off the top of the entrance.'

'I noticed.'

'It's melting!'

'And it will freeze a few more times before—' She stopped, staring at something moving on the slope on the right of the valley. 'Lyn, can you see that?'

He turned, shielding his eyes. 'Great Anthar . . . it looks like a man.'

The figure, dark against the snow, was struggling down the mountainside, sliding as the hard crust broke under him and plunged him into the soft drifts beneath. He righted himself, slid down, fell again, struggled on as if in a desperate hurry.

'He looks exhausted,' said Tanthe.

'We'd better tell Elrill.'

The man fell again in a tangle of long dark limbs, and this time he did not get up.

They watched him, Tanthe's hand poised on Lynden's arm. 'Come on, he needs help.'

As they floundered through the snow, Tanthe knew Lynden was right. The snow had been thawing by day, freezing by night. Spring would be a long time coming to the peaks, but it had begun. Perhaps they would be able to leave at Estrae.

The man was lying on his back in a drift, gasping for breath as he struggled feebly to rise. He was tall and all in black; breeches, thick boots, a heavy fur-trimmed coat. His long raven hair was tied back from a strong, almost ugly face with high cheekbones and a long chin. A sword hung against his thigh.

He was human, not Aelyr.

'Who is he?' whispered Lynden.

He meant, Tanthe knew, *what if he's an enemy?* Ignoring the question, she called to the man as they reached him. 'Hello? It's all right, you're safe. We'll help you.'

The man's eyes fluttered open. He looked at her, nodding in relief, too tired to speak. They began to help him up and he leaned heavily on them, nearly sending them all slithering down the steep slope.

'Thank you,' he gasped as the three staggered back towards Silverholm. 'It has taken me many a long day to reach this place. I can go no further.'

'It's all right. You're there.'

'Do you know Elrill?'

'Of course,' said Tanthe. 'He's looking after us.'

'But you two are not Shaelahyr . . .'

'Neither are you,' she said. 'It's a long story.'

He gave a hoarse laugh. 'Indeed.'

'I'm Tanthe, this is Lynden.'

'And I am a friend of Elrill's,' the man said. 'My name is Eldareth.'

Ysomir saw nothing of the King for seven days. Instead she lived in the Queen's chambers, not quite a maid, not quite a companion . . . more, she realised after a time, like a pet bird.

Mabriahna rarely left her rooms. Each day she would rise, bathe and take breakfast, all with the help of two

384

ladies-in-waiting who also attended Ysomir, rather to her embarrassment. Then the Queen would dress immaculately; she always looked regal, her hair and her lace cuffs stiff as silver. But after she was dressed, she seemed to step into a kind of limbo.

She would pace the large chambers, stare out of the windows, stand for an hour at a time on the balcony despite the chill weather. Restlessness and unused energy radiated from her. She made Ysomir almost as nervous as the King had done.

Ysomir felt she would rather still be slaving in the Tower than trapped and idle in this amber cage. And yet there was something charismatic and absorbing about the Queen, as there was about Garnelys.

After a day or two, feeling she had nothing to lose, Ysomir tentatively suggested that she might read to the Queen. Mabriahna was thrilled by the idea. Soon the Queen was spending most of the mornings and afternoons ensconced in a great gilded chair, her head tipped back and eyes closed in pleasure, as Ysomir read stories and novels and folk-tales of Aventuria until her throat was sore.

'I miss my granddaughter Helananthe so much,' Mabriahna said one day. 'She is such a dear girl. I fear, sometimes, that I will never see her again.'

'Surely you will, ma'am,' said Ysomir. 'I believe I will see my lover again one day, whatever happens.'

Mabriahna had no curiosity about Ysomir's private life; she had never even asked where she came from. 'When Helananthe was here, she brought the palace to life. It's so pleasant to have you here instead.'

'Do I remind you of her?'

The Queen laughed. 'No, you are absolutely nothing like her! She was a great, loud, argumentative thing! Always quarrelling with Galemanth. But Garnelys—' her face went rigid suddenly. 'Garnelys adored her.'

Ysomir, as happened a dozen times a day, had no idea what to say. It wasn't her place to be receiving the confidences of Aventuria's greatest family. How was she supposed to respond?

'I miss my mother,' she said.

To her surprise, Mabriahna placed a warm, consoling hand on her arm, 'Well, at least we have each other.'

That night, Ysomir woke in her bed to hear a soft, insistent sobbing coming from the Queen's chamber. Mabriahna sounded so desolate that Ysomir lay wide-eyed, not daring to intrude on her sorrow. But after a while the sound grew unendurable. Ysomir rose, crossed the living chamber, and cautiously entered the Queen's bedroom on the other side.

'Ma'am?'

Mabriahna was on her knees before a wall-shrine. In the centre stood a graceful statuette of Nepheter, surrounded by candles and smoking incense. The goddess looked impassively into the air, but the Queen knelt with her head bowed and her hair hanging dishevelled over her shoulders.

'What's wrong?'

Mabriahna reached out to Ysomir and pulled her down. She showed no embarrassment at being found in such a state. 'Oh, what isn't wrong?' she said. 'All women are potential priestesses, are we not? We speak directly to the goddess because we are each an aspect of the goddess, she resides in us and we in her . . .'

'Yes, ma'am.' Ysomir watched her anxiously.

'What is your name for her?'

'Breyid, ma'am. And Nephenie in her maiden aspect and Mahaa as the—'

'Ah yes, Breyid. Nepheter among the peasant women.' She held Ysomir's hand so tight it hurt. 'I know I am no better, no grander or greater than you, dear. You look like a princess in the clothes I give you. I could put on farmer's garb and pass unnoticed among you. We're all the same. I've always known it. The role of King and Queen is not to rule, but to serve. There is no point to our existence, except to protect and care for Aventuria. If that changes, then we may as well cease to exist. All our promises are broken, the Xauroma is dead.'

Ysomir was nearly crying. 'How can I help you?'

'I used to know what my purpose was. Garnelys and I loved each other, advised each other, carried out our duties together. The goddess manifested herself through me and I did all that was good for her sons and daughters. But now Garnelys has taken all my duties away from me. I am allowed to do nothing. Not because he wants me to have no power, but because he feels he must take everything upon his own shoulders.'

Ysomir swallowed. 'Have you – have you tried arguing with him?'

The Queen sat back on her heels. Her nightdress fell in folds around her bare feet. 'Oh, I have tried everything. I used to be strong and I feared nothing. Difficult to believe now, is it not? But he began to frighten me, so often and so badly, that slowly he wore all my courage away.'

'You still have courage,' Ysomir said. 'I do. We must.'

'You're still young, like a newly-made statue before the weather has pocked it and worn it away. No, I'm past it all now. I can't speak to my goddess any longer. I open myself to her as I used to but she no longer comes.'

Ysomir hugged her, at a loss. The two women remained there on the cold floor, holding each other, until at last she persuaded the Queen to go back to bed. Ysomir brought her a glass of wine, and sat with her until she fell asleep.

Now she knew what ailed the Queen, but there seemed to be nothing she could do about it. Days passed, in the same tense limbo. On the seventh day, Mabriahna and Ysomir were both infected by restlessness. Snow swirled against the windows and the blizzard made the whole Citadel moan. Ysomir thought of the conscripts in the tunnels beneath the Tower, Beorwyn in the mines. She felt guilty, so undeservedly warm and safe.

The Queen did not even want to be read to; Ysomir had

barely begun the first page when Mabriahna waved an irritable hand and said, 'Enough.'

'Shall I read something else, ma'am?'

'Nothing. I'm not in the mood.'

'Then how can I amuse you? A game?'

A smile ghosted across her tired face. 'My dear, nothing can amuse me. I no longer play metrarch; the game is tainted with blood. Just sit with me.'

The silence was heavy. The very fabric of the Citadel seemed to shudder and shift. Ysomir thought she heard human cries above the storm, while the great black sphere turned and shrieked in torment. So strange was the memory that she wondered if she had dreamed it.

Someone thumped on the double doors. Ysomir and the Queen both started up, staring wide-eyed at each other.

'It's him,' said the Queen.

The door opened. King Garnelys entered quietly, but his presence filled the chamber as if he had brought the bleak night in with him.

'I promised I would come for her,' he said.

He was like a dra'a'k, grey-skinned, hunched and towering. The two women clutched each other. Mabriahna was pushing Ysomir behind her, as if to shield her. The King frowned.

'Why do you behave as if you're afraid of me? There is no need for this fear! Come, Ysomir.' He held out his hand to her. She knew there was no point in resisting. If she tried, both she and the Queen would suffer.

As she stepped forward, Mabriahna caught her arm and cried, 'No!'

'It's all right,' Ysomir said soothingly. 'I have to go with him. You know that.'

The Queen seemed to diminish as Ysomir walked towards the King. His eyes glittered blackly down at her as he took her hand and looped it through his arm.

'You are a wise girl, Ysomir,' he said. 'I came to ask your forgiveness.'

He led her out of the chamber. As the doors swung shut, Ysomir caught a last glance of the Queen standing desolate in the centre of the room, one hand hovering as if to snatch her back.

The King led her slowly along the amber-walled corridors, just as if they were a royal couple on their way to a ball. Ysomir wondered where the walk would end. She felt numb, but oddly calm.

'What are you thinking?' he asked.

'That my life does not seem real any more.'

'Ysomir.' His voice was gentle, throaty with regret. 'If I frightened you, forgive me.'

'It's not my position to forgive you. I can't.'

'I don't blame you,' he said. 'All I ask for is your attention.'

'Why?' she hissed. 'I'm only your subject, your servant.'

'No. I am yours.'

'You're the King. You don't have to explain yourself to anyone.'

'No, you are wrong. I should have explained long ago. And now I must make you see.'

'Why?'

He stroked her cheek with a curved forefinger. 'You are like the daughter I never had. If you hate me, it matters. You are all my subjects, you are the spirit of Aventuria.'

Ysomir was dumbstruck. Was that how he saw her, an archetypical representative of his whole domain? Was that why he felt this compulsion to explain himself to her?

He took her through a vaulted hall that she had never seen before, a great chamber with an endless row of diamond-paned windows and a double throne adorned with blue jewels. The fabled Sapphire Throne.

'The Sun Chamber,' said the King. Ysomir had heard of it, of course; she looked around in silent awe. It took two full minutes to walk from one end to the other. When they reached the vast stained-glass window at the far end,

Ysomir looked through and saw a breathtaking view of the Heliodor Tower.

The light of Rose Moon and Lily Moon shone full upon it, casting a double shadow from its great hulk. The stone glittered, ice-frosted. The scaffolding was a mere jumble of ink-strokes around it, while against the dark sky the Tower itself seemed luminous. The sliver of Lily Moon hung above its unfinished walls like a diadem.

'Is it not beautiful?' said the King.

'Yes,' said Ysomir. And it was. Beautiful yet forbidding, too overpowering.

'I want someone to understand why I must build it.'

'But sire . . . Do you feel that people don't understand?'

'Don't humour me, Ysomir. Of course they don't understand. How could they, why should they? They have only seen me from the outside, the beneficent ruler. They have not been inside my mind, wondering . . .'

She waited, not daring to speak. After a few moments he went on, 'What have I done for Aventuria? I have forged no alliances between the realms. I did not win the War of the Silver Plains. I have not saved Aventuria from famine or flood, nor tamed the *roth* of the stones. I have been no more than an administrator. What reason have the folk of my kingdom to remember me?'

'How could anyone forget you?' she said in disbelief.

He spoke in a low, grave tone, as if to himself. 'I have always worshipped the beauty of the land over which I am fortunate enough to reign. Often have I wept to look upon its beauty. I would have laid down my life to preserve it. Yet now . . .'

'Sire?'

'Oh, the city lies below the Citadel in glory, as it always has. But now, for some reason, for some time . . . I cannot remember when or why it began to seem different . . . it means nothing to me. It looks flat to my eyes, meaningless. The gleaming roofs are a mere jumble of geometry. When the sun shines it is as harsh as brass. The rain tastes like dust on my tongue. Does it seem like that to you?'

'No. Parione is beautiful – or would be, if—'

'But you are young. I grow old. Not knowing whether I have a handful or a score of years ahead of me I have begun to ask myself this question. *How will I be judged after my death?*'

'As a good king, surely . . .'

'A good king? Is that enough? I have always struggled to be fair and kind, so that no one would find cause to speak ill of me. But is it sufficient to be merely *good*? My reign has been uneventful. I have never had cause to save Aventuria from enemies. Thus, I have never had a chance to prove my worth and to leave my signature on the history books.'

'But you will be remembered with affection!' She was more than shocked by his words. She felt sickened.

'It is not enough to be remembered with affection.' Garnelys stared out into the night, his sharp chin jutting. 'A true ruler should be remembered as glorious, noble, one who laid down his very life for the Nine Realms. A true King cannot afford to be less than perfect!'

Her mouth opened. Now was she expected to tell him he was perfect? Her lips clamped shut and she watched him, her eyes burning.

Garnelys sighed. His head drooped and he looked beguilingly human again. 'Ah, but I am very far from perfect. There is so much I should have done differently. I am flawed, Ysomir. My father Aralyth told me constantly that I would never prove equal to the task.' He turned to her, one fist against his breast, his face anguished. 'And if the King is flawed, so is everything around him! All that I once thought perfect, I now see is riddled with falsity.'

Ysomir drew back. His despair filled the whole chamber, and it terrified her. 'How *can* my people remember me as anything but a failed caretaker? If I die, you will judge me. And with what harsh contempt you will judge me! And you will be justified, and yet, some part of me rails against the unfairness of it, for I, with all my flaws, have tried so hard to please you!'

He stretched out a clawed hand, as if to touch her. His fingers hovered an inch from her shoulder. 'The prospect of your judgement terrifies me – and for that, I have begun to hate you. I fear my father was right – yet I have to prove him wrong! Unless I can achieve perfection before I die, and thus be judged and remembered well, nothing matters. It will all have been for nothing.'

'That's not true.' Her voice was a mouse-squeak. He didn't hear her.

'And since perfection is unobtainable, I am lost. My Tower, my Tower – that is my only hope. *That* will be my legacy. There is something that will never be ignored or forgotten, and generations will sing my praises!'

Gods, Ysomir thought. He really believes it.

'And yet, there are no guarantees, are there? I cannot control people's thoughts or actions after my death. Therefore – and the answer is quite simple, after all – I must not die.'

'What?'

'I have decided to live for ever. My heirs will not be needed after all, you see. The Tower is my offering to the Great Goddess Nuth and Her Consort Anuth; for as long as I go on building the Tower, higher and higher into the heavens, they will reward me with life everlasting.'

'And you—' her throat was dry as sand, 'you believe you can do this?'

His eyes flashed rage. 'It is not a matter of belief. It has been promised to me. It has already begun.'

'But no one's meant to live for ever, not even the King.'

'Answer me carefully, Ysomir, for you speak for the whole of Aventuria. You say that I am loved. Is it not to your joy, then, to have me ruling over you for ever?'

She clasped her arms around herself, a fragile shield. 'Not like this.'

392

'I cannot hear you.'

'No, it isn't,' she said clearly, letting her hands drop. She was shaking, soaring beyond fear into passion. 'Did you think that if you explained this to me, that would make it all right? That if I understood, all your subjects would understand too? If you were looking for permission, reassurance – I can't give it. What you are doing is cruel beyond belief. Why can't you see it? You were a good ruler, the best. Why, now, are you doing this?'

He glared at her. His eyes were black marbles with red flames at the centre. He seized her wrist, crushing the slender bones.

Then Ysomir knew. She was not the first whose approval he had sought, nor the first to answer him honestly. But all those who had gone before her had died for daring to speak out. Died in disbelief as their gentle lamb of a king turned into a snarling demon.

He dragged her with him through the Citadel to his private chamber where they had played metrarch. Through the inner door to the metal-smelling gloom of his secret chambers; the narrow tunnel, the uneven steps down into the dark. He thrust her forward and she fell and skidded on her hands and knees. The rough stones bruised her. Light flared; he was lighting a lamp. The glow fell greasily on the walls. She looked up and saw the post with the leather straps and chains, the smoky crystal shining banefully.

Someone was already tethered to the post.

It was Namane. The physician.

Ysomir found herself inches from Namane's feet, staring up at her plump form, loose-robed in dark material. The physician's mouth was slack with fear, her eyes wide with terror.

'Which of you shall it be?' said the King. 'I could free her and put you in her place, Ysomir. Would you save her life?'

'I don't care what you do to me,' Ysomir said, her voice cracking. 'She's more use to other people than me.'

393

'Don't be stupid,' Namane whispered. 'What did I cure you for? Not to see you die!'

'But don't think of it as death,' said Garnelys. He turned, his shadow leaping on the wall behind him. In his hand he held a long steel knife, and his eyes were rheumy and dark as molten sulphur. 'Think of it as giving your energies to the Xauroma – thus living for ever.'

He loomed over them. His hunger filled the chamber, tangible, beating like a heart.

'It shall be you,' he said, touching the knife to Namane's throat. She winced and closed her eyes tight. 'A sacrifice, as in the ancient days, to bless the land.'

He raised his hands and began to chant. The very walls seemed to rumble in response. Ysomir felt a ball of darkness forming, then beginning to rotate faster and faster, filling the room with a whirling power that flattened her to the floor.

Gasping, she began to drag herself inch by inch away from Namane's feet. The King was in a trance; Namane had passed out. Ysomir smelled the pungency of sweat and urine through the stormy tang of electricity. The knife danced over the physician's throat.

With a burst of strength, Ysomir dragged herself up and flung herself at the King.

'No!' she screamed.

It was like hitting a wall. He barely flinched. Instead his arm lashed out. Something struck her, she fell back; a moment later a burning pain began in her arm and she felt the wetness of blood. He'd slashed her just below the shoulder. The pain took her breath away, but as she gasped she heard another voice echoing her own; imitating her groans as sighs of pleasure.

She stared up at the entrance and saw, against the black archway, the figure of Laphaeome.

The whole chamber was spinning like a whirlpool. The dark quartz was sucking up Namane's pain, intensifying it, sending it lashing round and round the walls. She couldn't find her balance. Voices and a roaring wind deafened her; a tornado filled with flying things battered her.

She heard Namane give a strangled, bubbling scream. Saw the flash of the knife, a red cut smiling across Namane's throat; and the cut opened, and a voice came out.

'She is your conscience, O King. Kill your conscience lest it paralyse you!'

Ysomir was out of her mind. She was on her feet and running wildly towards the narrow stairwell that led down to the heart-chamber of the sphere.

The stairs veered horribly around her as she ran. Unseen, moaning things clawed at her, trying to pull her back. All that was in her mind was to get as far from the King as she could; she could see no means of escape.

Her chest heaving, she reached the deep chamber and stood for a few wild seconds, staring at the sphere. It groaned and rotated wildly, spinning this way and that in torment, throwing off flashes of blood-red lightning.

Suddenly the ghastly light flashed on a human face. He was there, Garnelys, reaching out for her with crimson, dripping hands; reaching after her even as she dropped into the well of unconsciousness.

Eldareth lay in bed in Elrill's own quarters, shivering though he was covered with layers of warm white fleece. Tanthe and Lynden, crowding in the doorway, watched anxiously as Elrill and Liyet leaned over him, talking softly, holding a tumbler of hot, fragrant tea to his lips. The cavern was spacious and its rounded walls gleamed like nacre. Two Zampherai were in attendance, holding a tray from which Liyet selected ointments and bandages to dress a wound on Eldareth's arm.

'You can go,' said Elrill, looking round at Tanthe and Lynden.

'I want to make sure he's all right,' Tanthe said stubbornly.

'He is.' Elrill waved as if dismissing a child; her hackles rose.

'We found him. He might have died on the mountain-side if we hadn't seen him and helped him.'

'Yes, and we thank you.'

'I would like to know who he is.'

The Shaelahyr lord turned an impatient face to her. 'Is it any of your business?'

'Of course,' she said. 'He may have news of the outside world.'

Elrill's lips thinned. 'So this is less concern for his health than self-interest?'

'Concern for my sister, in case you'd forgotten.'

Eldareth spoke, his voice creaking with tiredness. 'Oh, let them stay. They saved me. They're just being human, Rill. Besides, I want to question them, too.'

'Later, then,' Elrill said firmly. 'Not until you are well.'

'It's nothing a few hours sleep won't . . .' Eldareth's voice faded. His shivering stopped, and his breathing became a gentle snore.

'So, this Eldareth,' said Rufryd. 'We keep hearing his name, but who actually is he?'

It was evening. Tiny lamps sparkled in the vault of the main chamber. Moon and starlight glowed through the walls; streaks within the crystal walls glimmered like frozen smoke. The platforms, like upturned mushroom caps, floated in the semi-darkness. The Shaelahyr were filtering in to take their places for the evening meal, and the musicians were already playing their eerie, plangent music, which more than ever thrilled and unsettled Tanthe to the core of her soul.

'We don't know,' she whispered. 'That's what we're hoping to find out.'

Lynden's eyes shone. 'You know what this means, Rufe? If he could find his way here – we must be able to leave.'

396

'Yes, well, don't get too excited,' Rufryd said flatly. 'It's still winter. You told me what a state he was in when you found him. We can't take the horses out yet; melting and freezing ice will be even harder going for them than fresh snow.'

'I know that, but—'

'Shh.' Tanthe squeezed Rufryd's leg, trying to abort the quarrel before it started. 'Elrill's coming.'

They had not always been privileged to sit at Elrill's right hand for meals; usually they were on one of the lower platforms. Friendly as the Shaelahyr were, it was plain they did not think highly of humans. But this time, Cyl brought them to places beside Elrill and Liyet.

Eldareth was already there with the Shaelahyr leaders. He was wearing loose trousers and a long-sleeved tunic of shimmering pearl and, although he looked pale, he was clearly determined to ignore the effects of his ordeal. Tanthe admired him for it.

'Well, we know he's tough,' she whispered.

'Must have come from Riverwynde,' Rufryd said drily.

Around them were Elrill's favoured companions; snow-pale men and women who moved with gossamer grace. Half a dozen Zampherai came onto the disc to serve wine and savoury morsels. Most of them withdrew, but one, to Tanthe's surprise, remained.

Then Elrill spoke. 'Today, as you will have heard, our good friend Eldareth came to us after a long and perilous journey. Now he wishes to tell us the reason for his coming. Orque' – he indicated the Zampherai – 'will remain, as we believe this concerns us all, human, Aelyr and Zampherai alike.'

Eldareth exhaled, and rubbed his neck beneath the long black hair. 'It is not good news.' He looked at Rufryd, Lynden and Tanthe. 'Elrill has told me a little of how you came to be here; that you were trying to find your sister. I trust it is safe to speak freely in front of you. Indeed, the

397

more of us who have the blindfold lifted from our eyes, the better.

'What happened to your sister, alas, has happened everywhere, a thousand-fold worse in and around Parione itself. I think the King will not stop at using the children and the old, until every one of his subjects has been ground like meal in the grindstones to build this accursed Tower.

'Garnelys has built up a large army to enforce his will, which was the easiest thing in the world since his subjects are so unquestioningly loyal. But I helped to lead a small insurrection, and for that I am a wanted man. I was forced to flee the city, and I've been all over Aventuria trying to warn people.'

The Shaelahyr murmured in concern. Eldareth gave them a stern look and went on, 'Don't think that this is a human problem alone. I came here because no one is safe, and even Silverholm itself will not be inviolate if this madness goes unchecked. Garnelys seems bent on destroying all he once held dear.'

Tanthe felt Lynden's hand digging unconsciously into her arm. 'You've come from Parione?' Lynden said. 'And you've seen the – the conscripts there?'

Eldareth looked at him, his face sombre. 'Alas, they're being worked to death – if accidents or epidemics don't kill them first – but more are dragged in to replace them. The city is in a terrible state of fear. But nothing matters to the King, as long as his Tower is built.'

Lynden's head fell in misery. Tanthe hung grimly on to her tears; they burned her eyes and throat, but she fought not to break down. Rufryd put his arms around them both.

'I am sorry,' Eldareth said gently. 'I wish I could give you better news, but I cannot. Even in Parione no one understood how serious things were, until the King destroyed the Old Royal Theatre itself to make way for the Tower.'

'What?' Tanthe cried.

'Saphaeyender put on a play that criticised the King. It was an impudent play, a sarcastic play; wildly dangerous, given what we now know about the King's state of mind. But still, it was not reason enough to destroy the theatre. The theatre had done nothing to offend anyone. And the people of Parione had done nothing to warrant such an act of vicious, wanton destruction.'

Now Tanthe's tears flowed freely. She felt ashamed, that she had managed not to cry over her sister, but over the theatre she could not control herself. 'I dreamed of going there to see the great classic plays. I even imagined what it would be like to see a play I had written myself performed there. How ridiculous. It was fantasy, I know, but I promised myself – one day I will go to Parione, and mix with the great writers and poets, and I will go to the Old Royal. Now I never will.'

Eldareth stared at her in amazement. There, another one incredulous that a peasant could dream of such a thing – but she didn't care. Her heart was broken.

'I'm sorry,' he said. Awkwardly he passed her a napkin to blot her face. 'Many in the city wept as piteously, believe me.'

'Did you do nothing to save it?' she said savagely.

His angular face turned hard. He pulled down the neck of his tunic and showed her an ugly red scar on his shoulder. 'I received this, trying to save it. Others gave their lives, or were taken away in chains. When the battle was lost, I saved Saphaeyender, at least. I found him on the ruins, weeping not just for a lost dream but for bitter reality.'

'You saved Saphaeyender?' she cried. 'You know him?'

Eldareth gave a quiet laugh. He seemed bemused by the question. 'Yes, I know him.'

'What's he like?'

'Annoying.'

Tanthe gasped. How could he be so irreverent? 'He must be very old.'

'Ancient,' said Eldareth. He didn't look pleased at being sidetracked by her questions. 'Nearly a hundred and thirteen.'

She was trying to find another question, when Rufryd nudged her. 'Tan, shut up. This has nothing to do with anything.'

For once, she took his advice. Shaken by all she'd heard, she took a draught of wine and sat in silence.

'Theatres can be rebuilt,' Eldareth said heavily. 'Alas, the damage done to Aventuria is far deeper. It's rumoured that Garnelys had his own son put to death, while his granddaughter' – He stopped. His face was stiff, but the ropes in his neck convulsed – 'his granddaughter Princess Helananthe is lost at sea. A fishing vessel reported that they had seen her ship sucked into a great whirlpool. If it's true, his only surviving heir is Venirryen, who has been taken into hiding. The child could be in terrible danger.'

'From his own grandfather?' said Elrill.

'It sounds unbelievable, I know. But believe me; we have lived through it. And worse; they say that the King has turned to invoking *gauroth*, even shedding human blood to attune with dark energies that should never be disturbed.'

'*Gauroth*?' said Elrill. 'Oh, the fool!'

'Worse than that,' Orque put in. 'If he is ripping stones from the earth without the intervention and care of the Zampherai, he is doing more harm than we can begin to imagine.'

'And do you think your King will turn against the Aelyr?' said Liyet.

Eldareth shook his head. 'I couldn't say.'

'We can't take a stand against him,' said Elrill. 'We are too few, and my duty is to keep Silverholm safe. We have no wish to plunge the Aelyr and human realms into war!'

'Of course not. It would be desperately stupid of him to alienate his allies, but I would put nothing past him now.

400

I've travelled as far as Sepheret, trying to warn people before it's too late.'

Tanthe, Rufryd and Lynden exchanged looks. 'We heard,' said Rufryd. And he began to tell their story as, many weeks earlier, they had told Elrill.

Eldareth listened with his head in his hand. 'Bhahdradomen in Ardharkria,' he said, when the others had finished. 'I wish I could say this is a shock to me. But Lady Amitriya told me of it many months ago. This is one thing that is not Garnelys's fault; he merely inherited it. Small pockets of Bhahdradomen, allowed to live on the mainland for as long as they don't stray from their prescribed areas; they're more or less harmless . . .'

'Harmless?' said Rufryd. 'My brother was sick for days after he'd seen one! He was attacked and he nearly went mad.'

'Don't exaggerate,' Lynden muttered.

'And Amitriya showed me the forest from a high tower,' said Tanthe. 'The area where the Bhahdradomen live is like a great ink stain of dead forest. The stain is spreading. And they followed us and tried to kill us!'

'Wait, wait.' Eldareth held up his large hands. 'I was going on to say that, at least they *were* harmless. I'd heard rumours that the conscripting parties were being aided by dubious means. But yours is the clearest evidence I've heard yet.'

Lynden said, 'I saw a vision of the thing that killed Lord Arhan when he was trying to deliver your warning. And it was the same as the thing that killed Tanthe's uncle.'

'Ghelim,' Eldareth said heavily. 'Bhahdradomen that have been imprinted to look and behave like something else. In this case, dra'a'ks.'

'Gods, yes!' exclaimed Tanthe, remembering. 'When that one in the cloak argued with Beyne, he said he wanted Lynden because he'd injured this *ghelim*! Oh, goddess . . .'

Eldareth rested his head on his hand. He looked paler

than ever. 'Oh, this is worse than I thought. My warnings were in vain; poor Lord Arhan died for his trouble.'

'Sorry,' said Tanthe. 'We seem to have nothing but bad news for each other.'

'All along I have suspected the hand of the Bhahdradomen in this. Creeping in the shadows, like spiders. I don't believe they created this situation, but if they knew of it, it's the very thing they might use to their advantage.'

Elrill said, 'Yes – if they were stronger. They might *wish* to take advantage, but the truth is, the Nine Realms are still strong and united, while the Eaters are disempowered. They know that if they chanced an uprising, they would be crushed.'

Eldareth breathed out slowly. 'Thank you, Elrill, voice of reason. You're right. Their leader – Aazhoth, or whatever his name is – isn't an idiot. He knows what the consequences of an uprising would be.'

'But something's happening,' said Rufryd. 'We can't ignore it.'

'What are we going to do?' Tanthe asked.

To her surprise, Eldareth put his head back and laughed. His voice echoed in the vault. Some of the musicians stopped playing and looked at him, put out. 'Now there is a question and a half, Tanthe!'

Lynden said, 'All I wanted was to get Ysomir back and go home.'

'Yes.' Eldareth placed a hand on the young man's shoulder. The music rose again, as haunting and eerie as the white winter that glowed beyond the crystal walls. 'To wipe out this slight interruption to your lives and go on as before, as if nothing has changed. But you can't. Everything is changing, and it will never be the same again.'

Ysomir returned to consciousness on a couch in the metrarch chamber. Her head spun; then memory returned and she jerked in shock.

The King was leaning over her, pressing a damp cloth to her forehead. She recoiled; he took the cloth away. Then, to her complete astonishment, he fell to his knees beside the couch, gripped her hands and bowed his head in supplication.

'Forgive me,' he said hoarsely. 'Please, please forgive me. I cannot bring myself to harm you, Ysomir. Please don't fear me, for I never will harm you.'

She forced herself to look at him. His face! Darts of horror pierced her – not because he looked grotesque or terrifying, but because he did not.

He was different. His hands were dry and clean and he'd put on a fresh, yellow and silver robe – but it was more fundamental than that. Half-gilded and half in shadow, the planes of his face seemed smoother, his eyes direct and unclouded. All the lines of anguish had been erased. He looked younger. Even his hair was darker and glossier.

He looked like the man in the portrait. Strong, kind, innocent.

'You've changed,' she whispered. 'How?'

'I can't help it.' He was soft, imploring, sad and yet tranquil. 'The pressure – the darkness – it builds up within me until I can bear it no longer. All that releases it is the letting of blood. I have never admitted this to anyone except Laphaeome. I cannot tell the Queen.'

'Why are you telling me?'

'I don't know. You are different.'

'I have nothing to say to you. You killed Namane.'

'But their life force is never wasted. It strengthens the Xauroma, as it strengthens me. The King, the Xauroma, the land – we're inseparable.'

'And Laphaeome. I saw the energy going into him. He was smiling.'

'Please understand. I don't want to do this. I hate it. But I cannot help it. It's the only way, my only hope. Forgive me, Ysomir, I beg you.'

His eyes – soft, clear and beautiful – were begging her,

403

love me. And the dreadful thing was that she wanted to. She desperately wanted to love him, as her King and as a man, but she couldn't. She turned her head away. In shock and desperation she began to weep.

'I can't forgive you! If you hate it, you must stop. It's cruel, it's evil, it's pitiful.'

'I know,' he said. 'Yet I can't see any other way.' He touched the wound in her shoulder. 'I hurt you; I'm sorry. I'll get someone to dress it.'

'Who?' she said savagely.

He seemed taken aback. 'There are other physicians.'

'Until you destroy them all. Why are you trying to destroy Aventuria?'

The King blinked at her. She almost preferred his vulture-self to this oddly calm incarnation. At first she thought he was ignoring her question. Then he answered.

'There is no light without darkness. No life without conflict. We have had too much peace and so we need to be reminded that life is worth nothing unless we have to fight tooth and nail for it. This will be my legacy to Aventuria.'

Two days after Eldareth arrived, another snowstorm blew up, destroying Lynden's hopes of leaving. Rufryd began to understand how his brother felt. From being complacently happy in Silverholm, Eldareth's arrival had infected him with a desire for action. He felt as if they were trapped in a crystal bubble, while the outside world collapsed around them.

Tanthe felt the same, Rufryd knew. At night, lying in each others' arms, they began to make plans for the next part of the journey. It was all they seemed to talk about. The prospect of the journey seemed to be driving them apart, rather than bringing them closer together. They made love as passionately as before yet somehow Tanthe was not quite with him; her body, yes, even her emotions, but not her thoughts. Her eyes did not meet his. She always seemed to be looking at something above and beyond him.

They had begun to make preparations for the journey, so they could be ready to go as soon as the weather improved. The horses' tack was cleaned and oiled, their rucksacks re-packed, weapons and travelling clothes ready.

Rufryd, despite his natural suspicion of everyone, found himself liking Eldareth. He was blunt and straightforward; he was also the first person they'd met who understood their quest and wanted to help them. He was twice their age, and there was something reassuring about his experience and wisdom.

Eldareth practised with them in the sword arena, cursing his rustiness although he always bettered them; then, in the evenings, he would eat with them, entertaining them with stories of Parione and the Realms beyond.

'I'll be frank,' Eldareth told them. 'I hold out little hope of you finding your Ysomir. Oh, she may well still be alive; she's young and healthy, from what you say. But you would have to take her by force, and that's going to be impossible. There's far more chance of you being captured and set to work alongside her.'

'I'd rather that, than never see her again,' said Lynden.

'I know, lad.' Eldareth clapped him on the shoulder. 'But you could be sent to work miles from her, or put into the army . . . or even killed as you try to release her. That's assuming you find her. My advice would be to turn round and go home. How much chance is there of you listening to me?'

'None,' said Tanthe, before Lynden could speak. 'Absolutely none.'

'Will you come with us?' Rufryd asked.

'Part of the way. I have a slight problem; if my face is seen in Parione, I'll be a dead man. I've yet to decide what I shall do next. It all seems hopeless. Ah, if this situation was ended, your sister and all the others like her would walk free!'

The days began to lengthen, and warmer winds battled with the icy gales. Three weeks after Eldareth arrived, Shaelahyr scouts reported that the way down the mountains was becoming passable at last.

'Still not without risk, though,' said Eldareth. 'There may be late blizzards or avalanches to contend with.'

'I don't care,' said Lynden. 'We've been stuck here for long enough.'

They decided to leave the next day. While Lynden and Tanthe went down to check on the horses and make last-minute preparations, Rufryd and Eldareth went up to sit at the lookout window above the main entrance. The crystal pane was cloudy, and there was still little to be seen but whiteness. The path was fairly clear, but the high slopes of the valley were still thick with snow.

'Elrill's a cold fish, but I hope he's made you feel welcome,' said Eldareth.

'Apart from a misunderstanding at the start – we'd have died without him,' said Rufryd. 'And we've learned things we'd never have learned anywhere else.'

'Things?'

'How to fight, mostly. Funny, I thought the Aelyr were peaceable.'

'Yes – but they also have a great deal of foresight. They know we'll need those skills.'

A weird, ringing boom broke out, startling them both.

'What on earth is that?' Rufryd exclaimed.

'Someone at the door,' Eldareth said. He rubbed at the crystal pane with his sleeve; Rufryd looked down and saw two men in dark green cloaks at the entrance below them.

'Gods! Who are they? Not Aelyr?'

They jumped up and looked over the balcony at the entrance tunnel below them, just in time to see two Shaelahyr sliding back the great outer door. Elrill himself was striding down the corridor to meet the newcomers.

The two men came in, red-faced from the cold.

'We are here at the command of General Grannen and King Garnelys. We seek Lord Elrill of the Shaelahyr.'

'I am Elrill. How may I assist you?'

'We believe that you are sheltering a man named Eldareth. He is wanted for crimes against Aventuria.'

Rufryd looked at Eldareth; the older man's face was grim. Rufryd reached for his bow and arrow, but Eldareth stayed his hand.

'I'm afraid you've made a mistake,' Elrill said coolly. 'There is no Eldareth here.'

'We are also looking for three young humans, a woman and two men. They are wanted for the attempted murder of a Registat in Skald, for perversion of the King's commands and various other charges.'

Rufryd gasped silently. How could they have known we were here? Calamys? Surely not!

'Again, I have no knowledge of any such people.'

'There's no sense in protecting them, Lord Elrill,' said the officer. 'Give them up. We're giving you the chance to do so voluntarily.'

'I can't do so voluntarily, since they are not here.'

'If you don't cooperate, we'll take Eldareth and the others by force.'

As they were talking, Rufryd noticed two things. Below, the two Shaelahyr were sliding the door very softly and quietly into place. Outside a column of men, black as ants against the snow, was filing into the valley and taking up position outside the entrance.

'Force?' said Elrill. 'I thought your King was a friend to the Aelyr.'

'The King's quarrel is with Eldareth, not with you.'

'All the same, if you use force, we will take it as an act of hostility. Is that what you or your King want? To alienate their allies?'

'Spare me the political talk!' The officer and the soldier drew their swords; at that moment the tall stone door

407

slammed shut, and half-a-dozen Shaelahyr arrows flew from hidden niches. The soldier cried out and fell.

Rufryd fired too. His arrow flew and landed with a thud in the officer's shoulder; the man turned, stared upwards in shock, then fell. His eyes stayed open. Rufryd's was not the only shaft protruding from his body.

Eldareth swore.

Elrill came running up the carved steps to the lookout ledge, with eight Shaelahyr following him. Eldareth stood up to meet him; the two men stared grimly at each other, then turned to look through the crystal pane.

Out in the valley, a troop of sixty or so men were approaching the door. The other Shaelahyr spread themselves along the ledge, some of them climbing higher into rough niches in the rock.

'Is there any way the door can be opened from the outside?' asked Eldareth.

'No – unless they have brought a catapult or a battering ram, if they could have dragged such a contraption up the mountains. Still, you're not safe here,' said Elrill.

'*You* are not safe, as long as I remain here,' Eldareth replied. 'I am so sorry, my friend. I would not have brought this trouble to you for anything.'

Rufryd said, 'I don't think they need a battering ram. Look.'

The soldiers were hammering metal spikes into the stone of the door, using them to climb higher up its face. Then at the apex of the door, an iron loop was driven in and a rope attached to it.

'They mean to pull the door over,' said Eldareth. 'Will they succeed?'

'I fear so,' said Elrill. 'It may take them some time, but the door is not so thick that it's impossible to dislodge.' He turned and called a few words to the other Shaelahyr in their own language.

At once, the slender men and women – four of each – began to slither through tiny worm-holes cut in the clear

408

rock. Rufryd had not even noticed the holes before. He jumped up, clutching his bow, his heart pounding. 'Let me go with them.'

'Sit down,' Elrill said firmly. 'Those passages are too narrow for humans. And my people are not blundering out there with arrows and spears, to make easy targets of themselves.'

The Shaelahyr were hardly visible against the snow. They ran lightly up the slopes, four on either side of the valley, and towards the high ridges until he could no longer see them.

As he sat watching, Tanthe and Lynden came running up the steps to join him. They were out of breath.

'What's happening?' Tanthe said. 'The Shaelahyr are all heading this way with swords and bows—'

'They've come for us,' Eldareth said heavily. He and Rufryd explained what had happened. Meanwhile, the soldiers below them finished hammering more loops into the top of the door and stringing rope through them. Forming a dark wedge down in the valley, the troop began to heave on the ropes.

The door creaked. Down in the hall below, Shaelahyr were waiting silently behind rocks along the sloping walls, weapons at the ready. Tanthe and Lynden drew their swords. They both looked pale, but Rufryd felt excited; thrillingly terrified.

His ears began to hurt.

He felt the sound before he heard it; a high, thin vibration. Then the sound swelled growing louder, more complex; several piercing notes sounding in excruciating discord, setting up harmonics and thrumming vibrations.

'What is that?' said Tanthe in alarm.

'Look!' said Rufryd.

All along the tops of the valley, the Shaelahyr were singing. He could just see them, tiny pale figures against the grey sky; but each one shone like a star. Their arms were outstretched and their throats were open, each emitting a single, long, terrifying note.

As if in response, there was a deep cracking noise. All along the mountain slopes below them, great slabs of snow were breaking away and sliding downwards. Faster and faster they slid, flowing as easily as liquid, with a soft rumbling noise that drowned even the Aelyr song.

Tanthe clutched Rufryd's arms. 'Oh, gods, no!' she cried.

The soldiers began to look up, to point and shout warnings. Dropping the ropes, they turned and began to flee up the valley – too late. They had no hope of outrunning the avalanche. Tons of snow crashed down into the valley, filling it, crushing the soldiers.

Rufryd and the others watched in shocked amazement.

When it was over, the snow had filled the valley to the level of the lookout window. Only a strip of rock crystal at the top remained clear. Elrill stood up to peer through it.

There was silence. Eventually Tanthe said, 'Could anyone have survived that?'

Elrill turned to her. He looked shaken, but his voice was as calm as ever. 'Unlikely. The snow flows like a waterfall, but the moment it comes to rest it freezes like granite under its own weight.'

'Are – are your own people all right?'

'They were above the fall. I can see them coming back. Besides, unlike humans we can burrow and swim through the snow if need be.'

Rufryd stood on tiptoe to see the eight Shaelahyr running back towards Silverholm like ghosts over a snowfield that was barely below the level of his eyes. Tanthe was plainly stunned by so many deaths; so was he, but rather to his own shame his main feeling was one of relief.

Tanthe said, 'So, the entrance is blocked.'

'There's no other way out, is there?' Lynden said anxiously.

Elrill shook his head. 'This will not thaw quickly.'

'How are we going to leave?'

410

As Lynden spoke, the first of the singers began to squeeze back in through the worm-holes. They'd had to burrow through a couple of feet of snow to get back in. Lynden looked at Rufryd, who shook his head. 'Don't even think of it,' Rufryd said. 'We'd get stuck. And what about the horses?'

The first of the singers, a young man, straightened up and shook the snow from his clothes. 'Even if you could get out this way, you'd be better advised not to. There are more human troops on the mountains. We saw them, further down the valley.'

'Dyon's bollocks!' said Eldareth. 'Elrill, forgive me for bringing all this trouble to you.'

The Shaelahyr lord touched his friend's shoulder. 'I had no idea you were such a dangerous man. I'm almost impressed! Well, they will not get in now. And we have other ways to make the mountains spit them out.'

'All the same, I should leave. Rufryd and his companions should come with me.'

'Well, we're not staying behind!' said Lynden.

'But how?' said Rufryd.

Eldareth and Elrill looked gravely at each other. Elrill shook his head, in sorrow rather than denial. 'I would rather you did not. But you would seem to have no choice; you are not safe here and, although I love you as a brother, I would rather not put my people in state of siege to protect you.'

'And I would not expect it.' He gave Elrill's shoulder a quick, sad grip, then turned to Rufryd, Tanthe and Lynden. 'There is a way,' he said. 'But it is dangerous. We will have to pass underground, through the realms of the Azure Zampherai.'

Chapter Eighteen. The Azure Zampherai

Eldareth led Tanthe, Rufryd and Lynden to the lowest levels of Silverholm, through lightless passages they'd never entered before. Redbird walked calmly at Tanthe's side; Rufryd was in front of her, leading Sunhawk, and Lynden behind with Halcyon. The horses weren't in bad condition, despite their captive winter, thanks to the Aelyr's efforts to keep them fit.

The travellers were dressed in a mixture of clothing; the jackets, breeches and boots that had survived from Riverwynde, with soft Aelyr shirts underneath and their heavy cloaks on top. The garments from Luin Sepher, cleaned and mended, were stowed in their saddlebags. And before they left, Elrill had presented them each with an Aelyr sword.

It had been strange, saying good-bye to the Shaelahyr. Tanthe had kissed Cyl, Liyet, Thelliel, Alraen – even the treacherous Metiya – while feeling that she was no closer to knowing any of them. And Elrill had kissed her hand, still giving her the distant, guarded look he wouldn't explain. She hadn't been particularly pleased at the way Metiya had hugged Rufryd as they parted; but still, it was over now. And she felt a deep wrench at having to leave. A craving to know all the secrets whose surface she hadn't even scratched.

Elrill had insisted on sending a Zampherai with them, to guide them through the deep passages. It was Orque who came, the one who had taken part in their meeting the night Eldareth first arrived. Orque was a quick-witted, sharp-tongued creature, with skin like pewter, a head of thick black hair and large, dark-attuned eyes.

He was the only one who needed no light to guide him. The others were carrying small lamps, and glad of them as the tunnels grew deeper and darker.

'How long is this going to take?' asked Rufryd.

'We should be through within a day,' Orque replied, 'and out onto the lower slopes of the mountains.'

'I can't wait to see a tree,' said Tanthe. 'Just a leaf, just a blade of grass would do!'

Orque halted, bringing them to what seemed a dead end. He took from his tunic a spike of polished white quartz which he pointed at the wall. Misty energy flowed from its point, surging out like a tongue to lick the blank stone. Using it like a paintbrush, he swept the tongue of light over the stone and a glowing line appeared, delineating a door. At a touch from Orque's hand, the stone door rotated on its vertical axis, giving a narrow opening on each side. The tunnel beyond was pitch black. Tanthe and Lynden exchanged a nervous look as Orque beckoned to them.

'Welcome to the realm of the Azure Zampherai,' he said.

'Did you create that door?' Tanthe asked.

'No,' said Orque, deftly brandishing the quartz as he slipped it back into his tunic. 'This is the key.'

They walked through in single file. The horses made hard work of it, snorting and jibbing in fear, but as soon as they were through the stone door it span and closed, sealing them off from Silverholm. Eldareth held up his lamp to reveal a black, rugged passage, an irregular floor that was slippery and full of sudden dips and angles.

'The horses are going to hate this,' said Lynden. 'Are you sure it's passable?'

'Of course,' said Eldareth. 'I've been through here before, quite some time ago. There are no passages too narrow or too low for them. We will go carefully, and they will be quite safe.'

'What's the danger, then?' asked Tanthe.

Orque answered, 'Our cousins the Azure Zampherai

took issue with our decision to work with the Shaelahyr. Usually they keep themselves deeply hidden.'

Eldareth cleared his throat. 'So, no danger, as long as we keep our wits about us.'

Away from the gently heated atmosphere of Silverholm, the air grew piercingly cold. Their breath formed cloud-wreaths. The tunnel walls shone like coal in the lamplight as the floor angled down, twisting on itself.

For a couple of hours, which seemed tiring and endless to Tanthe, they made steady progress through the winding passages. Strange cavities all along the walls marked places, Orque said, where precious crystals had been carefully removed. But to her, the scars seemed to have a more sinister significance, like an alien alphabet. She fought down a rising sense of claustrophobia, and glancing round saw the same uneasiness on the faces of Lynden and Rufryd.

They stopped for a few minutes to rest and eat. The interior of the mountain was echoingly silent, brooding, leaning on them with its immense mass; impenetrable and black and glassy as obsidian. None of them cared to linger there. When they set off again, the tunnel widened into a cavern and they found themselves on a ledge above a deep chasm.

'Single file,' Eldareth said calmly. 'Plenty of room.'

They couldn't help but glance over the ledge. There was nothing to be seen but a steep drop into blackness. But very far below, so faint that Tanthe thought her eyes were deceiving her, the walls seemed to be painted with an eerie purple glow.

Once they were beyond the chasm, the passage became broad and smooth and they made brisk progress. Rufryd went ahead, Orque sitting on Sunhawk's back for a better vantage point. Feeling more cheerful, they talked and even joked as they went. Eldareth's laughter echoed loudly.

'Shush!' Orque whispered angrily. 'They won't let us pass in peace if you aggravate them!'

The passage bent to the right, narrowing as it did so. As they came round the corner, they saw with dismay that the passage was blocked. The barrier, from floor to ceiling, was formed by what seemed a mass of large smooth pebbles. These stones were black yet reflected glints of oily rainbow colour from their lamplight. Redbird's head came up and she snorted, trying to back away.

'This isn't good,' Lynden said. 'It won't let us through.'

Tanthe was swamped by an air of intense hostility, so powerful that it wasn't only Lynden who sensed it. She turned to Redbird, trying to keep her calm.

'Dyon's balls!' said Eldareth. 'This is the only way I know. Is there another, Orque?'

The Zampherai paused, staring grimly at the barrier.

'Can't we just break through it?' said Rufryd.

'No, don't!' Lynden exclaimed, but his brother ignored him.

'The stones look loose.' Giving Sunhawk's reins to Tanthe, he strode forwards and made to claw at the stones. Too late, Orque and Eldareth yelled 'No!'

The oily glow pulsed. It was as if a fist of energy repelled Rufryd, sending him sprawling at Tanthe's feet. Redbird and Sunhawk shied and tried to rear. When she finally managed to control them – battling to hold both horses and her lamp with one hand – she bent anxiously over Rufryd. He was curled up, groaning.

'Is he all right?' Lynden said anxiously, trying to soothe Halcyon.

'Yes, he's fine,' Rufryd grated. He struggled to his feet and stood hanging on to Tanthe, gasping. 'Gods. I feel like I've been hit in the stomach by a boulder.'

'Now you can see that we cannot demolish it,' said Orque. 'The Azure Zampherai have decided to have some fun with us after all. There are other ways, but only one is passable to the horses. It is a lot further. It means doubling back the way we have come and passing through the deeper layers.'

'Oh, no,' said Tanthe. 'I'm starting to hate it in here. How much further, exactly?'

Orque didn't answer. He turned and began to lead the party back the way they had come. After a few minutes he led them into a side turning, so narrow that they could not even walk alongside the horses but had to lead them from in front.

Lynden said quietly, 'If this is another dead end, it's going to be nearly impossible to get the horses back down it again. They won't be able to turn round.'

'Just keep going,' Eldareth said calmly.

'But there's something terrible down here. Pain. Can't you feel it?'

Unnerved, Tanthe said, 'Lynden, shush, please! You scaring the life out of us isn't going to help, is it?'

'I take it these Azure Zampherai aren't friends of yours, then, Orque?' said Rufryd. 'I thought you were all the same people.'

'We are different tribes, dwelling in different levels of these mountains. We were friendly once, until the Shaelahyr came. The Azures hate my people for helping them. They think we have sold ourselves into drudgery.'

'Have you?' asked Tanthe, startled.

Orque's tone was withering. 'That question barely deserves an answer. We work for the Shaelahyr as friends. It was our pleasure to create Silverholm for them, and to know they could not exist there without us. They value us for it. But our cousins insist that we have debased ourselves. Savages!'

The last word seemed to echo, as if a hundred faint voices were repeating it in the darkness. They looked about nervously. Tanthe felt something prick her ankle, like a thorn through her boot. Rufryd said, 'Ouch! What the—' and then Redbird went crazy, leaping and plunging in the confined space. It was all Tanthe could do to keep her from striking her poll on the roof. Pain stabbed at her knees and thighs, like tiny spear-points. She was breathing

416

hard with alarm and effort, her mouth dry.

Tanthe kicked out, made contact with an object. It was something alive, which gave an angry gasp. In the swaying lamplight she saw a small figure dodging between Sunhawk's legs, vanishing as if he'd melted into the rock itself. There was a burst of chattering laughter, then silence.

'They're here,' said Orque. He looked around, and Tanthe saw the fear in his large black eyes. She bent down to examine Redbird's legs, found a small wet stain on her near-fore pastern. Her finger came away red with blood.

'Keep going!' Eldareth barked. 'They're trying to unnerve us, that's all.'

Now the way widened a little, but it led ever downwards. Tanthe lost track of time, and felt they were spiralling towards the heart of the earth, never to escape. The horses were skittish and miserable. It was all she could do not to curse Eldareth for assuring them the horses would be safe.

'This is not the way I know,' said Orque. 'They've changed it!'

A fierce draught flowed into the tunnel. Thirty yards on, they found themselves stepping into an astonishing cavern.

Walls and floor gleamed with dull purple fire, above them was a yawning blackness. Tanthe stared at the walls until her eyes ached, taking in every inch, but she could see no way out except the tunnel by which they had entered.

The ledge they had crossed – it seemed a lifetime ago – was hundreds of feet above them. They were in the bottom of the chasm. And the strange cavern in which they stood thrummed with ghastly energies. Fugitive fires throbbed under the surface, hurting her eyes. Vibrations shook their whole bodies. Strange sounds echoed, like voices moaning in pain, only half-heard.

Lynden was clinging to Halcyon's head, as if trying to

protect himself as much as the horse. Eldareth cried out, 'What is this place? What's wrong with it?'

Orque didn't reply. He had curled up on Sunhawk's saddle with his hands wrapped round his head. And Tanthe knew, however badly the sour energies affected her, to the crystal-sensitive Zampherai it was a hundred times worse. She went close to Orque, wanting to comfort him, not knowing how.

A high, piercing voice said, 'You should know the answer to that question, human.'

They seemed to unfold out of the rock and the shadows, all around the chamber, a tribe of males and females, small and fierce. Like Orque their skin was darkest silver, but their black hair sprang in great plumes from their heads and it was streaked with bright blue. Spikes of crystal hung from the shoulders and belts of their short tunics. Their faces were painted with jagged black lines and their lips were pulled back from pointed teeth.

'I do not know,' said Eldareth, 'or I would not have asked.'

The speaker, a wiry Zampherai who looked immensely strong for his size, stepped forward and said, 'How dare you set foot in our realm?' His eyes were flat black pools in a crinkled face and his hair was a rainbow of black, ultramarine and bright blue fountaining halfway down his back.

Eldareth said, 'Our only wish is to find our way safely to the other side of the mountains. We apologise for intruding upon you, we would not have done so without the direst need. We wish no harm, we will disturb nothing. Please let us pass.'

'No.' The speaker pointed at Orque. 'One of your offences lies in bringing that among us.'

'*That* is one of your own people,' Eldareth said softly. 'He is our guide.'

'He's a traitor. But your worst offence, human, is this.' The Zampherai's gaze swivelled over the cavern. 'Even

418

you, the most obtuse of all races, must feel the pain of the very earth!'

'Yes, we feel it,' said Tanthe, 'but you can't blame us! We know nothing about it!'

'Don't you know why the *roth* in the stones is weeping?'

Orque uncurled himself and stood up on Sunhawk's saddle, glaring down at his enemy. 'They don't know what you're talking about, Vranof. And you know that none of us have done you harm. Let us pass.'

'How are they going to stop us?' Rufryd put in. 'Be realistic, Vranof or whatever your name is. In a fight you'd stand no chance against us. You can't fight giants.'

Vranof bristled with rage. 'You forget, this is our kingdom. You have swords and bows at your command. We have masses of rock, underground rivers and volcanic fires at ours. But we can be fair, if you will be fair also. If one of yours can defeat one of ours, you can go. If not . . . you will stay here until you die.'

'I'll fight you,' said Orque. He leapt down from Sunhawk's back and confronted Vranof. He was smaller, dull-coloured, almost puny against the leader's flamboyance. One of the other Zampherai threw him a spear, and the two moved into the centre of the floor.

'This is ridiculous!' said Rufryd, but Eldareth placed a hand on his arm.

'It must be so. I told you, it's a Zampherai quarrel.'

Tanthe and her companions watched anxiously as the two small men circled each other, dancing lightly on the balls of their feet. Then they rushed in, striking, lunging. Their weapons flickered so fast it was all she could do to see them. The glow of the pit flared violet behind them, casting them into frantic silhouette like shadow-puppets.

They crossed weapons, pushing, straining against one another, then broke apart in a flurry of striking, dodging, stabbing. There was a cry. Orque had fallen.

He lay gasping, blood flowing from a wound in his chest. Then the victor stood over him, his hair streaming like a blue flame and his spear poised to deliver the death-stroke.

Tanthe put her hand to her mouth. She hardly knew Orque, but couldn't bear to watch him die. She stepped forward; Eldareth firmly held her back.

The silence rang with the discordant faint moans of the cave. Vranof turned to them, his small face creased in triumph, and said, 'Victory to us.' Then he raised his spear and stepped back. Orque rolled on to his side and lay there, face squeezed with pain. Tanthe's breath caught on a surge of distress; she thought of Gazer, whom she'd had to leave for dead.

'This time, I spare the vanquished one's life,' said Vranof. 'But he lost; so here you stay.'

'This is crazy,' said Rufryd. 'You can't keep us here. I don't care what you say, there is no way you can defeat us. Come on, you've drawn blood. Isn't that payment enough?'

Vranof's face soured. 'You gave your word.'

'No, we bloody didn't.'

'Do you challenge us again?'

Eldareth was shaking his head, but Rufryd said, 'Yes.'

'It would not be a fair fight.'

'Well, tough,' Rufryd retorted. 'I can hit very small moving targets.' He lifted his bow and set an arrow to the string.

'Tough?' Vranof laughed. 'Indeed. I meant that it will not be fair on *you*.'

He put his head back and uttered a single, sharp syllable.

The chamber shook. It was as if part of the wall itself began to detach itself. A mass of crystal pulled itself from the rock like a great amorphous troll with a huge head set directly on a barrel of a torso, thick arms, legs like petrified tree trunks, formed all of dark bloodstone. It loomed over Zampherai and humans alike, looking blindly this way and that. Its fists were boulders; savage pain radiated from it, as from the walls that had birthed it.

'Gods, no!' cried Eldareth. 'Umbaroth! What have you done?'

'What in Breyid's name is that?' Rufryd muttered.

The blue-haired Zampherai drew back towards the walls as the stone-monster came lumbering forwards. Rufryd fired an arrow, which simply bounced off the impervious chest.

'Back into the tunnel!' said Eldareth.

Lynden was already on his way, trying to take Halcyon and Sunhawk with him. But the terrified horses resisted, and the bulbous stone fists came swinging at Eldareth.

Eldareth threw himself headlong on the floor and rolled out of its reach. As the creature turned, its attention fastened instead on Tanthe. A huge ball of rock, embedded in its head, glowed like a single purple eye. She froze. The tortured forces that emanated from it made her feel she was being crushed under a ton of stone . . .

Somehow she held onto the terrified Redbird. With her other hand she found herself reaching into her pocket, drawing out the Aelyr knife, holding it by its scabbard and pointing it pommel-first at the Umbaroth. The moonstone blazed so brightly it dazzled her. To her astonishment the lumbering creature stopped and stood where it was, transfixed by the moonstone like a baby by a shining marble.

'Put it away!' screamed Vranof.

Tanthe held out the *mnelir* with growing confidence. 'Get into the tunnel,' she told her companions. 'I'll keep it back as long as I can.'

'Put it away!' Vranof cried more fiercely, and now he came running towards her, straight between the stone creature's thick legs. He leapt up, trying to grab the knife, but she held it out of his reach.

'No,' said Tanthe. The creature was hypnotised, swaying gently with the slight movement of her arms.

'Not for our benefit, you fool! To protect the stone itself! As long as you brandish it like that, it will absorb

421

the foul energies of this place and be corrupted!'

'You're trying to trick me,' Tanthe said grimly.

'No,' said the warrior. 'For the *liroth*'s sake.'

And he meant it. Vranof cared more about protecting a single, exquisite stone than anything else, she realised in amazement. As if in reply, the jewel blazed brighter.

'You're wrong,' she said. 'It's an Aelyr stone. It has too much energy of its own to absorb anything negative. But I'll put it away, if you'll call this monster off and let us go! Please, Vranof. You've had your fun with us. You've defeated Orque! I suppose you can keep us trapped in here for ever – but if we use our Aelyr swords on you, none of us are going to win, are we?'

Eldareth came to her side and said, 'As you can see, my companions are as stubborn as your people. You've won your fight. So it won't compromise your honour to show us mercy, will it.'

Lynden was managing to calm the horses, speaking softly to them. Vranof struck the rock floor with the heel of his spear, as if in anger; then he raised his chin. 'Very well,' he said. 'Your reasoning is fair. Conceal your *liroth* stone, which is more precious than you can begin to imagine. You can go.'

Tanthe almost fell over with relief. Vranof uttered another word, at which the Umbaroth lost all signs of life. The light in its eye went out. Cautiously she put away the knife, watching the stone creature all the time; but it seemed as solid as some freakish stalagmite that had grown from the cavern floor.

'I don't trust them,' said Rufryd.

'We must,' said Eldareth. 'Look.'

Where the Umbaroth had pulled itself from the wall, it had left a deep hole; the mouth of a new tunnel.

'Come,' said Vranof, beckoning them past the Umbaroth's thick stone legs. Slowly the party began to make their way across the cavern.

Tanthe looked down at Orque as they passed. He lay

wounded where Vranof had left him. 'We can't just leave him!'

Orque feebly waved her away. 'Go. Honour among Zampherai is something humans don't comprehend. Go!'

'They will look after him, and return him to his own tribe,' said Eldareth. 'It might even stop them quarrelling, who knows?'

'This way,' called Vranof, sharp and commanding, waiting for them in the mouth of the new passage. His tribe stood around the walls, watching with glittering eyes. Once the party had sorted themselves out, each taking charge of their own horse again, the small warrior began to lead them into the darkness.

'What are you doing?' said Rufryd.

'You still need a guide, to find your way out of our realm. I have disabled one of your party. Therefore I must take his place.'

'There's no need.'

'It's not a question of need,' the Zampherai answered. 'It is my duty and my fate to replace your friend. Neither side has won, neither has lost. Therefore I call a truce between my people and yours.'

Eldareth stared at Vranof. 'Well, I can't argue with that part of it. We would be very glad of a guide.'

'That is what I offer as a sign of friendship. In return, I ask only that you observe and understand something about this realm. There is something you must see.'

'This sounds like a trap,' Rufryd said, grim and anxious.

'No. You will see.'

As soon as they set out along the tunnel, the sense of oppression and pain that they'd felt in the cavern was magnified. The walls shone with spikes of umber crystal, grown into tormented shapes. Fugitive lights danced inside them, chasing from one end of the tunnel to the other like snakes; there and gone. Tanthe's head began to ache.

She glanced round, saw Lynden behind her. His face

423

was white, tears flowing down his cheeks. It seemed pointless to ask if he was all right, but her heart twisted in concern. What was doing this to him – making him react as sensitively as the Zampherai to the atmosphere, making him see the true nature of the Bhahdradomen?

Unhuman moans throbbed in the air, growing louder. The earth itself seemed to tremble. The sounds of anguish and the bale-fire flickering in the stone grew stronger. Then as Vranof brought them into another cavern, the dark energies reached a crescendo.

'Pause here a moment,' he said in a savage tone. 'Never mind your own fear. Feel and understand.'

Rufryd came next to Tanthe and gripped her arm, as if to steady himself as much as her. The whole cavern moaned and throbbed like the inside of a tortured heart. It had a rawness, like a pit left behind after something valuable had been ripped out; the walls glistened darkly, giving Tanthe the impression they were oozing blood. Crimson lighting flickered under the surface. The screams sounded so human she wanted to fall to her knees and cover her head. Eldareth had his arm round Lynden's shoulder, supporting him, though his own face was grey with pain.

After a minute or so, the voices softened a little, as if she had begun to endure the atmosphere. Then Vranof spoke.

'Those great creatures, the Umbaroths, are born from the eggs of the earth. Every mineral has its own Umbaroth-form, born of its own peculiar properties. And every stone, base or precious, has its own special energies and characters. Treat them properly and their rewards are endless. But misuse them and they become distressed, enraged, tormented. But they have no mouths with which to cry out, no way to explain their pain! They only have the Zampherai to interpret for them, to fight for them.'

Vranof looked at the walls of the cavern. 'Two thousand years ago, a great mass of crystal was discovered here that resonated with a unique energy, that of the earth's spirit

424

itself, which we call *xauroth*. We gifted it to the humans to be placed in the Amber Citadel. My ancestors polished it to a perfect sphere – a gift of goodwill between Zampherai and humans. We did more for them than ever they did for us, for now they plunder the earth without care. But when the *xauroth* sphere was given, it was the most beautiful thing the earth has ever given up, the most perfect form that we have ever created. I have never seen it, but the stories say that it was clear as rock crystal, even as diamond, and within it were planes of gold and pale rainbows, and energies that looked like stars and swam like fish through the depths. The shaft through which it was removed we filled again afterwards, that this cavern would be preserved. For as the crystal resonated with joy at the heart of the Amber Citadel, sending out flashes of white and amber fire, so this cavern, although its fruit was long gone, resonated with it. This was a place of joy and beauty. Do you feel joy here now?'

'No,' said Tanthe. 'It's the worst thing I've ever felt. It's in agony.'

'Three years ago, the cavern began to change. We tried, but there was nothing we could do to heal it. It is in anguish because its egg, its child, is in anguish. Its pain torments us. Orque's people, cosily sealed up with the Shaelahyr, do not hear it – yet you wonder at my rage with them? *They* don't come here to comfort the weeping stone. Only we come. We can hardly bear it, but we must. It sighs and groans with pain. Blood oozes from the sides of the cavern. But do you know what this means?'

Tanthe couldn't speak; even Eldareth was lost for words. It was Lynden who answered, to their surprise.

'It's the Xauroma,' he said, staring red-eyed at Vranof. 'I felt it as soon as we came down here. I can see the sphere in my mind, but it's not clear any more; it's dark, and full of blood, like this. When the sphere screams, this cavern and everything around it screams too.'

'What else can you see?' Vranof said urgently.

Lynden leaned his head against Halcyon's neck. 'Nothing. It's gone.'

'But you are right. Humans have violated their agreement with us – with the very earth. This is the result. The earth cries in protest and she is not heard! Therefore all friendship between Zampherai and humans is ended!'

Eldareth broke in, 'Before you're too hasty to dismiss us all as enemies – yes, the covenant has been damaged. We know that. But some of us – most of us – are as unhappy about it as you are. We want to restore it. Vranof, we are not your enemies.'

'Are you not?'

'I swear. You've made your point. Look, my friends are weeping. Take us out of here, and I'll tell you what is happening in the outer world as we go.'

The warrior shook back his bright plume of hair. 'Come, then. I've punished you enough.'

They were deeply relieved to leave the groaning cavern at last. The rest of the journey, Tanthe remembered as a waking nightmare. They walked, rested a little, walked; on and on. The endless snaking tunnels, the groaning echoes, her claustrophobia, the image of Orque wounded and struggling . . . and all the while, Eldareth telling grim stories of King Garnelys.

When grey light filtered at long last into the end of the tunnel, she thought she was dreaming.

'You need me no more,' said Vranof. 'Cherish the stone.'

Tanthe did not know whether it was a Zampherai farewell, or a wish aimed at her. Vranof was gone, vanishing into the shadows – if not into the stone itself.

Then the realm of the Zampherai gave them up to the light. The passage emerged behind a tall boulder and a thick mass of bushes.

Pushing through the foliage, holding it back as best they could so the horses could get through, they emerged into brilliant daylight, blinking fiercely. Once Tanthe's eyes adjusted, she saw that they were on a slope that undulated down into a pine forest. The pines swept into the distance, as far as she could see, but the bulk of the mountains lay behind them. She looked back, saw sun glinting gold on the snow of the high peaks. The air was chilly, but here the snow was melting. She heard a stream rushing, birds chirping, and she smelled spring in the air. The horses shook their heads, snorted, dipped their muzzles to the grass.

Suddenly so joyful she felt like weeping, she turned to Rufryd and hugged him. He swung her round, laughing. 'It's good to see the world again,' he said.

'It feels like rebirth. And now we're even further from home!'

'And we still have a good distance to go,' said Eldareth. 'Let's get down into the forest and be on our way. We'll go on to the first stream we find and rest there. You may as well ride until then, if the horses are up to it.'

'What about you?' Lynden asked.

'Oh, I'm well used to walking. My legs are as long as the horses', in any case.'

They tightened girths, pulled down the stirrups, and mounted. As they rode down into the forest, Eldareth found a fallen branch and stripped the twigs off it to make himself a staff. The trunks were lofty red-brown columns stretching into the sky, the floor thick and soft with fallen needles.

They went without speaking for a time. Tanthe couldn't put the image of Vranof in the cavern out of her mind. Eventually they found the long-sought stream, and saw to the horses' comfort before stretching out on the soft bank to rest. Eldareth walked off some distance through the trees, to check what lay around them. Tanthe broke the silence. 'Are you all right, Lynden?'

'Fine,' he said. 'I wish you wouldn't keep fussing over me every five minutes.'

'I wouldn't, if you didn't look so awful!'

427

'Thanks. I'm all right. So you don't have to keep using me as an excuse.'

'How?'

'As in, "We'd better stop, Lynden's tired". I'm not five years old and we're all bloody tired.'

Tanthe gasped indignantly. 'Pardon me for caring about you. Gods, you're getting as bad-tempered as Rufryd.'

'Do you mind?' Rufryd exclaimed. 'I've been as nice as anything to you, since—'

'Yes, all right,' she said, colouring. 'I meant before.'

'Well, I'm sorry,' Lynden said, looking down. 'I didn't mean to bite your head off, Tan. But I keep seeing that sphere in my mind and I know it's where Ymmi is, and I just want to get there.'

'Don't we all.'

As Eldareth came striding back to them, Lynden looked up and asked, 'Can we head straight to Parione now?'

'Is that what you would have done without me?'

'I suppose so, yes.'

'Well, I can't tell you what to do, but I'd advise against it. What was your plan?'

There was an awkward pause. Eventually Tanthe said, 'I had an idea that we'd either sell the horses or hide them somewhere. Then we'd get into the Tower – I thought by volunteering as conscripts was probably the easiest way – and once we found Ymmi, we'd smuggle her out by night.'

'Not bad,' said Eldareth.

'But?'

'Impossibly risky.'

'But we won't get anywhere without taking risks, will we?' Lynden said hotly. 'Have you a better plan?'

'Not necessarily.' Eldareth looked thoughtfully up at the high canopy of branches. 'We don't know how much worse things have become since last autumn. I'd suggest you be a little patient for now and come with me. We're all in trouble with the King and we should help each other. I have some friends who will hide us while we consider the situation.'

'I'll go along with that,' said Rufryd. 'We trust you.'

Eldareth smiled. 'Thank you.'

Tanthe felt a touch uncomfortable. She trusted Eldareth too, but she couldn't help feeling that since he'd been there, they'd stopped thinking for themselves. His presence, his experience and certainty were reassuring, but it worried her that even Rufryd was leaving all the important decisions to him.

They were in Mithrain now, a realm of tall, ethereal pine forests laced with silver lakes and streams. For the next few days they passed through this eldritch landscape, making camp beneath great sheltering slabs of rock, catching glossy salmon from the lakes. There was something about the atmosphere that made Rufryd and Lynden jumpy, but Tanthe loved its eeriness; loved the way mists drifted over the pools and rose up from the surface in half-human shapes.

Eldareth was clearly at ease here, anyway. With fresh water, good grass and exercise, the horses soon regained their fitness; Tanthe was glad that Lynden had been there to soothe the animals after the terror of the mines. They were all in good spirits, relieved to be on their way again.

'We're travelling parallel with the road that leads from the Whiteveils to Paranios,' said Eldareth. 'Too risky actually to be on it.' They were sitting on the shore of a small lake, which was irregularly shaped as if a splash of quicksilver had been poured on to the dark, needle-crisp ground. Pines rose ghost-like around them; the far shore was almost lost in drifting vapours that glimmered violet in the last light of the day.

'The Meiondras Road,' said Rufryd. 'I know.'

'You haven't made this journey before?'

'No, but I've spent hours staring at the dratted map. Somehow I managed to guide us from Riverwynde to the Menroth Pass without getting us lost.'

'Only just,' said Tanthe, laughing. Rufryd pulled a face at her.

'I would say we have covered nearly two hundred miles since Silverholm,' said Eldareth. 'We have about another six hundred to go.'

'Not six hundred miles of these creepy lakes?' said Rufryd.

'Not all, no.' Eldareth laughed. 'They say you either love Mithrain or hate it.'

'There are *roths* here,' said Lynden. 'I can feel them . . . but they're not harmful. As long as you don't upset them, that is.'

'Wise lad,' said Eldareth. 'The most powerful *roths* of Mithrain are in the lakes, and all their deities are spirits of stone and of water. There is a legend that the hero Jhamian, in the time of Queen Hetys, came into Mithrain fleeing from the Bhahdradomen. A water sprite appeared to him and said that she would hide him from his enemies by enabling him to breathe underwater – if only he would trust her. But water sprites are renowned for enticing young men under the water and drowning them. Well, would you have trusted such a creature?'

Rufryd laughed. 'I doubt it.'

'But Jhamian had no choice; his pursuers were pressing hard on his heels. So he let her take him down into the lake, and she turned him into a fish, and so he escaped the Bhahdradomen. And when she turned him back to human shape again she revealed herself as the water goddess, Eshte. She told our hero that if he had refused to trust her she would, indeed, have drowned him.'

'That would have been the end of Rufe, then,' Tanthe laughed. 'I can just imagine Eshte rising from the lake. It's like a miracle to be travelling in other Realms . . . or would be, if it wasn't for Ymmi.'

Eldareth nodded. 'I've travelled in all nine, and they are, indeed, wondrous in their different ways. I always think each has its own characteristic colours; Mithrain is silver,

430

with touches of amethyst.'

'Yes, it is!' said Tanthe. 'And Sepheret is blue, black and ivory, although I imagine Breyid and Anthar dressed in leaf-green. Deirland was grey like dew, with autumn green and russet. In that landscape, their god and goddess could only be the stag and doe; human forms wouldn't have belonged.' She paused, remembering how those god-forms had surged up in front of her, pursued by the soundless hunt. 'I thought I was the only one who thought of things like that.'

'But to notice such things is to come closer to understanding the essence of Aventuria,' said Eldareth.

'Looks like you've found someone as mad as you are, Tan,' Rufryd said wryly.

'I don't care if we are mad,' she retorted. 'Eldareth, tell us what the other realms are like.'

He sat forward, hands loosely clasping his knees, his gaze resting on the lake. 'Well, Paranios would have to be green and gold, with the purple bloom of grapes, and their gods are those of rich living; Nepheter the goddess of creative intellect, her consort Dyon of fertility and revelry. Parione likes to think itself the centre of civilisation; they forget that Azura Maroc was first. A seductive place, the southern realm. Their great goddess is a cat, a wild cat like a lynx, but they accommodate many other sects and schools of rationalism, philosophies learned from the Aelyr. Now when I think of Azura Maroc I see deep reds and blues, sandy yellow and specks of gold, and the ultramarine of the night sky.

'And Noreya, in the north – I have a great deal of affection for their people, who know more of the *roth* of trees than you can imagine. Their colours would be darkest green, and pale yellow for their hair. They have great, sacred trees in which their god-forms reside. Many lesser tree deities, too.'

Tanthe put in, 'I heard that in Torith Mir all the forests are dead. Is that so?'

431

Eldareth gave a faint, quick grimace. 'Of course not. They have some forests that have turned to stone; they are something to behold. Torith Mir is beautiful, in a stark way. And all you hear of the people is not true, either. Yes, they can be belligerent, but in their own land they could strike you breathless with their hospitality and loyalty. Torith Mir's colours are black, grey and amber, with sparks of opal-colours. Did you know that they have deities in common with Thanmandrathor? A goddess of lightning and a god of thunder. In Torith Mir they're stern and warlike, in Thanmandrathor they're strong but gentle, standing more for justice than revenge. Deities with human faces.

'Eisilion, though, is a realm of animals; their goddess is the snake of wisdom, their god the fox of cunning. And they are a chamaeleon people, whose colours change as you look at them. Rainbows and iridescent dra'a'k scales. They've had to be clever and fugitive, stuck between Torith Mir and Paranios, between the Aelyr and the Bhahdradomen.'

'You haven't told us the colours of Thanmandrathor,' said Tanthe.

'Ah, that's hard. It's such a big country, the greatest of the Realms. But I would say emerald green, ochre and bronze; the rich and honest colours of the earth. They are a tall, graceful, steadfast people, who have suffered much from the Bhahdradomen, and now resent suffering at the hands of their King . . .'

He stopped. Rufryd said, 'You never told us which Realm you come from.'

'It's not important,' said Eldareth.

'If I had to guess,' said Tanthe, 'I'd say Thanmandrathor. Am I right?'

Eldareth's lips thinned; his expression set to stone. After a long pause he spoke. 'Yes, though I have never lived in one place long enough to call it my own. My mother was from Thanmandrathor . . . my father from Torith Mir. And that is all the detail I will ever give, so ask me no more.'

Tanthe sensed a barrier falling; like Elrill, Eldareth had secrets to keep. But there was pain shuttered in his dark eyes, terrible, buried pain; and for once, she felt that it was safer not to know its cause.

'Sorry,' she said softly. 'I didn't mean to be so insufferably nosey.'

'She just can't help it,' Rufryd added.

Eldareth gave a faint smile, but said nothing. On the lake, a roll of mist swirled up into a shape that seemed to be dancing slowly, watching them. The light of Lily Moon pierced it, casting an illusion of pale hair, long white arms, two glowing eyes; then, very gradually, the wraith lost its shape and was only mist, drifting away into the trees.

Leaving Mithrain many days later, they crossed the spine of the Serpentine Mountains, which proved kinder and greener than the Whiteveils. Their route brought them down into beech woods, verdant with new leaves and burgeoning undergrowth. The air sparkled green, gold, white and blue, and it thrummed with insects and birdsong. Winter and Silverholm, everything else that had happened, seemed far in the past.

'Welcome to Paranios,' said Eldareth. 'This, if anywhere, is home to me.'

Tanthe was enchanted. This realm, the very heart of Aventuria, really did seem different; lush and colourful and shimmering with life. She could imagine Aelyr slipping elusively through these woods. She thought of her mysterious red-haired friend, dreaming of meeting him in some secluded glade. But she never did.

It was now twenty days since they'd left Silverholm, and they'd become seasoned travellers, physically hardened to the rigours and the repetitive routine of their journey. They'd avoided all towns and villages, but now they were coming closer to civilisation; there were more human habitations to avoid, many well-used paths through the woods, cottages and hostelries along the way.

'I'm starting to have dreams about sleeping in a bed,' said Rufryd.

'Unfortunately,' said Eldareth, 'the closer we come to the heart of Paranios, the more we need to hide. My face is too well-known. But it's not much further, I promise.'

It was mid-afternoon. They were following a quiet woodland path, Eldareth striding ahead while the others walked their horses on a loose rein, when Lynden said suddenly, 'We're being followed.'

'What?' said Eldareth. He stopped, listened, climbed halfway up the knobbly trunk of a tree for a better view. 'I can see no one.'

'No,' said Tanthe, 'but Lynden does this sometimes. He senses things – and he's usually right.'

'Right. Get the horses into the undergrowth.'

Quickly they rode off the path, took the horses into a thick stand of bushes, dismounted and tethered them there. Then Eldareth had them climb up into the trees; he and Rufryd on one side, nearer the path, Tanthe and Lynden further back.

A few seconds later, a mounted party came trotting along the path. Three soldiers of the King in green and violet, half-seen through the lace of spring leaves. Riding glossy brown horses – like the ones on which Ymmi had been taken away – they seemed to be heading straight past; until Halcyon put his head up and whinnied.

'What was that?' The soldiers reined in and dismounted, drawing their swords as they came wading into the undergrowth. Two men and a woman, with leather breastplates and helmets. Tanthe watched from above as the soldiers found their horses, touched the lapis-chased saddles.

'Very nice,' said one of the men.

The first of Rufryd's arrows sank into his shoulder, killing him instantly. His second slew the other man, even as he span round to glare upwards. Tanthe aimed at the woman, missed. She looked up, drawing her sword; Tanthe took a flying leap out of the tree and landed on the soldier. They crashed to the ground; Tanthe swung her fist and knocked her out.

Rufryd and the others came slithering down from their hiding place. 'Come on!' called Eldareth. 'Wait for me, one second—'

Eldareth was taking one of the soldier's horses. Rufryd was already busy with Sunhawk.

Tanthe saw one of the fallen soldiers, the woman, struggling to rise, aiming her crossbow at Rufryd's back.

With a reflex faster than thought – as Alraen had taught her – Tanthe leapt forward, drawing her Aelyr sword in the same motion. The blade slashed through the woman's neck; she fell back, her bolt skimming off harmlessly to lodge in a tree trunk. The woman slumped back and she lay gazing at the sky, the crossbow lying loosely in her hands, her throat gaping red. Tanthe stared.

'Gods,' she said thickly. *I killed her. I killed her.*

'Come on, before any more come!' shouted Rufryd. Eldareth was on one of the powerful, glossy brown horses. 'Tan!'

Catching her breath, she sent Redbird galloping after the others. They sped on for ten minutes before they let the horses slow down, turning deeper into the woods, where they would be less visible. They walked the horses to cool them. Tanthe's mind was reeling.

'You all right?' Rufryd asked anxiously, riding alongside her.

'No. I killed one of them.' It was all she could say. 'The woman. I killed her!'

'Now you know how I feel,' he said tightly.

'I can't do it. I can't do it.'

'Too late, Tan. You'll have to harden up.'

'I can't! I thought I could but this is different, it's awful, it's like having my inside ripped out—'

'Stop it,' he said. 'Stop feeling sorry for yourself!'

She gaped at him. 'I thought you'd understand. Is that all the sympathy I'm going to get?'

435

'Yes!'

Rufryd's intransigence maddened her. All her feelings coalesced into a ball of ice. 'I see. If you must know, I was feeling sorry for her, not myself; she was only doing her job, serving the King—'

'Tan, shut up! I *don't* want to know!'

She bit her tongue, hating him, hating herself.

'It's still not safe,' said Lynden. He looked off to the right; Tanthe heard hootbeats, faint at first but growing louder. Then Lynden cried, 'Eldareth, look out!'

Just ahead, a horse bearing two riders was converging with them at a canter through the trees, as if to block their path.

'Oh, shit,' said Rufryd, seizing his bow and setting an arrow to the string. Tanthe began to draw her sword, now loathing the feel of it in her hand.

'No!' Eldareth snapped. 'Hold fire.'

'Yes, it's all right,' said Lynden. 'They aren't the danger.'

Rufryd turned angrily on him. 'How do you *know*?' His brother didn't answer.

The horse, a sturdily-built dark chestnut with rippling flaxen mane and tail, halted ahead. The rider in front was a bright-faced young man with curly brown hair; his companion, who held his waist, a red-headed woman with an attractive, freckled face. Both wore brown-green cloaks.

'It's all right. They're friends,' Eldareth said, riding forward to meet them. 'Mirias, Dawn! I can't tell you how glad I am to see you.'

'Eldareth,' said the man, leaning on the pommel of his saddle. 'You were being followed.'

'I know. We dealt with it.'

'Not completely,' said the woman, Dawn. 'There were another two soldiers, after the first lot; *we* dealt with them. But there may be more. We need to get you to the safe house.'

Eldareth gave a deep sigh. 'That is where I was taking

436

my friends. But the last thing I want is to lead the King's men there. Why is this wood crawling with them?'

'They have been all around Nachillei. They're growing suspicious about the level of resistance there. But we'll get you through, don't worry.'

Gazing through the trees with unfocussed eyes, Lynden said softly, 'The soldiers are moving away from the town. I can see them.'

'Who's *he*?' said Dawn.

'This is Lynden,' said Eldareth, with a weary but affectionate smile. 'And Rufryd and Tanthe. Some odd people I picked up on my travels. And this is Dawn, and Mirias. A couple of actors from Parione.'

'Ex-actors,' said Mirias. 'Now unemployed, homeless and wanted for insurrection.'

'What was your crime?' Tanthe asked.

'Trying to save a theatre,' he said.

Mirias and Dawn brought them by night to Nachillei; a town of high, narrow houses built into the sides of a horseshoe valley. Lily Moon shone. The valley was lush with orchards and chestnut trees bursting into leaf. Tanthe, soothed almost to sleep, hardly realised the town was there until she looked up suddenly and saw the handsome, tiered buildings riding haphazardly above her. Trees and bushes, heavy with white blossom, filled the steep streets. The scent was delicious.

'Almost there,' Eldareth whispered. He led them along a short lane and into a courtyard, quickly shutting the gate behind them. 'You can stable the horses here.'

The stables looked dilapidated, but clean and dry.

'We'll take care of the animals,' said Dawn, giving Tanthe a friendly smile. 'You go up with Eldareth.'

From the courtyard, Eldareth led them up a steep flight of steps that led up the hillside between the blank sides of houses.

'Is it safe here?' said Rufryd.

'As safe as anywhere,' Eldareth replied. 'We have friends here . . . I'll explain once we're inside.'

The steps brought them to a terrace. Above them towered a pale, narrow house with its back resting against a steep hill, almost a cliff. Eldareth avoided the front door but led them down some steps to a tiny side entrance. He gave a series of precise knocks; after a few minutes, a graceful old man with waist-length white hair opened the door and beckoned them in. They entered what seemed to be a small scullery. The old man quickly locked the door behind them.

'I bring friends,' said Eldareth. 'Mirias and Dawn are behind us.'

'Welcome, friends of Eldareth,' said the old man, beaming. His hair shone in the light of the lamp he was holding. Tanthe looked around and nearly sprang through the ceiling as she found, at her shoulder, another old man identical to the first.'

'We are twins,' said the old men, almost in unison.

'No, really?' said Rufryd. He sounded, Tanthe thought, unforgivably rude. She'd forgotten how angry with him she'd been in the wood, but that reminded her.

'I am Olberyd,' said the first man, 'and my brother is Olmion. Be safe and welcome here.'

Tanthe, Lynden and Rufryd followed Eldareth along a short corridor to a stairwell. He led them upstairs, but the twins did not follow. 'They very kindly give us use of their house, you see,' Eldareth said quietly, 'at great risk to themselves, if the King ever finds out they are hiding us.'

'Who else is here?' Tanthe asked.

'Several renegades from Parione.'

There were six flights; Tanthe counted them. She was shivering slightly with the cold of the night, with delayed shock and with anticipation. When they reached the top, they were not, apparently, in the main body of the house. Instead, Eldareth took them to what looked like to be a dead end with a large cupboard sitting against the wall.

But, to her surprise, he unlocked the cupboard door and beckoned them inside. There was just room for them all to stand. The darkness was absolute. Eldareth relocked the door, squeezed past them, and gave a coded tap on what she had taken to be the back of the cupboard.

After a few moments, the partition swung open from the inside. The interior was dark, but for the dazzling glow of a lamp; Tanthe could make out nothing. She stepped through after Eldareth, vaguely aware that the person who had opened the door to them was a dark-haired man dressed in white.

'Eldareth!' he exclaimed. 'Welcome, my dear friend. Gods, it's been a long time. Where on earth have you been?' The two men embraced. 'Ah. I scent horses, stables, woods, sweat – the outside world. Who are your companions?'

'Good friends,' said Eldareth. 'Explanations later. Refreshments first!'

'Of course. Come in. Welcome to my abode.' The man, holding the lamp in one hand, welcomed them in with a flourish. He was dressed in a tunic and loose trousers of white linen and he was about six feet tall, with long, full black hair, and the warmest smile Tanthe had ever seen. 'This is not as I would wish to receive you, but still, this is the place I am forced to call home for the time being.'

The room lay in shadow and she couldn't discern much, except that it was large, with recesses that seemed to lead to other rooms. She took a few steps and nearly went flying over an obstacle she hadn't seen.

'I'm sorry.' The man took her arm, helping her upright, holding up the lamp. She'd collided with the arm of a couch. 'I'll light some more candles. Are you all right, er . . .?'

'Tanthe,' she said. Now she looked up at him and saw him clearly. He was very handsome, she noticed with a start. Beautiful, almost. It was hard to tell his age but she guessed about the same as her father, in his early forties.

There were two slim wings of silver in the black hair, and deep creases around his warm dark eyes. He looked tired, and as if he hadn't shaved for a day, and yet startlingly attractive.

Eldareth said, 'And these two are Rufryd and Lynden. Like us; in trouble.'

The man raised dark eyebrows. 'Ah, what was your offence?'

'What was it?' said Eldareth. 'Oh, I remember. Trying to shoot the idiot official who conscripted Tanthe's poor sister.'

'Ah. Well done for trying.'

'Thanks,' Rufryd said sourly.

'Well, you're in good company. We are all wanted men and women here.' His eyes met Tanthe's, glinting with conspiracy. 'Aren't you going to introduce me, Eldareth?'

'Good gods, do you want a round of applause?'

'All right, I'll do it.' As he smiled, looking into her eyes, the most extraordinary radiance shone from his face. It struck Tanthe physically, a warm blow to the stomach. 'I'm Saphaeyender.'

Chapter Nineteen. Dream and Discovery

Tanthe felt as if the floor had fallen away beneath her. '*The* Saphaeyender?'

He gave a dry laugh. 'Well, *a* Saphaeyender.'

'The poet – the playwright?'

'The same.'

'I thought you'd be – much older.'

He looked stunned. 'Thank you, I think. It's nice to know you thought of me at all.'

She was becoming more embarrassed by the second, but she didn't know how to dig herself out. 'Eldareth said he knew you but I—'

Gazing at her, he blinked inscrutably, like a cat. 'You weren't sure how many Saphaeyenders he knew?'

'I didn't know what to think! He wouldn't tell me anything. He said you were over a hundred years old!'

'Oh, he did, did he?'

Tanthe turned to Eldareth, mortified. 'You didn't tell us!'

Eldareth only shrugged, grinning apologetically.

She felt herself falling apart, overwhelmed. 'I've loved your work since I was a little girl. I practically learned to read from it. When I heard what happened to the theatre—'

At that, Saphaeyender only stared at her, his warmth freezing. She felt Rufryd squeezing her elbow so hard it hurt. He propelled her forwards and she closed her lips before she made things any worse. Turning hot and cold all over, she went with the others like a puppet and sank gratefully on to the couch indicated by Eldareth.

A dark-haired woman had come in and was lighting lamps, illuminating a room about fifteen feet square. The walls and floor were grey stone and there was a smell of dust. The only adornment was a few rugs scattered on the floor. The furniture was shabby, musty with age. What Tanthe had taken for a long sideboard against one wall was actually a row of barrels, covered in a cloth.

'These were storerooms,' said Eldareth. 'No one searching the main body of the house would ever know they were here.'

'We make the best of it, but . . .' Saphaeyender raised his shoulders hopelessly. Tanthe imagined him living in halls of lofty marble, with fountains dancing in elegant pools. He didn't belong here. She longed to ask him a thousand questions, all of them inappropriate, if only she had dared to open her mouth.

'Give them some wine, Saph, while we get supper ready,' said the dark-haired woman. She was poised and attractive, with a voluptuous figure and small waist, a full red mouth, an unassailable air of confidence. Tanthe felt a spurt of jealousy. Another woman and two men came softly into the room from shadowed alcoves; they all had a look about them, a charisma and grace that was almost an affectation.

'Well, talking of the theatre,' Saphaeyender said, 'We are virtually all that's left of it. These were some of my actors; Ashtar, Sharm, Saliole, Evender.'

The actors came forward to greet them effusively but condescendingly, regarding the newcomers as if a stray cat had dragged them in. Tanthe bristled, hating the way they gazed down on her from their cool heights while she felt so awkward. This was worse than her humiliation in Luin Sepher. At least she had learned her lesson there, and was not foolish enough to try and prove her equality. But still she envied their knowledge and confidence, the ease with which they could address her hero, her god, as 'Saph'.

Ashtar was the voluptuous one who had lit the candles; in her late twenties, Tanthe guessed. Sharm was older, perhaps in her fifties, very grand and imperious with flowing fair hair and a seductive aura. Did anyone ever say no to her? Evender looked about thirty, though he was losing his curly blond hair. He was, she discovered later, Sharm's lover; and a joker who liked to be the centre of attention. Saliole was in his sixties, slim and energetic but as grand as Sharm. He liked to make extravagant hand gestures and humorous asides in a loud, rich voice.

Despite her irritation, Tanthe was already becoming fascinated by them. Saphaeyender's actors! Rufryd, apparently, thought them bizarre, but she wished he wouldn't wear his feelings so blatantly on his face.

'Gods, I'm tired,' Eldareth sighed, flopping down and dragging his boots off. 'Well, what's the news?'

Saphaeyender's eyelids swept down, showing long black lashes. 'It all grows worse, my friend.'

'We'll talk over the meal. Have you a change of clothes for us? Can we bathe before supper?'

'Of course. Evender will show our guests where everything is. There is no shortage of room to sleep, there are a dozen dusty larders where we can put down mattresses, but I can't vouch for the company.'

'Eh?'

'Spiders. Mice. Those little green lizards with the red frills.' Saphaeyender grinned, his gaze touching Tanthe's then dancing on, inscrutably, over Rufryd and Lynden.

They ate at a long, low table, sitting cross-legged on cushions. Mirias and Dawn had returned, so with the other actors, Saphaeyender and Eldareth's party, there were eleven. A cluster of thick white candles stood in the centre of the white cloth. The food was basic but filling; broth and bread, lamb and vegetables, goat's cheese and tiny dried-up apples.

Tanthe, although she was famished, found it hard to eat. She kept having flashbacks to the woman soldier lying dead with her throat slit open. Was she still there? Had more soldiers come to take the dead away and bury them?

She swallowed more wine, and tried not to think of it. Saphaeyender was the most extreme distraction she could possibly have had, in any case. She still couldn't believe this was real. He was sitting almost opposite her, mostly ignoring her, to her relief. Despite bathing in a wooden tub, in hot water piped up from the house, and changing into a loose white robe, she still felt travel-worn and scruffy. The others were talking so much there was no need for her to say anything; Rufryd and Lynden were quiet too, both looking exhausted but far more interested in food than conversation.

Throughout the meal, Tanthe watched Saphaeyender. It didn't matter how flamboyant the others were, how hard they competed for attention; only Saphaeyender shone, calm and quiet and dazzling as a moon.

As a child, when she'd first fallen in awed love with his work, she'd taken it for granted that he was centuries dead, as the great writers usually were. After her shock at Luin Sepher, discovering he was still alive, she had envisioned him as an old, old man. Eldareth, the rat, had done nothing to disabuse her. If she had been told that one of the twins who owned the house was Saphaeyender instead, she would have believed it more readily. But to find that he was no older than her father – and she never thought of her father as being either young or old – yet Saphaeyender was indeed so *young* to be such a genius, and to find that he was not only vigorous but beautiful and warm-hearted . . . her mind could hardly contain the revelation.

If I'd been born in Parione, she thought, I would have known all this and not constantly made such an ignorant fool of myself! She was envious of Eldareth and the other actors, so privileged yet not even aware of it.

He was graceful and good-mannered; effortlessly so. She couldn't imagine him ever descending to Rufryd's level of sour sarcasm. Beside him, Rufryd seemed an uninformed peasant, more plainly than he ever had beside Calamys.

Fair or not, she couldn't help comparing them.

'Conditions in Parione were becoming intolerable,' said Saliole. 'Streets full of mud, soldiers and skinny ruffians of conscripts. Damned blocks of stone being hauled everywhere; couldn't walk along the streets for the disruption. I was on Elm Hill one day when they lost control of a block, and it skidded down and crushed a conscript right in front of me. I heard his legs break. Nearly took me with it. Covered my robe with mud.'

'You poor thing,' Ashtar said drily.

'It gets harder all the time to find enough supplies,' said Mirias. He and Dawn were the only two who had no affectation about them. She liked them. 'You know why? Because so many of the farmers have either been put to work on the accursed Tower, or drafted into the army.' He pointed his fork at Rufryd. 'If you three had stayed at home, you would have been conscripted by now! They've been using this area to train the troops. Otherwise they might not have started to notice just how unhappy the people of Nachillei are about it.'

'They're not going to miss the fact that several of their number died today,' said Eldareth. 'Or fail to notice that a good-sized troop never returned from the Whiteveil Mountains.'

'They can't blame us for an avalanche!' said Rufryd, with his mouth full.

'I had no idea they were so desperate to find me.' Eldareth shook his head and poured more wine. 'I don't know whether to be alarmed or flattered.'

'Tell me more,' Saphaeyender said. 'Whatever have you been about, Eldareth?'

Eldareth told them about the Shaelahyr, how Lynden and Tanthe had saved him, how they'd escaped. Saphaeyender listened, as if making mental notes. She longed to ask, will you write about this, when it's all over?

'Now I think I understand something,' Saphaeyender said, when Eldareth had finished. His voice, too, was beautiful. Expressive and cultured. Everyone fell quiet to listen. 'They seem such brutes, these new people Grannen has recruited to the army, especially the officers. Grannen himself is a brute. Where are they finding such people in Aventuria, where our society has been one of compassion and love for so long? It's as if they have dug the bad ones from every community, placed them with their peers, and given free rein to their vilest behaviours. Without their family and friends around them to temper their impulses, they are lost, and we are suffering for it. But, since you told me about the Zampherai and the cavern of the sphere, now I see that it is something deeper. It's the Xauroma itself. It is not a few cruel people let loose, it could be any of us. I never realised before that if the covenant were broken, how utterly everything else would break down with it, even our very characters.'

Eldareth said, 'And now you have diagnosed the problem, do you have a solution?'

'You are familiar enough with my work to know that I do not answer questions, I pose them,' Saphaeyender said with a flash of annoyance. 'I don't know how it is going to end. All I can see is misery, starvation, the collapse of our civilisation. Villages and towns deserted, while the King sucks all his people slowly into the Tower and destroys them there like grains crushed in a grindstone.'

'This is why I love you, Saph,' said Eldareth. 'Your uncrushable optimism.'

No one smiled. Saphaeyender gave a faint grimace and lifted his glass to his lips; Tanthe noticed how long and fine his fingers were.

'However,' Eldareth said, 'None of you can wish to lurk in a storeroom while the Nine Realms collapse about you.'

'Not if you can show us somewhere more luxurious to lurk.'

'Hiding won't make it go away. The time has come to make a decision.'

Candlelight gleamed on their intent faces. Eldareth

446

looked slowly at each of them. Then he said softly,

'Are we going to hide and run and live in misery, while Garnelys tears Aventuria down around our ears? Or are we going to fight?'

Rufryd said, 'What exactly do you mean – fight?'

'I mean – take up arms against the King.'

No one made a sound; Tanthe held her breath.

Mirias said, 'That's open rebellion. Civil war.'

'No, we can't do that,' said Saphaeyender.

Lynden broke in, 'That's not what we came for! All I wanted—'

'Was to get your lover back, I know, but that is not going to be possible unless we bring the whole edifice down.'

Tanthe looked at Eldareth's glowing eyes, and shivered. The thought of not simply disobeying the King but trying to fight him, dethrone him, destroy him, filled her with terror. It was against everything she'd ever been taught. 'But the Xauroma works both ways,' she said. 'If the people turn against their ruler they turn against the land and its spirit is broken!'

'But it's already broken!' said Eldareth. 'We can hardly make it worse!'

'It would be wrong, my friend,' Saphaeyender said firmly. 'I am a writer, not an adventurer like you. All I want is for things to be back as they were.'

'It's too late! They will never be back as they were unless we make the change ourselves – and we are not going to do it except by force. Do you want to live in shame and fear for the rest of your life? Do you want never to write again, for your existing works to be burned and your name forgotten?'

'These are emotive words, Eldareth. I'm not going to rise to them. At this moment, I don't much care.'

Tanthe stared at Saphaeyender. She was shocked, but at the same time she saw the pain etched in his face, lying deep in his eyes. Her heart went out to him. Rufryd stared too, but with a touch of disgust on his face, which made

Tanthe angry. How dare he judge Saphaeyender, not knowing what he'd been through?

'Then it's just as well the rest of us care, while you are taking some time off from bothering, Saph,' Eldareth said caustically. 'What do the rest of your flock have to say?'

'They always do whatever I do.'

'Don't be too sure this time.' Eldareth's eyes glinted. 'It's frightening, isn't it? But we can't get to the other side of the fire without going through the heart of it!'

'I'm with you,' exclaimed Rufryd.

'In that case, so am I,' said Lynden. 'If it's the only way we're going to get Ymmi back.'

Tanthe was still looking at Saphaeyender, thinking, he was a god to me but here he is, a man, bereaved and suffering and all I want . . . She was almost on the verge of touching Saphaeyender's hand when Rufryd's voice snapped her back to reality. 'Tanthe?'

The soldier's throat hung open in front of her, bubbling with blood. 'No, I can't fight,' she said vehemently. 'I agree with Saphaeyender.'

'What?'

'It would be wrong! If you follow the goddess you believe that life is sacred. We'd be making ourselves as bad as the King, helping him to destroy the Xauroma, not healing it! It can only be a last resort. There must be a way to sort this out peacefully!'

Now everyone was looking at her. To her shock, the actors gave her a spattering of applause. She was shaken by her own passion. 'But,' she said more evenly, 'whatever we decide to do, we must all stick together. We're all we've got.'

'Well said.' Saphaeyender was looking straight at her, smiling warmly. Fire ran through her.

'And Tanthe is right, of course,' said Eldareth. 'So let us join hands and pledge loyalty to each other and to our cause; to stop the King's madness by force – only if gentle means fail us.'

They clasped hands above the candles, feeling the heat of the flames and of each other's palms; their hands and eyes burning with the enormity of their decision. 'We pledge ourselves to free Aventuria of the curse that the King has brought upon us. May Nuth and Anuth lend us their energy. As of this day, we stand firm.'

Saphaeyender's hand had been on hers; she didn't realise, until they broke apart. As they drank solemnly to their pledge, his gaze met hers over the rim of his glass.

'Tanthe, will you show me that knife?' he said. 'The magical knife that petrified the beast of stone.'

'Oh, yes,' she said, scrambling to her feet. 'It's in my jacket, I'll fetch it.'

'Tomorrow,' said Rufryd, standing up beside her and putting his hand through her arm. 'We've had a long day. If you'll excuse us . . . Come on, Tanthe, let's go to bed.'

The room was not as bad as it might have been. It was small and bare, but free from small intruders. Tanthe shut and latched the door, put the lamp down on a shelf, then lay down still dressed on the mattress. The material smelled musty. She was so angry she couldn't speak; the anger was a wall of ice between them.

'Aren't you going to get undressed?'

She didn't answer. Rufryd lay beside her, without touching her. After a long time, when the sounds from the living room had faded and all was quiet, he said, 'I can't believe you, Tanthe.'

'Why?' she said, trying to keep her voice low. 'What have *I* done?'

'Taking sides with that stupid poet.'

She drew a breath, outraged. 'How dare you!' she whispered.

'How dare I what?'

'Be upset with me after you ordered me to come to bed like that! You treated me like a naughty child in front of them. I don't belong to you.'

He sat up and leaned against the wall, arms folded. 'I thought I was being considerate.'

'No, you were being possessive. You were laying claim.'

'Someone you'd rather be with, is there?'

'No!'

'Really. The way that poet was flirting with you was revolting.'

'Don't be stupid, he barely took any notice of me. I don't know what's got into you, Rufe. You've changed so much.'

'*I've* changed?'

'I thought I might get some sympathy from you when I killed that woman. I thought you'd share how bad I feel. Instead you're telling me to harden up, and your eyes are lighting up at every mention of war. I think you're getting to like killing. What is it you're suddenly so eager to make war against?'

He gasped. 'Don't you understand? Against – people like my father, who just give in to whatever they're told to do, however cruel, however immoral, because they have little, tiny, dried-up souls and no imagination!'

'So really, this is a war against your father?'

Rufryd shook his head impatiently. 'It's against the sort of apathy that got us into this mess. The sort of rubbish Saphaeyender was coming out with.'

'Keep your voice down!'

'I don't care if he hears. But you agreed with him, Tan. Why? It's not you! You've always had guts. Then suddenly the great Saphaeyender appears and all you can do is sit gawping at him and going, "Anything you say, O Great One".'

'You bastard! That is not true!'

'He's a coward. You're too dazzled to see it.'

'You'd never say that if you'd ever read one word of his work. Gods, you're so jealous.'

'Of him? Come off it. I'm just sickened by the way you were drooling over him all night. I might as well have been invisible.'

'Oh, this after you lectured me on self-pity? I was wrong about you, Rufe. You've always been a nasty-minded, self-centred worm. My mistake was thinking you *had* changed.'

'My mistake, thinking your strength was anything other than pure selfishness,' he said flatly.

Tanthe felt more than angry towards him; she felt utterly cold. Still, it shocked her to find him equally intransigent. She scrambled off the bed, shook the creases out of her robe, lifted the door latch.

'Where are you going?' he said.

'To find somewhere else to sleep.'

'You needn't bother.' He lay down and turned his back to her. 'I wouldn't touch you if you were the last woman on earth.'

Tanthe stormed back into the living area, only to find herself in pitch blackness. She groped her way to the couch, meaning to sit there for a while until she could sleep. But as she reached out her hand landed, not on an upholstered seat-back but on a human arm.

Tanthe recoiled with a cry. A flame flared and illuminated the form of Saphaeyender, who was leaning forward to light a lamp on the table.

'I'm so sorry,' she said, her heart thudding. 'I didn't know you were there. That nearly scared me to death. I'm sorry if I made you jump, too.'

'You didn't. I could hear you wandering about in the dark.' He sat back, looking completely at ease, appraising her with dark, wise eyes. All his intelligence and experience seemed to fill the room, a cloak of light.

'Oh.' Again she felt hopelessly awkward. 'I can't sleep.'

'Nor can I. I rarely can, these days. Sit down, Tanthe. Have a glass of wine with me.'

Tanthe sat down beside him and accepted the goblet he offered her. The wine in the pale green glass was white, appley, rough-edged. She needed it. She couldn't believe she was here and sitting beside him.

Saphaeyender took a sip of the wine and pulled a face. 'Terrible stuff,' he said. 'But it's all we can get.'

'It's fine,' Tanthe said.

'You don't look well,' he said gently. 'You look very pale, very upset.'

'I'm all right. I – I had a quarrel with Rufryd.'

'He's your lover, I gather.'

'I don't think so. Not any more.'

'Ah. Can't it be mended?'

She was amazed that he was interested. 'Not this time. I'm not sure I even want to. It's worse than just a quarrel, anyway.'

'How?'

Her throat tightened. She rolled the stem of the goblet between her fingers. 'I killed someone today.'

'Oh.' He sounded shocked, but after a moment – to her astonishment – he took her hand and said, 'What worries me most is not that you are distressed, but that Eldareth *isn't*. He has no idea, no idea what he is asking when he talks so easily about fighting the King. Tell me what happened.'

She did so, haltingly, almost forgetting who he was. When she'd finished, he asked, 'Do you feel better for telling me? Unburdened?'

'A bit. But it's easy for me to feel better. I'm not dead.'

'Sharp, Tanthe. That's a trait I appreciate. Am I asking too many questions? Writers do that. Terrible habit.'

'No, I don't mind.' She glanced round, gave him a quick smile. He seemed to have moved closer to her. 'I feel I can talk to you. I never thought you'd be so easy to talk to, you sound like . . .'

He looked sideways at her, a smile creasing his eyes. 'Like what – or whom?'

'Just anybody, really. I thought you would—'

'What, talk in rhyming couplets?'

She laughed. 'Something like that. I thought you'd be very eloquent.'

'I can be. But it's my night off.'

Her face went hot; she hoped he couldn't see in the dim light. 'I didn't mean to be rude. You must think I'm such a peasant.'

'No, I don't. I don't. Eldareth was right about me, I'm only a man. Lazy, indolent and selfish into the bargain.'

'No. You're a legend.'

'Not in Riverwynde, surely. I'm amazed you'd even heard of me.'

'Why, because I come from the back-end of nowhere?'

He shook his head. 'Now I've insulted you. I didn't mean it like that. I meant that I am pleased my work meant so much to you, when you must have had more important things to think about.'

'Oh yes. Like cabbage and sheep-shearing.'

He laughed. 'Well, without those things, people like me would not have the luxury of writing poetry. But still, you care about literature – and about my work, as well.'

'Now, that's false modesty.'

'Actually it was a bad attempt at wit.' They caught each other's eye just for a moment.

'Riverwynde isn't that bad,' she said. 'The people are kind. My parents are wonderful.'

'I can tell. Do you miss it?'

'Not at the moment.' Again their eyes met and she dropped her gaze, turning hot. 'Anyway. I dreamed of going to Parione, and seeing one of your plays in the Old Royal—'

She choked on the words. Saphaeyender put his arm round her shoulder, rested his cheek on her hair. She felt his grief, and her heart ached for him. Yet she was on fire with wonder, feeling that they'd always known each other, that in finding him she had come home.

'I don't think we should talk about that, do you?'

'Sorry. The last thing I wanted was to upset you.'

'You haven't upset me, Tanthe. The King, and those

453

bastards Poel and Grannen – they're the ones who've ruined our lives.'

'I can't believe this is happening,' she said softly.

'What?' His other arm went round her. Her blood pounded harder.

'Any of it.'

He kissed her hair, then the top of her ear. His arms were warm, his hair clean and spice-scented. 'Strange,' he whispered, 'the moment you came in, I felt as if I knew you. You're so lovely, Tanthe.'

Washed away by disbelief, desire and sheer terror, Tanthe couldn't move. 'What about your, er . . . the woman who was lighting the lamps?'

He laughed. 'Ashtar? She's not my lover. None of them are. They're my friends, my actors. I've only ever been married to the theatre.'

Relief surged through her. 'Oh. Good.'

'So it's all right?' His mouth met hers and she opened her lips eagerly to him, hungry, tasting wine and fire. When it ended, Saphaeyender stroked her long, unkempt hair. 'We should go to bed,' he said.

Tanthe pulled back, flustered and not daring to believe he meant what she thought he did. 'Yes, I think I could sleep now. But I can't go back in to Rufryd.'

'Then don't. You can sleep on the couch. Or . . . you can sleep with me.'

She hesitated, hot and cold all over, while he only looked warmly at her, waiting. 'The couch,' she stammered.

'Very well.' He folded her hands together and kissed her lightly on the forehead. 'I'll bring you a blanket.'

In the morning there was herb tea, porridge with honey, eggs. Daylight fell through two high slits in the walls; there were no proper windows. Rufryd wouldn't meet Tanthe's eyes; she sensed him glaring at her, but if she tried to catch him out he would look away, his face like stone.

The white-haired brothers came and ate breakfast with

454

them, sitting at the two ends of the table and smiling benignly at everyone. When the meal was almost over, Olberyd said, 'We've heard there's a big gathering of troops north of here.'

Eldareth tensed visibly, eyes narrowing. 'Doing what? Looking for us, preparing to take more conscripts?'

'The latter, I expect,' said Saphaeyender. 'I'm sure we're not that important.'

'Well, we have to find out.' Eldareth rose, already in his dark travelling gear. 'I'm off on a scouting mission.'

'I'll come with you,' Rufryd said quickly.

'There's no need. I prefer to work alone. You need some rest.'

'No, I don't. I'm coming with you, I can't stay here.'

Eldareth sighed. 'All right.' He glared at Lynden, who was also starting to get up. 'Just Rufryd.'

'But I'd rather be doing something than sitting about!' Lynden said in dismay.

'The more of us who go, the longer it takes to get anywhere and the more likely it is we'll be seen. Stay and rest.'

'Sitting about?' Dawn said briskly. 'You'll be lucky. There's plenty to do around here, just to keep ourselves alive.'

Released through the hidden door, Tanthe and Lynden went down to the stables with Eldareth and Rufryd to feed the horses. The animals were pleased to see them, blowing into their hair and chewing their pockets. Tanthe fed Redbird a carrot.

'You should take my Aelyr knife with you,' she said to Rufryd, who was buckling Sunhawk's bridle. 'You might need it.'

'Thanks, but it's yours, not mine.' A pause. Then, 'How was your night with Saphaeyender?'

'I didn't spend the night with him. I slept on the couch. Not that it's anything to do with you.'

'Right.' He ducked under Sunhawk's neck and lifted the

saddle on to his withers, gently easing it back to smooth his coat in the right direction. 'Hope you didn't forget your little arkh-wood charm in your excitement.'

'You have really got a nerve!' She was struggling to keep her temper. 'What about you and that Shaelahyr girl?'

He turned and met her eyes, for the first time that day. 'I thought so! You're still angry about Metiya, after all this time. This is revenge, isn't it?'

'What's revenge? I told you, I haven't done anything! No, I'm not angry, Rufe. It's much worse than that. Since that day, part of me stopped trusting you.'

He looked stunned. 'You don't trust me – after everything we've been through together?'

He barged past her, leading Sunhawk into the yard and mounting. Tanthe couldn't speak. Eldareth, who'd been out in the lane checking that there were no soldiers about, came back and seated himself on the brown gelding he'd stolen the previous day. 'We'll probably be gone for a couple of days,' he said.

'Goodbye, Tanthe,' Rufryd said harshly. And he rode away briskly, not even looking back, leaving her hurt and furious. Wasn't he the one in the wrong? Shouldn't he be trying to apologise?

Lynden closed and locked the gate behind Eldareth and his brother. Then he strode up to Tanthe, looking distraught. 'What on earth is the matter with you two now?' he said.

'Leave it, Lyn.'

She headed for the steps but he came after her, pulling at her arm. 'I don't blame Rufryd! I saw the way you were with Saphaeyender! I've nothing against him but, gods, Tanthe, you made it so obvious! Have you forgotten why we're here?'

'No!' she said, turning on him. 'But all I can see is we've got ourselves into a hell of a mess and we're still no nearer to finding my sister!'

*

Riding through the green beech-woods beside Eldareth, Rufryd felt more human. He prodded carefully at the cold mass of anger he felt towards Tanthe. Yes, it was still there.

He loved her more than his own life, but he couldn't forgive her. And the strange thing – because he believed her – was that she hadn't actually done anything wrong. Only *looked* at that effete coward of a poet. But that had been enough.

He knew he'd lost her.

As strongly as he'd loved Silverholm, he hated the safe house. He needed to be in the forest again, just him and Lynden and Eldareth, riding, fighting . . . eventually rescuing Ysomir so Lynden could be happy again.

'Rufryd,' said Eldareth. 'I'm sorry about you and Tanthe.'

'Funny how everybody seems to have noticed.'

'It would have been hard not to.'

'Well. It's been going wrong for a long time. I don't think it was ever right, except for one or two nights.'

'But you love her very much.'

'I wish I knew how to stop. I thought she felt the same . . . now I find out I was fooling myself all along.'

'Blasted Saphaeyender.' Eldareth sounded grim. 'He's my best friend but sometimes I could hit him. He's always doing this.'

'What?'

'Falling in love with waifs and strays. Seducing them. He can't seem to help himself.'

A surge of rage gripped Rufryd. 'Bastard!' he spat. And yet . . . he didn't want her to get hurt, but a perverse hope rose that Tanthe might learn her lesson. He drew a breath and said, 'Tanthe's no waif, believe me. She's just as capable of using people as long as it suits her.'

The morning was pleasant. Eldareth, who seemed to know the land well, led the way into the low, folded hills south of Nachillei. Here they saw the green and violet of the King's troops everywhere; encampments flying the royal banner; men and women training on foot and on horseback.

'I don't like this,' said Eldareth. 'They look as if they might be planning to attack Nachillei. They certainly could, at a moment's notice.'

They circled back through the greenwoods, keeping off the main paths, manoeuvring carefully to avoid being seen. Rufryd managed to put Tanthe out of his mind; he was in his element. In the afternoon, they had ridden a long way north and west of the town, and Eldareth took Rufryd to the peak of a high escarpment.

From the top, they could see miles across Paranios; undulating land, rich with forests and rivers. As the sun moved, a bright flash of silver shone out. It was near the horizon, running east to west along a narrow plain; a long thread of silver with what appeared to be several wagons moving slowly along it.

Rufryd shielded his eyes. 'What's that?'

Eldareth gave a soft groan. 'That, my friend, is the rail that Garnelys had laid down, to take conscripts to their destination all the more swiftly. Like sheep to market. That rail, I believe, ends at Napheneth.'

'Where the quarries and mines are.'

'Yes. Looks like they're busy again after the winter.'

'I wonder if Ysomir was taken along there?' Rufryd said quietly. 'Poor Lynden. It's not knowing that's so hard for him.'

Eldareth turned his horse, heading down the slope again. 'Come on. We'll see if there's anything more to find west of here.'

They came to a ridge, which divided into two on either side of a densely wooded valley. Smoke rose here and there from the trees; there were piles of fresh manure on the path. Eldareth said, 'I need to know if these are troops or civilians. We'll cover more ground if we split up; you take the right-hand ridge, I'll take the left. Meet back here in about twenty minutes . . .' he pointed behind him, to a dip in the ground. 'In that hollow. It'll be easier to hide, if one of us is back first.'

'Fine,' Rufryd said, urging Sunhawk along the twisting, dark path between the trees. The horse still had lots of energy; he went eagerly, neck arched, nostrils flaring. Alone, Rufryd felt nervous, alert and full of excitement. The path was dark with drifts of old leaves but the sun gleamed through the canopy and birds chirped amid the rustling leaves.

He rode at a brisk walk for ten minutes or so, winding round treacherous tree roots. From the glimpses he caught of cottages down in the valley, he guessed that it was only a village. On the other side of the ridge he could see no signs of human life. Presently he discovered that he was desperate for a pee. It would only take a minute. Turning Sunhawk off the path, he jumped down from the saddle and went behind a tree to relieve himself.

He never saw his attacker coming; never heard him. One moment all was normal; the next, he was briefly aware of Sunhawk squealing, rearing; then a heavy blow across the back of his skull, and dark oblivion.

Although Rufryd and Eldareth had said they might be gone for two days, when night fell Tanthe began to worry. As she and Lynden helped to prepare the evening meal, she said gently, 'Lyn? Do you think Rufryd's all right?'

He gave her a troubled, sideways look. 'Do you care?'

'Don't be daft, of course I care! I thought you might . . . you know, feel something.'

He began to chop the vegetables he was cutting up rather too vigorously. 'Why? I'm not a Seer.'

'But those other things you were aware of . . .'

'I can't turn it on like a tap! What if I felt Rufryd was fine, and I was wrong? Or I felt he was in danger, but I couldn't help him? I'd rather not know! You can't use me like a telescope, Tan.'

She rested her hand on his arm. 'I'm sorry, Lyn. But if you did feel anything, you'd tell me, wouldn't you?'

'Of course. I didn't mean to snap at you. But this thing in my mind . . . I don't know what it's for, and I don't want it.'

'It's saved us, once at least,' she said, squeezing his arm. 'You still don't know what it is?'

Lynden looked around, to make sure no one else was within earshot. 'I talked to Liyet about it once. She said I'd picked up an *ethroth*.'

'What's that?'

'A sort of energy-form that floats about, especially where something violent has happened . . . like Lord Arhan being killed by the *ghelim*. She said there's nothing I can do to get rid of it, because it's only woken something in me that was already there.'

'Oh,' she said, shocked, not knowing what to say to him. 'It might be a good thing, Lyn. Help us find Ymmi.'

He smiled tiredly at her; she kissed his cheek. 'I hope so,' he said. 'But all I want to do tonight is forget about it.'

After supper, the actors lit candles all around the room, and in the bower of light they sat and recited scenes from plays – some of which she recognised, to her pleasure – bouncing the lines back and forth, laughing when they forgot. Later, Saphaeyender began to speak, his voice flowing like a low melody. It was one of his own poems, her favourite, an epic telling how King Maharoth won the War of the Silver Plains. Tanthe, sitting on the floor with her head resting back against his knee, closed her eyes and lost herself in the red glow and the beauty of his voice and words. For as long as this lasted, she was in paradise.

Lynden got drunk and fell asleep; when the others made their way to bed, she helped him to his room, tipped him on to the mattress and left him to sleep it off. As she came back into the living area, Saphaeyender was there on his own, snuffing out the candles one by one. He looked so beautiful as he turned to her, a slim white statue, his dark

460

hair flaring around his shoulders, that she could hardly breathe.

'Where are they?' she said.

'Eldareth can look after himself. I'm sure Rufryd can, too, can't he?'

'Yes, but . . .'

'Then don't worry. It won't help them.'

'I know. I can't help it.' She hugged herself.

'Are you cold?' He came to her and put his arms round her. She could feel the hard lines of his body through the loose fabric of his robe, his heat. She was held in the heart of an enfolding circle, as if she'd travelled for years and arrived home at last.

'I won't be able to sleep until they come back,' she said.

'Nor I. So we may as well not be able to sleep together.'

Her pulse quickened; her loins ached. 'Will you recite another poem for me? It was like a dream-come-true, hearing *The Song of Maharoth* in your own voice.'

'I'll write poems for you,' he said, kissing her neck. He parted the neck of her robe, lifted one of her breasts and kissed the nipple, so tenderly she thought she would faint with pleasure. 'I'll invent them while we make love. Mind, they will be absolutely dreadful.'

She laughed, stretching her hands above his shoulders, arching against him. 'Just make love to me, then.'

'It's much better than poetry.'

He led her into his room, and although it was as plain as the others, she found that he had a bed-frame, a silken cover, a small window through which Lily Moon shone.

'Luxury!' she said.

'They look after me, my beloved actors, and I try to look after them.' He pulled off her robe, then his own, and they stood naked before each other, slender, white as opal in the moonlight.

Their eyes absorbed each other; her rose-tipped breasts, the pale curve of her stomach, the dark cleft between her thighs. And his curved lips, dark hair falling around his shoulders, the narrow muscled abdomen, the long columns of his thighs and the phallus standing proud, dark against his paleness. And then, not only their eyes but their hands flowing over each other's skin.

She loved his scent, his feel, his gentle urgency. She never forgot who he was.

'Oh, you are strong, Tanthe,' he said, lifting her with him, lying her on top of him. 'Your skin is silk but such strength in these slim thighs, these arms. You're an athlete.'

'I am,' she said. She bent and kissed him, deep and hot, easing herself backwards to pleasure herself on the hard, warm shaft of his prick. She writhed there for a few minutes, melting like butter. Then lifted herself up and sheathed him, inch by inch, until he was completely within her. The wonder of it speared her. She was already on the edge of orgasm, engorged with moist fires. Closing her eyes she lost control and cried out, liquefying into white light.

Saphaeyender wept when he came. He rose over her, striving as if to lose himself in her as she in turn tried to drag him wholly inside her; both of them groaning in bliss; and then his seed spilling inside her, his tears falling on her face. Tanthe cried too. She had to pull away from him and curl up over her knees like a child, trying to stop herself shaking.

'What is it, what?' he said. 'Did I hurt you?'

'No, no, the opposite.' She was laughing and crying at the same time. Bliss so extreme she was caught there and couldn't come back. *Saphaeyender.*

'Come here. Hold me.' He drew her down with him and she lay boneless and ecstatic in his arms. 'You're trembling. So am I. Ah, goddess, what have we done to each other? You could amaze the moons, Tanthe. Tanthe, Tanthe.'

Slowly their trembling stilled. Her body was glued along the length of his with sweat. She wanted to stay there for ever, in the diamond centre of time.

'When this is over, I'll take you to my house in Parione.'

'Is it marble?'

'It is indeed marble, and onyx and opal, all the white stones and crystals except for a pattern of lapis lazuli in the tiling around the centre of the walls.'

'And you have a courtyard and a fountain.'

'How did you know that?'

'You look like a man who would. And plants, long green ferns like I've seen in books.'

'And white and orange flowers, and tiny birds like jewels.'

'I wish we were there.'

'We will be. I love you, Tanthe.'

She couldn't believe he'd said it. 'You've only just met me! I've loved you all my life. Why would you love me, when you have all these beautiful and clever people around you?'

'You're so new, like a fresh breeze, as different as an Aelyr from everything I know. And you are beautiful, Tanthe, and clever. You didn't have everything given to you, as these people did, you had to educate yourself – so you care about it more than they do.'

'And this really means something to you?'

'Well, of course it does. I have known writers and actors made of stone; they are all intellect, and the more people acclaim them, the more they pour scorn upon their worshippers. But I'm not like that. I'm flesh and blood. I respond very well to being loved.' He touched his lips and his tongue to hers, smiling.

'And I do love you. Oh, gods, do I.'

'And there's something about you,' Saphaeyender said, his lovely face near hers, his dark eyes shining. 'It doesn't matter that we've only just met. I feel I know you. I recognise you.'

Tanthe slept blissfully; she didn't think of Rufryd again until the morning. Then she awoke with a start;

463

Saphaeyender was still asleep. Trying not to disturb him, she dragged her robe over her head and ran out into the living area. Lynden, in the doorway of the room that served as a makeshift kitchen, looked up at her with wine-bruised eyes.

'They haven't come back yet?'

He shook his head. 'No sign of them.'

'Oh, gods . . . Well, they said two days. How's your head?'

He grimaced. 'Bad. I don't remember anything about last night – which is what I intended, I suppose. If Rufe isn't back by tomorrow morning, I'm going to look for him.'

'And if *you* get lost?' she said sternly.

'I won't. Dawn and Mirias will go with me.'

'Lyn, I'll go with you,' she sighed, leaning on the back of the couch. 'Don't exclude me.'

Lynden gave her a narrow look. 'I thought you'd rather stay here with Saphaeyender.'

She dragged her lower lip between her teeth. He added, 'You slept with him last night, didn't you?'

'I thought you didn't remember anything.'

'Oh come on, Tan. Apart from the fact you've just come running out of his room with your hair all over the place, it was blindingly obvious it was going to happen.'

'You're looking at me as if I've let you down.'

'It's not me, is it?' Lynden said hotly. 'It's Rufe. He was happy with you. I've never known him happy before. I couldn't understand him with that Shaelahyr girl and I can't understand you now!'

'Lynden,' she groaned. 'We can't all be as pure-hearted as you. We are talking about the man who, the night before he left, told me he wouldn't touch me if I was the last woman on earth?'

Lynden turned away; it was getting too confusing, too intimate for him, she could see. He said in a low voice, 'I just hope he hasn't done something daft, because of you.'

464

The second nightfall brought nothing.

'Two days,' Saphaeyender reminded her, as they passed a second, exquisite night in his bed. All day, they'd had to endure the knowing little jokes and arch remarks of Evender, Saliole and Sharm; Saphaeyender had basked in it, while Tanthe was irritated, embarrassed, yet secretly pleased. Ashtar seemed almost jealous. Now Tanthe had an edge of superiority . . . or at least, of equality. But when she was alone with Saphaeyender again, the others ceased to exist. 'Eldareth is notoriously vague about these things. I forbid you to worry until tomorrow night, at the earliest.'

The following day, it took all Tanthe's powers of persuasion to stop Lynden from rushing off in search of Rufryd. When the third night came without news, neither she nor Saphaeyender could hide their growing anxiety. Unable to sleep, they slid about each other's bodies in a bower of candlelight, clinging together as much in denial as passion.

'I'm sure they'll come back today,' Tanthe said over breakfast, holding Lynden's wrist across the table. 'You mustn't go anywhere yet. Imagine how Rufryd will feel if he comes back then has to set out again to look for you! He'll be furious!'

'All right,' Lynden said, glowering. He looked dishevelled, his eyes red with lack of sleep. He rubbed his face anxiously. 'But I don't think any of us can wait much longer. It's too hot.'

'No, it isn't. Are you ill?'

'No. I can smell smoke.'

Saphaeyender and the others were all looking at them in concern. Tanthe said anxiously, 'Lyn, are you having one of your visions? Tell me!'

As she spoke, there was an urgent, coded knock on the partition door. It almost made her leap out of her skin.

'I'll go,' said Saphaeyender. She stood up and went with him; as she opened the door, one of the twins staggered in, breathless, almost falling into her arms. Tanthe still found it hard to tell them apart, but she thought it was Olberyd.

'You have to leave,' he said.

'What?'

Ashtar, Evender and the others were gathering around Saphaeyender in consternation. Olberyd leaned on Tanthe's arm and caught his breath. 'The King's men are coming. The town is full of them. They're searching the houses for you, Saphaeyender, for those who killed the soldiers in the forest. Someone may have betrayed you!'

'Why?' breathed Saphaeyender. He'd gone white.

'Who knows? For money, to ingratiate themselves, to avoid conscription – I don't know. But you must leave immediately.'

'I can't understand why Eldareth hasn't come back to warn us,' Saphaeyender said. He, Ashtar and the others seemed frozen.

'Come on!' Dawn urged. 'Get ready, quick!'

'How are we going to get out without being seen?' said Tanthe.

'There is a passage that leads out of the storerooms, through the top of the hill and out onto the far side,' Olberyd said. 'You can escape the town that way.'

'The others can, but I can't,' said Lynden. 'What about the horses? I'm not leaving them. And what about Rufryd and Eldareth? They won't know where we've gone!'

'It can't be helped. Olmion and I will be here for them, if we are not arrested.'

Saphaeyender gripped the old man's hands. 'If the soldiers come, throw yourselves on them with gratitude. Tell them we threatened you, forced you to hide us. Say anything to protect yourselves!'

'I can smell smoke,' Tanthe said suddenly. She leapt up onto the rows of barrels and peered out of the window-slit.

Down the hill, despite her limited vantage point, she could see grey clouds pluming up on the lower slopes. 'Oh gods, they're setting fire to the houses!'

Chapter Twenty. Enhavaneya

When Tanthe said the word *Fire*, Lynden's unease flashed
into a clear vision; the wooden stables burning, the horses
screaming in pain, thrashing, suffocating on the smoke.
'I'm definitely not leaving the horses,' he said.

Tanthe stared angrily at him. 'I don't want to either, but
I don't see how we can get them out without taking them
down through the town where the soldiers are! Best to
flee, Lyn, and come back for them later.'

'No,' he said, dizzy with the pressure of the vision. 'Later
will be too late.'

There was a hesitation. Lynden saw that without
Eldareth there, no one was making a decision. 'Then I'll
come with you,' said Tanthe.

'No,' said Saphaeyender. 'It would be foolish to split up!'

Dawn said, 'Actually, we might have a better chance
that way. There are three horses in the stables, aren't
there? Mirias and I will go with Lynden. Tanthe, you go
with Saph and the others. If we don't find each other on
the far side of the hill . . .' she gave Saphaeyender a
meaningful look. 'You know where to meet us, don't
you?'

He nodded, looking pale.

'All right,' said Tanthe. 'I'm not happy about this, but
we've got to make a plan and just do it. You'll be safe with
them, Lyn. Now let's get ready, quickly.'

Carrying a hastily-packed saddlebag, Lynden ran down
the steep flight of steps into the stable yard, followed by
Mirias and Dawn. His feelings for Tanthe were so mixed –
he was annoyed at her for still treating him like a child,
thankful for her protectiveness, dismayed at her rejection

467

of Rufryd – that he was glad the others were with him instead. They were the only two of Saphaeyender's troupe who seemed to have any sense or courage about them.

Beyond the high wooden walls, he could hear voices raised in panic, shouts of anger, cries of alarm. Lynden wasn't sure how much was real, how much in his head. 'They're coming this way,' he said.

Working quickly, they tacked up the three horses and led them out into the yard. Dawn took Redbird, Mirias his dark chestnut. Just as they were mounting, harsh voices sounded raucously in the lane beyond the locked gate, shouting and laughing. Someone rattled it, then began to pound on the boards. 'Hey! Where's this lead?'

'Who cares!' yelled another raucous voice. 'Torch it!'

A fire-tipped arrow came arcing over the wall and struck a pile of loose straw. Smoke billowed out. The straw smouldered, beginning to catch. Two more arrows flew over, blazing.

Lynden and his companions stared at each other. 'What are we going to do?' he said. 'There's no other way out, is there?'

'Back up the steps,' said Mirias. He wheeled his horse round and urged it up the steep way that led back towards the house. Redbird and Halcyon leapt after him, climbing surefootedly. Lynden came last, with Redbird's ebony tail whirling and Dawn's cloak billowing in front of him. As the steps rose, he caught a glimpse of helmeted heads down in the lane; then the sides of houses concealed them from view.

Half a minute later, they were on the small terrace outside the house of Olberyd and Olmion. Walls rose all around them. A dead end.

'Now what do we do?' said Dawn, trying to control her prancing mare.

The two old men came rushing out of the front door. 'Come inside!' one cried, beckoning frantically. 'This way, quickly!'

They rode in through the front door, ducking under the lintel, and into the narrow hall. 'Follow us!' said Olmion.

The twins led the riders hurriedly through a kitchen, and out of a side door into a tiny enclosed garden that lay to one side of the house. A high wall at the rear was fused into the hillside, which rose steeply, thick with grass, bushes and fruit trees. But at one corner, the wall had crumbled away, and there was a gully of earth leading down to it as if part of the hillside had crumbled or been washed away.

Lynden set Halcyon at it. The horse took three short, bouncing strides, leapt, cleared the broken wall and scrambled for a purchase on the slope. Then he was climbing swiftly through the trees, Lynden leaning forward to ease the weight on Halcyon's hindquarters. He glanced back; the others were following. Redbird made the jump easily, the strong thickset chestnut with a prodigious leap.

High on the hillside, now above the roof of the safe house, they could glimpse what was happening in the town. They reined in to watch. The King's men were everywhere, some on horseback and some on foot; in the valley and climbing the steep streets that surrounded it, shouting, rampaging. Several houses were on fire. Lynden could taste the smoke, an acrid taint on the air.

'Gods,' whispered Dawn. Her face was flushed, her green eyes shining with tears. 'We brought all this trouble to them!'

'No, love,' said Mirias. 'The townsfolk sheltered us because they already hated what the King was doing. Look!'

Down in the orchards, a crowd of men and women were rushing towards a line of soldiers. It was hard to see clearly, but the crowd moved as if they were armed; leaning forward, intent. 'They're fighting back!'

Something pale, terrible, burning yet icy rushed up through Lynden's mind. He gasped and clutched his forehead. Trying to erase it. That sensation . . . the white madness of the Bhahdradomen . . .

'Lynden?' said Dawn. 'What's wrong?'

But he could only wait, paralysed, knowing what was coming. A few seconds later, the sky boiled, and out of it burst a huge dra'a'k-like *ghelim*. The loose skin of its wings snapped on the air, its tail thrashed as it sighted its prey.

Dawn and Mirias exclaimed in astonishment. 'What in Nepheter's name is that?'

The pallid creature circled, uttered a screech, lurched into a lethal dive. On the ground, the rebel crowd were screaming and scattering.

Lynden couldn't watch. Halcyon was already dancing in fear, his neck arched, foam flying from his mouth. He sprang away eagerly as Lynden turned him and urged him on towards the peak of the hill. Dawn and Mirias quickly caught up. They both looked horrified.

'What was it?' Dawn asked.

'They're called *ghelim*,' said Lynden. 'I've seen them before. One killed Tanthe's uncle, while we were trying to stop them taking Ysomir. One tried to attack me in a forest. I put an arrow through it, but it didn't die. They are Bhahdradomen creatures.'

'What?' said Mirias, riding closer to him. '*What?*'

He'd got used to saying the word. He'd forgotten that others found it offensive.

'You must be mistaken,' Dawn said, shaking her head.

Lynden said nothing. They crested the hill, and on the far side found a sharply descending slope, less steep than the town side, but thick with trees and undergrowth. He could see no sign of Tanthe and the others . . . easy to miss them in the foliage. But it was hard to think straight until the disorientating backwash of his visions bled away.

A dash through the warren of storerooms, a short climb up a wooden ladder, and a scramble through a trap-door brought Tanthe, Saphaeyender and the actors out into a thick green wilderness on the far side of the hill. She could hear nothing but birdsong. The sudden peace was eerie; it was hard to believe what was happening a few hundred yards away.

She paused, looking and listening.

'I think it's safe,' she said. 'Now, which way?'

The others – Ashtar and Sharm, Evender and Saliole – looked at her blankly. The clothes they had put on for travelling were hardly more practical than their indoor robes, with flimsy gold-coloured cloaks.

'I have no idea,' said Saphaeyender. He was all in white; he'd be plainly visible to an enemy.

'I thought there was something about knowing where to meet the others?'

He rubbed his forehead. 'We have an agreement with Eldareth, that if ever we were separated or forced to flee, we would make for a certain place.'

'Where is it?'

'I know the name of it. I know roughly where it's meant to be. How to get there – I haven't the faintest idea.'

Tanthe stared at him in dismay. 'You must have!'

'Dawn knows.'

'Well, tell me the rough part, then.'

'It's called Enhavaneya. It's in . . . Gods, I just can't remember. I can't think straight. Geography was never my strong point.'

Tanthe felt herself losing patience. If this had been Rufryd, she would have delivered all the insults she could remember. But he was Saphaeyender, she couldn't be angry with him.

'How can you say that, after writing *Eskadale*?'

Her tone was gently teasing, but the look in his eyes stopped her cold. A flash of imperious contempt, as if to an adoring sycophant who'd asked one foolish question too many. 'Research, of course. You seem to confuse the art of being a writer with the actual reality of my life.'

471

She shrank away from him, shaken and feeling two inches high.

'Well, we'd better start by going down the hill. Perhaps we can orientate ourselves better there.'

Tanthe strode off down the hill, in the strange position of finding herself in charge while feeling completely humiliated. Still no sign of Lynden . . . her heart quailed. Had they missed each other in the thick undergrowth, or had something happened to him?

As she went, she carefully worked out their direction, noting the angle of the sun, the growth of moss on the tree trunks. Presently she said, as lightly as possible, 'Has anyone remembered where it is we're meant to be going yet?'

'It lies in the forest of Lusaniah,' said Saphaeyender. 'We have to cross the Cherent River. It's west of here.'

'Well, we're going the wrong way, then. This is east. So somehow we have to get to the other side of the town . . . no, wait.' She closed her eyes, conjuring up an image of the map over which she and Rufryd had pored so many times. 'The Forest of Lusaniah is north-east of here. We are going the right way!'

'Are you sure?' said Saphaeyender. 'I thought it was west.'

The other actors looked at her suspiciously, as if wondering how she dared argue with Saphaeyender. 'I'm going this way,' she said. 'It's up to you if you come with me or not.'

'How can you be sure this is east?' Ashtar said with a touch of accusation.

'Practice,' said Tanthe. 'I go outside occasionally.'

She moved off and they went with her. Then she felt uncomfortably responsible for them; what if her memory had failed her, and Saphaeyender was right after all? None of them spoke to her; it was as if they were half-frightened and half-resentful of having to rely on her, and hating their situation they needed someone to blame for it.

472

They crossed a stretch of farmland, keeping to hedge-rows. Then another wood, which angled downwards until the trees ended on the bank of a narrow, looping river.

'Is this the Cherent?' she said.

'It must be,' said Saphaeyender. 'There's a bridge.' She saw the gleam of dark wood arcing above the water, two hundred yards down river to their right.

'Still no sign of the others,' she muttered.

As she spoke, Saphaeyender stepped out of the trees to make for the bridge, just as she caught the flash of a breastplate on their side of the river.

'Stop!' she hissed, seizing his arm and dragging him back into the foliage. 'There's a guard on the bridge!' She saw the helmeted head turn in their direction, and held her breath. But a second later, the guard looked away and returned to a nonchalant pose.

Tanthe took off her cloak and flung it on to Saphaeyender's shoulders. 'I'm not cold,' he said.

'No, but you are visible about two miles away.' He looked ruffled, but accepted the cloak without comment.

'How in the cleft of Dyon's balls are we going to get across the river?' said Evender. The profanity sat comically with his perfect enunciation.

Tanthe rubbed her forehead, trying to visualise the ink lines of the map. 'We'll go upriver round the loop, and then we'll have to swim. It's not that wide. If we are where I think we are, that's the start of Lusaniah on the other side.'

Saphaeyender's eyes hardened, but the others simply looked miserable. Tanthe was swiftly losing her awe of them, along with her patience.

In the event, the river was shallow enough for them to wade across, though the dark green water flowed to their waists. On the far side they walked on, wet and uncomfortable, through deep, dark gullies choked with bushes, overhung by gnarled and mossy trees. It was tough going, and the others were hard-pressed to keep up with her.

'Did Eldareth ever tell you how long it takes to reach this place?'

'Two days, I believe,' said Saphaeyender, miserably out of breath.

'Doubtless we're completely lost by now,' snapped Sharm. 'Gods, I hate the countryside.'

'I don't suppose it thinks much of us, either,' Saphaeyender said, giving Sharm a hard look. 'Enhavaneya is a disused fort from the days of Mounicaa; it was her base when she defeated the tribes of Torith Mir. Long abandoned and overgrown. I don't see how we'll ever find it.'

'Right,' said Tanthe. 'Perhaps we won't, since all I have to go on is guesswork.' She marched on, carefully watching the sky through the trees, using all she had learned during the journey, all she could recall of the map, and now looking for signs that might betray the way to such a fort . . .

Such as the path on to which they emerged a few tiring hours later. It was overgrown, but it cut straight through the woods to the north east.

'Why have you changed direction?' Saphaeyender asked.

'Oh, you noticed.' The last thing she wanted was to antagonise him, but the caustic words slipped out before she could stop herself.

'It's no pleasure for me to be forced to drag my people into this,' he retorted. His coldness upset her as much as it angered her.

'Drag them somewhere else, then! I'm trying to help you!'

Suddenly she saw movement ahead of them in the trees. 'Stop!' she whispered, thrusting her arm out so the others almost fell over each other. She held them back, peering through the trees. Horses grazing in a clearing, people moving about . . . A red-haired woman in a green cloak, turning and staring straight at her.

Tanthe slumped with relief. 'That's Dawn,' she said.

And now she could see the other two, Mirias and thank the goddess, Lynden. She hurried forward and they came to meet her, hugging her with relief.

'Thank the gods!' Dawn cried. 'I don't know how we missed you on the hill. The undergrowth was so thick we must have ridden straight past you.'

Behind them, to her surprise, she saw a score of strangers on foot.

'Well, we're here now,' Tanthe said, her arm round Lynden. 'But who on earth are they?'

'Some of the townsfolk. We met them, fleeing through the woods, and we brought them with us.' His voice fell. 'We saw one of those creatures again. *Ghelim.*'

'Oh, gods. Any trouble on the bridge?'

Lynden shook his head. 'Mirias knew where there was a ford.'

'Ford as in less than ankle deep?' He nodded. 'Sod it!'

The actors had followed her tiredly into the clearing. They sank down on the grass, moaning about blisters and thorns, but Saphaeyender hovered at her shoulder.

'I'm so glad you found your way,' Dawn said to her. 'Saph is so hopeless, I never thought he'd remember a word of Eldareth's instructions.'

'Mm.' Tanthe began to move away, not wanting to cause any more awkwardness by venting her feelings. But the poet caught her hand and said softly, 'I didn't remember, Dawn. It's completely thanks to Tanthe we found you. Left to me we would have gone thirty miles in the wrong direction by now.'

'Saph, really.' Dawn shook her head. 'Sit and rest. We're making camp here for a while. There's a spring, and since Mirias and I were the only ones who thought to bring any food, we'll share it out as best we can.'

As they busied themselves, Saphaeyender lifted Tanthe's hand and pulled her towards him. 'I'm sorry,' he said.

She looked up at him and realised that what she'd taken

for imperiousness in his eyes was actually fear; his way of veiling it, at least. 'It's all right.'

'No, it isn't. You saved my life today. Saved us all, in fact. And in return I was unforgivably rude.'

She met his eyes. He was so contrite, how could she stay angry with him? 'It was a bit uncalled for.'

'Completely uncalled for. But we were all born in the city, you see. Most of us never left it, until we were forced to flee. We're spoiled children, really, and we don't like it when someone else is proved cleverer than us. The truth is, we were all scared to death.'

'That's honest of you.' She sighed. 'To be honest back – I knew. I could have been more sympathetic, but I chose to make it worse. It's the way the others look down on me, like they're better than I am.'

'It's just their way. They like you, Tanthe.'

'Well. Rufryd will tell you what a dra'a'k I can be.'

'It's good to meet someone who speaks her mind, instead of hanging on my every word,' Saphaeyender said. 'Actually, I was annoyed with myself, not with you.'

'It's quite a revelation to find out that my great hero can be so bloody annoying,' she grinned, 'although Eldareth did warn me.'

'Both forgiven, then?' He smiled disarmingly, pulled her to him and kissed her. 'I don't want to sleep alone. I've never had to sleep in the forest before.'

'I'll look after you,' she said.

Two days later, they found Enhavaneya.

It would have been easy to miss; a broad green knoll that once had stood proud in the surrounding countryside. But now the forest had crept over it, dark and gnarled. The moat around its circumference was choked with weeds. Ancient walls rose here and there around it, thick with dark green ivy and creeping vines. They had to fight their way through holly bushes to make a path through to the hill itself, but as they came up at last through the undergrowth and the moss-covered trees to clearer ground, an astonishing sight greeted them.

'Stop!' said Tanthe. 'There are people here!'

Between the trees on the crown of the hill, there was a camp. There were brown tents, shelters built of branches, pieces of canvas slung between old walls, decaying wooden buildings roofed with twigs. Smoke drifted up from a couple of camp-fires. Men, women and children moved between the makeshift dwellings or sat on the ground, mending clothes, whittling arrows. They were dressed in an extraordinary assortment of garments; from peasant garb to fine city clothes now worn and grubby.

Tanthe and the others hesitated in shock. 'They don't look like the King's people,' she said.

'Indeed we are not the King's people,' said a sharp voice.

Figures were closing softly in on them from either side, arrows set to their bows. The one who had spoken moved in front of them, holding a spear. A tall, hooded figure, with strands of golden hair escaping from her hood.

'Who goes there?' she demanded. Her voice was powerful, her demeanour forbidding. Tanthe turned dizzy, wondering for a moment if they had encountered the ghost of Mounicaa.

'Er – we are not the King's people, either,' she said. 'Is this Enhavaneya?'

'It is.'

'We were meant to meet someone here. Eldareth.'

'*Eldareth*?' the woman said in amazement. 'Who are you?' Then she stepped forward, gazing past Tanthe and Lynden, suddenly seeing the actors behind them. 'Saphaeyender? Is that really you?'

The poet came forward. His clothes were now more grey than white; his hair was uncombed and his chin unshaven. The woman put her hood back and stared at him open-mouthed. Her face was strong, almost heavy; she couldn't be called beautiful, but she was very striking. 'My name is Vyne,' she said. 'You probably don't remember me.'

Saphaeyender looked equally dumbfounded. 'Of course I remember you,' he said eventually. He took the woman's hand and kissed it, never taking his eyes from her face. Tanthe's heart turned over with jealousy. Then he turned to the others and said, 'This is, er, Lady Vyne. Once a patron of our theatre. My lady, what are you doing here?'

The woman smiled. She signalled to her troop, who had lowered their weapons. 'The same as you, I expect. I know you had to flee from Parione, my lord Saphaeyender.'

'Yes, and we've just had to flee again.'

'Well, so have I.'

'You?'

'As you see.' Vyne turned to look at the camp. 'And here we are, refugees from the King. Have you and your friends come to join us?'

'It appears so.'

Tanthe and Lynden looked at each other. Lynden, for once, was bright-eyed with relief. We're no longer alone against the King, she thought. No longer alone!

'I'm glad,' said Vyne. 'You must have so much to tell me. Come, bring your horses; we'll find you somewhere to rest and sleep. You must be hungry.'

'Yes,' said Saphaeyender, still looking astonished. His actors, too, were exchanging curious looks. Tanthe wondered what was going on.

She said, 'I take it Eldareth isn't here, then?'

'No,' said Vyne, giving her a sorrowful look. 'Eldareth is not here.'

Rufryd returned to consciousness somewhere dark and dusty-smelling. Through the throbbing pain of his skull he perceived a wooden ceiling, a hard pallet beneath him, and heard others breathing, snoring, coughing in the darkness. Turning over with a groan, he saw a wooden floor. A long shed, filled with sleeping bodies . . .

A door creaked open at the far end and a figure stood in the shaft of grey gloom; a guard in cloak and breastplate.

His voice boomed out, making Rufryd wince with pain.

'Rise and shine, you lazy bastards! Another glorious day in the King's service!'

Moaning, the bodies began to stumble out of their beds and drag themselves into what seemed mud-covered rags. Rufryd couldn't move. The next thing he knew, the guard was striding towards him, lifting him bodily and shoving him on to the floor.

'Get to work!' he yelled.

Rufryd tried to protest, only to receive a kick in the back that left him gagging.

When the guard had moved away, the man from the next bed leaned down and helped him up. 'Come on, my friend,' the man said in a deep, slow voice. 'Do as he says or you'll get a beating, and worse.'

'Where the hell am I?' Rufryd gasped. 'What do they want me to do?'

He was still fully dressed from the day before, but his sword, bow and belt knife had been taken from him. The man who had helped him was nearly a foot taller, powerfully-built, with a mass of black hair, a thick beard, gentle eyes almost lost beneath tangled eyebrows.

'You are in Napheneth.'

'Where?'

'The quarries. Don't they tell the conscripts even that much now?'

'I wasn't conscripted!' Rufryd growled. 'Some bastard captured me. I can't even remember what happened.'

'They're getting desperate.' The man shook his big head. 'So many died over the winter, of colds or accidents. Stick with me, do what I do. What's your name?'

'Rufryd Arthryn-son.'

'I'm Beorwyn Athed-son.'

Bewildered, weak and sick from the throbbing pain of his head, Rufryd followed Beorwyn and tried not to attract any more notice from the guards. He'd been with Eldareth in the woods . . . someone had knocked him out . . . How

479

lucky am I, he thought, that I was sent here and not taken to some garrison and interrogated?

They were allowed fifteen minutes to visit the privies, to wash in troughs of ice-cold water, then to eat. Breakfast was taken in another shed next to the first. Rufryd couldn't face the thin porridge so gave his share to Beorwyn, but he drank several mugs of herb tea, so thirsty he barely noticed its flat, bitter taste. There were a hundred or so men and women crowded into the makeshift dining area. They looked physically strong but wiry, not a spare ounce of weight on them, and their eyes were weary in weather-lined faces. Yet he heard laughter. There was still a spark within them.

The guards were shouting again. Everyone began to move. 'Time to go,' said Beorwyn. 'Move smartish, then you won't get punished.'

'They do a lot of punishing here, don't they?' Rufryd muttered.

Outside, as the long snake of people trudged from the little valley in which the barracks lay, a ghastly landscape opened out. Rufryd cast his eyes over it in stunned dismay. They were entering a huge, gouged out valley of grey mud – less a valley than a trench, as if the hillsides had been ripped up by the claw of a gigantic, furious god. Long shelves tiered the hillsides where rock had been quarried at different levels; hollows in the valley floor were filled with sludgy water. The hillsides towered on every side, ravaged shells of pale chalk. Glints of amber-gold showed here and there beneath the ashen paleness of the rock-faces.

He stuck with Beorwyn as the workers were split into details, given appropriate tools. Rufryd received a hammer and a drill, and wondered what chance he stood of using them on the guard who had kicked him. There was a long, slippery climb into a basin lined with columns and ledges of rock, symmetrically marked by the blocks that had already been broken out . . . He wondered what had happened to Eldareth, to his horse. And, he thought, how

480

the hell am I going to get out of here and back to Lyn and Tanthe?

Gods, Tanthe and Saphaeyender . . .

A quarryman took charge, showing the workers where to drill holes in the rockface, a painstaking process of striking the drill with the hammer, turning it a little between each blow. Then wedges must be driven in, one inside another, until the force was great enough to rupture the stone. Others roped the blocks and lowered them to the wagons below.

The work was harder than Rufryd would have believed possible, made worse by the aftereffects of the blow he'd taken to the head. After an hour he was struggling desperately to keep going. After three, when the guard barked, 'Break!' it was all he could do not to collapse.

'Where are you from, Arthryn-son?' Beorwyn, completely unruffled, sat beside him on the ledge and passed him a flask of tea and a piece of flatbread. He had a slow, considered way of speaking and a way of fixing his eyes on Rufryd's that made him seem simple. But Rufryd suspected he was more shrewd than he seemed.

It was an effort to speak. His shirt was damp with sweat, clinging unpleasantly to him. 'Riverwynde. Sepheret.'

Beorwyn's small eyes lit up. 'I knew someone from Riverwynde once!'

'I doubt it. It's a bloody long way from here.'

'No, I did. The most beautiful girl I've ever seen. Her name was Ysomir.'

'You are joking.' Rufryd sat forward, forgetting his aches and pains. 'Describe her.'

Beorwyn gave an exact account of Ymmi's appearance and character.

'Gods, you're telling the truth,' Rufryd breathed.

'You know her – my Ysomir?'

'She and my brother were about to be handfasted before they took her – Hang on, what do you mean by *your* Ysomir?'

'I travelled all the way from Afthan Horn with her,' Beorwyn answered simply. 'I loved her.'

Rufryd scowled. 'Loved her, how?'

Beorwyn seemed upset by his suspicion. 'By protecting her. I protected her, as if she were my sister. What else could I mean?'

He answered so innocently that Rufryd had to believe him. 'So, where is she now?'

Tears came into Beorwyn's eyes. 'I don't know. We were separated; she was taken on to the Harpheneth mines, and I never saw her again.'

'Mines?' Rufryd exclaimed in horror. 'They made her work in mines?'

'There was a lot of trouble there, we heard. Bad air exploding in the shafts. Forced them to close the mines down for now, but not before a lot of the conscripts were killed. More will die, if they don't stop.'

Rufryd dropped his head onto his hands. He felt Beorwyn's big hand patting his shoulder. 'It's funny,' Rufryd said. 'We grew up together and I treated her badly, just because it was so easy to frighten her. I don't think I said a kind word to her in my life. But if I thought she was dead . . .'

'You treated her badly?' Beorwyn's fists were enormous.

'Only teasing. Childhood stuff,' Rufryd said quickly. 'It's in the past, all I want is to rescue her.'

The big fists relaxed. 'They took a few folk to Parione. Stone carvers, they needed. But I could never find out what became of her. All I know is she's not there now.'

'Ever tried to escape?' Rufryd whispered.

'Twice. First time they beat me and chained me. Second time they beat and chained my friends in front of me. So now I daren't try any more.' He added, flashing a quick smile, 'It took eight soldiers to hold me down, though!'

The guard was ordering them back to work.

'Good for you,' said Rufryd, dragging his protesting body into action.

When evening eventually came he thought he would never move again. After the unappetising evening meal, as the conscripts made brief preparations for bed, Rufryd made a quick check of the surroundings. The shed had solid wooden doors, locked and bolted on the outside; windows too narrow to escape through; guards on constant watch outside, and blazing torches stuck in the ground.

He sank on to his bunk, flexing his blistered hands.

'Sore?' said a youth with shaggy blond hair, on the other side of him.

'I don't think the Zampherai use drills and wedges,' said Rufryd. 'They coax the stone out of the earth with their fingers. Amazingly skilful. You wouldn't believe how small they are . . .'

Everyone was staring at him. 'The Zampherai are our enemies!' said the blond man.

'How so?'

'They have caused all the accidents; landslips, explosions, tunnels collapsing. Maggots! You're sitting there praising them? They're vicious little demons.'

Rufryd looked around at the accusing faces. He was thinking of the Zampherai in Silverholm, Vranof's rage. 'Yes, well, I think I understand why.' He began to explain what he'd seen in the realm of the Azure Zampherai. They listened in silence, riveted.

'It's not your fault you're here, upsetting the Zampherai,' Rufryd said. 'It's the King's fault. But you're the ones suffering for it. Isn't it time we put a stop to it?'

'How?'

'Refuse to work.'

They laughed cynically, but their eyes were wide in the gloom. 'We couldn't. If this is what the King wants of us, this is what we must do,' said one of the others.

'Even if the King has gone mad with power and no

483

longer even treats his subjects as human beings? Wake up. We've got to get out of here.'

'You're crazy. It's impossible.'

Another endless day followed. Rufryd watched how sluggishly the guards patrolled the ravaged hills, seemingly bored to death. But they were armed and trained . . . could he fight his way out with a hammer? What bastard had taken his bow, his Aelyr sword? He grimaced. Despair fell over him.

A third day. By then he was so tired he could almost understand how these people had no spirit to rebel. Easier just to do the work, fall into bed, not think. But again that night he talked to them, telling them everything he could think of to stir them. And they were beginning to ask questions. Once they began to talk, there was a veritable outpouring of grievances against the guards, resentment at being forced to leave their homes.

He actually fell asleep while they were still talking. He woke again suddenly in the depths of the night; all was silent, but for Beorwyn's snoring, yet he had the strangest feeling that someone had called his name. He lay listening, every sense electrified. And then he heard it. A sharp whisper.

'Rufryd!'

He sat up on his elbows. He couldn't make out where the voice had come from; it seemed to be down on the floor. 'Who is that?'

Something jumped up onto the bed, startling him violently. 'Hush!'

Rufryd started, his heart racing. 'Gods!' he whispered. The flickering light of torches outside the window illuminated the small figure. It was a Zampherai standing on the cover, with a plume of blue-streaked black hair, spikes of quartz round his shoulders and loins. Vranof. Rufryd stared at the tiny warrior, certain he must be hallucinating. 'Where did you come from?'

'I have stayed near Eldareth since you left our realm,

following him by the underground ways. He is outside. See.'

Dazed, Rufryd rolled off the bed and found Eldareth's strong, resolute face framed in the window slit. He was holding a blazing torch, apparently having torn it from the ground. 'Rufryd, thank the gods!' he said. 'It's taken us three days to find you. I found Sunhawk wandering loose; he's safely hidden with my horse. I discovered that a group of soldiers had been ambushing anyone they could find to bring here. Rogues!'

Rufryd felt like dancing with relief. Then alarm gripped him. 'Eldareth, there's guards patrolling out there!'

'I know, I've killed two already. Now, before more come—'

'The door's locked. There's no other way out. If we start trying to force it, all we'll do is have the guards down on us.'

'I know. So we have to make *them* open it.'

'What?'

'I'm going to pass you this torch. Wake the others, tell them what you're doing so they're ready to get out. Then set light to a blanket or something and yell *"Fire"*!'

'You're crazy!' Rufryd said admiringly.

'Wait, I've something else for you.' To Rufryd's astonishment, Eldareth passed a sword in a scabbard through the gap. His Aelyr sword! And then his bow and arrows, his belt knife, and half a dozen ordinary short swords. 'Pass these out,' Eldareth whispered. 'Vranof and I happened to discover the weapons store at the back of the guard house. Not much in there, but it will have to suffice.'

'You broke in?' Rufryd said, strapping the sword on.

'We didn't need to. Vranof slipped through a gap in the boards.'

'I don't know how to thank you.'

'Save it. You're not free yet.'

Rufryd woke Beorwyn first, then the other sleepers.

Many were already waking from the sudden flickering glow. Seeing Vranof, some of them reacted with disgust.

'Listen to me,' Rufryd said harshly. 'This is your one chance of escape. If we all work together, we can overpower the guards.'

'I have spoken with the Zampherai of Napheneth,' Vranof added. 'We are enemies only to those who go on defiling the earth. All those who want to flee, we will aid you. Go with Eldareth, and we will be your friends.'

'Eldareth?' said someone, as if he recognised the name.

'I'm here,' he whispered from the window, raising a hand in greeting. 'Question me later. But trust me now!'

The conscripts were struggling into boots, breeches, ragged work jackets. Rufryd had not undressed; however grimy he was, he felt better that way. 'Who can handle a sword?' he said, offering the six weapons, which were taken from his hands at once.

'Gather behind the door!' he ordered. 'Be ready to fight your way out!' And then he seized the blanket from his bed, bundled it on the floor, and torched it, yelling, 'Fire! Help us! Fire!'

Acrid smoke billowed into the room. Rufryd held his breath; what if the guards didn't respond? But almost at once he heard running feet; a few moments later, the sound of locks crunching, bolts shooting back.

Smoke and conscripts surged out of the open door, taking the few guards completely by surprise. Before they could draw weapons, blankets were thrown over their heads, swords stabbed into their sides, rocks gathered to strike their heads.

Drawing his sword, Rufryd ran to the women's hut and flung back the bolts. But there were locks he couldn't undo, so he began trying to break them, kicking the door hard with his boot. Beorwyn ran to help him. The women were already up, woken by the disturbance, and they helped from the inside; suddenly the door burst open, and Eldareth sprang into the doorway, a second torch held aloft. 'Rescue!' he yelled. 'Come with me now. Come out, I'm going to set it afire!'

The fire caught quickly as the women came rushing out, shouting and cheering. Now the conscripts were wildly excited, seizing torches out of the ground and using them to brandish against the guards who came running to challenge them. The torches were longer than swords. The guards' hut itself caught afire, orange flames and red sparks pluming into the night. The whole camp was in chaos.

A solid phalanx of guards and officers came surging towards the rebels, yelling orders. The commander himself was with them. Rufryd had only seen him from afar but he was a big blond man, bigger than Beorwyn and as pitiless as rock.

'Hold together,' said Eldareth. The rebels obeyed him. 'Torches at the front and sides!' Rufryd was there beside him, brandishing the long flame in his left hand and his sword in his right, daring them to try him. In the gap between the burning huts and the steep wall of a gully, the two groups confronted each other.

'Stop!' the commander yelled. 'Give yourselves up immediately!'

His guards formed up in tight lines around him. The front row had crossbows. Rufryd's mouth went dry; some of those bolts were bound to be fatal, but once they were all shot, the guards would never have time to reload.

Movement, boots pounding behind the rebel group; there was another division of guards there, cutting off their retreat. The rebels looked around wildly; they were beginning to lose their nerve, and Rufryd suddenly feared that, after all, their break for freedom had been doomed.

He glanced at Eldareth, but the older man only looked straight ahead, facing the commander with dark, hard eyes.

'No, commander,' Eldareth said. 'This is the end of the King's quarrying operation. It will soon be the end of the mining too. The Zampherai won't rest until it stops. And you men and women of the guard; you also know it is wrong! Come with us now, before it's too late.'

The commander's eyes spat rage. 'I don't know who you are, but I'll find that out at my leisure. Now, drop your weapons. Your punishment will be of the utmost severity. However, you will do yourselves a favour if you drop your weapons *now*!'

Rufryd sensed the rebels giving in. He felt he stood on a knife-edge over an abyss. Staring straight into the commander's eyes he carefully sheathed his sword; the moment seemed slow, coiled with tension. The commander's chin lifted; it was over. Then Rufryd flung his torch straight over the commander's head into the ranks of the guards, yelling at the top of his lungs, '*Fight*!'

In the same movement he swung his bow off his shoulder and set an arrow to the string. The guards ducked and shouted as the flaming torch arced down among them. Eldareth started forward, brandishing his own torch and sword, firing the rebels to action. In the same moment, the guards let off a volley of crossbow bolts.

Rufryd felt the shafts whistling past, but none hit him; he felt invulnerable. He fired his arrow, saw it sail sweetly to its target. It sank deep into the commander's chest, straight through his leather breastplate into his heart. The big man fell backwards, taking three guards down with him.

But alongside Rufryd, half the front line of rebels had fallen. He glanced round and saw Beorwyn lying on his back, staring at the smoky night, two lethal bolts protruding from his ribcage. Grief seized him, but he couldn't pause. He fired again and again, then when his arrows were exhausted he drew his sword and fought hand to hand.

Eldareth was striding through the ranks of guards, who were melting away in front of him. 'Sheathe your swords!' he was shouting. 'Your commander is dead! There's no need to stay here, come with me to freedom.'

And some of them were doing as he said, turning to fight their fellow guards. The rebels were halfway through their lines.

Someone shouted, 'Ware behind!'

The guards who'd trapped them were attacking at the rear. And they were tightly formed, under the command of a fierce-eyed female officer. Suddenly the rebel group was in chaos; those at the back rushing forward to escape, shoving their way through those at the front.

'No!' Rufryd bellowed, but he could do nothing to stop the rebels racing madly past him. He swore at them. But the guards came on; the disruption gave those at the front a chance to reform. They were lost. Rufryd began to back away after the others, suddenly finding himself alone with a dozen swords pointing at him.

Suddenly rocks came raining down, striking the soldiers' helmets and shoulders. The guards began to cry out in pain, dropping their swords to protect themselves. All over the gully wall above them, the Zampherai were hurling small missiles with effortless accuracy.

Some of the soldiers under attack broke ranks and came stumbling forward to escape the attack, trying to shield their heads with their arms.

'Now!' cried Eldareth. 'Rebels, to me! Stand firm!'

The rebels rallied to him and he stood in their centre, torch aloft, pouring flame and smoke into the obsidian sky. The Zampherai onslaught stopped; the guards stood dazed.

'It's over!' Eldareth called. 'None of you has any reason to remain in Napheneth. If you come with me, the fact that you fought against us tonight will not be held against you! But any who try to stop us – you will not prevail.'

To Rufryd's amazement, about a third of the soldiers sheathed their swords and came to join the rebels. Their officers looked on grimly, but even a couple of them went to Eldareth's side.

Eldareth grinned, more in relief than triumph. The Zampherai stood ready to defend his group, their hands full of sharp rocks.

'Come, then. Follow me, all who will.'

Rufryd looked back once, saw a score of corpses scattered on the ground, luridly outlined by the glow of fire. Beorwyn's great bulk was unmistakable. Would the remaining guards tend to those who had been wounded rather than killed outright? Gods, what a mess.

Passing a hand over his sore eyes, he turned his back on the scene. And Eldareth led the conscripts towards the long roads that would lead them out of Napheneth, their torch flames sweeping through the darkness and swathes of grey mud sucking at their feet.

Lynden was down at the spring below the western flank of Enhavaneya, filling buckets with the cool clear water where it came bubbling from the ground. He'd been up and down the hill all afternoon, filling the barrels that supplied the camp with drinking water. He needed a rest . . . but the longer he worked, the less time he had to think.

Lynden knelt on the bank and bent down to sip the glassy water. It was pleasant to be alone; so peaceful, just the water dancing over the stones and the green moss. When he straightened up, he found Saphaeyender standing on the bank beside him.

'They sent me to help you,' the poet said, smiling.

'There's no need,' said Lynden. He sat down on the bank, and Saphaeyender sat down beside him.

'Hard to believe the world can be in such chaos, here in the woods.'

'The chaos hasn't even started yet,' said Lynden.

'Are you afraid?'

'Not really.'

'I am,' said Saphaeyender. Lynden looked round. The poet's large dark eyes were fixed on him, and he saw the shadows behind the tranquil expression. 'I'm so terrified I can't sleep. Can't even breathe, sometimes.'

'Surely Tanthe helps.' Lynden tossed a pebble into the stream.

'You're upset about our being together, aren't you? I wish you wouldn't be. I love her. Yes, I forget while we are making love and that is a very good reason to make love as often and for as long as possible . . . but when it's over, the darkness hasn't gone away.'

Lynden watched the ripples from the pebble. He felt embarrassed. 'There's no use in being afraid, anyway. I used to be but not now.'

'Why not?' Saphaeyender moved closer, speaking very softly. 'Can you see into the future?'

'No.'

'But you have an ability . . . I've heard you talking about it. You see visions, you are aware of things before they actually manifest.'

'Sometimes. It's unpredictable.'

'When did it first begin?'

'When . . .' he paused, thinking. 'When I found Halcyon in the forest. I fell over the corpse of his rider, and I had a vision of how he'd died. That was the first time. Now I think back, that must have been when the *ethroth* entered me. I felt it; I went dizzy.'

'And since then?'

'It comes and goes. I never have any warning.'

'Useful, though.'

'No, I hate it! I can't see how it helps me, to have these horrible feelings in my mind!'

'That bad?'

'I think it'll drive me mad.'

'Not if you learn to understand the gift, to control it.'

'That's what Liyet said. But who the hell is going to teach me that?'

'Perhaps Eldareth will help you. He knows about these energies that can't be seen. At least, the Aelyr call them energies. We call them gods or spirits, but really they are just vibrations, ideas. Elementals is the best term for them, perhaps.'

Lynden was silent.

'You find it hard to talk to me?' said Saphaeyender.

'No. Just hard to talk to anyone. Ymmi was the only one who ever understood me.'

'You know, you are remarkable, Lynden. I've been watching you. If you went on the stage the women would adore you; the men would adore you, for that matter. I could write you such parts . . . You'd never do it, though, would you?'

'I shouldn't think so. I'd hate to make an exhibition of myself like that.'

'It's a shame.' Saphaeyender's voice was low, and Lynden sensed the dark eyes on him; could almost feel the gaze like heat. 'You keep so much of yourself hidden. Who are you, Lynden?'

'That's a daft question.'

The poet laughed softly. 'I expect it is. A writer's question. But can you answer it?'

Lynden shivered violently, without warning. 'No, I can't. A few months ago I would have said I'm Arthryn's son and I'm going to marry Ymmi and be a farmer. But I can't. Something's changed inside me. I feel as if there's somewhere I'm going, and I don't know where but I can't control it. That's why I'm not really afraid any more.'

'This is loneliness speaking. I know how that feels.' Saphaeyender put his hand on the back of Lynden's neck and rested it there, one finger stroking the skin. Lynden wanted to shake him off, yet he didn't. Oddly, the touch felt unutterably soothing. 'You seem as if you have not had the comfort of a lover for a long time . . .'

'Since they took Ymmi.'

'Ah. Could you love someone else?'

'I don't think so.'

'You won't know unless you try.'

There was a long pause, a strange, uneasy heat. Lynden

492

said, 'I think we had better take these buckets back.'

He heard a footfall on the grass behind him. Turning, he saw Ashtar there, her hands on her hips, looking archly at Saphaeyender. 'Dear Saph,' she said with a cool laugh. 'Nothing ever changes, does it?'

'You'd be surprised,' Saphaeyender said, straightening up, 'at how much has changed.'

Dawn was breaking, damp and misty, dropping diamonds of grey light through the woven-branch roof of the hut. Tanthe stirred under the covers, looking up at the light. She reached out for Saphaeyender, but he wasn't there. She exhaled heavily. Gone for another secret talk with Lady Vyne?

The hut was small and damp with weeds growing in the corners, but it was luxurious compared to the nights she'd spent on bare, rain-soaked moors. Saphaeyender wasn't happy here, she knew. He hated living like this, felt diminished by it. She didn't know him well enough to say the right things. It was only ten days since they'd met, and only now was she realising that there were great hidden tracts of his mind that she'd never be able to touch. Was I being ridiculously arrogant, she thought, assuming I could ever really know someone like him? But still, that didn't stop her being hopelessly besotted.

The mysterious Lady Vyne had been gathering refugees in the wildwood since the previous autumn, it seemed. Already they numbered nearly three thousand. There were many horses here, and as well as peasants from the land there were people who had money and arms, and could get more. But what was Vyne's power to draw them and hold them here? Saphaeyender knew, but he wouldn't tell Tanthe.

'Why won't you trust me?' she had asked the previous day.

'I do trust you, but she has asked me not to say anything to anyone,' Saphaeyender had replied.

'Was she your lover in Parione?'

'She was . . . a friend. More acquaintance than friend. But my lover, never.'

'Then why must you spend so much time with her?'

Saphaeyender had only looked at her with a kind forbearance that made her feel like hitting him. 'I'm not necessarily with her if I'm not with you. I may just as well be alone.'

'Alone, why?'

'It's just habit, love. I'm a writer, I'm used to spending time on my own. If you are going to stay with me, as I want you to, you're going to have to learn not to be jealous.'

'I'm not jealous!' Tanthe had said. But now she stretched uneasily on the thin mattress. What had he meant? Of what, or whom, should she be jealous?

The sweetness of their first encounter had been so overwhelming, she had wanted it to stay like that for ever, with no complications, none of Saphaeyender's past life to shadow the present. Impossible. She loved him and wanted him so much it hurt, and he seemed to feel the same, yet he would keep disappearing, and for as long as they waited here and Rufryd was still missing, their future together – if they had one – could not move or grow.

Outside, the camp was stirring. Tanthe lay listening to footsteps, horses' hooves, comforting sounds of activity. She must get up and attend to Redbird, then see about breakfast . . .

Someone was shouting. She sat up, trying to catch the words. It sounded like Mirias. '*Hoy! Company approaching!*'

Saphaeyender appeared suddenly in the doorway. He was smiling.

'Tanthe, come out and see this!'

She leapt up, pulling on her clothes and hopping as she dragged her boots on. When she got outside, the centre of the camp was already milling with people and she couldn't see anything. She edged her way through until she made

494

it to the front curve of the hill, where the trees were more widely spaced and gave a clear view for a short way down the slope. But the morning air was chill and moist, the holly bushes silver with dew, a mist clouding the air so it was impossible to see clearly.

Saphaeyender caught her hand, pulled her to his side. Lady Vyne was there, and the slim silent man who was often at her side, and the actors from Parione.

The first thing Tanthe saw coming out of the mist were Mirias on his chestnut; then Lynden on Halcyon, riding up through the trees. They'd been on dawn patrol. They must have galloped up to warn the camp, then ridden back down to accompany the strangers. A second later, a host of figures formed out of the greyness and came walking wearily towards the camp. Alarm gripped for a moment, until she saw at once that they were not the King's soldiers. They were grey as wraiths, as if the mist itself had birthed them.

She stood in shock for a few moments. All around, her companions watched in silence ready to draw their weapons. Then her gaze lit on the two leading figures, saw that their clothes were crusted with mud. But she knew their long, lean shapes and the way they walked, even before she could see their faces. Recognised the horses they were leading, walking tiredly beside their owners with heads down. She gripped Saphaeyender's hand and almost burst into tears with relief.

'Rufryd!' she said.

'And Eldareth! Oh, thank the gods!'

With them came a straggling line of strangers, but Tanthe hardly noticed them.

Beside her, Saphaeyender cried, 'Eldareth! Thank god and goddess!'

As the two men strode forward to greet each other, she was already running towards Rufryd, flinging her arms round him. He picked her up and swung her round into the air. When he set her on her feet, breathless, they clung tightly together, kissing each other's faces. 'I was so afraid for you,' she gasped.

'And we were, for you. When we went back to Nachillei we found the safe house empty and soldiers in the streets. I don't know how we avoided being captured a second time.'

'Didn't Olberyd and Olmion tell you we had to flee?'

'They weren't there,' said Rufryd.

'Not there? What happened to them?'

'I don't know. They just weren't there. But Eldareth said he had an agreement that if a crisis came, we'd all meet at Enhavaneya. So here we are.'

'But why has it taken so long for you to get here? Who are those people? What happened to you?'

Rufryd gave a sour grin. 'I got taken to Napheneth. They were actually kidnapping people from the nearby villages; some bastard clouted me on the head . . . oh, I'll tell you everything later. Tan, you should have seen Eldareth when he helped me escape! He was magnificent! Oh, and I met someone who had seen Ysomir!'

'What?' she cried in excitement, gripping his shirt. 'Tell me!'

'Don't get your hopes up. Don't say anything to Lynden. She was taken to another part of the mines. There were some underground explosions there and some of the conscripts were killed.'

'Killed?' Her excitement turned to dizzy fear.

'Yes, but she may not have been among them.' He held her tighter. 'We just don't know. No one's seen her since – but Tan, listen. Some of them were taken on to Parione. In particular, those who could carve stone.'

Tanthe pressed the heel of her hand to her forehead. 'So she might still be alive?'

'Yes. Let's hope.' He nudged her and said, 'Look at them.'

Tanthe turned, and saw Eldareth locked in a passionate embrace with Lady Vyne. She was almost as tall as him;

her hood had fallen back, unleashing her thick golden hair, and the two were hugging, gazing at each other, laughing and weeping and hugging again. There was a space around them; others were watching, smiling, but the two might as well have been alone. Tanthe laughed, thrilled not least to realise that when Saphaeyender said he was not Vyne's lover, he spoke the truth.

'Well, there's a turn up,' said Rufryd. 'Eldareth never mentioned a woman. Who is she?'

'Her name is Vyne,' said Tanthe. 'This is her camp. Some of the others seem to know her, but they won't tell me anything.'

'We'll soon find out.' Rufryd still had his arm round her. The smell of earth and sweat that hung about him was not wholly unpleasant, and his eyes shone softly as they used to when they were first lovers. 'Are you all right?' he said.

She nodded. 'You?'

'Fine. So, have we finished arguing?'

'I hope so.'

'Forgive me? I forgive you.'

'Of course,' she said. 'I'm just so glad to see you alive.'

He embraced her again and she responded, only to feel his arms grow tight and urgent. He made to kiss her, but she turned her head way. 'Do I smell that bad? You're none too fragrant yourself.'

'Rufe.' She half-smiled, easing herself away from his body. 'I'm sorry. I'm with Saphaeyender now.'

'Oh.' His hands fell away from her. '"With him" as in sharing a bed?'

'More of a mattress in a hut, at the moment.'

'So all that noble "I slept on the couch" stuff lasted how long? Just until I was out of the door?'

'I'm sorry. Don't be angry.'

'I'm not,' he said stiffly. He gave a hopeless sigh, resigned, exasperated. 'All this, because I made one mistake?'

'No, you don't understand. This isn't your fault, I'm not

punishing you. It's nothing to do with that Aelyr girl. I'm in love with him.'

'In love?' he said, as if naming a hideous disease. 'So all that stuff about Metiya was an excuse?'

'You made assumptions, and I let you. I was looking for an excuse, so I didn't feel quite so bad about it.'

She expected him to be angry, but he only looked downcast. 'I could see this was going to happen from the first moment you set eyes on each other. That's why I was so angry with you. You never loved me as much as I love you.'

'Oh, Rufe,' she said helplessly. 'Try to understand. I'll always love you, and I'm not doing this to hurt you. This is my dream come true and I can't not follow it. To be with Saphaeyender is everything I ever dreamed of.'

He sighed, pushing his hand through his hair. 'Not much I can do to compete with that, is there? Fine. We'll just be friends then.'

'Friends, yes,' she said, relieved.

He nodded, his eyes downcast, looking defeated. Then he spoke with an unexpected dignity that touched her. 'I'm glad you found your dream, Tan.'

She turned away, feeling upset although there was nothing else she could have done. Eldareth and Lady Vyne were still deep in conversation, but as Tanthe looked at them, Eldareth raised his head and addressed the crowd.

'Your attention!' he shouted. 'Lady Vyne and I have had a lengthy discussion—'

'With tongues!' someone remarked, to a burst of raucous laughter.

He held up his hand, grinning, 'And she now wishes to say a few words. Friends, please; this is very important.'

Vyne spoke, her voice carrying strongly across the encampment. Her face was radiant; previously Tanthe had not been able to look at her without the word 'hatchet' springing to mind, but now she was almost beautiful.

498

'Some of you have been with me for months, others only for days or indeed—' she indicated the rebels from the quarry – 'a few minutes.'

There was a ripple of laughter. She went on, 'You are very welcome. I gathered this camp in Enhavaneya as a refuge from the King's activities. It grows daily, and our existence cannot remain secret for ever; something or someone is bound to give us away, any day now. We must be ready to defend ourselves.'

Cheers of support. She went on, 'Many of you know the name of Eldareth; a man who has found fame as an actor, writer, adventurer, friend of the Aelyr and much more.' She laughed, resting her hand on Eldareth's chest. 'He is almost a legend! And he should be, as one of the handful of Aventurians who have stood against the King and survived. Now with him at my side, I know that we will stand firm against the darkness.'

A louder cheer rose and fell; sunlight touched the mist, as if to make tangible the mood of hope.

'Some of you know also who I am. I thank you now for keeping that information to yourselves; I wanted to win your loyalty for who I am as a human being, not for my title. I hope that won't change when I tell you the truth; for Eldareth and I have decided that you deserve no less than the truth.

'My real name is not Vyne. I'm Helananthe. I'm here because my father died for defying the King. And my father was Prince Galemanth, and my grandfather is King Garnelys.' Tears rolled down her cheeks as she spoke. 'I would rather be anywhere than here. But since it is so, I hope you can find it in your hearts to trust a member of Garnelys's family; to know that not all of us have turned our faces against Aventuria.'

The silence was absolute, shimmering with tension. She placed a hand on the shoulder of the slim man at her side, so quiet and unassuming that he had barely attracted any notice.

'I fled Parione, just as many of you did. I travelled to the Serpent Isles and brought back a Mediator, Rathroem, who may in the end be our only hope. He will vouch for me, if any doubt me. I'm one of you. I ask you to follow me, not because of who I am, but for Aventuria's sake.'

Chapter Twenty-one. Laphaeome's Web

For many weeks, Ysomir had sat watching the season change from the window of her room in the King's private chambers. She'd seen frost-flowers on the diamond panes, and, melting them with her breath, seen the ice frosting her windowsill, icicles lining the amber walls of the lower levels. Often she had watched snow falling and the guards' breath pluming on the air as they sluggishly patrolled the walls.

After the snow came days of icy wind and rain. And the rain turned warm, and the new leaves began to appear, and the sun turned the wet leaves to glittering crystal. The walls of the citadel shone as if crusted with billions of tiny yellow diamonds.

She remembered fleeing after the King had killed Namane. Running along the halls as if a winged black dra'a'k were chasing her, falling to her knees and hiding her head on the Queen's lap. Pouring out the horror of all she'd seen without noticing how white the Queen turned or how her sinewy hands gripped the arms of her chair.

'How much more can we bear, and do nothing, and not go mad?' Ysomir said.

'If we are not mad already,' said the Queen, stroking her hair. 'I lie awake and all night in the silence I can hear it groaning and crying out with pain . . .'

'You mean the sphere,' Ysomir murmured. 'I've seen it.'

'The Xauroma. Aventuria's spirit, bruised and broken. For have I not played my part in destroying it?'

'But ma'am, what could you have done to stop it? If you'd tried to act against the King, you would have been dead by now.'

'Better that, than to live with this guilt.'

A few days later the Queen fell ill. She stopped eating; nothing her ladies-in-waiting, the court physician or even Ysomir herself said would persuade her to take medicine or nourishment. Ysomir sat with her day and night, watching her turn paler and greyer. But her eyes shone with fragile luminosity.

'There must be something I can do to help you,' Ysomir said, distraught.

'You have already helped me more than you could know,' said Mabriahna. 'Through you I've touched the goddess again. She comes to me in the form of the Death Crone – but the Crone is gentle and wise. Her dark wings are soft and feathery. Her face is a shining light and she calls me to her.'

'It's the loss of her son,' whispered one of the ladies-in-waiting at Ysomir's shoulder.

'More than that. It's that her husband killed their son,' Ysomir replied, holding Mabriahna's hands as she drifted into sleep.

The next day, the Queen rallied. She asked to be placed on a couch, so she could look out of the window. While she was there the King came, dressed in a dark purple robe that billowed around him like a cloak; a great, gaunt bird of prey. He sank on one knee beside the Queen and laid his hand along her wasted arm.

He ignored Ysomir and since no one dismissed her she sat in silence, reluctantly overhearing their soft conversation.

'I know why you are ill,' he said. 'You have made yourself ill. There is no need for this.'

'No, it's the truth that has sickened me. That I failed to stop you while there was still time. That your own people will rise against you and against each other.'

'But we don't need those who refuse to share my vision! They're fools.'

'The old Garnelys would not have spoken of his subjects with such contempt. He would have listened to them.'

'The old Garnelys was weak. Such a man could not survive. He was burned away in the furnace of truth. But *this* Garnelys shall live for ever!'

'For ever?' Her head tipped on the cushion; Ysomir couldn't see her face. 'Can't you hear yourself?'

'The Tower holds the secret of my immortality. There's no reason for you not to share it, Mabriahna. Shake off this foolish illness. Stand at my side, pledge yourself to the eternal construction of the Tower. We shall be immortal together, husband and wife, king and queen, god and goddess.'

She rose up on one arm and now Ysomir could see her expression; utter disbelief. More than that; revulsion.

'No more, Garnelys!' Her voice briefly regained its imperious strength. 'The man I called my husband is long dead. Leave me to mourn him. I've no wish to spend another day with you, let alone eternity.'

The King looked at her, motionless. He rose and swept out, his face bleak.

'My bed,' the Queen called out, half-fainting, almost falling to the floor. 'Help me to my bed.'

She wanted no one but Ysomir near her; deep in the night, she smiled and whispered, 'You *are* the goddess, Ysomir. How your face shines! I'm glad you've come to take me. Glad.'

Ysomir had sat frozen by the bed for hours, while the physician and the royal embalmer and the endless officials came and went. At last, when all was quiet and the candles were glimmering in a circle around the bed where the Queen's body lay, the King came again.

He stood silently at Ysomir's shoulder, his hands folded in front of him, his deep eyelids lowered. Eventually his hand closed on hers, and he said, 'Come with me now.'

Since that day, the King had kept her in his own quarters.

From her window she could see the Tower; the endless coming and going of guards, overseers, workers. She saw new recruits arriving, innocent and bewildered, as she once had a lifetime ago. She saw carts winding down the hillside, carrying away the bodies of those who had perished.

True to his word, the King never hurt her.

She had her own room, luxurious as a jewelled casket, and he never came to her bed nor even suggested that he might. It was not his seed he wanted to pour into her, but his pain. Every evening, when his royal duties were done, he would seek her out and walk her endlessly around the corridors, the halls and balconies of the Amber Citadel, telling her all that had happened. Sometimes his mood was black, bitter, terrifying; sometimes he would seem almost desiccated with hunger, and then she knew he was near to plucking a victim from the Tower.

Near to it . . . yet clinging to her, clinging as if she could save him from himself. And she tried. Even held onto him physically until he would break from her with a dry shout of anguish, and she would see Laphaeome, as if he'd appeared from nowhere, smiling over his shoulder.

And the dreadful thing was that afterwards – after he had disappeared to his secret chamber and come back to her younger, soft-eyed, tormented with remorse – that was when she came closest to loving him.

'I am going to marry you, Ysomir,' he said softly, kissing her hand. 'You will be my Queen, and we will be immortal together.'

A few days after he had said it – with the Queen only fourteen days dead – he brought her to a tiny office where Laphaeome, Lord Poel and a priestess of Nepheter were waiting. The ceremony was brief and had an air of un-reality. Ysomir and Garnelys were, apparently, conjoined.

She felt no different. Her life did not change. Her days were spent, as before, recording every detail in letters to Tanthe that would never be sent. Her evenings, trying to survive the storm that was Garnelys. Her nights, battling nightmares.

When she tried to think of Lynden, she could hardly even remember what he had looked like.

As spring deepened, so Helananthe's hidden refuge grew. Each day, more rebels came from the surrounding towns and villages; young people fleeing the latest conscriptions, older people whose faith in the King had at long last broken. Now there were close to five thousand, swelling the camp amid the thick-leaved shelter of the forest. Life was hard, but there was an atmosphere of excitement.

Eldareth and Helananthe were training the rebels to fight. Rufryd was put in charge of the archers, Dawn and Mirias of the small band of cavalry. Tanthe and Lynden did their best to pass on the light, graceful and lethal method of sword-fighting that the Shaelahyr had taught them.

News reached them of other rebel pockets scattered about Paranios. A man named Masketh was trying, like Helananthe, to draw some of them together at a hidden encampment in the Serpentine Mountains, just north and west of Parione. Messengers came and went between them, at great risk. And there were rumours of an uprising in Thanmandrathor; too far away for the separate groups to help each other, but heartening news none the less.

Helananthe was a forceful, decisive personality, but strangely, Tanthe felt no particular awe of her. Perhaps it was the circumstances in which they'd met, but from the start she felt no qualms about arguing with her, princess or no. Helananthe was no delicate flower; she had spent time with the army, she had ridden and travelled as hard as anyone there. She never stood on ceremony and she liked a drink. By turns, Tanthe loved her, hated her, envied her, admired her.

'We don't *want* to fight,' Helananthe said, a few days after Eldareth had returned. She was holding a meeting over dinner in her tent, with Eldareth and Saphaeyender as her guests; and because they were there, Rufryd, Lynden and Tanthe were invited also, with Dawn and

Mirias, and a handful of others. The air was scented with crushed grass; lamps gleamed bronze, flashing gold from cups of wine. The Mediator, Rathroem, sat at her left hand, listening but saying little. 'However, we may be forced to it. It would be foolish to be unprepared.'

'And your aim?' said the Mediator.

'Rathroem, we talked about this endlessly on our travels.'

'You have talked to me, but not to these people.'

'Well, Eldareth knows. I don't want to throw my weight about. I don't mean to bring the royal edifice crumbling down. The one thing I mean to achieve is to speak to my grandfather.'

'Isn't it a bit late for that?' said Eldareth.

'I can't accept it! My father tried to reason with him and was killed; I tried and had to flee for my life. I know that if I went to the Amber Citadel alone, I would be arrested if I even set foot in the lower gatehouse. But if I arrive with a force of his own citizens around me, he will be forced to listen to me.'

'Do you really believe you can change his mind?'

'I don't know, but I must make a final attempt. I have some information now that I lacked before. Alas, it's dreadful news. The worst of news. But at least this knowledge, once made public, will make a difference!'

'Well?' said Eldareth. 'You've been chewing at this secret ever since we arrived. Is it so very hard to spit it out?'

Helananthe took a long draught of wine and her voice fell. 'The architect, Laphaeome, is no Mediator. I fear that he is Bhahdradomen.'

Eldareth put both hands to his head and groaned. 'Not this. Of all the things we feared, not this!' He struck the table in anger. 'How is it possible?'

There was a pause. Helananthe's mouth twisted wryly. 'The strange thing about that was not that you are so shocked, Eld; it's that the others weren't.' She looked

506

searchingly at Tanthe, Rufryd, Lynden.

'I am shocked,' said Tanthe. 'It's just that, after everything we've been through, I'm not particularly surprised.'

'Neither am I,' said Lynden. 'I've known it for a long time, your highness.'

'No titles,' she said. 'I've warned you about that before. How could you have known it, Lynden?'

'I don't know.' With his head bowed, lamplight shining gold in his chestnut hair, he calmly told her about their encounters on their journey. He was shaking by the time he finished; it was Saphaeyender, oddly, who touched Lyn's arm to comfort him. 'I think we've known from the very start, but none of us could admit it.'

Helananthe looked sombrely at him; as if, Tanthe thought, she realised there was more to peasants than met the eye.

'Since the Silver Plains, the Bhahdradomen have been too weak to launch an attack on us. They wouldn't dare. But somehow this creature has played on the King's insecurity and ego and now controls him; or indeed, he may well be obsequiously doing the King's bidding, but the end result is the same. The only way we are going to free the King is to break into the Amber Citadel, capture this Laphaeome and make my grandfather understand what has happened. Even if he won't speak to me, he must listen to Rathroem. The monarch is bound by ancient custom to give audience to a Mediator. When he sees a true Mediator, then he will understand.'

Tanthe said, 'How do you know he *doesn't* understand?'

'What do you mean?'

'Why are you so sure that the King hasn't done all of this of his own free will – that he's controlling the architect, not the other way round?'

Helananthe coloured. 'Because my grandfather is a good man at heart.'

'And wise, and strong?' Tanthe went on. 'That's what we were always taught and that's why it's like a knife through the heart to find out it's not true! If he was tricked, he can't be infallible. So, either he is good but feeble-minded, or he is canny and evil.'

There was a shocked silence; even Rufryd and Saphaeyender seemed uncomfortable. Helananthe stared hard at Tanthe, but she held the look.

'Well,' Helananthe said at last. 'That is something to ponder, Tanthe. I don't want to believe it, as you see.'

'No, I don't blame you.'

'We shall find out the truth when I see him face to face.'

'I'll tell you something else to think about,' said Rufryd. 'If all these folk are coming to us, it won't be long before the King's men know. And with these fires going every night, it won't take them long to find us, either.'

'Don't fear,' said Eldareth. 'The time is coming when we *want* them to find us.'

King Garnelys haunted the living quarters below the Tower, moving like a spectre through the dank caves and dungeons that housed his workers. The walls echoed with racking coughs, the dull murmur of voices, the occasional bark of a guard. Now and then he saw someone who was still succulent, not yet worn away by illness or roughened by work. He would catch their eye, but where he hoped for recognition and awe, he found only blank dread. Whispers followed him. *Old grey-bones.*

Agony, trying to choose one. But he must do it. Laphaeome and the Xauroma and his own dark hunger demanded it.

He saw no one to compare with Ysomir. No one who held, like a vessel of light, all that Aventuria had once meant to him. Still, there was only one Ysomir.

The conscripts were quiescent. Good. He had needed to see that for himself.

Earlier in the day, he had spent several hours in the Sun Chamber listening to the grim reports of his scouts and lieutenants. Lord Poel had been there with his aide

Derione at his side, attending gravely.

'Sire, we face a regrettable situation,' said General Grannen. His broad face was red with disgruntlement at having to deliver news that reflected badly on him, but at least he was honest. 'Some of your subjects are in open rebellion. Acting on information that the townsfolk were harbouring Saphaeyender and other traitors, we conducted a routine search of Nachillei, during which the townsfolk attempted blatant resistance. They were swiftly subdued, but a number fled.'

'And Saphaeyender was not found, I take it.' Garnelys exchanged a black look with Lord Poel.

'I'm afraid not, sire. Saphaeyender may have been the catalyst for this, but he's of no consequence now. We have graver problems. As you know, there has been a small-scale rebellion at Napheneth. We are doing our utmost to contain the situation, of course. But according to our scouts, the renegades of Napheneth and Nachillei are trying to form a rebel army in the Forest of Lusaniah and—'

'An army?' Garnelys cut him dead. His anger rose, scalding as molten lead. 'Pardon me if I am being pedantic over your choice of terms, General, but only I and certain of my dukes are allowed to form an *army*.'

'Forgive me, sire,' Grannen said flatly. 'The term I should have employed is "rabble".'

'However . . .' Garnelys leaned forward in his tall chair, saw the others stiffening as if he were a snake poised to strike. 'Terms are irrelevant, if you are telling us that a force is being created with the intent of defying us.'

'We must assume that that is their intent. I was about to add that I have had word of another such group forming north of Parione under the command of one Masketh, and other isolated pockets gathering across Paranios. Since there is the continuing unrest in Thanmandrathor to consider—'

'How dare they?' Garnelys was shaking, almost blinded by rage. 'They are my subjects. They know that all I do is

509

for them.' He waved at the window, indicating the Tower. 'This ingratitude is inexplicable. Intolerable!'

Lord Poel nodded. Grannen put back his shoulders, standing broad as a granite wall before him. 'Indeed, sire.'

'Then crush them. Nip this idiocy in the bud. I will not tolerate it.'

'Yes, sire,' the General said easily. 'The matter is in hand.'

'Good.'

Lord Poel's aide cleared his throat. 'Just one thing, sire. The implications . . .'

'What implications, Derione?'

The aide dipped his head apologetically. 'That you will be making war on your own people? Thus endangering the covenant . . .'

Garnelys stared at him, saw the man's nervousness turn to alarm.

Grannen broke in. 'This is not a war. It is restoration of order.'

'Quite.' Even as he spoke, Garnelys realised that he loathed the General. Hated his ruthlessness, his lust for blood and power . . . hated the fact that he needed such men. But there was no one left whom he loved . . . Love had become irrelevant to the endless vista of his life . . . except for Ysomir. 'Still, your point is taken, Derione. I shall give them one chance to surrender without violence. I want you to go to these fools in the forest, General Grannen, and find out what it is that they think they are doing.'

'And then?'

'Warn them that if they do not submit to me, they will die.'

The General's mouth firmed. 'Sire.'

'And all the resources you need shall be yours. Do whatever you must to defeat these traitors.' Garnelys turned his face away, struggling to suppress the black cloud of bitterness, that his own people could not understand him. 'They will rise against me and fall in a day, like moths. But I will endure for ever. When the Heliodor Tower reaches to the heavens . . . then they will fall down before me in awe and repent.'

The men in the room were silent.

'And you who are loyal to me – you shall be rewarded.'

They relaxed, bowing their head in promise and gratitude. Mutual understanding flowed between them; Garnelys raised his head, feeling strong again, ready to seize the new-forged sword of his power.

'One more matter, sire,' said Grannen. 'Although we have swelled the ranks of the army, since so many recruits are occupied on the Tower, I have only a force of twelve and a half thousand at my disposal. Therefore, I request your permission to summon Lord Serpeth of Eisilion and his Ducal army of two thousand. They have pledged their support. They are waiting for your word, just outside the city.'

'Yes, yes. Summon them. Go; carry out our commands.'

The men strode out, leaving Garnelys alone. He stood up, staring at nothing, motionless as a great spider watching his own roiling passion as if it were something separate from him, an insect struggling in the web. In the same state of mind he donned his disguise, a plain hooded robe, and went to the conscripts' quarters.

Quiescent, his workers. Should he reveal himself, assure himself of their loyalty? Would they fall down, kissing his hem in gratitude for letting them work on his great project? Or would they only recoil in terror? He saw the sullen fear in their eyes. It had haunted his dreams for months. It made him want to crush them like beetles under his heel.

'Sire?'

He was returning to the Citadel through the sub-terranean passage, empty-handed, when he became aware of a pale figure walking beside him. Laphaeome.

'Sire, you are troubled.'

511

'You always know,' the King said, soothed. 'My own subjects are plotting to make war on me!'

'But there is nothing to fear. If it comes to war, here and now I pledge you our support in battle.'

'Whose support?' Garnelys looked into the architect's soft, smiling face. 'The Mediators do not take sides.'

'The *Mediators* do not.' Laphaeome simply went on looking at him with that sinister, expectant smile, until Garnelys seemed to see right through the skin to the skull and the brain beneath. 'You have known for a long time, sire,' said the architect, 'what we really are.'

And now he realised there was a second figure beside him. It was the Mediator whom Laphaeome had originally sent to aid the army. Garnelys had only met him once and had never known his name; only the strange title by which Laphaeome had called him, Enabler. Yet that was not a Mediator title . . .

The second figure was taller, but rather stooped; vulture-like. And where Laphaeome was pale, the Enabler was camouflaged; greenish and greyish and shadowy, and his skin was not merely translucent but clear as glass, full of vessels and fugitive colours that came and went across the gel-like flesh.

Strange. Separately, they had not looked like this. Just unassuming quiet mages, wise and self-contained. But now he saw them together, they seemed to become something different, as if they fed each other with a sweaty energy, a nightmarish mutual glee.

Garnelys felt a stomach-sinking pain, but like all his emotions it was distant, lost in the void of his soul. He knew, had always known, but still could not admit it.

'My true name is Zhoaah. My colleague is Gulzhur. We tell you this in order to demonstrate our mutual trust and loyalty.'

'Zhoaah,' Garnelys echoed, turning the names over on his tongue. 'Gulzhur.'

'You have always dealt fairly with us, sire. Our leader

512

Aazhoth has always cooperated fully with the agreement. The Bhahdradomen are not your enemies. How could we be, since we have been at peace for two hundred and fifty years, and you have let us live without interference?'

'This is true,' said Garnelys. He felt the pain growing, spreading to his head, weakening his limbs. 'Aazhoth is wise. I know that you are not our enemy.'

'It's perfectly acceptable, then, for you to have taken us as your helpers.'

'Yes,' he said, thinking, *I have taken Bhahdradomen into my confidence, Bhahdradomen, and I knew what I was doing and yet the part of me that knew refused to connect with my conscious will and so this web of lies . . .*

As Zhoaah walked on his left and Gulzhur on his right, Garnelys became aware that lines of sticky light were flowing between them and that he was caught physically in the web they wove. He was tangled and floating. They carried him along in ropes of glue, of luminous venom, binding him tighter and tighter. And they grinned skull-grins.

'Sire?' said Laphaeome. 'Are you quite well?'

Pain squeezed his chest like a bruise. Sweat ran down under his robes. 'Quite well. Yes, clearly it is acceptable for you to work with me. Yet it is possible that others would not understand, that this arrangement is too . . . progressive for them.'

Gulzhur said, 'Quite so sire, which is why it must remain our secret. But I give you my pledge now that whatever battles you face, we will support you totally. As our *ghelim* have guarded your troops, so they will appear on the battlefield and crush your enemies. They will appear without warning, striking them down with terror. So, tell your General Grannen that he need have no fear. He will always have unseen reinforcements to ensure his victory.'

Garnelys felt that he was falling. Darkness howled around him and the end of the world had come. And yet, as he fell, a surge of elation came spurting up through the horror.

'Yes,' he gasped, reaching out to save himself and clasping the hands of Zhoaah and Gulzhur. Their limbs felt cold and boneless, but they arrested his fall. They raised him up; they had saved him. He had thrown himself body and soul into their hands, trusting them; and in return they would give him all that he wanted. The sweating nightmares seemed a small price to pay.

He felt he could see the whole of Aventuria laid out in front of him and he watched like a god, omniscient; while his people scurried, fought, died, swift and tiny as ants. Even the Bhahdradomen were insignificant. The world sloughed them off like flakes of skin . . . But the King, watching from his eternal vantage point, the Tower, would endure in dark glory for all time.

They helped him through the darkness as he spoke, hoarse-voiced. 'Until now I never realised the true value of your friendship, nor the risks you have taken to prove the sincerity of your intentions. For your pledge of support I thank you from the depths of my heart! Let this moment herald a new age of friendship between your people and mine. It's all falling into place. Garnelys the Kind may be forgotten, but Garnelys who built the Great Tower and first forged true friendship with the Bhahdradomen—'

'He is a King who will endure for ever,' said Laphaeome.

The festival of Firethorn was over, spring in full leaf, and Helananthe growing more anxious by the day. The messengers from Masketh and the other rebel groups had stopped coming; she'd sent out a young lad of her own who had not returned. Now she was sick with worry about him. Had he been intercepted, killed? What hope did she stand, in reality, of defying her grandfather?

The responsibility for all these lives rests on me, Helananthe thought as she watched her followers in the morning light; making fires, cooking, tending their animals. The struggle just to find enough food was endless.

'Can I really move them from here?' she said softly to Eldareth, as he came to her side. 'Let alone make them into an army?'

'Let's hope it doesn't come to that, Hel,' he said.

'I can see no chance that it won't. And I'm simply being realistic.'

They both turned at the sudden thunder of hoofbeats. Mirias, who had been patrolling the forest, came galloping up to them, his horse skidding to a halt before Helananthe. 'King's men, heading this way, ma'am,' he gasped. 'Thirty of them on horseback! They'll be here within fifteen minutes.'

'Thank you.' She looked at Eldareth, feeling surprisingly calm. Relieved, almost. 'Well, this may be the beginning of the end. Help me call everyone together.'

When the mounted party came jog-trotting up the slope to the crown of the hill – all shining leather breastplates, jangling bridles, rich emerald-coloured cloaks – Helananthe was ready. She and Eldareth stood ready to greet them, with Rathroem at her side, Dawn and Tanthe and a few other trusted ones gathered around her. They bore no arms, but she had positioned Rufryd and fifty or so bowmen in the undergrowth and behind walls. She had sent Saphaeyender and his actors to hide in one of the huts, in case they were recognised. The rest of her followers had gathered in an anxious crowd some yards behind her.

Helananthe had pulled the hood of her cloak deep over her head. She was not sure whether or not they would know her and she didn't want to reveal her identity. Not yet.

The man who led the party was a broad, barrel-chested figure, with cropped grey hair and an aura of self-importance. His horse was a dappled-grey destrier, a weight-bearing beast with a thick, arched neck and high-stepping hooves the size of plates. The lieutenant who rode at his side was tall, sallow, vinegar-faced. Seeing the King's insignia on their shoulders – the wheel, the tree and the jewel – she felt a wrench of regret.

'I am General Grannen, sent by King Garnelys,' the commander announced. 'I wish you good day.'

Although Helananthe had heard of Grannen, she had only seen him from a distance. She was glad; it meant he was less likely to recognise her. Oh, but she had heard so much about his ruthless nature, which went against all that Aventuria had once stood for.

'Good day to you,' Eldareth said drily, dipping his head in a polite greeting. 'How may we help you?'

'Lord Eldareth,' Grannen went on, his lips almost disappearing in his fleshy face. 'I might have known. You are an elusive man. And this is . . .?' He looked suspiciously at Helananthe, trying to see her face under the edge of her hood.

'My wife, Lady Vyne,' Eldareth said.

'I never knew that you had a wife. Full of surprises, aren't you? Not least that you are committing a crime of the gravest nature, inciting good subjects to rebel against their King. I have come to give you notice that it must cease.'

'We wish the King no ill will,' said Eldareth, 'but we refuse to be subject to conscriptions, either to build the Tower or to swell the army. To that end we are starting our own community.'

'You are *what*?' Grannen gave an incredulous laugh. 'You know that is impossible.'

Eldareth stood straight as a tree, his black hair tied back and falling long and glossy between his shoulder-blades; his rugged face composed, his tone one of easy authority. Helananthe felt proud of him. 'We do not seek conflict. We ask only to be left alone, and for any who wish to join us likewise to be allowed to do so.'

Grannen's face was toad-grim, but there seemed to be a

smile twitching at the corner of his mouth. He wanted defiance. He wanted a reason to crush them.

'Our action is peaceful,' added Helananthe.

'There is no such thing. Your action is unlawful, period. Disobedience to the King cannot be tolerated.'

'This is protest, not disobedience—'

'Under martial law,' he spoke loudly over her, 'I have the power to put your so-called "community" under immediate arrest. You'll be detained here until you can be taken away.'

'You are taking us nowhere,' Helananthe said passionately. 'We have a right to petition the King before you bring any action against us. It is our right to air our grievances before the King!'

'Under martial law, that privilege has been suspended.'

'Are you refusing our right to be heard?'

She and Grannen locked eyes; his were callously triumphant, hers burning with outrage. '*I* am not refusing. These are the orders of the King himself.'

Rathroem cleared his throat and stepped forward, putting back his pale hood. He looked vulnerable before Grannen, slender and pale as a sapling. 'General Grannen,' he said, 'since you and Eldareth's people are clearly unable to reach an agreement, might I offer myself to mediate between you until a compromise is reached?'

Grannen stared. For a moment he seemed completely thrown off his stroke. 'And you are—'

'Rathroem of the Serpent Isles.'

Grannen expelled his breath in an incredulous laugh. 'You have a Mediator? How?'

'How he came to us is of no relevance,' said Eldareth. 'He is here and even you must appreciate how much weight this adds to our cause.'

'It is one thing to refuse us,' Helananthe added, 'but quite another to refuse a Mediator. If you won't deal with us directly, then Rathroem will speak for us. This is one right that you cannot refuse.'

The ivory figure of the Mediator looked expectantly up at Grannen. But the general only looked away with a sneer. 'Can't I?' he said. 'The King already has Mediators working with him. He doesn't need any more.'

'Are you refusing my services?' said Rathroem.

Grannen leaned down, one thick arm resting across the pommel of his saddle. 'There's nothing to mediate, my friend. I haven't got time for it. Neither has the King.'

'Even the monarch does not have the power to overturn the laws of the land, General!' Helananthe said in fury. 'If you won't be reasonable, I suggest that you leave.'

General Grannen gave a curt, sardonic bow. 'We are going – for now. Meanwhile, you are commanded to stay where you are. Your refuge henceforth becomes your prison camp. Anyone who tries to leave here, anyone who attempts to use violence to defy the King, will be punished with the utmost severity.'

He shortened his reins and the destrier wheeled away, prancing, in a jangle of metal and creaking of leather. His troop turned in formation and jog-trotted after him down the hill.

In silence they watched the soldiers leave. Then Eldareth and Helananthe turned to the others. The bowmen came out from their cover, slinging their bows over their shoulders.

Tanthe said, 'I knew it was too much to hope that this could be resolved peacefully.'

'We did all we could,' said Eldareth, 'but it was inevitable from the start. Now we face a bitter fight, with likely defeat at the end of it. Those who remain – live or die, at least we shall not have failed to fight for the freedom of Aventuria! If you've no stomach for it – run after the General now and give yourselves up.'

No one moved.

'It's not over yet,' said Helananthe, flinging back her hood. She placed her hand at Rathroem's back. 'We're not staying here like sheep in a pen. I don't care what Grannen says. Once we reach the Amber Citadel, the King *must* listen to our Mediator!'

Early the next morning, Tanthe awoke with a start and a cry of pain. Something had burned her.

'What's wrong?' said Saphaeyender, waking up beside her.

The Aelyr knife was under her hand. She usually kept it beside the mattress; she must have grabbed it in her sleep, and the round moonstone was burning her palm. Trembling, she lifted the knife by the scabbard; the *liroth*-stone pulsed with brilliant iridescence.

'Gods,' said Saphaeyender. 'I didn't really believe it . . .'

But Tanthe was already scrambling from their bed, rushing outside wrapped in her cloak. It was still dark, a few streaks of silver fingering through the cloud. She almost ran straight into Lynden, who was standing outside the tent he shared with Rufryd, looking befuddled with sleep.

He saw the glowing knife and froze, wide-eyed. 'Tanthe, I've just had the vilest dream,' he said.

'We have to warn Helananthe,' she said, seizing his arm and pulling him at a run towards the princess's tent. Rufryd emerged, disturbed by Lynden, and followed them.

'What is it?' he said.

'What do you think?' she said, drawing the knife from its scabbard so it would be ready for use. The blade glinted like lightning. Then – just as Helananthe and Eldareth lifted the tent flap and peered at them from the dark interior – the knife went dead.

'Is something wrong?' Helananthe said, lacing her shirt and trying to tidy her tangled hair.

'I – I don't know,' Tanthe said. She looked at the dull grey knife, stunned; then slipped it back into the scabbard. 'Lynden had a bad dream.'

Her mouth twisted. 'You woke us up for a bad dream?'

'I, for one, take Lynden's dreams seriously,' said

Eldareth. He pulled his boots on, tucked his shirt into his breeches, and came out into the sharp morning air. Blue twilight was slipping down between the tangled dark masses of foliage. 'We had better have a look round.'

'I'm coming with you,' said Helananthe. 'So, what was your dream, Lynden?'

'It's hard to say,' he sighed. 'It's more a feeling than anything. A terrible feeling, like falling down a white tunnel, and these images just out of the corner of my eye . . .' he swallowed, shuddering. 'I hate talking about it. It's gone now.'

Helananthe patted him on the shoulder. 'Let's hope it was just a nightmare, eh?'

The five of them picked their way cautiously between the tents and makeshift dwellings, looking this way and that. Nothing seemed amiss; the camp was beginning to stir. Horses tethered by the tents had their muzzles down to the grass. Tanthe and her companions moved beyond the camp and into the woods, working their way in a circle around the hill-top. The woods were full of indigo shadow, their leaves black against the glimmer of dawn. And the stillness was almost too intense, as if the wood held its breath, and the birds dared not sing.

Helananthe saw it first. She caught her breath. Tanthe perceived something white on the ground, luminous in the gloom, a heap of fabric like a blanket thrown down.

They went closer. Eldareth bent to the heap, pulled back an edge of material, and groaned. 'Gods,' he said, closing his eyes. When Helananthe bent down to see what he had seen, she fell to her knees and wept.

It was Rathroem.

The Mediator lay dead, the whiteness of his robe stained with a splash of blood from throat to thigh. Tanthe's hand flew to her mouth; tears of shock filled her eyes. But Rufryd bent down to the body and lifted two frayed edges of material to reveal the fatal wound, a gaping crimson slot over his heart, as if whatever weapon had killed him had punched straight through his breast-bone.

'I've seen this before,' he said.

'What?' said Helananthe, glaring at him through her tears.

'This type of wound,' Rufryd said bluntly. 'It's what the Bhahdradomen do. They don't use a weapon. Just stick their hand straight in—'

'Stop,' Helananthe said. 'Please, stop. He was my friend. Oh, gods, Rathroem, I'm so sorry; I brought you into this.'

They were motionless around the small body, stunned.

'It's my fault,' said Lynden. 'If only I'd woken up sooner, realised what it meant!'

Tanthe slipped her arm round him. 'We weren't to know.'

'But what use are these stupid visions if I can't . . .'

'This is unheard of,' said Helananthe, opening her hands helplessly over the body in a protective gesture. 'Mediators are sacrosanct. No one kills them!'

'So what are we to make of this?' said Eldareth. He straightened up, folding his arms. 'The King is so hand-in-glove with the Bhahdradomen that Grannen sent one to do his dirty work?'

'The message is clear,' Helananthe said. She dried her eyes and rose, standing fierce and resolute over her fallen friend. 'This is war.'

Seven days later, Helananthe's company was on the march.

They'd been delayed a few days by the presence of the King's men in the forest, small patrols sent by Grannen to keep watch on the rebel encampment. Helananthe knew that the moment they broke camp, spies would be winging their way back to the General with the news. Then, strangely, the patrols had vanished. Called to another crisis – or hoping to lure the rebels out of their hiding place?

Whatever the reason, she could wait no longer. In

521

defiance of Grannen's orders, she was leading her followers towards Parione. Some had stayed behind, the old to take care of the children. But all the able-bodied left Enhavaneya, passed through the tangled woods of Lusaniah and on to the ancient Meiondras Road which wound through the lush green hills of Paranios to the city. Their number was just above four thousand.

Helananthe and Eldareth rode resolutely at the head of the long column. Their progress was slow; the majority were on foot, and to make and break camp each day was a laborious process complicated by the constant need to find fresh water and food.

She meant to head straight to the Amber Citadel and demand an audience with her grandfather. Their coming would be no secret, and everyone knew they would encounter obstruction and probably a full-blown battle at some stage. But they weren't afraid; better to meet their fate head-on than wait passively for it to crush them. Anger made Helananthe bloody-minded. If only they could join forces with Masketh, they might stand a chance against Grannen.

As they made camp on the fifth evening – still some six days' march from Parione – Helananthe felt a wrongness in the atmosphere. She'd felt it before, but never so intensely. She had no direct experience of the Xauroma; that was a mystery into which she would not be initiated until her coronation. All the same, she could sense it. Standing outside her tent on a slope above the wide valley, she looked up and noticed a weird purplish cast to the sky. Saw dra'a'ks hurtling over like leaves on a gale. Felt the land itself thrumming with distress, stretched to an unbearable tension.

The power of it rent her heart. To touch the earth's life-force was an awesome privilege and a terrifying burden. Too much for Garnelys . . . too much for anyone.

Then Helananthe saw the figure. A man, riding hard along the dusky hills into the camp. He was coming straight at her, his roan horse gaunt and stumbling with exhaustion, his clothes ragged and his face skull-thin. Eldareth and others saw him and called out, running to gather around her.

'My lady,' the man gasped, reaching her. As his horse stopped – head down and lungs wheezing – he did not so much dismount as tumble from the saddle in front of her. Keeping his feet with effort, he stood swaying, his raw eyes meeting hers. Then she recognised him. It was her lost messenger, the one she'd sent to find the other rebels, many days ago; bright-faced no longer but pallid and starved. 'My lady, Masketh is dead.'

He lurched forward and would have collapsed if she hadn't caught him. Eldareth and Rufryd rushed to hold him upright; but for a moment his young face had been an inch from hers, pouring all his despair into her. Helananthe felt a long cold wave of dread. 'What happened?'

'A terrible battle,' he said hoarsely, pointing in the direction of Parione, 'in the foothills of the Serpentines. Grannen brought his army, demanded that Masketh surrender, but he refused. Grannen's force was not as great as we had feared. Masketh's people were outnumbered, but only by a few hundred; they stood a fair chance. They fought once and Grannen's men seemed to be in retreat. But they reformed and turned to fight again, so the second battle began—' He broke off, struggling for breath. Tanthe brought him a cup of water, but he knocked it out of her hands and went on, wild-eyed. 'But something was wrong. The sky was a terrible colour, filled with boiling clouds. A – a *smell*, like metal or blood. A feeling of terror, far worse than just the fear of battle. Then – the two sides engaged and the sky exploded.'

'Exploded?' Helananthe said quietly, as he paused for breath.

'Flying creatures came bursting out of the clouds. I saw them. Shadows, terrible huge shadows of dra'a'ks. They swooped on Masketh's people – only on his, not Grannen's – and they killed and killed. Wherever Grannen's soldiers were not, the flying demons were. Slaughter. Between the King's men and the demons, Masketh's side were slaughtered. I saw it – I fled. I don't know how I found you. I'll never forget the sky.'

There was a deadly silence. Helananthe was speechless. The messenger looked at her with bewildered eyes, like a child whose world had turned to nightmare.

'What were they, my lady?' he implored. 'What did I see?'

'I don't know,' she whispered.

The man passed out, falling so heavily that he slipped from Rufryd's and Eldareth's hands and slumped face down on the grass. It was only then that they all saw the wounds in the messenger's back; six long red gouges, running parallel, as if a claw had rent him through clothes and flesh.

Chapter Twenty-Two. The Battle of Hethlas Rim

General Grannen sat gazing down at the battlefield in satisfaction, his gauntleted fist firm on the reins. Below him, the corpses of Masketh's rebels lay all over the churned valley; purple gore mingling with mud. Rags of cloud drifted like smoke over the silent field. Dra'a'ks were circling beneath the blood-red bowl of sunset, settling on the carrion; and Grannen could not even tell whether these were true dra'a'ks or the savage mimics sent by the Lord Mediator to aid him.

All across Paranios, bands of rebels were being crushed by the King's army in chaotic, nasty little battles. Not civil war, no. Restoration of order. The naive inexperience of the rebels hardly provided a challenge worthy of the label 'war'.

Masketh, though, had been of a different order – but he was dead. Those of his supporters who were not food for the dra'a'ks had surrendered. There was still Eldareth's rabble to deal with, however, and that should have been so easy . . .

Grannen's eyes narrowed in calculation. *Should* have been easy, if only he had not had to dispatch half his force into Thanmandrathor. The unrest that had bubbled there since the beginning had suddenly erupted into open rebellion; an unsuspected mass of them, eight thousand strong, pouring from the mountains to disrupt the perfectly legal business of the King. Grannen was still furious at the incompetence of those officers who had allowed such a force to gather in total secrecy. Too late; he'd had no choice but to send nearly seven thousand of his soldiers to deal with it. It was stretching his resources too thin. The King hardly seemed to care. His Royal commands must be carried out as if by magic; he'd become deaf to any suggestion of difficulty.

Now, because of the trouble with Masketh, Grannen could not rearm and move his troops to intercept Eldareth until the rabble were uncomfortably close to the city. Thank the thunder-gods, then, for Lord Serpeth's pledge of help. Grannen had learned to put aside some of his Torith Mirian pride and use anything and anyone that would keep him where he was; in favour with the King and in a position of unassailable control.

After what had transpired on the blood-stained sweep of the field below him, he had every confidence in the occult knowledge of the Mediators. So, let Eldareth's makeshift army come to the very edge of Parione. Grannen was looking forward to the encounter. He would relish seeing those hidden beasts of death spreading terror once more.

Now Helananthe's troops travelled in a mood of subdued anxiety, watching the skies like mice in fear of owls. Again she had given them the choice of surrendering to the King and thus (for a while) saving their own lives. But, as one, they had vowed to follow her into death rather than submit to Grannen.

Tanthe felt angry that she had even questioned their commitment, and told her so. Helananthe had borne her anger with grace and at last said simply, 'Then we go on, whatever happens.'

The journey had taken ten days so far, bringing them among the Hethlas Hills just west of the city. Some of their number – the unfortunate messenger included – had fallen by the wayside through illness or injury, though Helananthe always tried to ensure they would be looked after. Tanthe found it frustrating, mounted on swift Redbird, that they could only travel at the pace of those on foot. Lynden and Rufryd felt the same. Sometimes they discussed leaving, and making for Parione on their own . . . but although they talked of it, they knew their best hope lay in the strength of Helananthe's army. They were all more frightened than they would admit.

The Princess had explained that she meant to head directly to the Amber Citadel. So far, no one had come to stop them. Small patrols of King's soldiers watched them pass, so their coming was no secret; yet they met no resistance. It was unnerving, that they were being allowed so close; just as if Grannen were taunting them with the prize, teasing out their hopes to the agonising extreme.

On the tenth evening they came to a place Eldareth called Hethlas Rim; a long ridge running at one end into a high escarpment. Saphaeyender was riding beside Tanthe; Eldareth had found horses for him and his actors, though they were all only marginally happier on horseback than they would have been on foot. Ashtar, Evender, Sharm and Saliole moaned constantly so Tanthe kept out of their way; but Saphaeyender, at least, seemed to have learned his lesson about complaining.

As they rode onto the long summit of the hill, Tanthe caught a glint of gold on the horizon. It was too far away in the folded green hills to see clearly. 'What's that?' she asked.

'That, my dear, is Parione,' Saphaeyender said wistfully.

She gaped at him. 'Don't tease me. It can't be.'

'But it is, I promise you.'

'We're almost there! I can't believe I'm looking at it!'

'But will we be allowed to reach it?' he said gravely.

Parione lay east of Hethlas Rim. There, on the western slope of the ridge, they made their last camp. When they had put up their tents, lit campfires and eaten their evening meal, Tanthe waited until all was quiet. Then she slipped away on her own, took Redbird and rode towards the escarpment at the north end of the ridge. It curved east as well as north, taking her several miles nearer to the city. There she rode up onto a promontory, and saw a view that took her breath away.

The sun was setting, the three moons hanging low in the sky. Beneath them, on three great hills and innumerable smaller ones, lay Parione.

Her first sight of the city of dreams.

The plains were flooded with gold, and the city itself shone golden in the rich, fading light. She saw the vague shapes of buildings, sinking into violet shadow on the lower slopes while on the peaks their roofs still caught the light. And there was the Amber Citadel itself. A proud diadem on the greatest hill, its sheer walls and turrets gleaming, just as she'd imagined and yet different; distant, solid, poignantly real.

Tears filled her eyes. Just to see it . . . Gods, how she'd dreamed of seeing it; but never in such circumstances as these.

Right of the Citadel rose a gentler hill, crowned with a domed temple; the temple of Nepheter, patron goddess of the city. To the left of the Citadel she could make out the third hill, and what seemed a great stump rearing from it. It looked out of proportion against the grace of the city. Too big . . .

Gods, the Tower!

That was where the theatre should have been. She tried to blot out the dreadful Tower and to see the theatre in its place until her eyes watered. The accursed Tower . . .

Her stomach roiled. She felt the Aelyr knife turn hot against her breast. Suddenly afraid, she looked around, feeling that she was being watched. Was that a tree stump amid a stand of trees on the next rise . . . or a stooped, cloaked figure? Her heart froze. The shape was motionless and yet it seemed to be watching the road, the Meiondras Road that ran from Parione, weaving through the hills towards them.

She looked down at the road. It was growing dark, but the moons' light caught the loose, snaking movement of scores of men and horses marching towards the hills. The tree stump seemed to move and she saw two pale eyes blazing at her. The look turned her weak, like two sickly rays that drained all her spirit. In panic, she took the Aelyr knife from her pocket. The moonstone shone brilliantly; the figure made a faint hiss, and vanished.

Whatever had possessed her to come out here alone? Thoroughly alarmed, she turned Redbird, urged her into a gallop and flew back towards the camp.

It was still dark, an hour before dawn, but already the camp was stirring. Lynden had not been able to sleep; now, just as tiredness overcame him, he was forced to rise. He went outside to spend a few quiet minutes with Halcyon. There was a heavy dew. The horses were grazing softly between the tents but he could hear the sound of people rising, yawning, complaining. Then Helananthe's clear voice again, urging them to arms.

'Rise and shine, in the image of Anuth! Let us be ready before that sluggard Grannen has even opened his eyes!'

Thanks to Tanthe's warning the previous evening, they were ready. Grannen's troop had made camp on the lower hills on the Parione side, out of their sight. Last night, Helananthe and Eldareth had gathered the whole camp and discussed their battle strategy in detail. Now they were up early to take up position on the high ground before Grannen had a chance to get there first.

They had trained hard. They knew what was expected of them. But putting it into practice, with no second chances – that was a different matter.

The morning had an air of unreality. They ate a quick breakfast – Lynden sitting with Rufryd and Tanthe, Saphaeyender and Eldareth, just as they had for many weeks past. No one said much; the others were cheerful, but Saphaeyender looked ghastly.

Then Lynden and Rufryd went back into their tents and helped to equip each other. They'd decided to wear their black, ornate Sepher clothes for the battle; to go down in glory, if they must. Over this they put on leather breastplates and greaves, then their weapons. They each had their long Aelyr sword on the left, a short sword on the right, a bow and a quiver packed with arrows they'd fashioned themselves at Enhavaneya.

'Well, little brother,' Rufryd said, 'this is it. Got any weird feelings about today?'

'Nothing,' Lynden said, and smiled. 'That's a good omen, I think. I wish Father could see us.'

'He'd be proud,' Rufryd said, clasping Lyn's shoulders. 'Of you, at any rate.'

'Do you think we'll stand a chance?'

'Of course. If you're feeling scared, just keep one thing in mind; you might see Ysomir tonight!'

'I'm not scared, though,' said Lynden. 'That's the odd thing. I'm really not.'

Rufryd gave his shoulders a last squeeze, and turned away. He seemed upset, and trying not to show it. Lynden clapped him on the back, trying to encourage him in return, but there seemed nothing else to say. 'Breyid go with us, eh?'

'Mahaa is more like it,' said Rufryd. 'Or Anuth on our side and Nuth waiting for Grannen.'

Lynden laughed. 'You ought to show the gods a bit more respect, for one morning at least. I'm glad it's nearly over, aren't you?'

'Yeah,' said Rufryd, looking more cheerful. 'Yes, I am.'

Dawn was drifting violet above Parione, but the ground still lay in darkness. Tanthe was almost ready to mount Redbird when Saphaeyender came to her through the gloom. He looked strange in forest-green shirt and breeches, boots and breastplate, a sword at his side, a wooden shield in one hand. And yet he looked so elegant, so different that she felt a surge of desire for him, and an equal wave of fear.

'Ready?' she said.

He took a long, shaky breath. 'As I'll ever be. You look

magnificent, Tanthe. Don't get hurt, will you?'

She went to him and took his hand. She felt nervous, but he was trembling so badly his whole body shook. 'Oh, Saph, are you all right?'

'No, Tanthe, I'm really not,' he said, trying to sound flippant. 'I told you I was a coward. What I didn't expect was to feel quite this bad.'

'Gods, Saph, you don't have to fight. Saliole and Sharm are staying back at the camp; why don't you stay with them?'

'I don't want to be quite that useless,' he said.

'You wouldn't be. They need people to help with the wounded.'

'No.' His eyes were bleak; he wouldn't look at her. 'I must do this.'

'Why?' she said in sudden fear, holding his arm. 'What are you trying to prove? No one will think any the less of you for not going into battle. You're not a soldier, for the heaven's sake. You're not just *anyone*; you're Saphaeyender! If you die, what about all the wonderful things that you'll never write? You can't deprive the world of that!'

'Oh, Tanthe.' His arms went round her and he held her, his lips pressing kisses on to her hair. 'You don't understand. How can I presume to write those "wonderful things" if I haven't fought for the right to do it? If I want my world back as it was, I have to earn it.'

'No,' she said. 'I do understand. And will you please stop kissing me, it's making me want to cry.'

'Afterwards, then,' he said. And she could see how hard he was trying to seem brave; especially as Rufryd and Lynden came out of the shadows.

'This is it, then,' said Rufryd. 'Take care, Tan.'

'For goodness's sake, we'll see each other again in a few hours!' she exclaimed. He and Lynden hugged her in turn; she kept it brief, pushing them away with mock brusqueness. 'Stop it, this is horrible,' she said, uncomfortably close to tears. 'Battles are never anything like you expect, anyway.'

'How do you know?' Rufryd exclaimed.

'I've read about them in books,' Tanthe retorted.

By the time Grannen's vinegar-faced lieutenant rode out to Helananthe's encampment, her army were already in battle formation on Hethlas Rim. Blocks of infantry in the centre, lines of archers in front. The cavalry division commanded by Mirias was on the right flank; Tanthe was in the front row, Lynden further back on the outside. Rufryd was with Dawn's mounted division on the left flank. And Saphaeyender was with the infantry, near the rear, fighting alongside peasants who probably didn't even know who he was. Reluctant as Helananthe had been to let him fight, in the end she could find no good reason to refuse him.

It was good, high ground with wiry grass and a covering of trees, giving an excellent view of the valley below and the low hills opposite. When Grannen attacked, he would have to do so upwards, putting him at a disadvantage.

Helananthe and Eldareth, both mounted on dark brown destriers, were on a knoll behind and between the left flank of the infantry and Dawn's cavalry. This was their command position but they had raised no standard. Her banner was the King's, and since she was fighting the King, she could not in all conscience use it.

The lieutenant, as he came trotting up to the knoll on a thin chestnut, was obviously displeased to find the opposing army so well-prepared.

'I bear a message from General Grannen,' he said, addressing Eldareth, whom he believed to be the sole leader. 'Any attempt to enter Parione will be treated as an act of treason. Failure to surrender immediately will be regarded as an act of hostility. You have half an hour to lay down your weapons and give yourselves up.'

Eldareth laughed. 'I think not. If he wants hostility, we're ready for him.'

'I have a message for General Grannen,' said Helananthe, throwing her hood back and glaring into the messenger's sour face. 'This company is not being led by Eldareth alone. Tell him that his opponent is Princess Helananthe. Tell him that I will regard any attempt to defy a member of the royal family as treason! Let's see if he is still so eager for a fight!'

The first honeyed shafts of the sun were touching the hills as the lieutenant returned to Grannen's position. Helananthe and Eldareth now had leisure to take in the scene. She raised her telescope to her eye.

The King's army were still manoeuvring into position, in roughly the same formation as her own; archers and skirmishers in front, a tightly-packed phalanx of foot-soldiers behind, cavalry on the flanks. They were in the valley, Grannen himself up on a small hill behind them. She was too far away to recognise him, but she saw the standard rippling and shining as the red-gold sun found it. As the light slid lower, it drew gorgeous colour from the ranks of the King's army; green, purple, gold, leather dyed and burnished in violet and chestnut. Azure feathers on the officers' helmets. The shining dark chestnut horses with manes and tails of gold. Her own force were ragamuffins by comparison, arrayed in an assortment of garments, worn out and mud-coloured from months in the wildwood. Horses all different shapes and sizes. But they had passion . . . passion enough to compete with loyalty to Garnelys? *Or with shadow-demons that burst from the sky and perhaps are – no, don't think it!*

'How many would you say are down there?' she asked.

'I would estimate he has about four thousand foot and fifteen hundred cavalry,' said Eldareth.

'We are outnumbered,' said Helananthe, 'though not as badly as I feared we would be. It's even enough. We can win.' And the sky was clear; no hideous clouds nor stench of blood such as the messenger from Masketh's battle had described . . . no sense of anything sinister . . . but that had

533

not come until the second battle, had it? She drew a deep breath. The truth was, if the demons appeared, they had no plan to defeat them. Archers firing arrows into the sky, that was all . . . The only thing was to win this battle decisively and they could, they must.

And then she saw.

Several hundred yards over to Grannen's right, half-hidden by his command hill, there were another two thousand men. These were all in red and bronze, with flashes of bright blue, their horses black and powerful.

'Oh gods, Eldareth, do you see?'

She passed him the telescope. He cursed. 'That's all we need. What's their uniform?'

'Lord Serpeth of Eisilion,' she said. 'Lord Serpent, more like; he always was a slithery bastard.'

'You wouldn't be saying that if you were fighting on the King's side against a common enemy, Helan.'

She didn't answer. She felt no pride in what she'd brought to fruition. No bravado. She was only sick that it had come to this.

Her horse shifted. The lines were almost silent; a breeze rose and fluttered over them. Then the high note of Grannen's horn sounded, and his lines began to advance on hers.

Rufryd's heart was pounding with excitement. He saw Grannen's soldiers coming, uniforms glowing and weapons glinting in the right light; then the high note of Eldareth's horn, and their own archers unleashing shower upon shower of arrows. His fingers itched; he wanted to be down there with them. But he'd had to choose between fighting on foot or horseback and he could not give up Sunhawk to someone else . . .

Retaliation came from Grannen's archers. Arrows fountained darkly in both directions. Soldiers on both sides began to fall; his pulse accelerated, excitement twining with horror. He stood up in his stirrups to see better.

Their quivers empty, the archers were moving aside to let the men-at-arms through. Sounds of shouting filled the air; swords and shields clashed. Spears flew into the ranks of Grannen's men; they seemed to waver, but then they came on again, tightly-formed, their shields bigger and stronger than the rebels', so that they seemed impenetrable even though they were fighting uphill. The line of fighting swayed back and forth.

Then came the horn blast he'd been waiting for. The signal to charge. Dawn set off at the head, whooping, her hair a blazing copper beacon. All around him horses were leaping forward and Sunhawk was galloping with them. Rufryd's sword was in his hand; his ears were filled with the thundering of hooves, of his own heart. The King's powerful chestnut horses were charging to engage them. He wasn't afraid. Urging his horse on he opened his mouth and roared—

Glossy horses careened past him, attacking the riders on either side. He saw the rush of colour, violet and green, long carven faces under helmets, eyes narrow and teeth bared. He fixed on one and that man was going to be his first—

The steel flash of a spear came from nowhere. It happened before he could think, let alone act. Sunhawk ran straight on to it.

The horse squealed, did an arrested half-leap and fell, pitching Rufryd onto the grass. He fell heavily, winding himself. For several chaotic seconds, horses were galloping all around him, dodging, leaping clean over him. When a lull came, he took his arms from around his head and looked up.

Sunhawk was dead. The shaft protruded from his chest and blood pumped from the wound, turning his brown coat black; but his eye stared glassy at the heavens. Sobbing, Rufryd crawled towards him. At least he'd died instantly, not suffered.

He used Sunhawk's bulk to shelter him as he fumbled

for his bow and arrows. His shock hardened to rage. He began to fire one shaft after another, sending two men and two women flying out of the saddle, taking another two who were unhorsed. He was panting for breath, his lips drawn back from his teeth, sweat prickling his whole body. When his arrows were gone he threw the bow aside, took up his Aelyr sword, and ran towards the main crush of the battle.

On the far side of the field Tanthe waited, breathless. Time seemed suspended as the King's lines advanced, both sides in perfectly clean formation – and then came the first bombardment of arrows, falling like strange, clattering rain. Men and women began to die. The foot soldiers clashed, desperate shouts clamoured in the air, and there on the far side was Rufryd's division charging to meet the King's . . .

She was suddenly, desperately worried for all the others, knowing she couldn't reach them, that they were all on their own and this was for real. Nothing could stop it now.

Then came the signal for Mirias's riders to charge. All at once everything was happening too fast. Redbird leapt forward with the other horses, wildly eager, and they were galloping downhill, the wind surging into her face. Exhilarating, terrifying.

Something went wrong. The King's cavalry came charging into them in a tight wedge, splitting Mirias's division down the middle. Tanthe was on the inside, nearest to the foot-soldiers; Lynden a long way over to the outside, sundered: Tanthe stood no chance of seeing what had happened to him.

All became chaos. The horse next to her fell, run through by a spear. A soldier came charging straight at her from the right; Redbird shied and reared, and the next thing Tanthe knew she was on the ground.

Somehow she'd kept hold of the reins. Now a man was bearing down on her from the left. She ducked the swing of his sword, twisted round and up and slashed her longer,

536

sharper sword under his raised arm. She caught him across the belly in the gap under his breastplate. Blood poured from the slash and he doubled over the saddle, his horse carrying him away. Catching her breath, Tanthe vaulted up into the saddle again and sent Redbird flying after the main body of the cavalry. Wild energy filled her. Another rider in green bore down, his blade shining, intent on killing her; she tried to rally all the tricks Alraen had taught her. The Shaelahyr rhythm took her; she dodged and struck out and he fell, his head half severed. Her razor-sharp blade was red with gore.

Shock flashed through her but there was no time to indulge it. She was in the thick of battle and her blood hammering with fever. There was no order, no time to think nor to help anyone else. Every frantic mote of energy she possessed was channelled into keeping her horse and herself alive.

One moment Lynden was charging straight down the flank of the hill in formation. The next, the King's cavalry came exploding into their ranks and Halcyon was suddenly being forced aside, carried along with a knot of horses split from the main force.

The last thing he'd expected was this shambles. Halcyon was bolting; Lynden managed to get him under control, enough to glance back at the field of battle. He couldn't see the main action, only the rise just behind him where sundered cavalry were trying to turn back and engage the King's force. But it was hopeless; they were being driven out of the battle, riders and horses falling, others fleeing in Lynden's direction. He reined in; Halcyon came to a prancing skidding stop. Lynden was transfixed, flooded with horror at the sight of horses dying; pierced by spears.

His companions galloped on and he was left alone on the hillside, but he hardly noticed. His mind was whirling. *How mad, how stupid could I have been, to think that they would not attack horses?*

Helananthe's fleeing riders were trying to reform further down the hill. He saw a group of King's cavalry splitting off from the rear of the main force and riding in a curve to prevent the scattered riders from regrouping on the flank.

Lynden saw that he was going to be caught in it if he stayed where he was. Worse, Halcyon was going to be killed.

He jumped out of the saddle, turned Halcyon to face away from the field of battle, and gave him a hard whack on the rump. 'Get out!' he yelled. The horse fled, up and over the ridge in the direction of the camp; the last Lynden saw of him was his black tail whipped high by the wind.

It was growing fully light now, but the early shafts of sunlight had been obscured by a blank white mass of cloud. The day had turned flat, grey and shadowless. Lynden saw a mass of Grannen's cavalry bearing down on him and now he was on foot, with no swift means of escape. He began to run, straight across their path, heading for a clump of bushes that he could see a couple of hundred yards to his right, just where the land fell away at an angle to the main slope.

The King's party ignored him; they were intent on engaging some of his companions further up the slope. Lynden stopped, turned. He raised his bow and unleashed three arrows, one after the other. Only one met its target but the man fell heavily, glaring round astonished as he fell, as if he didn't realise where it had come from.

Lynden ran on towards the bushes. The fighting was spreading over the hill above, but it seemed to be mostly Grannen's men now. He meant to get his breath back, to do what he could with the rest of his arrows. After that – he didn't know. But he still had the Aelyr sword and he would fight his way through to Parione alone, if necessary. He felt exhilarated. He'd saved one life, at least; Halcyon's. And he could feel the weird *ethroth* energy whirling inside his mind, not nightmarish as it had been when it alerted him to the Bhahdradomen, but golden and soothing, as if something wondrous were close at hand. He was beginning to feel, for the first time, that it would be his friend after all.

Reaching the bushes he plunged down behind them and found himself rolling into a deep hollow on the hillside; its higher rim concealed by hawthorn and brambles. As he righted himself and got to his knees, he found that he was not alone in the hollow.

Saphaeyender was sitting six feet away from him. Pressed back among the hawthorns, weaponless, his face blanched.

'Lynden,' he said hoarsely. 'Is it over yet?'

Saphaeyender had tried. He'd stood in rank in his block of infantry, jaw gritted, stomach roiling; determined to see this through, to prove that he could live life as well as merely observe it. He had marched forward with the others when the signal came; thrown his javelin (which lodged uselessly in the ground) then drawn his sword. It was all right at first; just until the two sides interlocked and he found a tall, grim-faced soldier of the King facing him . . .

It was far worse than he'd ever dreamed it would be. His flight was a blur. He'd found this refuge and plunged down behind the bushes, fighting to get his breath. He was shaking so hard he could barely move. But he hadn't escaped; he could hear hoofbeats and shouts on the hillside above him. Close to hysteria, all he could do was curl up here while the battle washed over him. No choice. He was paralysed.

And then Lynden appeared, like a saviour.

'No, it's not over!' Lynden exclaimed, crouching like a leopard coiled to spring.

Suddenly a King's soldier strode up onto the lip of the hollow. Saphaeyender shrank back in terror, feeling the end of the world had come – but Lynden was on his feet, and the two men's swords were clashing. How cumbersome and slow the King's man seemed against Lynden's lethal, darting blade . . . A bubbling groan, and the soldier fell dead. Lynden pushed him with his foot as he fell, so the body rolled partway down the hill.

'Saphaeyender!' Lynden cried, crouching down beside him again. He wiped his dripping sword on the grass. 'What are you doing here?'

'He was going to kill me,' Saphaeyender said, his throat stiff with terror. 'This soldier on the battlefield. He hesitated; I'm sure he recognised me. He recognised me but he was still going to kill me! He flicked my sword straight out of my hand. So I ran. I turned and ran, I couldn't stop myself.'

Lynden gripped his wrist. The younger man's eyes were fierce and yet kind, full of light. 'It's all right. Calm down. But you can't stay here, there are King's men swarming all over the hills above us.'

'Leave me,' the poet gasped. He was close to passing out with fear. 'I can't be heroic.'

'You don't need to be, I'll defend you. Just let me get you out of here! I'll take you back to the camp.'

'I can't move. I'm sorry.'

'Hush,' Lynden said. 'All right, maybe if we stay here a while, they'll go past and not see us.' He put a hand on Saphaeyender's chest, pushing him back, while he crouched forward. 'Wait, while I see if it's clear – no, it isn't. Sit tight.'

They pressed back into the bushes together, Saphaeyender still holding Lynden's wrist loosely against him. 'Lyn, you don't have to do this,' he whispered. 'I'm going to die. Save yourself, at least.'

'Shut up!' Lynden hissed.

'No, this is important. I don't expect you to cover up my cowardice, but tell Helananthe I am sorry, and Eldareth and Tanthe that I love them more than life. And you, Lynden . . . I think you are the sweetest-natured person I ever met. You deserve more love than anyone can give

540

you; and I would have tried . . .'

'Saph, stop it, please,' Lynden whispered.

'You could have loved me a little in return. I know it.'

'I'm going to be with Ysomir soon. This isn't fair.'

Lynden's face was flushed, his eyes lowered in confusion. Saphaeyender touched his hot face, just on the cheekbone, but Lynden didn't push his hand away. 'I know you better than you know yourself.'

Running feet pounded past and faded. 'Right,' Lynden said. 'Let's have another try. Can't see anyone . . .'

Saphaeyender felt calmer now. Lynden edged further forward, until he was just peering over the grassy rim of their hiding place. 'Damn! Six more foot-soldiers coming,' he whispered. 'Stay quiet – I'll tell you when they've gone.'

Saphaeyender closed his eyes, trying to slow his breathing. Sweat was running down his back. He waited; there was the strangest noise, something like a whistle, followed by a clap and a grunting outrush of breath. 'What was that?' he said, opening his eyes.

Lynden didn't reply.

'Lyn?'

He was still where he had been, lying down to look over the edge of the hollow. Saphaeyender crawled forward, shook his ankle. 'Lynden!'

No response. His face was down on the grass, his chestnut hair spread like a halo with sparks of gold through it, his arms curved limply beside his head like a sleeping child. It was only when Saphaeyender moved up beside him that he saw the arrow-shaft protruding from Lynden's left shoulder.

It had gone straight in from the top, sinking deep into his lung. Saphaeyender stared at it, a deadly horror gathering in his chest. He touched the uninjured shoulder, gave it the gentlest shake. No reaction. He lifted him, trying to turn him over.

Lynden rolled heavily on to his back and lay there.

Frantic now, Saphaeyender pressed his ear to Lynden's chest, bent his cheek to his lips for the touch of warm breath. Nothing. Lynden seemed to be watching him from under half-lowered lids with eyes of blue glass; sorrowful, loving, sightless.

Saphaeyender screamed.

He shook the lifeless body, planted a kiss on the cooling lips, tugged at the hands and then pressed them to his mouth, soaking them with his grief. And then he looked up and saw a soldier in green and violet beside the bushes above him, just in the very edge of the foliage. The soldier was looking down and grinning.

Saphaeyender seized Lynden's sword and thrust upwards. The man fell with a gargling scream yet Saphaeyender thrust again and again, long after he was dead. And he looked up and saw nothing but blood-red mist. It was roaring in his ears, turning the hillside all to crimson flame; and into the fire he ran headlong, screaming.

Helananthe and Eldareth waited anxiously on their vantage point, watching the ebb and flow of the battle beneath them. It had all gone horribly awry on the right flank, but in the centre and left her army was holding firm. Grannen, though, was fighting fiercely, and she could see no easy end. As yet, he had not deployed Serpeth's force.

She had sent messages for the right flank to retreat and regroup. She sat holding her horse's reins with damp hands, her heart stuck grimly in her mouth.

'Gods, what have we done, Eldareth?' she said. 'Once Serpeth joins the battle, we'll be lost.'

'We've done what we must, love,' Eldareth answered, looking gravely into her eyes. 'Even if we fall today, the King will at least be in no doubt of our feelings.'

There was a surge on the wide slope below. 'Look!' she said.

The rebels were gaining ground. The cavalry on both sides made a new charge and Grannen's men were falling back, his infantry exhausted by the struggle of fighting uphill.

'We've got the upper hand!' she said. 'Wait – if they are retreating only to pull us into a trap, I'm not falling for that. Tell our side to hold back!'

'My thoughts exactly.' Eldareth raised the horn to his lips and blew.

General Grannen watched from a knoll as the battle raged along the hillside and the valley beneath. His fist was clenched on the reins, his face grim. The officers around him waited for his next command.

'The rebels are gaining ground, sir,' said his lieutenant.

'Indeed. What they lack in discipline they make up for in sheer bloody-mindedness. Good; all is going to plan, Kerowen. We begin a controlled retreat, sucking them forward. They rush all unsuspecting into Enabler's trap; meanwhile we move around behind them to cut off their retreat. It should be over within half an hour. I'll stand you all lunch!'

His officers laughed. After a time one said, 'Sir, the rebels do not appear to be taking the bait. They're reforming, moving forward very slowly.'

'Damn Eldareth's cunning. First he thinks he can undermine me with wild lies about Princess Helananthe . . .' Grannen huffed with irritation. 'I'd hoped to win this without Serpeth's help. Clearly that won't be possible. Rolin!'

The young herald rode forward. 'Yes, sir?'

'Ride down to Lord Serpeth and tell him to engage! It falls to him to cut off Eldareth's retreat!'

'Yes sir.' The herald galloped away, the King's standard fluttering from his saddle. Grannen waited until the boy was almost there. Timing was crucial. Then he said, 'Give the signal, Kerowen.'

Kerowen raised a horn to his lips and sounded the signal. A long note, pause, two short notes and another long note.

The signal to the Enabler, that would bring lethal winged monsters swooping down on the King's enemies. Hearing it, his troops down on the field also knew it was time to disengage, leaving the rebels to be massacred.

With a sigh of anticipation, Grannen looked up at the sky. He watched for boiling knots of cloud, tell-tale signs of the monsters bursting through from their own dimension. He didn't know how it worked; he left such arcane matters to the Mediator. All he wanted was the master-stroke.

But the clouds drifted on, smooth and oblivious. 'Sound it again.'

The notes rang out a second time. A third.

Nothing happened.

'Bring Enabler to me!' roared the General.

He waited; ten minutes later, messengers came flocking to him from all corners of the battlefield. All bearing the same news.

'The Lord Mediator Enabler is nowhere to be found, sir.'

Grannen thought quickly. He seized his rage, thrust it down into the pits of his being, and replaced it with cool logic.

'Try again. Don't stop searching until you find him. For now it all depends upon Lord Serpeth.' He looked down at the battlefield. Because his own troops had disengaged, they had been flung into disarray; they couldn't reform, and the rebels were routing them in every direction. 'What the devil is Serpeth waiting for?'

One messenger swung a large banner to attract Serpeth's attention, while Kerowen blew a succession of staccato notes. Grannen lifted his field-glass to his eye and watched Lord Serpeth intently. His ally did not move. He was looking straight at Grannen, he could not have missed the banner nor the horn, yet he did not move.

Then Rolin the messenger came racing back, belabouring his sweating horse.

'Sir,' he said, white-faced, 'Lord Serpeth refuses to

engage. He says the only agreement he ever made was to support the victorious side.'

'What?' Grannen yelled. He struck the messenger across the mouth, sending him reeling off his horse and on to the ground. 'Accursed opportunist! By the gods, he'll suffer for this!'

Now his fury came boiling up, but too late. Grannen watched aghast as the rebels came surging over and through his own troops, breaking their ranks, scattering them. He stuck his heels into the side of his horse and sent the beast thundering down the hill towards Serpeth's position. 'I'll speak to the treacherous rat myself! By the gods, he'll support me or die!'

Helananthe saw Grannen's grey destrier galloping towards Serpeth's position. Passion rose in her breast.

'The bastard's going to get Serpeth to aid him,' she breathed. And she swept her sword out of its scabbard, and gathered her own horse's reins.

'Helan!' Eldareth cried. 'We're winning!'

'We haven't won yet,' she said, her jaw set. 'There's one sure way to kill the body, and that's to cut off the head.'

'Helan!' he cried as she sent her mount skimming down the ridge, across the valley, racing desperately against Grannen. With a groan of defeat, Eldareth raced after her.

She intercepted the General yards from where Lord Serpeth stood with his standard-bearers about him. 'Grannen, you bastard,' she snarled, wheeling her lighter, faster horse in front of him so he was forced to stop. 'Did you not get my message? I warned you that to make war against me was an act of treason!'

His sweaty face broadened in a sneer. 'I don't know you, madam. Get out of my way!'

She pulled off her helmet. 'Now do you know who I am? We've never met, but you've seen my portrait. I am Helananthe.'

'And I don't care,' Grannen spat, drawing his sword. 'I

don't care if you are Queen Hetys, you are not my monarch!'

She raised her weapon. She rode at him, swinging her sword; he blocked the blow easily, jarring her whole arm. Rage possessed her and she struck again; but for all her passion and strength, he was so much older and stronger and more experienced. She was on the defensive, all her energy taken with blocking his blows and no chance to attack; and the world was filled with the stamping of hooves, the clashing of metal; banners fluttering behind her and Grannen's ugly face the last thing she'd ever see—

He raised her arm to slash at her again. But the onslaught never came. He stopped in that pose, uttering a strangled groan, then slumping forward to catch himself on the pommel. Eldareth had ridden up from behind and slashed him across the back.

Helananthe seized the moment. 'For what you have done to my people!' she yelled, and slashed his throat.

Still he did not die. Grannen looked at her in contempt, blood pouring from his throat, eyes rolling drunkenly. He rasped, 'All I have done is to be loyal to my King!'

Then Eldareth ran him through. Grannen pitched off his horse and lay dead. Helananthe and Eldareth backed off and stood for a moment, catching their breath; seeing Grannen's force routed and fleeing the battlefield.

Someone cleared his throat. She started and found Lord Serpeth beside her, fox-faced and smiling, coolly unruffled since he had done no fighting that day.

As she turned, Lord Serpeth leapt off his horse and knelt on one knee before her, offering up his sword. She sat looking at him, open-mouthed.

'I plight my loyalty to the victor, my lady. Princess Helananthe, most noble highness; my army, my life and all that I possess I place at your disposal.'

Behind her she heard Eldareth say, very faintly, 'Slithery . . . what was it?'

*

The battle was over.

Rufryd was wandering the battlefield, dazed to find he'd survived. He was exhausted, every bone aching and his skin sore with sweat. Helananthe's army was pouring joyously down onto the road towards Parione, but he had no urge to follow. First he must find Tanthe and Lynden.

He stumbled between corpses, seeing no one he knew. Some folk from the camp were on the field, carrying off the wounded. But his friends were not among them.

He saw dra'a'ks circling above the battlefield – but these were true dra'a'ks, not *ghelim*. He was almost glad to see them. They reminded him of home.

A riderless horse appeared over a ridge, its head high and its blue-roan coat dark with sweat. Rufryd would have known Halcyon anywhere. He called the stallion, approaching carefully so as not to frighten him off. But Halcyon knew him too and dropped his muzzle into Rufryd's palm, snuffing for a treat.

Rufryd gathered the reins and mounted. At least now he could explore the field faster. 'Where's your master, eh?' he said softly. 'Wandering about trying to find you, I'll bet.'

He rode to the far side of the battlefield, where Tanthe had been fighting. There were other riderless horses, but none of them was Redbird. Other casualties, but none of them her. He began to relax a little. Doubtless she was on her way to Parione with the others . . . He rubbed his face. Anthar's horns, how long was it going to take to round everyone up?

Where the hill angled to face more to the south, he saw a figure sitting on a rock. Rufryd rode closer. A tall, familiar figure with long black hair . . . Gods, was it really Saphaeyender?

Rufryd was right by him and jumping down from the saddle, yet the poet seemed not to be aware of him. A corpse wearing the King's uniform lay at his feet. But it was Saphaeyender's appearance that struck Rufryd dumb.

Blood stained him from head to foot, dripping in rivulets down a face that was blank with shock. The poet still held a blood-covered sword in his hand; an Aelyr sword. He was breathing raggedly, his eyes and his teeth showing white against the gore.

'Saphaeyender?' Rufryd said warily. He was afraid the man might attack him, but when he tried to take the sword the poet gave it up without resistance. 'It's all over. What happened to you?'

'I killed as many as I could,' he said woodenly.

'Gods,' Rufryd breathed. He followed Saphaeyender's gaze down to a clump of bushes, and saw on the intervening stretch of grass a scattering of bodies; six at least. 'Have you seen Lynden?'

'I'll take you to him.' Saphaeyender stood up unsteadily and with the same wooden demeanour led him down to the bushes.

Behind, Rufryd found a hollow. And there he saw Lynden.

He fell to his knees. The world turned to white flame. But when the dizziness subsided, Lynden was still lying there.

It was as if a block of ice had crushed Rufryd, driving all the breath out of him so he couldn't think, feel, cry, do anything. Eventually he managed to say, 'What happened?'

'I don't know whether the arrow was fired on purpose or if it was a stray. But he was trying to protect me.'

'Help me get Lynden onto Halcyon's back,' Rufryd said quite calmly.

Saphaeyender only stared at him.

'Come on, Saph, help me. I'll take you both back to the camp. You need help, it's no good you sitting about out here.'

'What is there to go back for? Don't you hate me?'

'No,' Rufryd sighed, lifting the body on his own and laying it across Halcyon's back. 'I don't hate you. I don't

548

feel anything for you.'

'You don't feel anything,' Saphaeyender echoed, a touch of life coming back to his eyes. His gaze touched Lynden despairingly; Rufryd couldn't understand why he was so distraught. 'Why aren't you weeping?'

'I don't know,' Rufryd said bitterly, beginning to lead Halcyon away. 'I can't.'

Ysomir had the dream again.

Above the dark roofs of the cottages, a single line of twilight remained in the sky. All else was black. Ysomir stood shivering on the village green, holding tightly to her lover's hand. Everyone was watching, waiting. They were terrified and there was no escape, nothing to save them.

Then it came. The darkness took shape and fell screaming upon them and it was Lynden who was snatched away from her, borne helplessly off into the night—

Ysomir woke violently, on the edge of a scream.

The darkness and the emptiness plunged into her and stuck there; a spear gouging a channel of howling, bleak winter.

'Lynden,' she cried. But she knew.

It was morning. She stumbled from her bed and flew into the King's living chamber, but he was not there; nor in his bed-chamber. Down the high golden corridors she ran, not caring that she was still in her night-shift; ignoring the stares of the palace staff.

She felt an air of doom on them. It lay on everything, like tar.

She came at last to the Sun Chamber and found the King there, a knot of officials surrounding him, talking urgently. They fell silent as she entered; Garnelys turned to her and his visage was gaunt, pallid and terrible.

He pointed at her with a gnarled finger, as if everything were her fault. 'Aventuria has made war on me,' he said. His voice trembled with accusation. 'After all that I've done for them – they've taken the Xauroma, thrown it down and shattered it. Will they not rest until they've destroyed us all?'

Chapter Twenty-Three. Rubies in Amber

The rebels poured through the streets of Parione.

Tanthe rode with them, tireless; they'd come so far she should have fallen down with exhaustion by now. But she flew with Helananthe's followers in a fire of excitement.

Around her the tall stone buildings flashed past in lines of pale gold and ivory; the great trees swayed and rustled, placidly oblivious to the chaos below. The streets seethed. Ordinary citizens came rushing from their houses; the scattering of King's soldiers were helpless to do anything but watch the rebels pass. Soon everyone was following the rebels in their headlong rush towards the Amber Citadel.

Helananthe rode at the head of the force, her hair a gold banner. Beside her was Eldareth, with Lord Serpeth and his colourful army just behind. But Tanthe was surrounded by strangers, she'd seen no one she knew except Dawn and Mirias – so they had survived, at least – but no sign of Rufryd, nor Saphaeyender, nor Lynden. Anxiety shimmered beneath her excitement, but she rode on, caught up in the exhilaration of victory.

The walls of the Amber Citadel loomed ahead. The sight overwhelmed her. Three great fortressed walls, one inside the other, and rising from the centre the palace itself; a melding of ancient walls and newer, more graceful structures, with long windows and turrets reaching delicately for the sky. All glowing, like the rich melting gold of the sunset gathered in a vessel of flaming crystal.

As they climbed the hill, the circle of the outermost wall towered higher and higher before them, until the rest of the Citadel was concealed behind. Set into the centre of the wall was a tall golden gate, its ornate fretwork set with lapis, azurite, amethyst; and in the centre of the gate, wrought in gold and amber, the wheel, the tree and the jewel.

Before the gate, the hillside had been flattened out into a huge square, lined with trees and pale golden mansions. Tanthe's heart was beating furiously as she eased Redbird around Serpeth's ranks to get as close to Eldareth and Helananthe as she could. But the tall gate was shut and guarded by a score of soldiers in the King's livery.

Helananthe drew her horse to a halt. She addressed the tall officer in blue and gold who stood before the entrance.

'I am Princess Helananthe, daughter of Galemanth, grandchild of Garnelys. I request to speak to my grandfather the King. His army is defeated, he cannot refuse me!'

'Your Highness, your request is refused. We cannot let a hostile force into the Citadel.'

'We are not hostile. But I'm not afraid to come in alone. I must speak to my grandfather.'

'Impossible. The King will see no one.'

'I must insist.' The officer shook his head, but he looked nervous. 'You don't seem to understand. This is my home. I have a right to come in. To prove my point, I have just defeated my grandfather's army.'

'The King has been informed. But still, he has commanded us not to let anyone in!'

'He can't stew in there for ever,' Helananthe said angrily.

'Wait, I know what to do,' said Eldareth. He gave the princess's arm a squeeze, then set off for a bell-tower that stood to the right of the square. The crowd parted to let him through. A few moments later, the bell began to sound, a sonorous single note.

Tanthe knew of its purpose. It was to summon the citizens of Parione to the Amber Citadel. Everything from her history books was becoming real.

Within minutes, an even greater crowd was pouring

into the edges of the square. The streets that led into it were seething. All along the top of the Citadel wall, guards were looking down. Tanthe saw the glint of crossbows, and shivered. Hadn't there been enough bloodshed today? She saw something else then; small shadows threading between the people, seeming to vanish into grass-covered niches where the outer wall joined the ground.

The bell ceased; Eldareth came back. Then Helananthe turned to face the citizens of Parione. She stood up in her stirrups and shouted at the top of her loud, commanding voice.

'Friends, citizens! I am Helananthe, heir to King Garnelys! Know you now that I am come not to usurp my grandfather, but to free *you* – you, my fellow countrymen of Aventuria. The slavery and tyranny under which you have suffered these past two years and more are ended. I have come, not to destroy your world but to restore it! The madness is at an end. Do I have your support?'

The cheer that went up was deafening.

'Then I ask your support in this. Help me persuade the officials of the Amber Citadel to let me in!'

A roar. A surge towards the wall.

Helananthe turned to Eldareth, then to the officer at the gate, her face flushed with victory. But there was movement behind the fretwork of the outer gate. The golden wheel split down the centre; the two halves of the gate opened; the inner doors, though, remained shut. On the threshold stood an official in a robe of white and blue; a stiff, stone-faced man with a tight-curled beard.

'Lord Poel,' said Helananthe. 'At last, someone worth speaking to.'

'The King will not see you, your highness,' said Lord Poel.

'He must. Poel, it's over. If you do not let us in we will break the gate down and nothing will stop us; not a few guards with crossbows, not even if they have vats of boiling oil or catapults of flame. Let us in.'

Lord Poel glared at her, intransigent. 'Serpeth, you traitor,' he said. 'What are you about? You promised yourself to your monarch.'

Lord Serpeth seemed unmoved by Poel's bile. 'I made a decision, a judgement, based upon what I believed was right for Aventuria. The King has lost his faculties. The future lies in other hands.'

'Traitor!' Poel snapped, his cold eyes revealing emotion at last.

Suddenly a rumbling noise began; part of the wall attached to the lintel of the gate began to sway; the guards looked up in alarm.

'What in Dyon's name is that?' Poel barked.

'The Zampherai,' said Eldareth. 'They are very angry, and they are underneath the walls. They can scoop the rocks out as if they were butter, and drag the whole edifice down around your ears. I'd move if I were you.'

As he spoke, a whole section of the wall toppled and fell in a thundering crash, dragging the side of the gate down with it. On the parapet the guards were shouting and fleeing in panic. Lord Poel leapt out of the gateway in horror; Helananthe went riding straight past him, and suddenly the rebels were pouring into the Citadel through the gap, horses leaping and those on foot scrambling over the rubble.

Tanthe, though, held back. She pressed Redbird in to the wall further along, waiting for the crush to slacken so she could get past them. She had seen something else.

Above the mansions and beeches of the square, there was the hill on which the Tower stood. Ysomir might be in there. She had to go and look at once. The Amber Citadel would wait.

She found herself riding against the flow, struggling to get out of the square and find the road that would take her to the other hill. It was a maze and she thought she'd never find her way. Then running towards her came people dressed in ragged grey garb. One or two at first, then scores, then hundreds.

She forced her way downhill, across the valley until she found her way to the path that twisted upwards toward the Tower. In contrast to the beautiful streets, this was a scene of devastation; flagstones awash in mud, trees torn down, grass churned to mud, and everywhere ropes and pulleys and blocks of raw stone. These people running past her were the conscripts, she realised.

The state of them shocked her. They were so gaunt, so ragged. How, how could Garnelys have done this?

Tears of anxiety burned her eyes. If she didn't find Ymmi now she never would. She took in every face that passed her, thinking, what if Ymmi's so changed I don't even recognise her? She tried to stop people, but no one would speak to her.

Finally she came to a squat entrance in the side of the hill. There were no guards there; they must have deserted in the chaos, or been unable to stop the conscripts breaking loose. Above her the unfinished Tower brooded, raw and heavy and deserted.

Tanthe dismounted and ventured inside. The dank corridors shocked her; the cells, the stench of illness . . . surely her sister had not been kept here? She wandered on in a trance, half-sobbing in stunned disbelief.

There were still a handful of people down there, grey and thin as wraiths. 'I'm looking for Ysomir,' she said as they passed her. 'Does anyone know Ysomir Ayniedaughter?'

Suddenly a pale, thin young man tugged at her sleeve. He looked at her with hollow eyes and spoke in a faint, broken whisper. 'I knew Ysomir. I worked with her here and in Harpheneth mines. I'm Lath.'

Tanthe spun round, gripping his skeletal arm. 'I'm her sister. Where is she?'

He shook his head. 'Old grey-bones took her before Hollynight.'

A sob of despair shook her. She thought he meant she was dead. 'Oh, gods, How – how did she die?'

Lath blinked at her. 'I don't know. I mean, I don't know for certain that she is dead. I expect she is, though, because the ones he took into the Citadel hardly ever came back.'

'The Citadel? So old grey-bones is – who?'

'Don't know. But everyone said he was the King.'

Tanthe paused a moment to control her fears, her impatience. 'Come on, Lath,' she said, putting her arm round his skinny form. She couldn't leave him. 'There's no need to stay in here now. Help me find out what happened to her, eh?'

Lath gave the ghost of a smile. 'She talked about you a lot.'

Ysomir only had the vaguest idea of what was happening that nightmarish morning. She picked it all up from whispers. Hushed waves of anxiety ran through the palace; the faces of the guards, officials and courtiers were grim.

After she had seen Garnelys in the Sun Chamber, and he had accused her of bringing the war, she had fled back to her own room. There she had dressed herself in a skirt of cream with a thin silver stripe, an overdress of violet with puffed sleeves slashed to show silver, a stomacher sewn with seed pearls and amethysts. Her fingers tangled numbly, but she persisted until it was done. At her throat was Serenis's moonstone locket; lastly she put on the long necklace of lapis and amber that Garnelys had given her as a wedding present. She did this for Lynden. She wished him to see her at her best, even though he never would.

She wondered where he had died. At home? Trying to find her? In the battle? One thing she knew for certain; however he had died, it was Garnelys's fault.

Dressed, she came forth again. Outwardly she was calm; inside her, the winter wind burned and wailed, but on the surface she was glass, serene and perfect. She went again to the Sun Chamber, and although Garnelys did not speak to her, he let her stay.

Messengers and officers came to him in an endless

556

stream, and she caught snatches of their urgent exchanges, and so she knew. A ragged uprising – led by his granddaughter who was supposed to have been dead – had crushed General Grannen's invincible machine. And out to the east, in Thanmandrathor, a horde of rebels had overcome seven thousand of the King's men by the sheer weight of their numbers, and were pursuing them in the direction of Parione.

Messengers came one after another, increasingly anxious and whey-faced. With each one the news grew worse. Grannen himself was dead, cut to pieces on the battlefield.

Garnelys did not take out his anger on the messengers. But with each one that came and spoke and departed, his dark restlessness grew. His face was lined and haggard, his eyes rimmed with fire. He shut out everyone but Ysomir, and then he paced around the great chamber, radiating a black energy that terrified her. She daren't speak; she could only sit and watch him.

'How could this be?' he kept saying. 'They promised, they promised!' And then, 'Why is Laphaeome not here?'

Outside, the sky darkened with thunder. She could hear the crystal sphere thrumming, groaning in the heart of the Citadel, even though she was too far away to hear it. The sound almost drove her mad.

At length Lord Poel came gliding in with his aide and officers on either side. Ysomir had grown to loathe him. 'Sire . . .'

'Well?' Garnelys pinned him with baleful, perilous eyes. 'What vile news do you bring this time?'

For all his composure, Poel looked ashen. 'Sire, I've gathered a clearer picture of what went wrong in the battles. Because Lord Serpeth thought that we were losing, he changed sides. And when the Lord Mediator's reinforcements were summoned, they failed to appear.'

Garnelys turned, all coiled rage. 'Impossible. They promised. How?'

'We don't know, sire. But it appears that the same thing happened in Thanmandrathor. Your troops were overwhelmed because the reinforcements let us down.'

'*Let us down?* No. No. I must speak to both Mediators immediately!'

Poel began visibly to shake. 'The whereabouts of their leader, Lord Mediator Enabler, are presently unknown. I understand that Grannen spoke to him before the battle and all was well. But when the moment came, he could not be found. We're still searching. The matter will be investigated, of course—'

'Bring me Laphaeome!' the King cried. 'Find him, bring him to me at once! I will hear no more of this until I have spoken to him.'

The aide and the officials bowed and swept out at speed, but Lord Poel remained, white and rigid.

'Well?' Garnelys said.

'Sire, the rebels are making their way towards Parione.'

'From Thanmandrathor?'

'No, sire – that is, if they do come from Thanmandrathor it will take them days – but Princess Helananthe's followers will arrive within the hour.'

'With what intent?'

'We do not know, but we can only presume that in the very worst case they mean to overthrow you by force.'

Garnelys laughed, as if bewildered. 'That would be an insane action.'

'Indeed, sire, but the unfortunate fact is that the bulk of our defence force is gone. We cannot stop them entering the city. All we can do is seal the Amber Citadel against them—'

'Then seal it! Get out! Do not come to me again until you have better news and my Lord Laphaeome at your side!'

Poel all but fled. When he'd gone, Garnelys took Ysomir's wrist and led her out of the Sun Chamber, along the corridors and into his private metrarch chamber. He felt safe there; she had learned that much about him. He paced the room while she stood rubbing her wrist, watching him, feeling the emptiness of Lynden's death sliding about inside her like floodwater and black ice.

'Why have they done this to me?' he said after a time.

'Would you like to play metrarch, sire?' Ysomir asked.

'What?'

'Metrarch. I thought it might take your mind off things.'

'Are you mocking me?' he said, so sharply she jumped. 'Be silent!'

The King took a knife from the sideboard – one with a long, curved blade and a jewelled handle – and stood weighing it in his hand. Ysomir watched him in growing alarm. Then he turned and gave it to her, handle first. 'Quarter an apple for me. My mouth is dry.'

'Yes sire.' She went to the small sideboard where the basket of fruit stood, and put an apple on to a small gold-figured plate. But fear made her clumsy; she couldn't wield the big knife, and half the fruit shot on to the floor.

'Let me,' the King said, snatching the dagger away from her. He began to cut up a second apple, went on cutting and cutting until it was pulp and the pips were scattered on the floor. Then he picked up the plate and flung it, so that it flew over the bier and smashed against the leaded window beyond.

'Why are they doing this to me?' he cried. 'Faithless subjects!'

'You know why!' said Ysomir.

He turned and advanced towards her, cloaked all in black, his eyes burning red in a skull-like visage. She was terrified, but even her own terror no longer seemed to matter; she'd felt it too many times. She held her ground and said, 'Kill me if you want. I don't care.'

He stopped, his pupils searing into her.

The door opened. He turned quickly, saying as he did so, 'Laphaeome?'

But it was Lord Poel again. Trickles of sweat were running down his temples.

'Sire, Laphaeome cannot be found anywhere. I have men still searching but alas . . .'

'Well?'

'Sire, the rebels are at the gates of the Amber Citadel. Your granddaughter is demanding to see you!'

'My granddaughter is dead!'

'It seems that she is not. The rebels demand entrance and I don't know how long we can refuse them.'

'I will not speak to these people!' Garnelys said indignantly. 'You are mad even to suggest it. Go down in person and refuse them!'

'Yes sire,' said Lord Poel, gritting his teeth.

Garnelys strode to the window recess, the one where he'd first played metrarch with Ysomir. Cautiously she followed him. Now she heard shouts from below, and saw chaos in the streets. Hordes of people were running along the road that led towards the Citadel, lost to sight as they passed beneath the bulk of the outer walls. A bell was ringing in the distance.

Garnelys slipped his hand round Ysomir's waist. 'This can't be the end,' he said, calm again in one of his lightning changes of mood. 'God and Goddess take many forms, but in the end they are all aspects of the great universal force; Nuth and Anuth. Have I not given everything to honour them with the great Tower? They understand that the Tower is merely a concrete symbol of my devotion. Therefore they must ensure that I triumph. It can't be otherwise.'

'When Lynden and I made love,' said Ysomir, 'that was the best honour anyone could give to them.'

He pushed her away from him, so roughly that she fell over the metrarch table. She dragged it over with her as she fell, landing heavily and bruising herself on the marble floor. She heaved herself to her feet. She wasn't badly hurt but the shock and the pain made her gasp. The pain ran all through her and it was not only physical.

Garnelys rushed to her and lifted her up. To her shock,

there were tears on his face. 'My dear, are you hurt?' he said, gripping her shoulders. '*I* would have made love to you, if only—'

A pounding at the chamber door. He let her go and she stumbled away to lean on the sideboard. This time it was not Poel who came in but his nervous aide, Derione, with three guards behind him.

'Sire, the rebels have broken through the first gate. They will breach the palace within minutes.'

'How is it possible that they are entering?'

'Sire, all has gone against us. We thought the rebels ill-prepared for war, but so were we. We were complacent, we put too many to the Tower and not enough to defence. We were not ready for battle because we never thought it would come! And the rebels have the Zampherai aiding them. The Zampherai have torn the very fabric of the stone—'

'Have you found Laphaeome?'

'No, sire.'

'Then get out, Derione,' the King said quietly.

'Sire, for your own safety, let us escort you to the innermost keep—'

'To be a prisoner there? No. I will not be held to siege.'

'Sire, please. Come with us or they will find you.'

'No. They will not find me, I assure you. Now go, all of you. Get out! Leave us!'

Derione and the guards fled, slamming the door behind them.

'It's not over, Ysomir.' He looked up, smiling; then he grabbed her wrist and pulled her through the door that led to his secret chamber.

Terror surged through her. She didn't know where it came from; she'd been almost numb, so close to death so often that she'd grown immune. But now, suddenly, her dread broke its bonds and she was certain he was going to kill her in one last blood-offering, one last attempt to fling a spear of dark energy at his enemies.

561

He dragged her across the torture chamber and down the spiral stair to the housing of the sphere. Halfway down, the screams of the crystal were already deafening; reaching it, the sound was unbearable.

The sphere was going wild, spinning so fast it gave off heat. Flashes of red lightning darted over the surface. It kept changing direction like a sleeper caught in feverish nightmare, giving off pulses of agony that brought Ysomir sobbing to her knees on the floor.

'Why?' Garnelys cried. 'I have fed so much power into the Xauroma, so much of myself. Why does it not aid me? It must aid me!'

Ysomir dragged herself to her feet. 'Because the sphere is not the Xauroma! There is no power in it. It's a barometer. All it's giving back to you now is a measure of how much pain the Xauroma itself is in – how much pain your land is in, because you had no faith in your own people!'

Garnelys reached out to touch the spinning globe. As he did so he cried out as it burned; a flow of black and red plasma surrounded him; then the sphere turned dull, and the King lurched away and fled, uttering heart-tearing groans.

Ysomir rushed up the stairs after him. She felt as if that fell energy was burning inside her too, turning all her self-restraint to ash so she had to speak the truth. He'd slammed the panel that led back into the metrarch chamber in her face, but hadn't locked it. She opened it furiously and went through, shutting it behind her. The King was pacing round and round, beating at his robes with his palms as if he were on fire. 'A barometer,' he said, stopping and glaring at her.

'Surely you knew that? Even I worked it out!'

'When I was a young man the sphere was silvery-white, and there were deep planes, whole worlds of gold and iridescent rainbows inside it. It used to sing. But when it began to turn dark I knew that I wasn't doing enough, that I must feed it.'

'No. It was when you began to doubt yourself that it began to turn dark.'

'How can you know such things, Ysomir? You're just—'

'A peasant? Is there anyone better to know what the land needs? You lie!'

'What?'

'You knew what you were doing. The Xauroma didn't take energy from all those people whose blood you shed. It only took their grief. But you didn't care! Even though there isn't enough power in the world to inflate your self-worth above the size of a pinprick – you wouldn't stop! Now it's crying out with Aventuria's pain.'

'I know,' he said hoarsely. To her shock, he turned towards her, his clawed hand imploring. 'The pain is in me now. Is this not punishment enough? Listen to them shouting, Ysomir. They're coming for me. Help me. I love you. You're the only one who can help me!'

He came staggering towards her. She stood frozen there in disgust, suddenly knowing how swiftly and violently love could turn to loathing. Garnelys the Beautiful, who had had Aventuria in the palm of his hand. Now Garnelys the Pitiful, who had crushed it all down to the level of his own inadequacy. And Ysomir pitied him, and couldn't bear to pity him. He had engineered all this misery. Her parents' faces as Riverwynde vanished behind her. Serenis buried in the mines, Ede dying pitifully of an illness that a warm bed would have cured. And Lynden, sweet Lynden whose face she'd nearly forgotten in her infatuation with the King . . . whose face she would never see again.

Garnelys came lurching towards her, begging for help, and all she knew was that she wanted to stop him.

The jewelled knife was on the sideboard near the fruit. Now in her hand. He reached out. Her hand flashed up and plunged the blade under his ribs, through his flesh, into his heart.

Blood spurted out, bright red, pulsing.

He didn't die immediately. Ysomir pulled the knife out

and stood aghast at what she'd done. He didn't fall; only stared at her as if he couldn't believe it, and clawed at the wound, so that his hands became, for once, red with his own blood.

She wanted to stop the blood, to end his pain before it infected her, to stop *him*. So she stabbed him again. Went on and on stabbing at his chest, his throat; following him even as he reeled away from her and collapsed on to a low couch. Stopped only when he moved no longer and the blood finally ceased to pour.

She stood and stared down at the body, the hilt wet in her hand. She hardly knew what it was she was looking at. Even as the voices grew louder and the pounding at the chamber door began, she barely even heard them. All she knew was that the sphere had stopped screaming.

Helananthe was the first into the chamber. She'd composed herself as she strode along the corridor outside; taking a deep breath, pushing her cloak back over one shoulder, raising her chin. Now she was ready to confront her grandfather.

But as she strode in – Eldareth just behind her – the scene of carnage before her stopped her in her tracks. Unbelievable. Hideous.

There was blood everywhere; streaked across the floor, spattered on the walls, dripping from the edge of a couch. And staining the garments of a young woman who stood in the centre of the room as if frozen. Her violet overdress and cream skirt were ruined with blood. Her mouth and eyes were wide; rubies of blood jewelled her face and her hair. In her right hand she clutched the hilt of a long, cruel knife whose blade dripped with gore.

And slumped across the couch was a tall figure in black and indigo. Blood lay on his throat and his chest, soaking wetly into his robes and the upholstery.

'Grandfather!' Helananthe screamed. She pointed at the unknown woman. 'Seize her!'

Four of Serpeth's men ran forward and grabbed the woman. She didn't resist; she seemed paralysed with shock at what she'd done. She gave up the knife without resistance, and stood blank-eyed between them as they dragged her arms behind her back and held her.

Helananthe approached the body slumped on the couch. 'Find a physician!' she snapped.

But it was too late. She could see he was dead before she even touched him. The hawkish face still troubled but sleeping now. A dozen rents in his clothing and hideous stab wounds all over his chest, stomach and neck – Gods, what kind of frenzy had the woman been in?

She touched her fingers to his hollow cheeks. Her grandfather's blood, already congealing, smudged her fingertips.

Helananthe cried out in anguish.

'Garnelys! No, no, no!'

She'd been cheated. Not only deprived of the grandfather she'd once loved, but cheated of her chance to confront him. All she'd planned to say and do, all her plans to show him that he was wrong and she right, and yet somehow to redeem him. All gone.

Her breath came in heaving groans. The others gathered sombrely around her but for a few moments she couldn't control her grief. Then she drew herself upright, strode over to the captive, and only just restrained herself from striking the woman across the face.

'You killed him!'

'Yes,' said the woman.

'Why?'

Now she only shook her head. Either she was in shock, or simple. A servant?

'Who are you?'

'Ysomir,' the woman mumbled. 'I was his wife.'

'What?'

Ysomir's head came up and she said, like a drunk trying to speak clearly, 'I was the King's wife.'

Now Helananthe did strike her, hard across the cheek. 'Liar, as well as murderer! You have killed the Land! Have you any idea, any idea what you have done?' She turned her back, unable to bear the sight of the woman's blank, beautiful face or the blood on her. 'Take her away, lock her up somewhere. I'll deal with her later.'

Eldareth was beside her, tentatively touching her arm. 'Helan, love, I'm sorry.'

'This is not what was supposed to happen,' Helananthe said, pressing a cold hand to her burning forehead. 'This is the end of everything.'

Rufryd came to the Amber Citadel hours later, so weary that he had lost all sense of urgency. He walked straight in through the ruined gate; up the broad path through the inner levels without once being challenged; and so at last into the palace itself.

Jaded as he was, the palace took his breath away. He'd never seen such beauty, such colour. The walls seemed almost on fire with it. And he felt like a rogue or a thief, oddly shamed that he dared to wander battle-stained through the monarch's pristine dwelling.

The corridors and halls were full of people; an uneasy mix of palace guards, royal staff and rebels. He stopped several times to ask where Helananthe's party had gone, but no one seemed to know anything, or if they did, they didn't intend to help him. Growing increasingly angry, he followed his own instinct.

The palace was vast and confusing, but it didn't take long to find the place. There was a great gallery, thickly thronged with people, and beyond it a large ante-room with folk sitting along the walls under portraits of kings and queens, or milling about in the middle. At the far end of the ante-room, he saw a gigantic pair of doors emblazoned with the King's insignia on top of a blazing, gold-leaf sun.

The doors were firmly shut. Guards stood in front of it.

That must be the famous Sun Chamber, he thought, and inside must be King Garnelys and Helananthe. And this lot are waiting to see what happens? Gods, why bother.

He turned, meaning to leave, when he saw Tanthe.

She was sitting on a marble bench, leaning against the wall, her eyes closed. She looked drained. 'Tan!' he cried, pushing past people to reach her. 'I've been looking everywhere for you!'

Her eyes flew open. She leapt up and flung herself on him, holding him so hard he could barely breathe. Yet he daren't let himself feel any joy. A stone barrier had come down inside him and his emotions were sealed away, and that was how he wanted it.

'Oh, Rufe,' she said, pulling him down on to the bench beside her. 'I'm so glad to see you. Where's Lynden?' Her lovely blue-green eyes were anxious, expectant.

He didn't want to tell her. He knew she would cry. And she did, and he held her – because he was obliged to, not because he wanted to – and he told her everything in a flat, emotionless voice as she sobbed.

'Someone took a pot shot at him – and that was it?' she said at last, wiping her stained face on his sleeve. 'It seems so pointless. So stupid.'

'Perhaps it's justice,' Rufryd said. 'How many people did I pick off with arrows today, feeling triumphant because I'm so good at it? It's no different. Lyn had no special privilege not to be killed. He wasn't even doing anything mad or reckless. He was just unlucky. That's battle, Tanthe.'

She gave him an excoriating look, wondering how he could be so cold, but not saying it. He added, 'It just gets me, that he died trying to save Saphaeyender.'

'But that's Lynden, isn't it?' Tanthe said. 'He would have done the same for us. Don't blame Saphaeyender, please.'

'Oh, and my horse died,' Rufryd said. 'It seems such a long time ago now. Poor Sunhawk.'

'Oh, gods.' She caught a sharp breath, and wiped her eyes again. 'I've really had enough of today.'

'Yeah. Anyway. We're still breathing. What are you doing here?'

'I'm waiting to see Helananthe. Haven't you heard?'

'What?' said Rufryd.

'Garnelys is dead. They're saying that Ysomir killed him.'

That struck some life back into him. He sat forward in shock. 'I don't understand.'

'When everyone was coming into the Citadel, I went up to the Tower instead, looking for her. I met a boy called Lath who knew her, and said she'd been brought into the Citadel weeks, months ago.'

'Why?'

'I don't know, Rufe. I have no idea what she was doing here because I can't find anyone who can tell me anything.'

'All right,' he said, holding her arms. 'Take your time.'

'So I came to the Citadel, but by the time I got here Helananthe had already shut herself in the Sun Chamber. She's holding audiences with palace officials, so I gather, trying to sort out this mess. I went round asking people if they'd seen Ysomir. And then one of the guards told me . . .' she swallowed, forced herself to go on. 'Garnelys was murdered, just minutes before Helananthe reached him. He'd shut himself in a private chamber with a young woman who was always with him. And that young woman had stabbed him to death; blood everywhere, the guard said. He was quite graphic. And he had heard that the woman's name was Ysomir.'

Rufryd paused, not comprehending. 'How common a name is it? It might not have been our Ysomir.'

'But if it wasn't, where is she? I'm sure it was her. The guard saw her being taken away; he said she had a beautiful violet and cream dress, but it was covered in blood, and she walked as if she was in a trance. Her height, her hair, her face; it sounded like her – but she was so gentle, I can't ever imagine her hurting anyone! And what was she doing with the King? It doesn't make sense.'

'Well, where have they taken her?'

'That's what I'm trying to find out. There must be a misunderstanding. I've got to speak to Helananthe, find out the truth! But they won't let me in, I was told to wait my turn with the others.'

Rufryd was furious. 'So – we live with her in a wood for weeks, we help her to win her blasted battle – and now she's too important to see us?'

'Looks like it.'

'Right,' said Rufryd, striding angrily up to the gilded door. Six guards – presumably Garnelys's former guards, since they were in palace uniform – formed a solid wall before him. 'I demand to see Princess Helananthe immediately.'

'That's impossible. We can let no one in.'

'Then tell Eldareth we're here! He knows us!'

'I'm sorry,' the guard said firmly, 'they are not to be interrupted until they give notice.'

A score of angry faces were raised to him. 'Wait your turn! We've been waiting hours to petition her! No queue-jumping!'

Rufryd turned away in disgust. He went back to Tanthe, took her hands and lifted her to her feet. 'Let's get out of here,' he said.

'We can't.'

'We're never going to see Helananthe tonight! Come on. We'll try again tomorrow. All I want now is to sleep.'

'Where?' Tanthe let him lead her away, resigned.

'I took Saphaeyender back to the camp, after I found him,' said Rufryd. 'Saliole and his other cronies were there. So we cleaned ourselves up, and then we all came back to Parione together. I – I brought Lynden, too. I couldn't just leave him. Saphaeyender took us to his house – it is quite a house, Tanthe – and then I came here looking for you. Anyway, he's asked us to go and stay with him. You know, I was tempted to tell him to stick his hospitality.'

'You didn't!'

'No. To be honest, I'm too bloody tired to care. Come on, I'll take you there.'

Saphaeyender's house stood on the third hill, a marble villa exactly as Tanthe had imagined and yet lovelier; it had a gentle atmosphere she hadn't expected, with cool airy rooms on different levels, lattice screens, a central courtyard with the fountains and the green ferns he'd described. It was like stepping into a sanctuary of blue shadows.

He came to greet them, looking dreadful. He'd bathed and washed his hair, which fanned glossily over his shoulders; she tried not to think of Rufryd's description of him, covered head to toe in blood. But Tanthe saw at once that he was changed. He moved slowly, as if in a sort of dream; there were dark shadows under his eyes and a fugitive darkness to his expression. Seeing Tanthe, though, he smiled and hugged her almost tight enough to crush her ribs.

'I'm so glad to see you. I couldn't have borne it – not you *and* Lynden—'

'I'm still here,' she said. 'Just bruised. I put Redbird in the stable with, er, Halcyon . . . is that all right?'

'Well, of course, Tanthe. Come, take some refreshment. Tonight you will both sleep in soft beds and bathe in marble baths—'

He stopped suddenly and sank down on a couch, his head in his hands. Tanthe sat down beside him; Rufryd stared at him, grim but unspeaking.

'Lynden died trying to protect me. One moment I was speaking to him; the next – a stray arrow and he was gone. And I – I don't know what I did after that. There is an old phrase, to see red, and now I know that it is more than a meaningless cliche. It was crimson fire that I saw, and black and white clouds of madness . . .'

'You killed at least six people,' Rufryd said bluntly.

Saphaeyender gazed for a few moments at nothing. He swallowed. 'Six? I only counted four . . . but I will take your word for it. None of it was clear. None of it was real, until you came and found me. Were they all the King's soldiers?'

'Yes. None of our own side, fortunately.'

Saphaeyender gave a short laugh. 'Well, how clever of me. Slaying people who until recently may have saluted me in the street and come to see my plays.'

'You fought bravely. You helped us win,' said Tanthe.

'Nothing brave about it. None of it will rebuild the theatre, none of it will bring back Lynden.'

In the golden-red light of evening, Saphaeyender took them to a wooded slope on the edge of the city. He had dispensation, he said, as an honoured citizen of Parione, to use the ground without asking permission of the authorities. The slope was on the south side of the city but it faced west; towards Riverwynde. And the slope was peaceful, each tree marking the resting place of a Parionian.

Here they brought Lynden, borne on the back of Halcyon, which was all the ceremony he would have wanted. Dawn and Mirias came with them; Tanthe was grateful. They were becoming true friends. Saphaeyender's other companions, Ashtar and Sharm, Saliole and Evender came too; for once sombre and subdued. The only one missing was Eldareth, so busy at the Citadel that they had not wasted any more time trying to contact him.

Ymmi should have been here, Tanthe thought. Gods, I shall have to break the news . . .

They dug the grave themselves and laid Lynden in it, his Aelyr sword at his side. Then Rufryd planted the birch sapling in the mound they made over him; the graceful silver tree in which his essence would continue.

Tanthe cried quietly all the way through. She couldn't stop. Only Rufryd was dry-eyed and grim; and because he either looked sourly at her or avoided her gaze altogether, she tried to hide her tears in Saphaeyender's shoulder. The poet hugged her, and he wept no less than she did.

On the way back she walked alone for a time, wanting no one. But then Ashtar came and walked with her, linking her arm through Tanthe's in silent sympathy. Tanthe was glad, thinking she'd misjudged her. After a while Ashtar said softly, 'Poor Saphaeyender. He's taken this very hard.'

'I know.' Tanthe took a deep breath. 'It's because he blames himself.'

'Oh no, it's far more than that,' Ashtar said in surprise. 'I thought you knew.'

'What?'

'He was very fond of Lynden.'

'I know that. Weren't we all.'

'No, Tanthe, more than fond. Saph always falls in love with anyone a tiny bit vulnerable, especially if they are beautiful too. He has to seduce them; well, you know that. But don't blame him. He can't help himself. He's had most of us, at one time or another.' She squeezed Tanthe's arm, giving her a look of warm, innocent sympathy. 'I thought it only fair to tell you.'

Numb, Tanthe looked back across the lush, peaceful hills; the horizon beyond which – two thousand miles away – Riverwynde lay. Then she looked forward at Parione, seeing it through a mist of tears and birch leaves, rising golden and elegant against the sky. Well, she thought, here I am.

In the morning, Rufryd and Tanthe returned to the Amber Citadel. The chaos was worse, if anything; more citizens had poured in, and now they could hardly force their way into the main gallery, let alone enter the anteroom.

'This is ridiculous!' Tanthe said. 'I'm not giving up!'

As they began trying to force their way through – ignoring the angry protests – a familiar figure came towards them from the other direction, pushing past the crowd.

'Eldareth!' Rufryd shouted.

He came straight to them, resting his large hands on their shoulders in relief. 'There you are! I've been trying to find you all morning. I'd almost given up hope.'

'Well, here we are,' Tanthe said, too agitated for pleasantries. 'Eldareth, we've got to see Helananthe at once.'

'You can't,' he said, pulling them to the side of the gallery. 'She's got several hundred officials, officers, priestesses, disgruntled council members and guild representatives all clamouring for her attention. Tanthe, she hasn't forgotten you. That's why I'm here. I've got some very bad news, I'm afraid.'

Her head jerked up in fear. 'More bad news?'

'King Garnelys was murdered yesterday. Helananthe's distraught, she is doing her utmost to deal with that and to restore order at the same time. The thing is that we caught a young woman, moments after the killing had taken place. Tanthe, I'm as sure as I can be that she is your sister.'

Tanthe slumped. 'So it's true.'

'You heard?'

'That's why I was so desperate to see Helananthe. I'm sure there must be a misunderstanding! Ysomir would not do a thing like that! Where is she?'

Eldareth cleared his throat. 'She was arrested and taken to a cell in the northern quarter of the inner wall.'

'A cell?' Tanthe gasped. 'What's going to happen to her?'

'I'm sorry, Tanthe,' Eldareth said gravely. 'Helananthe is devastated. She loved her grandfather, you know, whatever he had done. She'd pinned all her hopes on speaking to him. I'll warn you now, she is going to be intransigent about this. The automatic penalty for this crime is death.'

'Death?' Tanthe whispered.

'Garnelys's fate should have been decided by the council of the Sun Chamber; most likely he would have been taken away to rest, and Helananthe appointed as regent in his place. It wasn't Ysomir's place to take the monarch's fate into her own hands, was it?'

'I want to see her!'

'Of course. I'll take you to her.'

Eldareth led her and Rufryd into an older part of the palace, and across an enclosed bridge to the innermost wall. It was only now that Tanthe realised the walls were hollow and full of rooms housing Citadel staff; castles in themselves. But the area to which he led them was entered through a locked, barred gate, guarded by two warders in black. Inside there was a plain passage of sandy-yellow stone, lined with iron-clad oak doors. Glancing through the barred apertures in growing trepidation, she saw that the cells were all empty.

At last the female warder stopped outside one of the doors, fumbled with a bunch of keys, and let them in. 'Here is the prisoner, Lord Eldareth.'

Eldareth actually knocked politely on the open door before he went in, beckoning Tanthe and Rufryd after him. Then he stood back by the doorway to leave them to it. Tanthe was shaking. The cell was plain and bare, she saw, but clean, with one small, high window, a bed, a door leading to a separate privy.

Ysomir was sitting at a small table under the window, writing.

As they entered she looked up. Her eyes at first were dull, uninterested; then a shock of recognition ignited and she stared at them in astonishment.

Tanthe could hardly believe her eyes. Unbearable enough, to find her sister imprisoned; but more shocking yet was Ysomir's appearance.

She was in a loose brown dress, plain but for a ruffled gathering at the shoulders. Her hair, newly-washed, hung in an unkempt tangle over her shoulders, a mass of shining golden-brown. She looked ineffably beautiful and yet older, much older; no longer a sweet-faced girl but a dignified woman with haunted eyes.

'Tanthe?' She rose unsteadily and came forward.

'Hello, Ymmi.'

'Tanthe? Oh, dear gods, is it really you?'

'Yes, dear,' Tanthe said. Hesitating, then crossing the space between them in a rush, she flung her arms round her sister. They clung together, unable to let go. Tanthe cried bitterly, unravelling; it was Ysomir who was the calm one. She cried too, but when she dried her eyes she was immediately composed again.

'But what are you doing here?' Ysomir said, clinging on to her hands.

'We came in with the rebels yesterday. We came to get you back.'

'All the way from home?'

'Yes. Me and Rufe and Lynden. But Lyn can't be here. I'm so sorry, Ymmi . . .'

Tanthe blurted the words out, while she still could. Ysomir collapsed. Tanthe helped her back to the chair while Rufryd took a wooden goblet from the table and gave her sips of water. Eventually Ysomir sat back, loosely clasping Tanthe's hands.

'It's all right, Tanthe. I already knew. It was just such a shock, hearing you say it.'

'How did you know? Did someone else tell you?'

'No,' Ysomir said with a ghostly smile. 'I felt him die. That's why I stabbed Garnelys . . . I think. It's hard to say, there was so much in my mind. I couldn't bear it any more.'

'So you really did . . .'

'In a way it's easier that I don't have to face Lynden. There were things that would have been so hard to tell him.'

'I'm sure he would have understood.'

'Understood that I was married to Garnelys?'

Tanthe and Rufryd gaped at her, then at each other. Rufryd's expression plainly said, *she's gone mad*, and Tanthe was almost inclined to agree.

'You were married . . . to the King?'

'I know it sounds ridiculous. I don't even know that I can prove it. I don't know how much weight the ceremony carried; but Lord Poel was there, and that Laphaeome, and a priestess, so I'm sure it was legal.'

'Why would he marry you?' Tanthe said, struggling to understand.

Ysomir shrugged. 'The Queen died. He was lonely; I've never met someone so lonely. He said he loved me. I think he meant it. I loved him too, for a little while. The Princess wouldn't believe me, though. Tell her I only ever speak the truth, will you?' And Tanthe had never known Ysomir to tell a lie in her life.

'Did you really kill him?'

'Yes.'

'Are you sure? What if someone else did it, and put the knife in your hand?'

'That didn't happen.'

'But you could at least *say* it did. They can't keep you locked up if there's any doubt.'

'Tanthe, they caught me almost in the act. There is no doubt.'

'Why did you do it?'

Ysomir paused. The tip of her tongue touched her upper lip. 'To end his pain,' she said. 'And to end mine.'

Rufryd said, 'I think she did something incredibly heroic. I don't know what Helananthe's problem is! This conflict could have dragged on and on if Ymmi hadn't ended it!'

'We are going to get you out,' Tanthe said firmly.

'No,' Ysomir said firmly. 'You don't understand. Helananthe is right, what I did was unconscionable! I deserve to be punished. I don't want to be let out. I feel safe here. I don't think I can face what lies outside.'

'Gods, Ymmi, you've really changed. What's happened to you?'

In reply, Ysomir reached inside her sleeve and pulled out a sheaf of papers, adding to it the one she had just been writing. 'I wrote all these letters to you, Tanthe. I never thought you'd actually read them! But here . . . these will tell you everything.'

Helananthe pored over the papers for an hour and more, but her face did not soften. Tanthe waited anxiously. The princess had finally found time to see her and Rufryd, late at night, in her own private chamber.

In the dim lamplight she looked, as Eldareth had intimated, grieved and exhausted. But her demeanour was resolute and her eyes like steel. At length she looked up and said, 'Tanthe, I'm sorry.'

'What do you mean?'

Helananthe sighed, sitting back in her chair. 'I can see, from what your sister has written, that she was under great strain. But that is still no defence for what she did.'

Tanthe, horrified, fought hard to master her passion. 'She was afraid for her life!'

'Yet she admits in her own words that when she stabbed Garnelys he was not threatening her but begging her for help!'

'But – but – I know you are upset, Helananthe. You've been through a lot but so has she! She doesn't deserve to die. Please show her mercy!'

'Tanthe, I am showing her mercy. I was going to have her executed. Instead – because you are my friend, and you have spoken so passionately in her defence – I am commuting her sentence to one of life imprisonment.'

Tanthe was relieved for one second. Then shock washed through her. When she said mercy, she meant freedom. 'Life imprisonment! No, you can't! This isn't justice, it's revenge!'

'How dare you!' Helananthe stood up, her face

thunderous. 'I have no choice. Do you not understand the gravity of her crime? I would not release her if she were *my* sister. She has killed not just anyone but the guardian of the Xauroma. She cheated me – and when I say that, I mean that she cheated all of us of the chance to find the truth! This isn't a crime against me, it's a crime against Aventuria! And now all my hope is gone of discovering who Laphaeome was, or what was going on in my grandfather's mind. Can't you imagine for a moment how disastrous this might prove to us? No, I cannot release her. Just be glad she's alive. Now leave!' Helananthe turned away, dismissing them. Rufryd put his arm round Tanthe, urging her gently to the door.

'Come on. Enough,' he said softly. 'You've just saved her life, you know.'

Chapter Twenty-Four. Auriel

Helananthe wound step-by-step down the spiral stair towards the heart of the Citadel. All was dark, damp, claustrophobic; her lamp shone on crumbling stone and cobwebs. Eldareth was behind her; apart from their footsteps, all was silent.

Above, peace was returning to the Amber Citadel at last. She had heard all the petitioners, soothed their worries, restored order. Now everyone knew where they stood. She was in charge.

They reached the low, domed chamber and she saw it for the first time.

The crystal sphere, the *xauroth*, the gift of the Zampherai. The fiery jewel that mediated between earth and humans.

'I've never seen it before,' she whispered. 'I always heard whispers of it, but for all my childhood explorations I never could find it. Only the monarch is supposed to come here.'

The sphere rotated gently, emitting a faint hiss like a skate sliding on ice. The sound was somehow introverted, as if it murmured comfort to itself. It was twice her height, its surface polished to a perfect gloss. In colour a deep purplish brown, but even as she watched the colour seemed to be lightening by degrees, flashing iridescent planes of bronze and coppery-red.

Her palm hovered over it, but she did not touch it.

'It's amazing,' Eldareth breathed. 'Quite amazing.'

'It feels calm,' Helananthe said. 'It's not as Ysomir described, wild and full of pain. It seems to be . . .'

'Convalescent?'

She smiled. 'Yes, exactly that. Recovering.'

'Because the Xauroma is not broken,' said Eldareth. 'Garnelys strained it to breaking point – but the circle is unbroken. Aventuria has a new monarch. You are about to be crowned Queen Helananthe.'

She exhaled. 'Gods, what days these have been. I expected to become Queen as an old woman, after Garnelys and Galemanth were gone. Not so soon. I don't know whether I'm ready.'

'Helan, love, you are ready. The way you dealt with one phalanx of hysterical officials after another – you were born to it.'

'Funnily enough, that is literally true. Oh, I still have so much to think about. I gather the victorious rebels from Thanmandrathor are on their way to address their monarch; that should be interesting.'

'They are your allies,' Eldareth laughed.

'Gods, I hope you're right. Then there's soothing the Zampherai. Discovering the truth about those supposed "Mediators" who have now vanished from the face of the earth. I shall have to interview that damned Ysomir – if I can bear to look her in the face.'

'Must you be so hard on her?'

'I must. Don't feel sorry for her! She is a murderer, and dangerous, and more than a little unbalanced, and furthermore she is living quite comfortably at my expense! Oh, don't let me think about her now.' She turned to him, placing her hands on his arms, looking into his dear, travel-lined face. 'I don't care about royal protocol, Eldareth. I don't care that you aren't the right duke from the right family. When I'm Queen I am going to marry you.'

He clasped her in his arms and kissed her fiercely. 'Your majesty,' he said, with half-serious solemnity. 'I am at your service for ever more; as friend, advisor, lover, general, spy, ambassador, lover again – anything you want of me. But as husband – never. I have no wish to be king.'

She was taken aback. 'Oh – I thought – I assumed the only obstacle was my father. Now I feel quite the fool.'

'Don't. I should have made it clear before.'

Her temper rushed up. 'But Eldareth, I need you! Don't leave me to rule quite alone!'

'Helan—'

'If you cannot support me as I require, perhaps you had better leave altogether!'

Now he looked shocked and hurt. 'Don't take this so to heart, I beg you. In all my life I will love no one but you. But marriage, sitting beside you on the Sapphire Throne – I'd feel too ridiculous, like a dog dressed up as a priest. Don't ask that of me. Anything else.'

'Gods.' She leaned back against the wall; the sphere emitted what sounded like a note of questioning concern, *mmm*? She was stunned, disappointed. It was all too easy to forgive him, but she wanted to punish him a little. 'Very well, if you would have it so. I should have known you'd never settle, dear. In place of marriage, then, I accept your devotion. You are still restless? Then you can go and fetch my mother and my little brother Venirryen from Eisilion. Tell them it's safe to come home.'

'Has Helananthe read these?' asked Saphaeyender as he looked up, at length, from the letters.

'Yes,' said Tanthe. They were in a broad, cool chamber, open at one end to the courtyard. The fountain danced, reflecting sunlight, and the chamber was full of ferns and climbing plants, so that inside and outside seemed to be one. It was hard to believe that the battle had ever taken place. 'She said it makes no difference. Ysomir had been with Garnelys long enough not to be in fear of her own life. He was begging her for help when she killed him.'

'She can see no mitigating circumstances?'

'No. And neither can Ysomir. I've seen her again and she insists that she wants to stay in prison, she is perfectly content, she deserves it . . . Gods, I think it will take me years to understand her! Anyway, I thought . . . Well, that if you were going to write a play or an account of the last days of King Garnelys, Ymmi's letters might help.'

'I should write about it. One day I will. But not yet.'

'Why not?'

Every time he paused, looking darkly at nothing, she could only guess what he was actually seeing. 'It's too personal. I have never tried to write about anything so close before. How can I make a play out of something that nearly destroyed me, and watch it acted out every night?'

'Sorry. That was a stupid question.'

'Your sister writes wonderfully,' he said. He sat back and dragged his fingers through his hair, ruffling the silver and the black. 'But I can't use what she's written, because it's her story, not mine. It would be dishonest to use her work and present it as my own. It should be published just as it is, to tell people exactly what happened in the Amber Citadel. I can arrange it.'

'Oh.' Tanthe smiled. 'You know, you are a good man.'

'Honest, perhaps. I wouldn't say "good".'

'Saph . . .' She suspected what was coming.

'I might write a poem about a young man who lost all fear, because he knew he was going to die and yet didn't fear it. Who sent his own horse off the field of battle rather than put its life at risk. Who died, trying to save the life of a coward.'

'That would be a beautiful tribute. But don't torment yourself.'

'Rufryd blames me for what happened to Lynden. Any why not? I was cowering, he was trying to protect me.'

Tanthe went to him; he gathered her on to his knee, wrapped his arms round her.

'Is it true,' she said into his hair, 'that you seduced Lynden?'

His arms stiffened. 'Who told you that?'

'Someone who knows you better than I do. All those times I saw you with Lynden, all those times at

Enhavaneya when I thought you were on your own or with Helananthe . . .'

'I can't deny it. I wanted him. Tanthe, I loved him.'

'I thought it was me you loved.'

'I do!'

'Well, that someone also told me that almost everyone in the theatre company has been your lover at one time or another. That they stay with you after you discard them because they love you so much they'd forgive you anything. How long before you discard me?'

'I don't know, what time is it? Tanthe, I'm joking. Don't be angry with me.'

'Well, now Rufryd's really going to love you. You not only seduced me but his brother as well—'

'Ye gods, you're not going to tell him, are you?'

'Why not?'

'He scares me. I think he'd happily kill me, given half an excuse. Anyone who can be so emotionless over his own brother's death scares me.'

His words brought her up short. 'I know. I'm worried sick about him, if you must know. Of course I won't tell him. Someone else probably will, though.'

'Tanthe, I don't want to lose you. I've never discarded anyone. Things end; it was usually they who ended it.'

'Because you'd found someone else?'

'Sometimes. Yet they stayed my friends, most of them, it's true. Lynden was so alone, he seemed so in need of comfort and no one was there for him.'

Her throat tightened. 'We were there, Rufe and me.'

'I know, but he was still alone. Perhaps I could help when you couldn't because he didn't know me so well. Don't be upset, Tanthe. I fall in love very easily, I find it easy to feel affection for people and very hard to hate them; is that wrong?'

'No. I think you're twisting words somewhere – but no.'

'And making love to them . . . well, that's natural, isn't it?'

'Yes, but it still hurts! When you said you loved me, I thought I was special to you – I might have known it was too good to be true.'

'No, love. It is different with you.'

She said nothing. His long fine hands stroked her. He made it so hard to be angry, or even to think straight.

'Tanthe, nothing happened with Lynden.'

'Don't lie.'

'It's the truth. Yes, I wanted him, but all he could think about was Ysomir. So. If you want me to give up other lovers to keep you – not that I have any at this moment – I will. Anything. Marry me.'

She clasped him, her lips against the warm skin of his neck. She wanted so desperately to believe him . . . Saphaeyender's wife. The immortal Saphaeyender. Her name linked with his in the history books, *Saphaeyender and Tanthe* . . . but it lacked any ring of reality. 'No answer? That's ominous.'

'I don't know what to say. I'm in shock.'

'Well. Sleep with me tonight, at least.'

'Not tonight. Do you mind? I need to be on my own for a while.'

'Because of Lynden?'

'Not only that.'

'You still love Rufryd, don't you?' he said sadly.

She gave a strangled gasp of irritation, annoyed but laughing. 'Gods, why must it be another man? All I want is some time to think!'

She went to bed, early and alone, in one of Saphaeyender's many cool, quiet guest rooms. She lay for a time with her hands flung behind her head on the pillow, watching the light dappling the ceiling from the courtyard pool. Peace, of a sort . . . Then her door opened and Rufryd came in.

He walked slowly to the bed and stood over her. He seemed restless, hostile, his eyes glittering in the semi-darkness. The light feathered the edges of his chestnut hair and he looked so like Lynden, but for the cold fire of his expression.

'What is it?' she said. 'Say something!'

'Nothing to say, Tanthe, is there?' he said, his tone vicious. 'You got everything you wanted.'

'What? My sister in prison?' She sat up.

'At least she's alive.'

'Yes, but . . .' she didn't know what to say.

'You've got your poet. He can open all the doors into Parionian society for you, and all you had to do was sleep with him.'

Tanthe was furious. 'You spiteful rat! You've got nothing in your heart but spite.' She lunged at him, half-meaning to hit him, but he caught her wrists. Infuriated, she couldn't stop. 'You haven't shed a tear for Lynden. I don't think you ever cared about him. You're empty inside; you've got nothing, so you don't want anyone else to have anything either!'

'There's nothing for me here. That's a fact.' He held her wrists hard, his eyes glaring coldly into hers. 'What shall I do? I can't stay here. I can't go home.'

'Well, what do you want me to do about it? Do you think I have no feelings? I want to see my parents more than anything, but I can't leave, as long as Ymmi's here! What do you want me to do, Rufe?'

'Make love to me,' he said.

'What?'

'You heard.' He tried to kiss her, one hand holding her wrists, the other clamped round her back.

'Rufryd, no. This isn't fair.'

'Please,' he said, his mouth warm on her ear. 'I haven't been allowed to touch you for months. I can't stand it. Please, Tan.' And he held her hard, kissing her neck and cheeks until at last she let him find her mouth. He seemed so desperate that her own anger melted. She knew him too well ever to fear him, knew he would stop if she told

585

him to. But she didn't. He swept her along in a flood of emotion, sweet and bitter.

They fell together into the softness of the bed, Rufryd on top of her, pulling at his clothes. She was already naked. Breathing hard, she helped him; it had been a long time and she'd missed him. She couldn't control herself; her body was answering his excitement with a helpless ache of arousal. With Rufryd still half-dressed they joined urgently.

Release came swiftly for them both; sharp, molten, profound.

Then Rufryd wept at last.

He fell onto her with a groan; she rocked him, her hands in his hair, while for a long time he could only sob. And then he said only, 'Lynden, Lynden.'

When his grief subsided, a long time later, he said nothing else but only lay back on the pillow. Barely aware of her own tears flowing, Tanthe watched him, stroking his hair as he looked at the ceiling. He slept for a while but she stayed awake. A couple of hours later he woke suddenly and said, 'I should go.'

'You don't have to.'

But he sat up and replaced his dishevelled clothes without looking at her. 'No, it's better that I leave. You want to be with Saphaeyender, and I need to think.'

Stunned, she let him go.

In the morning she found that he had not only left her room, but left the house and taken his belongings with him. After she had searched the villa for him, she stopped on a cool verandah that gave on to the courtyard, trying to order her thoughts. She was more torn than ever. She still loved Rufryd, couldn't leave Saphaeyender . . . What in Breyid's name was she supposed to do?

Saphaeyender found her there, and slipped his arms round her waist. 'I missed you last night,' he said. 'I had some rather colourful nightmares I would have liked to share.'

'Oh, Saph.' She had been going to admit what had

happened with Rufryd; now she couldn't. 'Are you all right?'

'As all right as I can be, knowing what I know about myself.'

'Rufryd's vanished,' she said. 'Would you help me look for him?'

He exhaled tiredly. 'I can't. I have people coming; everyone who was involved with the theatre. Everyone who survived, that is. I want you to be there. Can't Rufryd look after himself?'

The meeting made her feel excluded. Suddenly Saphaeyender's house was filled with strangers who all knew each other, who had a prior claim on her lover and took him away from her. She began to wonder if she could ever be a part of it; if she even wanted to. It seemed meaningless, when Ysomir was in her cell and Rufryd in pain. But it wasn't meaningless to Saphaeyender. He was trying to piece his world back together and see if he could still live in it. Tanthe began to doubt that she had the strength to sustain him through it.

Here she was, with everything she'd dreamed of. And yet she would have given it all to see her mother and father again, to catch Lynden and Ysomir fondling each other in naive affection in a sun-washed meadow.

Ysomir dreamed.

She always slept well and deeply in her prison cell. She appreciated the plainness of the sandy-coloured walls, the simplicity of her clothes, the austerity of her routine. When the door opened, it was only to admit the female warders, who treated her well, or Tanthe, who came to her every day. No uncertainty, no passion or madness. She felt safe here. Luxury had only brought her misery.

All she asked for was ink and paper. In the day she wrote and wrote, not knowing where it came from. And by night she slept securely, clasping the only piece of jewellery she still had; Serenis's locket.

Ysomir dreamed she was Lynden. He didn't see the arrow coming, felt no pain, did not even know that he was dead; saw instead a golden tunnel whirling above him, the full manifestation at last of the *ethroth*. He rose into the tunnel, exhilarated, knowing that this was why he'd felt no fear. This was what had been waiting for him. Flight through the spinning golden light; and waiting for him at the other end, Ysomir.

She rose up to embrace him. They clung together in the glow, the whirling fire of jewels, and when she fell back he was inside her. Home.

She stirred, feeling his presence so vividly that for a few moments he was there, his silken skin and hair under her hands. But when she woke properly, there was only the flat hard fabric of the sheets against her palms. Her throat burned with tears. It was happiness, as well as sorrow.

Don't cry, Ymmi, said his voice inside her. *I found you. I'm here with you forever now.*

On a black plain, bisected by a black path under a black bowl of sky which glowed palely around the horizon, Zhoaah and Gulzhur waited.

They'd already come a safe distance from Parione before they slipped into the psychic plane. They'd made themselves scarce the moment the battle had begun, ignoring Garnelys's pleas for help, haunting the scene for just long enough to absorb all that delicious human pain. And then they had fled.

'Enabler!' said Zhoaah.

'Facilitator,' said Gulzhur. And they bowed to each other in mutual congratulation.

'Alas, Garnelys,' said Zhoaah, with his soft smile. 'He was easy meat.'

'It was indeed a beautiful day. Why lift a finger, when all we have to do with humans is whisper poison in their ears, then point them at each other?' Gulzhur gave his slow, grim laugh.

'It was a work of art. Mistrust, exploitation, civil war. Let me see; between us, you and I have killed less than a handful of humans. But of their own kind they have destroyed hundreds, thousands. Perfection.'

'Never perfection,' said Gulzhur, the cynical realist. 'We have much yet to do. This was merely the opening act.'

'Oh, give yourself a little credit. We achieved our objectives exactly: to set the humans fighting amongst themselves. And now basking in complacency, thinking they have won and restored peace; never having the faintest 'suspicion that we engineered all their misery.'

'The setbacks were only small ones, it's true. But humans are not completely stupid. We were discovered. It could have been disaster.'

'But it wasn't. And now we have vanished,' said Zhoaah. 'Ah, he died divinely.'

'The King?'

'Who else? Now, that I didn't foresee – yet I could not have envisaged a more exquisite end if I'd planned it myself!'

'But the best part was the betrayal.' Gulzhur nodded in satisfaction. 'Telling him what we were and still keeping his faith. Promising him the world then jerking it all from under his feet!'

'"Aazhoth is a wise leader, sire." Did I really say that?' Zhoaah giggled. 'Aazhoth is a dead leader, sire! And the Bhahdradomen are rising!'

Gulzhur nudged him. On the path a third figure had appeared; a slow-moving shadow, gliding towards them under the weird sky. The shadow flowed like a storm, blue-black and terrible, seeming to gather power about him like a tornado as he came. Even Gulzhur and Zhoaah trembled at the sight of him. 'He is coming.'

And they waited to impart their news to the one who would end their centuries of humiliation and exile; their new leader, he who had given them back their pride and power.

Vaurgroth.

Rufryd did not come back. Every day for four days, Tanthe went looking for him, growing more and more worried. Was he sleeping on the streets? She even went to Lynden's grave in search of him, but he wasn't there.

On the fourth afternoon, while she'd stopped to watch the stone masons repairing the gate of the Amber Citadel, she saw him. He was strolling along, carrying a sack of apples and pomegranates, as if he hadn't a care in the world. He almost walked past her; Tanthe caught his arm.

'Rufryd! I've been looking for you everywhere! Are you all right?'

'Surviving,' he said. A smiled touched his lips; his eyes on hers were no longer hostile, only haunted.

'For the gods' sake, come back and stay with us.'

'But you're with your poet.'

'Rufe, I'm not "with" anyone.'

'How d'you mean?'

She sighed in exasperation. 'He's like you, in a way. He's lost so much and I can't get it back for him; no one can. All he thinks about is his theatre company. He asked me to marry him and . . .' His gaze slipped away from her as she spoke. His mouth set in a line. 'I nearly ran away,' she went on. 'I can't see how it would work. It's not what I want.'

'Why not?'

'I don't know. Because I can't stop thinking about you.'

'Am I meant to jump for joy?'

'No. Gods, you're aggravating! Rufe, please come back with me. I can't bear to think of you being alone, with nowhere to stay.'

'But I'm not on my own.'

Her eyebrows rose. 'You're not?'

'I'm staying with someone.'

'Who?'

'Ashtar.'

'*Ashtar*?' Tanthe nearly choked. She recalled the actress, her thick dark hair, deep red mouth, voluptuous figure . . . recalled how she'd hung around Rufryd at Enhavaneya, though he had appeared not to notice at the time. 'You and Ashtar—'

Rufryd shrugged and gave an apologetic grin. 'She's been very hospitable. She's always liked me, apparently.'

'I'll bet she has!' Tanthe went hot with disbelief. 'Didn't take you very long to get over me, did it?'

'Just a bit longer than it took you to get over me.' He leaned forward and gave her an impersonal kiss on the cheek – mocking the way Parionians greeted their friends. 'So you can stop feeling guilty about me, Tan. I'm fine.'

'I can see that,' she hissed, turning on her heel. 'I don't know why I ever wasted my time worrying about you!'

That night, as she lay awake brooding, a figure moved into the room. He was silhouetted against the bluish light of the window, and at first she thought it was Rufryd, come back to her even after what he'd said . . . but no, his hair was too long. And it wasn't Saphaeyender, because he was in bed beside her, asleep. The stranger's hair had a reddish glow and his footsteps were silent.

A glamour lay on the room. Tanthe felt she was dreaming, and that Saphaeyender would not wake up even if she yelled for help.

It was the Aelyr male leaning over her, his face glowing with a light of its own. So close she could have kissed him. And as he leaned down, she was possessed by irrational terror of something she couldn't remember, of falling backwards into darkness and two figures, veiled from head to foot in grey and violet, fleeing; abandoning something precious.

Tanthe woke and sat up, drawing a deep, laboured breath. Her own reflection, in a long mirror by the far wall, made her jump. And then she saw his face again. He was inside the mirror, his fingers pressed to the inside of the glass.

'*You must come now,*' he whispered. His lips moved, but the voice was in her head. '*Time is running out.*'

'Who are you?'

He couldn't hear her, it seemed. '*Come to me, Tanthe. Now, before they capture me again. We need you. They're coming! Come and find me, please, before it's too late!*'

Urgency and fear flowed from him. The mirror darkened; he was gone. She sat up, looking frantically around the room. All she could see was a small bright moon; the pommel of the Aelyr knife, lying on the table beside the bed and almost dazzling her.

'Why are you doing this to me? How am I supposed to find you?'

She fell back with the sheathed knife clutched against her. It went on glowing, cold in her palm. Sleep would not come; at last she got up without disturbing her lover, dressed quickly, and wrote three notes; one for Rufryd, one for Saphaeyender, one for Ysomir.

'Well, Tanthe, how can I help you?' Eldareth had come down to meet her, in response to her message, at the gate of the Amber Citadel. Dawn was barely beginning to glimmer above the hills and the city had not yet begun to stir.

He was on foot; she jumped off Redbird's back to talk to him. 'I'm sorry to disturb you so early. It's really important.'

'I'm an early riser, as you know. I was already abroad.'

'I need help. I couldn't think of anyone to ask but you.' She took the Aelyr knife, now dull again, out of her jacket. 'This knife; I told you how I came by it. The Aelyr who gave it to me came to me again last night. He seemed so desperate, begging me to help him. I've got to find him, but I don't know how! You must help me.'

Eldareth rubbed his unshaven chin gravely. 'I'm flattered that you ask me, but I'm at a loss to explain these visitations. If you are sure they are not dreams . . .'

'They're not!' she said fiercely. 'Helananthe spoke of a Seer she had consulted. I thought he might be able to tell me what's happening.'

'Ah, Fox the Seer.' A glint of amusement. 'Yes, indeed, he *might*, if he is not by now too soaked in wine to remember his talents.'

'That doesn't sound very promising.'

'He is a good seer. The best. He will show you the truth; if you don't understand it, that is your failing, not his. That's what he will tell you, at least! But it's two long days' ride from here.'

'I don't care!' Eldareth studied her, looking dubious. 'Please. If I don't find out what this means, I shall go mad.'

'You'll be gone at least four days. Your friends will worry.'

'It's all right. I've left them notes, explaining I've had to go and look for something. Just tell me how to find him!'

'You won't find it alone. I'm not sending you to wander forever more in the wilderness, Tanthe. I'll come with you.'

She caught her breath. 'Are you sure?'

'To tell you the truth, I could do with getting away. Helananthe and I are not quite seeing eye to eye on certain matters. I'm bound to go on an errand for her, so now is as good a time to set out as any. Come to the stables with me; we'll take a quick breakfast, I'll saddle my horse, and we'll be gone. I'll just grab some wine and goodies to pacify the miserable sod.'

'Helananthe?'

'I meant the Seer.' He grinned.

She had new Parionian clothes now; a soft ochre-coloured shirt, breeches and a tabard of rich emerald cloth, boots of fine dark leather. The weather was too warm for cloaks. But Eldareth was in his old travelling gear of faded greens and browns, and his horse was the glossy dark brown he'd acquired when they first met Dawn and Mirias. That's his true self, she thought. Unassuming, unfettered.

The land into which Eldareth took her was breathtaking; fold after fold of steep green mountains, veiled in mist. Here and there a tree or a great rock stood sentinel. The valleys seemed depthless in the dawn and the peaks rolled away northwards as far as she could see, caught in a slanting silvery light that filled her with joy. These were the Serpentine Mountains, another legend becoming reality for her.

'It feels good to be on the move again,' she said.

'I sense that we're of like mind,' said Eldareth, amused. 'Both seeking escape from something or other. But I thought you were happy, Tanthe.'

'I should be, but . . . What are you supposed to do, when you love two people equally?' She found herself telling Eldareth all that had happened; it was easier because she was looking through her mare's ears, and not straight at him. 'I was that close, *that* close to taking Rufryd back, because in the end I have so much more in common with him than I'll ever have with Saphaeyender. I thought it was what he wanted; the next thing I know he's shacked up with Ashtar! I don't know what Rufe's playing at! Did he mean to win me back and then dump me, just to hurt me? Or is he being noble, giving me up to Saphaeyender?'

'But isn't it Saphaeyender you want to be with?'

'Yes, I worship him, but I'll never completely trust him. You know what he's like.'

Eldareth gave a bark of laughter. 'Indeed. But for all his faults, he's a good man at heart. He's loyal.'

'Still, it was no fun finding out that he loves me because he loves almost everyone.' Her tone was maudlin. 'He asked me to marry him, but I expect he says that to all the girls. And the boys.'

'Now that's interesting. To my almost certain

knowledge, he has never asked anyone to marry him before.'

'Really?'

'Perhaps losing the theatre has changed him more than I realised. It changed us all. Did you accept?'

'I couldn't. What would I be letting myself in for? I'd have to spend my whole life sharing him – with adoring admirers, if not with other lovers – and I don't know whether I could bear it.'

'You're under no illusions. That's good. But he thinks the world of you, Tanthe.'

'Yes, while I'm there . . . but I get the feeling that if I left him he wouldn't even notice I'd gone. It wouldn't break his heart. At least Rufryd cared fiercely about me. The strange thing is that Saphaeyender's never really hurt me; even when I found out about Lynden, I just forgave him. I wasn't even angry. So how come the slightest thing Rufryd does is like a knife through the heart?'

'I won't state the obvious. Your choice would seem to be between tranquillity and fire.'

'I can't choose! They're both driving me mad! Anyway, that's why I wanted to escape. You?'

'Oh, a small matter,' Eldareth said self-mockingly. 'Not a dissimilar problem to yours. Helananthe wants me to marry her. But I can't see it. Eldareth the Wanderer – King of Aventuria?'

'Oh,' Tanthe said. 'Well, that's shut me up.'

On the evening of the second day they arrived at the seer's hut. The dwelling stood high on a green slope, turfed with grass and wedded to the hillside so it was invisible until they were almost upon it. Late sunlight gilded the grass – she'd noticed how very soft the sky was above Paranios, unutterably beautiful like rose-petals – and the air was warm, heavy with scents of vegetation and animal dung.

Goats grazed on the roof, chickens pecked around the door. Tanthe laughed. 'A great seer lives in this hut?'

'He prefers it so, apparently.'

Eldareth knocked. The ramshackle door creaked open to reveal not a wizened mage but a small, suspicious looking man with a mane of red-brown hair streaked with white. He put Tanthe in mind of a woodland animal; a fox, certainly.

'Not more of you,' he groaned.

'Busy?' said Eldareth. 'There was been disruption aplenty.'

'At least you are not Aelyr, Eldareth. What is it you seek?'

'It is not for me, but my young companion.'

Tanthe began to explain, but the Seer moaned and put up his palms to silence her. 'No, don't tell me the details! Gods. You seek to know the identity of a mysterious figure who appears, asking for your help. Well, the crystal will show you what you need to know. Note, I said *need*, not want. Be warned. It may not be what you are expecting.'

'I'm not expecting anything,' said Tanthe, giving him the wine and food they'd brought.

'That's refreshing.' He looked pleased with their gift. He put the bundle to one side, then led her to the well in the centre. 'Sit down.'

She seated herself on a stool; Eldareth stood at her shoulder. The crystal disc that capped the well seemed to have a strange force to it; she felt it as soon as she sat down, and the milky striations seemed to be moving. Suddenly she was nervous.

'I need you to chant with me, like this . . .' he began to utter a low, rhythmic monotone. As soon as Tanthe caught it, he stopped her.

'Good,' he said. 'We shall begin. Don't lean too far forward. The crystal is very thin and the drop very deep.'

She felt as if the floor were moving up and down. Fear ran riot through her. She hadn't expected this, but it was too late to stop. The Seer began to chant and she followed. The sound echoed horribly in her skull, as if they had set up a resonance with something outside themselves.

The crystal was turning transparent. Within its circle she saw a point of blue-green light, a colour so deep and electric that she gasped at its beauty; and it sparkled like a beam thrown from a jewel. Far away at first, then coming closer . . . Rushing towards her . . . a beam of peacock light, and in the centre of its radiance a green glade, the grass curved and the trees bent in so they formed a sphere.

A woodland glade, but not of earth. The shapes were strange, the colours too intense. Saturated greens of a soft lushness she'd never seen before, strange feathery leaves, unknown flowers in the grass with blue petals and long inky tongues.

A figure stood in the glade. First he was distant; then, although he hadn't moved, he was close. Her Aelyr, in a tunic of grey silk, his arms and legs naked. Lean muscled limbs with skin of gold silk. Deep red hair flowing round his shoulders, his face aglow, beautiful as a god. He was reaching out to her, his fingers pressed to the other side of the crystal as if to the inner surface of water. Trembling, she stretched out her fingers to touch his.

And their hands met, and clasped, and he was really there.

Perspectives changed. He was below her in the crystal, and yet somehow he was in front of her at the same time and she only had to take one step forward . . .

She heard the Seer utter a cry. 'No! Gods, she's created a portal!' And she was aware, in the edge of her vision, that he and Eldareth were jumping up from their seats; but the image remained. The Aelyr was real, physical, holding on to her hands.

As he held her there was a memory. Falling backward into darkness. Figures in grey and violet, running into the night. Loss.

'You found me,' he said, breathing hard as if with exertion. 'At last! Come with me quickly. The portal will not hold for long.'

'Come with you – where?'

'Into my realm.'

'I can't,' she gasped, frightened, holding on to the earth she knew. 'Tell me who you are, what you want!'

'My name is Auriel. I don't want anything, as you mean it. To make you understand will take hours, days. You must come through. I can't come to you, I am bound here, and if you delay any longer it will be too late. We need you. We've missed you so badly, there's so much to explain. Come home, Tanthe.'

'Home?' Her heart hammered with fear and her mouth was desert-dry. She looked wildly at Eldareth. 'What does he mean, home?'

Eldareth looked stricken. 'Close the portal!' he shouted at the Seer.

'I'm trying!' snapped Fox. 'I can't!'

Other half-memories crashed through her mind. 'They were here,' she said. 'Those two Aelyr in grey – they were here! Who are they?'

'My parents, Tanthe,' said Auriel. 'They have been in terrible danger. They had to abandon me as a child. They had to abandon *you*. You're my sister, Tanthe. My sister.'

'No, wait. I'm human. You've made a mistake.'

'No mistake. You are human, and yet you aren't. Come, so I can explain!'

She felt Eldareth's hand on her shoulders. He was anchoring her, trying to keep her on earth, while Auriel pulled her towards him. 'Eldareth, help me! What does he mean?'

His eyes were sombre, his forehead creased. 'Tanthe, I don't know. The Aelyr can be tricksters. Let him go, let the portal close.'

'Tell me, Eldareth!' she blazed, tightening her grip on Auriel's hands. 'If you know something tell me!'

'Oh, Tanthe.' Eldareth frowned. 'All I know is something Elrill said to me. He said he looked into your eyes and saw an Aelyr spirit there.'

She was furious, remembering Elrill's inexplicable coolness towards her. 'Why didn't he tell *me* that?'

'What use would it have been, to confuse you?'

'I've got to know the truth.'

'Don't go! It's impossibly dangerous! You may never be able to come back!'

'Come,' Auriel said, desperate now. 'I gave you a token of trust, the *liroth* knife. You should have had another gift, a *silvenroth* mirror—' *Oh gods*, she thought, remembering. *The little mirror I lost! What* did *happen to it?* 'I've so much to tell you. Quickly. We're all in danger, Tanthe; all our family.' His face was imploring, magically alluring, his distress too tangible to be faked. 'Trust me.'

'Tanthe,' Eldareth said warningly.

She glanced up at him. 'I'm sorry,' she said, dry-mouthed. 'I've got to know what this means. Tell Rufryd and Ymmi and Saphaeyender I'm sorry, I'll come back as soon as I can, I love them!'

'No, don't!' he cried, but too late.

She pulled out of his grasp and stepped into the waiting arms of Auriel.

The Seer was right; the drop was indeed very deep. The world she knew closed up like a flower, and rushed away, and she was swallowed into a long green throat of light.

END OF BOOK ONE

EARTHLIGHT

A SELECTED LIST OF SCIENCE FICTION
AND FANTASY TITLES AVAILABLE FROM
EARTHLIGHT

THE PRICES SHOWN BELOW WERE CORRECT AT THE TIME OF
GOING TO PRESS. HOWEVER EARTHLIGHT RESERVE THE
RIGHT TO SHOW NEW RETAIL PRICES ON COVERS WHICH MAY
DIFFER FROM THOSE PREVIOUSLY ADVERTISED IN THE TEXT
OR ELSEWHERE.

☐ 0 6710 1783 7	Komarr	*Lois McMaster Bujold*	£5.99
☐ 0 6710 1607 5	Memory	*Lois McMaster Bujold*	£5.99
☐ 0 6710 1605 9	Escardy Gap	*Peter Crowther & James Lovegrove*	£5.99
☐ 0 6710 1784 5	Quicker Than The Eye	*Ray Bradbury*	£5.99
☐ 0 6710 1789 6	I Sing The Body Electric	*Ray Bradbury*	£5.99
☐ 0 6710 2207 5	Driving Blind	*Ray Bradbury*	£5.99
☐ 0 6710 1791 8	The October Country	*Ray Bradbury*	£5.99
☐ 0 6710 1790 X	Something Wicked This Way Comes	*Ray Bradbury*	£5.99
☐ 0 6848 4028 6	The Sum Of All Men	*David Farland*	£9.99
☐ 0 6710 1787 X	The Lament of Abalone	*Jane Welch*	£5.99
☐ 0 6710 1785 3	The Royal Changeling	*John Whitbourn*	£5.99
☐ 0 6848 5169 5	Sailing to Sarantium	*Guy Gavriel Kay*	£16.99
☐ 0 6848 5167 9	Beyond the Pale	*Mark Anthony*	£9.99
☐ 0 6848 5168 7	The Last Dragonlord	*Joanne Bertin*	£9.99
☐ 0 6710 2208 3	The High House	*James Stoddard*	£5.99
☐ 0 6848 5817 7	Superscience	*Michael White*	£9.99
☐ 0 6848 5828 2	Green Rider	*Kristen Britain*	£9.99

All Earthlight titles are available by post from:

Book Service By Post, P.O. Box 29, Douglas, Isle of Man IM99 1BQ

Credit cards accepted. Please telephone 01624 675137,
fax 01624 670923, Internet http://www.bookpost.co.uk or
e-mail: bookshop@enterprise.net for details.

Free postage and packing in the UK. Overseas customers allow
£1 per book (paperbacks) and £3 per book (hardbacks).